Maxim Jakubowski is a London-based novelist and editor. He was born in the UK and educated in France. Following a career in book publishing, he opened the world-famous Murder One bookshop in London. He now writes full-time. He has edited many acclaimed crime collections, and over twenty bestselling erotic anthologies and books on erotic photography. His novels include *It's You That I Want to Kiss*, *Because She Thought She Loved Me* and *On Tenderness Express*, all three collected and reprinted in the USA as *Skin in Darkness*. Other books include *Life in the World of Women*, *The State of Montana*, *Kiss Me Sadly*, *Confessions of a Romantic Pornographer*, *I Was Waiting for You*, *Ekaterina and the Night*, *American Casanova* and his collected short stories *Fools for Lust*. He compiles two annual acclaimed series for the Mammoth list: *Best New Erotica* and *Best British Crime*. He is a winner of the Anthony and the Karel Awards, a frequent TV and radio broadcaster, a past crime columnist for the *Guardian* newspaper and Literary Director of London's Crime Scene Festival. In recent years, he has authored under a pen-name a series of *Sunday Times* bestselling erotic romance novels which have sold over two million copies and been sold to 22 countries, and translated the acclaimed French novel *Monsieur* by Emma Becker.

Recent Mammoth titles

The Mammoth Book of Best New SF 25
The Mammoth Book of Gorgeous Guys
The Mammoth Book of Really Silly Jokes
The Mammoth Book of Best New Horror 23
The Mammoth Book of Undercover Cops
The Mammoth Book of Weird News
The Mammoth Book of the Best of Best New Erotica
The Mammoth Book of Antarctic Journeys
The Mammoth Book of Muhammad Ali
The Mammoth Book of Best British Crime 9
The Mammoth Book of Conspiracies
The Mammoth Book of Lost Symbols
The Mammoth Book of Nebula Awards SF
The Mammoth Book of Body Horror
The Mammoth Book of Steampunk
The Mammoth Book of New CSI
The Mammoth Book of Gangs
The Mammoth Book of SF Wars
The Mammoth Book of One-Liners
The Mammoth Book of Ghost Romance
The Mammoth Book of Jokes 2
The Mammoth Book of Slasher Movies
The Mammoth Book of Street Art
The Mammoth Book of Ghost Stories by Women
The Mammoth Book of Best New Erotica 11
The Mammoth Book of Irish Humour
The Mammoth Book of Futuristic Romance
The Mammoth Book of Unexplained Phenomena
The Mammoth Book of Quick & Dirty Erotica
The Mammoth Book of Pulp Fiction

THE MAMMOTH BOOK OF

Best British Crime 11

Edited by Maxim Jakubowski

ROBINSON

Constable & Robinson Ltd
55–56 Russell Square
London WC1B 4HP
www.constablerobinson.com

First published in the UK by Robinson,
an imprint of Constable & Robinson Ltd, 2014

A copy of the British Library Cataloguing in Publication
Data is available from the British Library

UK ISBN: 978-1-47211-186-9 (paperback)
UK ISBN: 978-1-47211-189-0 (ebook)

9 8 7 6 5 4 3 2 1

Printed and bound by CPI Group (UK) Ltd, Croydon, CR0 4YY

CONTENTS

Acknowledgements

THE HOLLYWOOD I REMEMBER by Lee Child © 2012. First appeared in *Vengeance*, edited by Lee Child. Reprinted by permission of the author and his agent, Darley Anderson Literary Agency.

ADVENT by Kevin Wignall © 2012. First appeared in *Ellery Queen's Mystery Magazine*. Reprinted by permission of the author.

TEMPUS FUGIT by Will Carver © 2012. First appeared online at *Dead Good*. Reprinted by permission of the author's agent, Samantha Bulos.

BASED ON A TRUE STORY by Paul Charles © 2014. Original publication by permission of the author.

DARKLING by Val McDermid © 2012. First appeared in *Ellery Queen's Mystery Magazine*. Reprinted by permission of the author and her agent, Gregory & Co.

THE WORLD'S END by Paul Johnston © 2014. Original publication by permission of the author and his agent, Wade & Doherty Literary Agency.

A TIME TO SEEK by Alison Bruce © 2012. First appeared in *Cambridge News*. Reprinted by permission of the author.

BILLY MICKLEHURST'S RUN by Tim Willocks © 2012. First appeared in *The Big Issue* and in book form with Editions Allia. Reprinted by permission of the author and his agent, A. M. Heath Ltd.

VERTIGO by Maxim Jakubowski © 2012. First appeared in *Off the Record 2: At the Movies*, edited by Luca Veste and Paul D. Brazill. Reprinted by permission of the author.

THE BAKER STREET CIMMERIAN by Rhys Hughes © 2014. Original publication by permission of the author.

HERE, THERE AND EVERYWHERE by Edward Marston © 2012. First appeared in *Murder Here, Murder There*, edited by R. Barri Flowers and Jan Grape. Reprinted by permission of the author.

A GOOD MAN by N. J. Cooper © 2012. First appeared in *Ellery Queen's Mystery Magazine*. Reprinted by permission of the author and her agent, Gregory & Co.

GOOD INTENTIONS by Michael Z. Lewin © 2012. First appeared in *Ellery Queen's Mystery Magazine*. Reprinted by permission of the author.

GOD'S LONELY MAN by Peter Guttridge © 2014. Original publication by permission of the author.

THE DAY OF THE DEAD by Mary Hoffman © 2014. Original publication by permission of the author.

FINNBARR'S BELL by Peter Tremayne © 2012. First appeared in *Ellery Queen's Mystery Magazine*. Reprinted by permission of the author and his agent, A. M. Heath Ltd.

TWO FLORIDA BLONDES by Kate Rhodes © 2014. Original publication by permission of the author.

RED ESPERANTO by Paul D. Brazill © 2012. First appeared as an e-book with Lite Editions. Reprinted by permission of the author and Desideria Marchi.

SHAME by Ros Asquith © 2014. Original publication by permission of the author.

MURDER UNCORDIAL by Amy Myers © 2012. First appeared in *Ellery Queen's Mystery Magazine*. Reprinted by permission of the author.

MIDWINTER INTERLUDE by Alexander McCall Smith © 2012. First appeared in *The Strand Magazine*. Reprinted by permission of the author's agent, David Higham Associates Ltd.

THE TIGER by Nina Allan © 2013. First appeared in *Terror Tales of London*, edited by Paul Finch. Reprinted by permission of the author.

THE LONG SHADOW by Peter Turnbull © 2012. First appeared in *Ellery Queen's Mystery Magazine*. Reprinted by permission of the author.

FOURTH TIME LUCKY FOR MICKEY LOEW by Jay Stringer © 2012. First appeared online at *Beat to a Pulp*. Reprinted by permission of the author.

NO FLOWERS by Martin Edwards © 2012. First appeared in *Ellery Queen's Mystery Magazine*. Reprinted by permission of the author.

LOST AND FOUND by Zoë Sharp © 2012. First appeared in *Vengeance*, edited by Lee Child. Reprinted by permission of the author.

EYES WIDE SHUT by Col Bury © 2012. First appeared in

Off the Record 2: At the Movies, edited by Luca Veste and Paul D. Brazill. Reprinted by permission of the author.

SECRET OF THE DEAD by David Stuart Davies © 2014. Original publication by permission of the author.

NO SHORT CUTS by Howard Linskey © 2012. First appeared in *True Brit Grit*, an e-book edited by Paul D. Brazill and Luca Veste. Reprinted by permission of the author.

LULLABY by Susan Everett © 2014. Original publication by permission of the author.

ANYTHING CAN HAPPEN by Christopher Fowler © 2014. Original publication by permission of the author.

THE HOTLINE by Dreda Say Mitchell © 2012. First appeared in *Vengeance*, edited by Lee Child. Reprinted by permission of the author.

THE ZATOPEC GAMBIT by Roger Busby © 2014. Original publication by permission of the author.

FUNERAL FOR A FRIEND by Simon Kernick © 2012. First appeared online at *Dead Good*. Reprinted by permission of the author.

A THREE PIE PROBLEM by Peter Lovesey © 2012. First appeared in *Ellery Queen's Mystery Magazine*. Reprinted by permission of the author and his agent, Vanessa Holt.

DEAD MAN'S SOCKS by David Hewson © 2012. First appeared in *Ellery Queen's Mystery Magazine*. Reprinted by permission of the author.

DAYTRIPPING by Gerard Brennan © 2012. First appeared in the author's e-book collection *Other Skies and Nothing But Time*. Reprinted by permission of the author.

THE END OF THE ROAD by Jane Casey © 2014. Original publication by permission of the author.

A NICE CUP OF TEA by Christopher J. Simmons © 2013. First appeared in *Fiction Feast*. Reprinted by permission of the author.

OUT OF BEDLAM by Stephen Gallagher © 2012. First appeared online at *Dead Good*. Reprinted by permission of the author.

BENTINCK'S AGENT by John Lawton © 2012. First appeared as a Kindle original e-book. Reprinted by permission of the author and his agent, Aitken Alexander Associates Ltd.

INTRODUCTION

Maxim Jakubowski

We are now well into the second decade of this anthology series in which, over the past years, I have endeavoured to unearth and discover the best criminal short stories of the year from the pens of British and Irish authors (including expatriates living as far afield as Australia and a handful of Yanks who have been resident in the UK for a long time). Few anthology series in the mystery field last this long and I must express my sincere thanks to our publishers past and present for continuing to support the project. Without David Shelley, Susie Dunlop, Peter Duncan and, holding the fort right now, Duncan Proudfoot, these books would not have seen the light of day and many crime writers would not have won a variety of awards by being published in *The Mammoth Book of Best British Crime*.

And still, year after year, our writers manage to come up with yet more ingenious crimes and solutions to crimes, together with a veritable landscape of atmosphere, emotions and sometimes chilling insights into the murky world that separates good and evil. But first and foremost, they continue to tell wonderful, gripping stories that have the ability to shock, delight and make you think twice, if not three times.

The mystery short story is a fertile field where all things go as long as the writer captures our imagination, and our contributors over eleven volumes have never failed to do so in splendid ways. And long may they continue!

Many regulars are with us again – both big stars from the bestseller lists and lesser known but no less worthy authors – but it's always a particular pleasure of mine to come across either new names or to be able to include writers who had not joined out little club before. So, a heartfelt welcome – in no particular order – to Will Carver, Christopher J. Simmons, Susan Everett, Tim Willocks (whose presence in the series was well overdue), Dreda Say Mitchell, Kate Rhodes, Rhys Hughes (from the shores of fantastic fiction with a rare step into mysterious pastures), Howard Linskey, Peter Guttridge (a fellow judge of mine for the Crime Writers' Association John Creasey Dagger and witty author in his own right, included here with a short tale which won the 2013 Graham Greene Festival story award), and two leading popular children's books authors shifting into a criminal mode, Mary Hoffman and Ros Asquith.

Sadly, Robert Barnard, a frequent contributor to the series, died just as I was making this year's final selection, and we salute his memory. He will be sorely missed. Nick Robinson, who started the publishing house that is now Constable & Robinson, also passed away recently. He was both a friend and a wonderfully supportive publisher for me over almost three decades, not just for this series but for many other books too. This volume is dedicated to the two of them.

So enjoy our tales of devious deeds, puzzles and twists in the tail that prove, once again, that crime indeed does pay!

The Hollywood I Remember

Lee Child

The Hollywood I remember was a cold, hard, desperate place. The sun shone and people got ahead. Who those people were, I have no idea. Real names had been abandoned long ago. Awkward syllables from the shtetls and guttural sounds from the bogs and every name that ended in a vowel had been traded for shiny replacements that could have come from an automobile catalogue. I knew a guy who called himself LaSalle, like the Buick. I knew a Fairlane, like the Ford. I even knew a Coupe de Ville. In fact I knew two Coupe de Villes, but I think the second guy had his tongue in his cheek. In any case, you were always conscious that the guy you were talking to was a cipher. You had no idea what he had been and what he had done before.

Everyone was new and reinvented.

That worked both ways, of course.

It was a place where a week's work could get you what anyone else in the country made in a year. That was true all over town, under the lights or behind them, legitimate or not. But some got more than others. You were either a master or a servant. Like a distorted hourglass: up above, a small glass bubble with a few grains of sand; down below, a big glass bubble with lots of sand. The bottleneck between was tight. The folks on the top could buy anything they wanted, and the folks on the bottom would do whatever it took, no questions asked. Everyone was for sale. Everyone had a price. The city government, the cops, regular folks, all of them. It was a cold, hard, desperate place.

Everyone knew nothing would last. Smart guys put their early paychecks into solid things, which is what I did. My first night's work became the down payment on the house I've now owned for more than forty years. The rest of the money came with a mortgage from a week-old bank. And mortgages needed to be paid, so I had to keep on working. But work was not hard to find for a man with my skills and for a man happy to do the kind of things I was asked to do. Which involved girls, exclusively. Hollywood hookers were the best in the world, and there were plenty of them. Actresses trapped on the wrong side of the bottleneck still had to eat, and the buses and trains brought more every day. Competition was fierce.

They were amazingly beautiful. Usually they were better-looking than the actual movie stars. They had to be. Sleeping with an actual movie star was about the only thing money couldn't buy, so look-alikes and substitutes did good business. They were the biggest game in town. They lasted a year or two. If they couldn't take it, they were allowed to quit early. There was no coercion. There didn't need to be. Those buses and trains kept on rolling in.

But there were rules.

Blackmail was forbidden, obviously. So was loose talk. The cops and the gossip columnists could be bought off, but why spend money unnecessarily? Better to silence the source. Better to make an example and buy a month or two of peace and quiet. Which is where I came in. My first was a superhuman beauty from Idaho. She was dumb enough to believe a promise some guy made. She was dumb enough to make trouble when it wasn't kept. We debated disfigurement for her. Cut off her lips and her ears, maybe her nose, maybe pull every other tooth. We figured that would send a message. But then we figured no LA cop would stand for that, no matter what we paid, so I offed her pure and simple, and that's how I got the down payment for my house. It was quite an experience. She was tall, and she was literally stunning. I got short of breath and weak at the knees. The back part of my brain told me I should be dragging her to my cave, not slitting her throat. But I got through it.

The next seven paid off my mortgage, and the two after that bought me a Cadillac. It was the eleventh that brought me trouble. Just one of those unlucky things. She was a fighter, and she had blood pressure issues, apparently. I had to stab her in the chest to quiet her down, and the blade hit bone and nicked something bad, and a geyser of blood came out and spattered all over my suit coat. Like a garden hose. A great gout of it, like a drowned man coughing up seawater on the sand, convulsive. Afterward I wrapped the knife in the stained coat and carried it home wearing only shirtsleeves, which must have attracted attention from someone.

Because as a result, I had cops on me from dawn the next morning. But I played it cool. I did nothing for a day, and then I made a big show of helping my new neighbour finish the inside of his new garage. Which was a provocation, in a way, because my new neighbour was a dope peddler who drove up and down to Mexico regular as clockwork. The cops were watching him too. But they suffered an embarrassment when we moved his car to the kerb so we could work on the garage unencumbered. The car was stolen right from under their noses. That delayed the serious questions for a couple of days.

Then some new hotshot LAPD detective figured that I had carried the knife and the bloody coat to my neighbour's garage in my tool bag and that I had then buried it in the floor. But the guy failed to get a warrant, because judges like money and hookers too, and so the whole thing festered for a month and then went quiet, until a new hotshot came on the scene. This new guy figured I was too lazy to dig dirt. He figured I had nailed the coat into the walls. He wanted a warrant fast, because he figured the rats would be eating the coat. It was that kind of a neighbourhood. But he didn't get a warrant either, neither fast nor slow, and the case went cold, and it stayed cold for forty years.

During which time two things happened. The LAPD built up a cold-case unit, and some cop came along who seemed to be that eleventh hooker's son. Which was an unfortunate confluence of events for me. The alleged son was a dour terrier of a guy with plenty of ability, and he worked that dusty old file like crazy. He was on the fence, fifty-fifty as to whether the floor or the wall was the final resting place for my coat, and my coat was the holy grail for this guy, because laboratory techniques had advanced by then. He figured he could compare his own DNA to whatever could be recovered from the coat. My dope-peddling neighbour had been shot to death years before, and his house had changed hands many times. None of the new owners had ever permitted a search because they knew what was good for them, but then the sub-primes all went belly-up and the place was foreclosed, and the hotshot son figured he could bypass the whole warrant process by simply requesting permission from whatever bank now held the paper, but the bank itself was bust and no one knew who controlled its assets, so I got another reprieve, except right about then I got diagnosed with tumours in my lungs.

I had no insurance, obviously, working in that particular industry, so my house was sold to finance my stay in the hospital, which continues to this day, and from my bed I heard that the buyer of my house had also gotten hold of my neighbour's place and was planning to raze them both and then build a mansion. Which got the hotshot son all excited, naturally, because finally the wrecking ball would do the work of the warrants no one had been able to get. The guy visited me often. Every time he would ask me, how was I feeling? Then he would ask me, wall or floor? Which showed his limitations, to be honest. Obviously the coat and the knife had exited the scene in the dope dealer's stolen car. I had put them in the secret compartment in the fender and left the key in the ignition when I parked the car on the kerb. They were long gone. I was fireproof.

Which brought me no satisfaction at all, because of the terrible pain I was in. I had heard of guys in my situation floating comfortably on IV drips full of morphine and Valium and ketamine, but I wasn't getting that stuff. I asked for it, obviously, but the damn doctor bobbed and weaved and said it wasn't appropriate in my case. And then the hotshot son would come in and ask how I was feeling, with a little grin on his face, and I'm ashamed to say it took me some time to catch on. Everyone was for sale. Everyone had a price. The city government, the cops, regular folks, all of them. Including doctors. I have no idea what the son was giving the guy, favours or money or both, but I know what the guy wasn't giving me in return. The Hollywood I remember was a cold, hard, desperate place, and it still is.

Advent

Kevin Wignall

The regional train from Düsseldorf pulled into Cologne's main station a few minutes behind schedule at a quarter to nine. Even this late in the evening the station was busy – people with suitcases killing time waiting for night trains, beggars searching out the sympathetic or gullible, passengers jumping on and off the regional trains which buzzed in and out like worker bees.

As the doors opened on the Düsseldorf train, forty or fifty people spilled out of it, charging along the platform at a brisk pace, none of them quite breaking into a run, but all of them eager to be where they were going. These were not people with luggage, but regular commuters returning home after a day at work, the station so familiar it had become invisible to them.

Karsten Groll, set against this backdrop, looked like someone walking at normal speed through a time-lapsed film. He'd stepped out of the front carriage of the train but walked so slowly that the passengers from the other carriages caught up with him, engulfed him, left him behind.

He hardly seemed to notice them, and anyone watching him might have wondered why he alone was in no hurry to be somewhere. Casually scruffy, but not homeless scruffy, he was wearing jeans and a military-style jacket, a beanie hat, a small, almost empty rucksack on his back.

Only the difference in his walking speed marked him out, but that in itself would have been enough to make the same observer question if everything was well in this young man's world. Did he have nowhere to go? Again, he didn't look homeless, but perhaps he'd only just walked out on his old life. Or was it that he didn't want to go where he was headed, and if so, why did he not want to go there?

That observer might have had misgivings about the young man from the Düsseldorf train, and they would have been right to be concerned. Karsten *was* on his way somewhere and was determined he would get there, but it was true that he was in no hurry.

Because Karsten Groll was walking towards his own death. He walked towards it with the same certainty that his train had travelled towards Cologne – a few minutes early, a few minutes late, but the destination never in doubt. He was resigned to death, too, a resignation which had developed its own steady momentum.

So Karsten walked slowly but deliberately, and knowing this was the last night of his life, he looked upon the station as none of his fellow passengers had done. In fact, he had chosen it – Messe would have been a little closer, but this station brought back memories of childhood visits with his mother and brother.

He glanced up now at the glass canopy arching overhead, at the orange glow of the lights and the darkness of the city beyond. He noticed a heritage train, the *Rheingold*, parked on a neighbouring platform – previously he might have sneered at something like that but now it looked wonderful and warm and inviting and filled him with a vague longing he couldn't quite identify.

He left the ordered hollow vault of the terminus with its tinny echoing announcements in German and English, and descended the steps to the more hectic retail area beneath the station. It was mainly fast-food outlets and cafés, but a few gift shops too – perfumes, chocolates, books – and Karsten guessed it attracted a lot of people who weren't even travelling because it was crowded with people at cross purposes, some loitering, socializing, others trying only to pass through.

He felt a little in both camps. He was passing through, but he came close to stopping a couple of times to look in one window or another, and finally did stop to look in the window of the chocolate shop. The display was full of advent calendars.

He and Stefan had both been given one as children, to avoid fights over who would have the chocolate behind each window, though he didn't remember ever fighting with his brother. Perhaps he just remembered it that way now, but seeing these calendars, some shaped like Christmas trees, he wished he could call Stefan to tell him about them, to ask if he remembered how excited they would get about opening each little window.

He wished, too, that some stranger would come and stand and stare at the same display, that they might strike up a conversation. It was never about the chocolates, he wanted to say to that person, but about the anticipation of opening the window, about the rhythm and the warmth that it gave to the Christmas season.

But no one came, and he walked on. He doubted all those calendars would be sold in the next six days, and after that they would be redundant. He wondered what happened to them afterwards. Maybe they were just thrown away. Like him, their time was almost up.

He left the station, out into the biting cold of this November night, across the concourse, climbed the steps and crossed the overpass to the cathedral. He was aware of it to his left, soaring above him like a gothic cliff face as he skirted around it.

This was the other reason he'd chosen to come to this station, so that he could also stroll for one last time through one of the Christmas markets. It was his earliest memory of Cologne but as he reached the far side of the cathedral he realized that dream would not be rekindled tonight. The fair was spread out before him, but unlit, and the shadowy activity filling Roncalliplatz was that of stallholders making last-minute preparations.

He walked through the almost completed market anyway, and as he overheard conversations about the opening the next day he regretted that his actions would fill the newspapers with something unpleasant, possibly even marring the atmosphere for a day or two. It was unfortunate, but he wouldn't change his mind.

Karsten was heading across the city, to Mohr's bar. Mohr would arrive there at nine, as he did every night to "check the books" – that's what Stefan had told him. Karsten would arrive a little later, kill Mohr and then get killed himself, not by choice but he was too much of a realist to dream up a plan that involved getting out alive.

Besides, there wasn't much left to stay alive for, only memories like this, tarnished forever now by loss and failure. This and the other markets would be full of families by this time tomorrow, and it filled Karsten with wonder and bitterness that his own family had been wiped out so succinctly by bad luck and bad choices – maybe the two were the same.

His father's death was so firmly lodged in the past that he struggled now to think of it as something that had not been meant to happen, but he guessed his father had known how tired he was before setting off on his last car journey. In truth, there had been nothing inevitable about it, only carelessness and perhaps a desire to be home with his family. Karsten had been only eight at the time.

There had been no choice in his mother's death, of course – no one would choose cancer – and it was still too raw for him to think about even five years later. What he did think about was the failed promise. He'd been twenty at the time, Stefan only seventeen, and Karsten had promised her as she lay dying, had promised that he would look after Stefan, make sure nothing happened to him.

He left the market behind and threaded through streets that were quieter, heading by memory and instinct towards the river and the Deutzer Brücke. On one of the side streets there was some building work going on and he had to walk in the road.

Stefan had made choices too, in getting together with Martina, in staying with her even when he realized she was a junkie, believing he could get her clean. But Stefan had failed in his bid to look after Martina, just as Karsten had failed to look after his brother.

His mind raced back, wishing Stefan hadn't warned her pusher off, wishing the pusher had listened, wishing Stefan hadn't gone round there and flushed his drugs and beaten him up. Stefan had known too well what would follow, which is why he'd bought the gun.

Even thinking of it made Karsten suddenly aware of the slight weight of it in his rucksack, a gun wrapped in a towel, lightly bouncing against his back as he walked. He'd test-fired it once in the woods, making sure he understood it, but only once, one single round, because he hadn't found spare ammunition and, unlike Stefan, didn't know where to get it. The remaining bullets in the clip were the sum of his armoury.

In the end, Stefan had left the gun with Karsten because he'd persuaded Martina to get away somewhere, hide out with him. That had been a choice too, and only an optimist in love could have failed to imagine that Martina would call her pusher as soon as the craving got too great.

As far as the police had been able to tell, they'd picked Stefan up on the street, driven him out of town. His body had been found a few days later. They'd beaten him to death, nearly every major bone broken, his skull cracked in three places, one eye ruptured, massive internal injuries. That's what those simple words concealed – he'd been beaten to death.

Karsten saw a girl huddled in a doorway, looking cold and strung out and lonely. She mumbled something as she looked up at him but he didn't hear her and didn't break his stride because the world was full of people like Martina and it always would be. Any sympathy he'd had, learned from Stefan, had long since disappeared.

But Martina was no longer one of those people – she'd died two weeks after Stefan, an overdose. One of her friends had claimed it was intentional, a grief-stricken suicide, and Karsten wished he could believe that, but he couldn't. Nor could he forgive her for confirming what he'd known from the start, that Stefan's death had been pointless.

He reached the bridge and started across its open expanse, cars tearing past, the tramlines in the middle. There were a few people cycling and walking on both sides too, but not many. The cold was raw and fierce out here with a wind whipping up off the river.

Even so, halfway across he stopped and looked back at the twin towers of the cathedral, illuminated against the night sky. He could just see, below the metal arches of the distant railway bridge, that the floating Christmas market was also being prepared for opening day.

It occurred to him that even though the news might be upsetting when it broke, he was actually about to give the city a gift, that the Christmas markets would open tomorrow and one of the city's biggest drug dealers would be dead. It wouldn't make the problem go away, of course, but it would be something.

That had been the excuse given by the police for not finding Stefan's killers in over two months, that the problem was bigger than Mohr. There were two big rival drug gangs, so maybe the other had killed him because dealings between these various gangs were complex.

He'd reminded them again that Stefan hadn't been in a gang, that the pusher he'd beaten up was one of Mohr's. "Trust us," they'd said. "Trust us, it may not look like it, but things are happening, we're investigating."

Why did they not see that Karsten had no trust left, that he had used it all up? A week ago he'd called them one last time and had been spoken to as if he were the criminal. No mention of the two rival gangs, of Mohr and the Turk, no mention of ongoing enquiries, just a curt reminder that they were busy, that his was not the only case, that there were many innocent victims out there.

Innocent had been said in such a way as to differentiate it from his calls, as if Stefan had somehow been part of the underworld that had killed him. Stefan had been able to get hold of a gun, he'd had a junkie girlfriend, but he'd been no criminal.

A long express train crossed the rail bridge heading into the main station, an array of lit windows passing behind the metal trellis, revealing in silhouette the countless pedestrians ambling along looking at the thousands of love padlocks that adorned the bridge.

Perhaps there were couples attaching their own padlocks as he stood there watching, an expression of their love and commitment. And though he felt a city and a lifetime away from that other bridge, it made him smile to think that good things were happening in the world, that good things would continue to happen after he was gone.

He walked on. A tram passed him and he involuntarily picked up his pace, as if trying to pursue it. The little illuminated universe of the tram grew smaller and smaller, merging with the other lights on the bridge, calling him on to his fate.

He checked his watch and walked faster still, spurred on, fearful that if he walked too slowly Mohr might have left again. By the time he reached the far side of the bridge, his eyes were streaming with tears from the cold wind, but he didn't stop, just wiped them on his sleeve and kept walking.

He turned right, cutting through side streets, and his pace only slowed when he saw the bar up ahead of him. It was open but looked quiet. It wasn't the kind of bar that attracted casual clientele and the regulars were mostly in Mohr's employ or hangers-on.

He steadied himself mentally as he walked, trying to look relaxed, like this was something he did every day. He had no fear of dying, not now, but he feared one last failure, failing to get to Mohr, being stopped before he was even close.

He pushed the door open and stepped inside. There was music playing, but it was nothing he recognized, some kind of rock from the 1970s. And it was so warm that for a moment he had to stand and collect himself – he felt almost instantly sleepy after the biting cold out on the street.

He walked into the main room then, a long bar down the left-hand side, tables and booths filling the rest of the space. Only a couple of the tables were occupied, fewer than a dozen guys in total, all Mohr's people. One table was playing cards, the other had been listening to one of them telling a story, but they fell silent when Karsten walked in.

He kept walking and looked at the barman as he passed and said, "I'm here to see Herr Mohr – he knows I'm coming."

The barman didn't respond at all, just stared blankly. Karsten had almost reached the door at the far end of the room, though, when he heard a voice behind him.

"Hey, kid!"

Karsten felt his heart perform a strange sickening manoeuvre. He stopped and turned as casually as he could manage. The dim lighting was the only thing masking his fear and the fluttering twitch that had started below his left eye and which he couldn't control.

It was the guy who'd been telling a story and he looked at Karsten now as if he was in the mood for sport. The others were all looking at the guy and smiling, and Karsten guessed this was one of the big men in the organization, maybe even the one who'd arranged Stefan's murder. It made Karsten wish that he had more bullets, that he could kill this man too, kill all of them.

"You're not Turkish, are you?"

The others all burst out laughing. Karsten looked anything but Turkish. It was a double joke too, because the Turk wasn't even Turkish, but an Albanian.

Karsten couldn't speak for a moment and responded by pulling his beanie hat off and putting it in his jacket pocket. He was too hot anyway, so hot he felt he might pass out.

The guy nodded in mock approval and said, "Now that is a fine German boy." He smiled at Karsten and said, "Don't look so worried, I'm just having some fun, but if you *had* been a Turk . . ." That seemed to be a punch line in itself because his friends fell about laughing again, maybe even laughing too hard, and so did the guys playing cards.

Karsten nodded and turned and walked through the door. There was a short corridor in front of him and then stairs to the upper floor. Even as he reached the bottom of the stairs he could see Mohr's bodyguard standing on the small landing at the top.

He tried a smile and stopped when he was halfway up the stairs and said, "I'm here to see Herr Mohr."

The bodyguard was heavily built, his head shaved, wearing a leather jacket.

"He's busy."

"He knew I might be coming tonight." As Karsten talked he eased the rucksack from his back and opened it. He clearly didn't look threatening because the guard looked unimpressed rather than suspicious. "I've brought him the payment . . . the money I owed." He was reaching into the rucksack now, and was pleased that it looked as if he was searching for the money instead of ensuring the towel was wrapped around the end of the gun, that his hand was firmly on the grip. "Three thousand, five hundred . . ."

Karsten held the outside of the rucksack with his other hand, pointing up at the bodyguard. He fired and his hand kicked backwards. The towel muffled the noise but the shot was still much louder than he'd expected. He'd been aiming at the bodyguard's chest but the bullet hit him in the side of the neck and blood sprayed out of it. The guy fell to his knees as he reached up, his hand blindly trying to address the fountain of blood which pumped deep and sleek around his fingers.

Karsten wasn't sure if he heard someone shout behind him – the music seemed louder now and he couldn't distinguish the sounds. They had to have heard something, surely. Either way, he wouldn't have long and knew he needed to move quickly.

The bodyguard toppled forward, a confused expression locked into his face. His body slid down four or five stairs before becoming wedged and crumpling awkwardly.

Karsten flew up the remaining stairs, jumping over the body. He could smell burning and pulled the gun out of the rucksack. He pushed the door open and stepped into the office. He dropped the smouldering rucksack on to the floor, pointing the gun forward as he kicked the door shut behind him.

Mohr was sitting there just ten feet away behind the desk. He had a shock of dyed hair, was overweight, wearing a shirt and pale grey suit – he looked like a car salesman. And amazingly to Karsten, he was actually going through the books in that there was some kind of ledger on the desk in front of him. There were no bundles of money or drugs, but then he guessed that was only in the movies.

Mohr almost instantly went to reach into his jacket but Karsten waved the gun at him and said, "Hands on the table or I'll kill you right now."

Mohr complied and Karsten reached behind and fumbled for the lock, turning it. He couldn't hear anyone coming yet, so maybe they hadn't heard the first shot. They would hear the others, but it wouldn't matter then. The rucksack was still smouldering and Karsten stamped on it a couple of times as he moved forward, never letting the gun stray from Mohr's body.

"You look familiar," said Mohr. "But you don't work for the Turk. Have we met before?"

Karsten shook his head. "I saw you once, from a distance, but we've never met."

Mohr shrugged and looked ready to speak, but Karsten only had a limited amount of time and this wasn't a conversation.

"I look like my brother, that's why you think I'm familiar. Stefan Groll, who you murdered."

He was expecting a denial, but Mohr nodded and said, "You know, in America they have something called suicide by cop, when a person wants to die and behaves in such a way that a policeman shoots him."

"Stefan didn't want to die – he wanted his girlfriend to live, that was all."

Mohr looked threatening as he said, "Did he honestly believe I would let him wreck my business? You call that wanting to live?" His voice got louder, and Karsten wondered if he was hoping his shouts might be heard from downstairs. "What did he think, that I would see the error of my ways and leave the drugs business behind? He left me no choice!"

Karsten couldn't hear anything, but he suddenly sensed as if by instinct alone that something was happening in the bar below, that there was some movement. He had no more time and realized anyway that he wasn't here for an admission of guilt, which was just as well, but for something much simpler.

He braced his arm and fired. The noise was deafening now. It hit Mohr in the chest and knocked him back in his chair. But there was no explosion of blood this time and Mohr looked damaged, winded, but no less threatening. His hands flailed about, and Karsten saw he was reaching for his gun in its shoulder holster.

At the same time Karsten realized Mohr wasn't as overweight as he looked, that he was wearing body armour. He aimed the gun a little higher, directly at Mohr's face. He squeezed the trigger, closing his eyes at the crucial moment, hearing a single word from Mohr, "No!", small and desperate and then the deafening bang and another and another until the trigger clicked beneath the pressure of his finger and nothing happened.

He opened his eyes. Mohr had slumped sideways, not quite falling out of his plush leather office chair. He was dead, his face barely recognizable. Karsten's ears were ringing with the gunshots, but he heard the rush of bangs and clattering and shouts as his own death came panicked towards him.

Then he heard a gunshot, but it was from the bar below. He walked to the office door, unlocked and opened it to look down the stairs. There were more gunshots. The door into the bar opened, the seventies rock pounding out, then a voice shouting, "Miki! The Turk!" A percussive thud followed, the sound of that same person having the air pummelled out of his lungs by the impact of a bullet. Karsten couldn't see him, but he guessed he'd slumped in the doorway, wedging the door open, because the noise level stayed the same and the gunfire became more insistent.

Karsten stepped back inside, locked the door again. He could see another door in the corner behind the desk. He picked up his rucksack and ran through it, into a long narrow corridor which had boxes of spirits lined up along one wall.

There was a window at the end of the corridor and he opened it and looked down. It was a yard below, with a couple of cars parked there. It was quiet too, though he could still hear the noise carrying up from the bar and perhaps a siren in the distance.

The window was narrow and he doubted any of the other people in Mohr's bar would have got through it. Karsten slipped the gun into the rucksack and threw it down, then pulled himself through the window, slinking his hips sideways to get out. There was a Mercedes parked almost below and he jumped, landing on the roof with a denting thud, and immediately to the ground from there. The car wasn't alarmed.

He picked up the rucksack, took the gun out again and slipped it into his jacket pocket. He walked along the side of Mohr's bar and out into the street. When he saw other people nearby looking on with concern, he adopted the same expression himself.

There were a couple of cars parked erratically outside the bar, and still the sound of gunfire, as if there were some kind of stand-off. There were more sirens now, too, and even as Karsten walked casually from the scene a couple of police cars came tearing past.

He dropped the rucksack into a litter bin a little way before the Deutzer Brücke, making sure he pushed it in all the way. And halfway across the bridge he stopped as he had before and looked at the cathedral and the trains passing on the railway bridge. He took the gun from his pocket and dropped it into the dark water below.

He stood for a moment longer, waiting for yet another police car to go hurtling over the bridge behind him. But he had no thoughts for the city now, nor for his family and his memories. He could think of nothing clearly because he was not meant to be alive.

What would he do now? He had no plans because he had imagined no future for himself beyond tonight. He was to return home, he supposed, but then what? Resume his studies, start again? He thought of an old Samuel Beckett quote he'd once heard – he couldn't remember all of it, only the end, *Fail again. Fail better.*

He walked on and, feeling the cold as his senses came back to him, he reached for his beanie hat and put it on again. Had he failed tonight? He had failed to die but that had never been part of his plan, just a consequence of it. He had killed Mohr and one other, deaths which sat remarkably lightly on his conscience, so in that at least he'd succeeded.

Perhaps, as it turned out, Mohr would have died tonight anyway, but Karsten had killed him, in a stand against Stefan's death, and against all the bad luck and bad choices that had beset their family and dragged it down. He had succeeded, for the first time in years, and it didn't matter that he didn't know how he'd succeeded, because neither had he ever understood the flowering of his failures.

He walked on, back the way he'd come, back to the market, and there for a few paces he walked alongside a middle-aged man carrying three cardboard boxes, an awkward load. Karsten was about to turn when he heard the man mutter something as the boxes slipped.

Karsten turned on his heel, grabbing the box that was in danger of toppling to the ground.

"I've got it," he said.

"Thanks," said the man, and was about to say something else when one of the other boxes slipped. Between them they managed to stop it falling to the floor but the top burst open and Karsten saw that it was full of wooden toys.

Once it was safely lowered to the floor Karsten smiled and said, "I loved these when I was a kid."

The guy smiled too as he stacked the open box on top of the other and picked them both up.

"I still do," said the man, then looked at the box in Karsten's arms as if at a complex puzzle.

"I'll carry this one for you."

"Thanks, it's only just over here."

They walked a short distance to his stall, the man talking briefly about the market and how long he'd been coming here. There were two people already at the stall, the guy's son and daughter he guessed, maybe a few years younger than Karsten.

He said hello to them and was thanked again for helping out.

"I was just there," said Karsten, and they shook hands and he said, "Well, good luck with the fair." He turned and headed towards the cathedral.

The man smiled and watched him walk off, but then for some reason he couldn't quite fathom, he became full of misgivings for the young man who'd just helped him. He wasn't sure why, but he felt in some way that it was important not to let him walk away.

He glanced at his son and daughter who looked back at him almost as if they knew what he was about to do. It was the way he was, he supposed, and they were long used to it by now.

"Hey, son!" He followed after him and as Karsten turned around he said, "I didn't even catch your name."

Karsten came back a couple of paces.

"Karsten Groll."

"This may be a strange question, Karsten, but do you have a job right now?"

Karsten shook his head and said, "I'm an art student, but I'm taking some time out."

"Art?"

He nodded and said, "Sculpture mainly. Some painting, but mainly sculpture." Over the past twelve months Karsten had almost forgotten art but suddenly felt the urge to go back to it, as if his old life were seeping back into him. He'd lost the will to create but could finally see that it would come back if he gave it time.

"Well look, my other son's travelling around the world, so we're one short this year. I can't pay you much, but it could be a good experience for an artist."

"You want me to work on your stall?"

"Why not?"

Karsten looked across at the son and daughter who were smiling expectantly, and he said, "I'm not sure what me plans are."

"It's only four weeks – Advent, that's all."

Karsten nodded and said, "I used to come here when I was a kid." He walked back as the man introduced himself and his family and talked about the opening tomorrow and what they might expect over the coming month.

Within twenty minutes it felt as if he had always been a part of this, or at least, as if nothing had come before. It was as if he had turned around on the Deutzer Brücke and not gone on and killed Mohr and his bodyguard.

Because this kindly man and his family had taken him in on a moment's trust, killer that he was. His future had been a blank, but now it seemed to him that the world had been made new again, and tomorrow night he would still be here when lights filled the darkness.

Tempus Fugit

Will Carver

It's just a Tuesday.

Nothing important ever happened on a Tuesday.

So, when Art Paler agreed to work late this evening, he could not have predicted the scene he now finds himself a part of. He could not have envisaged his wife sitting up, dead, on the tan leather two-seater sofa, her throat a broad claret smile. He could not have imagined his son, collapsed on the kitchen tiles, futilely attempting to hold in his guts as they spill on to unswept crumbs and spattered olive oil. And he would not have thought it likely that he could confront the stranger in his house. That he could chase him outside to the street.

That he could exact such revenge.

Not on a Tuesday.

Wind back a few minutes.

To a time when everyone was still alive.

The stranger approaches the Paler residence with a black clipboard in his left hand. That is the extent of his disguise but it implies enough for on-looking neighbours to shy away from their windows, wanting to avoid a petition or sales call or attempted religious conversion.

The only thing they sidestep is the opportunity to become a witness.

Art fumbles with his phone in the car, eventually stroking the correct icon to cut the sound of local radio from the speakers, replacing it with a short dial tone, followed by beeping, ringing, waiting. Then his wife's voice.

She says, "Hey, honey," and the stranger knocks on the door.

Art replies, "I'm minutes away," and his son has already been stabbed deep into his stomach twice.

"You want me to open some wine?"

The stranger has one hand over the boy's mouth as the dimpled, eight-inch chef's blade penetrates fat and muscle and organs another six times before dragging him into the kitchen to bleed out.

He is a victim. Another statistic. And he's only good for death.

The killer waits in the kitchen doorway for Mrs Paler to finish her phone call. It is neither calculated nor courtesy. The miserable heap of silent flesh to his left is taunted by this stranger's presence. But he can't call out, it's over for him. He does not have the option to warn the woman in the next room of her impending fate. He cannot tell her that he loves her one final time. There is no opportunity for life to flash before his eyes. No moment for him to consider his worth as a son. There is only time to fail and die.

Dial back a few moments.

Before an empty clipboard lay on a doormat, half covering the word *Welcome*.

Art Paler presses the button on his keys to unlock his modest hatchback in the car park. The final words of his boss seem to linger in his ear as he opens the car door, jumping in to escape the layer of cold that separates the sombre sky from the spattering of a falling autumn.

A bonus well earned.

With the engine turning and the heat blasting out at maximum, Art places his mobile phone into a cradle on the dashboard that connects it to the car's speaker system. He could call his son now, tell him that he can give him some money, help him out a bit, pay off that credit card that has had him so deflated these last few months. He could dial his wife and let her know that she should stock up on holiday brochures. But some things are best said in person, with a glass of wine in hand. It can wait, he tells himself.

At that moment, his boss exits the building with a coat-hanger grin and approaches the driver's window. Art lowers it by half. Warm air and hard work escape through the gap.

"Still here, Paler?"

"Just waiting for the windscreen to defrost, sir."

"Well get yourself home to that lovely wife of yours and give her the good news."

"That is my only plan for the evening."

"That and a bloody great drink, I hope." The older man laughs. "You deserve it, lad. A serious masterclass in closing a deal."

"Thank you." Art is drained and not as buoyant as his employer, whose own bonus will undoubtedly be considerably more substantial.

"And don't even think about coming in tomorrow before noon."

Art forces a smile, closes his window and drives off, his windscreen still partly frozen. He turns the radio to a local station.

And then his wife is on the phone asking whether she should open a bottle of wine, and Art says he'll *pop a cork on something fizzy* when he gets in and his son's heart is running out of blood to pump and the stranger waits for the woman to hang up the phone before clawing her over-styled hair from behind, pinning her head to the upright sofa cushion and swiping the sharp, bloodied blade across the front of her neck.

He does this four times. On the final cut he stops halfway and shakes the knife back and forth, gritting his teeth, almost growling. Like he hates her. Like he knows her. Like he is enjoying the kill.

Crank back a notch.

To the point where Art Paler is relieved that he has been asked to stay late by his boss. And he doesn't have to go home again to his wife and his son without that much-needed bonus.

So he doesn't have to detour via a bar and a bottle of Bordeaux he can't afford on the way back to his house. He doesn't have to pretend or confront. Or disappoint.

Art lets his wife know that he will be working late again this evening. It has become a part of his daily routine. So that she knows how long he'll be. How much time she has before he comes home. How long she has to wait to see him.

He'll be an hour.

She'll be waiting.

But she won't see him again.

Tick back further.

To the hour he first met his wife. When life was simpler and the future was not a spreadsheet loaded with numbers that didn't quite add up and new love meant that optimism could be found in the greyest of skies. And nobody had to lie.

Tock forwards to the birth of his son and the joy that only Art could feel. His wife was numb and down and sleep-deprived. And everybody said things would change. That she would get through. She would love him. He was her son.

Swing past the part where her only release was to cut through her wrists. Because not feeling anything was better than feeling the way that she had since two became three. Happiness died for Art Paler that day.

Wind on.

Beyond the difficult first years, when he did everything alone and he had need for nothing else. Stop at the point where he married his second wife, his current wife, and she vowed to love him for richer and poorer. When she promised to love his son like he were her own.

When everybody started to lie.

Move on.

Through the years of guilt and failure that Art Paler learned was now a part of life. Skim over the years where his second wife was a real mother to his son while Art allowed himself to drift effortlessly in and out of melancholy.

Now stop at the instant where she ceased being a mother and became something else. When Art Paler learned to hate his son as much as his first wife had.

Keep going.

To that day when he accidentally saw *that* phone message with *that* picture and he felt duped and saddened and foolish because the thought had never occurred to him. That it could happen again. Art's son would take his wife away. From that moment, everything became a suspicion. It all seemed so obvious. His phone call from work each day let *them* know how long *they* had. Together.

Click to now.

To the minutes following the calculated discovery of his murdered family and the stranger he had paid to kill them. There was supposed to be a struggle. *For authenticity.* But Art chases him down in the driveway. The stranger. The man with the clipboard whom nobody knows. The drunk who catered last year's office Christmas party and boasted some sinister information in his stupor.

Art pushes his full weight down on the handle of the knife that had killed his wife and son, plunging it into the chest of the stranger, going against the plan, ensuring he does not have to pay the other half of the money now the job is complete.

There is no trail. It is, a burglary gone wrong. Interrupted. A moment of temporary insanity caused by the bloody scene Art had returned home to. He had only just called his wife. There would be a recording. He would be free to start again. Or perhaps for the first time.

Art Paler should be frightened or in shock or repentant. He just wanted to be free. To feel relief. To make everything add up. What he actually feels is lucky.

Tomorrow is Wednesday.

And he doesn't have to be at work until noon.

Based on a True Story

A Mystery featuring Inspector McCusker

Paul Charles

"Inspector McCusker, I can't be held responsible for a person being shot while they were trespassing in my home."

"He wasn't shot," McCusker replied crabbily. He was never best pleased when he had to start work before breakfast.

"He wasn't shot?" Harry Reid, the owner of the house spat, losing his cool for the first time since McCusker had arrived, half an hour earlier. "Then what about all the blood splattered over the walls and on the ceiling in my study?"

"He wasn't shot, Mr Reid," McCusker replied again, firmly.

"So, what happened to him then?" Reid enquired, regaining his composure somewhat.

"We don't know exactly," McCusker admitted. "Our pathologist says it looks like the victim's head just exploded!"

Harry Reid looked like a collector and, if confirmation were needed, his Holywood house, merely a stone's throw from the Culloden Hotel on the main Belfast to Bangor road, certainly looked like a collector's house. You could look, but you most certainly could never ever touch. The room of death was shelved on all sides with deep-red, varnished, mahogany bookcases. Mostly the shelves were comfortably and carefully stacked. McCusker guessed Reid would by now have also collected, at the very least, his official retirement birthday. He was dressed head to toe in expensive black, and had well-groomed, traditionally styled grey hair and chin beard. His skin, particularly about his smallish nose, had the hue of a whiskey drinker. The skin of his hands, however, boasted the well-defined tan of a recent holiday location. His clear-varnished fingernails looked like they were manicured regularly, if not daily. He had the air of someone who clearly felt they had "done well", against the odds. He had an entourage of personal, live-in staff – Alan Henderson, PA; Ronnie Millings, chauffeur; Billy Harrison, security, and Eric Wilksen, chef – to prove this point to someone, if not to himself.

Reid and *his* people were very agitated because the SOCO team would not let them clean any of the blood and brain tissue from the valuable leather-bound books and the collection of priceless vases and decanters.

McCusker continued to linger by the door of the study. He was about to lean on the doorpost when he realized he'd probably get blood on his Saturday-night, dark blue, pinstriped suit. He looked, and acted, like a man from the country, with unkempt straw copper hair and red cheeks. He was solid rather than overweight, gangly, awkward and shy, but he wasn't the fool he might like others to think he was. He reckoned by the amount of human tissue splattered around the room, there couldn't be much of the victim's head left. All the Portrush-born-and-bred detective could see were two elongated denim legs in blood-splattered, fawn, Timberland boots protruding to the left of the desk along the royal blue carpet. McCusker noticed all of the SOCO team were stiff necked to ensure they avoided eye contact with the victim's remains. Even the dapper DS Willie John Barr was starting to look a bit green around the gills. They were all no doubt helped in their endeavours to avoid looking at the corpse by the distraction of a very large swan-shaped white vase sitting on top of the desk.

"Aruawareofathingmissinsir?" DS Barr asked.

Reid looked at McCusker's detective sergeant as though he came from another planet.

"I believe the policeman was inquiring if you were aware if anything was missing," Alan Henderson translated for his boss.

"Really?" Reid said, raising his eyebrows in disbelief. McCusker wasn't sure if Reid couldn't believe that was what Barr had said, or if he couldn't believe that his PA had understood.

"I believe so, sir," Henderson said. He, like the rest of Reid's "people", was dressed in a two-piece dark suit, with white shirt. They were distinguishable only by the different loud ties they wore. In another life, McCusker felt Henderson would have continuously rubbed his hands, tugged at his forelock and dipped his neck in respect to his boss.

"Nothing is missing," Reid declared.

"What?" McCusker replied. "With all of the stuff in this room, you don't need to do a thorough check to see if anything is missing?"

"I can assure you, nothing is missing from my collection, Inspector."

"What about the rest of the house?" McCusker asked.

Reid looked to Henderson who looked to Billy Harrison who said, "We believe there was only one intruder and he's—"

"Right," McCusker replied, certainly not needing the head of security to draw a picture. "Have you any idea how he gained access to the premises?"

"Yes, Mr Harrison," Reid began, without looking at his employee, "perhaps you could explain to the PSNI, not to mention myself, how anyone broke into my 'thief-proof' house. I've certainly got the bills, if not the certificate of guarantee, to testify to the system you put in."

Billy Harrison didn't look like the kind of person who enjoyed being the focus of Reid's attention, not to mention his wrath.

"Rest assured I'll find out for you," he said as he departed the room.

"Make sure you do, Mr Harrison, make sure you do," Reid ordered, surprisingly good-humouredly considering there were the bloody remains of a stranger on his floor. "Please rest assured, Inspector McCusker, that before the end of this day, I'll find out how our security was breached. I will of course pass the information over to you."

Reid and his people led DI McCusker and DS Barr into the conservatory just off the kitchen. Eric Wilksen, the chef, peeled off into the kitchen, as niftily as Lewis Hamilton taking a pit stop, and went about his business of preparing something.

Having settled into a luxuriously cushioned, basketwork sofa, all to himself, McCusker was just about to ask what it was, exactly, that Reid did when Alan Henderson opened the brown leather folder he'd been carrying under his arm since they'd first met and produced a single foolscap sheet of paper.

Top and centre was an embossed deep blue "H" and "R" squished together so they shared a limb, as it were.

By the end of the page, in four paragraphs of quite large typeface, Harry Reid's name had been mentioned seventeen times, and still McCusker wasn't sure exactly what it was he did. It appeared he owned companies who owned companies and these companies in turn were involved with other corporations who seemed to finance Mr Reid's complex endeavours. As far as McCusker could gather, the crux of Reid's business seemed to involve doing business with . . . his other businesses.

A man who does business with himself has no need for a conscience, was McCusker's golden rule. He was saved from having to ask an embarrassing first question of, "What exactly is it that you do?" when the chef, Wilksen, arrived with a platter full of bacon, eggs (fried and scrambled), sausages, fried tomatoes and – in McCusker's humble opinion, the US of A's No. 1 invention – hash browns.

Henderson sat down to join them and ended up "playing mammy" and dishing out everyone's ample helpings – everyone, that was, apart from Harrison, who had dry toast accompanied by black tea.

"He's pregnant," the chef jested and was flashed a very disapproving look from both Reid and Henderson for his efforts.

"Do you know if thieves have been working the area recently?" Reid began as McCusker tore into the food, his hunger overcoming the bizarreness of the situation.

McCusker nodded at his DS to reply.

"Nothing out of the ordinary," Barr replied, taking great effort to speak as slowly as possible. "Have you been broken into before?"

"No, positively not," Alan Henderson replied on behalf of his boss. "Mr Reid moved in here fifteen months ago when he relocated to Ulster. It's one thing to talk about regenerating the country, but it's another altogether to be here right in the middle helping the country get back on its feet again after all those years of conflict."

The PA's boast seemed to falter somewhat when McCusker asked, through munching on his packed bacon butty, "Ah, where do you come from, Mr Henderson?"

"My PA is from Chipping North, Inspector," Reid replied as he dabbed the corners of his mouth with a very expensive-looking lace napkin, "but I'm from just outside Belfast. I grew up not very far from here. I had five brothers and four sisters and we shared three rooms. I remember this house being in ruins for years and when I was a kid we'd all break in and play around the grounds. I'd tell everyone who'd listen that some-day this would be my house and I'd restore it to its former glory. I'll admit to you, Inspector, I'm very proud of what I've done to this house. I find there are not many pleasures one can take from wealth but restoring this house has certainly been one of the great pleasures in my life."

"Have you any idea, sir, what the thieves would have been after?" McCusker asked.

Reid laughed but didn't reply.

"What?" McCusker asked before finishing the remainder of his tea.

"You mean you don't know?" Henderson asked.

"You don't read the papers, or watch the telly, Inspector?" Reid added, with the exact same smile still painted on his face.

"Oh my good Go ... it can't be." DS Willie John Barr gasped like he'd just witnessed the four Beatles back together again in one room. "Mr Reid, that wasn't *the* White Swan in there on your desk, was it?"

Before Reid had a chance to reply, Barr rose from the coffee table, his napkin falling to the floor and under his feet as he sped out of the conservatory and back into the main part of the house.

A few minutes later they were all in the study again. This time Reid's posture was two inches taller with pride.

"It *is* the White Swan Decanter, Inspector," Barr kept repeating as they all stood looking at the brilliant-white, glass decanter.

The decanter, shaped like a swan, was about three feet tall, but unlike everything else in the study, it had not been splattered with blood; either that, or someone had wiped it down. So absolutely pure was the white of the glass, it looked to McCusker as if there were a 1,000-watt white spotlight shinning upwards from beneath the swan.

"Do you know who legend says this once belonged to?" Reid asked as the entire PSNI team and Reid's people gathered to study the unique swan.

The remains of the intruder were now completely ignored, apart from, that is, one member of the SOCO team who inadvertently ventured behind the desk to get a closer view of the swan, only to be seen running off, palm of hand blocking his mouth, in the direction of a flushable receptacle.

"Finn McCool," Barr replied.

"So they say," Reid replied proudly, and then, "He spent some time up around your way, didn't he, Inspector?"

McCusker wasn't sure if Reid was intentionally letting him know he was aware of the detective's homeland.

"I believe he played off a mean par up at the Royal in Portrush," McCusker offered, drawing an unsympathetic reaction from his audience. "Apparently he had a backswing that sounded like a thunderclap."

Barr was still too awestruck by what was before him to be drawn into McCusker's humour as easily as he normally was.

"There is a legend that anyone who comes into contact with the contents – supposedly McCool's acidic tears – dies a horrible death . . ."

At this point every head in the room swung in the direction of the blind side of the desk.

"Is that the actual legend Willie John, or is it maybe just the Eddie McIlwaine version for his column in the *Belfast Telegraph*?" McCusker asked.

Breakfast was concluded without any further revelations. Reid excused himself, saying Henderson would find a couple of windows of opportunity in the afternoon should the inspector have any further questions. McCusker tightened the Windsor knot of his Royal Golf Club tie into the crisp collar of his white shirt. This was his signal to his DS that he was ready to leave.

McCusker was in a much better mood as he and Barr drove back into the city centre. He'd long since given up on feeling bitter towards his (golf-widow) wife who'd scampered with all their nest-egg money. She had taken it all and just ran. There had been no vengeful letters, no rude "serves-you-right" telephone calls. She just arose, took up all of their money and walked (via Aldergrove) into the sunset. McCusker suspected she'd scampered off to America but he had neither the energy nor inclination to follow her. No, he had a much bigger problem he needed to address: the aforementioned heist had occurred four days before he was due to start his greatly anticipated retirement. He tried, unsuccessfully, to get his old post back in Portrush but his replacement had already started and consequently the only place McCusker could find an opening was in PSNI Donegal Place, Belfast.

That had been seven months ago and McCusker had, very reluctantly at first, started to fall in love with the city. He found there was an infectious energy and genuine enthusiasm from the people of Belfast. Slowly but surely he was discovering his watering holes and pit-stops for food and refreshments, one of which was the Linen Hall Library, just off Donegal Square. He had his young DS drop him off there.

McCusker wasn't great with computers, preferring instead to pick up all the information he needed amongst the hallowed bookshelves of the Linen Hall Library. Not just that, but their wee café did an amazing cup of coffee and an appetizing selection of nibbles to keep him fortified as he whiled away the hours working on his research. At least that was McCusker's story and he was sticking to it.

Today his research was focused on the legend of Finn McCool. History, McCusker firmly believed, was always written by the victors, and, thereby, much kinder to the authors than fact. For the truth you had to dig deeper. Were Robin Hood, William Tell, or Finn McCool, for that matter, real people? Or, were they all composites of people legend had been kind to because they'd unselfishly helped the poor over the rich; sided with the weak over the strong; battled for wrongs to be righted?

Tales of Finn McCool's life and times had been passed down, as far as the Linen Hall Library reference books were concerned, via the poems of his son Oisen.

As far as McCusker could make out, McCool acquired his wisdom when he burned his finger on a salmon cooking on a spit. He sucked the finger to ease the pain and, as there happened to be some skin of the salmon still stuck to his blistered finger, the young McCool swallowed the skin and thereby the salmon's wisdom.

His wife, Oisen's mother, Sadbh, who bred swans, was turned into a deer by "a dark man" and disappeared. McCool searched for her and waited patiently for her to return to human form. In the meantime he dallied with Grainne, the daughter of a High King, who promised Grainne to Finn for services rendered. But before Finn had a chance to take up the father's kind offer, she was whisked away by a young upstart called Diarmuid. Eventually, Finn forgave them both and they all became friends, until one day Diarmuid and Finn were out boar hunting together, and Diarmuid was very badly gored. One of Finn's special gifts was to be able to infuse healing powers into water simply by running his fingers through it. Diarmuid sent Finn off to find some water. Finn eventually found a river and scooped some water using his hands as a cup, but by the time he retraced his steps to Diarmuid all of the precious water had spilled through his fingers. Accidentally or on purpose, McCusker wondered. He erred to the opposite opinion of Oisen.

Finn, however, used the episode to his advantage. He continued to await the return of the deer that was his wife, Sadbh. He figured that when his wife changed from a deer back to a woman, she could suffer severe physical pain. He planned that, rather than risk her life by having to run to the nearest river, he'd always have some water in a container nearby. He also remembered his wife's love of swans, so he had a beautiful glass decanter made in the shape and lifelike size of a swan. Finn figured the beautiful white swan would attract his wife.

According to the three reference books McCusker studied, Finn McCool never died. Apparently, he is hibernating in a cave near Dublin and will be awoken in time to come and save Ireland in the hour of her greatest need. Perhaps it was this part of the legend which gave birth to the cavaliering attitude of the bankers and developers.

Conveniently, McCusker's coffee and banana muffin ran out at the same time as he completed reading the third book. He had another stop he needed to make on his way back to Donegal Pass. Within seven minutes he was on the opposite side of Donegal Square and hoofing it into Ross's Auction Rooms on Montgomery Street.

The novelty of Ross's still hadn't worn off for McCusker. He could happily spend hours in there wandering amongst the weekly changing collection. It wasn't that he was interested in buying. No, he just loved looking and wondering what stories the antiques could tell. What they couldn't or wouldn't tell, their ace auctioneer Ian McKay was always happy to hazard a guess at.

Ian McKay was everything Harry Reid aspired to be. Class is not bought; neither is it in the genes: it's in the brogues. In other words (McCusker's), it's there naturally or it's not there at all and, in either case, nothing can be done to successfully change the outcome. McKay was in his mid- to late forties; ruggedly handsome; distinguished with white, longish hair; dressed every inch the country gent and with a voice radio presenters would kill for.

"Long time no see, squire," McKay began, as he spotted McCusker walking towards his door. "Come on in and rest your weary bones. I'll order us up a fresh pot of tea and a couple of those door-stop egg sandwiches our canteen seems to specialize in."

McCusker did as he was bid and McKay closed the door to his office and ordered up refreshments on the intercom.

"I assume you're not in here just to discuss David Healy's form on Saturday again?"

"Right," McCusker said, taking the spare captain's chair in McKay's packed office. McCusker didn't make it clear whether Healy's form was on or off the agenda. "What can you tell me about Finn McCool?"

"Ah, you're on the Harry Reid case then, are you?" McKay offered in reply, moving the conversation into a different gear. "And you want to know all about his fast-becoming *legendary* White Swan?"

"Sorry?"

"Well, two auctions ago, Reid out-bid everyone upstairs to secure the absolutely stunning glass White Swan. But there was no way it was worth twelve and a half grand."

"Is that really what he paid for it?"

"Near enough," McKay admitted. "I'd put the reserve up to a top whack of £2,000 only because I was seduced by the powerful whiteness of the object. I thought it positively just glowed. But no sooner had Reid won the item and taken it out of the auction house than he was claiming it was Finn's original White Swan. The *Belfast Telegraph* took him at his word and stuck it on the front page."

"Ian, did such an item actually exist?"

"Augh, you know," McKay started expansively, "some say it did, and some say it didn't. But I'll tell you this for nothing, someone had been spreading the story around the auction houses recently, otherwise the big bird would never have reached more than the couple of grand I'd marked the reserve at."

"That's really all the reserve was?"

"Yeah and I thought I was chancing my arm at that. Tell me this, Inspector, did Reid by any chance have a UV light in the room he'd Finn's White Swan displayed in?"

"He did as it happens," McCusker replied as another piece of the puzzle dropped into place.

"Yeah, I did the same thing here. It just made the swan magnetic, made it stand out in our showroom. Anyway, Reid paid his twelve and a half grand, I was happy as a pig in . . . and then, before you know it, isn't it only all over the front page of the *Telly* claiming he'd discovered Finn's long-lost swan?"

"So why would he do that?"

"Well, let's just say that Harry has a bit of a reputation for honing in on items with a bit of an iffy providence and then he likes to rewrite history or even invent a history for said items, mostly a very expensive history."

"And do people really fall for it?" McCusker asked.

"People always want to believe in the supernatural, Inspector. It helps to make our daily lives acceptable."

"What else can you tell me about Harry Reid?"

"He's a Draperstown boy, born and bred, but about ten years ago he started to claim he was originally from Belfast, invented a wee history for himself, if you know what I mean. He's very clever though."

"How so?"

"Well, he'll never go for a scam where he could be contradicted. Let's take an example. In this instance, who is there amongst us to be able to 100 per cent claim this isn't Finn McCool's White Swan? It could even have been Marc

Bolan's White Swan. But don't you see there still are friends and relations of Mr Bolan who would have been available to positively contradict Reid if he'd made such a claim? Apart from which, Marc Bolan's White Swan, if such an item exists, is not going to get the big bucks Finn McCool's swan is going to get."

"Will he really get big bucks for it?" McCusker asked as the sandwiches arrived. The eggs were warm, exactly how McCusker liked them.

"Well, I can tell you I've had a few American dealers on to me already and one of them is prepared to go north of a million."

"Holy shit," McCusker replied, automatically and impolitely – he had his mouth full at the time. When he'd recovered he continued, "How did you come across the swan in the first place?"

"There was a house clearance up in your neck of the woods. Portballintrae. The usual thing, an old woman, Mrs White in this case, spends her whole life building up a collection of furniture, paintings and ornaments she loves and sees as her heirlooms and then, when she dies, the family trip over themselves to get rid of it all before she's even grown cold in her grave so they can put the house on the market and turn her life to their financial advantage."

"Tell me this," McCusker started in what was one of his favourite ways to ask a question, "would some dealers buy McCool's swan, even if it was a stolen item?"

"Not the particular American dealer I was referring to, but several others might."

"Really?"

"Well, just look at the story/providence/history of the item. Finn McCool, the man, the legend. The same man who created an island by scooping a hand-full of earth out of the heart of Ulster and hurtling it out to sea just so he'd have a stepping stone to get to Scotland when he was searching for his wife. The crater he created became Lough Neagh and the sod became the Isle of Man. The same wife by the way—"

"Who had been changed into a deer and disappeared."

"You've Googled it already," McKay said, breaking into a knowing smile.

"Better than Google, The Linen Hall Library actually," McCusker admitted.

"So, you know what purpose Finn had the glass swan made for?"

McCusker nodded positively, quickly.

"And did you know that McCool decreed that should anyone, other than Sadbh, ever use the water contained in the swan they would suffer the most horrible of immediate deaths?"

McCusker suddenly suffered a flash of the bloodstained walls of Harry Reid's library.

"Have any such deaths ever been recorded?" he enquired.

"Several," McKay whispered, "but then on the flipside there is another legend which says that Finn himself became eternal by drinking some of the water."

"Augh, away wit ye, Ian," McCusker moaned loudly.

"*And* even others claim that Finn created the Giant's Causeway while he sat on the coast edge weeping as he waited for his beloved wife to return. They say his acidic teardrops gave the rock-face its unique symmetrical shape."

"Tell me Ian, has anyone in modern times ever died from drinking the water?"

"No, not that I'm aware of."

"So," McCusker began slowly, "say for instance someone today, in search of life everlasting, was to die while drinking from the swan, what would happen to the price then?"

"I'd say, with a great deal of confidence, that the owner would then have on his hands an item to equal Hirst's diamond-studded skull."

"What, you mean £50 million?" McCusker shouted, totally losing his cool.

"Well, that depends entirely on which reports of the actual value of that particular item of Hirst's one believes. But in my humble opinion, under the circumstances you describe, then

McCool's White Swan would be up there and, at the very least, on a par."

Ten minutes later McCusker was being driven by DS W. J. Barr at a great speed back towards Reid's country pile close on the road to tranquil Bangor.

"So, let me get this straight," Barr said as they passed the George Best City Airport, "you think the headless victim we discovered in Reid's study was planted there?"

"Yes I do," McCusker sighed. "Don't you see, Willie John, the more Reid can add to the legend of Finn McCool's White Swan, the more he ups the asking price."

"But surely—" Barr started.

"In anyone's eyes £50 million, give or take a pound or two, is a hell of a lot of motive. I think once we discover the identity of the victim, if we dig deep enough into his life, we'll discover a connection with either Reid or one of his team."

"So, you're saying you think Reid had the victim murdered?"

"Yessir."

"But how?" Barr persisted.

"Well, I think we can rule the Four Horsemen of the Apocalypse from our suspect list."

"Yep, you're right there, sir," W. J. conceded. "I've already questioned them and they're all alibi-ing each other up, one for all and all for—"

"Wrong legend. You've inadvertently wandered into the Four Musketeers tale," McCusker interrupted, very deadpan.

"Oh yes, of course. But seriously, sir, surely it's just a wee bit too obvious. You know, renowned collector bags rare item for a steal. Item has a legend, it's sacred, protected; people die while in its company. A petty crook, we assume, dies while trying to steal it, thereby putting the value of said item through the proverbial roof."

"Fair point, Willie John, fair point, but perhaps Reid thought that the victim and his apparent crime would be the centre of our attention. A criminal with a record is caught on his premises. He probably figured we'd wrap the case up by dusk and not only that but also the taxpayers would be saved the cost of not only a trial but also the scallywag's prison upkeep when he was sent down."

"I'm still not convinced," Barr declared as they pulled into Reid's drive.

"Either way," McCusker replied, "we're about to have a very interesting conversation with the man in designer black, Mr Harry Reid."

When they entered the house it was still a hive of activity, thanks to the conscientious work of the SOCO boys and girls.

Alan Henderson greeted them outside the study and informed the PSNI officers that his boss, having gained permission from the SOCO team to remove his precious White Swan, had retired with said precious item to the folly at the foot of his two-and-a-half-acre garden. The folly was a life-size replica of the Mussenden Temple. The eccentric earl, Bishop Frederick Hervey of Derry, built the original in Down-hill, on the north Derry coast, in the eighteenth century. Like the original, Reid's was built overlooking the water. Apparently Reid had also built his favourite space for meditating as a completely secure panic room. Henderson claimed his boss had informed him that until the police were out of the house, he'd feel so much more secure down there with McCool's White Swan.

Henderson accompanied McCusker and Barr down the winding path through the mature garden. Due to the fact that the house had been built on a hill and the land between there and the folly dipped dramatically and was overgrown, in a cultivated way, with exotic trees and bushes, they didn't actually see the folly in its fully glory until they emerged from the dense undergrowth.

They could clearly hear some activity as the folly came into view. It sounded like someone beating a loose-skin drum several times, then there would be a horrific-sounding splat, then silence for a few seconds and then the same sound pattern would repeat over and over again, growing in volume the closer they got.

Henderson announced himself on the outside of the solid antique wooden door. The noise continued, louder now, but they still couldn't see what was creating it. Butumn, butumn, butumn, splat, silence.

Henderson clearly wasn't used to being ignored by anyone, including his boss, particularly with witnesses present, so he resorted to banging on the door. Still there was no reply from within and still the mysterious eerie noise continued from either the other side of the building, or the inside, McCusker couldn't be sure.

He climbed the thirteen steps to join Henderson on the threshold and put his hand on the antique bone doorhandle. Henderson put his hand out to stop McCusker. The faithful DS Barr hopped up the steps in a heartbeat to restrain Reid's PA.

The handle resisted McCusker's efforts.

"It's locked from the inside," Henderson claimed. "He always locks the door from the inside when he's meditating."

McCusker pushed his shoulder against the door.

Henderson laughed.

"It's solid oak," the PA stated, "and then steel-lined on the inside."

"What about the windows?" McCusker asked, wishing he hadn't tested his shoulder so.

Henderson had just started to laugh again when they heard glass smashing on the other side of the folly.

"That's totally impossible," a breathless Henderson offered as they all ran around the folly in the direction of the noise. "All the windows are bulletproof."

They all ran into each other as they reached the other side of the folly, the side from which they all thought they'd heard the sound of breaking glass. But the large window before them wasn't even cracked. It was dirty, very dirty, but not broken.

They all looked at each other as they heard an almighty racket from within. To McCusker it sounded like a troupe of banshees squabbling over the departing soul of the last man in the universe.

Henderson summoned Harrison on his mobile and ordered him to meet them immediately at the folly with the spare key.

McCusker thought that his imagination might now be playing tricks on him because he thought he could hear Reid walking around the wooden floor inside the folly.

"Fair play to you," McCusker said with a pat on the back to a hot and bothered Harrison three minutes later.

Henderson snapped the key from the head of security and ran, key first, at the door like a madman.

The key seemed to be meeting some resistance inside the lock as Henderson endeavoured to force it into its prime position. They all heard the other key, obviously on the inside of the door, fall to the floor. At the same time the noise inside the folly stopped.

Slowly Henderson turned the key and they all stood willing it to activate the tumblers in the lock and release the catch.

McCusker stepped up to the door, taking first place in the four-man queue. Henderson didn't object.

As McCusker opened the door, he was hit immediately by the trademark metallic smell of blood.

It seemed to the detective that actual particles of blood as well as the smell were making their way into his nostrils.

He gingerly pushed the door open further.

Inside, the folly was in darkness, apart from the daylight coming in from behind them and the unnatural amazing white glow from the glass swan, which had been positioned on a large circular table in the centre of the folly. McCusker checked all around him. This time there was no enhancing ultraviolet light, yet still Finn McCool's White Swan glowed.

Once McCusker's eyes familiarized themselves to the internal lack of light, he thought he saw something move on the other side of the table.

Instinctively he drew the door back towards him so now he was the only one able to see inside.

The next time McCusker refocused his eyes, the shadow, or whatever it was he had seen, had disappeared. He tuned into the eerie silence in the room. Then he thought he heard footsteps again on the wooden floor. He reckoned they were too light to be Reid's footsteps. They were more like the nimble pitter-patter of a large dog.

"Does Mr Reid have a dog?" McCusker asked, surprising himself that the question came out in a whisper.

"He can't abide them, won't let them near the house," Harrison whispered back.

The sound of footsteps had now completely disappeared. After a few moments of silence, McCusker opened the door again. This time he opened it fully and, aided by the daylight, they could all see clearly, in the beam of red-dusty light, a body lying face down in front of the table.

It was the comatose body of Harry Reid.

Henderson ran over to his boss and knelt beside him. W. J. Barr and McCusker followed quickly to see if they could be of any assistance.

Harry Reid lay in an ocean of his own blood and solid matter.

Barr slowly turned him over.

Henderson was physically sick on the spot.

DS Barr was somewhat more discreet; he rushed to the fresh air provided by the open door.

The last time McCusker had witnessed such carnage on a human being was as a result of a bomb.

He was convinced he could hear the sound again of someone, or something, in the folly.

A shiver ran up his spine.

He un-hunkered from beside the remains of Reid and walked slowly, carefully, closer to the brilliant white swan.

Then he saw the reason for the noise.

It wasn't the large dog he'd imagined he'd heard.

No, there before him was a deer, pacing proudly backwards and forwards on the other side of the table bearing the hallowed swan.

The deer looked up at McCusker.

Its giant eyes challenged the detective.

McCusker noticed blood generously, not to mention messily, splattered all around the deer's mouth.

Just before the deer darted past McCusker into freedom and daylight, she licked her lips.

McCusker reckoned it wasn't the lick of hunger or satisfaction of a hunger.

No, if McCusker had to describe the look in human terms, he would have said it was more the look of a woman desperate only to end the search for her man.

Darkling

Val McDermid

When the phone rings at seven minutes past two in the morning, I know I have to behave as if it's just woken me. That's what humans do. Because they sleep. "Whassup?" I grunt.

The voice on the other end is familiar. "It's DCI Scott. Sorry to wake you, doc. But I know how you like a fresh crime scene."

He's right, of course. The fresher the crime scene, the easier it is for me to backtrack to the moment of the crime. That's how I come up with the information that will help DCI Scott and his team to nail the killer. I'm a criminal profiler, you see. Once I realized my physical body was stuck in this place and time, it seemed like an occupation that would be interesting as well as being socially useful. It has the added advantage of having slightly vague qualifications and antecedents. And as long as I do the business, nobody enquires too closely about where I went to school.

I tell him I'll be there in fifteen minutes. I could make it a lot sooner, not least because I'm already dressed. But the last thing I want is to be too astonishing. I need to survive until I can resolve my situation. And that means not arousing suspicion.

When I arrive, the usual crime scene slo-mo bustle is under way. Forensic rituals round the back of an out-of-town strip mall. Tonight, for one night only, it's a theatre of the macabre.

The body's a pitifully young male, barely out of his twenties I'd guess. He's dressed in black, Goth hair to match. Silver in his ears and on his fingers. He's pale as paper and it takes me a moment to realize that's not make-up. It's because he's bled out from the two puncture marks on his neck.

"Vampires don't exist, right?" Scott says gruffly. "That's what I keep telling my girls. All that *Twilight* garbage."

"This isn't the first?"

"The third this year. We've kept the lid on it so far, but that's not going to last forever."

That's when I notice the writing on the wall. It's scrawled almost at ground level, but I can tell instantly it's written in blood. It'll take the technicians longer to confirm it, but I know I'm right. I crouch down for a closer look, earning a grumpy mutter from the photographer I displace. "Darkling," it says.

I step back, shocked. "Is this a first?" I point to the tiny scribble. "Was there something like that at the other scenes?"

"Nobody spotted it," Scott says. "I'll get someone to go over the crime scene pics."

I don't need them to do that. I know already it'll be there. I know because it's a message for me. Darkling is where I am, where I've been since I found myself trapped in this place, this time, this body. Darkling. In the dark. A creature of the dark. But now I've had a message from my own side.

And now I understand how to fight my enemy. I need to erase this darkling existence. If I can wipe the word from human consciousness, I'll be free again. Free to move through time and space in my full grace and glory, not the pale shadow existence I've had since I was jailed in this form. The murders will stop too. The three that have already happened will be undone, their victims back in their proper place in the world. That's an unintended consequence, but a good one nevertheless.

I say something, I don't know what, to get myself off the hook with Scott and melt into the night. I'm home in an instant, computer on, fingers flying over the keys. First recorded instance . . . Shakespeare. I can't help but smile in spite of the seriousness of my plight. Shakespeare. How bloody predictable is that? I take a deep breath, spread my fingers against the side of my head and will the transference.

The room is small, lit by a trio of tapers. In the flutter of light, I see a man in his late thirties hunched over a small wooden table. There's a stack of thick paper to one side of him. His sharpened quill is poised above the ink pot, his dark eyes on the middle distance, a frown line between the fine arches of his brows. His lips are moving.

"The hedge-sparrow fed the cuckoo so long,

That it's had its head bit off by its young.

So, out went the candle, and we were left darkling," he mutters.

If I was in my pomp, it would be no problem. Being physically present would offer all sorts of options for change and deletion. In extremis, I could kill. But I can only manifest as a voice. He'll think it's his own interior voice or he'll think he's going mad. Either way should serve.

"Not darkling," I say. "Sans light. It's the Fool speaking. Sans light, that's what he'd say."

He pauses, uncertain. "We were left sans light?" he says.

"Sans light," I say. "Sans light."

He twists his mouth to one side. "Not darkling. I cannot make a poet of the Fool. Sans light."

He dips the quill and scratches out the word and I dissolve back into my body. I'm amazed. Who knew it would be so easy to edit the great bard of Avon?

Next up, John Milton and *Paradise Lost*. My consciousness emerges in a sunlit garden where the great man is declaiming. There's no other word for it. But the poet is not alone. Of course he's not alone. He's blind. Somebody else has to write it down for him. There's a younger man scrawling as he speaks. I need to move fast. We're coming up to the line. Yes, here we go.

"As the wakeful bird sings darkling." Milton gives himself a congratulatory smile.

"Birds don't sing in the dark," I say. The scribe looks around wildly, wondering if he's just spoken out loud.

"Darkling," Milton says, a stubborn set to his mouth.

"They sing at dusk or at dawn. Not darkling. Do you really want people thinking you're an ignoramus? Think how it undermines the burden of your poem if the details are inaccurate. At dusk or at dawn, surely?"

"A correction," he says. "As the wakeful bird sings at dusk."

Two for two! I dissolve back into my body. These shifts out of body are exhausting. But now I've started I can't stop. The promise of being myself again is too powerful. And so I continue. Keats and his nightingale – "Darkling, I listen" becomes, "Obscured, I listen." Matthew Arnold's darkling plain becomes "a twilight plain" and Hardy's darkling thrush becomes "dark-bound thrush". *Star Trek Voyager* now has an episode called "Gloaming".

It's almost dawn and I'm almost drained. Darkling, I only have one more to go. Dr Samuel Johnson, the great wordsmith, the dictionary man. If I can remove the word from his dictionary, it will disappear for good.

I generate my final focus and emerge by the side of a fat man with a cat and a pile of manuscript paper by his side. I can read the words he has written. "Darkling a participle, as it seems, from *darkle* which yet I have never found; or perhaps a kind of diminutive from dark, as *young, youngling*. Being in the dark. Being without light. A word, merely poetical."

Then his eyes fix on where I would be if I was corporeal. "I've been expecting you," he says in his sonorous growly voice.

"You can see me?"

He laughs. "I was the doctor long before you aspired to the mantle, sirrah. And I will be the doctor again. You're trapped in a human life and when that body dies, so will you. I have fashioned darkling to hold you."

But as he speaks, the ink on the page starts to fade. The word and its definition are disappearing before our eyes. "Not for much longer. There are no citations. It doesn't exist anymore."

He glances at the page. I expect fear or rage, but I get a great guffaw of laughter. "But darkle does. The back-formation comes into being in the next century. Already, other poets have formed darkling and employed it in their verse. There is no escape from the power of the word. Did you really think it would be so easy? Darkling has taken you, boy. You are darkling forever."

The World's End

Paul Johnston

The footsteps behind me increased in speed. The man with the empty eyes and the knife was coming. I was limping, panting, desperately trying to get to the main road, but it was at least fifty metres away and I wasn't going to make it . . .

I was abroad for most of my thirties, the blood and spirit leaching out of me in the worst marriage since Charles Bovary's. I escaped by getting funding to do a master's in applied linguistics at Edinburgh University. I was born and raised in the city so it felt like I was going home, even though my parents had long moved away and I had to rent an attic room from the elderly sister of a family friend. I'd been teaching English as a Foreign Language for years and thought I'd improve my employment prospects by getting a degree in the subject. It turned out that the Edinburgh take on applied linguistics was much wider than language teaching, which I disliked intensely. I was able to study more challenging subjects such as literary stylistics, second language acquisition, bilingualism and psycholinguistics – the latter being just the thing for a budding crime writer.

It was June 1996 and we'd finished the taught part of the course – nine months of lectures, seminars, projects and exams. I was knackered because I'd also been rewriting my first crime novel since a positive meeting with an editor before Christmas, though no deal had been offered. The MSc was finished apart from the dissertation. I was pissed off because

I'd missed a distinction on the course work by one mark. Still, I went out boozing with some of my fellow students – four Brits (two called Mark), a couple of Greeks, a Russian, a Japanese and a Hungarian; the male/female ratio was about equal, but I might be wrong. I only had eyes for beer.

We went to various student haunts, where we stuck out as we were a lot older than the other denizens. We ended up in the World's End at the lower end of the High Street (you won't get me calling it the Royal Mile), probably at my instigation. The place had become notorious not long after I'd left school because of the murders that had inaccurately assumed its name: Christine Eadie and Helen Scott, both seventeen, were seen leaving the World's End after a Saturday-night pub crawl on 15 October 1977. They were found miles away in separate locations in East Lothian, both having been stripped, beaten, gagged, tied up, raped and strangled. Despite a huge investigation by Lothian and Borders Police – more than 13,000 statements were taken – their killers were never found. It was suspected that more than one murderer was involved as a witness had seen the teenagers talking to two men near the pub.

The World's End was built over the eastern extent of the so-called Flodden Wall, raised after Scotland's finest had been slaughtered at the battle of that name. Natives of Edinburgh back then were exclusive, as they still are; anything beyond the city walls was not of their world. For a local of my age the murders of the two girls still held a deep fascination. I wouldn't say that they made me a crime writer – underage viewings of *The Godfather*, *The Getaway*, *Dirty Harry* and *The Dirty Dozen* and repeated readings of the Sherlock Holmes stories were more inspirational – but they were part of my mental make-up. Things are hazy, but I imagine I held forth to the gathered company about the murders, doubtless to the disgust of the bar staff.

My memory started functioning the second a man brushed past me, grabbing my leather shoulder bag on the way to the door. It was a sign of my drunken idiocy that I'd put it on a stool at the outer side of our table, in clear view. The thing was, the bag was one of my most prized possessions, probably because no one else in Edinburgh had one like it. I bought it on a Greek island and it had slowly changed colour from pale yellow to deep brown. The leather was soft and the thick strap spread the weight comfortably across my left shoulder. I wasn't giving it up easily.

Although I hadn't run much in recent years, I was a lot lighter than I am now. I'd also been captain of the school athletics team, my events being the 100 metres, 200 metres and long jump. Pride was at stake, even twenty years after the last time I'd pulled on the vest. I was out of the pub about five metres behind the thief. He took his life in his hands by running across the junction of the High Street and St Mary's Street without looking. I did the same. My blood was up. The guy was piling down Jeffrey Street, the northern continuation of St Mary's Street, heading towards Waverley Station. And, worst of all, he was going away from me.

Three of my mates, the Marks and a Russian called Sasha, were behind me. My legs gave way and I tripped over the kerb, landing in an ignominious heap.

"Get him!" I gasped. "Get the bastard!"

They tried, but he was way ahead now.

Then something extraordinary happened.

The offside door of a parked car suddenly opened, forcing the thief to slow down, though he still hit it. By the time he got to his feet, he was held tightly from behind.

I stumbled after my friends, the skin from one of my knees having gone missing in action.

The guy holding the sprinter identified himself as an off-duty police officer.

"This is Jimmy Burns," he said. "He's well known to us."

I was still panting.

"He works out," the cop said, arms under Burns's oxters (armpits if you're not a Scot) and crossed over his chest St Andrew style.

"So do you," one of my mates said.

"Right, let's get to the bottom of this. I'm guessing the bag's the issue."

"Yes," I said, "it's mine."

"It isnae," said the thief. "It's ma gurlfriend's."

"Is that right?" said his captor. "So tell me what's in it."

"Em, a purse, some make-up and a Mars bar."

The cop turned to me.

"House keys, an empty water bottle, a file of notes and . . ." My memory returned in its full glory. ". . . a copy of *Bilingualism* by Suzanne Romaine."

"Oh aye? Let's have a look then." The bag was still in the thief's clutch. The cop undid the strap and looked inside. "What are you saying now, Jimmy?"

Jimmy was saying nothing.

"Do you want to press charges?" my saviour asked.

"Nah, forget it," I said, feeling nearer the top of the world than I should have. "Let the bampot go."

The thief glared at me, mortally offended that I'd failed to recognize him as a player.

"Right then, on your way, Jimmy," said the cop. "Next time you're for the high jump, mind."

"Thanks very much," I said.

"Not a problem, only doing my job. Get off home with you now. Burns is one to hold a grudge."

"No problem," I said, and danced back up Jeffrey Street with Sasha.

We'd been in the World's End for five minutes with a new round when the two Marks came in. They took me to one side.

"That nutter was following us, but we couldn't see him. He was saying bad stuff."

"Yeah, like 'I've gotta knife and I'll have youse all.' What do you want to do?"

I looked round at the group. I'd been telling them what had happened, seriously full of myself. Suddenly I didn't want any more beer.

"We could call police," Sasha said.

"They won't be able to see the guy any better than we can," I said. "We'd better split. We'll all go together, women in the middle. I'll tell them it's an old Edinburgh tradition after boozing on the High Street."

Which I duly did and they accepted, the foreigners in particular buying into the invented custom. We walked quickly up to the junction at the Tron Kirk and turned down South Bridge. Four of the group caught a cab and the rest of us continued on foot, splitting away one by one as we reached our turnings. I had the furthest to go, about another half a mile.

"I didn't want to tell you before," the taller of the Marks said, "but I heard the bastard again about ten minutes ago. He was saying, 'Ma blade's gonnae cut ye tae pieces,' over and over."

"Fuck," I exhaled.

"Do you want me to walk you home?"

I did, but I still retained some self-respect.

"It's okay. I can always make a hobble for it. See you at the class photograph tomorrow." He gave a hollow laugh, patted me on the shoulder and set off for his place at speed.

I looked around the empty streets and got walking before my knee stiffened any more.

Then I heard footsteps behind me. They were getting quicker. I turned down West Mayfield, hoping there would be some traffic on Minto Street at the end. I went into the middle of the road, intending to stop any car that appeared. None did. Had Embra suddenly turned into Tumbleweed Connection? I was breathing heavily, my vision blurred. But my hearing was fine – I could hear the sprinter's quick pace.

"Ma blade's gonnae cut ye tae pieces," came his mocking voice, not loud enough to attract attention.

The houses were all dark anyway. Even the main road ahead was more or less deserted.

"FUCK OFF," I yelled. "HELP."

"Bad move, ye shite."

He was on me in a split second. I felt the steel hiss of the blade near my throat and then asphalt against my face. My legs and arms were pounding at an incredible rate. I was running the fastest 100 metres of my life horizontally, but the tape was impossibly far away.

Then there was a squeal of tyres as a car drove up at speed. The weight on my body lifted and, looking round, I saw my assailant pelting down the street.

"Are you all right?" came a plummy male voice.

Hands helped me to my feet.

"Were you being robbed?" The man was heavily built and wearing a tracksuit.

"Em, no. Well, yes."

"You're confused. I'll take you to hospital."

"No, I'm okay. My lodgings are just round the corner. Could you . . . could you take me?"

"Of course. Jump in."

I didn't do that as my legs had decided enough was enough, but I managed to get them into the car. In a minute I was outside the house.

"If you could watch until I'm in the door," I said, feeling like a twelve-year-old.

The guy smiled. "No problem."

The key made scratches on the metal as I tried to get it into the hole. Finally I managed. I waved to my second saviour of the night, then pushed open the heavy door. We weren't supposed to apply the bolt, but I wasn't taking any chances. I stumbled up to the second floor and let myself into my room. It was at the back of the house so I couldn't see the street. Maybe that was just as well. If Burns had hidden in the vicinity, now he knew where I lived.

I washed my knee as best I could in the tiny basin in my room; the bath was on the first floor next to my landlady's bedroom and I didn't want to disturb her. Besides, the physical damage was minimal compared with the psychological. I sat at the table that served as my desk, elbows either side of the pile of printed pages that comprised my crime novel. It was full of disembowellings and eye removals, the hero a smart-arse private dick solving the crime of the century while exchanging scabrous repartee with his sidekick. Now it seemed as phoney as vegetarian haggis. I couldn't publish such a rucksack of lies, not even under a pseudonym.

I eventually passed out on my bed wearing only my pants, not an advisable course of action in Edinburgh, even in late June. I woke up shivering and buried myself under the covers, the sun already up. I eventually came round about midday, my stomach somersaulting when I remembered the events of the previous night. The class photo was at 2 p.m. Did I have the balls to leave the house? No, I didn't. I sat at my desk and started going through my novel, striking out the most egregious bits of flippancy. At least it took my mind off Jimmy Burns and his lifeless eyes.

I heard the doorbell and then heavy steps come upstairs. I was the only tenant, the other guy having disappeared a month earlier without a word. There was a knock on the door.

"You in there, mate?"

"Mark?" A wave of relief coursed through me. I opened the door and both Marks came in.

"So you got back all right?"

"Yeah . . . no problem."

"What are you doing?"

"Oh, fiddling with my novel."

"The big writer! Come on, the photo's in half an hour. We'll make it if we get a cab."

I found some reasonably clean clothes and followed them out. Even in the taxi I felt nervous. Was Burns lurking in a doorway, biding his time? Why had I dissed him like that? I didn't know as much as I thought about psycholinguistics, and I'm not being funny about psychos – I'm talking about how the brain processes language. I'd given the sprinting thief all the wrong language and he'd processed it in a way that had almost been terminally detrimental to my health.

We arrived in Buccleuch Place to find the staff and the rest of the class on the steps by the David Hume Tower. Many of the students broke into applause, then told the lecturers what had happened. I'm not smiling in the photo but everyone else is.

Afterwards I declined the offer of drinks and caught the bus home. I moved out of Edinburgh a week later, having spent all my waking hours fixing my novel. At least it wasn't the Famous Five with swearing, guts and gore by the time I'd finished. I only left the house twice, in the middle of the day, to buy food. There was no sign of my attacker, but I was still scared shitless.

I went to stay with my old man, wrote my dissertation, got a distinction for the overall degree and, a year later, saw the publication of my novel.

I was taken to Edinburgh for a day of interviews and photographs by my publishers. There was a lot of coverage in the local and national press, as well as on the radio. I often wonder if Jimmy Burns saw my photo above the jacket image in the *Evening News*.

I've no doubt what he would say if he had:

"Ma blade's gonnae cut ye tae pieces."

A Time to Seek

Alison Bruce

Simone guessed that the balcony measured something like eight-by-three feet, the same square footage as the bathroom then, and smaller than the kitchen and the other two rooms in the flat. But as long as the sun shone like this she knew it would remain her favourite spot.

She'd salvaged one cane chair and a matching side table from her parents' conservatory, pushed them both out on to the balcony and every day for the last week had come home to spend the first hour of the evening watching the Cam slip by. The river was one floor below and a hundred feet away; far enough to believe that the grass was green, the water pure and people who walked its banks were at a safe distance. Even when this Indian summer gave way to the bleakness of winter she imagined she'd still sit here.

The phone rang, she went inside and watched it flashing, Ollie's number showed on the caller display, but she didn't pick up. Until then the heat of sitting out there had almost felt too much, but now she guessed the sunshine wouldn't be enough to prevent her feeling chilled. She poured herself a glass of orange juice, then took it and the phone and returned to the balcony, placing the phone on the table but cradling the glass in her hand.

This glass was the sole survivor from a set of six, bought from the Sunday craft market just over a year ago. That day had been just as hot but, in the months since, almost everything had run cold, turning out to be brittle and fragile and ready to disintegrate. This glass was a rarity; there hadn't been much she'd salvaged from her and Ollie's old home. She guessed she could have gone back for more, fought for more, scrabbled around and come away with half a dozen more boxes of items that she could have argued as being rightfully hers.

She still wasn't sure why she hadn't.

A rowing team passed then, eight oarsmen plus the cox, pulling hard, their oars dipping in and out of the water. Focus and rhythm.

Focus and rhythm. Two of many things that she had neglected. In fact, she suspected that this balcony was the only place where peace and order existed in her life, everything else from her closest friendship to her career potential had been choked during this long and arduous year.

She picked up the phone and clicked down past Ollie's number, through the received calls list to the last call of yesterday afternoon. It had been unexpected. *Can you meet me at the Brunswick?*

Her gaze wandered upstream, where the bends in the river wove towards the expensive riverside apartments, towards the city centre and the pub she passed every day on the way home from work but had never stepped inside until yesterday.

The Brunswick: a quick drink had turned into dinner. Time had shifted until early evening had become closing time and could so easily have become daybreak. Thankfully it hadn't and her instinct today had been to avoid him until she'd had time to think, but now she decided that speaking to him might give her the answer. She found his number and pressed *call*.

He answered on the second ring. "I'm glad you phoned."

"I wasn't going to."

"I believed you when you said it. So what does this mean now?"

She watched the rowers slip out of sight before answering. "I still don't know. I've tried so hard to get myself back on track this year ... Do you realize the mess I'd be in today if last night had gone any further?"

He stayed silent but she could picture him, leaning forward, elbows on knees, staring down the length of the room until she was ready to speak.

Behind her the doorbell rang but, instead of answering it, she pushed the French window shut. She wasn't expecting anyone. And at this moment it didn't matter who stood outside.

"I can't afford to get in a worse mess than the one I'm already in. Do you understand?"

"You know I do. We've known each other a long time, right?"

"Right. Enough that I can see the look on your face right now." She half-smiled then, speaking to him hadn't made sense of it after all. She didn't know why she'd really expected that it might. "I need to go."

"Hang on, Simone. Can I see you? A drink or something?"

"I don't know." She stared at the glass again, "Look, I really need to go." Her smile had faded to nothing; what had she been thinking? "This is wrong," she muttered. She took a breath and spoke firmly, "Don't tell Tabby, all right? I need to get this straight in my head. I don't want to upset her."

"Why would I say anything?" He'd heard the change in her tone, and she found it easy to imagine the tilt of his head, the philosophical smile then the attempt at a playful dig. "Besides, nothing happened."

She didn't feel in the mood to be teased. "Nothing?" she snapped, "And I thought we were about thirty seconds away from doing it. Thanks."

She jabbed the red *hang-up-now* button and slumped back in the chair then closed her eyes for as long as it took to draw one slow breath. She needed to walk, to think, to tread carefully. She drained her glass and only then looked back towards the Cam.

Tabby stood in her line of sight, glaring up at the balcony, her hands wedged into her jacket and her feet planted squarely. She waited until their eyes met then turned away.

"Tabby. Wait!" Simone shouted but Tabby didn't look back. Simone ran down the stairs and out of her flat, replaying what

Tabby may have overheard with every step she took. *Shit, shit, shit.* But by the time she rushed outside her closest friend was nowhere to be seen.

9.12 p.m.
PC Sue Gully brushed the heel of her hand across her cheek. Almost two hours dealing with the aftermath of a relatively minor collision on Newmarket Road had exhausted today's quota of goodwill towards Cambridge's motorists – or at least the ones who felt being generally responsible citizens gave them the right to vent at each other once any delay ran to over about ten minutes.

The second of the two damaged vehicles had finally been winched on to the tow truck and she'd watched its tail-lights disappearing into the failing daylight. The buckled lamppost – the cause of all the cordoning off and diversions – now stood only as a three-foot-high sawn-off stump. The council truck took away the rest and, finally, this call was done.

The next came in immediately and that had been the cue for her to wipe her face, a symbolic gesture, a single moment to switch her mind from the chaos of one scene to the chaos of the next.

Unconscious female on Riverside.

As the last officer at this job she was almost certainly the closest and she had no doubt she'd beat the ambulance to the scene by several minutes. She activated the siren and moved into the traffic before swinging into the first of the side streets, weaving her way closer to the river. She saw no one until she approached the address despatch had given out; a group of eight or nine had gathered on the pavement outside a row of flats. They looked towards her as one. She felt her stomach tighten. They moved back enough for her to glimpse the injured woman. A heavyset man in a tracksuit spoke first. "She's breathing I think. We put her in the recovery position."

Gully nodded, knelt beside the prone woman and felt for her pulse. It rippled past her fingertips. And yes, the casualty was breathing. One jacket had been draped over her legs and another over her upper body.

"Can you hear me?" Gully asked, then leant closer and repeated herself more loudly. She looked up at the onlookers, "Step back a little please." They were more cooperative than the early evening motorists had been and moved enough for light from the nearest street lamp to hit the woman's dark brown hair. Blood glistened between the strands splayed on the path, a slowly swelling pool emerging from the back of her head. Gully spoke into her radio, "IC1 female, early 30s, head trauma, unconscious."

The radio crackled a response back at her. Tracksuit man moved closer again.

"Do you recognize her?"

He shook his head. "I don't know her name but she lives round here, I've seen her."

"That's Simone." A woman towards the back of the group had spoken. "She lives on the first floor at the other end of the block to me. Last name's Lewis, I think." She twisted slightly and pointed over her shoulder. Everyone's gaze followed. The building stood about a dozen feet away and the light shone from the second-floor window, illuminating the small rectangle of the balcony.

She spoke to Simone again. "Simone? Simone, an ambulance is coming. Just a couple of minutes. Can you hear me?" Gully slipped her fingers in and out of the front pockets of the woman's jeans. Empty. Gully could just pick out the siren; it had to be about a mile away. "Simone?"

She repeated the name, hoping that she could penetrate the woman's unconsciousness, but it was still unexpected when Simone's lips moved. Her mouth barely moved and the words were impossible to distinguish.

"Don't try to talk, we'll get you in the ambulance first."

Simone's eyes cracked open a fraction and the word *please* reached Gully who leant forward so that her ear was closer to Simone's mouth. The sentence began with a mumble then Simone slowed and the final words became clear. Her eyelids closed again.

Gully felt a hand on her shoulder then and looked up to find DC Gary Goodhew standing at her side. She had no idea how long he'd been there but, as ever, she wasn't surprised that he was. "What did she say?" he asked.

"I couldn't hear her clearly."

"Any of it?"

"Just the last few words . . . '*a time to die*'."

Goodhew had been about five minutes from the end of his shift when he heard the call. He wasn't the closest but found himself working out his arrival time and diverting in Gully's direction instead of returning the car to Parkside.

He arrived a couple of minutes ahead of the ambulance. Gully was tending the injured woman and the group of bystanders had already begun to disperse. One of them, a woman in her fifties, stood further back from the rest and only a few feet from the front door of the flats where the casualty lay. The woman wore unlaced shoes and a blank expression; she seemed like the best place to start. Goodhew introduced himself and gently turned her away from the scene.

"What's your name?"

"Mrs Hilton. Abigail."

"Do you recognize her?"

"Of course. She lives next door. But I don't know what happened, I heard someone shouting and looked out and saw her lying on the ground. I didn't realize it was Simone then."

"Do you know Simone's last name?"

"Lewis."

Goodhew pointed to the nearest balcony, "And she lives there?"

"Yes, and I'm next door."

"Does she live alone?"

"She split up with her boyfriend before she moved here. I see him sometimes though, and her friend Tabby. She was round earlier."

"What time was that?"

Mrs Hilton glanced at her watch as though that might have stopped at the precise moment. "At least a couple of hours ago. I was reading and my concentration broke because Simone called out to her several times. I was back from work about three, I had soup then planned to read for the entire evening. All I know is that I'd been sitting in that chair for a while when I heard her shout and I was there a while afterwards too."

"Okay." There was a gap of just a few inches between Mrs Hilton's balcony and Simone Lewis's. "Please show me."

She nodded and took him to the shared landing that both front doors faced. Simone Lewis's was locked. Mrs Hilton unlocked her own door and tilted her head towards the inside of her flat. "Just lean over."

The balcony led from the sitting room but, rather than follow him, Mrs Hilton remained in the doorway that led to the kitchen and watched him as he stepped outside. The blue lights from the ambulance were pulsing across the outside wall. He shone his torch across to next door but it took several seconds of staring through the flashing to pick out the full details. Shards of glass littered the floor and the base of a smashed tumbler lay in a puddle of liquid. Beside it a paperback was splayed open on its back. He swung the beam of the torch into each corner but there was nothing else immediately visible. Below him the sounds had quietened to just the clipped voices of the paramedics interspersed with the chatter of official radio communications. When he looked down he found Gully collecting details from potential witnesses. He directed his torch, making one quick sweep of the narrow flowerbeds outside the ground-floor window, and when he swung it back, away from where Simone had fallen, he caught sight of metal glinting in the adjacent garden's rockery.

Gully watched the ambulance doors close before turning to face Goodhew. "She regained consciousness briefly."

"Did she say anything?"

"Yes, that we shouldn't worry, no one pushed her. She said it a couple of times, too many for my liking."

"Anything else?"

"No, nothing."

"Hm." He held up the evidence bag. "I found her phone on the grass, just there." He directed his torch on to the spot where he'd pushed a Biro into the ground to mark the phone's original location. Then he pressed its buttons through the plastic and tilted the screen in her direction. "This is the last photo she took, timed at 6.43 this evening." An image of an open page of the Bible appeared. "*A time to be born and a time to die.* Is that what Simone Lewis was quoting?"

Gully read the first line and nodded. "For everything there is a season? Deep eh?" Gully ran her fingers up the side of the screen, then tapped at one corner. "Look at that, you can see the floor in the background. If you could zoom in I think you'd be able to see the tiles properly."

He hadn't noticed anything but the wording until then, but when he squinted the gold on dark terracotta tiles came into a better focus. There was something almost Celtic in their design and he recognized them immediately. "It's the Church of the Holy Sepulchre."

She frowned. "Where?"

"You know, the Round Church."

"And that means something?"

"We'll see. It'll be closed until the morning. Right now I need to find Simone's friend Tabitha."

Tabitha Whyte lived five minutes' walk from the airport and the Electoral Roll listed the only other occupant as Robert John Stanley. Goodhew could have rung ahead but he chose not to, even though it was now past 11 p.m. She'd been crying, he noticed that before anything else. He saw her surprise as she opened the door, then confusion next as he introduced himself.

"Has something happened?" Her eyes were puffy from tears, but tired too. She wore a cream cardigan wrapped across her body. She pulled it a little tighter. In another month she'd be thirty-one, but right now she looked older. "Is it Bobby?"

He shook his head, "Simone Lewis? She's a friend of yours?" He watched her closely.

She nodded.

"She's injured. She was found in the street, possibly a fall from her balcony."

"How bad is it?"

"She's in Addenbrooke's, but I don't know anymore yet."

"Has someone told her mum?"

"It's in hand."

She nodded slowly and looked beyond him, towards the head of the cul-de-sac. "You'd better come in."

She closed the front door behind them but made no attempt to move out of the hallway. "So, how did it happen?"

"You visited her earlier today? What time exactly."

"After five, maybe half-past. I hadn't seen her for a day or two, dropped by to make sure she was okay."

"And was she?"

Tabitha snorted as though one of them had just said something amusing. "Oh yes, she was fine." Despite their redness her eyes shone darkly. "She had this boyfriend Ollie. She'd been with him for about five years, thought it was the *real thing* until she found out he'd been at it with one of the temps at his work. What a cliché. Simone's beautiful and clever and he chucks it all in. Why do blokes do that?"

"I don't know." Goodhew shrugged, then thought of his own upbringing. "It's not just men though," he added.

"Oh, I realize that." She studied him and seemed to be weighing up what she should say next. He could have prompted her, but curiosity kept him silent. "Every time Ollie turns up saying he's made a mistake, Simone ends up in a mess."

"Because she still has feelings for him?"

"Exactly. And he's still with the other one. And when I went over today I thought Simone might be cut up and hiding away again. But she wasn't exactly—" She stopped suddenly. "She was on the balcony, on the phone. I didn't go up."

"So you don't know if she was alone?"

"I'm guessing she was, but no, I can't be sure." She glanced at her watch, then, instead of explaining anything further, she turned and walked through the door to the kitchen, "Coffee?"

"Sure."

She filled the kettle and switched it on but did nothing else towards preparing drinks. She leant back against the worktop. "I think she was on the phone to my boyfriend, Bobby."

"Which is why you've been crying?"

She didn't bother to reply. "She didn't know I'd be there and I heard her talking, telling him how I mustn't find out."

"Then what?"

"She saw me and I left. I guess losing your boyfriend to your best friend is pretty clichéd too. I came back here and waited, Bobby came back home and we had a huge fight." She clasped her hands in front of her, knitting her fingers together and studying the way they overlapped. "He left about ten minutes later and I haven't seen him since."

"And what time was this?"

"Just before eight. You think she was pushed then?"

"It's possible."

"All I wanted was for her to flush Ollie out of her system. I should have been more careful about what I wished for." Her gaze held steady for just a few more seconds. She blinked, suddenly fighting tears, and he saw her hands begin to tremble. "Who am I kidding? How could I want her hurt when I love her so much?"

To Goodhew it was the Church of the Holy Sepulchre; that had been the name that his grandfather had always used, but almost everyone else just called it the Round Church. He arrived a few minutes after the doors were unlocked and crossed the tiled floor towards the small information desk near the rear of the building. He'd been inside a few times. The first had been a primary school visit when they'd gone inside to make pencil sketches of the 900-year-old columns and arches. Then, as now, it struck him that the building looked far bigger on the inside than it did from outside.

There were two people at the desk, a man and a woman, both in their mid-twenties, pale-skinned as though neither saw daylight very often. He placed a 6 × 4 photo of Simone Lewis in front of them. "I believe this woman came here yesterday. Do either of you recognize her?"

The woman muttered something Goodhew couldn't catch and the man frowned, picked up the print and studied it closely. "I think you're right," he said to her, then handed it back to Goodhew. "There was a young woman who came in early yesterday evening. She seemed a bit disorientated and I asked her if I could help. She told me she just wanted to look round, asked if that was okay. I carried on doing something else then but Adrienne watched her . . ."

"Not because I thought I needed to, just because I was at a loose end. It's often quiet in here. I often watch people." Adrienne paused as if she expected Goodhew to comment. To Goodhew it seemed a pity that there were so many people that never bothered keeping an eye on the world around them, so he simply nodded and it was enough for her to continue. "When Josh was speaking to her I could see her looking behind him, trying to spot something. I guessed the Bible of course."

"There's a type of visitor who sometimes comes," Josh cut in, "not a tourist or a regular churchgoer but maybe someone whose circumstances drive them to end up here. For guidance."

Goodhew felt sceptical and it must have shown. Adrienne shook her head at him. "It happens you know. And this woman went over to the pews and picked up a Bible. She was decisive as she opened it, she didn't flick forwards or backwards, just photographed that one page."

"And then what?"

"She left." Adrienne nodded in the direction of the door. "She stood out there talking on her mobile phone for about half an hour."

"Are you sure?" Goodhew asked sharply.

"Yes. Next time I looked she'd gone."

"No, no, I mean the mobile. Are you sure she was using her phone?"

"Absolutely. Is that a problem?"

He shook his head slowly, "Actually no, I don't think it is." He saw the glimmer of the answer then, maybe not the whole answer but at the very least the next question to ask. Goodhew didn't need to recheck Simone's phone; he remembered the call history clearly and he knew that there had been no calls at all since her visit to the Round Church.

Goodhew had returned to Parkside and updated DI Marks. From then it had taken another two hours before the phone records had answered his questions. And now he waited in Ollie Maundrell's flat while Ollie's girlfriend Paula plied him with a third coffee.

"I can text him," she offered, also for the third time. She'd already assured him that Ollie would be back by one and it was still only five to.

The only conversation someone in Paula's position ever really wanted was the one that allowed her to ask why he was there, and instead the focus became time-killing small talk through each slow-moving minute. Paula heard his key in the door first and hurried across the room to speak to him. Goodhew had a clear view through to the short hallway. Maundrell had the tall and broad look of a rugby player. He tilted his head towards her as she quietly explained then tilted his head further still to take stock of Goodhew through the open doorway.

Maundrell pushed his jacket into her hands and walked into the front room. "What do you want?"

"We're investigating an assault on a former girlfriend of yours. Simone Lewis."

"We heard about it."

Paula slipped into the room behind Maundrell and stood quietly against the wall. She still held his jacket but more tightly now. During the first couple of questions her gaze remained pinned on Goodhew. "When did you last see

Simone?" he asked, and saw her focus switch to the back of her boyfriend's head.

Maundrell wetted his lips before speaking. "We broke up months ago."

"But that's not an answer to the question, is it?" Goodhew felt his own expression close down and his voice switch to a more clinical tone. "I'm asking when you last met with Simone."

Maundrell shrugged. "Months ago, Paula and I—"

"Telephone communication then?"

Maundrell's weight shifted on to the other foot. "Not as long, but still weeks back." Goodhew knew Maundrell was lying and, judging by her expression, Paula knew it too.

Goodhew glanced down at the sheet of A4 in his hand even though every detail on it was clear in his mind. "But yesterday evening Simone called your mobile."

"She might have tried, but I didn't speak to her."

"Who did then? The call lasted eleven minutes and forty-two seconds. I doubt she spoke to your girlfriend for that length of time, did she Mr Maundrell?"

Maundrell sighed. "No. Simone rang me." He turned slightly towards Paula, "It was the usual, begging me to come back. I didn't want to upset you with it."

She said nothing, her expression fixed with apprehension. Maundrell turned further towards her then, but she shrugged him away.

"He's twisting the truth," Goodhew spoke quietly. "Simone rang Mr Maundrell because she'd made a decision. It was never totally over between your boyfriend and Simone Lewis until last night. Simone spoke to him then deleted him from her phone. She ended it, Paula. And, in the end, it was nothing to do with you."

"Liar," she muttered. For a moment he wasn't sure where the words were aimed. "Psycho you called her." She flung the jacket at Maundrell. "You said she owed you. She was the reason we have no money, no life, that you're working every bloody hour paying off the debts she left you. Liar, Ollie. I found out it's all lies weeks ago, the texts, the emails, even the key to her flat. Why couldn't you just leave her alone?"

"I tried. But you and I have been fighting so much . . . I don't expect you to understand, but she has always been there for me."

"Oh, I worked that out," she snapped.

"Simone and I weren't getting back together."

"How could you when part of you had never left? Do you even know how often you mention her? Or compare me to her, or tell me about places you went together and the things you did?" Paula was leaning close to Ollie, her body rigid and her face just inches from his. "Do you even know how much she's hurt me?"

Maundrell's eyes widened. "What the hell did you do, Paula?"

"What do you think? I did what you'd promised me you'd done yourself. I've got her out of our life. I shoved her and she fell, and the only thing I regret is that she isn't dead."

Goodhew arrested her then. Maundrell just looked on in silence. "I'll need to take a statement from you, Mr Maundrell."

Maundrell nodded.

"Did Miss Lewis even know you had a key?"

"No, she didn't. I should have been more careful, Paula's always been so jealous."

At 3.05 p.m. Goodhew had called on Tabitha Whyte. She'd still been wearing the same jeans and cream cardigan as the night before and he would have thought she'd slept in them except it didn't look as though she'd slept at all. She'd eyed him warily, then held the front door open, expecting him to step inside.

He'd shaken his head. "Simone has regained consciousness," he'd told her, then watched as she'd pressed one hand to her face and drawn several slow breaths.

"Thank God," she'd murmured.

"I thought you might like to come to Addenbrooke's."

"Yes. Hang on." She'd reached back inside and grabbed a handbag from the hallway then stepped into the street, locking the door behind her. "Does she know what happened to her?"

Goodhew had waited until they were inside the hospital and close to the ward before handing her the same sheet of A4 that he'd carried for most of the afternoon. "How many of these do you recognize?"

There were four numbers on the list. She pointed to the bottom two. "Those are mine, home and mobile." She drew an invisible circle around the other two with the tip of her finger. "They look familiar but I can't think . . . hang on." She'd delved into her handbag and produced her own mobile phone. Then she'd scrolled through the address book for a few seconds "Okay, well, the top number is Simone's ex, Ollie's, and the second . . . oh." Her frown deepened. "Why is *he* on the list?"

"Who?"

"My brother Harry."

In the few seconds that had followed he'd watched deep furrows cloud her face and now, finally the realization that pushed them aside. "These are the calls to and from her phone?" she asked.

"Yes, in the last forty-eight hours."

Her skin blanched slightly and she shook her head. "My boyfriend's number isn't there, is it?"

"No."

She glanced at the door to the ward but, instead of going towards it, stepped back and dropped into the nearest seat. "I can't face her now, can I? What an idiot." She pressed her face into her palms. "What a complete idiot I've been. She was in pieces when Ollie cheated on her and I couldn't understand why she'd betray me like that." She leant back against the wall and looked up at Goodhew, "And, of course, she wouldn't."

Goodhew pulled up a second chair and sat beside her. "My DI spoke to her earlier. She remembers being pushed, but claims she doesn't know who it was."

"Well, it wasn't me."

"We know that, but I think she's scared it was."

"Well then, she's stupid," she said softly, and for the first time a small smile touched her lips. "And I guess we've been as stupid as each other then. Am I allowed to see her?"

Goodhew nodded. "We'll go in together. I need to tell her we've made an arrest."

Billy Micklehurst's Run

Tim Willocks

In the winter, Billy Micklehurst used to say, when the nights were bitter and long and you woke up before first light with your hair frozen fast to your collar, and when the hostels and dosshouses were crammed to the doors with the fallen – or when you just weren't in the mood for the company of the living – then Billy, in his raggedy suit and his laceless shoes and with his shoulders hunched against the wind, would make the long march from the nether world between Deansgate and the river, through the concrete bunkers of Hulme and the splendored decay of Moss Side, and past all manner of things upon the way, until he found the sanctuary he craved in the great necropolis of Southern Cemetery.

There were over a million graves in Southern Cemetery, said Billy. He knew this to be true for he had counted every tombstone himself – each and every one, he swore – and had read by moonlight the names and valedictions on more than just a few of them. Furthermore – and this next revelation he prefaced with a backward glance over either hunched shoulder, as if to exclude the unwelcome presence of eavesdroppers and spies – he claimed to be familiar with the still earthbound spirits of certain of those long entombed and poetically memorialized dead. The identities of these still-present dead he refused to reveal – to anyone, not even me – because, Billy said, they had entrusted him with some small but precious part of their soul, and it would have been a breach of that trust to identify those spirits who had elected him their guardian and saviour in this world.

Billy went to the cemetery because the vents from the crematorium gave off heat long into the night, and so if you slept on the vents you could curl up warm as toast. See, said Billy, burning bodies wasn't like burning wood or coal. No, burned bodies were like a kind of atomic power station. Even when the ashes were cold they gave off an invisible heat that you couldn't feel with your hands but which warmed your bones to the core. It was the spirits, see, fighting to escape from the earth. At this point – as if those very spirits were even now dancing in front of him – Billy's eyes would strain out from their sockets with a terror more pure and true than any I would ever see again. For, he explained, some of the spirits never did escape. They were trapped, for all eternity, in the Southern Cemetery. And later, towards dawn, when the warmth from the vents had faded, their ghosts would wake Billy from his sleep and torment him with their anguish.

The ghosts were real, he swore to God. He could see them as plain as he could see me. And solid flesh and blood they were too, not wispy and faint like they always were in the films. They were of all sizes and all ages – from withered old ladies who'd died alone, and big strong lads with their bodies smashed by cars, to a tiny little toddler boy scarred with pox. And they came from all times past, too – maybe fresh from just last week, or maybe from a hundred years ago or more. Billy's eyes would roll with an awful pity and his hands would flutter like broken wings. Because the most horrible thing of all was that none of them knew why they'd been left behind. They weren't bad people – and there'd been plenty of them put under out there, you could mark Billy's word; people who'd done all manner of terrible things. But how bad could a little toddler be? No, they were just people, that's all, who didn't know why they couldn't get out, nor why out of all the living there was only Billy Micklehurst to stand up in the dark and witness their suffering.

You see, they were counting on Billy Micklehurst to set them all free. And the source of Billy's torment was this: he did not know how this might ever be done.

To look at, Billy could have been ten years either side of fifty. Decades on the road, and unquantified gallons of Mann's brown, Yates's blobs and methylated spirits had forged his bone, skin and inner organs into an indestructible wreck. His face was remarkable for its eyes and its teeth. The eyes managed to be simultaneously both deep-set and ferociously protuberant; and whilst his lower jaw boasted a full set of yellowing stumps, his upper, scurvy-ravaged, gums could only field two – one canine and one incisor – which wobbled precariously and stuck out over his lip when he closed his mouth. Despite these handicaps he was quite a dapper fellow, in his way: his hair was still as black as oil and always slicked back in a greasy skein from his wide, scar-speckled brow. He always wore a suit – usually grey and double-breasted – its subtle pinstripe blotched with multicoloured stains of obscure and unsavoury origin. His shoes were rarely laced, as laces always broke and cost a fortune; and in summer – and many years before this habit became *de rigueur* amongst the self-consciously fashionable – he often appeared without socks to reveal feet as white as bathroom china and threaded with delicate threads of blue. His shirts tended to the threadbare and filthy, but were invariably brightened by a scarlet silk scarf with a gold-tasselled fringe, which he wore cravat-style around his throat.

He said – on several occasions; and always with some considerable pride – that the scarf had been given to him in 1963 by "a woman of means in Leicestershire", who herself claimed to have once slept with David Niven, during the war.

The first time I met Billy, in July 1976, he was perched like a vigilant gargoyle on a bench in St Ann's churchyard, elbows on his knees, fingers laced together, brooding on the time-polished paving stones at his feet and occasionally glancing up to sneer at the pedestrians emerging from the King Street passageway. I was seventeen years old and looking for somewhere to eat my dinner, and thought the little yard an exotic place to do so. It did cross my mind not to sit down beside the gargoyle and to find somewhere else to eat, but since this idea seemed both discourteous and cowardly I took my place on the bench a couple of feet distant from him. At this point – in this holy spot, and instilled as I was with the strictures, good and bad, of Roman Catholicism – the paper bag in my hand which contained a cheese-and-tomato sandwich and some salt-and-vinegar crisps suddenly seemed like an instrument of torture. The man had to be starving. He smelled like he was starving. Yet at the same time I didn't want to impugn his dignity by effectively saying: "Here, have a sandwich, you poor old bleeder." So I didn't open the bag. As I sat staring into space, pondering this unexpected moral conundrum, the gargoyle – elbows on his knees and fingers laced together – slowly rotated his head and looked up at me.

I looked back at him, into the deep-set yet protuberant eyes that had beheld a universe I would never know. I couldn't think of anything to say. He was lived life incarnate; and all I'd done was go to school and take exams. I just looked at him.

He said, "I'm Billy Micklehurst. And I don't give a fuck."

I raised my paper bag, as if it were an offering to a pagan idol, and said, "Do you fancy a sandwich?"

Billy squinted dubiously at the bag and said, of the sandwich within, "What's on it?"

I said, "Cheese and tomato. I've got some crisps too if you like. Salt and vinegar."

Billy said, "Go on, then." I produced the sandwich and Billy took it. When I offered him the crisps he shook his head. "Crisps give me wind."

He necked the sandwich down in huge bites that left strips of crust sticking out from between his gums and which he shoved home with the back of his hand, whilst proclaiming, with grateful references to Christ, just how good a sandwich it was. In seconds it was gone, and it seemed to me that because it had found its perfect resting place inside Billy's gut it was possibly the most perfect sandwich ever made. Billy pulled out a soiled rag and wiped butter, tomato seeds and slaver from his chin. With a magician's flourish, he snapped the rag free of debris and replaced it in his breast pocket.

"God bless you, Ginger," said Billy. He made a gesture with his hand that appeared to take in the whole world. "They're all over the place," he warned. "So don't you let 'em get their bloody hands on you."

"Who?" I said.

"Them as'll try to drag you down, and all manner of other things better left unmentioned," said Billy. He added: "You take my word for it."

And with that Billy got up from the bench and walked away.

That summer I seemed to run into Billy all the time. Sometimes he would be engaged in ferocious arguments with a ragged gathering of his brethren, waving his arms and shaking his fists and turning to spit in the gutter with disgust. On one occasion, this time in St Ann's Square proper, I saw him waltzing – with a surprising elegance and perfection of form – up and down the pavement outside Sherratt and Hughes with a can of Hofmeister held in either hand and a beatific grin on his face. On another I saw him standing rigid and mute at the exit to Victoria railway station. I smiled and said hello and asked how he was keeping, but Billy stared at me with a lack of recognition so complete that I might have been a creature from a distant galaxy. The very next morning he hailed me from the churchyard bench like an old friend, and offered me a drink of what smelled like Domestos, without the slightest memory of our encounter of the previous day.

Sometimes I'd walk round Ancoats with him and he'd show me the gutted factories and warehouses where a man without ties to bind him down might fashion himself a lair. On Sundays, sometimes, I'd go with him to the Mass organized by the St Vincent de Paul Society, in an abandoned church in the blitzlands east of the Erwell, where scores of men like Billy, and a handful of women too, would gather to hear readings from the Gospels and take communion in order to pay for the hot tea and sandwiches that followed hard on the last "Amen". You see, Manchester was "a good town for dossers", said

Billy. A good town. Much better than most. Occasionally Billy left for weeks at a time and headed south, "on matters of some importance best left unmentioned, now that they've been settled"; but he always came back, because Manchester was his town, and a good one. Why, Billy used to say, even the coppers were a soft lot in Manchester.

And so, in my imagination, and by way of Billy's tales and guided tours, another town arose more concrete and vivid than the one I thought I knew: a dark city. A ghost city. A city of outcasts stacked tall with broken majesty: an architecture of loss more monumental by far than the teeming triangle of shops and offices staked out by the train stations and unknowingly invested by the grandeur of its forgotten past. Billy's dark city was an epic whose purpose, conception and construction were far beyond the means – or dreams – of modern men, and had been built by a race whose like would never be seen again: vast and blackened red-brick hulks where generations uncelebrated and unnamed had toiled their lives away; crumbling Florentine confections which boasted of a long-vanished wealth both vainglorious and austere; wind- and weed-blown docks stacked from stones so large they might have graced the tombs of Memphian kings; vacant temples to insurance and exchange, storage and manufacture, exploitation and greed; scum-festooned canals, rusting incinerators, factory pulleys weather-welded to their chains; the silent geometry of railway arches and cobbles where feet no longer stepped; the Sharp Street Ragged School with its red and faded sign; and the chimneys slender and impossibly tall that would never smoke again. And all of it empty, vanquished, derelict, redundant and despised – by all except Billy, whose heart ached for its beauty and who knew that, like himself, this dark city's glory would soon be done and gone.

It was winter, February-winter, and bitter, and I hadn't seen Billy for months, when one evening I ran into him in Shudehill. He was matted and unshaven, sockless for all that the night was cold, and trembling from head to toe as he clung to a lamppost in a pool of yellow light and wept. He saw me approach and wrenched one hand free in a desperate invitation.

"Ginger," Billy cried. "Ginger! The game's up for Billy! The word's out! They're after me!" He paused and hissed and slaver spilled from his lips: "They're on my back!"

I took him in the Turk's Head and bought him whisky and beer, and Billy's trembles abated, though not the anguish and terror in his eyes. He stared into his glass, a man beset with demons in a world only he could see, and which he inhabited alone.

"I will tell you," said Billy, "they're never going to let me get away. Not this time. This time I'll swing, and that's a fact. You mark my words."

The tears returned to his eyes and Billy swabbed his face with the red silk scarf, whose gold-tasselled fringe was grey with dirt. He seemed shattered with confusion and grief. "And there's nowt that anyone can do," Billy whispered, as if even he who could believe in ghosts could hardly believe this. "Nowt at all."

At that time I had little idea what alcohol could do to the brain, nor any concept of the blind horror of psychosis. I didn't know that Billy's mind was the neurological equivalent of the derelict landscape he inhabited. The streets of his memory and hallucinated perceptions were randomly gutted and crumbling, bombed down and burnt out, shrouded in darkness, filled with rubble and infested with starving rats. The contents of his skull were like the scrambled fragments of innumerable jigsaw puzzles – soaked in meths, blowtorched by hardship, ravaged by malnutrition and disease – and assembled and constantly reassembled with shaking hands into fantastic pictures, distorted and yet punishingly real. Amidst those bits of puzzle forged from delusion, psychosis and a brain-damaged imagination propelled into dominions awful and unknown, there were without doubt great slabs of real memory, real events, real crime, atrocity and suffering. Yet which was which – which was real, which imagined and which the malformed offspring of the two – no one would ever know, least of all Billy himself. For Billy, all these things were as concrete as the table he sat at.

The game was up for Billy. They were after him. And he would swing.

Despite my ignorance, I did know that Billy was ill – very ill – and offered to get him up to the Royal Infirmary for a check-up and a rest; some clean sheets; a quick wash and brush-up, that's all. Billy lurched to his feet with alarm. He stared at me as if I were suddenly revealed to be one of "They". Then he turned, abruptly, and stalked off through the door.

I caught up with him outside, but Billy would have none of it. If he went to the Royal he was dead. The word was out for Billy Micklehurst. They were already on his back. The minute he lay down in that hospital bed "they'd 'ave me like that" – he snapped his fingers – and the next I'd hear of Billy his bones would be floating in the Bridgewater. No. It was now or never. He had to make his run while he still had the chance.

I didn't know what to do, and for all I knew Billy experienced these episodes all the time and always managed to escape their clutches, so I shoved a five-pound note in his pocket, which Billy seemed not to register at all, and told him to take care of himself.

"God bless you, Ginger," said Billy. And with that he disappeared into the night.

Standing there, I wished I had the guts to go with him. But it was dark and cold, and I was too sensible or scared or both. I didn't know if I would've lasted the night, even if he did. I assured myself that Billy's indestructibility would see him through to dance another day with a beatific smile on his face. But this wasn't to be the case.

Three days later, in St Ann's churchyard, one of Billy's fellow travellers, who introduced himself as "Brady", and whom I recognized and who knew me to be of Billy's acquaintance, collared me at the passageway to King Street.

"Billy's dead," said Brady. "I thought you'd want to know. He strung himself up from a cross in Southern Cemetery, with that fancy red scarf he always wore. You know."

Billy Micklehurst – the indestructible man – had killed himself. It seemed impossible and yet inevitable. Had he made his run to the graveyard with that bleak purpose in mind? Or had the ghosts of anguish woken him from his sleep and driven him to die alone in a vortex of isolation and fear? Whatever the sequence or intent, impenetrable despair had made hanging himself from a tombstone a more alluring prospect than the pain of the next day's dawning.

I told Brady I was sorry.

Brady nodded, and agreed that it was a right shame. But Brady walked the hard road too and he pointed out that these things happened, and that, after all, Billy Micklehurst had lasted a lot longer than most. And so we parted in the churchyard and left it at that.

I found out from the police that it was true. Billy had hung himself from a cross; no foul play was suspected. No one claimed his body and they buried him in a pauper's grave in Longsight, which in the end is as good a resting place as any other. Billy had lived his life the way he'd wanted to and the city – like all cities – had much darker tales than Billy's to tell. Yet I thought of him: every time I strolled through St Ann's Square, or up Shudehill, or passed through Ancoats on the 236. I couldn't get him out of my mind. So one night the following summer, after I'd been out late in Chorlton, I walked through Southern Cemetery to see if Billy's ghosts were still around.

They weren't, as far as I could see, though it was an eerie spot to be sure. I thought of Billy, encircled by the ghosts he could not free, and wished for some supernatural event or revelation of the kind I never believed in. No such event took place. So I imagined it instead. I imagined Billy's spirit arising – indestructible – from his pauper's grave in Longsight, and swooping down from the heavens like a raggedy Pied Piper to rally the earthbound dead who'd never done wrong. They all saw him coming and they cried out his name – "Billy!" they cried, "We're 'ere! We're 'ere!" – and Billy laughed and rolled his eyes and brandished the scarlet scarf from Leicestershire in his fist. And this time – now that he too was free, and had made good his run – the ghosts were able to cast off their bonds and follow him. They circled the necropolis once, with Billy laughing in the van, then he led them into infinity and they were gone.

No such exodus happened – or, at any rate, I wasn't there to see it – but it cheered me to think that it did; and it still does. So to this day, when I'm blue – when the game is up, and the word is out, and they're on my back – then I think of Billy Micklehurst, and the last run he made, and Billy helps free me from torment too.

Vertigo

Maxim Jakubowski

I kill people. That's my job.

I get paid for it. Well, I try not to worry about the moral implications of my trade, and I know that in the majority of cases the people I am eliminating are bad people if only because my employers are bad people themselves. Makes sense, no? Although I have actually never met the people who settle my bills. For security reasons, it's all done at one step removed, through the phone, the internet or by coded messages and left-luggage lockers in train stations or other places which attract discretion.

The little I see of my victims, whether on the photographs in the dossiers I am supplied with beforehand, or in the flesh, when I first track them down, observe their goings-on and plan the hit, normally confirms my assumptions: they look shifty, dishonest, dangerous and tick all the wrong points. And in some cases, they just look perfectly normal. It doesn't bother me either.

I do have certain rules and I stick by them.

No children, no witnesses, no one under police protection.

I entered the hitman profession by accident. But then isn't that how most careers develop?

I needed some cash fast. I have some expensive hobbies and collecting rare books is one of them. And when a title I lust after appears in a dealer's catalogue and if my funds are insufficient, that's when I indicate that I'm available for a job. In between books, I lead a normal life. I am not a greedy man, you see. I am pragmatic, dispassionate, logical. That's what keeps me out of trouble.

I even sometimes think of myself as something of an artist.

There are so many ways to kill a person. Many of them are vulgar, I find. If the client wishes the hit to be loud, spectacular, sometimes in order to make an impression, I comply. But in most instances they leave the minutiae to me, and that's the way I prefer it. I never use the same weapon twice, vary my methods. There are even cases where I can manage to make the death look accidental. Depends on my mood, the circumstances, the location. As I said, I'm a pragmatic sort of guy and I get a real kick out of improvisation. Which doesn't mean I'm neglectful when I make sudden changes to a plan. I still remain careful and go by my own rules.

On this occasion, a dealer in Belgium was advertising a first edition, not only in perfect condition and with dust jacket but also signed by both authors, which was pretty rare, of Boileau-Narcejac's *D'Entre les Morts*. I actually do read French, not that I soil any of the books in my collection by actually reading them. I already had a reading copy, a later paperback reissue of the title. The film is actually better than the book in my opinion. But my principal motivation was the fact that this thriller novel had later become one of my favourite Hitchcock movies and, actually, one of my favourite films altogether. The price the dealer was asking was outrageous, but as I said neither of the now-deceased authors was in the frequent habit of signing copies of any of their titles, and once I saw the listing, my lust for the book could not be sated.

Her name was Madeleine.

Normally I don't wish to know too much about the reasons behind the jobs. Makes things easier. But in this instance the dossier (which I had of course destroyed *Mission Impossible*-style after first carefully noting its contents) had spelled it all out. There's nothing new under the sun. Rich husband, unfaithful wife, money involved. The usual shitty reasons.

She was in the habit of cruising the plush hotels that circled the airport where she picked strange men up in bars. She didn't do it for money, which she was not short of. No amateur whore, she. She did it for the sex or whatever else she was after. Never went with the same man twice.

It didn't take much planning.

I followed her in my hire car from the moment she drove off from the mansion in which she and her husband (conveniently away that week at a trade convention in St Paul, Minnesota) lived in the plush suburbs of the city.

I'd been tracking her for a few days, checking out her habits, the hotel she liked to frequent. She flitted between a half dozen four-star establishments and I'd booked rooms in all of them beforehand under an assumed name and a credit card which couldn't be traced to me.

When I saw her drive her hybrid Prius into the underground car park of the Royal & Golf, I rang to cancel my other reservations pretexting a flight delay and parked across the Boulevard and was already checking in at the reception desk and picking up my electronic door card by the time she emerged from the elevator which connected the hotel lobby with the parking area. She went straight to the lounge bar.

I entered the dimly lit room in which a mediocre jazz pianist was tinkling the ivories in a corner with a repertoire ranging from Gershwin to Cole Porter and back to Gershwin again. Someone should have put a contract out on him long ago, I felt. But I didn't do jobs for free.

She was sitting at the bar and seemed familiar to the bartender. She never drank much, I knew. Just nursed a couple of glasses over a whole evening unless she connected with someone, usually businessmen passing through the city and stuck in the particular hotel between flights. Mostly gin and tonics, which was sort of more European than American.

I sat on a stool across from her. There were barely half a dozen people in the bar; it was still early in the evening. She was daydreaming. From observing her over the last few nights I knew she never took the first step. Which reassured the punters who might be nervous and feared they were dealing with a professional. She dressed elegantly but conservatively and did not look like a woman of the night, which was why she was not bothered by the barmen or hotel security staff. She could have been any business executive in town for meetings halfway between the coasts. Bored. Available.

She had style, did not throw herself at men. But there was an air of sadness about her, an emptiness that made you want to call her over and get her to lay her head on your shoulders while you stroked her long, lustrous dark hair.

"A drink for the lady," I beckoned the barman.

She acknowledged me with a faint smile.

Looked at me, the smile broadened. I was acceptable.

"Thank you . . ." Took a glance at my own glass. "What's that you're drinking?" she asked.

"Just Pepsi," I said.

It was always a good gambit to begin a conversation. A man who didn't drink alcohol. I never quite figured out whether the fact I did not drink made me appear more reliable or more remarkable. At any rate, I knew there were no rumours circulating about a Cola-drinking killer at large.

Her eyes were ebony black, deep wells of melancholy. Her lipstick just the right, discreet shade of red. Her cheekbones prominent and rouged to elegant perfection against the white tundra of her skin. She reminded me of Snow White. Her tailored suit top was open just one button down so you could catch a glimpse of the thin alley of her cleavage, and her breasts appeared to be milky white. Her voice was husky, a bedroom sort of voice. She didn't wear her wedding ring.

Normally, one would have conversed and quickly raised the subject of the unhappiness in her marriage, but I was aware she was on the prowl and knew all the normal preliminaries were quite unnecessary. I was the only willing male in the bar right now and I had passed her initial test of acceptability, it seemed.

"We could have a last drink up in my room," I suggested.

She agreed.

We were by now speaking the same language of things untold.

As we entered the elevator, I caught a whiff of her perfume. Anaïs Anaïs. I'd always had a nose for fragrances. Sometimes that's how I remembered women. Not just their bodies, but also their perfumes. Call me sentimental.

Her ankles were a thing of beauty, thin, firm, curvy, like a delicate sculpture of flesh, and the shoes she was wearing, heels just right, neither too short nor too high, like a showcase.

Constrained within the thin grey material of her suit skirt, her arse swayed gently over strong hips.

We had already kissed before we reached the top floor where the room I had booked was situated.

Yes, we fucked.

Some of you might feel that was taking undue advantage of her. That I could have done the deed without going to bed with her (although to be technical about the whole thing, not all of it actually took place on the bed . . .).

I disagree.

Now, I might not be God's gift to womankind but I did feel she deserved more than a peck on the cheek before I got around to the business of the night. If you feel that was an act of selfishness, then you are entitled to your own opinion and I won't come after you with a SIG Sauer or a dagger drawn if you persist in thinking that.

We made love.

She drew a deep sigh as I entered her for the first time and her fingernails raked my back as she held tight to me while I thrust inside her. Her legs circled my buttocks and gripped me in a vice of desire, inviting me to go ever deeper and reach her furthest sexual connection points.

When I came, and opened my eyes and looked at her face, I caught a few tears pearling down her pale cheeks.

"Are you okay?" I asked.

"Yes, I'm fine," she reassured me. "It's silly. I always cry a little when I'm fucked. Just the way I am. Don't let it bother you." And she attempted a feeble smile.

We lay together in the darkness a long time.

Madeleine didn't want to talk.

Neither did I.

Maybe this surprised her, as all the men she picked up on her lost evenings no doubt bombarded her with the customary questions as to why she did this, why she was unhappy, if they were sensitive enough to the situation, or just treated her disdainfully once they'd enjoyed the fuck they were seeking and found her eminently disposable.

She gave me a few curious glances, peering through the penumbra of the room, expecting some form of reaction.

I was different.

It was the middle of the night by then. Soon, I knew, she would want to leave. She never stayed with any of the men she slept with until morning. It would have been too intimate.

"You know, the view from the balcony is incredible. Did you know you can see the whole city and its lights? It's really great. Let me show you."

She hesitated one brief moment then consented and rose, regally naked, from the bed. At the sight of her body, my heart seized a little. She now looked smaller without the heels, the clothes, like a little girl lost in a deep, dark forest.

I took her hand, slid the window open. It was a summer night.

"It's okay," I said. "No one can see us this high. Know we are naked." I kissed her neck as we stepped across to the balcony rail. My hands held her waist. Her skin was warm and ever so soft.

"It is beautiful," she agreed, taking in the view that stretched for miles until the horizon of night and electricity just faded into nothingness. She shivered a little, as the breeze caressed our undressed bodies.

"Good," I said as my hands left her waist and rose.

One sharp push and she tumbled over the balcony rail and fell into the void.

Her white body flying downwards through the night was like a broken butterfly in flight.

She didn't even scream.

By the time she reached the ground I was already back in the room and it only took me a couple of minutes to dress, gather her clothes, her bag and the bed's crumpled sheets, dust the few surfaces I knew I had been in contact with and make my way to the ground floor through the service stairs and find my car. It hadn't even been ticketed.

I scattered her belongings in dumpsters throughout the next city fifty miles down the highway and caught the first morning shuttle flight out to the East Coast after returning the rental car.

In all likelihood it would be reported as a suicide.

Job done.

And if you were expecting that on my next assignment I would meet another woman in a bar who would have looked just like her but wearing her hair a different way and in a different colour, and calling herself Judy, you'd be sadly mistaken. Life is not that ironic.

Death is.

And if you really want to know about the next hit, well it was a slimy Cuban in the drugs business and I slit his throat.

The Baker Street Cimmerian

Rhys Hughes

"By Crom, my dear Watson!"

The man who uttered this exclamation sat awkwardly in a chair by the fireplace and his blue eyes glared moodily at the page of a newspaper that he was holding open at arm's length.

"Yes, Holmes? What seems to be the bother this morning?" Dr Watson spoke with a mildness that was forced.

The barbarian squinted. "This article here says that something devious is afoot somewhere and that police are baffled. Perhaps I should offer my services as usual, and employ my superior intellect to solve the case!" He clenched his rugged jaw and brooded.

Dr Watson licked his lips. "I hope you don't mind me pointing this out but you're holding it upside down again."

"Bah!" The man called Holmes tore the newspaper in half with barely a twitch of his mighty biceps, then he stood and bellowed, "Something is afoot whether you like it or not. And here's the evidence!" And he hurled a severed bloody foot on to the carpet.

"I see," meekly answered Dr Watson. He spooned three sugars into his teacup and stirred the sickly-sweet beverage for several minutes. Then he asked, "Where did you get this one from?"

"Some vile dog that was busy inserting square pieces of paper through the horizontal slit in the front door not long after dawn. I was outraged by such behaviour and pursued him along the street. He didn't get far before he was forced to hop the rest of the way."

"Ah, the postman." Dr Watson swallowed a mouthful of tea unhappily and the teacup rattled on the saucer in his hand. He added, "Did you keep the letters? They may have been important."

"By no means. I made the fool eat them before I let him go."

"But there might have been a tax demand."

"Sorcery and magic, I call that!" snarled the barbarian, pacing up and down the room in agitation. His broadsword stood leaning in a corner, so he snatched it up and began practising thrusts and swipes against invisible foes, his reflexes inhumanly fast, his loincloth flapping disagreeably as he danced with astonishing grace on the balls of his bare feet, the muscles of his naked chest rippling in harmony with each other. Dr Watson observed this performance nervously but also in awe.

There was an abrupt knock on the door. Before he could stop himself, Dr Watson had shouted, "Enter!" as a reflex. The door opened and a man nimbly stepped over the threshold at the exact instant that the barbarian was executing a particularly long thrust. The wide point of the blade went through his breastbone with a crunch. The new arrival opened his mouth soundlessly and his bulging eyes went blank.

"Oh dear, Holmes! That's the police commissioner!"

"Impossible, by Crom! I killed the fellow you refer to last week with a spear when he loomed unwisely out of the fog."

"This is his replacement, the *new* police commissioner. You should try to be more careful. They don't grow on trees!"

The barbarian immediately rounded on Dr Watson. "Have you seen a man *grow on a tree*? It is ancient despicable witchcraft, I warrant, and I'll have no gentle dealing with the dark arts."

"Just a figure of speech, Holmes. Calm down!"

The sword was withdrawn with a squeak and the body collapsed, thick gore pulsing and watery blood spurting from the large wound. Dr Watson kneeled down by his side and tried to hear the message that the expiring man was gasping, but it wasn't until he applied his stethoscope to the blue lips that he was able to decipher the words.

"There has been a theft of jewels . . . Lady Muffintop was burgled last night in her mansion . . . The window was forced and so was her virtue in her own bed . . . Rubies, emeralds and diamonds, precious heirlooms taken by some heartless villain . . . Who could have done such a thing! . . . He also slashed the framed portraits on the walls . . ."

The black-haired giant laughed and wiped his massive sword clean on the dying man's trouser leg. "It was me, by Crom! She was a fine wench and with the talons of a hawk! My back is raked free of all the itches that your cursed 'soap' gave it. And when I had finished with her, she begged me to ravish her again! As for the gems, they belong to any man with the heart to take them. That is the true law."

"Oh, Holmes! You should try a little restraint . . ."

The icy blue eyes flashed in quick anger. "Bah! I spit on the values of your so-called 'civilization'. What do your decadent and perfumed virtues mean to me or to any Cimmerian? The 'barbarian' was alive aeons before the urbanite and will persist aeons after."

Dr Watson nodded resignedly. "You may be right."

"Ha! By Crom, you are a sly fox, changing your mind whenever it best suits you, and you lack merely the hook nose and curled blue-black beard to be a Shemitish counterfeiter! Truly you would have thrived in my own world in one of the decadent eastern cities."

"But, Holmes, we've talked about this before. Until we discover just how you got here, *this* is your world now—"

But the barbarian was daydreaming, his mouth curling in a vast grin of lustful nostalgic delight. "Those eastern cities with their eastern women! Wide hips and generous bosoms. Ah, the wenches of Zamora, of Khoraja, Zamboula, Khauran, and that nameless city-state where I helped Murilo defeat the pet ape of Nabonidus! The sweetness of their lips crushed into mine, the firm duskiness of their thigh flesh and the rosy freshness of the aureoles surrounding their russet nipples!"

Dr Watson was embarrassed; his cheeks flushed, he cleared his throat and brushed a few loose grains of sugar off his coat. "That doesn't sound very appealing to *me*, I must say; but the morning is halfway gone and we haven't even started on solving a case yet!"

The barbarian brooded and he sighed profoundly.

"In fact," continued Dr Watson, "we haven't solved a case since 'The Adventure of the Neglected Cake Tin' two weeks ago. That's a very poor showing. Why the dry patch, Holmes?"

"I lack inspiration, perhaps that's why. By Crom, I am bored cooped up in these lodgings like a pig awaiting a butcher's knife. I should be on a fine steed lashing out with axe and sword, splitting the thick skulls of the warriors of Vanaheim and Asgard! Soft living has befuddled my mind. I need the clean air of the mountains, the scent of blood in my nostrils, the glitter of frost on the bones of my enemies."

Dr Watson said cautiously, "Well, Holmes, perhaps you should try the cocaine? It's about this time of day when you habitually take a dose. I'm sure it will give you the required inspiration."

"Bah! That effete white powder! I saw the effects of the pollen of the grey lotus on the minds of men, turning them into cannibals gnawing the flesh off each other in demented fury, when I was but a young thief. I'll have nothing to do with any powdered drugs. I'll stick to honest ale like a trueborn Cimmerian! Which reminds me that I do indeed have a gigantic thirst! Let us hasten to the tavern, Watson!"

And before the other man could raise an objection, the barbarian was out of the door, down the stairs and in the street, oblivious to the chaos his presence was having on pedestrians and traffic. Dr Watson hurried to catch up. Along numerous sidestreets they went until they reached a pub in one of the seediest quarters of the city.

Striding inside, the barbarian cried out to the landlord, "Ale, by Crom! The darkest and strongest brew in the house!"

"A glass of grapefruit juice for me, please," added Dr Watson.

The landlord pulled a pint of frothy stout.

"Bah! That's a glass for a child!" roared the barbarian. "Give me a real drinking horn fit for a warrior!" ("They don't do drinking horns around here," hissed Dr Watson ineffectually.) "I spit on this transparent thimble of weasel milk!" But he drained the pint in a single gulp and leaned over the counter. "There! That flask will suffice!"

"It's the cleaner's bucket, sir," retorted the landlord.

The edge of the broadsword came down hard on the wooden counter, embedding itself half a yard deep, and it was withdrawn with a wrenching noise so horrible that everyone present covered their ears with their hands while the landlord hastily removed the mop and filled the wooden bucket to the brim with Guinness. The barbarian took the bucket, threw back his head and inverted it over his gaping mouth.

Dr Watson wore an apologetic expression as he watched the throat of the drinker throb, though much of the brew spilled down his scarred chin and over the rippling muscles of his chest. At last he held aloft the empty bucket and cast it aside heedlessly, belching an astoundingly loud belch, wiping flecked lips with the back of a hand.

"By Crom, now I need a piss!"

And without any shame whatsoever, he lifted his loincloth, relieved himself where he stood and grinned. The arc of yellow rose high, came down on the brass foot-rail of the bar, splashed over the trousers of Dr Watson, who moved a few steps to the side, while the barbarian loosed another barrage of belches in mid flow.

"That's better! Now I feel ready to tackle a case!"

There was utter silence in the pub.

A man in the corner came forward through the gloom. "You are the famous Sherlock Holmes? You don't look the way I imagined, but that doesn't matter. Perhaps you can help me? Shall I tell you a little about myself and the trouble I am experiencing?"

Dr Watson interrupted at this point. "No need. Holmes can work out those things for himself. It's his speciality." And he nudged the barbarian in a meaningful way, but the barbarian only blinked, scratched his mane of black hair and clenched his huge fists.

"Go on, Holmes," Dr Watson urged. "Remember what I told you, how I showed you to make logical deductions?"

"Yes, yes!" growled the barbarian, studying the newcomer with a gaze so blue and piercing it seemed more like the twin prongs of a bident made of an amalgam of steel and lightning ("I've heard of a trident, but never a bident!" complained the landlord to Dr Watson, who shushed him) than a look that one man might bestow on another.

"Well then, what do you *deduce*?" urged Dr Watson.

The barbarian struggled to speak. "There is a bulge in the fellow's hat, which means he is concealing something there, perhaps a barometer, and this suggests he has red hair and a fondness for dog biscuits, or maybe he is contributing to an encyclopaedia of snakes that . . ." An enormous frown runnelled the barbarian's brow. "No, start again. There is a blister on the third toe of his left hand, or the fourth finger of his right foot, which can only mean that his sister's brother's wife's parrot is a . . ." He ground his teeth together in agitation. "Let's see. The stain on his trousers logically suggests that his bank manager desires . . ."

The effort was too much. With a demented howl that would have sent all the wolves of London baying in savage harmony, had there been any in the city at this time, the barbarian snatched up his sword again, swung a mighty blow at the newcomer and lopped his head clean off. The head jumped over the bar, landed with a sound like half a coconut, rolled along the floor and somehow got under the feet of the landlord, who tripped and fell and banged his own head on a cask.

Blood flowed into the sawdust. The barbarian could not ignore the call of its aroma and patterns. He went wild, swinging his sword in a blur of death, cutting off the heads of every customer present in the pub. Only Dr Watson was spared as usual. Then the berserker fit left him and he ceased mowing down the regulars. None was left.

"You didn't handle that as well as you might have done," ventured Dr Watson meekly, "but no matter: you tried your best and that's all anyone can ever do really. Next time you might get the hang of it; but I suggest we leave this establishment now and go elsewhere. Perhaps we ought to lie low in the park for a couple of hours?"

The barbarian said nothing in reply, gave no indication he had heard the words, but allowed himself to be led out of the pub and along various streets to the gates of a spacious area of greenery, where couples strolled arm in arm and ducks circled on a lake.

They sat on a bench and Dr Watson said, "Have you given up on the deerstalker and pipe, Holmes? You really should try to get used to them if you want to fit into your adopted role."

The barbarian thrust his sword into the soft earth between his gaping legs and let it stand there, vibrating with a curious enigmatic note. "What use is that cloth helmet against the arrows of Hyrkania or the spears of Stygia? As for a pipe: I care not to fill my lungs with noxious fumes, for they are already clogged with smogs. By Crom, the air of this city stinks like the breath of a Kushite toad god!"

"But they are necessary props for your present role."

"I'd sooner disembowel you than perch that thing on my head." The nostrils of the barbarian flared. Then something caught his eye, a child sailing a model boat on the lake, and his dangerous mood was gone in an instant. He leaped up and gestured.

"What's the matter?" Dr Watson murmured.

"A ship! A ship with sails!" came the excited answer. "I recall when I sailed for Bêlit, queen of the black coast, a pirate with the compassion of a panther! We prowled and slayed for many moons and sank innumerable merchant vessels and burned scores of villages. Bêlit was voluptuous but lithe, slender yet formed like a goddess!"

Dr Watson said meekly, "Was she *the* woman?"

The barbarian turned and glowered. "What do you mean by that? Yes, she was a woman. Do you think she might have been a man in disguise? I say no! Despite her thirst for the blood of weaklings and a hunger for the property of chiefs and kings, she was a lady, but a filthy whore in bed all the same! Wenches by the hundreds I have known, and she-devils by the dozen, but Bêlit most assuredly had ivory globes in the top twenty breasts ever witnessed by these eyes, which have roved over the chests of fairest womanhood from Aquilonia to Khitai!"

Dr Watson kept his mouth shut and watched the boy and the boat. He was taken by surprise when his companion suddenly ran and jumped into the lake, landing among the startled ducks and creating a huge wave that sank the model and washed over the boy, who scarpered off howling. Dr Watson watched the display with dismay.

"Control yourself, Holmes, for the sake of decency!"

"Bah! I am no pampered catamite to live according to the rules of any master. I make my own destiny. It does a true man good to have a bath on occasion. You should try it yourself, Watson. But we are wasting time! It seems to me that we must find a new case."

"My thoughts exactly," sighed Dr Watson.

The barbarian splashed to the shore and stood there, gleaming dully in the weak sun, his eyes like blazing sapphires.

"Over here, my dear Watson. I spy villainy in progress."

"It's an ice-cream stall, Holmes."

"A man who can make ice scream? A wizard or enchanter! In the dim fastness of remote Hyperborea I met such vermin and extinguished their lives with honest cold steel. Like this!"

"Restrain yourself, Holmes. The man is innocent."

But the barbarian had already dragged the vendor out of his booth and was stamping on his head with his iron-nailed boots, while casual strollers took a detour around the spreading circle of crimson. Then the barbarian knelt and sawed at the man's neck with a serrated knife until his mangled head rolled free. He stood triumphantly and Watson led him away while the severed head rolled hollowly across the path, over the grass verge and on to a lawn where some youths were kicking a football about. Somehow the head got mixed up with their sport and was kicked into an improvised goalmouth with a splat. Nobody cheered.

"That was gratuitous, Holmes. You're not playing the game properly. I am starting to think you don't really want this opportunity at all, that you regard it only as a nuisance. I suggest we forget about solving new cases today and go and visit Arthur instead."

"Bah! He asks too many questions. I dislike him."

"This is how we make our living." Dr Watson lowered his voice. "We tell him what we've been up to, he writes it down, publishes it as a brand-new tale and shares the payment with us."

"I would prefer to live on plunder and booty!"

"Yes, well I'm not so adept at such things as you. I rely on cash from Arthur to pay the bills. Come on, let's go and see him and tell him about that very peculiar case we solved last month. I've given it a title, 'Twenty Thousand Red-Headed Leagues Under the Sea', but I'm sure he'll change it. He always does. This way, Holmes . . ."

"He doesn't seem to trust me. One day I shall be compelled to send his flabby soul to whatever hell he believes in."

Dr Watson sighed. "Of course he trusts you. It's just that you haven't been an especially profitable substitute for the real Sherlock. Try to see it from his point of view. And remember that his middle name is the same as your own. So you are kindred spirits."

Defeated by this logic, the barbarian allowed himself to be led to the house of Arthur, who received them politely and eagerly. Dr Watson told the story of the case mentioned above, hugely embellished, while Arthur made notes. The barbarian endured all this with barely tamed impatience, his eyes roaming the room, looking for possible plunder. One dark night it might be worth breaking in here and—

Something caught his attention, a flickering shape in the corner. Like a large moth it fluttered among the shadows between the grandfather clock and a cabinet. The barbarian peered more intently. It was a tiny woman with wings! Drawing a poniard from his belt, he estimated the range and angle and with a snap of the tendons of his forearm, as fast as the crack of a whip, hurled the blade through the air.

It struck the creature and pinned it to the wall.

"My fairy!" shrieked Arthur, jumping up and running to the scene of the slaying. He was unable to draw out the poniard and clenched his fists in anguish. "You killed her! My only concrete proof of the afterlife! Why did you do such a thing? Why, you brute?"

"I am a Cimmerian. I was born on a field of battle. The screams of the dying are sweet music to my ears. Slaughter and rapine are the best things in life. That is why," the barbarian replied.

Arthur slumped and his eyes shone with tears. "Why did you come to our world? Why did you have to take the place of the real Sherlock? It's so unfair. What happened to him? Did he end up in your own world? Did you swap places thanks to some cosmic mix-up no better than a bad joke? I want him back, I want the real one back . . ."

The barbarian shrugged. "I have already told you what happened. One moment I was in the forest of the Pictish Wilderness, attempting to outrun the band of painted warriors who were pursuing me, seeking a vantage to make a stand and sell my life dearly to them, when I burst into a clearing in the centre of which stood a stone circle."

"A temple of the people who were chasing you?" Arthur was intrigued despite his grief. The barbarian shook his head.

"It was very ancient and no work of the Picts. Perhaps it was as old as Atlantis or older. To reach the far side of the clearing I had to run through the circle. As I passed the outer ring, the air shimmered, everything went black and a moment later I found myself standing in a room of that cursed Baker Street lodgings with no way back. I was furious and yet too dazed at first to respond as I should have, by slicing with my sword through the neck of the man who occupied the room."

"I was even more dazed than you were," said Dr Watson.

The barbarian ignored him and continued: "By what agency I know not, we became friends and he persuaded me to play the role of this 'Sherlock', who had been standing in the spot that I arrived at. But I now believe I made a mistake. I should have killed him and taken my chances alone in your world."

Arthur rubbed his nose and mused aloud: "And the real Sherlock, I wonder if he succeeded in your world? With his immense intellect and mastery of logic I have no doubt that he quickly dominated the primitive locals and became the ruler of his own kingdom, perhaps the mightiest king ever to reign."

"Unfortunately we'll never know," said Dr Watson.

The man in the deerstalker hat stumbled on the rough grass, regained his balance and puffed on his pipe. "I appear to be standing inside a stone circle of unique design. What's this?"

The first painted warrior dashed into the clearing.

"Ah, a naked savage covered in woad. From the gore that is crusted on his tomahawk I deduce that it has been employed in splitting numerous skulls in recent days. The blood is pale and anaemic, which means that it belonged to persons who had been deprived of adequate nourishment for many weeks. Doubtless his captives.

"But why keep them as starved prisoners before killing them? There must be a ritualized element to their deaths, perhaps a religious sacrifice to a pagan god. There is a vomit stain on his knee, which suggests that something he ate at a feast disagreed with him. The presence of human hair in the vomit indicates cannibalism."

More warriors entered the glade and stopped to eye with implacable hatred the man in the stone circle, who had touched his fingertips together and was blithely continuing to cogitate.

"One of the hairs has a sheen that suggests it has been lavished with expensive lotions and therefore belongs to a rich merchant. Clearly this is not a mercantile land, so he must have travelled from afar. The scent of this lotion is reminiscent of a certain spice that comes from the southern part of the subcontinent. One moment."

Removing a magnifying glass from his pocket, he stooped to examine the hair in greater detail. "Ah yes, the merchant was a fat man with a limp in his left leg. He had a wife who was conducting an affair with the seller of melons in the market. His favourite colour was mauve. On the fifth day following his fifty-eighth birthday he—"

With a bellow of primal bloodlust, the first painted warrior unleashed himself on the speaker, splitting the deerstalker in half with the tomahawk and rending the cranium beneath in twain. The superlatively clever brains of Sherlock Holmes flopped on to the floor like dough from a cake-tin that a baker had neglected to put in the oven.

With a chorus of howls, the other warriors approached and danced on the grey mess, spreading it with their bare feet over the glade like mind jam, thinning forever the abnormal cerebral powers of the famous sleuth. Then they went home in savage single file.

Here, There and Everywhere

Edward Marston

Steve Long was like a lot of young men – alert, willing, well-educated, conscientious and chronically unemployed. When he graduated in Modern History from Manchester University, he'd assumed that he could walk into almost any profession that he chose. But the jobs market seemed to shrink by the day and he found himself taking on all sorts of temporary employment just to keep his head above water. He sold plastic flowers, delivered pizzas, worked in a biscuit factory, stacked shelves all night at a supermarket, had stints as a bartender, spent a dispiriting month in the kitchens of a hotel and, worst of all, acted as a dogsbody for a major political party and lost any belief in the essential goodness of human beings.

The one job he actually relished was with an organization that provided security for public events. There was always something going on in London at the weekends, whether it was supervising a big sporting occasion or manning the barricades at the Chelsea Flower Show. Tall, well-built and supremely fit, Steve thrived on action and was equally at home breaking up fights at a football match, helping to protect some showbiz icon or throwing out gatecrashers at an arts ball. It was varied work that allowed him to attend events he could never afford to go to as a member of the paying public. And since he was prepared to work outside London, he got more and more calls from the security firm.

"Ever heard of Westonbirt?"

"Isn't that where the National Arboretum is?"

"Got it in one," said the voice at the end of the line. "How are you fixed for next Saturday?"

"I'm free and available," replied Steve, mentally cancelling a visit home to see his parents. "What's the deal?"

"Get yourself to Westonbirt by 4 p.m. for acclimatization."

"Why?"

"You need to get the lie of the land. You'll be acting as a steward at an event organized by the Forestry Commission Live Music. They get big numbers at these things so you'll be very busy."

"Who's performing there?"

"Status Quo!"

"Jesus!" exclaimed Steve. "Are they still alive? I mean, my *father* still talks about going to concerts to hear the Quo."

"There'll be lots of people just like him in the audience. The band has a strong nostalgia appeal. Do you know how to get to Westonbirt?"

"I will do by Saturday. Who do I report to?"

"Charlie Kavanagh."

"Great – I've worked with him before."

"Then you'll know he appreciates punctuality."

Charlie Kavanagh also appreciated alcohol but Steve wasn't going to mention that. Work was work and Kavanagh was one of the best and most efficient bosses he'd ever known. That was all that mattered. Steve was elated. A warm ray of sunshine had suddenly brightened up a hitherto barren week. Instead of going all the way to Newcastle on Saturday, he'd be controlling the multitudes flocking to the National Arboretum to hear a legendary rock band. It would be well-paid fun. What his contact had failed to tell Steve was that he'd also be involved in a murder investigation.

Steve got to Westonbirt hours before the appointed time. When he parked his motorcycle and removed his crash helmet, he was instantly recognized.

"Hey!" said Charlie Kavanagh, bearing down on him. The

big, paunchy, amiable Irishman squinted. "I know you. It's Steve something, isn't it?"

"Steve Long."

"You're early. You don't get paid until 4 p.m."

"I wanted to get the feel of the place."

"Good thinking."

"What will I be doing this evening?"

"Hold on," said Kavanagh, flipping over a page on his clipboard and looking down the list of names. "You'll be wasted on the car park. You've got a sharp eye and sharper instincts. I remember you caught someone shooting up at Lord's. We can't have heroin addicts at the home of cricket. Yes, and I seem to recall you defusing a nasty situation at Wembley Arena last Christmas. See? Impress me and you get rewarded."

"Does that mean you're doubling my wage?"

Kavanagh laughed. "No, Steve, it means that you'll be doing something more elevated than parking cars and taking tickets. I want you on the gate as a watcher."

"What am I watching out for?"

"Trouble. Drugs, drunkenness, knives and anything else that might make people potential dangers. Even in a mature audience like the one we're likely to get, there are always a few idiots bent on livening things up. Pick them out early on."

"I'll do my best."

"We need to have eyes here, there and everywhere."

"I know the ropes."

"You're partnered with a guy called Phil Denton."

Steve shrugged. "Don't know him. What's he like?"

"Useful man. Retired boxer. He works well – just like you. Report back here this afternoon and I'll issue detailed instructions."

"Thanks, Charlie."

"By the way, do you like Status Quo?"

"I don't *dislike* them," said Steve, "but they're not in my Top Ten. My father, on the other hand, worships them. I was supposed to see my parents this weekend. They were dead peeved when I cried off. The only way Dad will forgive me is if I get him a programme signed by Rick Parfitt and Francis Rossi."

"I'll see if I can arrange it," said Kavanagh. "I'll even ask them to put OBE after their names. How many people get an Order of the British Empire for their services to music? We're in good company here this evening. These fellas are pop aristocracy."

Westonbirt intrigued Steve. After a snack at the restaurant, he explored 600 acres of trees and shrubs from all parts of the world. Wherever he looked, there was something to make him gape in wonder. The arboretum housed the National Japanese Maple Collection along with many other striking collections. Pride of place went to a 2,000-year-old lime tree. Steve gazed at it for minutes.

"Amazing, isn't it?" asked a voice.

"Yes," said Steve, turning to see a tall, lean, angular man in his twenties. "It's been here for two millennia."

"That's almost as long as Status Quo have been around." They shared a laugh. "I saw you talking to Charlie Kavanagh early on so you must be one of the stewards. So am I." He offered his hand. "Nick Hooper."

Steve shook his hand. "Hi, Nick. I'm Steve Long." He'd heard the soft burr in the newcomer's voice. "You sound as if you come from somewhere in the Cotswolds."

"I was born and bred in Cirencester," explained Hooper. "That's less than half an hour away. Gloucestershire is a wonderful county. It's got everything. We even have Charlie, living down the road."

"Charlie Kavanagh?"

"His Royal Highness, *Prince* Charles. He lives at High-grove."

"I'd forgotten that. You must know Westonbirt well."

"House *and* arboretum."

Steve looked around. "I don't see any house."

"It's on the other side of the road," said Hooper, pointing. "It stands in its own estate and is now an upmarket girls' boarding school. I heard the Eagles there."

"I can't believe the Eagles would play at a girls' school."

"They didn't. They played right here in the arboretum. I had a girlfriend at the school. Her parents lived abroad so she stayed on alone at the school for a few weeks in the summer. I climbed in one night and we left the window open so that we could listen to the concert for free. When we weren't otherwise engaged, that is." He wagged a finger. "We'll have to watch out for that, Steve."

Steve was confused. "People climbing into the school?"

"No. I'm talking about those who just won't pay for a ticket. The arboretum closes two and a half hours before the concert but some clever buggers hide in the trees then sneak up close when the music starts and listen for free. We have to flush them out."

"You've obviously done this before, Nick."

"I've been here for lots of gigs. They're always terrific. There's plenty of pussy to go round and there's never a shortage of gear."

"We're supposed to confiscate any hard drugs."

"I always turn a blind eye," said Hooper, airily. "That way, you get stuff slipped to you by way of thanks. Let's face it, you don't go to a pop concert to stay stone-cold sober. And you don't leave until you get laid. That's my motto, anyway."

It wasn't an attitude that Steve shared. He took his duties very seriously. He'd smoked a little pot at university but – having seen the horrors that cocaine and heroin could inflict on people – he'd kept well away from hard drugs. Nick Hooper was clearly a user.

"You been to the Old Arboretum yet?" asked Hooper.

"I thought this was it."

"No, this is Silk Wood, the main part. Come on – I'll show you the other bit. It's close to where the concert is being held and has one big advantage over Silk Wood."

"What's that?"

"No dogs are allowed in there. *This* is where the bow-wows always come for exercise. They crap all over the place. You'd never bring a girl here, Steve. Take her to the Old Arboretum. At least you know it's safe to lie down on the grass. Off we go. I'll show you some of the places *I* always use."

Preparations had been thorough. A high perimeter fence had been erected on the Downs and a stage put up with a huge awning over it. The roadies went through their sound checks and – after all the visitors had left – Status Quo had a brief rehearsal, piercing the silence with their plangent harmonies. Steve was exhilarated by the pulsing rhythm of their music and had to make a conscious effort to listen to Charlie Kavanagh's orders. A small army of stewards had now assembled, dressed in yellow jackets and issued with instructions. Charlie warned them what to look out for and said that anyone caught slacking would have his wage halved. That helped to concentrate their minds wonderfully.

As the hours slipped by, they took up their posts. The early trickle of cars became a steady flow before turning into a veritable flood. Those in charge of parking the vehicles were working at full stretch. Tickets were scrutinized carefully at the main entrance. Steve was a little distance away, studying people for any danger signs. His colleague, Phil Denton, was a short, stocky man in his late thirties with the broad shoulders and craggy face of someone who'd spent a lot of time in a boxing ring. After talking to extroverts like Kavanagh and Hooper, Steve found him refreshingly taciturn.

Expecting a largely mature audience, Steve was surprised to find so many younger fans flocking to the concert. He gave them a welcoming smile while he appraised them. Denton was equally vigilant though his intense gaze did tend to stay longer on the young women. One trio caught the attention of both stewards. They were three students who'd hitched a ride from Cardiff to see the band and had clearly come for a good time. They were already pleasantly drunk and ready for banter with the stewards. Two of them were attractive but they were overshadowed by the third girl, a shapely creature of middle height with the face of an angel and blonde hair that hung down her back. She had tattoos on her bare shoulders and her name – Angie – was on a large silver pendant around her neck. Steve was struck by her but Denton couldn't take his eyes off Angie. He watched her for minutes and only broke off when Steve nudged him.

"That guy over there," said Steve. "Recognize him?"

Denton shook his head. "No – should I?"

"He looks very much like someone we had to throw out of a concert at Regent's Park for pestering women."

"Sure it's him?"

"No – but it could be."

"He's doing no harm now. Let him go."

Steve looked hard at the man. He was a slim individual in his twenties with an arrogant swagger. It was the confident grin that Steve felt he'd seen before. The man was with a male friend and they carried blankets and a shoulder bag apiece. As they picked their way through the crowd, they looked for somewhere to sit. Spotting the three girls who'd arrived earlier, they settled down on the grass nearby. When he saw that the trio of students had been targeted, Steve felt almost parental. He wanted to go and warn Angie and her two friends but it was not his business to do so. Denton, by contrast, clearly thought it *was* his business. Gaze locked on Angie, he was consumed by envy. It was as if he'd already designated the girl as his and feared that he'd be dispossessed.

"Keep your eyes on the gate," warned Steve.

Denton turned round. "What?"

"That's what we're supposed to do."

"Oh, yes."

Denton returned to his duty but kept glancing over his shoulder at Angie. Hundreds of people had already arrived. Some chose the seating provided but most had either brought their own chairs or preferred to squat on blankets. Food and drink were already being consumed. A faint aroma of cannabis hung over the whole audience. Still they came and still they were checked by Steve and Denton. Only a few people had to be turned away. One man was so hopelessly drunk that he collapsed and was carried out. Two shifty-looking youths were questioned and made the mistake of resisting when Steve tried to search them. Denton felled one of them with a punch. Both were carrying knives and sachets of drugs. They were handed over to the police. Steve watched them being taken away. Denton was far more interested in the way that Angie was being drawn into conversation by the slim, aggressively confident man whom Steve thought he'd identified as a troublemaker.

"Ever heard them before?" asked Steve.

"Who?" said Denton, turning to face him.

"Status Quo."

"I worked at Glastonbury last year. They were there."

"What are they like?"

"Loud."

A musical thunderstorm hit the arboretum. The quiet glades and dignified avenues of trees trembled at the booming explosions and the flashes of psychedelic lightning. Status Quo were like a force of nature, sweeping all before them and transforming a well-behaved, largely middle-class audience into a howling mob of dervishes. They could not get enough of the band and hailed each song with a standing ovation amplified by shouts, screams, whistles and an occasional firework. Collective madness reigned.

It was difficult for Steve to keep his mind on his duties but he did his best, patrolling the outer edges of the concert in search of any trouble. Though Denton was supposed to stay with him, he drifted back time and again to a position from which he could see Angie at the heart of the crowd. As light began to fade, Steve lost sight of him. He felt a firm hand on his shoulder.

"What gives?" asked Charlie Kavanagh, raising his voice above the tumult.

"Nothing much to report," replied Steve. "We only had to turn three people away. This lot are yelling their heads off but you expect that. Everything is very much under control."

"That's what I like to hear, Steve. Where's Phil?"

"Oh, he wandered off."

"He's supposed to be with you."

"I think he went to the loo," said Steve, trying to cover for his colleague. "We all have to do that at some point."

"That's exactly where I'm sending you now." Kavanagh indicated the long line of portable toilets. "You know the drill – only one person to one cubicle. If two men go in together, it's a drug deal. If a male slips into a cubicle with a female, then it's copulation."

"I'll get over there right now, Charlie."

"Remember what I told you earlier."

"We need to have eyes here, there and everywhere."

"Good man," said Kavanagh, slapping him on the arm. "Now go and find Phil Denton. Make sure he earns his money."

Kavanagh went off to check with stewards stationed at key points inside the perimeter fence. Steve obeyed his orders but saw no sign of Denton. It was as if his colleague had disappeared. The band got progressively louder, the mood more excitable and the lighting effects more spectacular. Steve was still lurking near the toilets when he caught a glimpse of a yellow jacket in the midst of the audience. Next minute, somebody was hauled to his feet and frogmarched through the crowd. Phil Denton was escorting the slim young man whom Steve had picked out earlier as a sex pest. The man struggled hard to escape but Denton's grip was firm. He pushed his captive towards Steve.

"We're slinging this joker out," said Denton.

"What's he done?" asked Steve.

"Nothing!" protested the man.

"He was molesting a young woman," said Denton.

"That's rubbish. She was up for it. Everything was going well until *you* interfered. Can't a bloke have a free grope when it's offered to him on a plate?"

"Open the door, Steve. Let's get him out."

Steve led the way to a gate in the fence. He and Denton had already been given the combination of the locks on the exits.

While Steve was finding the numbers, the man continued to yell and struggle. Denton silenced him with a couple of punches. Steve opened the gate and his colleague flung his prisoner unceremoniously out before locking the gate again.

"Who was he pestering?" asked Steve.

"Angie," said Denton.

"Did she ask for help?"

"That bastard was all over her and she was trying to fight him off. Something had to be done. Angie came here with her friends to listen to the music not to get jumped on by that animal." He peered through the chain-link fence at the young man who was dragging himself to his feet. "And don't you dare show your face in here again," warned Denton, "or I'll murder you!"

Denton stalked off, leaving Steve with two thoughts. The first concerned the evicted man who was now skulking off into the trees bordering Mitchell Drive. He'd be back. His type never gave up. He'd get back inside the compound somehow in order to cause some real trouble. Angie might be spared, but another girl would fall into his clutches. Steve resolved to pass the word around the other stewards to look out for him.

The second thought was more disturbing. In a crowd of that size, Denton must have got very close to Angie to be able to see that she was in distress. That meant he'd abandoned his duties altogether. Throwing out a troublemaker was no routine assignment for Denton. There'd been real hatred in his voice. He looked and sounded as if he'd wanted to kill the man he'd ejected. Steve was very worried about his colleague. What on earth was eating Phil Denton?

Even after four decades, Status Quo could still generate an immense amount of energy, connecting with their audience at a deep level and leaving them in a state of ecstasy. When the gig finally ended, the applause went on for almost a quarter of an hour. It was time for the stewards to click into action, shepherding the band offstage, guiding the punters back to their cars, calling for medical aid to the inevitable minority too drunk or drugged to move, and generally helping to clear up the mess left behind. It was well past midnight before Steve was signed off. He'd parked his motorcycle near some trees and was upset to see that it had been knocked over. After hauling it upright and putting it back on its stand, he noticed some marks gouged out in the turf. It was as if someone or something had been dragged over the grass and collided with his machine on the way.

There was enough light for him to follow the channels in the earth as they snaked towards the trees. Once there he was in relative darkness and picked his way forward with care. When he came to a clearing, moonlight broke through to reveal a hideous sight. Stretched on the ground with her clothes ripped off was the body of a beautiful young woman with long, fair hair. Though he could see no telltale pendant around her neck, Steve identified her at once. It was Angie.

After handing everything over to the police, Charlie Kavanagh talked to the two students who'd come to the concert with Angie. Steve was close enough to his boss to smell the whisky on his breath but it didn't seem to affect Kavanagh's ability to do his job. He was as brisk and authoritative as ever. One of the girls dissolved into tears, but the other one – Rachel by name – wanted answers.

"Where is Angie?" she demanded.

"There's been an accident," replied Kavanagh, unwilling to tell her that her companion had been strangled to death after a sexual assault. "You have to stay well clear, Rachel."

"Can't we go to her?"

"Not at the moment, I'm afraid."

"But she's our friend."

"Even so."

"Why are the police involved?"

"They'll explain that in due course," said Steve, wanting to do some detective work of his own. "When did you last see her, Rachel?"

"It was ages ago," she said, brushing away tears. "Angie went off to the loo and never came back."

"Didn't you go looking for her?"

"Well, no. I mean, we didn't want to spoil her fun. All the lads chase Angie. She's drop-dead gorgeous. If she's in the mood, she sometimes picks one out. That's what we thought she'd done."

"What about the young man sitting close to you?"

"Oh, he was horrible!"

"Did you get his name?"

"Jez," she said. "He told us to call him Jez. Not that he took any notice of Helen and me. All he wanted to do was to touch up Angie. He just wouldn't leave her alone. We were so glad when he got thrown out by one of the stewards. His name was Phil."

"Yes, I know."

"He came back to tell us that Jez wouldn't bother us again."

"What did Angie say to that?"

"She was grateful – very grateful." The wail of a siren made her jump. "An *ambulance* – is it that serious?"

"Yes, it is," said Kavanagh. "Look, why don't we see if we can find a cup of tea or something for you and Helen? You've had a terrible shock." He walked away. "Stay here with Steve."

"You said that he came back," noted Steve, resuming his questioning. "When he'd kicked Jez out, you said that Phil came back to speak to you."

"He wanted to reassure Angie, that's all."

"Was she that upset?"

"Oh, yes. Jez was a real pest. His hands were all over her."

"Why didn't you move?"

"We did, but Jez and his mate followed us."

"Then Phil came to your rescue?"

"That's right."

"What exactly did Angie say to Phil?"

"She thanked him, of course."

"Anything else?"

"Yes," said Rachel. "She gave him a big kiss."

*   *   *

After he'd given a full statement to the police, Steve was free to go. Returning to his motorcycle, he sat astride it and brooded. When he'd first stumbled on the corpse, his mind had been racing. One obvious suspect occurred to him. Jez was persistent. He was also vengeful. It wouldn't have been impossible for him to climb back in. The area around the stage was well lit but there were shadows around other parts of the perimeter. Somebody as lithe and determined as Jez could have slipped back in unnoticed. Steve's theory was that Jez would have loitered near the toilets on the off-chance that Angie would go there sooner or later. He'd pounced, enticed her out of the compound and, when she resisted, overpowered her and dragged her off. In the deafening blast of sound from the band, nobody had heard the girl's desperate cries for help.

Steve was now examining another suspect. Phil Denton. He and Jez had something in common. Both were obsessed with Angie. Phil had abandoned his duties in order to watch over her, and had used unnecessary force to eject his rival. The difference between the two men was their appearance. Jez might be a nuisance but he was a handsome young man with a seedy charm. Denton, however, was coarse, ugly and almost twenty years older than Angie. On an impulse of gratitude, she might kiss him but he'd have no other appeal for her.

Denton had two advantages over Jez. As a steward, he was in a privileged position that allowed him to move where he wished. More to the point, he knew the combinations of the locks on the gates. If he'd encountered Angie on her way to the toilets, he could have let her out through the fence and spirited her away. Nobody would have stopped them. When they saw a man in a yellow jacket hustling someone away, they'd have assumed that she was being thrown out for a good reason. The more he thought about it, the more Steve became convinced that Phil Denton had to be the prime suspect. Jez was eager to have sex with Angie but he wouldn't kill to get it. Denton was a retired boxer who didn't know his own strength. He could easily have misinterpreted Angie's kiss as a promise and – when she rejected him – taken her by force. Steve could almost see the scene being enacted before him.

Putting on his crash helmet, he gunned the engine and drove off. When he got to the main road, however, he didn't turn right and ride towards the motorway that would carry him to London. Instead, he turned left and went the short distance to the huge entrance gates of Westonbirt School. Steve dismounted and peered through the wrought-iron bars. Set in the middle of extensive grounds, the school was some distance away but Steve got a glimpse of it through the trees that lined the long, curving drive. Silhouetted against the sky, the building was a perfect example of Victorian Gothic and looked rather like a haunted house in a horror film. Its size was daunting, its solidity impressive and it sported hundreds of extravagant decorative touches. As he studied the school, it occurred to Steve that anyone who climbed into one of its upper rooms would have to be something of an athlete.

Another name suddenly came into contention as a major suspect. Steve remembered how Nick Hooper had boasted about taking drugs and having sex at every pop concert where he'd worked. Because he'd lived so close, Hooper knew the arboretum intimately. He'd be aware of the nearest and best place to take a girl for privacy. As a steward, he'd been assigned to duties inside the compound so he wouldn't have failed to see someone as gorgeous as Angie arriving there with her friends. Again, he'd have the combination of the locks on the gates. He'd be able to slip away in the shadows. Jez might have assaulted the girl out of revenge and Denton would have been driven by lust. Neither of them would have been able to lure Angie away.

Nick Hooper was different. He was as handsome as Jez and had infinitely more sex appeal than Denton. Steve remembered his earlier conversation with Hooper. Women, drugs and booze were there for the taking. That was his philosophy. Hooper was powered by a sense of entitlement. Whether it was in an exclusive girls' school or in a clearing in the arboretum, he expected to get what he wanted. If there was resistance,

Hooper would feel insulted. Even a girl as lovely as Angie couldn't be allowed to get away with that. She'd have to be punished. While the band was still pounding away nearby, Hooper had taken his chance.

Who was the killer – Jez, Phil Denton or Nick Hooper? It took Steve only a matter of seconds to pick out one name. Taking out his mobile phone, he dialled 999 and asked to speak to the police.

It was days later when Steve got a call from Charlie Kavanagh. He recognized the Irishman's rich brogue immediately.

"Hi," said Charlie. "Can I speak to Sherlock Holmes?"

"Hello, Charlie."

"I've just talked to the boys in blue. After grilling Nick Hooper until he cracked, they've now charged him with the murder. Her full name was Angela Wilbourne, by the way. I dare say you picked that up from the papers. Thanks to you, the crime is solved. You were the one who first fingered Hooper."

"It was something he told me," said Steve. "It stuck in my mind. But I can't take all the credit. It was really an educated guess."

"And a bloody good one at that," said Charlie. "They didn't catch him with a smoking gun exactly but they got something just as good. When he was arrested, Hooper was carrying a silver pendant with her name on it."

"That's what made me think of him, Charlie. He took me for a walk around the Old Arboretum and pointed out places where he'd had sex with various women. Hooper bragged that he always took away a little souvenir for his collection. In this case," said Steve with a sigh, "it was the girl's pendant."

"To be honest, I thought it might have been Phil Denton."

"So did I at first."

"He was acting so suspiciously once the murder came to light."

"He did pay Angie a lot of undue attention."

"Nick Hooper got there before him. It's a pity," said Charlie. "I know that Hooper was a randy so-and-so but he was one of my regulars. From now on, he won't be on my payroll for a long, long time. I'll have to replace him with someone who knows how to keep his eyes peeled and his wits about him." He tried to sound casual. "Know anyone in need of a more permanent job?"

Steve was thrilled. "Funny you should ask that," he said with a laugh. "When do I start?"

A Good Man

N. J. Cooper

It's people you leave, not places. I'd been wrong about that, too. For years, I'd told myself it was this empty landscape I'd hated. Only the shushing of the wind in the willows and the calling of birds broke the silence, and they'd never been any use to me.

I gazed at the garden, still a big semicircle with the grass bordered by flowering shrubs and the odd fruit tree among the willow saplings. Whoever the current owners were, they must have shared his taste for nature only barely tamed.

The river still ran along the bottom of the lawn, with the orchard on the far side and the wet empty fields beyond. I could just make out the distant hills, and I thought of how I'd hated the flatness and the loneliness.

A big white bird flapped down on to the rickety bridge he'd made when he'd bought the land for the orchard, and I heard his rich deep voice echo in my head: "That's an egret, Kim. Have you ever seen one before?"

How could I? Only six when I'd first come here, but already the dangerous victor of eight failed fosterings, I'd never been outside a city.

This place had seemed like a prison, and he my jailer. I'd known he must be weird from the start. If I hadn't hurt so many of the other children, I'd never have been sent here. He'd been the carer of last resort, a man who'd had some success with tough boys in the past. This time, when they'd run out of options, they'd given him a girl. Me.

The egret lifted itself from the bridge up into the sky. Today the great space above the wetland was clear bright blue. I didn't remember that, any more than I remembered the wild flowers that were turning the fields ahead of me into a yellow and white froth. Everything here was beautiful. Why hadn't I seen it then?

The low-built old farmhouse had friendly looking green-painted windows in its sturdy white walls, and a steeply sloping roof of terracotta tiles, rippled like the sea.

"Double romans, they're called, Kim," he'd once said, always teaching, pointing things out, trying to make me someone I wasn't.

There were no cars at the front of the house and neither sound nor light from inside, so I let myself push open the side gate and walk right into the semicircular garden. If anyone challenged me, I could pretend I thought the house was for sale. I saw at once that someone had changed the scrubby vegetable patch into a neat set of raised beds, beautifully kept and showing pristine rows of new growth.

I thought of the slugs, horrible squelchy things, that I'd collected once when he'd pissed me off, nagging about my homework or my clothes or hair. I must have been eleven by then. The slugs had seemed fair revenge for the nagging and the way he'd fallen asleep in his chair, leaving his mouth open . . .

A cloud sidled across the sun and took away even the thin, inadequate English warmth I'd felt on my face, making me shiver. Or was that memory? Or guilt?

The slugs had been the least of it. I saw so much now, more or less the age he must have been when he'd taken me in. I hadn't understood any of it then: how badly I'd needed him to be safe and kind and so how hard I'd pushed him to make him reveal himself the opposite.

I'd never known an adult who couldn't be cruel. All those failed fosterings had proved to me that any one of them, however calm they'd seemed at first, could be driven to take off their masks of kindness. Only he had resisted nearly everything I'd tried to make him do.

None of my malice or my violence had made him hit me or lock me up. I still don't know what a sight of my true feelings might have done because I'd never let him see those.

I used to watch him, tall and upright and shabbily dressed, smiling at me as he calmly talked on and on, using words as reins and bits and goads and whips. Now I wondered what would have happened if I'd howled and told him what it had been like before and flung myself into his arms. Would he have picked me up and cradled me and made it all safe and different?

Or would he have stuck to his line of teaching me the things he liked, trying to make me into what he wanted?

Sometimes I had tried. But never for long. Waiting for horror to descend had been unbearable. I'd always rather have done something to bring it down quickly and get it over.

"He's a good man," my social worker said. One of my social workers. I don't remember which. They blurred at this distance.

I walked now across the lawn, remembering the opportunities for rebellion the grass had given me. I'd refuse to mow when he asked me to, or mess about with the straight lines he'd left on the lawn, or hide small dangerous stones in the longer grass to bugger up the mower blade and give him trouble.

Standing at last on the edge of the river, I wondered if I'd see the kingfisher today. I never had. I don't think I'd even believed it existed. I'd thought he was lying about that too.

"You have to be quiet, Kim. And very still. And you have to watch. Once you've seen one for the first time, it'll get easier. You'll learn to recognize the flash of greeny blue, just above the water. Once they've let you see them the first time, they seem to slow down for you."

Not for me, I'd thought then. I thought it still. No beautiful wild thing would change its course for me. Why should it? I'd always been a lost cause. The source of endless trouble for anyone who'd ever been lumbered with me. That's what one set of foster parents had said. Dangerous, too.

In England anyway. Out in Australia, I'd learned to be different. Someone else. I'd had friends and work and my own money. Never much money. With a messed-up education like mine, you didn't get well-paid work. But I'd done okay. I'd even found a bloke. He *was* a good man, as well as the reason why I was here now, smelling the wetness of the peat and clay all around me, the squashed grass, the horses in the far field, and the sweetness of the wildflowers, remembering.

"You'd better go back, Sally," Sam had said a week ago, using the name I'd chosen for myself when I'd run away to become someone else. "Something's not right in you and you're talking more and more about England. Go back and lay the ghosts. Make your peace with your memories, whatever they are. I'll buy you an open ticket so you can take your time. We can afford it. Don't come back until you're ready."

"When will that be?" I'd asked, standing on the beach, with the sun drilling down into my shoulders, my ears full of the crashing surf and the shrill calls of happiness from the unknowing people all around us. I'd felt sullen in a way I'd almost forgotten, ready to dump it all on someone else again.

"You'll know when you're ready," Sam had said, tucking stray wisps of hair behind my ears under the sun hat. "I can't tell you."

When I was six my hair had been white blonde, then it had darkened. Later I'd dyed it all kinds of colours, chosen to make him angry. By the time I'd stolen the passport at Heathrow, I'd had a mousy-brown ponytail, like the girl I'd picked out of the London-bound taxi queue as my target. The Aussie sun had bleached it since.

Looking back, I can't see why I wasn't afraid at Heathrow. I'd had a bagful of his money – all I could get from the house and the cash machines – and the nicked British passport. Why hadn't I been afraid a report of what I'd done might get to Sydney before me so that I'd be arrested on the plane? Why had I felt cocooned in some transparent casing no one would be able to break?

I still didn't understand it, but once I'd got to Sydney unmolested I chucked the passport into the sea, then found the kind of bar where they're happy to give you work for cash, even if you haven't any proof of identity. It was also the kind of place where people who offer fake ID documents can be found. I'd waited till I was sure of one, then paid his price without letting him know how much I hated him. Once I'd paid I was free. For the first time in my life, I was free.

No one could do it now. Not with CCTV cameras everywhere, and DNA and email.

It was the first thing I'd ever done well. I'd tried to make it the start of someone I could like. Sally. For a time I'd thought I'd won. But memories had grown in the dark silence until they'd devoured my sleep and my health.

He walked with me everywhere now, and his face hung over me as I lay in bed. I couldn't forget the warmth in his dark eyes when I'd done something that pleased him, or their hardness when I'd failed.

He must have been lonely, too. I can see that now. But then he'd seemed all-powerful, without feelings or fears or needs.

I turned my head away from the river. His voice sounded again, bumping around in my mind, as smooth and comforting as rich hot chocolate:

"Sometimes they say that only people who deserve it actually see the kingfisher, but I think that's sentimental, Kim."

"Then I am sentimental," I said aloud to the space he'd once inhabited. "I don't deserve it."

I turned my back on the river and walked at last towards the rhubarb patch, where we'd had our last encounter. It was a mound, carefully sloped to make the water drain away so that it wouldn't rot the crowns. How well I remembered the care he'd lavished on those red stalks and their poisonous yellowy-green leaves. Bending down over them, he went on talking to me even as he weeded around his acid, horrible fruit.

"I know you'll be legally free to go on your birthday, Kim. But you can't. You may be nearly old enough, but you're not fit to live alone. Not yet. One day, I'll help you go. But for now you must stay here. And I . . ."

He'd never managed to say whatever it was he'd do because I'd raised the old iron bar like an axe above my head and brought it crashing down on to the back of his head and then his spine.

Now I looked at the scarlet stalks of rhubarb, asking the old questions that had come to torture me: Had he died at once? Who had found him? Could he have been saved? Why hadn't they come after me?

Tyres squeaked on the paving, like something out of one of my nightmares of retribution. I thought of hiding, or climbing the wall into next door's garden. But I had to face it. I'd always known it would come. And better here than in Australia with Sam. At least Sam would never have to know who I really was, what I'd done. I turned to face it.

A wheelchair came to a stop just by the rhubarb bed. He raised his head, white-haired now and stared right at me. His dark eyes were the same. His voice, too:

"Thank God you're safe, Kim."

Good Intentions

Michael Z. Lewin

It seemed like the rain would never stop. I was getting cabin fever and I wasn't even in a cabin. Had I *ever* been in a cabin? I mean, a *cabin*? I couldn't remember one. I wanted to go to a cabin. Experience Cabinness. Be thoroughly cabined. The rain seemed like it would never stop.

I was bored. There is only a certain amount that a private investigator can do constructively when he is without clients, even in a fascinating, action-packed city like Indianapolis. I'd done it and it wasn't even noon yet. We do get rains like this here but not usually in November. Or is it common in Novembers? Had the incessant rain washed my memory away?

So it was with pleasure that I thought I heard footsteps on my office stairs. Normally I'd dismiss such sounds as self-delusion – so few clients ever arrive without an appointment. And then there was the rain. I *mean* . . . Could I *really* be hearing footfalls among the plops of those endless raindrops?

As it turned out, I could. There was a knock at my door. Even the most savage rain doesn't do that. I dashed to respond. The last thing I wanted was for a prospective client to dissolve away.

The last thing I expected was to open the door and recognize the prospective client. My repeat clients always call, make appointments, even summon me to come to them. But then again this prospective repeat client was not a normal kinda guy.

"LeBron," I said. "Come in. Get out of the wet."

I stood back but he didn't cross the threshold. At first I

thought he was being contrary, but then I saw it was hard for him to move at all. One arm hung loose at his side. His clothes were torn. He was standing askew.

"LeBron, what's wrong?"

Faintly he said something. When I leaned forward and asked him to repeat it he said, "It's Wolfgang now."

It took a while but eventually I sat him in my Client's Chair. He groaned with each step. I sat on my desk facing him. "How badly are you hurt?"

He didn't respond.

"How badly are you hurt, Wolfgang? Should I call an ambulance?"

"We heal quickly."

I didn't like the way he held himself in my chair. I didn't like the sound of his breathing. I didn't like the sight of blood dripping on to my floor. I picked up the phone.

"No."

"Yes."

He passed out. I dialled 911.

1

St Riley's emergency department was full, which surprised me. Ice and snow produce broken bones, but rain? What were they all here for? Near-drownings? Mould?

Whatever the answer, the emergency crew jumped Wolfgang to the head of the line. "So what happened to your friend?" asked the nurse when I followed him to a cubicle.

"I have no idea."

"What's his name?"

"Wolfgang."

"Wolfgang," the nurse said. "Interesting." She turned to him. "Wolfgang, my name is Matty. Can you hear me?"

He made a sound. I couldn't make out, like, a *word*, but Nurse Matty seemed happy with the noise itself. She turned back to me. "Has he lost consciousness since it happened?"

"He passed out when he arrived at my office, just before I called 911. Before that I don't know."

"How long ago did this happen?"

"I don't know."

"You don't know much, do you?"

"No, ma'am, I don't."

"Did you do this to him?"

"No."

"You know *that*, do you?"

"He came to where I live, dragged himself up a flight of stairs and knocked at my door. That was about . . ." I looked at my watch. "Fifty-seven minutes ago, when I called 911. I don't know what happened before he got to me, where it happened, when it happened or how he got to my place."

"He's . . . your boyfriend?"

"He's not a friend of any description. Two months ago he hired me to do a job for him. I haven't seen or spoken with him since."

"That was September?"

"Yes. I finished the job for him in a day."

"You're not a plumber by any chance?"

"No. Sorry."

She sighed. "So, why did he come to you?"

"Once you and your colleagues put Wolfgang Dumpty back together again, maybe he'll tell me."

"That's his last name? Dumpty?"

"I have no idea what his last name is. When I worked for him he called himself 'LeBron James'. If he's 'Wolfgang' now, chances are that the rest of his handle was Mozart. He has an interest in prodigies."

"What's all that supposed to mean?"

"He changes his name sometimes."

"He changes his name?" She looked from me to him and back again. "Why?"

"I'd rather he told you himself."

"Is he crazy? Is that it?"

"Personally, I think he's unusually sane. But he does have some quirks."

"You're not helping me here."

"I'm helping you as much as I can."

"Does he have medical insurance? Wait, let me guess. You don't know."

"I can probably remember his address."

"But he was rich enough to hire you for a day in September?"

"Yes."

"Are you cheap?"

"I'm fabulously expensive and worth every penny."

"A doctor will be here in a minute. I'm going to check his pockets now. They might have some ID that will help."

She checked his pockets. They were empty. Which surprised me because when he came to my office in September he was carrying a lot of cash. So maybe he'd been robbed.

"Go tell them what you can at the desk," she said.

"And will you let me know when you find out what's wrong with him?"

"You're waiting around?"

"Yeah."

"Even though you're not a friend?"

"I give good customer aftercare."

She made a face at me.

I left to deliver a second batch of "I don't knows" at the reception desk.

2

I expected to be left to my own devices in the waiting room for a long time, but Nurse Matty came to get me less than a quarter of an hour after I picked a seat.

"You *are* still here."

"Didn't you expect me to be?"

"Not after we found your friend – no, your non-friend – has stab wounds."

"That's not nice."

"No it's not."

"And you thought I was the stabber and had made a run for it."

"Look, can you come with me and go through what you know with our head of security?"

"While you wait for the cops to come and have me go through what I know with them?"

"Or hunt you down like a stray dog if you don't stay. Your call," she said with a bit of a smile.

"Why don't you tell me something about Wolfgang's prognosis?"

"The doctor found two wounds in his belly before I came to look for you. Neither looked deep or in a vital place but they'll take him up to an operating theatre in a few minutes to make sure."

"And has he said anything about what happened or who did it?"

"He's been mumbling things. Maybe an old friend like you will be able to understand him better than I can."

I followed Matty into the treatment labyrinth. I wasn't sure what to tell the security people – or the cops. When I knew him, Wolfgang's fickleness about names wasn't his main peculiarity. That honour fell to his insistence that his father was an extraterrestrial.

But with me he behaved rationally and paid cash. By no means all the terrestrials I deal with do either.

The security guy was a woman who was taller, younger and arguably more muscular than I am. She waited for me at the foot of Wolfgang's bed, but as I was about to introduce myself, the patient spotted me and tried to sit up.

He said, "Albert."

It was quiet but clear enough for Nurse Matty to ask, "Is that you?"

I nodded and went closer to his head.

"Four of them," he whispered.

"Who were they?"

What he'd already said seemed to have left him exhausted. But then he made one last effort and said what sounded like, "Terrorists . . ."

3

Once the magic "t" word was passed on to the police it wasn't long until two officers in uniform homed in on me like I was the door to their future careers. By then Wolfgang was in surgery.

I followed the cops to a visitors' room but it didn't take long for me to repeat my collection of "I don't knows". However, it was long enough for Nurse Matty to stick her head in with an update. "Sorry to bother you, officers," she said, "but the surgeon upstairs believes that the two abdominal wounds were done with different knives."

The uniforms looked at each other. I said, "How do you tell something like that?"

"Think about an ordinary knife," she said. "One side sharp, one side blunt."

"Okay."

"And think about it being pressed through skin. Once the point goes in, one side of the wound is cut by the sharp edge but the other is just rubbed by the blunt one. Maybe torn open a little, but not cut. The result is that the two ends of the wound look completely different under magnification."

"Sounds reasonable," I said.

"Apparently one of the blades that cut him had *two* sharp edges, whereas the other had only one. That's what he says. He also says that he can't be completely certain without doing an autopsy."

I leaned forward.

"But he doesn't think it'll come to that," she said. "Oh. And they found another cut. On his back. Not as deep. He didn't say if he thinks it was done by one of the original two knives." She left.

"She says there were three wounds, not two?" the smaller of the two cops asked.

I nodded. Poor ol' Wolfgang.

The smaller cop crossed something out in his notebook and wrote a correction.

The larger cop just said, "What's he expect?" He was a big guy who looked the age and size of a high-school lineman.

"What do you mean?" his colleague asked.

"He said it was terrorists," the lineman said. "If he's going to mess with terrorists . . ." He looked from his colleague to me, looking for support.

I said, "If someone is attacked by terrorists, *they're* responsible?" I shook my head. "You're saying the 9/11 people were *messing* with terrorists?"

"I just said . . ." the lineman began. But he stopped.

His colleague smiled and shook his head slowly.

I said nothing more. And at least they had treated me as a witness rather than a suspect, probably because Nurse Matty had stressed that I stayed around after Wolfgang came in.

But with the patient in surgery and the uniforms unable to think of more questions for me not to know the answers to, I began to consider leaving. However, then a southside detective, Imberlain, showed up. So I got to do it all again.

By which time Matty had a further update. The surgeons had found a fourth cut. They were now putting Wolfgang's spleen and liver back together. So I decided to leave, at least for the time being.

I'd followed the ambulance in my car, so I had wheels. But instead of using them to go back home, I went to Wolfgang's house.

Wolfgang had showed up at my office about eleven-thirty. Now it was nearly four, and still raining. I didn't know when he'd been attacked by the "terrorists" but he'd been away from home for many hours.

Though when I got there it didn't seem like the house was empty. Through the rain I could see some lights on inside. But not behind curtained windows. I could see them through the wide-open door.

I parked and went to the porch. It was then that I discovered the door wasn't wide open after all. It had been pulled off its hinges.

4

I had no idea what Wolfgang had been doing in the two months since I'd last seen him. Then he was hale and hearty – not a single stab wound. He had talked optimistically about the future, wanting to create a project to help the people he described as society's "invisibles".

And when I'd last visited his house, the interior was immaculate. Wolfgang – though then he was LeBron – had converted the conventional interior into a large space. He'd done all the work himself, having trained as a carpenter. And he'd painted pictures and designs on the walls. There wasn't much furniture when I'd been there, just what a half-alien gentleman would use when living on his own.

But now, coming through the open doorway, I saw pieces of furniture everywhere. Most seemed once to have come from beds, and there were also mattresses ripped open.

This was clearly a matter for the police, though none was on the scene.

Which left me with a decision to make. I ought to call Imberlain, who'd given me his card. But my impulse was to call my daughter. She was a cop just off her probationary year. Sam didn't work southeast but Wolfgang's house wasn't far from the southwest sector where she did work. And she, at least, was used to me. She wouldn't ask me endless questions about why I'd gone to Wolfgang's house instead of going home.

"Why did you call me, Daddy?"

"You're a cop. This is a police matter."

"Call 911."

"It isn't an emergency. The house isn't on fire. The front door's been ripped off its hinges. The owner's in hospital with four stab wounds. There are a few lights on but I don't know if anyone's inside. I didn't want to go in without somebody knowing where I am and what I'm doing."

"So naturally you called me."

"My daughter, the cop. Naturally," I said, "I'm not asking

you to drop whatever you're doing and rush out here, but would you stay on the phone while I go in?"

"You shouldn't go in. It's a crime scene. You should call the police."

"I did call the police. And what if someone's in there, and injured?"

"Call 327 3811. That's the number for non-emergencies."

"I'm going in." I was already inside the front door, but dwelling on details would be pedantic.

"Call the number, Daddy."

"Just hang on while I look around."

"Daddy!"

Slowly I walked into the middle of the open room. The room was chaos. A large television set had been tipped off its mounting. DVDs were scattered over a whole corner. In the kitchen area large pans were on the floor. More and larger pans than I would have thought a man living alone would have. Mind you, there were pieces from a lot of beds – I counted what looked like half a dozen without trying. How many people were sleeping here? Had Wolfgang set up an open-plan B & B?

"Daddy?"

"I'm here, honey. Just hang on."

"I'm hanging up."

"Please don't do that."

Given the beds, I was interested in what I didn't see. Which was evidence of people – their bags, their clothes . . . Such things might be underneath the wreckage, but I saw nothing on top.

I made my way to the back door. That was still on its hinges but it swung loose in the bits of breeze that passed through the house.

I didn't get it.

"Daddy, I'm hanging up."

I was about to say okay and that she should get back to whatever or whomever she was doing when I heard a whimper.

"Hang on. I hear something. Or someone."

"Who?"

"I'm looking."

I followed the sound. I found its source in the bathroom. It was a child. "It's a little boy."

The kid looked up sharply. He had tear-stained eyes. "I'm a girl," he said.

"I mean a little girl."

"How old?" Sam asked.

"About . . . seven."

"I'm ten."

"I mean ten. She's about ten. And her name is Jane."

"Nicole," the girl said.

"I mean Nicole. And she's resting in the bathroom because she just broke all the furniture here and destroyed the place."

"I'm hiding," Nicole said. "I was scared."

5

Sam arrived about half an hour later. She wasn't wearing her uniform.

"Thanks for coming," I said. "I didn't know what to do."

"I hope you didn't disturb anything."

"I had to think of Nicole." Nicole looked up from a chair she was using as a table in the kitchen area. "She was hungry."

"Thirsty," Nicole said.

"And thirsty. I made her a glass of water."

"You don't *make* water," Nicole said.

"And I *made* her cinnamon toast." I stuck my tongue out at the child. She laughed. I turned to Sam. "Like I used to make for you."

"Is that your wife?"

"My daughter."

"Is that *really* your daughter?" Nicole asked.

"My lovely daughter, of whom I am double-proud."

"Why double?"

"Proud of her as an outstanding police person and proud

of her as a wonderful human being who has come through a lot of difficulties in her life."

Nicole frowned. "She's police?"

"Sure as shootin'."

Sam drew me aside. "What do you know about her?" I shook my head. "Or about what happened?" I shrugged.

"I waited for you before asking questions," I said.

Sam looked at her watch.

"Do you have to be somewhere?"

"I called this in on my way. Some uniforms should be here soon." She knelt beside Nicole's "table". "I'm Sam," she said.

"That's a *boy's* name."

"My father wanted a boy. He didn't realize that girls are better."

That pleased the child, who acknowledged it by taking a giant mouthful of the toast, as if no mere boy could eat so much at one time. She choked a little but got it down.

Sam said, "I need you to tell me what happened here, Nicole."

"Men came and wanted money. Wolfgang wouldn't give it to them so they looked everywhere for it. Then they took him away."

"Wolfgang?" Sam asked.

"He owns the house," I said.

"The men broke everything," Nicole said. "It wasn't me."

"Who else was here?"

"Two of the mothers." Nicole thought. "Tara and ... I can't remember her name."

"They were staying here?" Sam asked.

"We all stay here."

"Why is that?"

"Our husbands and boyfriends aren't good ones. They hit us." Her face wrinkled. "Not me. But Mom. Harvey does that."

"Is Harvey your dad?"

"No." Her frown suggested that the less she had to do with Harvey the happier she'd be.

"How many women are staying here?" Sam asked.

Nicole counted on her fingers. "Seven."

"And children?"

"Only me and a couple of babies."

"Where are they all now?" Sam asked.

"Tara and the other one ran away when the men came. Two others . . . Janine and Stephanie . . . They came back later but they left. I think it was because their kids were about to get out of school." She thought. "That's Harry after the prince of England 'cause he's got red hair, and Chloe."

"They go to school?" Sam said. "I thought you said only babies stayed here."

"Harry's six and Chloe is seven. They're *such* babies."

"And," Sam said, "where is *your* mother, Nicole?"

After toughing it out for a moment, Nicole's face puckered up. She began to cry. "I don't know. She left this morning and said I should wait here."

"And you haven't seen her or heard from her?"

"I *told* her I should have my own phone."

"Why aren't you at school?"

"The one I go to is too far away. Mom said we'd get a new one soon."

"She wasn't here when the men came?"

"No."

"Do you know where she went? To work, maybe?"

"She used to work at Denny's but then Harvey found her. I don't know if she found another job yet." Another pucker. "But she always comes back at night. I wait here for her." She looked up at Sam. "Do you think Harvey found her again?"

"I don't know," Sam said quietly, "but I'll try to find out. So Harvey wasn't one of the men who took Wolfgang away?"

"I don't know. They had masks on."

"What kind of masks?"

"All over their faces, with holes for the eyes."

"Did you recognize any of the men?"

She shook her head.

I said, "Do you know Harvey's last name?"

"Peterson, I think."

"Does Harvey know you and your mother live here now?"

"I don't think so. But we've only been here . . ." She thought. "Three nights. But even if Harvey comes Wolfgang promised he won't get in."

"How does he make sure of that?"

"He locks the door and he's the only one who answers it." The face puckered again. "But when the men came, they just pushed him out of the way. Wolfgang shouted for everyone to run and he jumped on one of the men, on his back."

"You must have been scared, Nicole," I said.

She nodded.

"But you didn't leave with the other women?"

"Mom said to wait here."

There was noise at the front of the house. We turned to look and saw two cops coming in through the aforementioned – but absent – door.

Sam put her arm around Nicole and took control.

I took flight.

6

I headed back to the hospital. The answers to most of my questions were knocking around somewhere in Wolfgang's head. Wolfgang, the half-alien formerly known as LeBron James, Wolfgang, the half-alien born in Santa Claus, Indiana, under the name of Curtis Nelson.

I did know *some* things.

As I drove I thought about what Nicole had told us and I wondered what kind of place Wolfgang was running. The Wolfgang I'd known didn't seem a first-choice candidate for defender against angry terrorists, or boyfriends. He wasn't big – just an average kind of guy. And when I knew him he didn't even have secure locks on his doors.

However, at that time he'd lived alone. Now he lived with seven women and three children. Maybe other things had changed too.

Once inside the hospital I was waylaid in the crowded waiting room. The rain hadn't stopped and people continued to flood into Emergency. However, I said magic words. I asked for Nurse Matty by name. Moments later she appeared before me.

"You're back," she said.

"Your powers of observation continue to dazzle."

"I thought this Wolfgang guy wasn't a friend."

"He's not. However, I've just been to his house where the cops are sifting through the wreckage of all the furniture."

She leaned forward with her eyes wide open. "*Wreckage?*"

"There was also a ten-year-old girl hiding there who doesn't know where her mother is."

"This is Wolfgang's . . . girlfriend?"

"Unlikely, but he's the only person I can think of who might have an idea what's up with mom. And if he's anywhere close to conversation-enabled, I need to see him."

Nurse Matty tilted her head. "So, does that make you a cop?"

"No. But my daughter is."

She blinked a couple of time. "Does *anything* you say make sense?"

"I've been asked that before."

"I'm going to take you to see him anyway."

"Thank you."

"But you've got to promise not to stab him. We've sewn him up enough for one day. We found a fourth cut – in his shoulder from the back. Did I tell you that before?"

"Not where it was."

She turned and we walked. "He's in a recovery room."

"Not intensive care then?"

"He should be fine. Only one of the abdominal wounds was deep. There were perforations in his liver and pancreas, but not big ones. The shoulder will give him trouble for a long time, but your Wolfgang is a very lucky boy."

"I wonder if he sees it that way yet." After a couple of turns, I said, "Were the four wounds all with different knives? Could they tell?"

"I don't know."

"They didn't find he has two hearts by any chance, did they?"

She stopped abruptly and looked at me. "What is *that* supposed to mean?"

"Don't mind me."

"That he loves you but he loves somebody else too?"

"I know nothing whatever about his love life, if any."

"I don't know if he's going to make much sense yet," she said, "so you should be a perfect pair."

"This whole situation doesn't make any sense," I said.

"No?"

"Like, why did he come to *me*?"

Outside some drawn curtains, Matty said, "Remember, people take different lengths of time to come around after a general anaesthetic." She opened a gap in the curtains and I went in.

7

Wolfgang was not looking his best. The side of his head was bandaged – though I hadn't heard about a head injury – and there were enough drips and tubes and machines to make Baron Münchhausen envious.

But he responded to the noise of my arrival and he moved to sit up while I pulled a chair close. "Mr Albert Samson," he said. "Greetings."

"Mr Wolfgang . . . would that be Mozart?"

"It would." Not too spaced-out to smile.

"How's it going?"

"I've felt better. But we heal quickly."

"You told me that before. Do you remember?"

He thought. He didn't remember.

"Have you healed enough to answer some questions?"

"I'll try."

"Your house is a wreck."

"That's not a question."

"Why are seven women and three children living with you?"

"Not *living*."

"They have – had – beds. They come home to your place after they finish work. What do *you* call it?"

"Visiting."

"Silly me."

"It wasn't my plan."

"Women, some with children, just started appearing at your door?"

"It began with one. I was walking around and I found this woman leaning against a fence. She'd been beaten up."

"You *found* her?"

"About two miles from my house – in fact a little closer to yours than mine."

"So you dialled 911?"

"She didn't want me to do that."

"Why not?"

"Do you know anything about the psychology of battered women?"

"Do you?"

"I've been reading up on it. Anyhow, I brought her home. I got her a bed. The idea was that she could stay for a few days, until she felt better."

"When was this?"

"Second week in October."

"And is she still visiting you?"

"Well, yes."

"And she happened to have some buddies who also got beaten up?"

"I guess. Or some kind of word started spreading around. Women, and children . . ."

"But there are shelters in the city, Wolfgang. Organized places with much better facilities than just having beds scattered around an open space, all sharing one bathroom."

"And one kitchen . . . I know. Dayspring, the Julian Center . . . I have a list and I tell them. And some have gone to them. But a lot don't want to."

"They all stayed on?"

"A lot have gone back to where they came from." He shook his head sadly.

I said, "Back in September you talked about doing something for 'invisible' people."

"This wasn't what I meant. I want to do something to *help* people with problems. But now all I do is squeeze more beds in and try to keep them all from squabbling. I hate raised voices."

He paused. I just waited. Any group of people crowded in together isn't going to last as happy families. The *Big Brother* television shows made fortunes on that principle.

Wolfgang said, "I don't want my house to be a refuge for anyone but me. And I'm sure the neighbours don't like it. But if people are in trouble, how can I say no to them?"

"Practice makes perfect," I said.

"But the best part . . ." He smiled with some life in his eyes.

"What?"

"Sometimes they hold my father's handprint and they say it makes them feel *better*."

I knew all about the "handprint", supposedly left by his extraterrestrial father. In the real world it was a piece of limestone with some grooves in it that looked like the fossilized veins of a leaf.

"They feel 'better'?"

"It calms them. They say it makes them more positive about life and the future. Sometimes we sit in a circle and pass it around."

"The psychological equivalent of homeopathy?"

"They tell me they feel something. I feel something. Maybe if you'd hold it you'd feel something too."

"I guarantee I'd feel whatever a guy giving me a safe place to sleep and food to eat wanted me to feel."

He tilted his head with a world-weary smile.

I said, "I didn't see the stone in the wreckage."

"It wasn't out. I keep it in a safe place."

"So the police in your house won't be in danger of feeling better by stumbling across it."

"Police?"

"You were cut up. Your house is a wreck. What do you expect?"

"I guess."

"Wolfgang, what *happened*? You were stabbed four times, maybe with as many as four different knives. Did everyone want a piece? Like when the Brutus gang hit Julius Caesar?"

"They weren't trying to kill me. They were trying to get me to tell them where I keep my money."

"What *happened*?"

"Four men came to the door wearing masks. I wouldn't let them in, but they broke the door down and grabbed me and said they wanted money."

"So it was money rather than being connected to the women you were sheltering?"

"Yes and no." He smiled.

"Will I get a straight answer if I whack that bandaged shoulder with a saline drip bag?"

He didn't like the sound of that.

"When I asked you before, you said it was terrorists."

He shook his head.

"It's what you told me," I said.

"They had terrorists' *masks*."

"I only heard 'terrorists'. So we're talking about their masks, not them?"

He nodded.

"Because I didn't hear the apostrophe, the city of Indianapolis is on a rainbow alert."

"They just wanted money. For some reason they thought I keep enough money around the place to be worth robbing me."

"Do you keep a lot of money around?"

"You never know when you're going to need cash. Especially with a lot of mouths to feed."

"And beds to buy." He nodded. "How many women have stayed in your house since October?"

"Maybe twenty. Twenty-five."

"Do you keep records?"

"Of what?"

"Well, like their full names and Social Security numbers."

"I'm extraterrestrial, not anal."

"And do you get a lot of men coming to the door?"

"A few. Husbands and boyfriends. A violent girlfriend once too. Not often."

"So what happened when the four guys in terrorists' masks demanded your money?"

"I wouldn't give it to them."

"Why not?"

He smiled. "Guess?"

I stood up and threatened his shoulder. But as he winced I put it together. "You keep your money in the same place as the handprint?"

"Yes." A smile.

"So you got yourself cut to pieces because you were protecting that damned chunk of rock."

"Whoever told them about the money might have told them how much the handprint means to me. I couldn't bear to lose it."

So he'd rather die. I guess I just don't understand extraterrestrials . . . "They wanted money. You wouldn't give it to them. What happened then?"

"They showed me the knives but when I still wouldn't do it the leader cut me – not deep, but enough to draw blood. There were a couple of women in the house and that set them off screaming and they ran. The men started cutting up mattresses and couches and everything they could see that might have money in it. But eventually the leader said they should take me with them, so they bundled me into a car."

"Right there, in front of your house?"

"Yes."

"What kind of car was it?"

"Quite large. Quite old. Light green or maybe light blue."

Not a description to conjure up a car with, but the kind of neighbourhood Wolfgang lived in would probably provide the police plenty of witnesses.

"Where did they take you?"

"They just drove around."

"And continued to cut you in the car?"

"They didn't know what else to do. But then . . ."

"What?"

"They gave up. The shoulder was bleeding so much the driver complained about the car upholstery and how they'd never be able to clean the DNA off it. He said he didn't want to burn his car and they started arguing with each other."

"Obviously a gang of master criminals."

"So they dumped me out, behind the Murphy building and I recognized it."

The old Murphy five and dime was across Virginia Avenue from my office. That was one question answered.

"So you came to me," I said.

"I didn't have a phone. They took the stuff in my pockets."

"What was in them?"

"The usual things. Keys, wallet, phone."

"Much money?"

"A couple of hundred."

"The police are going to want to hear in detail what these guys said, anything you can remember about the car, and maybe names of the women staying with you."

"You don't want those things?"

"Are you hiring me?"

"Well, no. But I thought . . ."

"The cops probably won't have much trouble tracking down your assailants. And when they find them they'll have the advantage of the power of arrest."

"I see."

Which made me wonder something. "Wolfgang, could the guys who attacked you have been neighbours of yours?"

"Neighbours?" A deep frown.

"From families who don't like the idea of your opening your house to waifs and strays."

"Well . . ." He thought about it. "I don't know *who* they were."

"Did they say anything about your moving somewhere else, say?"

He shook his head. "It seemed to be all about the money. I've had some problems with my neighbours but I can't imagine . . ."

"Okay," I said. Though there seemed to be quite a lot he couldn't imagine, at one time or another. Why people didn't just accept him as an extraterrestrial, for instance. "I do want something else."

"What?"

"I found a little girl in your house. She was hiding and must have been there for hours."

"Who?"

"Nicole? She's ten."

He nodded. "Elaine's little girl."

"Elaine hasn't come back."

"That's surprising. She's a very attentive mother."

"Nicole was surprised too . . ."

8

I had no reason to think that Elaine was in the kind of trouble that would lead her to court. But a woman desperate enough to run with her child from a boyfriend was not going to leave that kid unattended if she could help it.

The police would get on to it eventually, no doubt. But as long as they could drop the kid into the welfare system they'd focus first on the wreckage and the stabbings. That's how police prioritize. Even those related to me by blood. Unless given a little guidance.

I had no specific reason to connect Elaine's absence to the attack on Wolfgang, but I don't believe in coincidence much more than I believe in extraterrestrials. One way or another there was a connection. And the only person I knew who could tell me more about Elaine was Nicole.

I called Sam.

"Where are you, Daddy?" she asked.

"Funny thing. I was about to ask you the same question."

"A detective named Saul Imberlain wants to talk to you."

"I already talked to him, at the hospital."

"He wants to talk to you again, so I gave him your address and phone number."

"I haven't been home. But look, sweetie, I need to talk some more with the little girl, Nicole. Do you know where she is?"

"She's still here."

"Wolfgang's house?"

"I'm waiting with her till someone from the Department of Child Services shows up. Which won't be long."

"So her mother hasn't appeared?"

"No."

"Just don't let Nicole go anywhere before I get there, okay?"

"Why not?" I could hear her not saying she wasn't on duty.

"Because I'm trying to find her mother and if I can do that it'll save the poor kid some grief."

After a moment Sam said, "Okay."

What a good girl.

9

Wolfgang's house looked lit up like a roaring fire now that the light was fading. The cops seemed to have turned on every light in the place.

Which is not to say there weren't a few lights aglow elsewhere along the street. Dim ones, with just enough illumination for neighbours to find their cigarettes and lemonade without making a mess as they watched the goings-on from behind their curtained windows. The neighbours were curious, but were they hostile?

A carpenter was at work on a temporary repair to the front door as I went in. Sam sat with Nicole in the kitchen area. A tall guy with a brown and grey beard stood behind them. Sam got up when she saw me. The tall guy pulled out a notebook.

Sam said, "This is Whitney Moser of DCS. Department of Child Services."

Moser offered a hand.

I shook it. I like to give people the benefit of the doubt.

Sam said, "Mr Moser is going to take Nicole to where she can sleep tonight."

"I need to ask her a few questions," I said.

"And she needs to get settled for the night so she can get some sleep," Moser said. "You can't treat a child the way you might treat an adult."

I crouched to be on a level with Nicole. Admittedly, she looked sleepy. It wasn't all that late, but she'd had a shocking day. "Hi," I said.

"Hi."

"Which would you rather do, Nicole?" I asked. "Get some sleep or help me find your mother?"

"Daddy!" Sam said as Moser said, "Honestly, Mr Samson."

"Help find Mom," Nicole said. She was plenty awake now.

"I need you to tell me some things that no one but you knows."

"Okay."

"Do you know the address where you and your mom lived with Harvey?"

"Who's Harvey?" I heard Moser whisper to Sam.

Nicole said, "3117 Hincot Street."

"Good girl. And does your mom have any friends around there?"

"Laurie across the street."

"Right across the street?"

She nodded. "With the orange door. Mom wanted one but Harvey said no."

"Shall I get you an orange door for Christmas?"

She nodded, vigorously considering how tired she was.

"What school did you go to before you and your mom moved here?"

"Ninety-three."

"Did you like it there?"

Nod.

"I bet they liked you there too."

A little shrug. Then a nod.

"What's your mom's name?"

"Elaine."

"Elaine what?"

"Warren."

"And are she and Harvey married or is he your mom's boyfriend?"

"No."

"No?"

"He *was* her boyfriend. We don't put up with him anymore."

"And does your mom have any brothers or sisters that you know about?"

"Bobby. But he died."

"Oh, I'm sorry to hear that."

"He did magic. He found an egg in my ear."

I took a close look at one of her ears. "Yeah, I'd say there was room for an egg in there."

She smiled as she rubbed the ear in question.

I said, "And how about your mom's parents? Do you know them?"

A nod.

"Where do they live?"

"Crawfordsville."

"Are their names Mr and Mrs Warren?"

A nod, but then uncertainty. "I guess."

"Do you know their first names?"

"She's Lily. He's . . . Um. Oh, he's Wayne."

"And do you like them?"

A nod.

"My grandmother used to make pies, just for me," I said. "Does Lily do that for you?"

Shake of the head.

"Well, I'll tell her to get her act together," I said.

"Yeah!" Nicole said. Then she yawned.

I said, "I'm going to let you go sleep now."

Nicole looked from me to Moser and back to me. "I want to stay here, in case Mom comes home."

"I'll see what we can arrange." I gestured to Sam to take over distracting the little girl.

I led the social worker a few feet away. "Look," I said, "I know you want to get this all settled."

"I want what's best for Nicole," Moser said.

"If I can find her mother in a reasonable amount of time, that would be best, wouldn't it?"

"As long as she's able to provide a safe environment."

"Can you hang on here for a while?"

"Do you know where Elaine Warren is?"

I was tempted to say yes just to get the guy to agree but I saw Nicole paying attention to us. "Not for sure, but I have an idea. And I'll give finding her a damn good try. Plus, you've seen that Nicole doesn't want to leave. I'd appreciate it if you'll give me some time."

Moser looked at his watch.

I said, "Think about all the paperwork you'll save if I'm successful."

Moser turned out to be one of the good ones.

10

Whitney Moser began to gather bits of bed and bedding to make Nicole a place to sleep and I took Sam to the front porch. "He's going to stay here with Nicole while I can have a crack at finding Elaine."

"Where is she?" Sam said.

"I have no idea."

"Great."

"But I might know someone who does."

"I want to help, if I can, Daddy."

"Officially or as a caring human being?"

"Can you stop being you for a moment and just tell me what you have in mind?"

I had a moment in which I visualized Wolfgang the extra-terrestrial in his hospital bed, bandaged and receiving drips. My feeling of isolation from the world I inhabit can be as self-created as his. "Sorry. I'm going to try to become a better person."

"Perhaps you can postpone that too," she said, looking at her watch.

"I want to start by looking at 3117 Hincot Street. If I can find it."

"Want to follow me and my GPS?"

Hincot was a short, dead-end street behind an old shopping centre a couple of miles south of the city's centre. It didn't appear to be a bad neighbourhood, but then again it didn't *appear* much at all. The GPS had brought us to a dark stretch between two streetlights that didn't work. Or that had been shot out. I've never owned a gun in all my years as a PI but for a moment I was glad Sam-the-cop was packing.

However, the only trouble we encountered was not being able to see the house numbers without our flashlights, what with the darkness and the rain.

But we found 3117, which turned out to be the top half of a duplex. Both halves were dark.

"What do you think?" Sam asked.

"I'm going to walk around back in case Harvey's sitting in his kitchen drinking himself silly by candlelight. You could make a note of the licence plate numbers of the cars parked nearby along the street."

"You think one of them is Harvey's?"

There were only a few cars on the street, none parked in front of the duplex, so the chances weren't good that they were relevant. But who knew?

My squishy stroll around the property did not reveal Harvey lit up round back. Or any evidence of occupation at all. There were also no cars on the alley pull-in space behind the house. Maybe everyone was out partying.

But when I returned to the front Sam's was not the only umbrella over the sidewalk. She was talking with a woman.

Sam said, "Daddy, this is Laurie. She lives—"

"Across the street and has an orange door." I stepped forward with a hand extended. "Nicole told us about you. Once we checked to see whether Harvey was at home we were going to come over and see you."

Laurie's hand was soft and warm, both pleasant qualities to experience when you're standing under an umbrella on a cold, rainy night.

"Are you a cop too?" Laurie asked.

Sam said, "Laurie came over because she thought we looked like we were police."

"I leave the weighty burden of badge-carrying to the youngsters," I said.

"I thought maybe you were here because you'd arrested Harvey and wanted to check out his house, that kind of thing," Laurie said.

"Laurie," I said, "why do you think Harvey's done something to be arrested for?"

"Can you see my face?" she asked, and turned her head.

Sam lit Laurie's face with her flashlight, revealing puffy bruising around her left ear and cuts that looked like scratches on her neck.

"Are you saying Harvey did that?" I asked.

"He certainly did."

"Why?"

"He thought I knew where Elaine was, that I was holding out on him."

"When was this?"

"This morning."

"And did you report the assault to the police?"

She hesitated, maybe working out that her answer could be checked. "No."

"Why not?"

"He said it would be my word against his and that if I told the police he and his friends would come back and *really* hurt me."

Sam said, "And do you know where Elaine is?"

Laurie hesitated over this too.

I said, "Elaine's with you, isn't she?"

"What?" both women said.

"Elaine is in your house right now," I said. "Isn't she? That's why you couldn't to do anything that might result in Harvey coming back and coming in."

Elaine Warren met us just inside the orange door. "Has Harvey been arrested?" she asked Laurie. "They're cops, right? He's been arrested, right?" She looked from me to Sam and back to Laurie. None of us spoke. "What? What?"

"The girl's a cop," Laurie said. "And, no, Harvey hasn't been arrested."

"Why *not*?" Elaine was clearly agitated.

Laurie put her arms around her friend and made a face at us to say we shouldn't upset her more.

I wasn't that worried about upsetting her, but I said, "That's a lovely daughter you have, Elaine."

"What?" She looked up and pulled away from Laurie's support.

"Nicole. Bright, funny. A real credit to you."

"Is she all right?"

"She's fine. We've left her with a guy from Child Services."

"Child Services?" New panic. "But Wolfgang said he'd look after her," Elaine said.

"Wolfgang is in the hospital, Mrs Warren," Sam said. "He was attacked by four men and stabbed several times."

"No," Elaine said, with disbelief. "*No!*" she cried.

I said, "So the Child Services guy is waiting with Nicole at Wolfgang's. They both hope you'll come back tonight to pick her up."

"How can I do that?" Elaine was more agitated than ever. "Where could we go? If Harvey sees me, I'm a dead woman."

"You think he's still looking for you?" Sam said.

"Unless you people lock him away."

"Elaine," I said, "when we came in, why did you ask if Harvey'd been arrested?"

"Because he's dangerous, and evil. Look what he did to Laurie."

"But the police didn't know what he did to Laurie."

Elaine looked from me to Sam to Laurie. "I just thought . . ."

"What?"

"Oh, I don't know. I don't *know*. I need to get Nicole. But I *can't*. If he sees me . . ."

"You think he'll be waiting for you outside Wolfgang's?"

She thought. "He could be. He probably is. Oh God!"

"Well, suppose we bring Nicole here for the time being."

Sam looked at me uncertainly.

"Would you?" Elaine said. She sounded more hopeful than at any previous time in the conversation. "Will you? Please!"

11

As soon as Laurie's orange door closed behind us, Sam said, "Whitney Moser's not going to let us bring Nicole here. Not with a dangerous guy on the loose who's already threatened to come back to Laurie's."

"No?"

"I wouldn't."

I said nothing.

"Daddy?"

"Yes, dear?"

"What are you up to?"

"Tell me, if you were Harvey and you were looking for Elaine, where would you wait for her?"

Sam considered. "Wolfgang's maybe."

"Once you've seen the cop cars there? Given that Elaine all but told us that he was one of the gang that stabbed Wolfgang?"

"She did?"

"She expected him to be *arrested*, honey. Even Wolfgang the extraterrestrial doesn't claim to read minds, and if he can't, then the police sure can't. Arrested for what, since Laurie didn't report him?"

"If he *was* part of that," Sam said, "then he wouldn't hang around while the cop cars were there."

"So what would be your second choice as a place to wait for Elaine?"

"Well," Sam said, "here, I guess. If he thinks Laurie is helping her."

"And tell me, did you get a chance to look at the cars parked along the street?"

"Yes. But I haven't called them in."

I said, "Were the windows of any of the cars fogged up with condensation?"

12

Sam and I got in our cars and drove away.

Around the corner and then another block for luck. Sam called for a couple of squad cars to join her, stressing that they must do it quietly and must avoid Hincot Street.

The rain might have brought a lot of people out to the ER but it seemed to have kept most of Indy's malfeasants at home. Patrolling cops were bored. The call for two cars brought five.

Under Sam's guidance a couple of them drove up the alley behind 3117 with their lights out. Once they were in place at the end of the street, Sam and the other patrol cars filled the street from its open end.

I walked back to the corner to watch. While I waited for Sam to give the go, a gust of wind blew my umbrella inside out. Then another gust righted it, but left me with a droopy corner – the umbrella would never be the same again. Was it a metaphor for life? We survive our trials but we're never quite the same?

Suddenly the six cars leapt into action, lighting the street with head, spot and blue-revolving lights. Moments later Harvey's car was surrounded with guns brandished by cops in raincoats. I saw his car's door open a crack. The first thing out was his hands held high and in plain sight. Once he was standing by the car, even from a distance he looked like he didn't know what had hit him.

I wondered if Harvey figured that his windows being steamed up would make him inconspicuous because no one could see him in the car. Wrong. His being the only car on the street with opaque windows made it more conspicuous, not less. Poor Harvey. Not one of nature's deep thinkers, at a guess.

Elaine didn't *think* Harvey had a gun, but in Indiana you can never be sure. Hence the aggressive posture of the bored police officers. As it turned out, he was as unarmed as he was unaware. They didn't even find his knife.

While the assembled representatives of law enforcement secured him ready for transfer downtown, I crossed and went back to Laurie's orange door, my umbrella's new flap flapping in the wind.

13

Whitney Moser was sitting on a kitchen chair, concentrating on his phone. Either he was dealing with weighty matters of child protection or he was playing on one of his game apps. Nicole was asleep at his feet, curled up on a nest of mattress leftovers.

Elaine followed me into the house, but as soon as she saw Nicole she rushed to her and took her in her arms.

"Mom?" Nicole said as she rubbed her eyes and opened them.

It would have broken my heart if she'd woken up like that for anybody else.

Moser and I stepped away and I explained that the abusive boyfriend was now in custody, that Elaine and Nicole could go safely to the duplex where they'd been living or stay with a friend across the street.

"That's just as well," Moser said, "because I couldn't allow them to stay on here."

I thought he meant because of the lack of whole beds, but that wasn't it.

"The guy who owns this place," Moser said, "what's his name?"

"Wolfgang. I'm not sure what his full name is." By now he might have changed it again, to that of someone else whose precociousness he suspected of identifying a fellow extrater-restrial.

"Well, I've checked the address and he doesn't have any of the permits he needs to run a refuge, *especially* one with children."

"I don't think Wolfgang intended this place to become anything formal. He just took in people who asked him for help."

"Well, he'll have to learn to say no," Moser said, "unless he goes through the authorization procedure. But even if he gets personal clearance, his chances of being approved for one big open-plan room . . ."

"He means well," I said. "I can't say more than that."

Moser gave me a card. "Have him get in touch with me if he wants to talk about his options."

I took the card.

But my lack of enthusiasm for bureaucracy's facility for stifling generosity must have shown, because Moser said, "I'm not one of the bad guys, Mr Samson."

"I worked that out before," I said.

"It's just the way things are."

14

I didn't return to the hospital until the morning. The heavy rain had stopped at last. Impenetrably grey skies were drop-ping no more than a drizzle.

Sam met me there, curious to see the guy who was at the centre of the action. And I was pleased to see that Nurse Matty was on duty again. Or was it still? "Don't you ever get time off?" I asked her.

"I volunteered for a double," she said, "which tells you something about my private life."

"It tells me you're a wonderful, caring person who's prob-ably stockpiling her money in order to open a charitable foundation."

"Me and Bill Gates." She eyed Sam up. "So, who's your friend? Or is this a non-friend too?"

"She is, indeed, a friend. As well as being my daughter."

"The cop?"

"Yes."

"And she's *your* daughter?" Matty tilted her head. "Her mother must be very, very beautiful."

I declined to respond. "How's the patient?" I asked.

"He's making me a little uncomfortable, to tell the truth."

"Because of his endless demands for attention and enhanced comforts?"

"Cut up like he is, he should be restless and trying to get more pain relief out of us. But instead he just lies there."

"And that's a problem for you?"

"He watches everyone come and go, and then he smiles a little smile whenever someone takes his blood pressure or fluffs up his pillows."

"And says thank you, I bet."

"Every time. It's creeping me out. I'll be glad when we get a normal patient back in that bed."

"Matty, have you had a personal chat with him?"

"*Personal?* Is that man-code for something I don't understand?"

"Asked him about himself, his family?"

"No." She peered at me. "Why?"

"Well, don't, if what you like is normal."

"Okay, now you're creeping me out too." She shook her head. "You know where he is."

"Yeah."

"Nice to meet you," she said to Sam and went about her business.

I led Sam to my non-friend.

Wolfgang was not asleep. He gave us a little smile when we came in. "Albert," he said. "And a stranger." He peered at Sam. "Are you two related? Daughter?"

"Thanks for acknowledging my genes," I said. "This is Sam."

"How do you do, Sam?"

"Nice to meet you, Mr . . . Mozart?"

"Just call me Wolfgang." He turned to me. "I thought you told me your daughter is a police officer."

"She is."

He stared at her. "Okay, I can see it now. But there's something . . . more. You're an unusual person, Ms Samson."

"Is that unusual-good or just unusual-different?" Sam asked.

"Good. Definitely good. You will do things in your life."

"No need to butter her up. She's not here to arrest you," I said.

"We'll see how it goes," Sam said. "No promises."

I said, "They're complaining about you out there. They say you should be trying to get more morphine out of them."

"It's only pain," Wolfgang said.

"There have been developments since I was here yesterday."

"Do I want to know?"

"Probably not, but there will be consequences for you." I sat beside Sam to tell the story of the previous evening. As it went on, Wolfgang looked increasingly weary. Weary and unbelieving.

"*Elaine* is responsible for what happened?"

"I don't know how the law will interpret it, but hers was the big bang from which the rest of yesterday's universe followed."

"But *why*? I took her in. I fed her. Her and her child."

"It was about her, Wolfgang, not you."

He absorbed this. "Okay. I can see that. I'm thinking narrowly."

"She was desperate to get rid of her boyfriend. She never intended for anyone to get hurt. And, like yourself, she hasn't had a good experience with the police."

He glanced at Sam, who said, "So she went to her best friend. She got the friend to ask Harvey, the boyfriend, what it would take to get him to leave Elaine alone once and for all. Harvey said money."

Wolfgang shook his head slowly, sad about the way human nature plays out. Maybe he was wishing his dad had taken him along to Planet Other.

"So Elaine and the friend hatched up a plan," I said. "The friend told Harvey that you keep a lot of money around the house. Elaine *thought* he'd go to your place alone and that between you and the women there you'd subdue him and he'd be arrested."

I paused while Wolfgang revisited what had happened in his house the previous day. "When I saw the four masked men," he said, "I shouted for all the women to get out. Everyone ran out the back door."

Except for Nicole. I said, "Maybe Harvey smelled some kind of rat when Elaine's friend became cooperative. But for whatever reason he recruited some friends of his own for the visit to your house. Friends willing to rough you up for some easy money."

"All wearing those terrorists' masks." Wolfgang shook his head, looking wearier and wearier.

Sam said, "We have Harvey in custody, Mr Mozart. I hear that he gave up the rest of the 'terrorists' in about five seconds."

"They're sad, silly men," Wolfgang said. "I've been thinking about how they acted when they had me in their car. They were childish and squabbly. And if they needed money so badly, they should just have asked. I'd have given them some."

"That's not how things are expected to work on Planet Earth," I said. "And chances are it was greed rather than need anyway. For which they'll all go down, for assault with deadly weapons."

"I won't press charges."

"What?"

"I won't testify against them. I should have talked more with Elaine. I should have learned more about *her* problems. I should have worked out some way to help her. I could have talked with this Harvey."

"Had him hold your stone and let it make him see the light?"

"You think I'm crazy, don't you?"

"I'd say you are otherworldly, but you'd just agree with me," I said.

Sam said, "Your refusal to testify won't keep them from being charged, Mr Mozart. They'll testify against each other. The medical records here will establish the injuries. They'll plead out. And they will go to jail. They're dangerous and they need to be prevented from hurting more innocent people."

I said, "Why wouldn't you help punish idiots who are willing to stab people to get a few bucks?"

"Because jail is not the answer. We have a higher percentage of our population in jail than any other country in the world and things like this *still* happen."

"You could ask the judge to give them twenty-five years of community service."

Wolfgang sat up in his bed. "I want to talk to them." He looked at me but then settled on Sam. "Can you make that happen, Officer Samson? I *need* to talk to them. All of them."

15

Sam and I stood in the parking lot before we went our separate ways. "Weird guy, your friend Wolfgang," she said.

"He's not my friend."

"Why does he want to talk to Harvey and the other idiots?"

"I think he believes he can spread peace on earth, one peace at a time."

"Is he a megalomaniac?"

"He's got this piece of limestone that he thinks has his extraterrestrial father's handprint on it. Wolfgang believes that people who touch the stone feel better. Maybe even become better people."

"If they do let him talk to Harvey," Sam said, "they won't let him take a lump of stone into the interview room. They'd be afraid your Wolfgang would just whack him on the head with it."

"That'd make *us* feel better, in his place," I said. "But then again you and I are not extraterrestrials."

"I suppose I should be thankful that you're human, no matter what Mom says."

"She was never *that* beautiful," I said. "It was her brains I went for. But then they ran out."

"Why didn't you tell Wolfgang that he can't run his house as a refuge anymore?"

"Maybe he'll pass his handprint around Children's Services and they'll sign him up and everyone will live happily ever after."

"You think?"

"With him I don't know what to think," I said. "Will Elaine face charges?"

"She and Laurie didn't tell Harvey 'Go stab', but they provided information knowing it was likely to result in a felony crime. Most judges won't like that much, especially in an election year."

"Maybe Wolfgang will want to fund a high-priced lawyer for her."

"Has he got a lot of money?"

"I have no idea."

"Will you go back in there now and tell him that Elaine might be in trouble?"

"Do you think I should?" I said.

"Maybe for Nicole," Sam said.

"Yeah, all right. Good kid, isn't she?"

"Yeah."

"Like you," I said. And she didn't even smack me for calling her a kid.

God's Lonely Man

Peter Guttridge

The wind rocked the car and spray broke across the traffic-lanes and misted the seaward window. Falcon kept the black limousine in view through the swish of his own wipers. He glanced at the ruined West Pier, buffeted by the unusually high sea. He wondered if this was the day it finally sank beneath the waves.

The limousine pulled off the promenade on to the narrow drive in front of the Grand Hotel. The doorman hurried to open the rear door with one hand, unfurling with a sweep of his arm the umbrella in his other. Falcon's target took a moment to exit the car then climbed the steps into the hotel.

Falcon picked up the book from the passenger seat and climbed from his car, his stiff left leg caught up in his clothing. He cursed as spray spumed over the promenade railing and slapped him in the face. He hated Brighton.

Wiping the stinging saltwater from his eyes, he hobbled across the road, anger rising as he saw the doorman give him a look that mixed amusement, contempt and pity.

"Don't I get your umbrella?" Falcon snapped as he drew level.

"Bit late for that," the doorman said, gesturing to Falcon's wet hair plastered to his head.

Falcon fought down the urge to drive his fist into this man's stupid, smirking face.

"What room?"

"Four thirty," the doorman said, the smirk replaced by fear as he saw something in Falcon's eyes. "His driver is parking."

Falcon hauled his leg up the steps, limped across the extravagant foyer and stood aside as the lift doors opened, disgorging a boisterous trio of women. They walked to the bar, arms casually draped about each other's shoulders, glancing back at him and giggling.

Falcon had never known that kind of camaraderie with men and certainly not with women. He'd never known intimacy with a woman except as a transaction. Instead of love he'd only known loss.

He entered the lift, praying for the doors to close before anyone else joined him. As they were closing, a long-fingered hand thrust between them. Falcon's face contorted for a moment. He had expected God to abandon him, given his line of work. What he hadn't expected was that God would keep spitting in his face.

A petite blonde wearing a slash of red lipstick, a short skirt and an apologetic smile stepped into the lift. She looked Falcon up and down. Falcon looked straight ahead. The woman stood too close, her perfume engulfing him. Falcon watched her reflection in the polished brass, his emotions shifting between longing and loathing.

The lift stopped at four. He brushed past her the moment the doors opened and set off down the corridor. The corridor was thickly carpeted, but at 422 he realized there were soft footfalls behind him. He paused, fiddling with the book in his hand.

Her perfume preceding her, the woman walked past him, hips swaying. When she'd gone a few yards ahead he followed more slowly. He passed 424, 426. She continued along the corridor.

He stopped at 430. The woman had slowed, looking at a piece of paper in her hand. Falcon hesitated, his fist half-raised to knock on the door. She came back down the corridor and stopped beside him. She laughed throatily.

"This should be interesting," she said as she reached over

to rap on the door. She pointed at the Bible in his hand then touched her breasts. "Which do you think he's going to go for, Father – The Good Book or the Bad Girl?"

Falcon gave her a tight smile and stepped to one side, his cassock swishing against his legs. He gestured for her to move directly in front of the fish-eye glass set in the door.

"I'm s-sure he'd rather s-see you than me," he said.

He heard the chain being removed on the inside of the door. The woman glanced at him then moistened her lips.

Falcon took the gun from the Bible's hollowed-out pages and let the book fall to the floor. He barged the opening door with his shoulder and shot the man through the right eye.

The man slumped to the floor as Falcon turned the gun on the woman. She was terrified, he could see, but she didn't make any sound. She held his eye as she reached for the door and pulled it shut.

He should kill her. He gestured to the lift as he stooped to pick up the Bible. She walked ahead of him. She watched him as he pressed the button. He examined her face. Longing or loathing. Love or loss. He had four floors to decide.

The Day of the Dead

Mary Hoffman

Just because he was wealthy, obnoxious and had a much younger wife, everyone assumed he was American.

That was what he wanted people to think. He had been born Dick Sams in the Peabody Buildings Estate in Clapham Junction, London. But once he moved to the States he soon realized that it was a liability to be known as "Dick", in spite of Cheney, Nixon and Van Dyke – or maybe because of them.

The USA was just a distant dream when Dick Sams married his first wife, Barbara, as they both turned nineteen. He hadn't done much at school, left as soon as he could without any qualifications and got a job in a mate's garage.

But Dick's real life happened in the evenings, when he roadied for a band at the local town hall. "Roadied" was a misleading term, since they never went on tour, but they still needed someone to shift amplifiers and other heavy equipment and Dick was strong and wiry, though not brawny.

It was at the local town hall that he got his big break, meeting Tony Calloway, who was the band's manager. Tony liked the way Dick worked, tirelessly and without moaning, so enlisted him to help with another band, one that really was going somewhere.

It was a long, hard road and he and Barbara had two kids by the time he got there, but Dick, by sheer force of desperation to get out of the shabby life in rented accommodation he foresaw before them, made a new career in the recording industry. He watched and learned the whole time, hungry for information the way he had never been at school.

He asked questions, met the right people, learned how every piece of equipment in the recording studio worked, and worked long hours for the overtime.

But there was a cost. His children scarcely knew him and Barbara complained she never saw him.

It was so unfair.

"I've been working my balls off to make life better for us," he said. "To buy us somewhere to live, to give you and the boys everything you want. Can't do that if I spend my evenings watching telly with you, can I?"

He wanted to take her to America with him when the offer of a job in a New York studio came up. They left the boys with Dick's mother and went for three weeks.

After that, Barbara came home and started divorce proceedings, having discovered that when she did spend time with her husband, she found she didn't like him much. And she hated America.

Dick was the opposite; he loved every bit of it, especially the big bucks he made at his job. He changed his first name to "Rich" and his surname to Samson. Rich Samson soon owned the studio he worked for, having persuaded a beautiful young black woman to let him manage her singing career, which went global.

That was wife number two.

It was wife number three who was with him in Mexico. Rich's power cruiser, named the *Peabody* to remind him how far he had come, was moored in the marina at Bendita Cruz.

She was sleek, expensive and a status symbol. Like Rich's third wife, Leontyne.

Rich himself now had an American accent, a perma-tan and a very expensive haircut, which was supposed to make him look like a silver fox. In fact he more closely resembled an ageing ferret, but he had enough money for that not to bother Leontyne.

He wasn't very demanding in the bedroom – prostate

problems – and he was a generous husband, even though he was paying alimony to two previous wives.

It was their second visit to Bendita Cruz in the autumn – Rich said he had to have a bit of real sun before facing a New York winter – but the first time they were going to be in Mexico for the Day of the Dead. Their holiday this year had been delayed by some negotiations Rich had been involved in with the latest sexy teen sensation he had found on YouTube.

"It's a bore, babe, but he's going to be the next Justin Bieber," he had explained to his wife.

Since they had arrived in the marina, he had been making it up to her. It was just a pity everyone else found him so repugnant. But they all loved Leontyne in Bendita Cruz. The marina staff remembered her from the year before and how they had wondered then how she could put up with a man like Rich.

"She doesn't seem like a gold-digger," they would say. "Too nice."

"And too good for him."

This autumn there was a new assistant manager at the marina who was particularly smitten with Leontyne. Maybe it was because she began to see her husband through Chilo's eyes, but Leontyne was becoming critical of the way he treated other people.

"I don't know what you see in that dago," said Rich. "Greasy-looking devil, like all these Mexicans."

He was grumpier and nastier than his wife had ever known him. Maybe because his YouTube sensation was proving awkward to mould to his will and Rich was spending a lot of his holiday on his smartphone. Maybe because he really was jealous of Chilo, who was as physically fit as Rich was flabby, and had a full head of black curls.

"Do you have to be so unpleasant?" asked Leontyne. "Chilo is a perfect gentleman – and why are you suddenly so against Mexicans? You were very enthusiastic about coming down here again."

"I like Mexico," said Rich. "I like the heat, the food and the tequila. I even like the music. I never said I liked *Mexicans*, though, did I?"

They were sitting in a restaurant on the seafront, one of the upmarket venues that had sprung up recently in Bendita Cruz. It was getting further and further from its roots as a fishing village but was not yet completely spoiled; unlike Puerto Vallarta, it had no airport.

Rich had ordered fish tacos – good Mexican peasant food made with locally caught mahi-mahi – but he ate them with a bottle of the best Chablis the restaurant could provide. Leontyne picked at her shrimp and avocado salad and drank papaya juice.

"Sweet Jesus, he's followed us here!" said Rich, pointing to a nearby table, where the man from the marina was also eating his lunch.

Leontyne blushed under her bronzed skin.

"I suppose he has a lunch break like anyone else. Or maybe it's his day off? I'm sure it's a coincidence."

But she smiled at Chilo and gave him a little wave, while her husband glowered.

As they set off back to the boat, someone lurched into their path, knocking them both off balance. There was a real danger that all three of them would end up in an unseemly tangle of limbs on the cobbled street. But in an instant, Chilo was beside them, steadying Leontyne on her strappy high heels and brushing dust off Rich's cotton jacket.

"Get your fucking hands off me, you filthy wop!" growled Rich, reverting to the accent and vocabulary of his childhood.

Chilo flinched. "Are you okay, Senora Samson?" he asked. "Take no notice of Juan Luis – he is a village character, not . . . not quite right in the head you understand."

Juan Luis was joining in the brushing down, much to Rich's disgust, who threw him off roughly.

"May every day be the thirteenth of the month for you," said Juan Luis, wandering off, whistling tunelessly.

"Bloody psycho!" muttered Rich. "All right, all right, we

don't need you fussing round. She's okay, aren't you, babe?"
His American accent was returning.

They walked back to the *Peabody* in silence, both a bit
shaken. Chilo watched them go, his handsome face inscrutable.

The cruising community was a loose-knit one, but one
thing they had in common was a distrust of wealthy amateurs
like the Samsons who had paid crew and staff to look after
them. Many were retired couples who had dreamed of using
their savings to buy a boat and sail round the world and were
now living the dream.

Others were youngsters travelling in their gap years before
university. In between were those who had somehow managed
to chuck in their jobs, some selling houses to buy their boats
and raise young families aboard ship.

They met up with each other in different marinas and on various islands, sometimes teaming up to take a boat through the
Panama Canal or to celebrate a birth or a wedding on a beach. To
swap bits of equipment or outgrown baby clothes or just pieces
of gossip and sea-lore. There was an easy camaraderie that Leontyne envied. She and Rich had few people they could count as
friends, either in New York or when cruising: just one or two
couples with boats as expensive as theirs, and she suspected that
didn't count as either real friendship or really travelling the sea.

No one who would look out for their boat if they went away.
Among the real community a boat owner might leave a vessel
for some months to go back "home" and work for a few
months to get enough money to finance the next leg of the
trip. The boat would be locked but there was always someone
to look out for it and make sure it wasn't damaged by a freak
storm outside hurricane season.

The Day of the Dead celebrations were approaching and
the small town was filled with improvised shrines and decorations, each glowing with the bright colours of marigold petals,
painted crosses, candles and paper flowers of vivid purples,
blues, deep pinks and oranges.

November the 1st was dedicated to dead children, Los
Angelitos – "the little angels".

"Morbid, I call it," said Rich, who had been drinking even more heavily since the encounter with Chilo and Juan Luis, and did not identify with people who had lost children. After all, he had his boys, healthy and grown up, though he didn't see them, and a daughter by his second wife, whom he also never saw, but who cost him a lot in maintenance.

But Leontyne thought of their baby that she had miscarried at three and a half months and wanted to visit the cemetery.

The town cemetery was the focus of the Day of the Dead rituals. Although every house had its improvised shrine in honour of ancestors and family members recently passed, it was at the cemetery that the main commemorations took place.

In Bendita Cruz, on the first day of the festival there was dancing, in multicoloured dresses and shirts, before the more macabre images of the day for adult remembrance set in. Leontyne hadn't known and went to the cemetery dressed in a black sundress and a black straw hat with a pink ribbon.

It broke her heart to see all the little meals laid out on small graves smothered with flowers and photographs of the dead children. Whole families sat and picnicked with their missing loved ones, breaking off every now and again to dance to the haunting music that seemed to be playing all over the town.

And they were kind and hospitable too, approaching her with special dishes and sweets that their children had loved to eat. And they drew her into the dance, holding her hands and smiling at her as if they knew the secrets of her heart and could see that her loss was recent and painful.

They wouldn't have been so nice if Rich had been here, thought Leontyne.

"Thank goodness she didn't bring her horrible husband," they said in Spanish behind their hands.

She went home feeling tender and vulnerable but unexpectedly happy. Only to find her husband very drunk and abusing the staff, who were paid a fortune to stay on Rich Samson's boat.

"Where the fuck have you been?" he asked, thrusting his face aggressively into hers. "You been with that dago? I bet you have. Well, I'm not having it."

"I've been to the festival of the dead children," she said. "And I was happy – till I came back here. Why do you have to spoil everything?"

That night she slept in the spare cabin, which was hardly less luxurious than the master cabin suite. She dreamed of the little girl she would have had, wreathed in marigolds and dancing with the people in the street. Only the little girl had black curls like Chilo's.

I'm not going to let him take that away from me, she thought when she woke.

Rich rose late and hungover, and had eggs and Bloody Marys for breakfast. The boat's chef was used to his master's habits and his temper.

The couple didn't meet again till the early afternoon; Leontyne went swimming in the pool that had been built at the marina since their last visit. Rich slept and showered and changed into his new Day of the Dead outfit.

One thing they still had in common was a love of dressing up.

Leontyne was going as the elegant skeleton lady Catrina, with a skull mask and an elaborate orange dress trimmed with leaves made out of green silk. Rich was a bit more of a generic skeleton – a disguise that did not fit his stocky figure well – with violently coloured jacket, trousers and hat.

The costumes helped them to tolerate each other, and by the time they left for the cemetery, when it was already beginning to get dark, they had more or less made up the row of the night before.

The dancers were out in force, brightly costumed figures going from house to house and winding through all the streets of the town to the big cemetery. There were so many skeletons and skulls that Leontyne soon got used to it, so that it startled her to see an ordinary face without white paint or a mask.

Once or twice they got dragged inside a house, and invited to admire the memorials made for the dead. In one such house, they saw Juan Luis, holding a bunch of bananas, which he was arranging artistically along with some bright red chillies around the edge of an existing shrine.

"A few sandwiches short of a picnic, that one," said Rich, a bit too loudly.

"Picnic," said Juan Luis. "Let's have a picnic in the rainbow field."

He made to grab Rich's arm, but they pulled away and went back out into the street.

Soon after that they got separated. There were so many people dressed like them and it was getting really dark now. The cemetery was all lit up with candles, with an especially large crowd of people round the graves of those who had died in the last year – "the Fresh Dead" they called them.

"Fresh Dead, fresh fish!" someone was shouting. Leontyne thought it was probably Juan Luis.

She couldn't see Rich but she was sure that a man dancing with her was Chilo. He had curly black hair between his white-painted skull-face and his colourful hat, but it might have been a wig. Her partner fed her candied pumpkin and sugar skulls.

Once Leontyne thought she saw Rich drinking from a bottle of tequila left on one of the graves for a dead man to enjoy. To be fair some locals were doing the same – after all, the dead don't drink – but she nevertheless felt ashamed of him and turned away.

It was a bizarre night, hot and hectic in spite of the dark, everywhere filled with light and colour chasing away the fear from death. But towards the early hours there was a change in the atmosphere and Leontyne felt a chill at the sight of so many skeletons and skulls in the candlelight. Greetings and embraces that had felt just friendly before now seemed more sinister.

As the festivities wound down, some families left blankets and pillows on graves and Leontyne thought at first they were going to sleep there but it was just in case the dead woke up and needed somewhere more comfortable to sleep than the hard ground, someone explained to her.

It might have been Chilo; she had lost track of the different dancers and had been given a fair amount of tequila herself. Faces swam in and out of her vision, all with the gaping horror of a noseless death's head. She gave up thinking she would find Rich and wobbled unsteadily on her green wedge-heels as she left the cemetery. The candles were almost burnt down and few people remained. She was sure she saw one settling down on a "grave bed" and thought longingly of how she would like to sink down on one.

There was no sign of her husband back on the boat. The staff had gone to bed and Leontyne stripped off her mask and sank into the master bed as wearily as she would have done on a grave. It had been changed with fresh sheets since Rich's drunken stupor of the night before.

She slept long and well, but when the maid came in with her hot tea the next morning, she sat up and was aware that she was alone in the bed.

"Maria," she called. "Where is Mr Samson? Did he sleep in the spare cabin?"

"No, madam. He didn't come home last night."

Leontyne didn't worry straightaway. Rich was a bit of a law unto himself. After her shower and breakfast of freshly squeezed oranges and limes, wholewheat toast and coffee, she walked over to the marina offices.

They were attached to the Yacht Club, and the air-conditioned lounge, which Leontyne had scarcely used since their cruiser had its own artificially cooled air.

"Your husband did not come back?" asked the manager. "It was a good party, wasn't it? Chilo has not showed up for work this morning either."

Was it then that Leontyne felt the first chill? The first frisson that all was not as it should be?

She was wearing espadrilles this morning and white slacks with a red bikini top and poppy-flowered shirt. Large shades obscured her eyes and hid any trace of a hangover that her breakfast coffee hadn't chased away.

She retraced her steps to the cemetery with a mounting

sense of dread. There were several mound-like shapes on the graves and she uncovered each one, fearful of what she might find. One was Juan Luis, clutching a papaya to his chest like an unyielding teddy bear, and snoring heavily. There were two empty bottles beside him.

The cemetery looked so squalid with all the candle stubs, crushed flowers, squashed fruit and empty bottles. Leontyne hoped that the families would come back in the day and tidy it all up soon.

None of the figures was Rich – or Chilo – and all were definitely alive, if comatose.

By mid-afternoon she was very worried and went back to the manager to get him to call the police.

But it was two days before anyone else was really concerned. Neither Rich nor Chilo had been seen since the Day of the Dead evening.

"You say your husband was jealous of Chilo," said the officer who had taken Leontyne's statement.

"A little," she said, twisting her wedding ring. "It was nothing serious – just a mild flirtation."

"And do you think Chilo was jealous of your husband?"

"I can't answer that," she said. "I scarcely knew him."

But she had known that Chilo didn't like her husband, didn't think him worthy of her.

Gradually, the investigation had morphed from being a missing person's enquiry into a murder probe.

Leontyne couldn't believe what was happening. Day after day no news of Rich. She called his cell phone but it was dead. Was he? Should she try to get hold of his mother in an old people's home in the UK?

And Chilo had not returned to the marina. His family lived in Puerto Vallarta but they had heard nothing from him either.

After a week, the police seemed to have decided that Rich was dead and Chilo was on the run.

"But that makes no sense," said Leontyne. "If he killed my husband – which I don't believe for a minute – your theory is he did it to be with me. So why wouldn't he contact me?"

"He got scared," said the officer. "There is no other suspect, is there?"

But by morning they had pulled in Juan Luis.

"We can't get anything out of him," the policeman told Leontyne. "He just goes on about the Fresh Dead."

Two days later she was asked to identify a body.

There was a man in the town called Miguel who had lost his wife just one week before the Day of the Dead festival; she was the freshest of the Fresh Dead, her grave still a mound of newly turned earth. It was one of the ones that had been laid out with pillows and blankets on the night of the festival.

Miguel had cleared the bedding away next morning and hadn't noticed anything amiss, but when he had returned a week later to put fresh flowers on his Carmelita's grave, he had seen a foot.

It was a man's foot and it now stuck out, together with its partner, from under a sheet in the improvised morgue that was a cordoned-off part of the air-conditioned lounge in the Yacht Club.

Leontyne held her breath as the sheet was removed from the other end of the corpse, but the face was still unrecognizable under its white paint.

Even so, she could tell from the hair that it wasn't Rich. It was Chilo.

"This is not your husband?" said the policeman.

"No. Please – I need the bathroom."

She ran to the ladies' room and was sick in the toilet. Leontyne had never seen a corpse before. But she had been braced to look at Rich's dead body – not Chilo's.

When she had composed herself, she went back. She was now icily angry; the police must have known this was not the body of a man in his sixties. They had been trying to provoke a reaction.

"Mrs Samson," said the officer. "Do you know where your husband is?"

"I do not," she said, trying hard to keep her temper.

"Then you'll have no objection to our searching your boat?"

"Please do," she said.

When they found no Rich hiding in any of the cupboards or in the bilges, they emerged regretfully from the *Peabody*.

"We shall now apply for a warrant to search all the other vessels in the marina," said the officer in charge. "This is a murder enquiry."

"How did Chilo die?" she asked quietly.

"A blow to the back of the head."

Later that same afternoon there was a shout from one of the empty boats in a slip several jetties away from where the *Peabody* was moored. Leontyne came up on to the deck and saw two officers dragging up a man she could scarcely recognize as her husband; a corpse would have looked more like him.

He was thin and unshaven, ragged and dirty. Later she learned he had lived on cold tinned food and canned soda for over a week, as the owners of the sailboat he had broken into had turned off their fridge and water filters. He was still wearing the colourful Day of the Dead jacket and trousers but they were now dull and filthy. There was no sign of the hat.

"What the fuck do you think you've been doing?" she raged at him, as they dragged him past his own boat. Leontyne followed them to the Yacht Club. She wanted to kill Rich with her bare hands.

"Sorry, babe," he said, trying to raise his hands in the air, but the policemen had him by the wrists. "Hiding."

"What happened?" she begged, running alongside the police and their prisoner, tottering in her high-heeled sandals.

But it was a while before the whole story came out. Rich was taken in a police car to a jail in Puerto Vallarta. Leontyne learned later that Chilo's family and friends had gathered outside the jail, baying for her husband's blood.

She had gone back to the boat and packed a bag with fresh clothes for him and some things for herself, sobbing all the time. A taxi took her to P.V. but it was hours before she was allowed to see her husband and there was no crowd round the jail by then.

He looked even worse close up and smelt terrible.

"I brought you some clothes and your razor," she said.

"I'm not staying," he said.

"What do you mean?"

"It's obvious, isn't it? It's a bloody third-world country. When they know what I'm worth, they'll let me go."

"What you're worth? You don't look worth much at the moment."

"It can all be settled with money," he said. "I'll put it right with the wop's family."

"You admit it then? You killed him?"

"It was an accident. I saw you dirty dancing with him and I'd had enough so when you moved on I took a swipe at him."

"Hit him on the back of the head? What with – a bottle?"

"It wasn't like that. I socked him on the jaw and he fell on a headstone and cracked his skull. I tried to get someone to help him, but you know what it was like that night. Everyone seemed to go a bit mad. Only that loony would help me."

"Juan Luis?"

"Whatever. I realized the guy was dead and the village idiot showed me that the grave next to where he was lying was all piled up with soft earth, so I buried him under it."

"And no one noticed?"

"There were people fighting and dancing and snogging everywhere and only candles to see by. I don't think anyone could have seen anything clearly."

"By why did you run away and hide on a boat?"

"I panicked. I realized what I'd done and I found an empty boat and broke the lock."

"Did you think you could stay there forever?"

"I stopped thinking, but I see it all clearly now. Once these buggers know how much money I've got, I'm out of here."

"That's what you think, that because you're rich – and because you're Rich – you can kill a man and get away with it?"

"Are you saying I can't?"

They glared at each other.

Leontyne got up.

"It's over as far as I'm concerned, Rich. This marriage is now one of the Fresh Dead."

She took another taxi back to Bendita Cruz. The car passed Juan Luis, who was wearing a battered hat she recognized as the one Rich had worn on the night that Chilo died.

"Butterflies!" he shouted as the taxi passed. "Beautiful bright butterfly."

She wished with all her heart that she lived in a world as simple as his.

Back on the boat, she put in a call to a lawyer in New York. But not a criminal one. Rich could take care of his own defence; she was going to get a divorce.

Finnbarr's Bell

A Sister Fidelma Mystery

Peter Tremayne

"This is an act of . . ." the elderly abbot paused, searching in his mind for the appropriate word. "It is an act of sacrilege!"

Sister Fidelma raised a quizzical eyebrow.

"Sacrilege? I was told that it was merely the theft of a bell."

Abbot Nessán frowned in annoyance.

"Not just any bell, Sister. It was the bell which our founder, the Blessed Finnbarr, used to summon the faithful to his little chapel here. Its value to our community cannot be placed in terms of temporal wealth. With Christ's Mass to be celebrated in two days from now, it is a tragedy. This bell has been used to begin the celebration of that Mass every year since Finnbarr established this abbey. That is why, when I heard you were visiting, I sent my steward to seek you out. Your reputation as a *dálaigh*, and for solving such matters, is known throughout the kingdom."

As a *dálaigh*, a junior Brehon or judge, Fidelma had been instrumental in resolving many mysteries which had been thought insoluble. The High King in Tara had even consulted her on the occasion of the theft of his ceremonial sword of office.

Fidelma sighed softly.

The purpose of her journey through the great marshland of Muman, stretching across the River Laoi, had been to visit the

Brehon Sochla of the Cenél mBéicce with whom she had studied at Brehon Morann's law school. She had been invited to
spend the celebration of the nativity of Christ with her friend
and she had no intention of staying at the abbey of Finnbarr
whose sprawling buildings lay on the south bank of the river in
an area which took its name from the marshland – Corcaigh. It
was only lack of familiarity with the route that had caused her
to pause and inquire at the abbey for the road to the home-
steads of the clan of Béicce.

The excited steward, hearing her name, had asked her to
wait while he hurried off, only to return in a moment with the
news that Abbot Nessán desired to see her urgently about a
stolen bell.

In truth, Fidelma was a little irritated at delaying her journey for such a seemingly paltry thing as a missing bell.

Now it appeared that the bell was extremely valuable to the
community of the abbey. She had heard that Finnbarr, who
had died a few years before she had been born, was venerated
in many parts of the kingdom of Muman. He had built a
community on the banks of the Laoi that had quickly grown
into an ecclesiastical school that was being compared to those
great schools at Darú and Cill Dara.

The garrulous steward had explained to her that the current
abbot, the elderly Nessán, had been one of Finnbarr's followers as a young man and, when he died, had become *comarb*,
Finnbarr's successor, as abbot.

She glanced at the agitated abbot thoughtfully.

"You say the bell is missing. From the way you choose your
words, I would deduce that you believe it has been stolen with
some deliberate intent."

Abbot Nessán made a cutting motion with his hand.

"Everyone in the abbey knows how valuable that bell is," he
replied sharply. "Not in mercenary terms but of its symbolic
value to this community. We need to find it before Christ's
Mass."

Fidelma hesitated a moment or two before giving in to the
inevitable. She could not refuse to undertake the investigation

requested by the abbot. There were politics to be considered for she was sister to Colgú, King of Muman, who ruled from Cashel. She was duty-bound to respond to a request that impinged on the welfare of his people.

"Then tell me the details of the matter as they are known to you, so that I may begin to investigate."

The old abbot looked relieved.

"The matter, as I know it, is quite simple. With the celebration two days hence, Brother Merchar was sent to clean the bell among other items we use at that time. It was Brother Merchar who had reported that the bell was missing."

"Very well. I shall need to speak with him. However, describe this bell to me."

"It is a cast-metal bell of brass, a mix of copper and some other ore," he added pedantically. "It was an old cow bell which Finnbarr had picked up in his travels but then utilized as a hand bell to summon the faithful to his services. There was nothing outstanding about its appearance. It was almost square in shape, and fairly flat to hang about the cow's neck. There was a pattern on it that is easily recognizable and Finnbarr had his name engraved on it by our smith many years ago."

"And where was it kept?"

"It was kept in a recess near the altar in our chapel. Finnbarr is buried under our altar," added Abbot Nessán, "and we keep many items that he used in this life in that chapel."

"And when Brother Merchar found the bell missing, he came straightaway to report the matter?"

"He did. For over fifty years that bell has summoned the faithful to Christ's Mass. That it will not do so this year is a tragedy."

"In what way apart from the break in tradition?"

"You may not be aware, Sister, that not all the peoples of this kingdom are fully converted to the Faith. Some prefer to continue to follow the old gods."

Fidelma knew that fact well.

"How does that relate to this matter?" she pressed.

"To the southeast of us is the land of the Cenél nAeda and they follow the old ways, the old gods and goddesses. But Aed, their chief, has finally accepted to attend this Mass with the influential members of his clan. This loss will be looked upon as symbolic and we may lose all the work we have done in bringing him to the point where he and his people will convert to the Faith."

Fidelma pursed her lips.

"Would such a theft have such influence?"

"Knowing Aed as I do, I am sure he will claim it is a sign that his people should stick to the old ways. In fact, he is being pushed reluctantly to this conversion by other members of his clan and would seize this opportunity to maintain his own beliefs. I would not put it past him to have been responsible for the theft himself."

"That is a serious accusation."

Abbot Nessán sniffed.

"I make no accusation but only point out a possibility."

"And since you do so, are there any other possibilities?"

The old abbot hesitated a moment or two before replying.

"There is one . . . and I have known the man for forty years and so I am loath to contemplate the idea."

"But?" snapped Fidelma. "Your voice has a 'but' in it."

Abbot Nessán nodded slowly.

"Brother Riaguil joined the abbey forty years ago. He is . . . shall we say . . . eccentric and claims that we celebrate the Christ's Mass on the wrong day. He even refuses to participate in the celebration. Finnbarr tolerated him for he was a brilliant astronomer when he was young and," the abbot shrugged, "I have followed that example of toleration for in all other things Brother Riaguil is a pillar of our community. But when it comes to feast days, he argues astronomical matters that make my mind go dizzy with their obscurity."

Fidelma looked intrigued.

"Are you saying that you suspect him of the theft of the bell because he disagrees with the celebration of the Christ's Mass?"

"You asked me for possibilities."

"But why would he wait until now to make such a protest if he has argued against the date of celebration for forty years?"

Abbot Nessán shrugged.

"I have resigned myself to not being able to see into the mind of all my flock, Sister."

"Very well. Let me begin at the beginning with Brother Merchar."

Brother Merchar was a nervous young man who had not long joined the community. He had a prominent Adam's apple and punctuated his speech by swallowing, causing it to move up and down in a distracting fashion.

"When did you notice the bell was missing?" inquired Fidelma.

"I was sent to clean the relics yesterday morning," the young man replied. "It was not cold for the time of year; the sun was bright and so I thought I would be better able to perform the task of polishing the brass outside the chapel rather than in its gloomy interior. There is a bench outside and so I laid my polishing rags outside and went into the chapel and removed those items which were to be polished."

"Including the bell?"

He nodded quickly.

"I sat awhile and polished the items and then came the summons to the *prandium*, the meal house, for the *eter-shod*, the middle meal."

"And you went for your meal leaving the items on the bench?" interposed Fidelma.

The young man looked defensive.

"Who would imagine that anyone would take anything from the bench outside the chapel? We are in the midst of the abbey grounds here with a wall around us. No strangers could pass in, or so I thought. Here we trust everyone."

"In spite of that, when you returned to your work at the bench, the bell was gone?"

"It was. It had been taken in my absence."

"And was any other item removed?"

"It was the only item missing."

"And you reported it?"

"At once to the *rechtaire*, the steward, who reported it to Abbot Nessán."

"You saw no one near the bench before you left or nearby on your return?"

"No one who should not have been there."

Fidelma sighed impatiently.

"That is not the question that I asked. Who was in the vicinity?"

"Several brethren passed by on their way to the *prandium*."

"I presume that Brother Riaguil was among them?"

Brother Merchar flushed before nodding agreement. "I know that the abbot suspects him. But the steward has questioned everyone."

"Was there anyone else?"

"There was the young *bóchaill*, Iobhar the cowherd, who was leading a cow to the kitchens to be slaughtered ready for the feast on the eve of Christ's Mass."

"On my way here I observed a large herd of cows on the hills to the east of the abbey. Do those beasts belong to the abbey?"

"The abbey does not possess a large herd," replied Brother Merchar, with a shake of his head. "We have a small herd but, as the abbey lands adjoin several grazing lands, we join with others in what is called *comingaire* or common herding in which one herdsman is employed to attend to all the cattle where they can graze together."

Fidelma was aware of the Brehon Law text in the Senchus Mór which stipulated that those owning cattle should be "in brotherhood with each other" and that a man, while especially looking after his own cattle, must have a care of those belonging to his neighbours.

"And those were the only people you saw?"

"Well, there was the pagan chieftain, Aed. He and two of his men had come to speak with the abbot about their acceptance of the Faith. But I am sure they were accompanied by Brother Ruissíne, the *rechtaire*, the whole time they were in the abbey."

Fidelma found Brother Riaguil in the *scriptorium* of the abbey engaged in examining some ancient manuscripts. He was elderly, sharp featured with a prominent nose and close-set eyes that gave him an unfriendly appearance. He glanced up at Fidelma and it seemed that his anger deepened.

"I know you, Fidelma of Cashel. I studied with Brother Conchobhar and keep in touch with him. He believes that you are a sharp-witted young *dálaigh*."

Brother Conchobhar was the apothecary and astronomer who had served her family at Cashel since the time that her father, Failbe Flann, had been King of Muman. Before she could respond, Brother Riaguil continued sharply:

"I know why you are here. That old fool Nessán thinks that because I disagree with him about the dating of Christ's Mass, I would stoop to steal poor Finnbarr's bell as some sort of protest. The man is an idiot."

Fidelma smiled patiently at his indignation.

"It seems you had the opportunity to pick up this bell from the bench while you were passing on your way to the *prandium*. Abbot Nessán suggests that you might also have had the motivation."

Brother Riaguil made a sound that was half between a laugh and an ejaculation of anger.

"Is there no room in this Faith of ours for debate? When the Blessed Columbanus argued with Gregory the Great, the Bishop of Rome himself, over the dating of the Paschal celebration, was he accused of high crimes? I adhere to the old computistics which are based upon thousands of years of observation and not some arbitrary date decided by a council of abbots and bishops."

Fidelma seated herself on a nearby stool.

"I am interested in such matters. Tell me why you disagree with the holding of Christ's Mass on this particular day?"

"I am an astronomer."

"That is not enough explanation."

"It is the explanation. When did we start this celebration on this day? I will tell you. Three centuries ago Liberius became Bishop of Rome and decided that all the various dates on which the peoples of the Christian world celebrated a Mass dedicated to the Christ should be centred on one date. And what was the date he chose? Remember that he was a Roman."

"I presume it was the date on which we now celebrate it," observed Fidelma. "The twenty-fifth day of the month that the Romans called the tenth month in their ancient calendar."

"Exactly so, December, the tenth month. But why? Because throughout the Roman world they celebrated the feast of the birth of the pagan god Mithras on that date. The feast of Saturnalia. They converted a pagan feast which was entrenched in people's minds because they knew it would be easy to establish it in the Christian calendar of feasts. It happened with many other pagan feasts."

"And this is why you object to celebrating the Christ's Mass because it was formerly a pagan ceremony?" queried Fidelma.

The old man shook his head.

"I told you, it is because I am an astronomer."

"I still don't understand."

"All our ancient and major celebrations were fixed by the stars in the heavens and the position of the sun and the moon, by the equinox and the solstice."

"That I know."

"Our feast of Samhain was once fixed at the winter solstice. Our astronomers were once so accurate with their observations of the skies that they could construct great buildings in alignment with the movement of the sun and moon. In the great valley of the Boann are buildings that have openings so carefully aligned that the sun will return to those apertures exactly on the winter solstice or the vernal equinox. I have seen them with my own eyes."

The old man shook his head.

"Then we started to accept the New Faith and believed all new knowledge emanated from Rome. We accept the Roman calendar, which I am told was devised by a general called Julius Caesar. A general! Not an astronomer! The calculations are out of synchronicity with the movement of the planets. Indeed, I have calculated that with every 128 years, the calendar is one day out in accuracy. So now the feast days that were once celebrated in accordance with the calendar of the heavens, at the solstices and equinoxes, are many days adrift. This is what Columbanus argued when rebuking Rome for fixing a new date for the vernal equinox at which time the Paschal fires were lit. This is, indeed, what many of the Irish church argued at the council in Northumbria. This is why I refuse the arbitrary dating to celebrate."

He sat back and glared at her determinedly.

"But even though I hold this view it is an affront on my honour that I be accused of theft, and theft of a bell that was once owned by a saintly man that I admired."

Fidelma shook her head with a soft smile.

"You are not accused, Brother Riaguil. However, when a theft takes place, you must know that an investigation must follow. Therefore, it would reflect on me if I did not question everyone who was in the vicinity near the time the object was stolen."

She stood up.

"I thank you for your time, Brother Riaguil. Moreover, I will reflect on what you have said about the calendars which begin to govern our affairs."

It was the steward, Brother Ruissíne, who directed her to the rath of Aed, chief of the Cenél nAeda, which, in fact, was in the green hills overlooking the abbey to the southeast. It was within a comfortable walking distance and the way lay through the herd of grazing cattle that spread themselves over the hillside. As Fidelma walked up the hill towards the distant rath she saw a young boy sitting on a large grey rock staring moodily out across the grazing cows below him. He seemed deep in thought because he did not appear to notice her approach.

The path led just by the rock and she called out a greeting to him.

The boy started nervously and scrambled to his feet. He seemed relieved when he saw her.

"You have a fine herd there," she said, correctly assessing he was the *bóchaill*, the cowherd.

"If they were mine, they would be fine enough," replied the young boy. He was about thirteen or fourteen.

"Ah, they are the abbey's herd, I suppose. And you must be Iobhar."

"They are. I am," replied the boy.

Fidelma suddenly peered closely at the boy's features. He had an ugly bluish bruise on his forehead.

"That looks nasty. Did you have a fall?"

The boy shook his head, raising a hand automatically to the bruise. Suddenly one of the cows let out a plaintive bellow below them and began to move across the hillside with a tinkle of the *bó clag*, the cow bell, hanging round her broad neck. Fidelma turned to watch the magnificent beast who was obviously the leading cow of the drove, for the others began to follow her.

"That must be the pride of the abbey's cows," she smiled at Iobhar.

The boy shook his head, his hand moving again to the bruise.

"The cow belongs to my master, not to the abbey. Most of the herd belongs to him. But she is heading for the small runnel. I must head her off."

Before she could saying anything further, he had leapt from the rock and was trotting down the hill at a rapid pace. She paused a moment, listening to the jangle as the drove moved sedately off across the slopes. Then she sighed, turned and continued her path up to the rath that dominated the hills.

Aed was a big burly man, muscular with a full beard, his features swarthy and his hair black. He was every inch a warrior but given to quick outbursts of emotion, ranging from raucous laughter to fiery anger.

"Of what am I accused, Fidelma of Cashel?" he demanded, his eyes angrily dark and his features grim.

"You are accused of nothing," replied Fidelma quietly. "You are merely being asked to help with some information."

The thin-featured man seated by the chief sniffed uneasily.

"It sounds very much to me that my lord is being accused of *gat*, of theft by stealth."

Fidelma regarded the man, who had been introduced as Aed's Brehon, scornfully.

"Have I said as much?" she demanded. "If I make an accusation I will state it clearly and not imply it."

The man, Rumann, flushed.

"I am Brehon and will not stand—"

Fidelma interrupted him with a motion of her hand.

"I am qualified in law to the level of *anruth*."

It was just below the highest degree that law schools could bestow. Rumann fell silent. Fidelma had guessed that she was better qualified than a rural lawyer. It seemed, for a moment, that Aed, the chief, almost enjoyed the discomfiture of his legal advisor.

"You may accept it from me, Fidelma of Cashel, that I did not take this magical bell nor cause it to be stolen by anyone in my service."

"That is good to know," replied Fidelma solemnly. "Tell me, when you were visiting the abbey yesterday, did you see the brother cleaning objects outside the chapel."

Rumann made to speak, but the chief cut him short with a grimace.

"I am capable of answering Fidelma's questions, Rumann. And the answer is that as the abbot's steward escorted us to see the abbot, I was aware that we passed by the chapel and someone was seated outside engaged in some work. But who they were and what they were doing I could not say. I saw no bell nor would I be interested in such things unless it was the sound of bells on my herd going out to pasture."

Fidelma knew that the chiefs measured their wealth in the number of cows they owned.

"You own a large herd?" she asked absently.

"Alas, not as large as the Cenél mBéicce to the west of the great marsh or even the Muscraige Mittine to the northwest. No, my people and I are of modest means and I am content to let my herd graze in common with that owned by the abbey."

Fidelma glanced across the hill to where the herd of cows was grazing.

"So you jointly employ Iobhar as your *bóchaill*, your cowherd?"

Aed was surprised.

"So you know the young scallywag?"

"I saw him as I ascended the hill to the rath. So he looks after both the herd of the abbey and your own herd?"

"He does, and a bad job he can make of it."

"So bad that a sharp clout is needed to punish him?" Fidelma demanded sharply.

Aed gazed at her thoughtfully.

"When a dog behaves badly, a good hit will teach it manners. So it is with a boy. He has to be brought into order or he gets worse."

Fidelma regarded him with distaste.

"Your Brehon should advise you that the Bretha Crólige imposes heavy penalties for an injury inflicted on a young child no matter what social class he or she belongs to."

"He is my son," protested Aed.

"It makes no difference. Being over seven years of age, the boy's honour price is half that of your own and that is his legal worth . . ."

Her voice trailed off as the thought came to her. Without a word, she turned and left the astonished chief's presence. As a *dálaigh* of her rank as well as sister to the King of Muman, it was her right to be so dismissive of the chief of the Cenél nAeda. She was hurrying back down the hill at a swift rate and making for the distant herd of cattle.

Iobhar, the cowherd, having turned the cattle away from the runnel where they might have stumbled and caused themselves injury, was standing near a tree and saw her swift approach.

Yet it was not towards him that she was making but to the large cow that was the leader of the drove. She reached forward and seized the bell that hung around its neck and let out a great sigh before swinging round.

"Do not run away, Iobhar," she commanded, seeing the look of fear on the boy's features. "Tell me why you did this?"

The boy stood undecided for a moment and then spread his arms as if in surrender to the inevitable.

"I did not think anyone would care about an old cow bell," he muttered.

"You do not know what this bell is?"

"I saw it lying on a bench. An old brass cow bell. That's all."

"But why steal it?"

He hesitated and again his hand went to the bruise.

"The beast lost her metal bell," he said, indicating the cow. "I searched all over the pasture for it. I did not know what to do. I was so fearful."

"Fearful? Of your father?"

The boy was wide-eyed.

"You know of him?"

"I know that Aed seems quick with his hand and forgets the law. Yet would he punish you over the loss of a bell?"

"He would. That was why, when I saw the bell lying there, I did not think anyone would mind if I took it and replaced it on the cow. Now he will beat me doubly."

There was a whine of anguish tinged with terror in his voice, which caused Fidelma to moved forward and pat his shoulder.

"No one will hurt you. You have my word. We will take this bell and return it to the abbey where we will explain to the abbot the circumstances. Your father shall be summoned and stand to be judged before me. Is your mother alive?"

The boy shook his head.

"And have you reached fourteen summers?"

"I have," Iobhar said tremulously.

"And you have not been in fosterage and received your education?"

"My father said he would teach me all I needed to know."

"Then as a son of a chief you should have been in fosterage from the age of seven until seventeen. It is time for you to catch up and you will go into fosterage and no longer be a cowherd. If there is no one to foster you for *altramm serce*, for affection, then we shall find someone to foster you for the fee of three *séds*, according to law. And that fee will be the fine imposed on your father."

"But I took the bell," pointed out the boy.

"You took it because the fear of punishment made you do so. According to the law, that makes your father responsible for the theft," smiled Fidelma grimly. "Aed of the Cenél nAeda will have much to answer for."

She turned and removed the brass cow bell from the unprotesting animal and set off down the hill with a light step, followed by the young boy. She was now looking forward to celebrating Christ's Mass with her friend Brehon Sochla in the country of the Cenél mBéicce.

Two Florida Blondes

Kate Rhodes

The air conditioning in Frank's hire car had failed as he passed Orlando, and now he was driving with the windows open, sweat coursing down his sides. All he could see in the mirror was a blur of headlights on Highway One. It was impossible to tell whether he was still being followed, but he had no regrets. The man he'd killed in Miami had been responsible for the deaths of both his brothers, and countless others who had dared to challenge his business empire over the years. Frank had always known that a mob would come after him, and their style was cat and mouse. If they caught him, they would take him to a warehouse and make a video for his nearest and dearest, while they sliced him apart. Frank's mug shot had featured on Fox News, so he'd missed his chance to use his false passport and fly home to London. He'd shaved off the moustache he'd worn for ten years but he was still much too visible. Now all he could do was keep driving south, with nothing fuelling him except panic.

At dawn he drove past the entrance to the Everglades National Park, a huge plastic alligator throwing its shadow across the road. A ribbon of ocean kept appearing between the condos, unreasonably blue. But Frank would happily have traded beauty for safety, even though the bridges between the islands were fine as the links on a coral bracelet.

It was breakfast time when he parked his car in Key West, the humid air refusing to stir. He locked himself into the first hotel room he could find, then stretched his long frame across

the bed. By afternoon he was aware of sounds. Tourists laughing on their way to the beach, and a motorbike buzzing around
the island, high-pitched and insistent as a wasp. There was a
metallic taste in his mouth when he forced himself to stand
under the shower, legs trembling. Instinct told him to carry on
hiding, but by now he was weak with hunger.

The sunlight burnt Frank's eyes when he stepped outside,
but it was a relief to find the hotel veranda empty. He slumped
into a deckchair, and when he looked up again, a neatly
dressed young man was standing in front of him.

"What can I get you?" he asked.

"A club sandwich and a beer, please."

"Sure."

Florida seemed to be full of people who were sure; every
shop assistant and bartender existed in a state of unquestion-
ing certainty. The waiter busied himself behind the bar,
levering the top from a Budweiser. It was difficult to guess his
age. Thin and blond and tanned, all of his movements were
fluid and deft.

"There you go," he placed the glass of beer on a napkin,
and Frank took several long gulps.

"Thirsty?" the waiter laughed.

"Parched."

"I know the feeling, I come from Seattle." He nodded at the
cloudless sky. "Sun comes out twice a year there, if you're lucky."

Frank took another swig from his drink and the man carried
on watching him. There was something unexpected about his
face. Maybe it was his eyes? So pale it was hard to judge
whether they were green or blue.

The waiter took a step backwards. "Let me know if I can
get you anything else."

Frank scanned the street nervously. A straggle of sightseers
were traipsing from bar to bar, and a sign outside Sloppy Joe's
was advertising frozen margaritas at three dollars ninety-five.
Two boys stood on the sidewalk close to Frank's table. They
were bare-chested, arms slung round each other's waists.

"Want a sundowner?" the taller one asked his friend.

"No. Let's go back to the hotel."

Before Frank could look away, the boys were kissing, holding each others' faces with their hands. A year ago he would have been disgusted, but he'd forfeited the right to question other people's choices. Suddenly his gaze snagged on a familiar face. The man who'd been following him in Miami was twenty yards away, wearing a Hawaiian shirt, with a hula girl dancing across his chest. Before Frank could move, the hired goon took a photo with his phone, then grinned at him and sauntered away. A surge of fear rose in Frank's chest. Now it was only a question of time; his only chance was to find a safe way out of town.

He was about to return to his room when the waiter set down a pitcher of beer on his table.

"Compliments of the house."

"Any particular reason?"

"You're my only customer. There's a deal on at La Te Da's."

"Where's that?"

"Two blocks away, free drinks till midnight." The waiter eased himself into the deckchair beside Frank's. "Want to know a secret?"

"What?"

"I'm moonlighting. I work nights there, through till four. I'm saving for my own place."

"Yeah?" Frank watched him pour beer into two glasses. "I can't imagine living here."

The waiter laughed. "You know what the Key West motto is? Anything goes and everyone's welcome."

"Even ex-policemen from London?"

He grinned. "I'll bet you looked great in that uniform. Exactly how tall are you?"

"Six five."

"Oh my God," he giggled. "We need you. The island team has the worst quarterback you ever saw."

Frank tried to raise a smile. The non-stop chatter was soothing, even if the guy was hitting on him, but it was hard to focus. He had to find a place to hide before the goons returned.

The waiter glanced at him. "You seem distracted. Is something wrong?"

"You wouldn't believe me if I told you."

"Try me." The man's pale eyes seemed to invite secrets.

"My brothers got involved with a bad crowd, and I had to organize their funerals last week. I took things into my own hands, and now I need to get off the island, fast as I can."

The man looked shocked, then nodded in sympathy. "Give me twenty minutes, then meet me here."

The waiter rose to his feet and disappeared into the hotel. Frank was tempted to pour himself another beer, but the sky was already two shades darker, and his life depended on keeping a clear head. He wandered out on to the sidewalk, looking for the Hawaiian shirt. There was no sign of him, and the street was thronging with tourists, all searching for the perfect holiday. In the distance a flotilla of dive boats were scattered across the ocean like breadcrumbs. He knew that someone was watching him, the heat of their gaze searing the back of his neck as he reached Mallory Square. Street performers were gathering to welcome the sunset: flamenco dancers, sword swallowers and fire jugglers; and somewhere in the thick of it, the hired man with his Colt 45.

When Frank got back to the hotel a young blonde was standing by the bar. She sashayed towards him, her figure good enough to take his breath away as she slipped into the seat beside him. Her short dress revealed an expanse of smooth brown thigh.

"You prefer me this way, don't you?" The woman laughed quietly and Frank's vision blurred. "I told you," the waiter examined the newly applied nail polish on his left hand. "When I finish here I do a shift at La Te Da's."

The transformation was so convincing Frank could only stare. He recognized the waiter's gentle, unsettling eyes, but everything else had changed. A woman's face looked back at him now, high cheekboned, pale lips shimmering.

"What do you call yourself?" he stammered.

"Danielle." The waiter's voice was an octave lighter, almost girlish.

"And they make you wear that get-up, do they?" Frank tried not to imagine his mates' faces, if they could see him now.

"Sure. It's a drag club. Boys become girls, that's the deal." Danielle pointed across the street. "And there's the main event."

Frank twisted round in his chair. A carnival was passing the hotel, bystanders gathering to watch. A dozen showgirls were decked out in peacock feathers, sequins glinting under the streetlights. One of them looked like a supermodel, her skirt slashed to the hip, balancing on stilt-like heels.

"And they're all . . ."

"Men," Danielle confirmed. "Of course, sugar. Friday's cabaret night."

She was gazing up at him. No one had paid him that much attention in years. His ex had hung on his every word at the start, but by the end she hardly bothered to meet his eye.

"Come up to my room."

Frank knew he was stupid to trust her, but he was running out of options. Even the town's architecture had started to look temporary; pastel houses so thin-skinned it looked like they were made of tissue paper.

Danielle led him to a small room and made him sit still, while she applied creams to his face, touching his eyelids and lips with small brushes. Her potions smelled of the gardenia perfume his mother wore when he was a child. The scent made him long to be young again, before all the violence and killing started. Danielle knelt in front of him and studied his face intently.

"You'll never be Greta Garbo, but you'll have to do."

She led him to a mirror and Frank stared at himself open-mouthed. A hard-faced blonde gazed back, ten years older than Danielle, her wig an extravagant mass of curls. The glittering shawl draped around his neck disguised the heft of his shoulders.

"There's no way I'm going out like that."

"What choice do you have?" she whispered. "We're only going a couple of blocks. You can borrow my friend's shoes."

It was dark when they got outside. Honky-tonk piano spilled from the bars, and crowds milled on every street corner, swapping information about trips on the marlin boats. Maybe it was panic that made everything shine, but the neon signs outside the cafés were a dazzle of red and gold. Frank's mouth was so dry that his tongue felt like it had been welded to the roof of his mouth. The goon in the Hawaiian shirt would be easy to spot, but others would be lurking under the surface of the crowd. Gradually his confidence began to revive. The mob would be looking for a dark-haired ex-cop with a thuggish scowl, not a transvestite with a Tammy Wynette hairdo. Danielle led him across the intersection, weaving between cars.

"We're breaking the law, Mr Policeman."

"How come?"

"Jay walking. They'll slam us in jail."

Frank didn't reply. He had broken more laws than he could count since he'd touched down in Palm Springs: housebreaking, assault, homicide. He tried not to think about it as he followed her down a narrow path to the docks. There was no one in the marina, the crowds drinking the night away in the centre of town. Dive-boats and dinghies were moored side by side, lobster creels piled on the jetty. The Hawaiian shirt was sitting on the harbour wall, smoking a cigarette. The man's gaze drifted towards him then darted away again, towards the sea. Frank couldn't resist tottering over on his high heels.

"All alone, sugar? A big boy like you?"

"Fuck off, you freak." The goon shot him a look of disgust then took another drag from his cigarette.

He must have inhaled deeply, because when Frank slipped the knife between his ribs, a line of smoke streamed from the wound. The goon tipped backwards, speechless, and Frank eased the gun from his pocket, then piled lobster creels over the lifeless body.

Danielle was already starting the motor on the fishing boat she'd hired from a friend. When she reached up to kiss him, Frank responded without questioning why. Kissing a man turned out to be much like kissing a woman. Danielle was small and soft-skinned in his arms, her perfume enough to send him giddy. He couldn't forecast what would happen when they reached Key Largo, but for the time being, he was safe. Anyone gazing across the harbour would see two Florida blondes piloting a boat across a calm sea, under a glitter of off-white stars.

Red Esperanto

Paul D. Brazill

The winter night had draped itself over Warsaw's Aleja Jana Pawla like a shroud, and a sharp sliver of moon garrotted the death-black sky. I was in the depths of a crawling hangover and feeling more than a little claustrophobic in Tatiana's cramped, deodorant-soaked apartment.

I poked my trembling fingers through a crack in the dusty slat blinds and gazed out at the constellation of neon signs that lined the bustling avenue. Sex shops, peep shows, twenty-four-hour bars, booze shops and kebab shops were pretty much the only buildings that I could see, apart from the Westin Hotel, with its vertigo-inducing glass elevator. Looking at it always made my stomach lurch a little.

I fought back the acrid bile that burned my throat as I watched a black taxi jump a red light and cut across the road, narrowly missing a rattling tram. A police car's siren wailed and pierced my pounding head like a stiletto. Another cop car joined the chase, quickly overtook the cab, swerved and screeched to a halt in front of it. The taxi driver tried to stop but the taxi skidded back across the icy road, just missing another tram, before eventually stopping on the pavement outside a garishly painted peepshow. A tall blonde dressed only in red high heels and suspenders looked out of its front door, saw the police cars and went back inside, slamming the door behind her.

A massive, bull-necked man with a bald head and wearing a black leather jacket raced from the taxi towards the front of

Tatiana's apartment block, but before he could get close to the front door, a swarm of policemen swiftly surrounded him and dragged him down on to the snow-smothered ground, attacking him with truncheons before handcuffing him and hurling him into the back of a police van, giving him the occasional kick.

I turned back toward Tatiana. She handed me a glass of bourbon. The smell made my stomach roll. I took a furtive sip and balked.

"Not a Maker's Mark fan?" she said.

"I prefer Jack Daniels," I said. "With coke. But, to be honest, I usually only drink whisky when I'm so drunk I shouldn't be drinking anything at all. When I've drunk the pint of no return."

Tatiana grinned as I persevered with the drink. After a while, the burning sensation was cleansing. I turned back toward the window. A mob of English football fans wearing only T-shirts was staggering down the street singing a song about three lions.

Tatiana came up behind me.

"When the last pope – the Polish one – died, the whole of the street was lined with multicoloured candles, in tribute," she said, looking almost tearful.

Her English was perfect but her Ukrainian accent was as dark and as bitter as the Galois that she deeply inhaled. "It was a thing of rare beauty," she continued, a halo of smoke floating above her.

She switched off the flickering light and switched on a small lamp with dusty red bulb. My mouth was dry and I felt as if my heart were caged tightly within my chest and ready to burst free. Tatiana finished her drink and carefully placed the glass on the rickety bedside table.

"Ready?" she said.

I nodded and she dropped her crimson silk kimono to the floor and stepped over it. Her skin was white as the snow that fell outside her window like confetti. Her stockings and pant-ies were black, her short-cropped hair blonde. She picked up her snakeskin handbag, took out a lipstick and traced her blood red lips.

I took out my wallet and fished out a handful of notes. I placed them on the bedside table. Unsteadily, I sat down on the edge of the bed. Throbbing with guilt, I could hear the thump of a bass line coming from one of the pubs across the road and for a moment I wished I was there.

Tatiana dropped to her knees and licked her lips as she crawled toward me. She spread my legs and placed her scarlet painted talons on my hard penis. She dug in her nicotine-stained fingers so deeply that I suppressed a groan. Then she shuffled closer, her head above my crotch. She smiled warmly as she unzipped my fly, took out my erection and kissed my cock before licking it all over.

Ten minutes later, as she poured me another drink, there was loud banging on the door. I stumbled to my feet, zipped up my black jeans and picked up my black sweater from a rocking chair.

"Who the hell is . . . ?"

Tatiana put a finger to her lips.

"Quiet. It's only Bronek. Wait," she whispered.

"Who?"

"Oh, he's just a customer who has problems separating business from pleasure."

The banging continued. And then the shouting began. Well, it was more like the cry of a wounded animal. Repeating Tatiana's name over and over again.

She shook her head and leaned close to me.

"Wait until he has gone, eh?"

She kissed my cheek and poured the last of the bourbon into my glass. She held up a finger and stepped into the bathroom

Tatiana showered and dressed in a black polo-neck sweater and leather skirt. She cracked open another bottle of bourbon, sat next to me and we slowly drank in silence until, just before midnight, the noise stopped.

"I think you can go now," said Tatiana, standing, stretching and yawning.

"Are you sure? Is it safe?" I said.

"Yes. He will be at Mass now, and then he'll return home to his wife and children."

I stood up, a little unsteady. Tatiana produced a handful of business cards from her bag and sifted through them.

"Maybe we can get a taxi together?" she said.

"Safety in numbers, eh?" I said, and I forced a smile which Tatiana didn't return.

"Oh, I think we're outnumbered where Bronek is concerned," she said, with the hint of a smile.

I took the last of my notes from my wallet and stuffed them into the taxi driver's sweaty paw while Tatiana wiped the white powder from her nose and pulled a Zippo from the pocket of her black PVC raincoat. She lit another French cigarette, dissolving into the darkness as the flame flickered out.

"We made it in one piece, then," she said.

"Just about," I said. My nerves were shot.

Before I'd come to Warsaw, I'd heard stories about "The Night Drivers". Legend had it that they were a group of amphetamine-pumped young men who, each midnight, tied fishing wire around their necks, and the cars' brakes, and then raced each other from one end of the city to the next.

So, when I saw the cut marks on the taxi driver's neck and his red, red eyes, I didn't exactly have the Colgate ring of confidence.

I was relieved, then, when, minutes later, we pulled up outside the Palace of Culture and Science, Josef Stalin's unwanted neoclassical gift to the people of Warsaw, which loomed over the city like a gigantic gargoyle keeping evil at bay. A large red banner was stretched across its entrance advertising an avant-garde jazz concert.

"So, same again next month, then?" she said.

"Yes, why not?" I replied, to the fading sound of her high heels click-clicking on the palace's wet, concrete steps.

I waited a moment until she was inside and then rushed across the road into Rory's Irish Pub. I ignored the wrinkled, old cloakroom attendant and headed straight into the putrid smelling toilets to puke.

"Out with the old, in with the new," said a familiar, well-spoken, sandblasted voice from the next cubicle.

I wiped my mouth with toilet paper, flushed and walked up to the basin. As I splashed my face with water, Sean Bradley stumbled out of the cubicle.

"We are all in the gutter but some of us are looking at it through the bottom of a rather nice glass of gin and tonic, eh?" he said.

He swayed as he zipped up his fly, waved to me and walked out the door.

Sir Arthur Conan Doyle once described London as being a "great cesspool into which the flotsam and jetsam of life are inevitably drawn", and the same thing might reasonably be said of the world of TEFL teaching. A Teacher of English as a Foreign Language can usually be described as either flotsam – perhaps a fresh-faced young thing taking a break from university – or jetsam – the middle-aged man with the inevitable drinking problem and enough skeletons in his closet to keep a palaeontologist happy for months.

And, I'll make no bones about it, Sean fitted rather snugly into the latter category. I literally stumbled into him the first week I arrived in Warsaw. After that, we seemed to orbit each other more than somewhat. Sean was a permanently drunk, dapper, nicotine-stained example of jetsam, who supplemented his teaching income by chess hustling.

I walked into the half-empty bar, ordered a beer and shot of vodka to cleanse my palate.

"Oh, bollocks," I said, as I realized I had no more folding money left.

"Can I pay by credit card?" I said.

"Yes, of course," said Blanka, the tiny barmaid with the statuesque, purple Mohican haircut. "But there's a minimum amount you have to spend."

"Fair enough," I said. "I'll run up a tab."

And then I headed toward oblivion like rainwater down a storm drain.

I sat at a checkerboard table with Sean and watched Yankee-Doodle-Andy, a big, dumb-looking American I'd seen shuffling around the expat pub circuit, play pool with Rory, the owner. Rory was a pallid, ghostly, prune-faced old man with all the charm of a pitbull.

"Evening gents," I shouted.

Rory glanced up, irritated.

"For fuck's sake," he grunted, by way of a greeting.

Like I said, he wasn't well known for his charm. But, in his favour, he was equally ignorant of the smoking ban that had been introduced in Poland's bars and restaurants. The air in the bar was as thick as pea soup. Little blue clouds of cigarette smoke hung below the green lamps that dangled from the low ceiling.

The sound of Van Morrison's version of "It's All Over Now, Baby Blue" crept out of crackly speakers as a nicotine-smudged TV screen showed an episode of *MacGyver*.

Andy sat at the seat opposite Sean, sipping a Diet Coke and keeping an eye on the door.

"The thing is, some people absolutely loathe the place," said Sean, jabbing a yellow finger at a postcard of the Palace of Culture and Science that Andy had been using as a beer-mat. "The locals call it the Russian Wedding Cake, you know? And, indeed, that's what it looks like: a wedding cake plonked in the middle of the road."

"I see what you mean," said Andy, who quite clearly didn't.

The night staggered on. Andy bailed out pretty quickly and then the cloakroom attendant left. Sean and I were soon in our pots, sitting at the end of the bar smoking cigarettes and drinking whisky, watching the ice cubes glimmering and shimmering in the wan light. Blanka had gone home, too, and Rory clearly wasn't enjoying Sean and I exploiting the Polish tradition that a bar can only close when the last customer has gone. I was about to order another round of drinks when I heard a loud bang that seemed to send seismic tremors through the pub.

I turned and saw a stunningly beautiful blonde woman burst through the frosted glass door and rush into the bar bringing a trail of snow behind her. Her wet hair hung down like party streamers.

Even in my drunken stupor, just looking at her was like lightning hitting a plane. She was tall, with long blonde hair and a slash of red lipstick across her full lips. She was wearing a long black raincoat which flapped in the breeze behind her.

"Ding dong," I said. "Who's that?"

"Oh. That's C. J. Crazy Jola. Better watch out for her," said Sean. "She's eaten more men than Hannibal Lecter."

"Looks like a pretty tasty morsel herself," I said.

"No, really, she's trouble. She's a married woman, for a start," said Sean.

I shrugged.

"That's not the greatest of sins."

"Yes, but she's married to Robert Nowak. You do know who he is?"

I shook my head.

"He's a twat, that's who he is," said Rory, as he went over to Jola's table.

"He's a mid-level gangster who owns a lot of property in the area. He's also a second-hand clothes baron," said Sean.

"Who and a what?" I said.

Sean finished the last of his drink and shuffled off the bar stool. He staggered close to me and, even as pissed as I was, he stunk of booze. I recoiled.

"He's a mid-level gangster, basically," said Sean.

"Yes, you said that."

Sean tried to gather his thoughts.

"He owns a couple of bars. Peepshows. And another one of his business enterprises is to get Poles that live abroad to collect donated clothes that have been left outside charity shops overnight in, say, London or Dublin, and ship them back to Poland to sell in second-hand shops. You can get some damn good stuff, actually," said Sean, pointing to the Hugo Boss label on his shirt.

"The only crime is getting caught," I said, shrugging.

"Yes, but if a butterfly beats its wings in the forest a one-handed man claps and a tree falls down," said Sean, and he stumbled off in the direction of the toilets.

I ignored him and tried to catch Jola's eye. Rory was placing a drink in front of her. She said something to him and, for the first time since I'd known him, I actually saw him laugh. Though when he turned back to me he had the same grimace he always wore.

Jola took out her mobile phone and began sending a text message. Fuelled by Scotch courage, I walked over.

"Would you like another drink?" I said, swaying a little.

Jola looked up and tried to focus on me, as if she were attempting to take in a magic-eye painting.

She sipped her drink and shook her head.

"Well, I would but I really shouldn't," she said, with a fake-sounding transatlantic accent. "I should go home and hit the sack. I've hit the bottle enough for one night."

"Maybe one for the Ulica?" I said.

She laughed.

"Fantastic use of Polish. You're a regular polyglot. I'm guessing you're an English teacher?"

"Surprisingly not," I said. "Do I look like one?"

"Well." She took in my worn leather jacket, scuffed Doc Martens boots and frayed jeans. "You certainly don't look like a businessman."

"Which means?"

"Hack?"

"Bingo!"

"So, do you work for one of those shitty rags that dig out all the sleazy tales about Poland and sell them to the English tabloids for shock-horror stories?"

"No," I said. Although I did do that sometimes. "I'm freelance but mostly I work for *EuroBuilder Magazine*."

I gave her a sweaty business card.

"Heard of it?"

"Yes, of course. My asshole husband has a lot of property

in this city so he buys it and reads all of those fascinating articles about warehouses and shopping malls."

"All my own work," I said. "Well, some of it."

She looked at the card. "Luke Case. That's a cool-sounding name."

"Not that cool," I said. "At school, my nickname was head."

"I don't get it."

"Oh, I'm sure you do," I sniggered.

Jola stared blankly at me.

"Never mind. So?" I said, gesturing toward the bar.

"Oh, why the hell not?"

I ordered another whisky for me and a gin and tonic for Jola.

"Gin makes you sin," I said as I put the drinks on the table.

"Oh, I don't need a drink for sinning," she said.

Sean had disappeared and we were the only customers in the bar.

I put some money in the ancient jukebox, sat down and asked her where she was from.

Thin Lizzy's Phil Lynott sang about someone with a "Bad Reputation". Something that always attracted me to a woman, of course.

Jola sipped her drink and seemed to hold on to the table to steady herself.

"Your home town?" I said.

"Well," she said, knocking back her drink in one. And then her words staggered out like drunks at closing time. "I'm from the industrial wastelands of the east," she said, playing with a lighter with a picture of a matador on it. "Bialystok. Heard of it?"

"Amazingly, I have." She looked as if she didn't believe me. "It's true. I had a friend from there. He showed me a photograph of a big Soviet tank in the town centre that was painted a very camp pink."

"That's the one," she said. "Not the most exciting place. A real 'one-whore-town', as they say. So, as soon as I could, I got out of there fast."

"And you came here to Warsaw?"

She shook her head.

"No. First, I headed off to Chicago for a couple of years. And then to London. Which is where I met my wonderful husband."

"Where in London?"

"Ealing? Know it?"

"Yes," I said. "I worked there for six months back in the eighties, looking for the streets that are paved with gold. Still looking, mind you."

"Well, there's a golden shopping mall here in Warsaw, as I'm sure you know, but the streets are as grey and cold as anywhere else."

Jola took out a Marlboro from a battered pack and I lit it with one of my Embassy Regal.

"What line of work are you in?" I said.

"I manage a bar. Robert, my husband, is the owner. The Emerald Isle? It's over in the Esperanto district. Do you know it?" said Jola.

I nodded.

"Another one of Poland's authentically Irish pubs," I said.

Jola laughed. "Well, there are pubs in Ireland selling Polish beer and food, so, why not?"

"Why not, indeed."

I shifted in my chair.

"Is it fun?" I asked.

"The pub or the marriage?"

"Both."

"They serve their purpose."

"Which is?"

She rubbed her fingers and thumb together.

"I suppose marriage to Robert was what you would call a marriage of convenience," said Jola. "Though it's not so convenient, these days."

"Better to regret something you've done than something you haven't done," I said.

"Indeed."

Leaning close to me, Jola put a hand on my shoulder and looked me up and down, like she was deciding on whether or not to buy a second-hand car.

"You'll do," she said, dragging me out of the bar by my tie and through a metal door that was marked "Private".

I looked over at Rory, who was lighting a cigar, took a glance and ignored us. I got the impression that he'd seen this sort of thing many times before.

Jola locked the door behind her and switched on a strip light that flickered and buzzed before it blanched the tiny room, which was stacked with crates of Johnny Walker and metal beer barrels. On the wall was a dartboard with a poster of Stalin hanging over it. Three darts perfectly placed between his eyes. I sat down on one of the crates.

"Won't Rory mind?" I said, as Jola pulled down her knickers and took off her black leather skirt.

"Not a chance," she said. "Robert ripped him off in a big business deal a while back. He despises my husband so much he lets me get away with murder."

Before I could take off my jeans, she pulled out my dick and slowly masturbated me before she slid herself on top of me. I pushed a hand under her sweater and tweaked a nipple.

"Well, everything but that," she gasped. "So far."

At some point during the night I woke up in my own bed, soaked in a cold sweat, with no recollection of getting there. Jola, naked, was smoking and gazing out of the bedroom window. The tip of her cigarette glowed bright red and then quickly faded to black. I closed my eyes and let the sea of sleep enfold me.

In the morning, slivers of sun sliced through the blinds and slashed across my eyes, stinging like a knife blade. After a moment, I focused and looked around the room. Jola was gone.

Days bled into weeks and then months. I visited Tatiana with the same regularity but increasingly less enthusiasm. Sometimes we just talked until the early hours. She told me of her lesbian lover with the violent husband. And how they were saving enough money to get out of Warsaw. She fell asleep and I left.

A warm spring dusk was struggling to break free of winter as I left her apartment block in a daze which, for once, wasn't due to the booze. I'd been drifting through the weeks like a phantom, with thoughts of Jola haunting me. For whatever reason, I couldn't get her out of my mind. I knew I had to see her again.

As I walked along the deserted street a massive figure suddenly stepped out of the shadows and in front of me. He was a real behemoth, with a shaved head and wearing a black leather jacket. His gigantic fist grasped a knuckle-duster that slammed into me and sent me sprawling backwards until I smashed into a kebab shop window, setting off a burglar alarm.

I sank to the ground, blood oozing from my burst lip, as the giant shouted and screamed at me. My head was spinning and my limited Polish was never too good but I recognized one word that he said before storming off down the street. Tatiana.

A small group of old women wearing mohair berets surrounded me, speaking too quickly for me to understand.

I struggled to my feet and did the best thing I could think of to do. I went to the twenty-four-hour pub.

Nursing a beer and a shot of vodka, I phoned Tatiana and explained my predicament.

"It's Bronek," she said. "My former client. He's getting crazier. He started following me. Watching my clients. He's got it into his head that you are going to marry me and take me away to England."

I drifted out of her conversation and thought that maybe it was better to be hung for a sheep than a lamb. Hanging up, I ordered another shot of vodka.

The Emerald Isle was far from emerald. The walls were painted garishly red. The furniture pitch black. The atmosphere grey.

John Martyn's version of "Glory Box" whispered through

the sound system as Robert Nowak, well dressed and over-weight, with what seemed like a constantly constipated expression, drank whisky and played chess with a statuesque Indian girl.

A small group of fashion students sat sharing two beers, occasionally topping the glasses up with the contents of a bottle of supermarket vodka, while keeping a furtive eye on Robert.

I sat by the window drinking my second Warka Strong. I briefly turned my gaze outside to where the morning rain poured down in sheets and the wet pavement reflected a nearby kebab shop's flickering neon sign. Police sirens screeched through the roaring wind.

Jola came down a staircase at the side of the bar and briefly paused when she saw me. She helped herself to a drink and headed outside with a pack of cigarettes in her hand. She stood under a grubby umbrella smoking as if it was the last cigarette on earth.

I waited a few moments and joined her. Turning my collar to the rain, I sat in a grubby white plastic chair and lit up.

"You shouldn't have come here, you know? Robert is a very jealous man," she said, lighting a second cigarette, not looking at me.

"Does he know about us? About that night?"

"Of course not. But he has his suspicions. All sorts of suspicions. Especially when he's snorting cocaine from morning to night."

"I . . . just wanted to see you again. I thought you might want to go out somewhere, sometime."

She turned slightly and looked at me. Closed her eyes. Smiled.

"Oh, why the hell not?" she said.

I grinned like a schoolboy.

"When?"

"We can meet tomorrow night, if you want. Somewhere out of the way, though?"

I thought for a moment.

"What about my place?"

"Cut to the chase, eh?"

I smiled.

"In for a penny, in for a pound," I said.

The night was like a thunderstorm of drinking, smoking, sex and conversation. In the early hours, we lay on my bed in the wan light listening to an old mix tape that I'd brought with me.

Gandalf's version of "How Can We Hang On to a Dream" eased into a Bobby Womack song and Jola turned and looked me in the eye.

"You know," she said. "Life with Robert is like a living death these days. I really do want to get away. Escape. I've managed to save some money but it's not enough. Anyway . . ."

And in the space of that short pause, the thought of running away with Jola was like the lone, beautiful whore in a rundown brothel, teasing and tempting.

I said. "Can't you divorce him?"

"Ha! He's a Catholic. He'd never let me divorce him. He'd never let me leave him," she said, stroking the bruises on her neck.

As a mild spring trudged on into a scalding hot summer, our meetings became more frequent and dangerous thoughts hovered over us like a hawk ready to strike its prey.

And before long, thought congealed into action.

The plan was simple enough. We were to wait until New Year's Eve, and when Robert was as drunk as a skunk, Jola would drug his drink with some cheap cocaine and take him to bed when he passed out. And she would smother him with a pillow until he was dead. Then, after clearing the safe at the Emerald Isle, and Robert's bank account, Jola and I would head off out of Poland, towards Spain, or who knows where.

The hope was that during New Year's Day, people would think that Robert was sleeping off the previous night's indulgence, giving us plenty of time to head out of the country. And when he was found, the police would put it down to a drug overdose. Simple? As simple as Chinese algebra.

It started to snow and fireworks filled the sky as I headed through an alleyway and into the Emerald Isle. The place was stuffed with drunken, overdressed people celebrating the New Year.

Robert was clearly already drunk, holding court to a group of no-necked skinheads. Jola was already on her way upstairs to the safe.

The fire exit was propped open with a fire extinguisher and I eased my way through.

I took out a cigarette and lit up. Feeling all too confident.

And then a familiar behemoth stood in front of me. And this time, he seemed to growl.

Robert indifferently smoked a large cigar, his bleary eyes glaring at me.

"So, you are the one Bronek was telling me about, eh? The kurwa that is stealing my Ukrainian whore from me. Eh?"

Robert and Bronek stood either side of me. Grinning. Putting on knuckle-dusters.

"My brother Bronek can be very protective about our property," said Robert, "and he has taken far too much interest in little Tatiana. But that is his right as my brother. So, it really wouldn't do for us to let you take her away, would it?"

I couldn't agree or disagree. I couldn't say a thing and I couldn't move. I'd taken a beating and I was slumped in the oak and leather armchair like an insect trapped in amber. It was all I could do to wipe the glass from my eyes and ignore the burning before the brothers raised their fists and the world turned red.

The hospital stank of antiseptic. Not that it bothered me that much. The morphine was working, and the last few days I'd been feeling stronger. Able to move around. And to check my emails on my iPhone. The usual crap, of course. Spam. Jokes.

And one from Tatiana. A photo of her on a beach. With Jola. Thanking me for creating a diversion and allowing them to get away. And hoping that I get well soon.

I lay back on the small bed, closed my eyes and let the sea of self-loathing enfold me. And then I slept.

Shame

Ros Asquith

It started with a roll of the dice. What had made Sam choose a number that landed him freezing in a ditch, deafened by a helicopter's roar? Everything had been going just fine, just so fine.

Not that it was supposed to go fine for him. No folks and no prospects were never a fine thing for a boy, nor a girl neither. True, the girls he knew succumbed, depressed, cut themselves up. The boys got to cut up other people and that was bigger trouble. But Sam was always going to be different. Yes indeed. Gifted, that was Sam. He could beat his head teacher at chess, and him just seven years old! *The kid's a prodigy.* How often had he heard those words?

Shame. It's a crying shame. Then more phone calls would be made, the same old, same old. Murmurings about paperwork and funding. And he'd hear the words *gifted* and *shame*.

He'd got quite a bit of kindness, no doubt about that. But never from the same person, or not for long. Dave and Karen were the best. He'd been there two whole years, seemed longer, too, in a good way. As if all his happiness had been condensed, bottled in those two years – a bottle he could still drink from. Karen and Dave had got him great haircuts and trainers with lights on and they read him stories at night. He remembered not letting on to them that he could read – he was only four years old back then – so they would go on reading to him. He'd thought maybe the reason he had to leave was because he'd lied about his reading. But later, by the time he'd moved around a bit, he reckoned it was because Karen had had twins. It sometimes worked, he now knew, for foster parents to have their own newborn babies. But twins. That meant foster kids had to move on, more than likely. He could remember Karen crying when he left, and Dave had said they'd always keep in touch and to remember he was a great kid, the best. And Karen definitely sent him a card when he was seven. He knew that, because he still had it. *For a great boy who is seven*, it said. And she'd written "All our love" inside. But by the time you've been moved about a bit, a few more fosterings that didn't work out, and you're ten years old, at a children's home, you're past your sell-by date for adoption. Even fostering's tougher by then. It's only natural to want a sweet young kid and at ten Sam was way too tall to look sweet.

Who else could he remember? Who could he possibly call who would believe him now? The whirr of the helicopter blades scythed into his brain . . .

Well he could surely remember someone? Not the tall thin man at the children's home who always wore a grey suit, who kept asking boys to search his pockets for sweets. But one of his pockets wasn't lined, it was just a hole cut in the side of the grey trousers, so your hand went . . . Sam wasn't keen to think of him. Nor that distracted lady who'd kept promising to get him on a music course. She'd thought music would come naturally to Sam, she thought drumming and jazz would keep him out of trouble. He'd accepted the casual racism; liking Mozart was something he kept even from other kids.

As Sam flicked through his memories the kind, anxious faces blurred into one another. And the not-so-kind. He could feel the wind of the blades.

For a boy for whom nothing good was going to happen, a lot had happened to Sam. First, he had got exam results his schoolteachers only dreamed of. Then a scholarship to a Great University. He had, surely, beaten the odds. The "freezing negative" dealt out to Hardy's Obscure Jude had been conquered by Sam. He lived in a time when native wit and application were recognized. Britain was a meritocracy now. And he would graduate in law and make it better still. For Sam, learning to curb his temper, turning every negative thought into a positive, had become a way of being.

He had left behind the peeling corridors, the curses and graffiti. He had risen above it. Another face from his past solidified. *Rise above it, Sam.* Ed had stuck by Sam after the third set of foster parents dropped out. He'd seen him every week for nearly eighteen months. Sam knew he was a mentor, now. But back then he'd thought of Ed as a friend. It was continuity that counted, said Ed. He wrote to Sam, too, twice, after he got a better job. He wanted to keep in touch, he really did.

And then Sam had rolled the dice. That's what kids did in the children's home, whenever they played dares. It was a habit that stuck with Sam and he'd argued in his Oxford interview that it might be the best way for a jury to judge some cases, the law being as loaded as it was and juries being so often at a loss. He'd thought the dons would like that. Quirky. Original.

He hadn't settled in Oxford's halls, felt too different. Wanted a room of his own. *Room to rent. Suit student.*

There were plenty to choose from.

"If it's a six," thought Sam, "I'll take this one." And the die came up with a two and a four. He liked the room, paid a deposit, started to unpack. And then he opened the drawer.

Could he have lived in the room for three years without opening that drawer? Probably. It was the bottom one in a five-drawer chest and it was a weird thing to have opened that one first. But he opened that drawer and that was when freedom evaporated for Sam. There were no choices after that, as far as he could judge.

The drawer was lined with fading newspaper.

Sam raised his head from the icy water. "Come out with your hands above your head," roared the police megaphone.

Wait, there had been a moment of choice after opening the drawer. He didn't *have* to have read the yellowing newsprint.

Why did he read it? But had there, really, been a choice? For a child to whom reading had been the first, the only, thread of hope? For a boy for whom Camus made more sense as an author than a footballer? Well, he read it, naturally.

"HARRY'S HOOKER SHAME" the faded headline screamed. And there was a picture of a handsome white man and a beautiful black woman. And the woman was the woman whose photograph Sam had kept for as long as he could remember.

Shaking, Sam read on. He read how Harry was a dazzling young politician tipped for high office. He read how Harry had been caught with a prostitute and how Harry's career was in the balance. He read about how someone so happily married, with such a lovely young family, could descend to the gutter to risk everything for a moment's sordid gratification. He read how Harry was mortified. He read some crude details from the police report. He read how nothing more was known about the beautiful black woman, except her name, which was a different name than the one on the back of the photograph that he kept in his wallet alongside his card from Karen and his letters from Ed. On the back of the photograph was written, in a spidery, fragile hand:

To my darling Samuel Josiah Darwin,
Love is too small a word, Ma.

The newspaper was dated 10 September, nineteen years ago. Just nine months before Sam was born.

The moment, you could say, changed Sam's mind. His scholarship, his talent for research, was unleashed to one purpose and in just two weeks he unearthed all he needed to know. Sam's father, the dazzling young Harry, had escaped the paparazzi by putting a gun to his head six weeks after his indiscretion was first blazoned across the tabloids: "TRAGIC HARRY'S FINAL ACT." There was a picture of a startled widow, protecting two small boys. Sam had two brothers, then: Charles and Henry. Sam's own mother had died, as he had always been told, shortly after his birth. That remained true, and the truth remained bitter. But the carefully constructed story of her life which she had entrusted to his first care-givers and which, he was now amazed to realize, he had never doubted, had been entirely false. She had been neither married, nor tragically widowed. She had not been a nurse, but a hooker. She had not even been English, but American. She had conjured the father's name on his birth certificate. It must have been almost *her* final act, her last attempt to confer some dignity on her son. The blaze of publicity surrounding her encounter with Harry had led her to flee London, change her name and make a bid for a quiet life. Morning-after pills must have been the last thing on her mind. She resisted offers to sell her story, just disappeared.

"Come out with your hands above your head," repeated the voice from the megaphone. But Sam's mind raced.

Supposing he hadn't rolled the dice? Opened that drawer? Read the old newsprint? He could have just crumpled it unread. He could have left the drawer closed for three years. The truth would have smouldered silently in the very room he slept and studied in. Could that have happened? Wouldn't he have smelled the burning ink? But he had opened the drawer. And then he had to dig and dig. There had been no choice after.

Samuel Josiah had completed his research fourteen days after opening the drawer. One day later, on a golden Sunday morning, in a sleepy Gloucestershire village, in a chorus of birdsong, he raised the heavy brass of a lion's head on a door. Once, twice, three times.

The door was opened by a small, elderly man.

The small, elderly man saw a tall, black stranger and heard him say:

"You killed my father."

The small, elderly man saw the stranger reaching inside his jacket for a gun.

Samuel Josiah reached into his jacket, to pull out his sheaf of newspaper clippings. He hadn't meant it to be like this, not so abrupt as this. The fear on the little man's face unnerved him. He had witnessed two stabbings at the second children's home. They had been easier to watch than this small man clasping his heart, staggering, flailing, falling, uttering a small, surprised cry as he fell. Sam looked away, overwhelmed by shame. And when he looked back, he saw blood trickling from the little old man's temple, where he had cracked his skull open against the stone step.

Sam had seen two dead bodies. He knew.

Sam did not read the papers the next day, or the day after that. He dared not show his face. He was an animal now, running, hiding in a barn one night, a ditch the next.

So he didn't read of the dreadlocked thug who had cracked the skull of a defenceless old man in his own home in a picturesque English village. Nor did he see the artist's nightmarish impression of the mindless killer pieced together from a neighbour's description.

In the ditch, Sam felt only rage and shame.

"Come out, with your hands raised."

Sam came out, too fast. Freezing mud streamed from his hair, his teeth were startling in the sunlight. The youthful policeman, panicky, saw an animal, not a man, leaping. Luckily for him, shooting murderers was not frowned upon in those parts any longer. Not when the murderer was a mindless thug who had slaughtered without motive.

No one who knew Sam's "victim" remembered that it had been his tireless pursuit of Harry Engerfield that had led to the promising young MP's suicide nineteen years before. If they had remembered, they would have said that digging the dirt on MPs was a tabloid reporter's duty. That if people didn't like heat, they should stay away from kitchens. And who, in that peaceful village, would have connected the young black killer with the dazzling, talented, white Harry?

And how could the legitimate children of Harry Engerfield know that the mindless killer on the run, who had caused them to double-lock their doors for a week to protect their infants, was their brother?

Days later, the smallprint reported that the mindless killer had been a most promising, indeed brilliant, student. Drugs were blamed for his apparent personality change. The young police officer who shot him received counselling and the consolation that he had acted as anyone else might have. It was no crime, was it, to kill a killer?

No connection was made between the faded newspaper photograph in Sam's lodgings and the picture in his wallet. The authorities tried to contact Karen and Ed, but both had long since moved on.

In the absence of any family, it was thought proper that the children's home should send a mourner to Sam's funeral: a tall, thin man in a grey suit.

Murder Uncordial

Amy Myers

There was something seriously wrong. One did not serve oyster forcemeat with a delicate guinea fowl. Auguste Didier despaired of the modern standards of cuisine. Worse, Tranton Towers, the stately Kentish residence of Lord and Lady Bromfield, seemed to be a most mysterious mansion. Instead of concentrating on the delights of a menu prepared by Master Chef Auguste Didier, his lordship's household seemed far more interested in politics.

It was a small comfort that the dinner, for which Auguste's services as chef had been specially arranged, was in honour of the President of the French Republic, during his return journey to Paris. The reason for his visit to England had been to seal the knot of friendship between the two countries with the Entente Cordiale, and so the menu for the evening demanded the best of Auguste Didier's art. But that, he fumed, would not be possible with the assistant chef with whom he had been provided. Oyster forcemeat? Non, non, *non*.

"Why not?" assistant chef Françoise Dagarre had asked demurely.

Usually Auguste was only too happy to work with women in his kitchens, especially attractive ones like Mademoiselle Dagarre. After all, this was 1903. Nevertheless he drew the line at those who pretended to be chefs and were not. She was a good cook, yes, but a chef? No. He had even considered the possibility that she was a secret agent, a spy, as the reason for today's banquet was that the German ambassador would also be present. It was generally known that the Kaiser viewed the Entente Cordiale between France and England with deep suspicion, and the Foreign Office had suggested this gesture to show that he had nothing to fear from this new rapport between its two rivals. All three nations were, and would be, the best of friends.

Auguste tried to convince himself that with the ambassador's presence, the French would not require a spy in Tranton Towers, as the President would not only have his entourage with him, but would be accompanied by Scotland Yard detectives throughout his visit. Nevertheless all sorts of fearful visions filled Auguste's head, from assassination to his delicate Swan of Savoy à la Chantilly being smashed by an intruder in his kitchen bent on ruining this important occasion.

It was not too late to prevent catastrophe, as Monsieur le President and the other guests would not be arriving until five o'clock this afternoon. He must take his concerns to Lord Bromfield immediately.

"A spy?" Lord Bromfield roared. "By heaven, Didier, this is *England*, man. We don't hold with spies here. Not gentlemanly."

"But Mademoiselle Dagarre is not what she seems, sir."

"Nonsense. What would she be spying on, might I ask?"

"I don't know, sir." It seemed obvious to Auguste, but Lord Bromfield was the politician, not him.

"Well, I do know. Nothing. Stick to your trade and cook." Then he added a conciliatory note. "Look here, Didier, you're a good fellow, but you're French."

"Half French, sir."

This was waved aside. "You don't understand the way we do things here. This is a *private* dinner, so as a matter of honour politics are left at the dining-room door."

Not in Auguste's experience, but he maintained a diplomatic silence.

"Good Lord, what's that?" The monocle dropped from Lord Bromfield's eye in his astonishment. He had been standing by the window and something was clearly amiss in the forecourt below. Auguste hurried to join him.

Drawn up in front of the pillars of the grand entrance to Tranton Towers he could see a horse-drawn charabanc, towards which the butler, Mr Jennings, was hurrying as fast as his dignity permitted. One of his lordship's grooms was bemusedly holding the reins, and out of the charabanc spilled surely the strangest array of people ever to grace the portico of Tranton Towers.

Auguste's fascinated eyes fell on a thin man busily donning a one-man-band harness, jangling cymbals, trumpets, a drum and sundry other instruments; a well-rounded gentleman in a large checked suit and battered top hat; a dapper man with moustache and melancholy expression, clad in dinner suit and huge bow tie; a large solid man of many muscles; a lady of middle years and girth who seemed to be covered in purple feathers waving from her costume and hat; and a young – no, not so young – lady clad in a tight bustled white dress with pink frills and sporting a large and very flowery hat. She was grasping the leads of three small yapping dogs. Behind her streamed several others, including a lady in male attire. In all, Auguste counted twelve unexpected visitors.

Whoever they were, they were not the President of the French Republic.

"Look here, your lordship." Mr Check Suit was obviously the leader, Auguste noted, and was only too happy to explain their presence. "Charlie's my name. The Great Charlie, I am, and what we're all here for is what you promised." He gave a hearty chuckle, as he waved a letter in front of his surprised lordship's eyes.

Mr Jennings, having been forced to summon higher authority to deal with the calamity, stood by ashen-faced at this challenge to his ability to deal with any domestic emergency. Since no one seemed to object to his presence, Auguste edged closer to Lord Bromfield whose face had assumed a bright shade of red.

"That's my writing paper," he roared.

"Course it is." The Great Charlie sounded surprised. "So here we are, straight from the Wapping Palace of Varieties. Daisy, dear, introduce yourself."

"Pleased to meet you, your lordship," trilled the lady in the tight frilly dress. "Sweethearts," addressing the dogs, "bow to his lordship." Her charges reluctantly stood on their hind legs, wobbled and dropped down again.

"And this," Charlie said proudly, "is the Wapping Blackbird, Miss Emmeline Foster." This was the large lady with the feathers – an apt stage name, Auguste thought, as the Blackbird kissed his lordship's hand, much to his horror.

The one-man-band, Joachim Schmitt, made no attempt to follow suit, being laden with jangling musical instruments, but managed a toot on the trumpet to acknowledge Charlie's introduction. The dapper gentleman was introduced as "our own, our very own Caruso, Soulful Songster Stefan Meyer". Joe Jones, the strongman, looked all too eager to crush his lordship's hand but Lord Bromfield hastily backed away. The rest of the group took their turn, as his lordship struggled to give vent to his feelings.

At last he found his voice: "What the blazes are you doing here?"

Charlie looked puzzled. "Come to take a tour of the house, dine with you and perform for a few guests. That's what you asked in your letter, sir." He waved it again, and this time Lord Bromfield snatched it.

One glance and he'd seen enough. "Not my writing. Looks like it, but it's a forgery. My apologies, Mr Charlie, but you've been grossly deceived and so have I. Mr Jennings . . ." The butler approached him almost in tears. "Kindly arrange for these good people to be recompensed and see them off the property."

The faces of the good people promptly changed from cheerfulness to dismay, and rebellion looked likely to break out as they murmured angrily amongst themselves.

"Can't do that, your lordship," the Great Charlie said

firmly. "A contract's a contract, and who's to say whether it's your writing or not? What's more, it's against the professional code of Wapping Palace of Varieties not to perform when contracted so to do."

"And what about our grub?" Joe, the strongman, demanded.

"Looking forward to our little tour, I was," Daisy wailed tearfully, thus making the dogs yelp again and the Wapping Blackbird move forward to the attack.

"*I* was to sing," she informed Lord Bromfield with heaving bosom. "Are you telling me that the Voice of the Wapping Blackbird is not good enough for your guests?"

Soulful Songster Stefan hurried to support her. "Meine Liebling has the voice of an angel."

He was swept aside by the Wapping Blackbird's dismissive hand, which indicated she could fight her own battles.

His lordship, Auguste thought, highly amused, looked as though speedy retreat would be his preferred tactic in the fight, but he managed to stand his ground.

"Kindly leave," Lord Bromfield almost squeaked in response, but in vain. The mutiny was growing in strength. It was time for his own version of diplomacy, Auguste decided.

"Your lordship, suppose we served an early luncheon on the south lawn for these artistes, followed by a short conducted tour of the house? Your guests do not arrive until five, and if the charabanc leaves by two o'clock no one need be incommoded."

"Yes, yes." Lord Blomfield clutched at this compromise. "You'll make a politician yet, Didier."

The Great Charlie still looked doubtful. "What about our show? We got a contract."

Lord Blomfield took a firm stand. "So have I, and mine's with Scotland Yard. Personally, I would of course have greatly enjoyed your performance, but I have already given the Yard a list of those who will be attending today, and due to this misunderstanding it does not include you. Another time, perhaps."

There followed a brief consultation between Charlie and

his colleagues. "We get our dosh and our tour then?" he finally
asked his lordship. "And grub?"

"Jellied eels," Daisy eagerly demanded.

"Victoria sponge," requested the Wapping Blackbird.

"Kugelhopf," the Soulful Songster pleaded.

"And booze," Joe added firmly.

"Plenty of *everything*," his lordship assured them.

At last the magic hour of two o'clock arrived. It had taken its
time doing so, Auguste thought, breathing a sigh of relief as
he watched the well-fed and well-oiled uninvited guests
lurching their way out of the servants' wing towards the charabanc. Fortunately Mademoiselle Dagarre had not only
superintended their luncheon and drinking requirements
(only the Kugelhopf proved a problem), but she had offered
to help Mr Jennings escort the group round the house, an
arrangement with which Auguste had eagerly concurred. Not
only had he been able to continue with the delightful preparations for the banquet ahead, but he had been relieved of the
anxiety of superintending his assistant chef's every move in
the kitchen – particularly any threat of her moving towards
his guinea fowl or Chantilly Swan.

The tour had duly taken place, ending with a second visit
to the servants' hall to reclaim any property left there and
also – in Mademoiselle Dagarre's discreet words – to prepare
for the journey home. A wise precaution, Auguste thought, in
view of the copious amount of drink consumed.

Auguste decided to follow the eventual exodus, if only to
support Mr Jennings who was still glassy-eyed with shock.
Just as it was rejoining the charabanc, however, the party
decided to stop to express its thanks.

"Let's have a song for his lordship," shouted a bleary-eyed
Great Charlie.

His lordship had not appeared, but they sang it all the same,
perhaps under the illusion that Mr Jennings had been elevated
to a position of rank. "Goodbye Dolly Gray" was their choice,
and an enthusiastic rendering took place. They were still

singing it as they climbed on to the charabanc, and with Charlie taking the reins, the horses were turned and made their merry way down the drive.

But surely there was something wrong . . .

Belated realization sent Auguste running after the charabanc yelling "Stop." No one heard him, or if they did, no one took any notice. Mr Jennings was pulling him back, shouting, "Are you mad?" and between that and "Dolly Gray" Auguste's pleas went in vain. "Dolly Gray" grew fainter and fainter.

Auguste groaned, to Mr Jennings's annoyance. "What is wrong with you, Mr Didier? His lordship instructed that they all depart by two o'clock. It is now five minutes past."

"Everything is wrong," Auguste replied. "They did not all depart."

"Are you inebriated, Didier? We saw them go."

"Twelve arrived, but only eleven left."

Lord Bromfield was instantly summoned, but a ten-minute search of the house failed to find Joachim Schmitt, for which his lordship appeared much relieved. "Obviously," he announced, "the fellow has decided to walk into the village and get the train back. What was his name?"

"Schmitt, sir," Auguste replied. The one-man-band harness and instruments had been found in the servants' hall, where they had been left before the tour began, and to him this discovery would seem to rule out his lordship's theory. Auguste's visions of calamity came back with a rush.

"German, eh?" Lord Bromfield looked momentarily taken aback.

"It is not uncommon in music halls," Auguste tried to reassure him.

"That is so, your lordship. The Soulful Songster fellow is also German." Mr Jennings too was anxious to calm his master.

Lord Blomfield seemed slightly cheered. "Mere coincidence that there are two of them then. Anyway, this Schmitt isn't in the house now and the other fellow's left, so that's that.

Besides, the German ambassador's dining here himself, so he can report to the Kaiser on what's going on. That puts paid to any of your damned spy nonsense, Didier."

Auguste nerved himself. "The French too might have their spies. There is—"

"You're out of your mind, Didier. The French don't have spies any more than we do," Lord Bromfield interrupted crossly. "Like us, they're gentlemen." He thought about this. "Almost."

Should he mention the possibility of assassination? Auguste wondered frantically. As the German ambassador was hardly likely to leap up in the midst of a Didier-inspired menu to kill the President personally, a hired killer would be required, and thus Herr Schmitt should be tracked down without delay. But with his lordship's present attitude, he could say nothing. In any case his attention had been caught by what he could see outside the morning-room window.

"Good thing Scotland Yard's accompanying the President, eh?" Lord Bromfield added a forced laugh.

Auguste cleared his throat. "It is indeed, sir. However, it appears to have arrived here already."

The charabanc was once again coming to a halt outside the Towers, with eleven noisy occupants, some crying, some angry, some shouting. Auguste was more interested in the carriage following it, however. Two men were stepping out of it, one of whom was very familiar. It was Detective Chief Inspector Egbert Rose. Lord Bromfield hurried outside to greet the other man, and Auguste promptly followed him.

Egbert's face registered a mixture of pleasure and wariness when he saw Auguste. "Trouble," he said gloomily. "Wherever you are, I find trouble. What is it this time?"

"A missing man."

"Not this Schmitty that this lot are on about? Got left behind, did he?"

"I hope that is all, but he hasn't yet been found, and his one-man-band instruments are still here."

Rose frowned. "Good thing, I came down early. Monsieur Lapelle here is one of the President's private secretaries. He's convinced someone is out to slaughter the President, and he wants to go through the house with a toothcomb before the main party arrives. First thing we found was this charabanc blocking the gateway as they argued over whether to come back or not. Back, I told them. No one leaves this house without my permission, I said, or my governor will have my guts for garters. Now you're telling me you can't find this German bloke. Got drunk and lay down for a snooze somewhere?" he asked hopefully.

"I think not. It's at least possible that he planned to stay behind and has hidden himself all too well. A thorough search is needed, and, Egbert, there is something else." Auguste passed on his doubts about his assistant chef in a discreet whisper.

To his annoyance Egbert chortled. "Probably planning to jump out of a cake in pink tights and do the dastardly deed herself."

"Perhaps she is," Auguste replied with dignity, with a nightmare vision of his Swan of Savoy being so desecrated.

"You're right," Egbert said hastily. "We'll get this search going. Can you look after this mob for me?"

Auguste faced the prospect with sinking heart. "We can entertain them in the servants' hall."

This was easier said than done, as Daisy and Emmeline had to be restrained from rushing into Tranton Towers immediately to conduct their own searches for the missing Schmitty. Lured by the promise of tea and cakes, however, they meekly followed Auguste back into the servants' hall.

"Poor Schmitty," wailed Daisy, dabbing at her eyes with a delicate handkerchief with one hand and restraining her dogs with the other, "what's happened to my poor darling?"

"That's not what you were calling him last night," the Wapping Blackbird snapped. "Not when you found out he has a wife and children back in Germany."

"Nor you." Joe rounded on her in Daisy's defence. "You

didn't like it, Emmeline. Fancied your own chances, did you? Some hopes."

Blackbird Emmeline went very pale, and decided to side with Daisy, throwing a comforting arm round her. "We were both betrayed," she said mournfully. "I too was betrothed to him before I found out The Truth."

Schmitty seemed a busy man, Auguste thought, juggling not only his one-man-band instruments but sweethearts too.

Soulful Songster Stefan took advantage of the situation to do his own comforting, slipping a manly arm round the Blackbird's purple-feathered dress. "Meine Liebling, do not fear. I am here to protect you."

The Wapping Blackbird did not seem to appreciate this offer. "Joachim will explain all when he returns. This story about a wife was surely a misunderstanding. And you," she whirled round on Auguste, "where are those cakes we were promised? And tea."

"And Kugelhopf," the Soulful Songster added hopefully.

The latter at least would still not be forthcoming. Auguste had never been able to see the attraction of this concoction, which to him was merely a doughy brioche with raisins and almonds added to make it edible. He ignored the request. "The police will require a photograph of Mr Schmitt? Does anyone have one?"

"Of course," the Blackbird declared grandly. "Next to my heart." Under everyone's fascinated gaze she drew on a silver chain, a locket jerked itself up from her bosom, and she handed the photograph inside it to Auguste. It was unpleasantly warm.

"That's not Joe Schmitt," Egbert Rose snorted, taking one look at the photograph. He had been conferring in the morning room with Lord Bromfield and Monsieur Lapelle, who owing to the tension of the situation did not seem to think it unusual that a temporary chef should apparently be working for Scotland Yard.

"This Schmitt might be a one-man-band," Egbert continued, "but his trade is killing. His real name is Carl Halbach, and he does the dirty work for the Camarilla. Heard of them?"

Monsieur Lapelle had, and he looked grave. "That is the name given to the group of parasites that surround the Kaiser," he explained. "They dream up ways to please their master, and assassinating the President of France could well be one of them. Mon dieu, and he will soon be here."

His lordship paled. "You know all about this fellow, Rose. *Find him.*"

"We will," Egbert assured him, with more confidence than Auguste had. "It seems clear enough that the Camarilla arranged for a sight of the German ambassador's invitation to forge one for the Wapping Palace of Varieties – including Halbach. I only know about this Halbach through the *bureau noir*, your lordship. The French spy service. They sent me a photograph of him a month or two ago."

Auguste drew great satisfaction from the sight of Lord Bromfield's face as he took in this confirmation that the French did not play by gentlemanly rules.

"We must find Halbach before the President arrives," Lapelle lamented. "If we cannot, I must stop the President from leaving the train at Bexley."

Auguste was aghast. Cancel the dinner? After all his work on the Chantilly Swan? It could not be allowed to happen.

Mr Jennings seemed to have abandoned all hope of a life that did not feature the Wapping Palace of Varieties, as an intensive search was ordered and he and Mademoiselle Dagarre reconstructed their tour round the house, closely followed by Egbert Rose, Pierre Lapelle and Auguste Didier. The tour for the Wapping group had been a brief one, Auguste realized, the bare minimum to satisfy it. Only the library, the dining room and the famous long gallery had been included. When Egbert questioned the charabanc party in the servants' hall there had been no consensus as to where Schmitty, as they continued to call him, had last been seen. The Great Charlie remembered seeing him last in the library, the Soulful Songster spoke to

him in the dining room, and the Wapping Blackbird claimed
to have seen him in the long gallery examining the fireplace.

Auguste hoped that her testimony was a reliable one, as
the gallery had been the final stage before the Wapping
group returned to the servants' wing. The library offered no
possibilities for secreting Herr Schmitt and neither did the
dining room, but the corridors in between the destinations
had opportunities aplenty for anyone trying to slip away
unseen.

Even Egbert Rose was daunted by the time the small party
reached the long gallery, and Auguste began to despair. Was
there room in the chimney for a man to hide? Investigation
proved not. Nor was there a closet with enough space for
Schmitty to conceal himself in even temporarily. The Blackbird had either been mistaken or lying.

Then his eye fell on a large aspidistra adorning a low table
which was covered with a red plush cloth. Surely it was too
low even for an occasional table . . . He looked at the aspidistra again – a plant he had always hated – lifted it off and picked
up a corner of the cloth, conscious that his heart was beating
loudly. It proved to be no table that lay beneath, but an antique
wooden chest.

Hearing his cry of triumph, Egbert was quickly at his side.
"Get ready, Auguste. He'll fight, and is probably armed." He
stood guard, as Auguste took the corner of the lid. "*Now!*"

The chest was empty.

"Search the whole house, every corner, every cranny, every
damned mousehole," roared Lord Bromfield. Monsieur
Lapelle was quick to follow him, beckoning Egbert Rose to
come with him, which left Auguste and Mademoiselle
Dagarre alone.

The answer to the problem of the disappearing one-man-
band was tantalizingly close. Auguste was sure of it. But where
to start with so little time left? He decided to speak out directly
to his new assistant, as they hurried back to the servants'
domain in the basement.

"You know nothing of this man Halbach, mademoiselle?"

Françoise looked so innocent that he could almost believe her to be so. "But I am a mere cook. An assistant chef."

Auguste's eyes gleamed. So she wanted to play games – and at such a time. "And yet you made oyster forcemeat. A risky choice for adopting the role of an assistant chef."

"Merely a slight mistake," she purred, "which only a master chef such as yourself would recognize." She paused. "If a mere assistant chef may make another suggestion, it is wise to study the ingredients of every recipe for life – and, monsieur, for death also."

No game, now. "What ingredients would you recommend I study immediately?" he asked gravely.

"If I knew, I would tell you, but I do not. My task is to return to my work which is to ensure that no impure ingredients are lurking there."

Recipe for death? The master guiding plan for assassination? His mind began to work, as with a whisk of her skirts, she left him standing in the servants' corridor. Not for him the delights of the kitchen yet. Those impure ingredients – had she been speaking metaphorically, or of the food to be served to the President? The latter possibility was too terrible to contemplate, and first he must deal with the ingredients of the missing Carl Halbach problem.

Question: why did Halbach leave the one-man-band instruments in the servants' hall if he intended to disappear? A glaring mistake for a would-be assassin. Every ingredient is included in a recipe for a reason. What was the reason here? *Answer*: to make his pursuers believe that he was hidden in the main house, whereas . . . Auguste's eye wandered round his many-roomed temporary basement domain.

Question: why would Halbach want to hide in the servants' quarters, when in the main house he would be much closer to the President? *Answer*: there was something here that he needed.

Question: how did he plan to get close enough to the President to kill him? *Answer*: by appearing to be a servant . . . a footman, who would have best opportunity to be close to the President.

The last two ingredients melted into one another like a roux of butter and flour. *Answer to the roux*: Halbach needed a spare livery.

Summoning up his courage, Auguste walked towards the room where the footmen changed into their livery, and where there were usually spare sets. He held his breath as he gently pushed open the door, but there was no one to be seen and no closet large enough to hold a man. Then his eye fell on a chest underneath the window. This time he was more cautious. Even if the chest did contain his quarry, he must remember that he was likely to be armed, and there was no Egbert Rose here now. But there was also no time to waste if his Swan was to be appreciated this evening.

He flung open the lid. Inside lay Carl Halbach's body. There was a gun beside him, and he had been strangled.

The would-be assassin had become a victim.

It was 3.30. The body of the unfortunate Halbach had left Tranton Towers, Lord Bromfield, Pierre Lapelle and Egbert Rose were in conference, and Auguste Didier was pacing between his twin responsibilities not knowing which offered the least comfort – the sight of a kitchen where the Chantilly Swan only required the last-minute addition of spun sugar to attain its full glory for a President who might never see it, or the sight of the Wapping artistes in tears, tempers and shock. He manfully chose the latter responsibility.

"I just cannot believe it, I really cannot," exclaimed the Wapping Blackbird. "That dreadful man was only a nasty spy who might have killed us all in our beds."

"I always said there was something odd about him," Daisy sniffed, at last in accord with Emmeline.

Joe looked puzzled. "But someone killed Schmitty, he didn't kill no one."

"He *meant* to," the Soulful Songster said. "He meant to kill the President."

"And to think I hired him for the Palace," the Great Charlie mourned.

"A disgrace to his fatherland," declared the Songster.

"But who killed him?" Joe persisted.

Auguste retreated. He would see if Egbert Rose could be found. There was little doubt that the assassin would have been Halbach, but even if the slightest possibility of danger remained it was his duty to help Egbert in his task. He found him alone in the morning room.

"I had my eye on the other German chap as Halbach's murderer," Egbert grunted, "but that doesn't add up. If he was an accomplice, he wouldn't go and kill Halbach instead of the President, would he?"

"Among the Wapping visitors there are several with personal reasons for wishing this man removed," Auguste said. "Have you considered them? Two ladies, both falsely believing themselves betrothed to the so-called Joachim Schmitt, discovered last night that he was already married, and two gentlemen, the strong man, and Stefan Meyer were extremely jealous of him."

"Doesn't seem like a woman's job to me. Of course, it's possible, if it was done from behind with a garrotte of some kind. But I prefer the sound of these two gents, especially Meyer, who could have been Halbach's accomplice and also had personal reasons for wanting him out of the way."

"But Meyer would surely wait until *after* Halbach had killed the President if he was his accomplice. Why kill him before that, and make the job more difficult for himself?"

Another grunt. "Very well. Back to his personal motive – flimsy though it is. It would have been easy enough for any of that Wapping lot, perhaps the Great Charlie himself, to follow Halbach on the spur of the moment. Tell you what, Auguste, that's what I don't like about that theory. Too spur of the moment."

"What's wrong with that?"

"Too straightforward for a case you're mixed up in."

Auguste let this slur pass with dignity. "So I take it that you think my assistant chef might still be planning to jump out of a cake."

"Ah," said Rose. "Matter of fact you were right about her. Lapelle told me she works for the *bureau noir*, and so indirectly for him. She was under strict orders not to draw attention to herself; her task was to watch in case someone poisoned the President's food."

Auguste was aghast. So Mademoiselle Dagarre had not been speaking metaphorically. There had indeed been a risk to his exquisite food. The full horror of such an outrage terrified him. He had much to thank the attractive Mademoiselle Dagarre for. At any other time . . .

"I keep coming back to this other German chap," Rose said. "Accomplice and jealous lover."

"But they do not fit, mon ami," Auguste said patiently. "They are impure ingredients together—"

"Beg your pardon?"

Auguste thought hard. "The ingredient for murder that does not fit."

"Hurry up, man," Rose said urgently. "If you're going to have an idea, have it quickly. Time's fast running out. Halbach may be dead, but if there's still a killer running around, we need to know."

"Kugelhopf!" cried Auguste in triumph. "Stefan Meyer is *not* German."

Rose regarded him blankly, and Auguste hastened to explain. "Meyer's favourite food. But Kugelhopf is an Alsatian dish, not German."

"Alsace is in Germany," Rose snapped.

"No, mon ami. Not to those who live there. They still belong in their hearts to France, and wait only for an opportunity to be free of the tyrant that has governed them since 1870. Meyer is an Alsatian name too. Furthermore, when speaking of Halbach, Stefan Meyer spoke of *his* fatherland, not *our*— Halbach's fatherland is Germany, but not Meyer's."

"Then he wasn't Halbach's accomplice?"

"He pretended to be, but only to foil the plot to kill the man whom he regards as his President."

A pause. "I'll give the good news to Lapelle."

Auguste walked back into the kitchens, eager to find his assistant chef. "I think, mademoiselle, you need have no fear now of impure ingredients. Our recipes will be presented to the President tonight; we will forget such matters as forcemeat, and," he took her hand, "soon perhaps we may spin sugar together?"

Françoise blushed prettily. "I did my best," she sighed, with downcast eyes that failed to hide the twinkle in her beautiful eyes, "but working with a master chef such as you, how can my best be enough? Monsieur . . . Auguste . . . to spin sugar, to float through the heavens with you . . ."

Auguste kissed her hand, and soon, he hoped, her lips. "How shall we enjoy our Entente Cordiale, Françoise?"

Midwinter Interlude

Alexander McCall Smith

Ulf Varg was a Swedish detective. He was very well aware of just how fashionable it was to be a Swedish or Danish detective, and was amused by the extraordinary degree of interest shown by the rest of the world in Scandinavian crime. "It's entirely unrealistic," he said to his friends. "People must believe that Scandinavia is a hotbed of criminal activity – with bodies everywhere – whereas in fact we have a very low crime rate compared with other places. It's the same with English villages: they have a sensational murder rate, if you believe those novels – which, of course, one does not. Real life is very different. There are no clichés in real life."

That, of course, is where he was wrong. Sweden may not have a very high crime rate, but it has plenty of detectives who are exactly as they are portrayed in fiction and on the screen – rather morose, a bit enigmatic, inclined to drink too much, perhaps a bit depressing. There are undoubtedly Swedish detectives who are not like that at all, but there are many who fit the mould very well. Ulf himself was one of these.

His name, of course, was absolutely right for the job. If Philip Marlowe was a perfect choice for a laconic Los Angeles gumshoe, and Hercule Poirot an ideal name for a moustachioed Belgian, then Ulf Varg was an entirely fitting name for an inspector with the Malmö criminal investigation department. Ulf means "wolf" in Danish and Varg translates as "wolf" in Swedish. Ulf Varg was therefore a name that would make most malefactors think twice before engaging in criminal activity. One would not wish to trifle with somebody called Wolf Wolf.

Yet even if the name Ulf Varg was one that might discourage criminals, Ulf himself was a gentle and sympathetic man. He was prepared to be rough, of course, when toughness was required, but he understood the role of mercy and forgiveness. On more than one occasion, Ulf had turned a blind eye to a matter that a harder detective might have pursued to its conclusion. He understood that people did things they might regret; that even the worst of men might have within them some qualities worth cherishing. "That is what our civilization stands for," he explained. "If we cannot exercise forgiveness, then what have we learned over the last thousand years or so?"

On one occasion, when he was attending a police conference in Stockholm, he responded to a question from the speaker in terms that surprised the other detectives present. The speaker had talked about the qualities of a good detective and had concentrated on intuition and a willingness to be painstaking and methodical. Ulf agreed that these were important elements in police work, but when the speaker had said, "And is there anything else?" Ulf had put up his hand and said, "Forgiveness." The other delegates had all turned in their seats to look at him; there had been sniggers and one or two people actually burst out laughing.

"I'm serious," said Ulf. "Without forgiveness, our life is an empty cavern of ice."

This remark had brought silence.

"Possibly," said the speaker, after a while. Then he had added, "However, I would query whether it is for us, as detectives, to forgive."

Again there was silence, and then an inspector from a northern city, a place of winter darkness, had said, "You can forgive them after they've served their sentence; not before."

Ulf lived by himself in an apartment in the centre of Malmö. He had been married, but his wife had gone off with an accountant who worked for a car-hire firm. He was lonely, and his colleagues, sensing this, had attempted to match-make. Ulf was used to being invited to dinners at which he would find himself seated next to a recently divorced or sepa-rated woman – quite coincidentally, of course – but he had never found that any of these people appealed to him. He had had one or two relationships after the break-up of his marriage, but none had lasted. His work made it difficult, of course; a detective inspector keeps strange hours, often being called to a crime scene in the small hours of the morning and then finding himself on duty for twenty hours or more. "Never leave a crime scene too early," Ulf said to his assis-tant. "Leave no stone unturned. Clues are like fish: they go off after a while."

"Yes," said his assistant, who agreed with him on all points. "I'll bear that in mind."

"Don't only bear it in mind," said Ulf. "Practise it."

"Of course," said the assistant.

Ulf's assistant was named Markus. He was thirty-two and was married to a paediatric nurse named Tekla. She came from the northern town of Örnsköldsvik, where her father had been an ethanol engineer. She preferred Malmö, where there was more light. "No wonder Swedish films are so dark," she once said to Markus. "All that darkness, all that cold. No wonder Bergman made the films he did."

"We are not meant to notice such things," said Markus. "If you are Swedish then darkness and cold are natural. We do not notice them."

"I do," said Tekla.

Ulf liked Tekla and she liked him. Every two or three weeks she invited Ulf to join Markus and her in their apartment for a meal of raw fish, washed down with Finnish vodka. After they had finished their meal, they would sit in silence, gazing through the window at the clouds moving slowly across the sky.

Shortly before Christmas one year, Ulf invited two of his junior colleagues to a special lunch in a restaurant near the headquarters of the Malmö CID. This restaurant was owned by a man whom Ulf had known since he was a boy in Gothenburg. They had enjoyed many adventures together, some of them rather dangerous. It had been their habit to hide in the bushes at the Liseberg amusement park, watching a particular ride in which people were strapped to a garishly painted gondola that then swung backwards and forwards on a long metal arm before doing a complete circle. The performance of the circle meant that the people taking the ride were briefly and stomach-churningly turned upside-down, and it was at this point that Ulf and his friend, Fabian, would run out from their hiding place and retrieve the money that fell out of the pockets of the suspended thrill-seekers.

On one occasion, Fabian was not quite quick enough in getting out of the way of the descending gondola. He had seen a ten krona coin fall from somebody's pocket and he had dashed out to rescue it. Sensing danger, Ulf had called him back, but Fabian had disregarded his friend's warning. The gondola caught him on the right leg and broke it in three places. Thereafter Fabian walked with a limp.

Ulf had learned a lesson too. Greed, he thought, is the downfall of many. And that lesson had been of great assistance to him in his police work. Time and time again he saw it: greed led people to take one risk too many; greed, he was convinced, was the most useful of all the handmaidens who danced attendance on Nemesis and helped her in her work.

The two junior officers whom Ulf took for this Christmas lunch were his assistant, Markus, and Stig, a young detective from another department.

"This is very kind of you," said Stig. "My boss never gives us a Christmas lunch. Never."

"Mr Varg always does," said Markus. "And I am very grateful to you, sir."

"I enjoy it too," said Ulf. "At this time of year it is very pleasant to sit in a restaurant at lunchtime when outside it is cold and inhospitable."

"And there is a wind blowing down from those cold northern quarters," added Stig.

Fabian gave them a warm welcome and allocated them the best table. "I have some very good things on the menu today," he said. "*Julskinka* – Christmas ham in a special sauce I have developed myself; *Janssons frestelse* – potatoes with anchovies; and *fläskkorv* – pork sausage. – All of this is very delicious, I assure you."

Ulf rubbed his hands in anticipation of the feast ahead of them.

"Tekla says I'll have to go on a diet after this," said Markus.

Ulf laughed. "You could go to the gym instead."

That reminded Stig of something. "I had to make an arrest in a gym the other day," he said. "When the suspect saw me coming he forgot that he was on an exercise bike. He pedalled faster and faster to get away, but of course he did not move at all."

They all laughed. You have to have a sense of humour if you are a detective, or you would rapidly become overburdened by the nature of the work. Especially in Sweden.

Halfway through the ham course, Ulf said, "Don't give any indication. Don't stare, but I've recognized somebody at that table over there. Or I think I have."

Both Markus and Stig were too well trained to look in the direction of the table in question.

"Who is it?" asked Markus, sotto voce.

Ulf toyed with his ham. "Not a major criminal, but one we know all about. Andersen – I forget his first name. He's a big pickpocket."

Stig raised an eyebrow. "Hardly big stuff." He bent down to retrieve the napkin he had deliberately dropped on the restaurant floor and in so doing glanced in the direction of the other table. "Railway stations? Airports? That sort of thing?"

Ulf shook his head. "No, our friend Andersen is a cut above all that. He moves only in the best of circles. He masquerades as a waiter and gets into classy receptions. He's only interested in big pickings."

"I suppose it's easy if he's serving drinks and so on," said Markus.

"Yes," said Ulf. "And there's a warrant out on him."

"I suppose we'll have to arrest him," said Stig. "Shall I go over and take him in?"

Ulf thought for a moment. Then he shook his head. "It's Christmas in two days' time," he said.

"What's that got to do with it?" asked Stig.

"Rather a lot, actually," replied Ulf. "Andersen's mother's pretty ill. I know that because my secretary lives a couple of doors from them. She says that she's not long for this world, I'm afraid, and so this probably means her last Christmas."

Stig glanced at Markus. "But is that—" he began.

"Yes, it's relevant," Markus said.

Stig shrugged. "He's lucky it's you here rather than some of the other inspectors. Very lucky."

While they were waiting for the cheese course, Ulf rose from his chair to visit the washroom. Andersen saw him then, not having noticed him before. The pickpocket froze, a forkful of food on the way to his mouth, suspended now midway.

Ulf hesitated, but then walked firmly over towards Andersen's table. There was one other person seated at it – a woman wearing a small fur stole.

Andersen began to rise to his feet, but Ulf had already reached him and pushed him gently back into his chair.

"I hope you're enjoying your Christmas lunch," Ulf said.

Andersen looked down at his plate. His expression was one of misery.

"How's your mother?" Ulf asked. "I hear that she's not been too well. I do hope that you've got a good Christmas lined up for her."

Andersen looked up in surprise. "Yes," he stuttered "I—"

Ulf cut him short. "I'm glad to hear it," he said. And then, with a polite nod to the woman, he went on his way.

They rounded off their meal with coffee and liqueurs. While they were doing so, Andersen suddenly appeared at the table. He, too, was heading for the washroom, but evidently wanted to say something to Ulf. Ulf looked up, bemused.

"Yes, Andersen?" Ulf said.

"I just wanted to thank you Mr Varg," said Andersen. "There are plenty of people in this world who are mean inside – really mean – and – then there are some who are not."

Ulf said nothing, as he was inclined to feel embarrassed by emotional exchanges. Nor did he say anything as Andersen bent down to embrace him.

"Thank you, Mr Varg," the criminal muttered. "Thank you for being human."

Ulf never had to pay at Fabian's restaurant. He gave Fabian fish he caught on his fishing expeditions throughout the year, and these gifts offset the cost of any meals he had in the restaurant. So he did not need to reach for his wallet until he was walking home after the meal and stopped to buy an evening paper. Realizing that his wallet was not in his pocket, he stood quite still for a moment. The sky was heavy with snow, and a few flakes, drifting, blown by the wind, had started to fall.

"I have been very foolish," he said to himself. "Human nature is human nature."

There was no point in going back to the restaurant, he thought; Andersen would be long gone, and it would only embarrass Fabian, who never liked any fuss. So he continued his journey home, planning to phone from the apartment and cancel his credit cards before Andersen or his fence could do anything with them. The snow was falling faster now and his shoes, inadequate for the purpose, were beginning to let in water from the slush underfoot.

He heard someone coming up behind him. He turned around. It was Andersen. "Mr Varg," he said. "Thank goodness I found you. You dropped this in the restaurant. I only noticed it a couple of minutes ago."

Ulf took the wallet and slipped it back into his pocket. "Thank you," he said.

Andersen nodded. He smiled.

Somewhere not far away a street musician had started to

play a tune. A child ran past, pulling a sled. On the other side of the road, a man for some reason was holding a flashlight and its beam was weaving through the night, a cone of yellow gold in the darkness.

The Tiger

Nina Allan

There is a bed, a wardrobe with a large oval mirror, a built-in cupboard to one side of the chimney breast. The boards are bare, stained black. There is a greyish cast to everything. Croft guesses the room has not been used in quite some time.

"It's not much, I'm afraid," the woman says. Her name is Sandra. Symes has told him everyone including her husband calls her Sandy, but Croft has decided already that he will never do this, that it is ugly, that he likes Sandra better. "I've been meaning to paint it, but there hasn't been time."

She is too thin, he thinks, with scrawny hips and narrow little birdy hands. Her mousy hair, pulled back in a ponytail, has started to come free of its elastic band. Croft cannot help noticing how tired she looks.

"Don't worry," he says. "If you can let me have the paint, I'll do it myself."

"Oh," she says. She seems flustered. "I suppose we could take something off the rent money. In exchange, I mean."

"There's no need," Croft says. "I'd like to do it. Something to keep me out of mischief." He smiles, hoping to give her reassurance, but she takes a step backwards, just a small one, but still a step, and Croft sees he has made a mistake, already, that the word mischief isn't funny, not from him, not now, not yet.

He will have to be more careful with what he says. He wonders if this is the way things will be for him from now on.

"Well, if you're sure," Sandra says. She glances at him quickly, then looks down at the floor. "It would brighten up the walls a bit, at least."

She leaves him soon afterwards. Croft listens to her footsteps as she goes downstairs, past the entrance to the first-floor flat where she and Angus McNiece and their young son live, and into the pub where she works ten hours each day behind the bar. Once he feels sure she won't come back again, Croft lifts his luggage – a canvas holdall – from where he has placed it just inside the door and puts it down on the bed. As he tugs open the zip, an aroma arises, the scent of musty bedsheets and floor disinfectant, a smell he recognizes instantly as the smell of the prison, a smell he has grown so used to that he would have said, if he'd been asked, that the prison didn't have a smell at all.

No smell, and no texture. Being outside is like being spun inside a centrifuge. He keeps feeling it, the enthralling pressure on his ribs and abdomen, the quickfire jolts to his brain as he tries to accustom himself to the fact that he is once more his own private property. Just walking from the station to the pub – the long, straight rafter of Burnt Ash Road, the blasted concrete triangle that is Lee Green – gave him a feeling of exhilaration so strong, so bolt upright it still buzzes in his veins like neat whisky, like vertigo.

The pub is called the Old Tiger's Head. Croft has read it was once a coaching halt, a watering hole for soldiers on their way to the Battle of Waterloo. More recently it was a tram stop, where trams on their way down from Lewisham Junction would switch from the central conduit to overhead power. Photographs of Lee Green in the early 1900s show the place when it was still a village, a busy crossroads between Lewisham and Eltham, creased all along its corners, faded, precious.

He begins to remove his clothes and books from the canvas holdall. The clothes will go in the wardrobe. He tries the door to the built-in cupboard but it appears to be locked. Croft wishes the woman, Sandra, had felt able to stay with him in the room for just a few minutes longer.

Why would she, though? What is he to her, other than the sixty pounds each week she will get from him in rent money?

Croft wonders what, if anything, she has heard or read or been told about his case.

The child, Rebecca Riding, lived less than two miles from the place where he is now standing. A decade has passed since she died. In an alternate world, she would now be a young woman. Instead, she went to pick flowers in Manor Park on a certain day, and that was that.

Abducted and raped, then murdered. Her name had joined the register of the lost.

Did Croft kill Rebecca Riding? The papers said he had, for a while they did anyway. He has served a ten-year prison sentence for her murder. Even now that the charges have been overturned, the time he has spent living as a guilty man is still a part of reality.

He is free, but is he truly innocent?

Croft cannot say yet. There are too many things about that day that he cannot remember.

His first meeting with Symes consists mainly of Symes cross-examining him on the subject of how things are going.

"Did you manage to sign on okay?" As if penetrating the offices of the Lewisham DSS was a significant accomplishment, like shooting Niagara Falls in a barrel, or scaling Everest. Perhaps for some it is. Croft thinks of the faces, the closed and hostile faces of free people who through their freedom were unpredictable and therefore threatening. In prison you became used to people doing the same thing, day after day. Even insane actions came to make sense within that context. In the offices of the Lewisham DSS, even getting up to fetch a cup of water from the cooler might turn out to be a prelude to insurrection.

All the people he encounters make him nervous. He tells Symes everything is fine.

"It was lucky about the room," he adds, as a sweetener. "I'm grateful to you."

The room at the Old Tiger's Head was Symes's idea. He knows Angus McNiece, apparently. Croft dislikes Symes intensely without knowing why. In prison you come to know a man's crime by the scent he gives off, and to Croft Richard Symes has about him the same moist and fuggy aroma as the pathetically scheming lowlifes who always sat together in the prison canteen because no one else would sit near them, suffering badly from acne and talking with their mouths full.

Symes wears a lavender-coloured, crew-necked jersey and loose brown corduroys. He looks like an art teacher.

That Symes has been assigned to him by the probation service to help him "re-orientate" seems to Croft like a joke that isn't funny.

Symes is telling Croft about a group he runs, once a week at his home, for newly released offenders.

"It's very informal," Symes says. "I think you'd enjoy it."

Offenders, Croft thinks. That's what we are to people. We offend. The idea of being in Symes's house is distasteful to him, but he is afraid that if he refuses Symes will see it as a sign of maladjustment and use it against him.

Croft says yes, he would like to attend, of course, it would be good to meet people.

"Here's my address," Symes says. He writes it down on one of the scraps of paper that litter his desk and hands it across. "It's in Forest Hill. Can you manage the bus?"

"I think so," Croft says. For a moment, he imagines how good it would feel to punch Symes in the face, even though Croft isn't used to fighting. He hasn't hit anyone since he was fifteen and had a dust-up in the schoolyard with Roger Burke by name, Burke by nature. Croft has forgotten what it was about now, but everyone had cheered. He imagines the blood spurting from Symes's nose the way it had from Roger Burke's nose, the red coating the grooves of his knuckles, the outrage splayed across his face (how fucking dare you, you little turd), the pain and surprise.

Symes is finally getting ready to dismiss him.

"Tuesday at eight, then. Are you sure you don't want me to email you directions?"

"There's no need." Croft isn't online yet, anyway, but he doesn't tell Symes that. "I'm sure I can find you."

"I'm just popping to Sainsbury's," Sandra says. "Can I fetch you anything?"

The supermarket is only across the road, Croft can see the car park from his window. Sandra knows Croft could easily go himself, if he needed to, but she asks anyway because she's like that, kind, so different from her husband, McNiece, who hasn't addressed a single word to Croft since he moved in.

Sandra has her boy with her, Alexander. He gazes around Croft's room with widening eyes.

"You're *painting*," the boy says.

White, Sandra bought. A five-litre can of matt emulsion and a can of hi-shine gloss for the woodwork.

The smell of it: bright, chemical, clean, the scent of new. It reminds Croft of the smell of the fixative in his old darkroom.

"That's right," Croft says. "Do you like it?"

The boy stares at him, open-mouthed.

"Don't bother Mr Croft, Alex," Sandra says. "He's busy."

"It's no bother," Croft says. "And it's Dennis." The presence of the boy in his room makes him more than ever certain that Sandra McNiece does not know what Croft was in prison for. If she knew, she would not have brought her son up here. If she knew, she would not have allowed Croft within a mile of the building.

She will know soon though, because someone will tell her, someone is bound to. Croft is surprised this hasn't happened already. Once she knows, she will want to throw him out, though Croft has a feeling Angus McNiece won't let her, he won't want to lose the extra income.

"I could do with some teabags," he says to Sandra. "If it's really no trouble."

*   *   *

"Were you really in prison?" the boy says. *Alexander*. He sits on the edge of Croft's bed, swinging his legs back and forth as if he were sitting on a tree branch, somewhere high up, in Oxleas Woods perhaps (do kids still go there?) where it is said you can hear the ghosts of hanged highwaymen, galloping along the side of the Dover Road in the autumnal dusk.

"Yes," Croft says. "I was. But I'm out now."

"What were you in for?"

"Does your mother know you're up here?" Croft replies. The idea that she might not know, that the boy is here in his room and that nobody has given their permission, makes Croft feel queasy. Or perhaps it is just the smell of the hardening gloss paint.

"Yes," the boy says, though Croft can tell at once that he is lying, that the child has *sneaked upstairs to see the prisoner*, that in the boy's mind this is the bravest and most daring feat he has ever performed. Croft wonders if Sandra realizes she has given her son the same name as her. Perhaps she does, perhaps the boy was named after her.

Alexander the Great.

Alexander Graham Bell.

Alexander Pushkin.

In Russian, the shortened form of Alexander (and Alexandra) is not Alex, but Sasha. Pushkin was shot in a duel. He died two days later in some agony from a ruptured spleen. He was thirty-eight years old.

"Shouldn't you be in bed?" Croft says. The boy looks at him with scorn. How old is he, exactly? Six, seven, eight?

"What did you do before you were in prison?"

"I took photographs," Croft says. "That was my job."

"Would you take one of me?"

"I might," Croft says. "But I don't have a camera."

The boy reminds him of someone, the lad who betrayed him, perhaps. The boy is younger of course, but he has the same bright knowingness, the same hopeful aura of trust as the lad who seemed to become his friend and then called him a murderer. Croft wonders what his Judas – Kip? – is doing now. Has he become a photographer himself, as he intended, or is he cooped up in some office, serving time?

Croft never dreamed in prison. The air of the place was sterile, an imagic vacuum. The outside air is different, teeming with live bacteria, primed to blossom into monstrosities as soon as he sleeps. In his dreams of Rebecca Riding, he begins to remember the way her hair felt, under his hand, the soft jersey fabric of her vest and underpants.

"Will you take me home now?" she says. Croft always says yes, though when he wakes, sweating with horror, he can't remember if this really happened or if it's just in his dream. There's cum on the bedsheet, still tacky. He steps out of bed and goes across to the window. Outside and below him, Lee Green lies hazy in the light of the streetlamps. In the hours between two and four there is little traffic.

His legs are still shaking.

If he waits until five o'clock a new day will begin.

Croft opens the window to let in the air, which is crisp, tinged with frost, the leading edge of autumn, easing itself inside him like a dagger. The orange, rakish light of Lee Green at night reflects itself back at him from the oval mirror on the front of the wardrobe.

Croft wishes he had a camera.

If he cannot have a camera, he wishes he could sleep.

The bus to Forest Hill is the 122. They run every fifteen minutes, approximately. There's a stop more or less opposite the pub, at the bottom end of Lee High Road. It's the early part of the evening, after the main rush hour but still fairly busy. When Croft gets on, the bus is half empty, but after the stop at Lewisham Station it's almost full again.

Croft moves upstairs, to the top deck. He does not mind the bus being packed, as Symes seemed to think he would. The crush of people, the sheer weight of them, makes him feel less observed. None of them knows who he is, or where he is going. Friends of his from before, police officers and journalists living north of the river (Queen's Park and Kilburn, Ealing and Hammersmith, Camden Town), liked to joke about southeast London as a badlands, a no-man's-land of scabby takeaways and boarded-up squats. Croft looks out at the criss-crossing streets, the lit-up intersections and slow-moving traffic queues. Curry houses and fish-and-chip shops and eight-till-late supermarkets, people returning from work, plonking themselves down in front of a cop show, cooking supper. All the things that, once you are removed from them, take on an aspect of the marvellous. He feels southeast London enfold him in the darkness like a tatty anorak, like an old army blanket. Khaki-coloured, smelling of spilled beer and anti-freeze, benzene and tar, ripped in several places but still warm enough to save your life on a freezing night.

The sky is mauve, shading to indigo, shading to black, and as they pass through Honor Oak Park Croft thinks of Steven Jepsom, who once lived not far from here, in a grubby base-ment flat on the Brownhill Road. It was Jepsom they arrested first, but a lack of real evidence meant they had to let him go again.

Whereas in Croft's case, there were the photographs. It was the photographs, much more than Kip, which had testified against him.

Now, it seemed, Steven Jepsom had been Rebecca Riding's killer, all along.

Croft remembered Symes's first visit to the prison, Symes telling him about Jepsom being rearrested, almost a year before he, Croft, had been set free.

"It won't be long now," Symes had said. He gave Croft a look, and Croft thought it was almost as if he were trying to send him a signal of some kind, to claim the credit for Croft's good luck.

"Is there new evidence, then?" Croft asked.

"Plenty. A new witness has come forward, apparently. It's strange how often that happens. There's no time limit on the truth, Dennis."

Croft dislikes Symes's insistence on using his first name. Using a first name implies familiarity, or liking, and for Symes he feels neither. He has always tried not to call Symes anything.

He tries not to think of Steven Jepsom, who is now in prison instead of him.

A guilty man for an innocent one. Straight swap.

Richard Symes lives on Sydenham Park Road, a residential street leading off Dartmouth Road, where the station is, ten minutes' walk from the bus stop at most. The house is unremarkable, a 1950s semi with an ancient Morris Minor parked in the drive. The porch lights are on. As he approaches the door, Croft thinks about turning around and heading back to the bus stop. There is no law that says he has to be here – the group is voluntary. But Symes won't like it if he doesn't attend. He will like it even less if he finds out that Croft turned up at his house and then went away again. He will see it as a mark against him, a sign of instability perhaps, an unwillingness to reintegrate himself into normal society. Could Symes report him for that? Perhaps.

That would mean more meetings, more reports, more conversations.

More time until he's off Symes's hook.

Croft decides it is better just to go through with it. It is an hour of his time, that is all, and he's here now, anyway. It's almost more trouble to leave than it is to stay.

He rings the bell. Someone comes to the door almost at once, a balding, fortyish man in a purple tank top and bottle-glass spectacles.

"You're exactly on time," he says. He steps aside to let Croft enter the hallway. Croft notices that in spite of it being November and chilly the man is wearing leather sandals, the kind Croft used to wear for school in the summer term and that used to be called Jesus sandals. Croft feels surprise that you can still buy them.

The Jesus man has a front tooth missing. The light of the hallway is sharp, bright orange. Croft follows the Jesus man along the corridor and through a door at the end. By contrast with the garish hallway, the room beyond is dim. The only illumination, such that it is, appears to be coming from a selection of low-wattage table lamps and alcove lights, making it difficult for Croft to find his bearings. He estimates that there are eight, perhaps ten people in the room, sitting in armchairs and on sofas. They fall silent as he enters. He looks around for Symes, but cannot see him.

"Our mentor is in the kitchen," says the man in the sandals. "He's making more drinks." He has an odd way of speaking, not a lisp exactly, but something like it. Perhaps it's his adenoids. Each time he opens his mouth, Croft finds himself focusing on the missing front tooth. Its absence makes the man look grotesquely young. *Our mentor?* Does he mean Symes? He guesses it's just the man's attempt at a joke.

A moment later Symes himself appears. He is carrying a plastic tray, stacked with an assortment of mugs and glasses. Croft can smell blackcurrant juice, Ribena. For some reason this cloying scent, so reminiscent of children's birthday parties, disturbs him.

"Dennis, good to see you," Symes says. "Take this for me, would you please, Bryan?" He eases the tray into the hands of the Jesus man, who seems about to overbalance. "What are you drinking?"

"Do you have a beer?" Croft says. His eyes are on the Jesus man, who has recovered himself enough to place the laden tray on a low wooden bench. The thought of the Ribena or even coffee in this place fills him with an empty dread he cannot explain. A beer would at least be tolerable. It might even help.

"Coming right up," Symes says. The baggy cords are gone and he is wearing jeans, teamed with a hooded sweatshirt, which has some sort of band logo on the front. His wrists protrude awkwardly from the too-short arms.

He's dressed himself up as a kid, Croft thinks, and the idea, like the thought of the Ribena, is for some reason awful. Symes tells him to find himself a seat, but all the sofas and armchairs appear to be taken. In the end he finds an upright dining chair close to the door. The chair's single cushion

slides about uncomfortably on the hard wooden seat. Croft
looks around. He sees there are more people in the room than
he thought at first, fifteen or twenty of them at least, many of
them now talking quietly amongst themselves. Immediately
opposite him an obese woman in a brightly coloured smock
dress lolls in a chintz-covered armchair. She has shoulder-
length, lank-looking hair. Her forehead is shiny with grease,
or perhaps it is sweat.

Her small hands lie crossed in her lap. The hands, which
are surprisingly pretty, are adorned with rings. The woman
smiles at him nervously. Quite unexpectedly, Croft feels a
rush of pity for her, a sensation more intense than any he has
experienced since leaving the prison. He had not expected to
see women here.

"Hi," Croft says. He wonders if the woman can understand him, even. There is a blankness in her eyes, and Croft
wonders if she's on drugs, not street drugs but prescription
medicine, Valium or Prozac or Ativan. There was a guy Croft
knew in prison who was always on about how the prescription meds – the bennies, as he called them – were deadlier
than heroin.

"They eat your fucking mind, man." Fourboys, his name
was, Douglas Fourboys, eight years for arson. Croft had liked
him better than anyone, mainly because of the books he read,
which he didn't mind lending to Croft, once he had finished
them. He had an enthusiasm for Russian literature, Dosto-
evsky especially. Douglas Fourboys was a lifelong Marxist,
but at some point during the six months leading up to Croft's
release, he had found God. He claimed he'd been sent the gift
of prophecy, though Croft suspected this probably had more
to do with the dope Fourboys's girlfriend occasionally
managed to smuggle past security than with any genuine apti-
tude for seeing the future.

"You've got to be careful, man," Fourboys had said to him,
just a couple of days before his release. "They're waiting for
you out there, I can see them, circling like sharks."

Fourboys had definitely been stoned when he said that.

He'd reached out and clutched Croft's hand, then tilted to one side and fallen asleep. Croft misses Fourboys, he is the only person from inside that he does miss. He supposes he should visit him.

"We know who you are," the woman says suddenly. "You're going to help us speak with the master. We've seen your pictures." She smiles, her thin lips slick with spittle. Her words send a chill through Croft, though there is no real meaning to them that he can fathom. The woman is obviously vulnerable, mentally challenged. Clearly she needs protection. Croft feels anger at Symes for allowing her to be here unsupervised.

Suddenly Symes is there, standing behind him. He pushes something cold into Croft's hand, and Croft sees that it's a bottle of Budweiser. The thought of the beer entering his mouth makes Croft start salivating. He raises the bottle to his lips. The liquid is icy, familiar, heavenly. Croft feels numbness settle over him, an almost-contentment. Whatever is happening here need not concern him. It is only an hour.

"I see you've met Ashley," Symes says. He squats down next to the armchair, leaning in towards the fat woman and taking her hand. He presses his fingers into the flesh of her wrist as if to restrain her, as if she is something dangerous that needs to be managed. The woman shifts slightly in her seat, and Croft sees that her eyes, which appeared so dull, are now bright and alive. He cannot decide if it is wariness he sees in them, or cunning.

She doesn't like Symes though, this seems clear to him. Join the club.

"Ashley is my wife," Symes says. He grins into the face of the woman, a smile of such transparent artifice it is as if both he and the woman are playing a practical joke at Croft's expense.

Suddenly, in the overheated room, Croft feels chilled to the bone.

Is Symes serious? Snatches of words and images play themselves across his brain like a series of film stills: Symes's grin, the woman's slack features, the sticky word "wife".

You're wondering if they fuck, Croft thinks. Is that all it is, though? He takes another swig of the beer and the thoughts recede.

"Would you excuse me, just for a moment?" Symes says. "There's a phone call I need to make. I'll be right back." He stands, and walks away. The woman in the armchair looks after him for a second, then strains forward in her seat and puts her hand on Croft's knee. Croft can smell her breath, a sickening combination of peppermints and something else that might be tuna fish.

"You know him," the woman says, and for a moment Croft imagines she's talking about Symes, though the words that follow make his supposition seem impossible. "Even though you don't know it yet, you know him. He'll steep all his children in agony. Not just the agony of knowing him, but true pain." She tightens her grip on his knee, and Croft realizes that she is strong, much stronger than she appears, or than he would have believed.

The mad are always strong, Croft thinks. He does not know how he knows this, but he knows it is true.

"Who are you talking about?" Croft says quietly. "Who is the master?"

The woman leans towards him. Her face is now so close to his that her features seem blurred, and Croft thinks for a confused moment that she is about to kiss him.

He sees himself, straddling her. Her mounded flesh is pale as rice pudding.

"He is the tiger," she says. She grins, and her grin is like Symes's grin, only just like the Jesus man she has a tooth missing. The sight of the missing tooth fills him with horror.

"I need to get out of here," he says. "I mean, I need to use the bathroom." The room feels unbearably hot suddenly, stifling with the scent of unwashed bodies. He places his half-drunk beer on the coffee table, and as he makes his way back to the hallway he finds himself wondering if the woman will take advantage of his absence to taste the alcohol. He imagines her thin lips, clamping themselves around the mouth of the bottle in a wet, round "o".

He can hear Symes's voice, talking softly off in another room somewhere, but Croft ignores it. The staircase leads upwards to a square landing, with four doors leading off it, all of them closed. Croft tries one at random, not through any logical process of deduction but because it is closest. By a stroke of luck the room behind it turns out to be the bathroom, after all. Croft steps hurriedly inside and locks the door. He sits down on the closed toilet seat, covering his face with both hands. The room feels like it's rocking, slowly, back and forth, like a ship in a swell, though Croft knows this is only the beer, which he is unused to, he has barely touched a drop of alcohol since leaving prison. He presses his fingertips against his eyelids, savouring the darkness. After a minute or so he opens his eyes again and stands up. He lifts the toilet seat, pisses in an arcing gush into the avocado toilet bowl. He washes his hands at the sink. His face, in the mirror above, looks pale and slightly dazed but otherwise normal. It is only when he goes out on the landing again that he sees the photographs.

There are six of them in all. They are arranged in two groups of three, mounted on the blank area of wall at the far end of the landing and directly opposite the bathroom door. He had his back to them before, Croft realizes, which is why he didn't see them when he first came upstairs. He recognizes them at once. He thinks it would be impossible for an artist not to recognize his own work. One of the photos is of Murphy, or rather Murphy's hands, secured behind his back with a twist of barbed wire. The Kennington case. Four of the other photos are also work shots, all photos he took for the Met in the course of his twenty-year career as a forensic photographer.

Lilian Beckworth, an RTA.

The Hallam Crescent flat, gutted by fire.

The underpass near Nunhead Station where the Cobb kid was found.

The sixth photo, not a work one, is of Rebecca Riding. The police believed it had been taken less than thirty minutes before her death.

Croft told his lawyer and the police that the photos they found at his house were not taken by him. His camera had been stolen, he said, and then later returned, placed on his front doorstep, wrapped carefully in a Tesco bag. Whoever left it there had not rung the bell. When Croft later developed the film, he found pictures he remembered taking at various sites around Lewisham and Manor Park. He also found the photos of Rebecca Riding.

"The photos are good though, aren't they, Dennis?" the cop kept saying. "They're no amateur job. You're a professional. You remember taking these, surely?"

Croft said he didn't, and kept saying it. In the end he could hardly remember, one way or the other.

It was true that they were very fine photographs. He'd spent some time working on them in his darkroom. The excellence of the results surprised even him.

Croft turns away from the photographs and goes back downstairs. In the stuffy living room, they are all waiting, and for a moment as he returns to his place near the doorway Croft gets the feeling that he has been lured there on false pretences. He brushes the thought away, sits down on the uncomfortable wooden chair. The hour passes, and at the end of it Croft cannot remember a single thing that has been said. People are standing, going out into the hallway, pulling on coats. As Croft moves to join them, he feels a hand on his arm. It is Richard Symes.

"Some of us have clubbed together to buy you this," he says. "Your work means a great deal to us here. We're hoping this will help you find your feet again."

He hands Croft a package, a small but heavy something in a red-and-white bag. He knows without having to be told that it contains a camera. The gift is so unexpected that he cannot speak. Symes is smiling but it looks like a snarl, and finally it comes to Croft that he has been drugged, that this is what has been wrong all along, it would account for everything.

Drugs in the Bud.

Bennies in the beer.

It's the only thing that makes sense. Fourboys was right.

Outside, he feels better. The air is cold, bright as a knife. The sensations of nausea and unreality begin to recede. Croft walks smartly away, away from the house, along Sydenham Park Road and all the way to the junction with Dartmouth Road. He stands there, watching the traffic, wondering how much of the past hour was actually real.

The camera is a Canon, a top-of-the-range digital. It is not a hobby camera. Whoever chose it knew exactly what they were getting.

He has given up asking himself why this has been done for him. Having the camera in his hands is like coming alive again. He remembers the dream he had before he was in prison, his idea of giving up the police stuff and going freelance

He has been taking photographs of the boy, Alexander. They are in the old Leegate shopping precinct just over the road. The boy is in a T-shirt and clean jeans, it is all perfectly harmless. When Croft returns the boy to the pub afterwards, Sandra is behind the bar. There is a complicated bruise on her upper arm, three blotches in a line, like careless fingerprints.

Croft has a bank account now, with his dole money in. He has filled in a couple of application forms for jobs. One is for a cleaning job with Lewisham Council, the other is for a shelf stacking job at Sainsbury's. He can afford to buy a drink at the bar.

"Why is the pub called the Old Tiger's Head?" he asks Sandra McNiece.

"It's from when it was a coaching inn," says Sandra. "Tiger used to be a slang word, for footman. Because of the bright costumes they wore."

"Is that right?" Croft says. Croft briefly imagines a life in which he asks Sandra McNiece to run away with him. They will travel to Scotland, to Ireland, wherever she wants. He will take photos and the boy will go to school. He does not dare to take the daydream any further, but it is sweet, all the same, it is overwhelming.

"That's boring," Alex says. "I think it's because they once found a tiger's head inside the wardrobe. A mad king killed him and brought him to London, all the way from India."

Sandra laughs and ruffles his hair. "What funny ideas boys have," she says. "What are you doing in here, anyway? You should be upstairs."

Croft buys a small folding table from the junk shop at the end of Lee Road that sells used furniture. He places objects on the table – an empty milk carton, two apples, an old Robinson's jam jar filled with old pennies he found at the back of the wardrobe – and photographs them, sometimes singly, sometimes in different combinations. He places the table in front of the wardrobe, so the objects are shown reflected in the oval mirror. Croft experiments with taking shots that omit the objects themselves, and show only their reflections. At first glance, they look like any of the other photos Croft has taken of the objects on the table. They're not, though, they're pictures of nothing. Croft finds this idea compelling. He remembers how when Douglas Fourboys was stoned he became terrified of mirrors and refused to go near them. "There are demons on the other side, you know," he said. "They're looking for a way through."

"A way through what?"

"Into our world. Mirrors are weak spots in the fabric of reality. Borges knew it, so did Lovecraft. You have to be careful."

"You don't really believe this stuff, do you?" Croft knew he shouldn't encourage Fourboys, but he couldn't help it, his stories were so entertaining.

"I believe some of it," Fourboys said. "You would too, if you knew what I knew. There are people who are trying to help the demons to break through. They believe in the rule of chaos, of enlightenment through pain, you know, like the stuff in *Hellraiser* and in that French film, *Martyrs*. They call themselves Satan's Tigers." Fourboys took a coin out of his pocket and began swivelling it back and forth between his fingers. "If you knew how many of those sickos were on the loose it would freak you out."

The next time the boy comes to visit him in his room, Croft shows him how to set up a shot, then lets him take some photographs of the Robinson's jam jar. Afterwards, Croft takes some photos of Alex's reflection. He has him sit on the edge of the bed in front of the mirror.

"Try and make yourself small," Croft says. "Pretend you're sitting inside a cupboard, or in a very cramped space."

The boy lifts both his feet up on to the duvet and then hugs his knees. In the mirror shots he looks pale, paler than he does in real life. It's as if the mirror has drained away some of his colour.

"What's in there?" Alex says. He's staring at the chimney alcove, at the built-in cupboard that Croft has been unable to open.

"I don't know," Croft says. "It's locked."

"Perhaps it's treasure," says the boy.

"If you can find out where the key is, we can have a look."

"I know what it'll be." Alex grins, and Croft sees he has a tooth missing. "It'll be the tiger's head." He throws himself backwards on the bed and makes a growling noise. "I bet that's where they've hidden it."

"Isn't it time for your tea yet?" Croft says.

"I'm scared of tigers," the boy says. "If they come on the TV I have to switch off."

That night, Croft dreams of Richard Symes. There has been a break-in at Symes's house and there are cops everywhere. They're trying to work out if any valuables have been stolen.

Symes's throat has been cut.

There is no sign of Ashley Symes, or anyone else.

At his next meeting with Symes, Croft is able to tell him he's been offered the shelf-stacking job. Symes seems pleased.

"When do you start?" he says.

"Next Monday." He wonders if Symes will say anything to him about a burglary at his home, but he doesn't. Instead, Symes asks him how he's getting on with his new camera.

"It's great to use," Croft says. "The best I've had."

"Why don't you bring some of your work with you to show us when you come on Tuesday? I know Ashley would love that. Bring the boy with you, too, if you like."

How does Symes know about Alex? For a moment, Croft feels panic begin to rise up inside him. Then he remembers Symes knows the McNieces, that it was Symes who found him his room. "I couldn't," Croft says. "He's only eight. His mother wouldn't allow it."

"What she doesn't know won't hurt her. It would be an adventure for him. All boys love adventures."

Croft says he'll think about it. He thinks about himself and Alex, walking down the road like father and son. On his way back to London Bridge Station, Croft buys Alex a present from one of the gift shops jammed in under the railway arches near Borough Market, a brightly coloured clockwork tiger with a large, looped key in its side. It is made of tin plate, made in China.

The journey from London Bridge to Lee takes seventeen minutes. As he mounts the stairs to his room, he meets Sandra, coming down.

"I've just been trying to find you," she says. "I found this. Alex said you were looking for it."

She holds something out to him, and Croft sees it is a key. "It's for that cupboard in the chimney alcove," she says. "We've not opened it since we've been here, so God knows what's in there. Just chuck out anything you don't need."

"That's very good of you," Croft says. He searches her face, for tiredness or bruises, anything he can hate McNiece with, but today he finds nothing. He thinks about asking her to come up for a coffee but is worried that his offer might be misconstrued. He closes his fingers around the key. Its hard, irregular shape forms a core of iron at the heart of his hand.

It is some time before he opens the cupboard. He tells himself this is because he has things to do, but in reality it is because he is afraid of what he might find inside. Late afternoon shadows pour out of the oval mirror and rush to hide themselves in the corners and beneath the bed. As the room begins to fill up with darkness, Croft finds he can already imagine the stuffed tiger's head, the mummified, shrunken body of a child, the jam jar full of flies or human teeth. When he finally opens the cupboard it is empty. The inside smells faintly sour, an aroma Croft quickly recognizes as very old wallpaper paste. The wallpaper inside the cupboard is a faded green colour. It is peeling away from the walls, and in one place right at the back it has fallen down completely. The wooden panel behind is cracked, and when Croft puts his fingers over the gap he can feel a faint susurrus of air, a thin breeze, trapped between the wooden back of the cupboard and the interior brickwork.

Croft puts his whole head inside the cupboard and presses his opened mouth to the draughty hole. He tastes brick dust, cool air, the smell of damp earth and old pennies.

He closes his eyes and then breathes in. The cold, metallic air tastes delicious and somehow rare, like the air inside a cave. He exhales, pushing his own air back through the gap, and it is as if he and the building are breathing together, slowly in and out. It is then that he feels the thing pass into him, something old that has been waiting in the building's foundations, in the ancient sewer tunnels beneath the street, or somewhere deeper down even than that. Its face is a hideous ruin, and as Croft takes it into himself he is at last granted the knowledge he has been fumbling for, the truth of who he is and what he has done.

Strange lights flicker across the backs of his closed eyelids, yellow stripes, like the markings on the metal tiger he bought for the boy near Borough Market.

You are ready now, says a voice inside his head. Croft realizes it is the voice of Ashley Symes.

*   *   *

And in the end, it is easy. Both McNieces are downstairs, working the bar. Alex is alone in the living room of the first-floor flat. The carpet is a battleground, strewn with Transformers toys and model soldiers. The tin-plate tiger is surrounded by aggressive forces. The TV is playing quietly in the background.

When Croft sticks his head around the door and asks if Alex would like to come on an assignment with him, the boy says yes at once. The boy knows the word "assignment" has to do with photography, because Croft has told him so.

"Where are we going?" Alex says. It is getting on towards his bedtime, but the unexpectedness of what they are doing has filled him with energy.

Croft knows that unless he is very unlucky the boy's absence will not be noticed for at least three hours.

"To visit some people I know," Croft says. "They keep a tiger in their back garden."

The boy's eyes grow large.

"You're joking me," he says.

"That's for me to know and you to find out."

The boy laughs delightedly, and Croft takes his hand. The journey passes uneventfully. The boy seems captivated by every small thing – the pale mist rising up from the streets, the lit-up shop fronts, the endlessly streaming car headlights, yellow as cats' eyes.

The only glances they encounter seem benign.

When they arrive at Symes's house, Alex rushes up the driveway to the front door and rings the bell.

"And who is this young man?" Symes says, bending down.

"Dennis says you've got a tiger, but I don't believe him," says the child. He is beginning to flag now, Croft senses, just a little. He is overexcited. The slightest thing could have him in tears.

"We'll have to have a look, then, won't we?" Symes says. He places a hand on the boy's head. Croft steps forward out of the shadows and towards the door.

Once he is inside, he knows, it will begin. He and Ashley Symes will kill the child. The rest will watch.

"You have done well," Symes says to Croft, quietly. "This won't take long."

"Will there be cookies?" Alex says.

Croft stands still. He can feel the thing moving inside him, twisting in his guts like a cancer.

He wants to vomit. Croft gasps for breath, sucking in the blunt, smoky air, the scent of macadam, of the hushed, damp trees at the roadsides and spreading along all the railway lines of southeast London. The fleet rails humming with life, an antidote to ruin.

He smells the timeswept, irredeemable city and it is like waking up.

Above him, bright stars throw up their hands in surprise.

"Come here to me, Sasha," Croft says. He is amazed at how steady his voice sounds. "There's no time now. We have to go."

"But the tiger," the child whimpers. He looks relieved.

"There are no tigers here," Croft says. "Mr Symes was joking. Come on."

The boy's hand is once again in his and he grips it tightly.

"Will we be home soon?" says the boy.

"I hope so," Croft replies. "We should be, if a bus comes quickly."

He does not look back.

The Long Shadow

Peter Turnbull

Arresting.

It was the only word that the man could think of to describe the sensation. He was strolling past the shop window, not paying any particular attention to the items for sale, when he stopped in his tracks, arrested, as if his subconscious eye had seen, rather than his conscious eye. For there it was. About six inches in height, a greyish brown colour, "dun" being the proper name for the hue, as was his favourite pub "The Old Dun Cow" in his village. And it was *the* figurine, the small chip at the base said so. The man stood and stared at it. It was like meeting an old friend, yet a friend with whom unpleasant experiences had been shared. So how many years had it been. Eighteen, nineteen? He stood and smiled despite painful associations and said, "Well, well, well, and where have you been all this time?" It was Sunday, in the forenoon, the Minster bells peeled joyously over old York town, echoing in her alleyways and snickets, and the shop was shut. But tomorrow he would return. As soon as the shop opened he'd be there, like the alcoholics who can always be seen standing outside the pub doors in the city centre just before opening time, then when the doors are flung open they stampede to the bar, happy to drink stale beer which has spent the last twelve hours in the pipes. Tomorrow he'd be at the shop, he'd be the first customer over the threshold, anxious to buy the figurine or he'd lose it forever.

Oh, and he'd bring the police with him. He thought he'd better do that. He thought he'd better ask the police to accompany him, because eighteen or nineteen years ago his parents had been murdered during the course of the theft of the dun figurine of Dresden china. During the same burglary, quite a few other items had been removed from the house. The robbers quite calmly carrying item after item out of the house, past the dead or dying bodies of his parents.

The man returned home, said little to his wife and nothing about the figurine, though their relationship was warm and well. He spent the evening in his study and that evening he retired early.

The following day, the last Monday of that merry month of May, the first people to enter Lashko's Antiques, Micklegate, close to the medieval walls of the ancient city, and met pleasantly by Julius Lashko, were a middle-aged, prosperous-looking man with a pleasant and fulfilled countenance and, behind him, a much younger man who was trim and muscular. Julius Lashko thought that they were father and son.

"Mr Lashko?" The young man spoke, and instantly Lashko realized that the first two customers that day were not father and son. In fact, they were not even customers at all.

"Yes, 'tis I."

"I am Detective Constable Sant, City of York police. This is . . ."

"Mr . . ." said the older man.

"Mr Toucey," Sant continued.

"Oh, yes. How can I help you?" A note of concern had crept into Lashko's voice. He was a small man with a pointed nose and a weak chin, and wild, woolly hair. Sant felt that antiques dealers are not dissimilar to second-hand car dealers in that at one end of their way of business they nudge criminality, at the other they are above reproach. Sant, while keeping an open mind, felt that Lashko fell into the latter category.

"By allowing us to look at that figurine in the window."

"Certainly," Lashko said after a pause. He moved to the

window and removed the figurine from where it stood between two Edwardian clocks and handed it to Sant. Sant handed it to Toucey, who held it lovingly.

"Yes," Toucey said. "This is she all right, one of a pair, in fact . . . it's the small chip on the base that identifies it. It's rare, eighteenth-century Dresden, quite valuable as it is. Without the chip on the base, and with her partner, she would be very valuable indeed."

Lashko looked on in silence, paling slightly. Sant addressed him. "Mr Lashko, can you tell me how you came to obtain this item?"

"I bought it from a man who came into the shop about ten days ago. He didn't seem suspicious . . . I have to be careful, some shifty types come into the shop, usually young, usually in pairs, wanting to sell stuff that they don't know anything about. Clearly proceeds of a burglary. I decline to purchase from such people and notify the police as soon as they have left the shop. The police often pick them up before they get far. But the chap who offered me the figurine didn't fit that type at all. He came in a few days earlier, asked me to value it, something a thief wouldn't do. He also seemed to know something about it . . . he correctly identified it, said it had been in his family for some time and he seemed reluctant to part with it. He was giving off all the right signals and I felt that I had no reason to be suspicious."

"Well, unfortunately, we have reason to believe that it has been stolen."

"Oh, I'm so sorry." Lashko seemed to Sant to be genuine. "It does happen. I've been in the business a long time and there have been one or two previous occasions when, to my shame, I have found that I have bought a proceed from a burglary. It's an occupational hazard, and I lose, because having bought it, I have to surrender it and chalk up the loss."

"As may be the case here. I'll have to take this into custody of the police in the first instance."

"Of course," Lashko nodded. "You'll let me have a receipt?"

"Yes. Did the person who brought it to you wear gloves at the time?"

"No. Not that I recall. But if you're hoping to lift finger-prints I think you'll be out of luck – the whole shop is given a good dusting every other day. Got to keep them dust free if I'm going to sell them."

"It's worth a shot, though," Sant placed the figurine in a large envelope. "Did you buy anything else from him?"

"Him? Oh, the man who sold me that, no I didn't . . . don't think so . . . certainly not a regular. There are people from whom I buy regularly; one lady is trickling antiques on to the market to provide herself an income in her declining years. I have one or two other customers like her. I also have custom-ers who have money and are putting it into antiques, and so, like all businessmen, I have my regular customers. But that chap was not one of them."

"Can you describe the man?"

"Well, it's going back a few days now . . . but I did see him twice and he did deal with me, unlike the sort who treat the shop as though it were a museum, just wander in and look around and then wander out again. That's another occupa-tional hazard. So the man . . ." Lashko shut his eyes. "He was middle-aged . . . slim build . . . he hadn't put on a lot of weight as many men of his age would do. He had an appearance which I have heard described as 'genteel shabby'."

"Genteel shabby?"

"I take the expression to mean a person who has been used to the finer things in life but who has fallen on hard times and, while trying to keep up appearances, has become a little threadbare, but what was threadbare was still of the best qual-ity. He had a calm manner, he seemed warm about the eyes . . . he seemed emotionally fulfilled. He wore a ring." Sant scribbled on his pad.

"Dark hair . . . not greying and hadn't lost any of it. Had worn well for his years, he'd retained much of his youth. Can't think of anything else about his appearance to report . . . carried himself proudly, erect, like a former soldier. He had a soft

Yorkshire accent, as if moderated by education . . . not a broad Yorkshire accent of the football terraces, but a softer version, of the golf club or the boardroom. Oh, he was left-handed. I paid him cash and he held out his left hand."

David Sant accessed the file on the murders of Daniel and Olivia Toucey of The Limes, Harrogate Road, York. He settled down with a mug of coffee in hand and read it. It was a story of a burglary and murders which he felt was passing brutal. The elderly couple, he a retired barrister, she a retired pathologist, lived in well-earned luxury at The Limes, a rambling mid-Victorian mansion, sufficiently large that when it was sold, it was sold to White Rose Care Ltd, who turned it into a nursing home for the elderly. White Rose Care Ltd was, to the best of Sant's knowledge, one of the newly formed companies that had jumped on to the money-spinning bandwagon of "granny farming", as a response to Britain's ageing population, a consequence of which was that Britain now had one pensioner for every person in employment, all of whom had to be provided for. But eighteen years ago, the Touceys lived in The Limes, having given a lifetime of unblemished public service and successfully brought up three children, by then away from home and consolidating their own careers. One fateful night in the autumn of the year, their house appeared to have been stormed by at least four men . . . Mr Toucey had died of a head injury; Mrs Toucey had died of a heart attack induced by the shock and trauma. A removal lorry had then been reversed up the drive and the house stripped of all valuable contents. It was a crime which had shocked York and its environs. Hardly surprising, thought Sant, who at the time would have been just starting to read.

There was little for the police to go on. Known housebreakers all had good alibis, the felons had all worn gloves, no fingerprints "alien to the crime scene" had been found, and none of the items stolen from the raid had surfaced, until now, in the form of a six-inch-high figurine, dun-coloured, of the finest Dresden porcelain.

So now where? Sant stood and walked over to the table by the window on which stood the electric kettle and the coffee jar and the teabags and the powdered milk and the mugs. He made himself a second mug of coffee. It was his pattern, when in the police station, to drink endless mugs of coffee, until he was awash with the liquid, and then he would drink nothing for the rest of the shift. He glanced out at the Ouse, glistening in the sun, the rowing skiffs and the pleasure boats. All that the police had to go on was the description of a man, who seemed down at heel, who might have come across the porcelain figurine quite legitimately, not knowing it to have been stolen, and who may not have had anything to do with the murder of the elderly Touceys, but also who would have been a youth eighteen years ago, probably hot-headed, whose local accent had been subsequently modified and softened by education.

David Sant finished the shift at 2 p.m., signed out, and walked into the warm afternoon air, just the weather for a light jacket. He drove home to his cottage in Thornton le Clay, parked his car in the drive, and checked his telephone answering machine; just one message, from his wife, confirming his access visit to their son later in the week. When they had separated, he hadn't contested custody in return for a generous level of access. He had never seen the purpose of wanting custody; it was, he felt, a legal state which didn't affect the relationship between parent and child, but access did, for it was during the access that bonding occurred and relationships developed. In the evening, he felt the urge to go for a short walk.

A short walk to the Queen's Head, which stood on the edge of the village green and had an ancient pair of stocks outside, sometimes used for charity fundraising events, as had recently happened when the community constable had been placed in the stocks for an hour so that the villagers could throw cream cakes (donated by the baker) at him, one pound for five cakes. Fifty pounds had been raised to help keep the village play-school open.

That evening, the pub was quiet, as it most often was on Monday evenings, a few old boys playing dominoes, the landlord (who had amply rewarded the good humour of the community constable with not a few pints of strong beer once the cream had been washed off) involved in a game of darts, leaving his wife to pull the pints. Not an onerous task, for on Mondays the frequency of pint-pulling is perhaps one every ten minutes. Sant asked for a pint of Timothy Taylor and stood at the bar. He pondered the postcards which had been sent by the regulars and enjoyed the low hum of conversation, the rattle of dominoes, the thud of darts into cork, and in the winter months there would be the crackling of the log fire. This, he felt, was how a pub should be; not for him the crush and loud music of the city-centre pubs.

"I don't believe him," Sant said to himself, but loudly so.

"Sorry, love?" The landlady smiled at him.

"Nothing." Sant returned the smile. "Nothing at all. I was just speaking aloud."

"Don't believe who, love?" For the landlady of the Queen's Head was like a dog with a bone where gossip was concerned. She was, in fact, considered second only to the post-mistress as a source of gossip. She was quite good at it too, so it was thought, and well she ought to be, because before she and her husband had taken the pub they had had the post office in the neighbouring village.

"Oh, just this fella," Sant said, thinking that he'd get a better pint if he gave the woman something. "Fella I spoke to this morning. I believed him at the time, but now I don't."

"No?"

"No . . . not now. Sometimes it's like that, you know, looking back over time, only a bit of time sometimes. You see that you've been fed a pork pie and this was a convincing pork pie as porkies go, but now I see it as just too pat."

The landlady reached forward and took Sant's half-empty glass and replenished it and handed it back to him. "A crime, was it?" she said.

"A witness." Sant took his glass of beer. "Thanks, that was good of you."

"Just taking care of my regulars. Witness, you say?"

"At the time I thought so . . . now I think a change of status from witness to suspect is probably appropriate."

"Serious crime?"

"Double murder."

"Serious enough."

Sant drained his glass and walked home, aware that he was on duty at 6 a.m., which meant he had to be up at five. He didn't think he'd given the landlady anything that compromised his integrity or the investigation, but he'd given her enough to lubricate the machinery of his standing as a "regular" in the Queen's Head. It is, he thought, the way the ball bounces, the way the world goes round. He enjoyed the walk home, the rural night air, the scent of herbs and crops. In the sky he was able to pick out the Plough and Orion.

"I just didn't believe him, sir." Sant sat in front of Leif Vossion's desk. "I mean, the description of the man seen only twice about ten days ago, his 'genteel shabby' appearance, left-handed, local accent moderated by education . . . for heaven's sake . . . it just doesn't ring true. It's fiction."

"Putting us off the scent, you think?"

"That's what my intuition tells me."

"So, shall we go with your intuition?" Vossion looked keenly at Sant, with steely blue eyes.

"I think I'd like to."

"First step?"

"Interview him, sir."

"Do you think so?"

"I can't see another way forward."

"Can't you? He handled the figurine yesterday, didn't he?"

"Yes!" Sant's eyes brightened. "Latents. Of course."

"That's your first step. The murders are eighteen years old, so forensics won't give your request priority. Carmen

Pharaoh and Simon Markov have a city-centre stabbing which is still less than twenty-four hours old, Ken Meninnot is up to his eyeballs in requests for forensic analysis, but if there's a result to be had, they'll get it for you."

There was, in fact, a result to be had, though because of the backlog, it took Forensic Science Laboratory at Weatherby three weeks to process Sant's request. But he thought the wait well worth it. The fingerprints on the figurine, once his and Toucey's had been isolated, didn't belong to Julius Lashko. In fact, they belonged to a man called Shane Cody. When Sant entered Cody's name and numbers into the computer, he came up with gold dust. Cody had graduated from petty theft to the safer, less violent, but prosperous crime of receiving stolen goods. He was, in criminal speak, a "fence".

"Well, well, well." Sant peered at the information which had appeared on the monitor screen. The implication was that the entire contents of Lashko's Antiques, Micklegate, York, were "hot". The fuller implication was that Cody may well have had a part in the double murder of the elderly Touceys eighteen years ago.

Vossion listened with interest to Sant's verbal report. "How do you want to handle it?"

"Bring him in for questioning. Itemize the contents of the shop, it's probably an Aladdin's cave of stolen goods."

"Does he live over the shop?"

"No, sir. So closing the shop won't compromise his living quarters."

"Convenient, eh?" Vossion smiled. He rarely smiled these days and Sant was pleased that he had been able to do so.

"I think that's what you do. Obtain warrants to search the shop and his house. You'll need help . . . I wonder . . . no . . . first things first. Bring Cody in for questioning . . . I'll find someone to go over the shop with a manifest of items taken from high-profile burglaries in the Vale of York for the last . . . twenty years. Who knows what we'll find?"

* * *

Cody looked worried. Sant pondered him and noted the worried look, the paling of the complexion, the furrowed brow, the nervous twitch. Sant took two audio cassettes, tore the cellophane from them, and slipped them into the recording machine and pressed the record button. The twin spools spun, the red light glowed.

"The date is the twenty-first of June, the time is 10.30 a.m., the location is Friargate Police Station in the City of York. I am Detective Constable David Sant. I am now going to ask the other people present in the room to identify themselves."

"PC Howie, Friargate Police Station."

A pause.

"Will you please state your name for the purposes of the tape?" Sant spoke to Cody.

"Shane Cody."

"Right, Mr Cody. Is it true to say that you are also known as Julius Lashko?"

"It is."

"And you are the proprietor of Lashko's Antiques, Micklegate, in the city of York?"

"I am."

"And you have waived your right to have a solicitor present during this interview?"

"I have."

"Thank you. Do you have any other aliases?"

"No."

"How long have you been in the antiques business?"

"About twenty years."

"Always at the same address?"

"Not always. I started with a stall in the market, then I had a shop on Nunnery Lane. I moved from there to Micklegate premises about five years ago."

"All right. Now, Mr Cody, you have a number of previous convictions, going back quite a few years, but latterly for receiving stolen goods."

"Yes, but I'm going straight now."

"Yes . . ." Sant echoed wryly. "Mr Cody, the statuette, the figurine which we removed from your shop a few weeks ago, has been positively identified as having been stolen in a burglary which took place eighteen years ago during which an elderly householder and his lady wife were murdered."

Cody gasped. "I didn't know that."

Sant smiled inwardly. He knew then that the case was about to crack wide open. "It happens to be true. Two people who had given a lot to the city and the Vale of York, two professional people. The issue would be the same if it had been an elderly couple who'd been chronically unemployed all their days, but because it was a retired barrister and his wife who was a retired pathologist, well, it just seems worse somehow. It just does. The other thing is that because the piece of porcelain has been positively identified as having been stolen, we have obtained a warrant to search your business premises. This is being done at the moment. Our officers have with them a manifest of all unrecovered items taken from major burglaries in the area in the last twenty years."

"I didn't know you could do that."

"We can. And we are doing so. A warrant to search your house has also been obtained."

"You can't do that! There's nothing there."

"So there is something at the shop?"

A pause. The twin spools spun silently. The red light glowed.

"Look, Mr Cody." Sant leaned forwards. "Take my advice, will you? And I'm not just saying this because I want to wrap this up: If you're caught bang to rights, put your hand up to it, play with a straight bat. Don't try to wriggle off the hook in the face of overwhelming evidence as to your guilt. If you do that, you just dig yourself deeper and deeper into a hole. In this case, your best bet is to cooperate fully with the police enquiry."

"That'll help me?"

"It will."

"Okay. How about a coffee?"

*   *   *

Sipping coffee, Cody said, "Well, yes, I knew the piece of Dresden was bent, and a few other things that you'll find in the shop, particularly in the cellar, but you've got to believe me when I say I didn't know anybody had been topped during the burglary ... I also do want to go straight ... and have been doing so, in the main."

"In the main."

"Well, there's always one or two people who have something to hold over you and who want favours. You can make enough straight pennies without having to make bent ones as well. I suppose I'm finished now."

"I think you are, Shane. So tell me what I want to hear."

"I bought the piece of Dresden about fifteen years ago for about a tenth of its actual value, put it down in the cellar where all the bent stuff goes, with a little label on it with the date I acquired it. I have a fifteen-year rule, fifteen years after the purchase, if it's bent, it goes on sale. After that length of time, it might not be recognized during the few weeks, even days, that it's on display. I used to see bent stuff as long-term investments. That's how it's done, wait till you think it's safe and then trickle it back on to the market."

"That right?"

"That's right. You'll find some stuff in my cellar from the big burglary last year."

"The farmhouse?"

"Yes, the farmhouse. They cleaned it out."

"I know." Sant leaned back in his chair. This case was really cracking open.

"Sometimes you can't ever sell them. Too famous. Not openly, anyway. Can't put a stolen Van Gogh in the shop window."

"I've often wondered that, you know. What is the point of stealing a famous painting?"

"A lot of point, really. People think that famous works of art that are stolen are sold to private collectors who keep them for selfish reasons, but that isn't the case, because private collectors can't get rid of them so easily and private collectors like showing off their collections. No . . . what happens is that they're sold and re-sold in the underworld, from generation to generation, and eventually the time distance from the theft and the distance of the descendants from the original owners is so great that ownership is difficult to challenge, and if the present 'owner' claims he found it, he can claim 'Treasure Trove'. It will be given to the nation, but he will receive its monetary value. Famous paintings stolen 150 years ago will start to emerge in a hundred years' time."

"Well, you live and learn." Sant drained his coffee and tossed the plastic mug into a waste bin. "So, tell me about the figurine. How, or from whom, did you acquire it?"

Cody took a deep breath. "This will help me?"

"It won't harm you."

"I'm forty-five, getting too old to do serious time."

"Implicated in a double murder. That's very serious time."

"I didn't know it was *from* that murder. I bought it four or five years after that murder."

"So, spill the beans."

"Hickman. He's the man you want."

"Hickman?"

"Hickman. I see him around the city from time to time. He hasn't offered me anything for a while now."

"First name?"

"Sid. Sidney Hickman."

"Address?"

"I don't know – that's the gospel truth, but you can find it, he's got form for burglary. Don't know his numbers but he's in his forties. Tall, thin guy, neatly turned out. Drives a flash car, a yellow Mercedes."

"I've seen him!"

"I'm certain you have, the original Flash Harry, always posing in his yellow Merc."

"We'll pick him up quickly enough." Sant was pleased with the progress that had been made. "He sold you the figurine?"

"He did. And a few other items you'll find in the cellar."

"Right little treasure chest you've got, isn't it? And I dare say you'll be keen to tell me about all the other felons you've been receiving from."

"Yes . . . yes . . . at my age I can't go to prison."

"Oh, but you can, though the likelihood of doing so diminishes in direct proportion to the level of cooperation we receive from you. In fact, it isn't impossible for the Crown Prosecution Service to grant immunity from prosecution depending on what hard and verifiable information you have to offer, and what evidence you are prepared to give in court. But that is another matter, for another day. Right now, all I'm interested in is Sid, Flash Harry, Hickman. That burglary was a mob-handed affair, at least four guys."

"Only he can tell you what happened. I only took the bent stuff off him, and only after he'd been sitting on it for years, so I wouldn't connect it with *that* burglary."

Sidney "Sid" Hickman was indeed well known to the police. He was arrested at his prestigious house on the Shipton Road, on the very outskirts of the city of York, and conveyed to Friargate Police Station.

For the second time that day, Sant tore cellophane from new audio cassettes and placed them in the recording machine and pressed the record button. The twin tapes spun slowly, the red light glowed. After stating the date, time and location, and after identifying himself, Sant said, "I am going to ask the others in the room to identify themselves."

"PC Daltry, Friargate."

"Sidney Hickman," said in a surly manner.

"Mr Hickman, you have been arrested and cautioned in connection with the double murder and aggravated burglary in the Toucey household, eighteen years ago. Mr Shane Cody has given a statement to the effect that you offered him a porcelain figurine and other items stolen during the burglary. The figurine has been positively identified as stolen from the Toucey household."

"Him and his big mouth."

"So you concede you perpetrated the crime?" Sant tried to hide his surprise.

Hickman shrugged.

"Please answer for the benefit of the tape."

"Aye . . . yes, yes, yes, yes. Is that all right? . . . a thousand times yes, for the benefit of the tape."

"That'll do," Sant said. "That'll do nicely."

"Tell you the truth, I'm quite relieved. I've done the crime, but I don't do violence. It just isn't on my agenda."

"So what happened at the house that night?"

"We thought they were out, so when we rang the bell just to be on the safe side, and the old guy answered, Billy Lear smashed him one helluva punch and he hit his head going down . . . The old lady, she came into the hallway and cried out, then stumbled into a side room clutching her chest, sort of folding up as she went down. Then we emptied the house."

"With two people lying dead or dying?"

"We were young then. It didn't seem to bother us. Death only happened to other people."

"Now?"

"Now it haunts me. Now I've reached the age where I know death will happen to me . . . now that night haunts me. Even criminals can feel bad. I didn't know there was going to be violence that night."

"Carried on with the burglary though, didn't you? Didn't flee the scene as soon as Billy Lear punched the old boy, did you? Makes you just as guilty as if you had felled the old gentleman yourself."

"That'll be something to talk over with my lawyer."

"I told Cody that a full and frank confession will help him. It'll help you too."

Hickman nodded. "There was me, Billy Lear, Tom Ingrow and Charlie Pitt. We were young bulls, especially Billy Lear and Charlie Pitt. Me and Tom, we never did violence."

"Where will we find them?"

"Billy's got form, you'll pick him up easily enough if he isn't inside at the moment, he never did stop duckin' and divin'. Tom Ingrow and Charlie Pitt have gone straight, both married with families, never got caught, so didn't get any form. Calmed down and went to university. Tom's an accountant now and Charlie's a schoolteacher. I can tell you where they live."

Sant groaned. Arresting a professional man of standing in the community at 7 a.m. for a crime committed a long, long time ago was never easy. Sometimes he envied the Americans their Statute of Limitations, even though he knew it didn't apply to the crime of murder. But it was not unknown in the United Kingdom, nor in Sant's relatively brief experience as a police officer, that an act committed in a person's twenties was not traced to him, with life-ruining consequences, until he was in his middle years of life. The long shadow of the past, as it is known.

Simon Toucey, who a few weeks earlier, whilst walking in Micklegate one Sunday morning, had spied a piece of dun-coloured porcelain in an antiques shop window, stood and climbed into his black gown, and then, with a practised flourish, placed the wig upon his head. Later, in a hushed room, he turned to a thin-faced youth and said, "You have, in my opinion, quite properly been found guilty of the crimes for which you have been charged. You have ruined the lives of your victims and I have been observing you throughout this trial and you have not shown the slightest trace of guilt or remorse for your actions. I sentence you to life imprisonment."

Fourth Time Lucky for Mickey Loew

Jay Stringer

Renée and Dion had waited all night for the perfect catch. The heat was keeping people indoors; even as late as midnight the only people out on Delancey were locals running to the deli with pocket change. Nothing worth hitting. They had already taken three pizza breaks with their third fisher, Marlo, and were about ready to call it a night.

Renée was on the opposite corner, leaning against the shutter of the closed opticians, her own name sprayed on it with red paint. Dion was resting against the stoplight and, further down Delancey, Marlo stood in the darkness of the abandoned storefront.

Just after midnight they caught one, a woman walking up Ludlow toward them all alone. Dressed in motorcycle boots and tight black jeans, her eyeliner matching her short dark hair, Dion figured her for a tourist who'd walked too far down.

Perfect.

Dion watched out of the corner of his eye as she walked up Ludlow on his side of the street, then crossed over before she got to him, toward the shadows of the opposite corner. He nodded at Renée, who caught the message and headed down Delancey a few steps ahead of the target, walking casual. Dion pushed off from the stop sign and followed a few metres behind, nice and slow.

As they reached the storefront, Marlo stepped out of the shadows and pointed his gun at Renée, making it look like she was the one being mugged. As the real target took a step back,

Dion stepped in behind her with his own gun ready. The target moved fast, grabbing Renée from behind and whispering something in her ear that made her shudder. Marlo must have caught something in her eyes, because he lowered his gun and then dropped it to the floor. Dion stepped in again looking for a fast control of the situation, but the woman whirled on him and grabbed his gun hand in a vice grip. She twisted his hand until it felt like his wrist would snap, and then lifted the gun out of it with her free hand. All the time her dark smile stayed in place.

All three would-be muggers stood and watched as she continued her walk along Delancey, whistling and swaying her hips.

"How's Williamsburg working out for you?"

"It's hip. Too hip, you know? All coffee shops and baby strollers now."

"Yeah? When I was a kid the only people who lived out there were Jews and arsonists."

"They have barmen now, too."

"Is it as hot over there as it is here?"

Toby looked over the bar at Mickey. "It's this hot everywhere."

Mickey had been coming in once or twice a month for four or five years. Toby knew him by name, and knew that he was some kind of lawyer, but left it at that. Mostly because it reminded Toby that he'd been running the bar for the past five years, and he tried to forget.

Nestled on Mott Street, just around the corner from Prince, he'd been discreetly trying to offload it ever since his father had passed away. If the bar had been twenty feet further south, he'd have been able to sell up to make way for some clothes shop or deli. But nobody wanted to touch a dive bar hiding behind a church on Mott. Case in point; still a couple of hours until closing and he only had one customer.

Mickey finished his drink and signalled for another, working through them in a hurry, "You know what this heat reminds me of?"

"Yes, you say it every time."

"Well it's true, don't it remind you of that night?"

"Everything reminds me of that night."

"TV saying, leave your A/C switched off because of the dust, the whole city is sweating?"

"Yeah," Toby passed the drink across the bar top. "It got hot, all right. My cat still got asthma."

"You know? I hear that a lot. Could be a lawsuit in it."

"Who you gonna sue?"

Mickey shrugged. "I'd find somebody. You in a bad mood?"

Toby shrugged, said no, then nodded, "Yeah. I don't know. I just got this feeling like, I don't know. You superstitious?"

"Nope." Mickey rubbed his beer belly, "Only things that lead me around are down here."

Toby smiled, thought about leaving it, then, "I am. Little things, not ladders and shit like that. My A/C broke? Last time that happened, my old man passed."

"You think the A/C is out to get you?"

Toby shrugged, wished he'd left it. A couple of minutes later Mickey was signalling for another. Usually he signalled by pointing down at his empty glass and looping his index finger round in a circle. As the night had worn on, his signals were getting more elaborate. This time he pretended to shoot the empty with both hands turned into guns. Toby poured another and then, "You celebrating something?"

"Yep. Got a big one through the court today, fourth time of asking."

"Fourth?"

"His lawyer kept finding an excuse to postpone it, get more time. Just stalling though, they knew the minute we got them in court it was done."

"Big case?"

"You don't read the papers, huh? Irish guy, Quinn?"

Toby paused, his mouth did a wobble before finding the words. "Shit, that was you?"

Mickey put his drink hand up in the air as if celebrating a

goal. "Yep. Took me four attempts, but he's down. Pushing for the lethal."

"Wow. Big day then, huh?"

"Yeah, just don't tell your A/C. It might get ambitious."

They both paused, drawn to look out into the street. The city down here had a way of telling you when to look, like a sixth sense. A guy walked past outside, naked except for a pair of briefs and a guitar case. He seemed oblivious to the stares he was attracting, bopping down the street with iPod earphones in. Nobody could see where the iPod was tucked.

After everyone in the street turned back to look for a new thing, a woman walked into the bar. Toby and Mickey both noticed her, cute ass in tight jeans, motorcycle boots. Toby's head filled with a hundred different song lyrics, but he didn't have a pad to write any of them down.

"Get you a drink?" he said.

Mickey slid across the three stools between him and the woman. "Whatever she wants," he said, "on me."

She didn't decline or feign politeness. She just took the drink and stared down into it for a second. Toby noticed a few freckles on the bridge of her nose, then stopped himself before he got annoying.

"Not seen you in here before?" Mickey tried again, all his frustrated charm amounting to nothing more than a mumble.

She turned to meet him, smiling a little at his failed attempts at suave. "You're Michael Loew, right?" Her voice was low and cracked slightly, a genuine Irish accent in a city that could fake it with the best of them.

Mickey was not one of the people who could fake it, and his attempt to say, "Aye" in an Irish accent died at the back of his throat, came out more like, "Arr."

Great, Mickey the Pirate, Toby thought.

The Irish girl reached into her handbag and pulled out a large gun. She'd pumped four rounds straight into Mickey before Toby had time to blink. She turned to point the gun at him, holding it there while she downed the drink. She wiped her mouth with her sleeve, smudging her dark lipstick ever so slightly, and toasted Toby with the empty glass, "Sláinte."

Toby didn't let out another breath until she'd turned and walked out.

Dion heard the gunshots and then a moment later saw the woman walk out of the bar and head away from them up Mott. She was walking calmly, not worried that police sirens might cut the air at any moment. Dion liked that, it was cool. He tucked his hands into his pockets and walked with his head down low, trying to look casual, as he followed her up the street. Halfway up, she slowed down and then stopped. Still not worried about police, amazing. She kicked off her boots, the main thing Dion remembered about her, and threw them over the wall into the churchyard. Out of her handbag she pulled a small pair of slip-on shoes and stepped into them. Next she pulled out a small hat, one of those old-school things that all the white women were wearing, and slipped it on at an angle.

At the top of Mott she crossed diagonally, heading for the subway. Two blocks down Dion could see Marlo, walking slowly away from them on the other side of the street. Renée would be somewhere out of sight, he could feel it.

Detective Marcus leaned against the squad car, its blue lights bouncing off the back of the church wall like an old French film. He watched his partner come out of the bar and cross the road to him, ignoring the reporter who was buzzing around them like a housefly.

"What you get?" Marcus said.

"Nothing useful," Doyle said. "He just keeps talking about his A/C being broke. He did say something about an Irish woman with freckles. It was like talking to you."

Marcus laughed and waved away Doyle's joke. He watched as she turned to talk to the reporter, quietly telling him to get to fuck. She would surprise folk, a dark and attractive native woman with an Irish name; it seemed to throw them off.

Marcus was an old Jewish man with a Jewish name, didn't seem to surprise anybody.

"Let's take him over to the fifth," Marcus said once Doyle had scared off the crime tourist, "Get him some coffee and a cell. You never know, might turn out he's our guy."

Doyle cocked her head to one side and shot him a look, "You even looked in there? No way he climbed over the bar to shoot Loew from that angle. And where's the gun?"

"I'm just saying. Wouldn't it be nice an easy?"

"When is it ever?"

Marcus nodded at that, then his thoughts drifted for a second, snapped back, "So, this Loew, he's a city lawyer, right?"

"Yes. Part of the team who did the Quinn case today."

"No shit? I never heard his name before?"

She shook her head. "Wasn't a big part. Did some of the paperwork, research. I talked to his boss, he says Loew was their go-to guy for the smallprint. He got round the delays from Quinn's defence team."

"Okay. And the barman says the shooter was an Irish woman, right? No way is that coincidence. We should put someone on the other members of the legal team."

Doyle shot him that look again. "You think I'm new at this?"

"Already done it?"

"Already done it."

One of the uniforms stepped close, looking nervous around the two detectives. "Uh, we got another one, up on East Houston. Gun-related, figured you'd want to see it."

Doyle leaned low over the body; its glassy eyes still staring up at the railing of the subway entrance. A nice-looking hat lay nearby, looking like it had been knocked off the woman's head as she fell.

"No coincidences, huh?" Doyle stood back up and walked over to where Marcus was catching the story from the uniform who'd caught it. "You sure about that?"

Marcus smiled thinly and nodded, then he took a turn to

look down at the woman's body. First thing he noticed were the bullet holes across her chest and abdomen, four of them, probably fired fast at point blank. Second thing he noticed were the freckles on the bridge of her nose.

"So you reckon if we check her ID she'll be Irish, huh?"

Doyle nodded to the nearest squad car and said, "Let's find out."

The shooter was cuffed in the back of the car, caught straightaway by one of the squad cars that had been on its way to the bar. Two other youths had been seen at the scene, a girl with blood all over her nose and a black male running on a nasty-looking limp. But the cops had prioritized catching the third one, who'd been stood holding a gun and a woman's handbag.

"What's the shooter's name?" Doyle asked.

Marcus rechecked his notes. "Uh, Dion. DeWhite Dion. Name rings a bell."

"Related to Black Top Dion?"

"I bet you he is. Say, a beer after work?"

Doyle looked him up and down with a faint smile then said, "Yeah, okay. Only if we're right, though."

They both bent to look on the front seat, where the victim's bag was lying. Her ID lay beside it. Margaret Quinn, twenty-seven. Definitely Irish. They both stayed silent for a long time and then Doyle said, "This is fucked up."

"Yeah."

"If she's the shooter from the bar, where's her gun?"

They both looked to where the murder weapon lay, in a plastic bag on the hood of the car, at pretty much the same time they both said, "Can't be."

Then Marcus looked back along East Houston toward the corner of Mott. After a moment he said, "What you reckon we go back to the bar, see if we can't convince that A/C guy of yours that his shooter was a young black kid?"

"Think you can do it?"

"A dinner after our beer says I can?"

"You're on."

No Flowers

Martin Edwards

Sunlight burst through the arched windows. For an instant, Kelly was blinded.

"Unbelievable, isn't it?" Brett asked.

"It's . . . amazing."

Despite the sunlight, the house felt chilly. As she shaded her eyes, she couldn't help shivering.

"I knew you'd love it!" He nodded towards the brilliant light. "Those aren't the original leaded windows, but triple glazing in precisely the same style. There was never any stained glass in St Lucy's, but no expense has been spared, promise."

"St Lucy's?"

"Name of the old church. The developer changed it to Meadow View. More appropriate, truly rural."

"And you want to move in soon?"

"Today!" Decisiveness was a quality he prized. "The deal is done, contracts were exchanged simultaneously with completion."

"Already?"

"I had to keep my plan secret, in case negotiations broke down."

"You're so thoughtful." She hugged him. "And it really is ours?"

"Down to the last maple floorboard." He lowered his voice, and for a few seconds it was almost as if the house were still a church. "I only hope it goes a little way towards making up for – you know . . . what happened."

Churlish and ungrateful to say nothing could make up for what happened. She was thankful that he cared so much. After she lost the baby, he might have abandoned her. But in his way, he had tried his best to offer comfort.

"I want to put your name on the title deeds," he said. "We can sort the paperwork once you give the landlord notice to quit your flat."

"I don't care about title deeds," she said. Financial and legal stuff meant nothing to her, she was happy to leave bureaucracy to him. He was the banker, after all. She only worked in a florist's. "But . . . is there a bus route nearby? How will I get to the shop?"

"I'll buy you a car," he said, "though really, sweetie, you don't want to stay stuck behind a counter all day."

"I like the job," she said. "You know I love flowers."

"Why not design a floral arrangement for the sitting area? This space calls out for a splash of colour, make a contrast with the potted palm."

"A customer once told me palms symbolize the victory of the faithful over enemies of the soul." She gazed at the exposed rafters of the ceiling. "How old is this place?"

"A hundred and forty years old."

"When did it stop being a church?"

"The last service was held three years ago." He shook his head. "I bet there were scarcely half a dozen old folk in the congregation. The church authorities realized St Lucy's was uneconomic. In the end, five parishes were merged, and the redundant churches put on the market. Sound business decision, the figures never added up."

"Sad, though."

"There comes a time when you have to rationalize," he said.

For a moment, she recalled those endless nights, crying herself to sleep in her poky flat, when she feared he might rationalize her out of his life. Foolish of her, she should have shown more trust.

"The conversion was a labour of love," Brett said. "St

Lucy's was bought by a man called Dixon. He was born round here, but moved to London with his family. I gather he dreamed of coming back to the village. Not that there was much of a village left to come back to."

"How do you mean?"

"The school closed, along with the post office, and the pub was knocked down. Most of the cottages on the main street have become second homes or a base for commuting couples. According to the estate agent, hardly anyone has lived in the village more than five years."

"Pity."

"Progress, sweetie. By all accounts, the whole area cried out for an upgrade, investment was required. Don't fret, there's a retail park ten minutes away by car, they sell everything you could wish for. You won't have to depend on some grubby little village shop for over-priced groceries."

She squeezed past the potted palm, which was nearly as tall as Brett, and sank into the clutches of a leather sofa, one of three stationed at right angles to each other. An enormous television screen completed the square.

"You can't see the wiring," he said. "It's cleverly concealed, but we have the latest cinema sound system."

At a flick of a remote, the screen sprang to life. A rock band, performing in concert. Kelly didn't recognize their contorted faces; flowers were her thing, not music. The sound deafened her, the strobe lights made her want to shut her eyes.

"The equipment is all to the highest specification," Brett said, as he silenced the acoustic guitar. "Hot water underfloor heating. Zoned thermostats. And it's environmentally friendly, with a bio-treatment sewage system. Come and see the mezzanine gallery."

As she followed him up the stairs, he maintained a running commentary on their surroundings. "Matching maple treads, see? The black strings are made of steel. The safety glass meets the highest standards."

As they reached the top, Kelly found herself facing an enormous four-poster bed.

"Silk curtains as well as sheets," he said. "Over there is our en-suite bathroom. Mahogany-framed Shoji screens for privacy – not that we need worry about that when we don't have guests to stay."

"Guests?"

"Sure, you know how important it is for me to entertain clients and colleagues. My progress up the ladder depends on keeping them satisfied. You'll enjoy the company, honestly."

Kelly said nothing. Brett's best clients were from the Middle East, rich men who traded in oil. They oozed charm, but she didn't care for the way they looked at her.

"Seriously, you'll be able to experiment." He paused. "You know, you can try out all the appliances in that wonderful kitchen downstairs."

She gazed across the living space to the gleaming breakfast bar and state-of-the-art stainless-steel units at the far end of the house. She and Brett might have boarded a starship, where no germs and grime could survive.

"This is where the organist used to play," Brett said, waving towards the matching bedroom cupboards. "But when the place was converted, of course the organ had to go."

Later, Kelly took herself out for a walk while Brett made a few calls. He always had calls to make, he liked to say that he made sure his clients always got whatever they wanted. The grounds of Meadow View were smaller than she'd expected, though as Brett said, that wasn't a problem, since neither of them was a gardener. She could plant a few flowers at the back. He'd dig out a border to keep her happy.

There were no gravestones. Another selling point of the property, Brett explained; it was rare to find an Anglican church in this part of England without accompanying grave-yard. St Lucy's cemetery once sprawled behind the rectory, he'd heard, but the parish allowed it to become overgrown, a haunt for the village's few indigenous teenagers to misbehave with each other and take drugs at night when no adults were around. The planners insisted it was tidied up as part of the regeneration project. Now the gravestones lined a neat formal garden that linked the lane to the main street. Brett wasn't sure if the remains were left under the redeveloped land or re-interred elsewhere, but the whole garden was monitored by CCTV and the gates were locked as soon as darkness fell. Much more respectful.

Beyond the meadow, a string of industrial units lined the horizon. Sun glinted on their dark metal roofs. A throaty rumble came from vehicles queuing on the slip road, although the new motorway was invisible. Across the lane from Meadow View stood a large building almost as old as her new home. At first she thought it was another house, and wondered what her new neighbours would be like, but then she saw the front garden had been turned into a car park with spaces marked for half a dozen cars, and spotted a freshly painted board announcing the place as headquarters of Old Rectory Technology Solutions. A sign indicated the way to the Meadow Memorial Garden, but Kelly ignored it. The memory of her lost baby was too raw for her to wish to confront fresh reminders of mortality.

The lane was narrow, and lacked a pavement. Three times in as many minutes, Kelly pressed herself into the hawthorn hedge as a lorry raced round the bend on the wrong side of the road, taking a short cut to the business park. At least there was no need to worry about traffic noise in the house. Brett said the triple glazing made it soundproof.

A couple of hundred yards further on, the lane dog-legged and Kelly saw the junction with the main street that ran through the village. A shame the school had closed. A quiet place in the countryside was perfect for bringing up youngsters. She wanted to try again soon for another baby, even though her pregnancy had been an accident. To begin with, she'd dreaded Brett's reaction when she broke the news. He admitted thinking he was still too young for fatherhood, but after that first fraught conversation, he'd never raised the possibility of abortion again. The miscarriage was the worst thing that had ever happened to her, worse even than her mother's death from cancer – Dad had deserted them when she was five, and she'd never heard from him since – but at least she had Brett. He wept when she lost the baby, though he soon seemed to get over it. She rid herself of any impression that his generosity was tinged with relief. Her mother used to be fond of saying that everything happens for the best in the long run, though Mum's own troubled life scarcely proved her point.

"Are you the new person?" a hoarse voice asked.

Kelly's thoughts had wandered, and she hadn't seen the old woman leaning on the gate of a dilapidated cottage close to the junction. The woman's white hair was untidy, and her lined face reminded Kelly of parchment. Her misty grey eyes were fixed on some point far away. She wore an ancient black overcoat that seemed too big for her. An unlikely soulmate, but if the village was to become her home, Kelly must make friends, and this old biddy would have forgotten far more about the neighbourhood than incomers would ever know.

"My partner and I have just bought Meadow View, yes."

"Meadow View?" The woman closed her eyes for a moment, as if determined to shut out the here and now. "St Lucy's, you mean."

Kelly hated causing offence. Better make it plain that she was an ignoramus. Most people liked to give help to others who were in need. It made them feel superior.

"I wasn't even aware there was a saint called Lucy," she said with a friendly smile. "Sorry, I wonder, can you tell me if—"

"You don't know about St Lucy?" The woman shook her head. "And we didn't have partners in my day, either. You either lived in wedlock or sin, and that was an end to it."

Kelly said hastily, "This is such a lovely part of the world. I feel so lucky to be moving here. Becoming part of the community."

The old woman resumed her contemplation of an invisible

spot in the distance. "We used to call the church a house of God. Not any longer."

"The man who designed our house made a spectacular job of it," Kelly said. "Would you like to come and visit us, have a look round? We'd be happy to offer a cup of tea and scones."

The woman coughed. "You don't understand."

Kelly felt a nip of wind on her bare cheeks. "Well, I mustn't keep you. But it was nice to say hello. I'm called Kelly, by the way. Sorry, I don't know who you are?"

"My name is Honoria," the woman said.

"Lovely." Kelly stretched out a hand. "Pleased to meet you, Honoria. And I look forward to seeing you again. Don't forget to look in next time you're passing, the tea and scones are a standing invitation."

The woman stepped back from the gate, and ignored Kelly's hand. "Do not sleep in that house tonight."

Kelly stared. "Sorry?"

The woman limped back up the path towards her front door. The garden was a mess of nettles and ground elder, and the house cried out for a lick of paint. One of the ground-floor windows was cracked.

The sun disappeared behind a cloud. Kelly hurried back in the direction of Meadow View.

"If you insist," Brett said.

"It's not a matter of insisting," Kelly said. "Only, I didn't expect any of this. I have stuff to do back home."

"This is your home now."

"Yes, I mean the flat." She stroked his hand. "Look, it's only for one night. If you run me back, we can stay over . . ."

He sighed heavily, and she knew she had persuaded him. What she didn't know was why a stray remark from a stupid old woman had bothered her, so that she didn't want to spend tonight in their new dream house. Honoria must be jealous of them. Two young people with their lives ahead of them, everything to look forward to. The old cow would be reduced to a meagre state pension, surrounded by strangers in a village that had changed beyond all recognition. No wonder she was bitter, and prepared to spoil the innocent pleasure of others.

But spoil it she had. Kelly was determined not to stay here tonight. Of course, she couldn't explain to Brett. He would only laugh, and say she was a gullible fool. It might make him wonder again what a tall, handsome Rhodes Scholar from Sydney had in common with a shy English girl who worked in a florist's shop. Things would be different in the bright light of morning. Honoria hadn't warned her against sleeping here in future, she reasoned. Nor would the woman have a second chance to make a nuisance of herself. From now on, Kelly meant to give her a wide berth.

When they were in the car, she asked, "Who was St Lucy, then?"

"I looked her up," Brett said, as he zigzagged past smaller vehicles into the fast lane of the motorway. He always relished parading his knowledge. They had first met twelve months ago, in a posh London bar when she was on a night out with a friend from school. Brett captained the winning team in a quiz, and he bought the girls champagne to celebrate his success. He was six feet seven, with bleached blond hair and the bluest eyes Kelly had ever seen. That night, he and Kelly made love for the first time. They had been together ever since. "I like to do my homework. Lucy is patron saint of the blind."

"Never heard of her."

"She was a Christian martyr who consecrated her virginity to the Lord." He sniggered. "When her marriage to a pagan bridegroom was arranged, she turned the fellow down. He took his revenge by denouncing her to the magistrate. She was ordered to burn a sacrifice, and when she refused, her sentence was to work as a prostitute."

"Poor wretch!"

"Yes." He considered her, blue eyes gleaming. "But the guards found they could not move her, even when she was hitched to a team of oxen. In their anger, they gouged out her eyes with a fork."

She put her hand to her mouth, too shocked to speak.

"You did ask," he said. "Maybe she should have been more cooperative. Anyway, it's good to know the history of your own home. If we don't understand the past, how can we prepare for the future?"

For a few miles, Kelly did not say another word. Something puzzled her. When they were a couple of streets away from the flat, she asked. "How come you managed to buy the house so quickly? I heard on the news that the property market is depressed."

"This is a buyer's market," he said. "I put in a basement offer, non-negotiable, with a twenty-four-hour deadline. The woman who was selling had to make her mind up on the spot. Take it or leave it, yes or no. She said yes, and that was that."

"I thought you said the house was converted by a man called Dixon."

"Yeah, but my vendor was a woman called Hitchmough, all right?"

"How long had she lived there?"

"I don't think she ever moved in."

"What do you mean?"

Keeping his eyes on the road, he said, "Have you been listening to gossip in the village while you were out on your walk?"

"No, I don't understand." She fought to keep panic out of her voice. "What sort of gossip?"

He exhaled. "It's only that someone died there."

"Where? In our new house?"

"Listen, there were protests about the regeneration of the village. The not-in-my-backyard brigade caused a load of trouble. A lost cause, obviously, but John Fryer, the old bloke who used to play the organ, decided to stand in the way of progress. He blocked the path of the builders' trucks. When the police were called in, he took shelter inside the church."

"Sanctuary?"

"Stupidity, more like. He was wasting his time, obviously. When they told him the church authorities wanted him out, he went berserk. He was a widower, and he reckoned the church and its organ were all he had left. Whatever happened to the afterlife, uh? Sounds to me like his so-called Christianity was only skin deep."

"What did Fryer do?"

"Threw himself from the loft on to the ground."

"Oh no!"

"No maple floorboards at that time, needless to stay. The church floor was solid stone. His head was smashed up, as you might expect. Utterly ridiculous. What was he trying to prove?"

"Yet the conversion went ahead?"

"Thank goodness it did, from our point of view. Not that it did Dixon much good."

"Why do you say that?"

"Fryer's death may have spooked him more than anybody realized. Then again, maybe he was just exhausted. The project was almost complete, he'd been working at it night and day, when he slipped off a ladder and fractured his skull."

"He died too?"

"'Fraid so. The place was on the market for a year or more, until the Hitchmough woman bought it from Dixon's family."

"You mean two people met their deaths in our house?"

"What's so unusual about that? Not everyone dies in hospital, you know." His lips tightened. "That unborn baby of yours died in your flat, have you forgotten?"

Kelly bit her tongue, did not say a word.

"This is how things get snarled up, when people react emotionally." He clenched his fist, trying to keep control. "For some reason, Hitchmough got the wind up herself, that's why she never moved in."

"But it took her a long time to sell?"

"Blame the economy, sweetie. Hitchmough was desperate, that's why she bit my hand off even at a massive undervalue. One person's misfortune is another's slice of luck, that's how life goes."

"So not a single person has slept in the house since it stopped being a church?"

He gave her a sideways look. "Exciting, isn't it, sweetie? We have our very own virgin home. You and I are the first real occupants."

They returned to Meadow View at noon the next day. While Brett busied himself with calls to clients on his mobile, she tiptoed into the porch, closed the double door without a sound, and set off down the lane towards the village.

Soon she arrived at the cottage where she'd met Honoria. She'd changed her mind about avoiding the old woman. Sometimes you needed to confront your fears, that was why she'd asked the doctor whether she was going to lose the baby. She was due a break. If she interrogated Honoria about what happened to John Fryer, and Dixon for that matter, chances were, she'd find there was nothing to worry about. Accidents happen every day, you can't allow your life to be taken over by fear.

The garden gate was latched, but nobody was in sight. Kelly pushed open the gate, and strode up to the door. When she pressed the bell, nobody answered. She knocked furiously, until her knuckles hurt, but with the same result. The cracked front window was festooned with cobwebs. Peering through the grimy panes, Kelly saw that the room was empty. Yellowed newspapers covered the floor, but there was no furniture. Honoria must live in the back. It wasn't uncommon for old people to confine their living quarters to small portions of their homes, when the whole house became difficult to manage.

Kelly trudged back to Meadow View to find removal men hurriedly unloading her possessions. Brett's mobile was still clamped to his ear, and big boxes full of her bits and pieces were strewn across the rear part of the ground floor, between the sofas and the steps to the gallery. By the time the removal men departed, she'd emptied a couple of packing cases and at last Brett was off the phone.

He wrapped her in her arms, and lifted her off the ground. "Time to celebrate!"

"I thought I would cook us a nice meal this evening. If you can pick up some food and champagne . . ."

"I read your mind!" he crowed. "A couple of bottles of Bolly are cooling in the fridge. I'm expecting a delivery van from the hypermarket on the retail park. It's due in an hour, bringing everything else we could possibly need."

"You're wonderful!" She kissed him hard, determined to push the image of miserable old Honoria out of her mind. "See the silver candlesticks I left on top of that packing case? They are heirlooms, they belonged to my grandmother."

"Very nice," he said absently, "we can use them some other time, once you've given them a polish. There are fresh candles in a holder for the table in the delivery I ordered."

"You think of everything," she murmured.

"Trust me, sweetie. It's all about getting the details right. Like I say, we have an hour before the van arrives, and I know just what to do in the meantime."

She nuzzled his ear. "Tell me."

Laughing, he swung her over his shoulder and carried her up the staircase, towards the mezzanine gallery and the four-poster bed.

"How does the underfloor heating work?" she asked later.

"Digitized utility control panel in the porch. I switched the system on before the delivery arrived."

They were lying on the bed, his long, long limbs entwining hers. As soon as they'd unpacked the food delivery, he'd hauled her back up to bed. She felt exhausted, and right now, the warmth of his flesh mattered more than the pleasure of intimacy.

"But the place is freezing!"

Amused, he said, "You're not wearing any clothes, that's why."

"Even so!" Her teeth had started to chatter. "Are you sure the heating isn't broken, if the house hasn't been occupied?"

Brett scowled as he disentangled himself from her. "Better hadn't be broken. Otherwise, I'll be on to my lawyer, first thing tomorrow."

She jumped off the bed and threw on a gown retrieved from the packing cases. Her stomach rumbled, reminding her to start preparing their meal.

"What's this?" she said, pointing up towards the ceiling.

"Didn't I tell you?" He roared with delight. "How could I forget? Up there is the bell tower, and that is the pull-rope. We can ring our very own church bell!"

Kelly couldn't sleep. Perhaps it was the champagne. Brett had downed most of it, but she'd drunk more than usual, and although he started snoring the moment his head touched the pillow, her thoughts kept racing, and she found it impossible to slow them down enough to enable her to drift out of consciousness.

Cocooned by the duvet, her feet no longer felt like ice. During their meal, they had needed to resort to using her old electric fan heater. Even then, she'd worn a thick sweater. Brett, made of sterner stuff, remained in shirt sleeves. Although he'd grown up around Sydney's surfing beaches, cold weather amused him, as if it presented a challenge a strong young fellow must overcome as a matter of honour. Besides, Meadow View was fully insulated, and the roof weatherproofed with the latest materials. Not a single crack for the night air to creep in. As he drained his glass, he told her that the coldness was all in her mind.

Her imagination was too vivid, according to Brett, though sometimes she feared it wasn't vivid enough. It failed her whenever she tried to picture St Lucy's as a place of worship. How many years had John Fryer played the organ here, to the deaf ears of people who were close to death? She fancied she could hear the strains of the Toccata and Fugue, echoing in her brain. Did they often play that in rural churches? She could not recall the names of hymns from her childhood.

The darkness was absolute. Brett had been diligent about turning off even the standby lights on their electrical equipment. It was a ritual with him, as close as he ever came to religious observance. It wasn't about saving money; he could afford to keep lights burning all night, every night, but he insisted on doing his share to save the planet.

Her throat felt dry and scratchy after the alcohol. She should have drunk more water, and despite the cold outside the bed, she'd better go downstairs and pour herself a glass. She reached out through the curtain and fumbled for the bedside light, but when she pressed the switch, nothing happened.

She swore under her breath. If the power supply had failed, she ought to check the control panel in the porch. Brett had mentioned some kind of fail-safe gizmo, but she'd better not disturb him. He would be furious if anything went wrong on their first night in his dream home.

That was the point, she realized, as she put one foot on the chilly floorboards. This was his dream, not hers. Not yet, anyway. Surely she could not allow old Honoria to ruin things forever?

Easing herself out of the bed, she pulled on the gown. Thankfully, its fleecy lining kept out the chill. Better be careful, venturing down those steps with open treads. It was all very well for Brett to brag about safety features, but when you could not see a thing, you needed to take care.

One foot in front of the other. No rush, she reminded herself.

At last she reached ground level. Her soles were freezing, but a couple of kilims were stretched out on the floor near the sofa. As she padded across them, something brushed against her cheek. Something cold and slithery; it was like being stroked by the thin fingers of a creature from another world.

She couldn't help jumping back, and the movement knocked over the pot containing the tall palm whose fronds had touched her. The pot smashed on the floor, and she screamed with the shock of it.

Not even Brett could sleep through that. The sound of movement came from upstairs.

"What's happening?"

He sounded groggy, no wonder after drinking so much. She wanted to call to reassure him, but her throat had dried, and when she tried to shout, no sound came.

"Kelly, where are you?" He swore viciously. "What have you done to the lights?"

As she heard him clambering out of bed, she found her voice at last.

"Brett, it's all right!"

"Were you trying to get away?" he bellowed. "What did they tell you about this place?"

"Nothing, nothing." Had she woken him from a savage nightmare? "It was only an old woman . . ."

"You bitch, why did I ever think you would have the guts?" He sounded frantic, unreasoning.

She heard the crash of the bell in the tower. He must be pulling on the rope. His rage terrified her. She needed to get back to the mezzanine gallery, and calm him down, but she dreaded cutting her feet on shards from the plant pot. Fear rooted her as the bell stopped clanging, and she heard him thunder around on the upper floor.

"I can't see you, but I know you're there!"

"Brett, why . . . ?"

Something happened, so quickly that afterwards she found it impossible to describe. A terrible crash ripped through the silence, and she knew at once that Brett had fallen from the gallery. Despite the rails and safety panels, it was easy for such a tall man to pitch over while flailing around in the dark, and plunge to the ground.

Only when she found the switch to restore the power, and bright lights banished the darkness, did she realize that one of the wooden packing cases had broken his fall. But it had not saved him. The impact must have been horrific. Worst of all, he had fallen head first, straight on to her precious silver candlesticks.

She dared not look as she dialled 999, but when the ambulance arrived, one of the paramedics threw up the moment he tried to shift the body.

His colleague told Kelly what even a man familiar with death found so shocking.

The candlesticks had taken out both of Brett's eyes.

As her strength returned, Kelly worked on a tribute. White lilies, white roses, and white gerberas, with green ferns for contrast. When she had finished, she thought it the most beautiful wreath she had ever made.

Time for her last journey to the village. She took a taxi from her flat, not wanting to brave the motorway. A "For Sale" sign stood outside Meadow View. The car stopped at the gate to the memorial garden, and she asked the driver to wait while she laid the wreath.

It did not take long for her to find the grave she sought. Not Brett's, of course. There had been a cremation in London, which she was too unwell to attend. No flowers, by request, but donations to his favourite ethical causes. Everyone agreed, it was as he would have wished.

Kelly felt a lump come into her throat as she stared down at the small black stone bearing John Fryer's name.

In the act of bending to lay the wreath, she halted.

John Fryer's wife had been buried with him. An inscription said simply that she had fallen asleep.

It was her Christian name, and the date of her passing, that caused Kelly to scream.

Honoria Fryer had died three months before her husband.

Lost and Found

Zoë Sharp

He waits. No hardship there – he's waited half his life. But now, tonight, finally you provide him with that perfect moment.

The one he's been waiting for.

In the alley, in the dark, just the distant glitter of neon off wet concrete. And he's so scared he can hardly grip the knife. But anger drives him. Anger closes his shaking fingers around it, flesh on bone.

He tries not to know what the blade will do.

But he knows. He's seen it too many times. He remembers them as only a slur of violence, swirled with a lingering despair.

And he can't remember a time before you. A time when he was innocent, trusting. You taught him misery and guilt, and he's carried both through all seasons since. A burden with no respite.

Tonight, he hopes for respite.

Tonight, he hopes finally for peace.

There should be lights in the alley, but he's taken care of them. Something else you taught him – not to let anyone see.

It's fitting you should die here in the dark, amid the rats and the filth and the garbage. You are what they are – the detritus of life.

And he is what you made him.

He hopes you're proud.

But right now he just hopes you're ready. That he's ready. He's dreamed of this so often down the years between then and now he feels suddenly unprepared, naked in the dark.

Shivering, he's a seven-year-old boy again, with all the majesty fresh ripped out of him, howling as he's punished for truth, punished for faith.

Punished for believing, when you told him you would take very special care of him indeed.

He's punished himself and those around him ever since. Lived a life stripped to base essentials, where *refined* means cut with stuff that's only going to kill you slow.

Lost.

And now he's found you again, and he thinks, if he does this right, he may find himself again, too.

He hears the footsteps, familiar even loaded by the drag and stagger of the years. He folds his hand tighter around the knife, takes in the sodden air, feels the pulse beat in his fingertips.

Feels alive.

It's a privilege only one of you can share.

Attuned, he sees your figure sway into the open mouth of the alley, hesitating at the unexpected gloom. A stumble, a smothered curse, but he knows you won't play it safe. You never have. Going around will take time, and you're loath to be away from your latest pet project, whoever that might be.

He wonders if he will be in time to save them – not from what's been but from what's to come – even as he steps out of the recess, a wraith in the shadows, the knife unsheathed now and eager for the bite.

At the last moment you hear his lunge of breath and you begin to turn. Too slow.

He is on you, fast with the lust of it, strong with the manifestation of his own fear. His hand grasps your forehead, tilting your head back for the sacrifice. Is it instinct that tries to force your chin under, or do you know what's coming?

Too slow.

He can smell soap overlaying sweat and tobacco, the garlic of your last meal. Garlic that failed to keep this vampire at bay.

The knife, sharp as a butcher's blade, makes a first pass across your stringy throat. It slips so easily through the skin that for a moment he almost believes you are the demon of his childhood nightmares and to be slain by no mortal hand.

Then he remembers a laughing boast – that the first cut is for free.

The second cut, though, is all for himself.

He goes in deep, hacks blind through muscle, tube, and sinew, glances across bone. The blood that gushes outward now is hot, so hot he can almost hear it sizzle.

Your legs run out on you. Shock puts you down and sheer disbelief keeps you there. He steps back, hollowed out by the skill, watches your eyes as the realization finally sets in. *Your heart still pumps but you are dead, even if you don't know it yet.*

He expected a fierce joy. He feels only silence.

He turns his back, not waiting for your feeble struggles to subside, and walks away. At the mouth of the alley he drops the knife into a drain, and walks away.

The rain starts up again, like it's been waiting, like it's been holding its breath.

The rain cleanses him. His feet take him past the gang tags, the articulation of alienation that forms the melody of his daily life, to the crumbling church. Not the same church, but another very like it. They have all become one to him – a place of undue reverence. A place where he was found and lost, and maybe found again.

A penance. And now a place of twisted sanctuary.

Approaching the altar, he makes jerky obeisance, slides into the second row. The wood is polished smooth by long passage of the tired and the hopeful. And the building smells of incense and velvet, wax dripped on silver, and the pages of old books lined with dusty words.

Still damp from the rain, he finds no warmth here.

Still restless from the act, he finds no comfort.

He wonders if he was expecting to.

You first came upon him sitting alone like this, all those years ago, scuffed and crying, pockets emptied and pride stolen. You comforted him then. He remembers a pathetic gratitude. *Salvation.*

The blood rises fast in him. His hands are clasped as if for prayer, the knuckles straining to release a plethora of fury and regret.

There was no release then. He had nowhere to take it other than the river, was so close to letting go when strangers wrestled him, a child demented, from the railing's edge. They were shocked at his vehemence, his determination.

They brought him back to you.

And you smiled as you told him suicide was the gravest sin. That he would go straight to the depths of hell, where he would be raped by every demon up to Lucifer himself.

So he chose to live rather than die, although it seemed to him that there was little to choose between one and the other.

Lying jumbled in the alley, the truth of what's been done finally descends on you, soft as snow.

You see the lights of passing cars, buttoned tight, oblivious. Flashes of coloured sound made distant by the glass wall of your dysphonia. Out of reach. Out of touch.

You are nearly out of time.

But still you grip the coat-tails of life with the stubborn savagery that is your nature. Logic tells you that you should already be dead, that somehow the blade has missed the vital vessels. You have gotten away with too much to believe you will not get away with this, if you want it badly enough.

After all, you have survived exposure, excoriation, excommunication, by will and nerve.

Someone will come.

A stranger, a Samaritan. Someone who doesn't know you well enough to step over your body and move along through.

If he *doesn't come back to finish you first.*

Only a fatalist would believe this is some random act of

violence, but not knowing *who* scratches at the back of your mind. There are so many likely candidates.

You are troubled that he did not speak. You expected the bitter spill of self-righteous self-pity. Of blame.

See what you made me do, old man.

Killing you without triumph is pointless.

But the face . . . you don't remember the face. You are not good with the faces of men, although it's different with the boys. Unformed and mobile, fresh . . . you have never forgotten one of your boys.

Your special boys.

It tore your heart out to have them taken away from you. To be taken away from them. But they underestimated the number, and few came forwards to be counted.

They called it shame.

You call it love.

Maybe that is the reason you are lying here, bleeding out into a rain-drummed puddle smeared with oil, in an alley, in the dark, alone.

Maybe he loves you too much to see you with anyone else.

He is on his knees when the cops come for him. They shuffle into the church snapping the rain from their topcoats, muting radio traffic, hats awkward between their fingers. Like they've seen too much to believe in the solace of this place. Like they're embarrassed by their own lack of devotion.

For a moment panic clenches in him and he teeters on the cusp of relief and outright despair. He should have anticipated this.

He rises, crosses himself – a reflex of muscle memory – and turns to them with empty hands.

The cops don't need to speak. Their faces speak for them. It is not the first time they have come for him like this. Not here. He doesn't stop long enough to pull on a coat before they hustle him out, through the slanted rain to the black-and-white angled by the kerb, lights still turning lazily.

The ride is short. The cops exchange muttered words in

the front seat. He reads questions in their gaze reflected from glass and mirrors but has nothing to say. This is the place of his choosing, and they cannot understand the choice.

He stares out through the streaked side window at the passing night, at the tawdry glitz of hidden desperation.

The rain comes down with relentless fervour. Water begins to pile up in the gutters, flash-flooding debris towards the storm drains. *If only sins were as easily swept clean away.*

The car slews to a halt beside two others just outside the crime tape. The lights zigzag in and out of sync with more urgency than the men around them.

Hope plucks at him.

The cops step out; one opens his door. They lift the tape to duck inside the perimeter, though there is nobody to keep at bay. Violence is too common here to draw a crowd in this rain.

A detective intercepts them with a doubtful glance, hunched into the weather. He has a day's tired stubble above his collar, and a tired suit beneath his overcoat.

"This him?"

One of the cops nods. "All yours."

"Let's go." The detective steps back with a spread arm, an open invitation tinged with mocking – for what he is, for what he represents.

"Wallet was still in the vic's hip pocket – how we knew he was one of yours," the detective says as they walk toward the alley. "But we would have made him sooner or later."

The detective waits for a response, for a simple curiosity that's not forthcoming.

"I do what needs to be done."

The detective shrugs. "Sure you do. For the sinners as much as the saints, huh?"

"That's always been the way of it."

"Sure." The detective's face bulges, bones pressing against his skin as if engorged. "This guy's a convicted pederast. He fucks boys – kids. The younger the better. And he was a priest when they sent him down. A goddamn priest."

"He'll be judged."

They reach the throat of the alley and the detective stops, as if to go farther will leave him open to contamination.

"Well, I'd say he's had his earthly judgement." And if the voice is ice, the eyes are fire. "All that's left for him is the fucking divine."

Adrift in your own circle of confusion, you catch only snatches of words you recognize but can no longer comprehend.

". . . amazed he's lasted this long . . ."

". . . nothing more we can do . . ."

". . . had it coming . . ."

And you're colder than the sea, locked inside a faltering body and a breaking mind, locked into a tumult of regret and the terror of going to meet a vengeful Maker.

The medics rise, retreat, leaving the clutter of their futile effort strewn around you.

You want to cry for them not to leave you, not to let you die alone, but you lie muted by the blade, stilled by the approaching darkness. Darker than the alley, darker than the earth. The devil prowls the shadows, waiting without tolerance, watching with lascivious eyes. Soon he will engulf you, rip apart your body even as your last breath decays, and devour a soul already rotten.

Unless . . .

". . . he's here . . ."

Your eyes flutter closed.

Thank God.

It takes effort to open them again, to see the priest approaching. The medics have moved back a respectful distance, clustering with the detective at the mouth of the alley, superfluous. The priest bends over you.

You prepare yourself for Penance, Anointing, Viaticum. He'll hear no spoken confession from your lips, but absolution assuming contrition surely must be granted.

You prepare yourself for a ritual worn with consoling familiarity. One you carried out often enough, back in a former life.

But as the priest bends low, you catch sight of his face, and this man's face you *do* remember, from behind the blade right the way back to his boyhood.

He was a special boy, all right.

Your first temptation on the path of sin.

And now your last.

The fear writhes in you, but he touches your forehead with a gentle finger and when he speaks, his voice is gentle too.

"God, the Father of mercies, through the death and resurrection of His Son, has reconciled the world to Himself and sent the Holy Spirit among us for the forgiveness of sins; through the ministry of the Church may God give you pardon and peace . . ."

Impatient, your mind runs on ahead:

. . . and I absolve you from your sins in the name of the Father, and of the Son, and of the Holy Spirit.

But the expectation is not fulfilled. The essential words do not follow.

Your eyes seek his, frantic, pleading. The devil growls at your shoulder, taking shape out of the umbra, exulting as he solidifies. Closer. You feel his talons pluck at your vision, begin to pull the fetid shroud across your eyes. You are sinking.

Quickly! Finish it!

The priest bends closer still, his voice a whisper in your closing ear.

"You found me, and I was lost. Now *you* are lost, because *I* found you . . ."

Eyes Wide Shut

Col Bury

Castro caught a red tear, trickling down the flushed cheek, with the muzzle of his Browning 9 mm. "Aw . . . poor O'Shea. We all get our comeuppance eventually, don't we, Jack?"

The reply was muffled by a duct-taped mouth, but the panicky eyes and frantic head shakes translated as "guilty" to Castro.

"That you begging for forgiveness, Jack? Well, you won't be getting any from me," Castro spat, his gold incisor accentuating a sneer behind the neatly trimmed goatee. "Fancy agreeing to come for a pint with me. As if I'd tell you anything. I'm no grass, ya fuckin' sucker. Thought your lot always had your eyes wide open." Castro took a small bottle from his jacket pocket. "He-he. You'll know it as Rohypnol, but we call it 'Roofies'."

Jack O'Shea still appeared groggy, but his vivid blue eyes widened on seeing the bottle, the head-shaking more frenetic.

Castro thrust the single-action Browning to O'Shea's left temple. "I see you've pissed ya pants too. Is that the piss of a guilty man?"

As he shook his head, O'Shea's eyes gestured desperately at his wallet on the adjacent desk.

"What? I've already taken the hundred quid. It'll come in handy that, thanks a lot, buddy. The credit crunch even affects us guys you know."

O'Shea indicated again, more pointedly this time by using his head.

"Oh, you want me to look inside?"

O'Shea nodded.

Castro used the muzzle of the pistol to open the wallet and studied the photo of O'Shea with his three children. Beaming smiles all round; his two young sons in their Manchester City kits, one with a foot propped up on a football. The older girl had headphones on, her long strawberry blonde hair lit by the sun glistening off the vast lake splitting a backdrop of two mountains.

"This you trying to convince me then, Jack?"

He shrugged, blinked exaggeratedly.

"Well, it's not working, man. The only thing this has done is give me a fuckin' semi-on looking at your daughter."

O'Shea's eyes hardened.

"Tell me, Jack . . . does she take it up the arse?"

He wriggled on the wooden chair, jerking it briefly off the badly tiled floor, the leg and wrist ligatures binding him and the chair as one.

"I'll take that as a 'Yes' then, buddy. Or at least she will do when I've finished with her." A throaty laugh revealed the gold tooth.

Muffled cursing followed, pleading eyes widening again.

"You really love 'em don'tcha, Jack?"

His head dipped.

Castro pointed at the snapshot with the pistol. "Look at you with your daft smile and that twinkle in your eyes. Aw, big daddy Jack O'Shea, the family man, eh? Hey, have you ever considered . . . you know . . . with her?" He pointed the gun at O'Shea's daughter.

O'Shea glared at him, fixedly.

"What?" Castro shrugged, chuckled. "You must've considered it, even for a split second. C'mon, man, admit it."

Ignoring Castro, O'Shea looked up and scanned the room; desk to his left, the open window, a metal cabinet in front and the door to his right . . .

Another guttural snicker then he asked, "You gotta have seen her naked over the years . . . seen her maturing . . . an' then, a guy like you must've been tempted?"

He continued to scrutinize the sparsely furnished room, particularly the wide-open window beyond the desk.

"Don't fuckin' ignore me, ya low-life piece of shit!" yelled Castro, pistol-whipping him on both cheeks.

The chair jolted noisily off the floor and O'Shea shook his head violently, as if to clear the pain somehow. It didn't work. His jawbones throbbed like hell and he felt dizzy.

"So, let me put a scenario to ya, Jack . . . there's these two cops on patrol. It's late at night, not much happenin'. To relieve the boredom they cruise over to the red-light district, near the arches on the edge of town. They see this fit piece of black meat and decide to have some fun, get her into the back of the van. She's cold, right? And she trusts the cops. They ask a few cop-like questions, but no worries, par for the course in her line of work, so nothin' untoward there, right? Then she's threatened with arrest cos she's already had her quota of street warnings. But she don't wanna spend the night in a cell cos she's rattling an' clucking, cold turkey, right? So they notice this, and the conversation turns to . . . 'What can you do for us?' . . . Right? One cop climbs into the back an' whips his cock out . . . an' she gets down to it. But, no, he's not happy with that . . . he wants to feel this whore, taste her. But she's not happy with that, and so the second cop pins her down. Then they both abuse their positions big time . . . and of course, the girl. Afterwards, they just laugh and dump her back on the streets . . . the piece of meat she is, right?"

Jack motioned an emphatic "NO" with his head.

"So, what do ya think of that scenario then?" he asks, almost casually, before ripping the duct tape from O'Shea's mouth.

"Aaargh! Fuck . . ."

"Bet that's what you said on the night, innit?"

O'Shea opened his mouth, stretching his aching jaw and stinging facial muscles. His mind still foggy, he tried to speak, but just croaked. He cleared his throat with a cough. "I didn't . . . do anything . . . I swear."

"Bullshit, bitch!" Castro forced the Browning into O'Shea's mouth, the muzzle clattering against his teeth, making him heave. "Just cos some bullshit internal enquiry says you did shit, don't make it so, ya punk-arsed pig. I want a fuckin' confession. Now!"

O'Shea just eyeballed him, had no choice. He could feel the metallic tang, the grind of metal on teeth. The sickly taste of the gun's last discharge made him heave again. He wondered who it had been used on. Castro yanked the pistol from the cop's mouth, scraping a molar on its exit. A sharp pain was followed by a hint of blood oozing on to the back of O'Shea's tongue.

Ignoring the pain, and the banging headache, he tried to compose himself, think straight. With a deep breath, he said, "Believe what you want . . . but I know the truth."

"The truth? The fuckin' truth!"

"Yeah . . . and I . . . did nothing that night."

"Nothin'?" Castro's dark eyes flared. "You raped ma fuckin daughter, ya cunt!"

"She was lying, Castro . . . and what the hell are you playing at anyway . . . pimping out your own flesh and blood like that?"

Castro suddenly became quiet, his eyes narrowing. He turned his back, shoulders sagging. Smoothing his braided hair, his voice hushed. "But times have been real hard. It's a fuckin' jungle on the street, man. And, anyway, she was more than willing . . ."

O'Shea's senses continued to slowly kick in, and he realized just how musty the room was, increasing his nausea. He couldn't quite place the smell, but it was familiar. "Imagine how hard times will be . . . if you kill me. A life sentence, fella."

Castro pivoted, grimacing, pointing the Browning toward O'Shea's forehead. "Yeah, but it'll be worth it. I'd be a hero inside for killin' a pervert cop."

"Whoa. I'm not so sure about that, Castro. Pimps are classed as sex offenders in prison . . . just like the paedos."

"Don'tcha fuckin' compare me to no nonce, man!"

"Well, my daughter's only fourteen, you know." He gazed at the photo on the desk.

"That's well different. You smartarse cops always twist things. This isn't about me, man . . . it's about you." Rushing forward a pace, he raised the gun, pointing it at O'Shea, whose head flicked from side to side. Leering, he inched closer, pressing the pistol into the cop's brow.

O'Shea winced, thought of his family.

"Thirteen rounds in this magazine, Jack. Well, there was. Unlucky for some, eh?"

Was? O'Shea glanced at the wallet photo on the desk. He tried to stop his voice from trembling, but being parched wasn't helping. "But . . . but what's the point, Castro, when I honestly did nothing wrong? The judge threw it out of court, remember?"

The gun remained pressed against O'Shea's forehead, creating a ringed imprint. "Rah, rah, everyone knows you all piss in the same pot. Confess or die, you cunt!"

"Pleeease! You know that's . . . not the case. Loads of bad guys get off with shit . . . including you."

Castro lowered the gun. "You're pecking ma head, man. You smartarse muthas do ma box in." He turned, picked up the duct tape from the desk.

"Look . . . before you do that . . . please, just let me tell you about that night."

Castro hesitated, glared. "It better be fuckin' good, pig."

O'Shea glanced out of the open window, the view of roof-tops in the distance telling him he was high up, the blue sky and wafting breeze teasing him. "Please, hear me out . . ." he began. "It was a cold night, very cold. My partner, Webber, saw Shannice standing on the corner. She was freezing, had no coat on. He shouted her over. We took her into the van, flicked the heater on and chatted. Suggested ways she could get off the brown. Rehab programmes, drugs workers and all that. I even gave her a coffee from my own flask to warm her up. We were with her for about twenty-five minutes, half-hour tops, when she insisted on hitting the streets again, saying she was losing money for every second spent talking to us. So we dropped her off, told her to be careful. She even thanked us for caring . . . for God's sake."

"Not good enough, O'Shea. Nice touch blaming Webber for shouting her over, though. That lying piece of shit." He noisily yanked duct tape from the roll, bit a strip off.

O'Shea briefly considered his partner. They spoke daily. Surely he'd be out looking for O'Shea by now. He had to keep stalling. "Okay then. If it's as you said, then why did Shannice not get examined at the hospital? She refused, remember?"

He held the strip of duct tape outstretched, aloft, his right index finger resting perilously on the Browning's trigger. "It was too late."

"Exactly. She left it too late. I mean, five days later she reports it."

The pimp stepped forward a pace. "She was scared of repercussions."

"I'm not having that, as it's the easiest thing to do. Contrary to popular belief, and unlike with the public, if you accuse a cop of anything, he's guilty straightaway, until proven otherwise. Because no one likes a dirty cop, including other cops. I've already been through hell these last eighteen months."

"Nice speech, O'Shea. Even I'm beginning to believe you. No wonder you got off with it."

"Okay, why didn't Shannice hand over the clothes she wore that night?"

"She'd already washed them."

"Surely it was worth a shot though, if not for DNA, then fibres."

"You're twisting again. Don't wind me up, you mutha! Or you'll end up like . . ." He fleetingly turned to the cabinet.

"Like what . . . who?"

Castro ignored him, screwed up the duct tape, went to the window and stared outside.

O'Shea's fuzzy mind drifted back to his children. They were too young to lose their daddy. He cursed himself for trusting this career criminal, saying he had "info of interest to the police". Should've taken Webber with him, dammit. He glanced at the door to his right, then back to Castro. He heard traffic below, emanating from the gaping window. He tugged on the ligatures. No use. *Think!*

He swallowed, then said, "My guess is that Shannice, like many others, saw an opportunity. The chance of getting off the streets by winning a shed-load of compensation, and even selling her story to the papers and then living happily ever after."

"Fuck this, man!" yelled Castro manically, passing the metal cabinet and banging the butt of the gun on it in anger. The left cabinet door slowly opened behind him, as he turned and forced the Browning into O'Shea's gob again.

This time Castro leaned in real close, his contracting pupils inches from O'Shea's. He was so close that O'Shea could smell his breath. It smelt like dog shit, a reflection of its owner.

O'Shea could just about see the left cabinet door, now fully open. His heart somersaulted and he double-blinked in a rush of panic. Webber was squashed inside, eyes staring like a dead salmon, but seeing nothing. The bullet hole in his forehead ensured that.

Castro seemed to notice what O'Shea had seen and glanced behind for a second. O'Shea bit down hard on the gun's barrel. With a twist of his neck he yanked the pistol from his kidnapper's grasp and flicked it overhead. The gun clattered on the floor. Castro's eyebrows shot up to his creasing brow, as O'Shea lunged forward, still tied to the chair. The cop's gaping mouth impacted Castro's neck, forcing him backward on to the desk. O'Shea clamped his teeth down, feeling the skin giving then splitting. The taste of blood, bitter and metallic, flooded warm in his mouth, spurted up into the air as he rocked his head side to side and ripped at the flesh like a hyena on speed. He felt Castro's desperate punches thudding on his head. But O'Shea continued, tearing into the pimp's throat, survival instinct and desperation driving him on, until Castro's screams became a pathetic gurgle.

O'Shea was standing in a painfully awkward crouch, the chair sticking out behind him. He yanked repeatedly, ripping bloody tendrils out, feeling them rubbery between his teeth, Castro now offering silent screams, his vocal cords in bits. O'Shea re-clamped his aching incisors and dragged Castro inch by painful inch along the desk closer to the open window. Castro's dark, bloodshot eyes swamped with fear and tears, his leg kicking out like a giant, upturned insect. O'Shea struggled with the weight, so unclamped again and sank his blood-dripping teeth into the pimp's thigh. The punches hitting him now were like that of a child's.

Half out of the window, Castro's head jerked up and O'Shea looked into those dark, defeated eyes one last time, showing their true cowardly colours as they pleaded mercy. Ignoring the pain in his gums and neck, and the increasing weight of the chair, O'Shea swiftly switched his grip. He bit hard on to Castro's belt, before heaving him that crucial last few inches, the slippery blood-drenched desk O'Shea's ally.

Relief flooding him, O'Shea peered over the window's sill . . . and mentally waved "bye-bye" to the cop killer, whose eyes bulged in disbelief as he plummeted.

Seconds later, O'Shea heard screams from below and sank backward, clumsily into the chair still strapped to him, knowing his colleagues would soon be here.

Breathlessly, he surveyed the bloody scene; incredible how much of the fluid covered the walls, desk and floor. He, himself, was soaked from head to toe in Castro's claret. He prayed that the pimp hadn't dipped into too many of his girls. He spat sprays of Castro's sickly fluid repeatedly on to the floor in disgust.

His best mate, Webber, eyed him. How could he possibly tell Webber's wife and kids about this? His emotions bubbled and he saw his open wallet on the floor, the blood-spattered photo of his own three children staring back up at him. It was all too much. He cried red tears.

As he heard the sirens, he reflected. He knew the world would be a better place without Castro. And, as a vampiric smirk formed, he also knew that bitch, Shannice, had enjoyed it. He could tell by her eyes.

Secret of the Dead

David Stuart Davies

It was Reuben Flowers, landlord of the Shoulder of Mutton, who found Annie Lincoln. She was floating in the village pond. Flowers had been taking his retriever for its early morning constitutional when he spotted a body lying face downwards. He recognized the old woman's plaid shawl, which was spread out on the still water like bat's wings. Stepping into the pond, he grabbed Annie's ankles and heaved her body on to the grass bank.

"She's a dead 'un, all right," he said, turning the body over and gazing down at the pale lifeless face. "Silly old girl. She must have missed her footing and gone in head first," he murmured, addressing the dog. The hound stared back inscrutably.

"Hello, I'm Sherlock Holmes."

Richard Cuff stared at the tall thin youth who stood on the threshold of his little cottage. He had a cadaverous, intelligent face with a long nose and dark expressive eyes. His manner was polite but there was something about him, thought Cuff, which radiated a confidence and a certain amount of arrogance beyond his years.

"Oh?" responded Cuff and waited for further data.

The youth shifted his feet. "I've come to help you."

"Have you now? I wasn't aware that I needed any help."

"It was my aunt's idea. I'm staying with her for the summer. My parents are in Europe with my brother."

"And who might this aunt be?"

Holmes ruffled his hair, suddenly aware that he was not explaining himself very well. "It's Mrs Dryfield, up at the Grange. She said that you were a keen gardener but now that you've been struck with a bad attack of sciatica you weren't able to . . ." The boy's voice trailed away.

Cuff smiled. "So she sent you down to be my assistant. My under gardener."

Holmes returned the smile. "I suppose so."

"Well, that is mighty thoughtful of your aunt. Indeed, she is a thoughtful woman. I have had reason to thank her for her kindnesses in the past but in this instance I don't really think—"

"Oh, please Mr Cuff, do let me help. I'm awfully bored up at the Grange. I've read all the books I brought with me and there's nothing to do there. I just need something to occupy my time. And, for another thing . . ."

Cuff's face shifted into a gentle inquisitive frown. "Yes?"

"Well, I believe you used to be a detective."

"I reckon it's time you came in for a cup of tea, young man. I think you've earned it." Cuff had been standing at the end of the vegetable patch for some time unobserved by Sherlock Holmes who was busy turning over the earth and creating furrowed rows in readiness for the planting of potatoes.

Holmes looked up, ran his sleeve across his brow and nodded.

"My aunt tells me you were a policeman in London," he said as he lifted the large mug of tea from the rough wooden table in Cuff's kitchen. He scrutinized the man opposite him, the grizzled head bowed, with bright intelligent eyes and long white fingers now somewhat gnarled with age.

"Your aunt is quite correct. But I came up to Yorkshire to investigate the strange affair of the Moonstone diamond . . ."

"Oh, yes, I've read all about that. It's an honour to meet you, sir. The history of crime is a passion of mine."

"Well, I liked the county so much I came back up here to

live when I retired. The air is much sweeter than in the metropolis."

"Don't you miss the detective life? Solving crimes, unravelling mysteries?" Holmes asked after taking a sip from the mug of very hot, dark brown tea.

Cuff chuckled, his eyes steel sharp. "It's not like it is in stories. Investigating crime can be tedious and boring at times as well. Ah, but you're right, I suppose. I do miss it. Police work gives you an appetite for folk."

Holmes gave him a puzzled frown.

"I like to know how people tick and what's going on up here." He tapped his forehead. "What a person says is often different from what they think, but little things give them away. You for example."

"Me?"

"Yes. I can tell that you are interested in chemistry, you make use of that old punchbag Mrs Dryfield keeps in the outhouse and that you are somewhat jealous of your older brother swanning off to Europe with ma and pa."

Holmes smiled.

"Am I right?"

"I suppose so. How did you know?"

"By using my intelligence and my eyes. I deduced, you see. A young lad with chemical stains on his shirt and jacket, especially in the school holidays, must have some interest in the subject of chemistry. I've seen the old punchbag and I've seen your bruised knuckles. You're obviously an active fellow who likes to keep fit."

"And me being jealous?"

"Ah, well spotting that comes with practice. Interviewing people for all those years one learns how to interpret not just words but tone and expression. You fathom the ways of men and women. When you told me about your brother your eyes narrowed momentarily and there was a cool timbre in your voice and a slight purse of the lips. That spoke volumes to an old sleuth hound like me."

Holmes clapped his hands together in appreciation.

"Excellent," he said. "Now, perhaps I could reciprocate and tell you something about yourself."

"That would be most interesting." The old man gave him an indulgent smile.

"Well," said Holmes, "I should say that you have misplaced your spectacles this morning and that you've recently lost a pet dog, probably through old age."

Cuff's eyes widened in surprise. "Well, Master Holmes, you are quite correct. Now you tell me how you arrived at these conclusions."

Holmes rubbed his hands with pleasure. "It is clear that you normally wear spectacles. The red rim across the bridge of your nose and the indentations on either side proclaim as much. But you are not wearing them at present and yet I observe this morning's paper, folded and unread on the table. Similarly your post remains unattended to, two envelopes unopened because you cannot read the contents without your spectacles. And finally, you are wearing odd socks."

"Very smart and hitting the bull's eye. What about the dog?"

"There is a blue rubber ball in the hearth. It is pitted with teeth marks, probably made by a small dog in play. Adhering to both your trouser legs are some stray hairs which I would surmise are of the canine variety. They are white, which suggests an old dog. There is no sign of a creature now so it seems appropriate to surmise that he has only recently died."

Cuff nodded. "Sammy, my little Jack Russell. I had to have him put down last week. Liver disease."

"I'm sorry."

"But that was a master class."

"I'm afraid it's second nature to me. I see, observe and reach conclusions. I suspect it is the same with you."

"Not quite. I have a natural facility for taking notice but I had to train myself to interpret what I see."

"Not many unsolved crimes here though."

"Maybe. But if the truth be known I'm puzzling on a little matter at the moment."

"An investigation?"

"Not exactly. It may just be my fancy . . ."

"Do tell me about it."

Cuff shook his head. "No. As I say it may be something and nothing."

Holmes leaned forward over the table, coming perilously close to knocking his mug of tea over. "But if it's not . . . Wouldn't it be useful to explain your thoughts out loud? It might help you to reach some conclusions."

"Explain my thoughts . . . to you?"

"Yes. Who better? A relative stranger. Besides I am intelligent and . . . I believe I have the makings of a great detective."

Cuff burst out laughing.

"I'm only fifteen but in ten years' time I expect to have established myself as an important detective in London."

Cuff retained his amusement. "King of Scotland Yard, eh?"

"Oh, no. I intend to be a private consulting detective."

"Ah, solving the problems of the rich."

"No, my fees will be reasonable. The crimes will be what will determine whether I take the case or not. So try me out. Tell me about your little matter."

Cuff paused for a moment and scrutinized this odd youth once more. "Why not? If nothing else it'll teach you that sorting the wheat from the chaff in crime is no easy matter. Right then. There was a death in the village last week."

"A murder?"

"If you are going to interrupt me at every verse end, I'll clam up, Master Sherlock."

"Sorry."

"It was regarded as an accident. Old Annie Lincoln was found drowned in the village pond. It was assumed that she was making her way home after dark, missed her footing and fell in."

"But you're not sure."

Cuff shook his head.

"Evidence to the contrary?"

"Very little. Annie has lived in the village all her life. It seems strange to me to believe she'd be foolish enough to fall in the pond. I reckon she could have walked around the place blindfold without putting a step wrong. I saw her in the afternoon of the day she died. She was in a hurry but she stopped briefly to talk to me. She said she'd call in at my cottage the next day because there was something that was troubling her and as I was 'an old policeman' she wanted to see what I thought."

"She gave no clue as to this thing that was troubling her?"

"Not really. She was in such a hurry, I didn't have the chance to question her. She was off like the wind. Her last words to me were, 'See you in the morning.'"

"But by the morning she was dead."

"Yes."

"And you think that . . . perhaps her death wasn't exactly . . . natural. That perhaps she was . . . murdered."

"It sounds so brutal, so ridiculous when you say it out loud."

"But . . . ?"

"The thought had crossed my mind."

Holmes wriggled in his chair, his dark hair falling across his brow. "Oh, this is most interesting. Have you *any* idea what she was going to tell you?"

"Not a clue."

Holmes was not convinced by this response. Cuff's wrinkled features were immobile but the slight furtive movement of those still bright light grey eyes suggested to the youth that the old man was not being completely honest.

"What was Annie like as person?"

"She was a busybody and a gossip. Nothing happened in this village that she didn't know about. If Mrs Matthews's cat had kittens Annie would know. When Parson Phillips received a small inheritance from a distant aunt, it seemed that Annie was cognisant of the fact almost as soon as the cleric himself. She had a keen nose for finding things out."

"So she may very well have discovered something of significance that put her in danger."

"If that is the case, she didn't quite know how dangerous it was."

"Were you the usual audience for her tales?"

"No, not really. That's another thing that makes me suspicious. I reckon she wanted to tell me because of my history – because I'd been a detective, a solver of crimes. She always referred to me as 'Sergeant C'."

"When you saw her, did you notice where she was going?"

Cuff thought for a moment. "I really didn't take much notice at the time. To be honest, I saw no real importance in what she told me. I expected that she wanted to be the first to reveal who was expecting a child or whose marriage was in difficulties." He closed his eyes as though bringing the moment to mind. "She could have been going to the village shop . . . or maybe to see Doctor Randle—" Cuff suddenly let out a short exhalation of breath. "Yes, it would be to see the medic."

"How can you be sure?"

"She walked oddly. I'll bet her old rheumatism was playing up. When you get into the sear and yellow like me, you recognize such symptoms in others."

Holmes thought for a moment, assimilating all the information he'd learned from Cuff. "If this lady was an inveterate busybody who, it would seem, had some very interesting gossip to pass on to you—"

Cuff finished Holmes's thought. "Might she not tell the doctor as he was doling out his pills?"

Holmes beamed. "Exactly."

"I think you may be right. Anyway, a quick chat with Randle will clear that matter up. Would you like to come along with me?"

"I certainly would," cried Holmes rising from his chair. "But first, I think there is something that you haven't told me. Something that makes you think that Annie had dangerous information and that her death may not be an accident."

Cuff stroked his chin. "You're a canny lad. Maybe you will be king of Scotland Yard or some other famous detective after all."

Holmes tried to restrain his smile but failed. "Well . . . ?" he said gently.

"Annie's was the second death in the village within the month. Andrew Barrett also met with an unexpected accident. Well, perhaps not quite unexpected in one sense. He fell headlong down his staircase when in drink and broke his neck. He was frequently in drink so there were only a few raised eyebrows, including mine, on hearing the news. But now one begins to wonder. Two accidental deaths in one small village in a matter of weeks. Is it a dark coincidence or is there human treachery afoot?"

Cuff locked his front door and he and Holmes made their way to the village green. "Andrew Barrett was a retired judge. He lived in that imposing Georgian house on the outskirts of the village, Botham Lodge. You'll have seen the large stone gate-posts to the long drive as you came into the village. He lived there with his daughter Emilia. Apparently she has formed a romantic attachment to Albert Dawson, a newcomer to the village. Quite the whirlwind affair."

"Can you think of any circumstances in which there might have been foul play?"

"I'm an old policeman, Master Sherlock, of course I can think of several but they'd all be fancy without some hint of tangible evidence or some clue."

"Well, perhaps Doctor Randle can provide it."

If Sherlock Holmes were in the theatre business and he wished to cast an actor as a village doctor in one of his plays, he would have chosen someone who looked exactly like Doctor Joshua Randle. He was a gentleman of middle height, plump around the middle, with rosy cheeks, and a pair of twinkling grey eyes which peered nonchalantly from behind a pair of golden pince-nez. His hair, sandy in colour but going grey, gave the impression of exploding from his scalp. It stood wildly on end as though it had not seen a brush or a comb in many a day. He appeared kindly but astute, amenable but no fool.

The doctor seemed bemused to find both Cuff and a young stranger entering his surgery.

"Good day to you," he said, rising from his chair and offering his hand to Cuff. "What can I do for you? You're not both ill?"

Cuff shook his head. "This is a young friend of mine, Sherlock Holmes. We are both in the pink, Doctor. We come for a rather different purpose than our health. Together we're a little puzzled over the death of Annie Lincoln."

"Really? Well, she drowned, you know. In the village pond. A very sad occurrence."

"Indeed," said Cuff. "Did she visit you on the day she died?"

Randle narrowed his eyes and looked a little wary. "She did."

"Rheumatism?"

"Up to your old detective tricks, eh, Cuff? Yes, she had bad attacks quite often. She was a regular customer of mine. I gave her some powders to alleviate the pain. It's a condition that cannot be cured, you know."

"I do know. Annie was a real teller of tales."

"Aye, she was."

"Did she confide any gossip when she visited you?"

"Oh yes, often. She had all kinds of silly theories about people."

"What about on her last visit to you?"

Randle frowned. "What is this all about?"

Holmes, frustrated at this circumlocution, took a step forward. "We think perhaps Annie was pushed into the pond. Drowned deliberately because she knew something. We think she may have told you what she knew."

It was clear to Cuff from Randle's expressions that he didn't know whether to smile or grow angry. "Is this some kind of jest?" he asked.

"No", said Cuff. "My rather impetuous young friend is right. Did Annie have some juicy gossip to relate when you saw her? Believe me, Doctor, this is not an idle enquiry."

Randle scratched his head. "This is all very strange. The truth is, Cuff, that I often do not listen to my patients when they ramble on about things not connected with their ailments."

"It may have been something about old Judge Barrett," said Holmes.

Randle narrowed his eyes and scrutinized the strange youth who seemed to have an unnatural confidence and maturity.

"She said nothing directly about Judge Barrett as I recall. She did however . . . No, no. I do not see it my place to repeat such things."

"I wouldn't ask you to if it wasn't important. You have my word on that," said Cuff, lowering his tone to emphasize the seriousness of the matter. Holmes thought it a most impressive ploy.

Randle stroked his chin pensively for a moment. "Oh, very well. It is something and nothing after all. Annie asked if Emilia, the judge's daughter, had been to see me about her bruises. Apparently Annie had observed that the girl had some nasty marks on her wrists. I think that she was suggesting that Emilia had received some rough treatment from that young man of hers."

"Albert Dawson."

Randle nodded.

"Had Annie seen this 'rough treatment'?"

"She implied that she had and that she believed there was something not right about Judge Barrett's death. I believe that she'd done a bit of spying."

"What gave you that idea?"

"Oh, I don't know. It's not what she said but how she said it. I got the impression that she'd been seen by Miss Barrett and Dawson. But as I say I let all this tittle-tattle wash over my head."

"Regarding Judge Barrett's death, I gather you attended to the body," said Cuff.

Randle's face adopted a more sober mien. "Yes, I did. A sad business. The fellow drank too much, I know, but he didn't deserve such a fate."

"Can you tell us about it?"

"For what purpose, Cuff? Are you manufacturing mysteries out of people's accidental deaths?"

"Just trying to get at the truth. Please indulge us."

Randle sighed resignedly. "Very well. What do you want to
know?"

"Exactly how he died," piped up Holmes.

"Late one evening Emilia sent me a message saying that
her father had had an accident and could I go up to the Lodge
immediately. I did so and found the judge lying at the bottom
of the stairs with his neck broken. Emilia said that he'd been
drinking heavily and had tripped and fallen the full length of
the staircase."

"Was Albert Dawson present?"

Randle shook his head. "I'm not sure. I only saw Emilia and
Buckley the butler. It was he who brought me the message."

"How was the judge dressed?" asked Holmes. "Was he in
his night attire?"

"No. He was dressed for dinner and he did smell heavily of
alcohol. Now gentlemen, if you don't mind, I have real patients
waiting to see me . . ."

"What do you know of this Albert Dawson?" asked Sherlock
Holmes as he nursed a glass of lemonade between his hands.
He and Cuff were sitting on a bench outside the Shoulder of
Mutton in the warm sunshine.

Cuff wiped a thin moustache of beer froth from his upper
lip before answering. "Not much. I believe he is a solicitor
with a firm in York, Gammidge and Brown if my memory
serves me right. I've never met him personally. Just seen him
in the distance. He's only been in the village six months or so.
It certainly seemed as though he made a beeline for young
Emilia. Well, not so young. She must be approaching thirty
now. A sturdy lass but rather plain, if you catch my meaning.
Since her father's death, Dawson seems to have spent most of
his time at Botham Lodge. It's raised the eyebrows of some of
the ladies of the village."

"If he is courting her, why would he ill-treat her?"

"That, my dear Holmes, is the key question."

The next day found Sherlock Holmes on an investigative mission on his own. He had travelled to York to seek out the firm of Gammidge and Brown where Albert Dawson was employed. After some fruitless perambulations around the old city, he discovered their offices down a side street near the Minster.

On entering the gloomy building he found himself in an outer office where a young clerk – not much older than himself – sat perched on a high stool at a wooden desk scratching away at a large ledger.

The youth's face folded into a superior sarcastic sneer as he observed Holmes.

"Yes?" he asked in an imperious manner.

Rather than being intimidated, Holmes was rather amused by the air of self-importance that the young man had wrapped around himself.

"I wish to see Albert Dawson," he said simply.

"Do you now? Are you a friend of his?"

"I wish to see him on business."

"And what kind of business is that then? Embezzling business?"

"I'm sorry," replied Holmes, appearing more confused than he actually was. His quick brain responding instantly to the clerk's brusque intimation, which prompted a series of potential scenarios to flash into Holmes's mind.

"Embezzling business," repeated the sneering clerk. "He's good at that is Dawson. Well, actually not all that good. You see he got caught. Fiddling the funds. He was damned lucky he didn't get choky for it but we didn't want that kind of stink associated with the firm. He just got sacked instead. He was a spineless, cowardly mouse. Good riddance, I say. So, I'm afraid you can't see Albert Dawson 'cause he ain't here."

Holmes smiled. "Thanks for your help," he said smartly, turning on his heel and leaving.

*   *   *

While Holmes was on his mission in York, Cuff was carrying out an investigation of his own. He had decided to visit Botham Lodge to see Emilia Barrett. As he walked down the tree-lined drive with his stiff arthritic gait, he wondered what he would say when he rapped upon the door. He had only the vaguest of ideas of how he would provide a reason to secure an interview with the girl.

As he neared the house, he paused by an iron gate to peruse the walled garden beyond. It was a riot of roses, his favourite bloom. As he breathed in the warm scent on the summer air, he relaxed and for a brief time all troubled thoughts left his mind. With some difficulty he pulled himself back to the task in hand.

Moments later he rang the bell at Botham Lodge. The door was opened by the old butler, Buckley.

"I've called upon Miss Emilia concerning a matter of the greatest import," Cuff said sotto voce.

"I am afraid the mistress is resting," came the response.

Cuff smiled and leaning forward touched the old retainer's arm. "Come on Buckley, it's me, Cuff, not some stranger calling out of the blue. Did you hear what I said? 'A matter of the greatest import.' Private and serious. In those circumstances, you shouldn't be preventing me from seeing your mistress, should you?"

Buckley failed to hide his discomfiture, his features clearly mirroring his indecision. Cuff stared past the butler into the gloom of the house and caught sight of a dark figure skulking at the far end of the hallway. It was Albert Dawson who, aware that he had been observed, disappeared quickly into the shadows.

"You place me in a difficult situation, Mr Cuff," said Buckley, at length. "Stand in the hall, please, and I will relay your sentiments to my mistress."

Cuff gave the old retainer a warm nod of thanks and did as he was requested, closing the door behind him.

The butler returned some minutes later with the announcement that, "Miss Barrett has agreed to see you."

Cuff was shown into the sitting room where Emilia Barrett was reclining on a chaise longue by the window. He was once again reminded how plain a girl she was. Her features, tending towards the plump, were bland in the extreme with small eyes and a nose that seemed too small for her face. She made a movement as though to rise but seemed to think better of it.

"Mr Cuff or rather Sergeant Cuff as we all think of you, how nice to see you."

"The feeling is mutual, Miss Barrett. I hope I don't disturb you."

"Of course not. Do take a seat."

Rather than sit on the large sofa facing the girl, Cuff dragged a chair up towards the chaise longue.

"I know this is a sad time for you. Losing your father . . ."

Emilia Barrett put her hand to her mouth and stifled a little sob. Cuff noticed the dark blemishes – bruises, indeed – that mottled her wrist. "Yes," she said, tearily. "Sad and strange. To be honest I have a mixture of emotions coursing through me at present. To lose my beloved father and yet gain the love of my life in the same period . . ."

Cuff's apparent lack of comprehension prompted the girl to explain further.

"Mr Dawson and I are to be married in a few days' time. He was a dear friend before my father's unfortunate accident, but he has been such a great support to me since and we have grown very close."

Cuff tried hard to conceal his surprise at this news. "I . . . I am most happy for you, my dear."

"Thank you. This house needs a master as well as a mistress and Mr Dawson will make an excellent job of managing our domestic affairs. Fortunately my father has left me comfortably off."

Cuff nodded, but made no comment.

Miss Barrett turned her gaze on her visitor. It was sharp and piercing. "And so what is the purpose of your visit, Sergeant Cuff?"

"Just to enquire after your health, my dear. What with your father's passing and . . ."

"And?" The voice rose in tone and hardened.

"Well, poor Annie Lincoln told me that she had seen you in the village and you . . . you looked far from well."

"Oh, that old busybody. I am as well as can be expected. I am in mourning of course and that certainly affects one's pallor and demeanour."

"Of course. I called only out of neighbourly concern. Just to be sure that you are . . . safe."

Miss Barrett looked at Cuff for a moment. "Safe," she murmured and then forced a smile. "Of course. I assure you there is no need for concern." She rearranged her dress awkwardly and then turned her attention to the window through which she could glimpse the garden. It was an act of dismissal. Cuff acted upon it. He rose, replaced the chair and backed towards the door.

"I'll take up no more of your time," he said. "I am pleased to see you are bearing up nicely. And . . . er . . . congratulations on the forthcoming nuptials."

"Thank you," she replied softly, still viewing the garden.

Cuff made his way down the hall but stopped outside one of the rooms where the door was slightly ajar. He heard a movement within. He knew he had to enter. Such instincts always guided him.

The room was a small library and he discovered a young man sitting in a leather armchair holding a large glass of whisky to his lips. It was Albert Dawson.

"Oh, I am sorry to disturb you. I thought I would find Buckley in here."

Dawson peered at him. The watery, bleary eyes clearly indicated that the man was drunk.

"He's not here. Who are you?"

"Just one of the villagers paying a visit on Miss Barrett."

"Good for you."

"I believe congratulations are in order."

Dawson's brow puckered. "What?"

"Your forthcoming marriage."

"Oh, that. Yes. Hooray for the nuptials, what?"

"I am sure you will be very happy."

Dawson gave a strange laugh which was tinged with bitterness. "Do you? Well, cheers then." He took a drink before turning away.

Cuff left him and made his way home, his mind awhirl with conflicting thoughts.

That evening, Cuff and Holmes dined at the old policeman's cottage on rabbit pie and cider while they each related their adventures of the day, piecing together what evidence they had gleaned.

"Well," said Cuff after the plates had been scraped clean and he sat back by the fire with his old clay pipe, "I am more convinced than ever that there is some strange game afoot."

"Indeed, no doubt about that," flashed Holmes eagerly, consulting his notebook in which he had jotted down all the relevant details concerning the case. "As I see it, we have two mysterious deaths: Annie Lincoln and Judge Barrett. The strange behaviour of Barrett's daughter and her fiancé help to suggest that his death is as suspect as the old woman's. We know that Dawson is a thief and now has no income. It would be very fortuitous for him to marry the heiress to Barrett's fortune."

Cuff nodded in agreement. "Once the judge was out of the way."

"A gentle push."

"Indeed. Dawson obviously found it easy to woo such a plain girl as Emilia. Probably done so he can get his hand on her inheritance."

"That theory fits the facts, certainly," said Holmes thoughtfully. "But you've stated that Emilia is far from being a shrinking violet. Could she be coerced into agreeing such a plan?"

"Not coerced, Master Sherlock, but threatened. Remember the bruises."

Holmes pursed his lips and nodded. Cuff could see that the youth was not quite convinced by this theory. "Whatever happened, Annie Lincoln may have suspected the truth and paid with her life."

Cuff puffed on his pipe and nodded.

"We need to know more about Judge Barrett's death," said Holmes at length.

"You are right. We require more data. We cannot make bricks without clay. Let's ponder on this further and make plans on the morrow. And now," he scooped his pocket watch from out of his waistcoat pocket and scrutinized the face, "you'd best be off or your aunt will wonder what on earth has happened to you. Call round at nine in the morning."

Reluctantly Sherlock Holmes took his leave of his new friend.

It was a warm moonlit night and as Holmes reached the crossroads at the far end of the village, instead of turning right on to the road home, on impulse he turned left and made his way towards Botham Lodge. All the disparate facts of this mystery were floating about in his brain and he focused on both the practical sides of the investigation, while allowing his imagination to provide bridges between them. Gradually he built up a very convincing picture of what he believed had actually happened, one that did not quite tie in with Cuff's theory. Dawson's character was the key and this bothered him. Cuff's encounter with the fellow at the Lodge and that clerk's assessment of Dawson as "a spineless cowardly mouse" failed to fit Cuff's assessment of this case. Holmes now believed that he saw the matter more clearly. His face grew taut with excitement and he quickened his pace. All he needed was some further clear evidence to support his assumptions. "No," he murmured, correcting himself. "They are not assumptions; they are deductions." He grinned broadly at his use of the word.

He made his way up the driveway of the Lodge, taking care to keep close to the foliage at the side and in the shadows in case he was seen. He passed the gate to the walled rose garden, and as he rounded the bend, the great house loomed up, a dark silhouette against the starlit sky. There were several lighted rooms downstairs, including one with a large bow window that overlooked the lawned garden. He crept closer to this, crouching down as he did so. Cautiously he peered over the lip of the windowsill into the room. It was occupied by two people whom Holmes judged to be Emilia Barrett and Arthur Dawson. What he witnessed made his heart beat faster and his eyes sparkle with excitement. It confirmed that he had been right.

He turned to go but froze as he heard a noise in the shrubbery nearby. Was it a nocturnal animal? he wondered. The answer to his question came in the form of a blow to the head. Darkness flooded his senses and he collapsed to the ground.

When Sherlock Holmes woke, with a thundering headache, he found himself lying on the floor of a small attic room where the glimmer of dawn could be observed faintly through a small dusty window high above him. As his mind shook off the torpor of unconsciousness, he realized that his hands were tied behind him by a thin, coarse rope. With some effort he managed to pull himself to his feet, his head spinning slightly with the effort. Unfortunately, the window was too high for him to peer out of and even if he could have tried to open the door, he was certain that it would be locked.

He was a prisoner.

What on earth was going to happen next, he asked himself.

The answer came quickly. He heard footsteps outside the room and the key turning in the lock. The door opened slowly to reveal Albert Dawson.

"Hello, old chap," he said softly. "I'm glad to see you're awake. I've brought you some water." He held out a glass.

"I am afraid I am somewhat encumbered," said Holmes, turning round and raising his bound hands.

"Of course. So sorry." Placing the glass of water on the floor, Dawson proceeded to untie Holmes. He had just managed to loosen the bonds when Emilia Barrett appeared in the doorway behind them. She was carrying a pistol.

"What on earth do you think you are doing, Albert?"

"Letting the boy free. This thing has gone too far, Emilia. You cannot go on harming people to satisfy your desires."

The woman's eyes widened. "I can do whatever I want," she snapped, her face flushing with anger. "As well you know it. Don't think you can start taking the law into your own hands now." She turned her attention to Holmes, with an expression of malice. "It seems we have another busybody like old Annie Lincoln here. Poking and prying into other people's affairs. He will have to learn her lesson that snooping is bad for the health."

"He's only a young boy."

"But a dangerous one, eh, Miss Barrett?" said Holmes, dropping the ropes that bound his wrists to the floor. "One who knows the truth."

She sneered and gave a little laugh. "And what is the truth?"

"That you murdered your father to get your hands on his fortune, and then Annie Lincoln when you realized she suspected the truth. You bullied Mr Dawson here into going along with your plans, promising him half the fortune that would become yours on your father's death as long as he married you. You were desperate for a husband. You saw your youth slipping away and there were no respectable suitors on the horizon. Dawson was desperate for money and so he complied."

"A very nice fairy story. I don't know where you get your ideas from."

"Annie saw your bruises and thought at first it was Mr Dawson who was ill-treating you. But then she must have observed your treatment of him and put two and two together."

"To what end?"

"You are the violent one, not Mr Dawson here. You gained those bruises as you fought with your father at the top of the staircase when you managed to push him all the way down, breaking his neck."

"Clever little fellow, aren't you?"

"You learned that Annie had worked this out, too, so she had to be silenced."

Emilia nodded. "Just like I'm going to silence you." There was madness in her features now as she raised the pistol and aimed it at Holmes.

"No, no. You cannot do this, Emilia," Dawson cried, stepping forward to shield Holmes.

"You fool, stand aside."

Dawson shook his head. "Not this time. All too often I've bowed to your demands and let you have your cruel way. I will not let you kill this young boy."

He rushed forward and made a grab for the pistol. His hand fell on Emilia Barrett's wrist and the gun went off, the bullet embedding itself into the wooden floorboard with a dull thud.

"Get away from me, you fool," cried Emilia as Dawson struggled with her. The pistol went off again and both figures froze. They remained immobile for a few seconds and then with a groan, Emilia Barrett fell to the floor, a bright crimson mark staining the front of her dress. While Dawson gaped in horror, Holmes knelt down and cradled the girl's head with one hand and felt for her pulse with another. He could not find one.

"Oh, my God!" cried Dawson. "Is she dead?"

"Yes, I fear so," said Holmes.

Dawson dropped to his knees and began sobbing. "What have I done? What have I done?"

Holmes observed another figure standing on the threshold of the room. It was Buckley the butler. His eyes wide with horror on seeing the grim tableau inside.

"I think you'd better let me go now and inform the police," said Holmes firmly, approaching the butler.

Buckley opened his mouth to speak but for some time shock robbed him of speech. Eventually, he was able to nod his head. It was clear to the young sleuth that Buckley was another fragile pawn in Emilia Barrett's game. It must have been Buckley who had hit him over the head last night.

Holmes hurried from the room and within minutes he was flying down the drive of Botham Lodge. As he reached the gateway, he almost collided with Cuff.

"Ah, there you are," cried the old policeman. "I've had your aunt on my doorstep early this morning wondering where the heavens you were after not getting back last night. She's been terribly worried about you. I might have known you'd be snooping up at the Lodge."

"There's been a tragedy," cried Holmes, almost out of breath. "We need to get the police."

"I think after all your efforts, you deserve a taste of real ale rather than tame lemonade," chuckled Cuff as he placed a pint pot on the kitchen table in his old cottage. It was late afternoon and the sun was streaming through the tiny windows of the cottage. Dust motes danced merrily in the fierce beams.

Sherlock Holmes smiled but then looked apprehensively at the foaming beer.

"Come on lad, get some down you. You've a tale to tell."

Holmes took a drink and smiled.

"You saw more than I did," confessed Cuff. "I want to know how you reached your conclusions.

"Well," said Holmes, after a brief pause, as he assembled his thoughts, "we both believed that there was dark mischief afoot and that Annie Lincoln had been drowned because she had discovered that Judge Barrett had been murdered. It certainly looked like handsome Albert Dawson had agreed to marry plain Emilia, the judge's daughter, on the proviso that he could share the judge's fortune."

Cuff nodded. "Agreed. And that fortune would only be available once the judge was dead."

"And so he was killed. And it would seem obvious that Dawson would be the perpetrator of that deed. But certain things troubled me about that conclusion. I remembered what the clerk at Gammidge and Brown called him: "a spineless, cowardly mouse". A mouse, note you. He wasn't even elevated to status of a rat. Just a feeble, skulking timid creature. You also related how Dawson seemed an ineffectual drunk. Certainly he needed money and saw an easy way to get it through marriage to Emilia, but had he the brains to plan such a deed and the courage to carry it out? I thought not. When I went up to Botham Lodge last night and looked through the window, I had the proof I needed."

Cuff leaned forward eagerly in anticipation but said nothing.

"I saw Emilia standing over Dawson berating him about something, and at one point in her tirade she hit him across the face. He cowered under her attack. The man was obviously dominated by her."

"He was her puppet."

"Exactly. She was the strong one. The one who pushed old Annie Lincoln into the village pond. After all, Emilia, a long-time resident, would know all about Annie's prying ways. Probably the wily old bird had seen Emilia bossing Dawson or even ill-treating him and put two and two together."

"And the bruises on Emilia's wrists?"

"No doubt they were the result of her frantic struggle when she grappled with her father on the top of the stairs before she managed to push him to his death."

"The heartless creature."

"Indeed, she was. She ruled that household, make no mistake about it. Even Buckley was in her thrall. When he knocked me out – thinking I was an intruder – she decided that I must die also."

"The woman was mad."

Holmes nodded. "I think she was. How she hoped to explain my death . . . It was my imprisonment that was the last straw for Dawson. I think he was about to allow me to escape."

"Well, Emilia Barrett met her just desserts in the same violent manner as she dealt it out to others. And the law will deal with Albert Dawson and Buckley. They may have been reluctant associates but they were in effect accomplices to murder and they must pay the penalty."

Holmes took another gulp of ale. He found he rather liked it. "Five lives ruined because of one woman's desire for a husband and wealth."

Cuff flashed his young companion a bitter smile. "You've learned a valuable lesson, Master Sherlock: human nature can be cruel, dark and corrupt. You'll find that more and more as you pursue your detective career."

Holmes beamed. "So you think I have the makings of a good sleuth."

"I do indeed. You were able discover why poor old Annie Lincoln was murdered, to discover the secret of the dead and solve the case with a flourish. I raise my pot in a toast to you. Here's to Sherlock Holmes, master detective."

They both laughed before draining their drinks.

Cuff walked his new young friend to the garden gate as dusk was falling.

"You love your garden, don't you?" said Holmes softly.

"I do. I shall be glad to get back to it. I reckon this will be my last investigation. I'm happy to turn my thoughts and attention to my beloved roses. They are special, y'know. Our highest assurance of the goodness of Providence seems to rest in the flowers. All other things, our powers, our desires, our food, are really necessary for our existence. But a rose, a beautiful rose, is an extra. Its smell, its colour are an embellishment of life, not a condition of it. It is only goodness that gives extras, and so I say we have much to hope from the flowers. Remember that."

"I will," said Sherlock Holmes, shaking the old man's hand.

No Short Cuts

Howard Linskey

My feet were on the ledge. I couldn't move, my arms were pinned behind my back, held fast, no point even struggling. One push and I'd be over the edge, a dead man for certain. I could hear Tatty next to me and he was sobbing uncontrollably, shitting himself; we all were. There were four of us in our crew and right then we were all as helpless as each other, praying that this lot wanted to talk about what we'd done to them, to give us the chance to make amends. I didn't want to think about the alternatives because I couldn't see any way out of this now but down; about 200 feet on to rock-hard concrete. And all I could hear in my mind were my dad's words, over and over again, "There are no short cuts, son."

I felt the hand on my back and suddenly I was pitched forward and I screamed, as the ground seemed to lurch up towards me, but the big bastard behind me pulled me back by my belt at the last moment, then he actually laughed at me. He was just shitting me up; this time.

The soles of my trainers skidded on the metal top of the ledge and he had to support me or I'd have gone over. The fear was like nothing I'd ever experienced. I was powerless, on the wrong side of the metal barrier put there to prevent people from accidentally falling off the top floor of the high-rise. Terrified, I tried to catch my breath, then a big, booming, horribly familiar Geordie voice told us, "I don't want any of you to be under any illusions lads. You're all going off this roof."

* * *

The last time the four of us were all together, we'd been in the pub, happy as pigs in shit, listening to Carey spouting off about Kevin Keegan and his complete lack of managerial credentials, "I'm telling you man," he reminded us between sips of his pint, "the world's gone daft. He has never managed anyone before. The man's spent the last eight years on a golf course in fucking Malaga and now everyone's acting like he's bound to be a success. It's all bollocks. He was a great player but so was Ardiles and look what a disaster he was as manager."

Carey had a point. Since Kevin Keegan was made manager of Newcastle United a few weeks back, the world had indeed gone daft, our corner of it at least, and Carey was probably adding a bit of much-needed realism to dampen the euphoria, but I hoped he was wrong for once.

Carey was undoubtedly our leader. He was older than us, a man of twenty-three, could pass for twenty-five maybe thanks to the coarse stubble on his chin and his short, buzz-cut hair, and he's been about has Carey. He's seen stuff, knows people, considers himself a bit of a player and I didn't think he was bullshitting all that much. Not after the stunt we all just pulled together. It was like something out of a film, honest it was, and it was all his idea, all down to Carey. He takes the credit; 100 fucking per cent. We were still buzzing with adrenalin. You see we were the boys who'd only just gone and ripped off Bobby Mahoney; the man who runs . . . fuck that . . . the man who *owns* Newcastle.

"Everything all right?" I asked Carey as soon as he arrived that night.

"Kula Shaker," he told me, looking cucumber cool, and I was bloody relieved. It was three days since we burst into that bookies with two sawn-off shotguns, an ancient Webley revolver that used to belong to Carey's granddad and a base-ball bat. We marched out of there a few minutes later with a little over twelve grand in cold, hard untraceable cash and knew we'd arrived. We were in the big league.

Three pints later and Carey had warmed to his subject. "Bobby Mahoney is like Ardiles," he told us firmly, "finished in this city. I mean, he's in his forties man." And we lapped up every word.

"What does that make you like? Kevin Keegan?" Tatty was giggling like a little girl with a crush on Carey. There's some hero worship going on there because Tatty, aka Andy Tate, is only eighteen and he doesn't understand the meaning of playing it cool. Clarkey and me, well we're just that bit older, we've seen a bit more than Tatty, so we know to disguise our admiration for Carey. Don't want anyone thinking we're a bunch of benders.

"So what's our next move?" asked Clarkey, trying to sound like the veteran gangster he wanted to be.

"I'm on it," Carey assured him while dragging on a cigarette, "I've set up a meet."

"Who with?" I asked him.

"Anderson," he told me, without giving us any more, and I got the impression he wanted me to ask, "Who?" so of course I didn't. Clarkey did it for me, though, and Carey told us, "Only the biggest face in Liverpool. He's well connected. Heard a whisper about us and called me up; wants to put a bit of business our way."

That night we had a cracking time. One of those evenings when you just know the world can't touch you cos absolutely every-fucking-thing is going to plan. Somehow, I even found the balls to flirt with the lass behind the bar, who I would normally see as seriously out of my league but maybe Carey's ambition is beginning to rub off on me. She was blonde and as fit as fuck, older than me too, at least twenty-four I reckoned, and I asked her, cool as you like, if she fancied going out one night, "Maybe to the pub or the pictures or something."

"Maybe," she smiled at my cheek, "I fancy seeing that new one with Sharon Stone."

"*Basic Instinct*?" I asked her, trying not to look too bloody excited.

"That's the one," she said, and I gave her my best crooked smile like that was cool with me, but inwardly I was wondering, because I never would have had the nerve to suggest we went to see a film like that together.

"Fuck me," said Clarkey afterwards as we walked home, "doesn't she get her fanny out?"

"The barmaid?" asked Tatty excitedly.

"Not the barmaid," said Clarkey, cuffing Tatty around the head with the palm of his hand, "Sharon fucking Stone."

"I don't know," added Carey, "she might."

"Might what?" asked Clarkey.

"Get her fanny out," said Carey with a grin, "the barmaid; if he asks her nicely." And he winked at me and, just for a moment, I felt like the cock of the north.

It was cold and windy on the afternoon of our meet with Anderson, like it always seems to be in Newcastle. We drove up there in Tatty's knackered old Vauxhall Chevette. It was a purple car with a green bonnet and he was desperate to trade it in for something better, but Carey wouldn't let him spend any of our stash because it would draw attention to us all. "And that's a big fucking no-no in this game," he'd warned us. He'd put all our money in a safe place and we didn't question it at all. I didn't question any of it, in fact; why Anderson was calling us up for a meet, why it was happening on the roof of an empty, dilapidated high-rise that'd been condemned by the council and just what work a Scouse gangster was planning to put our way in Newcastle. I was happy to leave the thinking to Carey, mastermind of our big heist down at Bobby Mahoney's bookies. Carey had inside information on that one. He knew Mahoney used the bookies to launder some of his cash and he didn't see why we shouldn't just smash our way in there and take it all.

We walked up hundreds of stairs because the lifts were out then stepped breathlessly on to the roof of the high-rise. I didn't even see the blow coming. I just got a monumental smack around the head from something heavy and fell face first on to a hard surface. By the time I came to my senses I had already been picked off my feet by someone much bigger and stronger than me. He effortlessly pinned my hands behind my back and frogmarched me to the edge of the building, then lifted me over the railings like a child. I screamed because I reckoned I was going straight over, but at the last moment he stopped and I desperately scrambled with my feet until my trainers finally got some traction on the slippery ledge. I couldn't move, though. Carey, Clarkey and Tatty got exactly the same treatment; each one of us trapped on the ledge, held by blokes much bigger than us; proper big-time gangsters.

"It was the Webley that gave you away," Bobby Mahoney told us, right after warning that he was going to chuck us all off the roof. I knew it was Mahoney, even though he was behind me. Everyone from our neck of the woods knew the man. He was a legend in our city and right then he didn't sound as if he was finished. "You don't see too many of them around these days. I made a couple of enquiries and someone whispered your names in my ear."

The man holding on to me spoke then. "Why are we wasting valuable drinking time on these little queers?" he asked. "Let's just chuck 'em over." He sounded serious and Tatty squealed in protest. They'd chosen the right location. The whole estate had been condemned, so there was nobody around to see us fall and the wind was blowing about us, so you wouldn't even hear us scream on the way down.

"Let us go," demanded Carey, "or you'll be fucking sorry." But he didn't sound too confident about that.

"Careful Jerry," warned Bobby, and I realized the psychopath holding on to me must have been Jerry Lemon, one of Bobby's main men. "I hear these lads are protected. A little bird told me they were connected to that Scouse hard-nut Anderson." And Jerry Lemon just chuckled.

"You'd better fucking believe it," said Carey, "you don't want to go to war with Anderson and we are well in there."

"Really? Are you Anderson's best little boys then?" asked Mahoney, but he didn't sound convinced. "What's he promised you, eh?"

"We work for him now, exclusively," Carey was blagging, like he was bluffing at poker with a really crap hand. "We're protected. No one can fuck with us without him straightening them out."

"Oh, I see," said Mahoney, "well I'm quaking in my boots. I can just imagine Anderson telling you that, can't you Jerry? I wonder how he sounded when he said it."

"Ooh I don't know Bobby," answered Lemon, "maybe he sounded a bit like this, 'Alrigh' La', I hear you're da guy who stood up to Bobby Mahoney, what a fucking Billy Big Bollocks you must be eh? You should work for me son, if you want to earn some real money dat is.'"

I listened to Jerry's comedy Scouse accent, which sounded like he was a bad London actor playing a bit part on *Brookie,* but I was looking at Carey, whose head had slumped, his eyes screwed tight shut, and he looked like he was about to cry like a bairn, and I realized the stupid, dumb bastard's been had. It was Jerry Lemon who phoned up Carey offering him work, not Anderson, getting him to admit he's the man who ripped off Bobby's bookies then luring him into a trap up on the roof of a derelict high-rise. I can't believe the leader of our crew could have been that stupid. All at once, I realized the only man on this roof who was dumber than Carey was me, for following him up here. All I wanted now was to go home and lock my door, climb into bed, pull the duvet over my head and never go out again. My dad warned me when he heard I was hanging around in a gang. "There are no short cuts son," he told me. He meant I should settle down, get a shit job like his and be a *normal person* as he called it. I thought that was crap advice at the time, but now it's all I keep thinking about.

Bobby confirmed my new view of Carey. "Not the sharpest knife in the drawer, are we son?"

"Fuck off," snapped Carey, but there wasn't much conviction behind it. Bobby took immediate offence.

"Tell me to fuck off again and see what Finney does to you," he told Carey. Finney, who was one of the biggest blokes

I had ever seen in my life, gave Carey a shake and put the shits up him proper. Carey fell silent, which was the only smart thing he had done this week.

"Now you are going to tell me where my money is. Otherwise it's a quick shove and a long goodbye for all of you."

"I'm saying nowt," Carey replied, and I couldn't believe what I was hearing. I was thinking our only chance of avoiding being thrown off this building, to our certain deaths, was to tell Bobby Mahoney where his money was, get it back to him very quickly and beg him to let us off with just a serious beating for offending him. Even then I reckoned our chances were somewhere between slim and nil. Not telling him was insane.

Before Bobby Mahoney could reply, I shouted, "Tell him, Carey, for fuck's sake!"

"Fucking shut up!" Carey screamed at me. "Tell him and he has no reason to let us go."

Surprisingly Bobby Mahoney stayed calm, "I can see your dilemma, lads. Young Carey here is right. If you tell me where my money is I might order my boys to throw you all off the ledge. Then again, if you don't tell me, I *will* order my boys to chuck you over."

"Then you'll never see your money," warned Carey.

"True," admitted Mahoney, "but then this isn't really about the money, son. I have enough money. You taking me for a few grand is like you losing fifty quid out of your wallet on a Saturday night. I mean it's annoying but, in the grand scheme of things, it doesn't matter shit. No," he continued, "the most important thing is ensuring that other cocky little cunts like you think twice before they try and steal from me, which means making an example of you lot now doesn't it?"

None of us said a word. None of us had the courage to speak. Mahoney waited patiently.

Eventually he said, all matter of fact, "I don't think these boys are taking us seriously enough." There was another long pause and, out of the corner of my eye I watched Mahoney take a look at us all, one by one, as if he was weighing us up. Then his eyes rested on Clarkey, who hadn't said a word up to now, and he nodded at the other enormous bloke who was holding my friend and said, "Joe."

I'd seen Joe Kinane around town. He made the bouncers on pub doors look tiny by comparison to his bulk. He straightened and let go of Clarkey who automatically brought his free hands out from behind his back. Clarkey frowned his incomprehension but soon learned why he had been released. Kinane gave him a push and he shot forward. My old school mate went face first off the building, flailing his arms out to his sides, desperately trying to grab something, anything, to save him but he was too far out for that and all he had left to claw at on the way down was air. He seemed to fall so slowly. He didn't scream but instead just carried on pedalling his arms against the cold air, all the way down, right up to the end until finally he hit the concrete with a sickening sound like fruit being thrown against a wall.

"Oh God! Oh God!" Tatty was sobbing and gasping. Carey was repeating the same thing over and over again; just saying "Fuck . . . fuck . . . fuck."

Me? I couldn't say anything. I was too terrified to utter a word. I just stood there on the ledge with my mouth open, looking down at Clarkey's smashed body, expecting him to climb to his feet in a moment and run off like it's all been a big joke. But he didn't. I was trying to get my head round the fact that my friend was actually dead, properly gone and wasn't ever coming back.

"Who's next?" asked Bobby Mahoney.

"Don't!" I found a voice from somewhere but I didn't sound like myself anymore. I sounded like the little boy I had suddenly reverted to. "We'll tell you where the money is."

"Shut up!" ordered Carey, but he stopped being the leader of our crew when one of us went off the side of a building. "Don't tell him!"

I couldn't see how not telling Bobby would save him but I think I understood why he was desperate to keep me quiet. Mahoney undoubtedly knew he was the leader of our crew and likely to face most of the older man's fury, but I didn't care about that now. I'd forgotten all of that bollocks about friendship and brotherhood. All I cared about was saving my own life.

Carey was shouting at me. He was louder than me and Bobby was frowning like he was hard of hearing and couldn't make out what I was saying.

"Shut up," he said quietly and we both stopped. "We'll get to the money. First I want to know who hit her."

And I stared at Bobby Mahoney like I had no idea what he was talking about, because I *had* no idea what he was talking about. "The girl," he prompted me, "the girl behind the counter, twenty she is, and one of you cunts hit her in the face with a gun, broke her nose and knocked her teeth out, messed her up proper, ruined her looks, because she wasn't quick enough filling one of your bags with my money. So," he took a breath, "who did it?" Then he turned his attention to me. "You," he said, "tell me. Tell me now."

I opened my mouth but the words wouldn't come out. Bobby looked impatient. "Was it him?" and he nodded at Carey. I glanced at Carey too and he had a desperate look on his face like he knew what was coming and couldn't do anything to prevent it but was still praying for a different outcome. I'd seen Carey go behind the counter while we kept the punters covered with the shotguns, but I hadn't seen him hit the girl and he certainly didn't tell us anything about it afterwards. I couldn't believe he had done that. Not to a young lass.

I caught Carey's eye then I turned to Bobby Mahoney and nodded. Mahoney glanced over at Finney and nodded too like he was getting no pleasure out of this but it was just something he had to do. Carey looked right at me as Kinane pushed him off the building. This time I closed my eyes because I didn't want to watch him fall. I waited for what felt like an age before I opened them again and glanced over the edge and there was Carey's body smashed up and twisted on the ground way below us. When I saw Carey go off the edge of the building I felt sick but I couldn't help wondering, praying in fact, if

Bobby Mahoney would be happy now. After all, this was Carey's idea, all down to him. You could say it was his fault I was standing there, soiling myself and pleading for my life.

"Now then, ladies, that just leaves the two of you," said Mahoney. "Since I'm in a good mood today I'm going to be extra generous. I'm going to let one of you live." Tatty started sobbing again but I was concentrating hard because I believed Bobby Mahoney was telling the truth. He would let one of us live and I was damn certain it was going to be me.

"Whoever tells me where the money is will walk away from here."

"I don't know where the money is!" screamed Tatty, "I don't know where it is! I don't!"

Bobby looked at Tatty dispassionately and said, "I believe you, son." Then he nodded at the bloke holding him. "No!" screamed Tatty desperately, but he was already being pushed over the edge and I could see his terrified eyes as he was pitched over the side. His scream was high-pitched like a little girl's and it got quieter but somehow more shrill as he fell, only finally silenced when his body hit the edge of a skip and bounced off, landing hard on the ground next to it. He didn't move.

Bobby looked at me. "It's in a lock up," I told him quickly, "in black plastic bags in a garage on the Sunnydale estate, number 37. It's got a green door and a padlock on it but you could break it off easy. Carey had the key."

Bobby looked at me for a minute that stretched out in front of me. Then he said, "All right, son," before adding, "A deal's a deal. We'll let you walk." And I couldn't tell you how sweet those words sounded or how relieved I was to be walking away from this nightmare. I swore I would never do anything stupid or dangerous again. I knew right then and for sure that I'd do exactly what my dad told me to do. I'd get a job, marry a nice girl, have kids and never cross any one like Bobby Mahoney as long as I lived. I'd just disappear forever.

Jerry Lemon let go of my hands and I straightened but almost fell off the edge. I desperately regained my balance and

I was about to step slowly and carefully back down and away from the edge when Lemon said, "Course we will." But he said it in a nasty, sarcastic way and straightaway I knew what was coming next. I felt a shove in my back and I was pushed out into thin air.

As I fell, I didn't even bother to flail my arms or scream because I knew there was nothing I could do to save myself. My life did not flash before me but I did see that barmaid's face as I closed my eyes tight so I didn't have to watch it happen, and I remembered my dad's words again, "No short cuts, son."

"What the fuck did you do that for?" demanded Bobby.

"What?" asked Jerry Lemon. "I thought you was joking."

"Joking?" Bobby Mahoney was furious. "I don't joke, Jerry. I gave that lad my word, told him he could walk and you just shoved him over the edge? Fuck you think you're playing at, man?"

"He was a witness to three fucking murders and we were all in the frame for them," Jerry was defiant. "He had to go."

"You won't hear any argument from me," said Joe Kinane.

"Who asked for your opinion?" snapped Bobby and he turned back to Jerry, "I gave him my word. That might mean fuck all to you, you simple cunt, but it means something to me." And he bared his teeth at Jerry.

Jerry Lemon finally realized the trouble he was in. "I'm sorry Bobby. I didn't mean to . . . I never thought . . . I just figured."

"Don't think, don't figure, leave that to me. Just do what you are fucking told in future!"

Jerry nodded like a simpleton. "Yeah, yeah, course, sorry Bobby. Hey, it won't happen again. I promise."

"It had better fucking not," said Bobby, and he seemed to calm down, then he jabbed a finger at Jerry Lemon, "but you're buying the beers tonight, and I do mean all night."

Kinane and Finney both laughed at Lemon then.

"Fucking hell, that's a bit harsh Bobby," said Lemon, "the way these cunts put it away." He jerked his head at Finney and Kinane but Bobby silenced him with a look.

"Very generous of you, Jerry," said Kinane. "Think I might have a few of the top shelf tonight, since you're paying."

"Aye," added Finney, "let's go from one side of the optics all the way across the bar to the other."

"That's settled then, Jerry," confirmed Bobby, "tonight's on you," and his eyes took on a mischievous sparkle because to him the punishment had begun to fit the crime.

"You're a chiselling bunch of bastards, the lot of you," said Lemon. Then he glanced over the edge of the building. "That last little bastard just cost me big time. I hope he's happy."

"Yeah," said Kinane, "he's looking down from his cloud right now Jerry and he's laughing his little cock off at you."

They all laughed as well. Except Jerry Lemon. "Ha-fuck-ing-ha," he said.

Lullaby

Susan Everett

There is a man outside in a blue car. He is trying to steal my baby. I first noticed him three days ago, when he parked, sat, waited, and then calmly drove away. I knew that he'd come back. I recognized his face.

I am not being paranoid, though I may be quite hormonal. I wonder how he tracked down my address.

The doorbell rings.

Angry.

Abrupt.

Accusing.

I feel my throat tighten. I pad slowly down the wooden floorboards to the door. Part of me wants it to be him.

I must be free of him. We must be free of him.

The door to number 47 opened a fraction when the postman arrived with a parcel. Her face was blocked, but he could see the curve of her hand on the doorframe. He could not make out if she was wearing a wedding ring.

The door closed and the postman walked away. Ian started to hum an old song by the Carpenters, but it clashed with the sounds of his FM radio and made him feel quite ill. He didn't think that he would ever hear another song that had the power to make him smile. He clicked the stereo off. Silence. Bar the buzz of a passing bike, its metal spokes spinning, reminding him of school days, happy days, sunny days. Not now.

Cars passed by, children ate crisps and dropped the pack-
ets, an untended dog spat a shit out of its arse.

He made a note on his off-white pad.

10.22. Nothing to report.

That didn't seem worth reporting. He made more of an effort.

Occupant in the house.

Occupant?

He pushed the car door open as the postman strode along.

"Excuse me?"

The postie looked back at him, put on his workmanlike
smile.

"D'you know the name of the lady in number 47?"

"Sorry?"

"Number 47?"

The postman chewed his upper lip, contemplating
company policy.

"Sorry mate, I don't know if I should . . ."

"Can you tell me if she's pregnant?"

"Um . . ."

"You've just seen her. Please."

The postman's bag slid off his shoulder as he shrugged.
"Dunno. She were fatter before."

"Is there a baby?"

The postman's boots clicked against the pavement as he
quickly walked away.

"Please! Is there a baby?"

The postmark is from Leicester. I peel off a layer of brown
sticky tape and find another layer beneath. I imagine the
sender sealing it up with extra care. Folding the contents in
her warm, bread-baked hands, one sleeve first, and then the
other. Left over right. Flipping it up to bend the bottom half
into a sandwich made of little legs in the softest terry cloth.

I pull out the romper suit and place it on the table. It is a
paler blue than I remember from the advert, with a navy
anchor on the right side at the front. It looks like a pocket, but
it isn't. I lift it up and smell it, expecting to smell babies, baby

talc, baby sick, baby breaths – but there's just the strong odour of Lenor, mixed with stale air that travelled miles within the bubble wrap.

I cannot tell if this was ever worn. The eBay advert didn't specify, and presumably you'd pay more if it was new, not that I paid much at all.

If it's new, why was the vendor selling? Perhaps an unwanted gift, one of many showered upon her by friends and relatives. Perhaps her baby was so chubby he was too big for it from birth. Perhaps she had a girl, but had bought both blue and pink before she knew the sex. Or perhaps her baby fell asleep and didn't wake. Or died before he took a breath.

It isn't good to think about these things. It isn't good to think.

10.48. Nothing to report.
Apart from he was hungry. He missed his wife's cooking, and even though he used to groan when she scraped leftover meat, veggies and gravy straight into the dogs' bowls without asking if he'd finished, he vowed never to pull a face or sigh again. No more arguments about him coming in second place to her beloved dogs, with their photos and trophies spread around the house, taking over every wall and mantelpiece. The only photo of him was from their wedding day, and the only thing he had ever won was a runner-up prize for sprouts.

He'd left her before – twice. He came back with his tail between his legs. She promised to change, he promised to change, and they carried on the same. But the last time, he had an ultimatum. He knew that the dogs were like her children, but he wanted a human child.

A baby.

A baby boy.

A beloved baby boy.

My baby was born by Caesarean section. Some women opt for these for lifestyle reasons, but with me there was no choice. There would simply be no life.

Years ago, my grandma died in childbirth. The baby sucked the life from her, wedged inside her belly, kicking, kicking, but never getting out. Her husband would not let anybody come into the house. No onc kncw for ovcr a wcck that they were dead in there. Home births are not safe.

People get it wrong about the Caesarean myth. Those women chit-chatting in cosy pre-natal sessions, thinking that Julius Caesar was the first, hence the impressive name, and their own impressive impending child, the future mayor of Bingley, the manager of Leeds United or B & Q. They're all wrong. It wasn't Caesar, but an ancestor of his, who was ripped from his dead mother, and given the nickname as a reward. The lie became the truth.

Caesarean derives from Latin. To kill. To cut.

Caedo.

Caedere.

Cecidi

Caesum.

There are internet sites about it, with photos, explanations. It is good to do research. You can get a practical grasp of the process, its combination of sharp instruments and blunt dissection. It is not for the faint-hearted or the squeamish.

It begins with the multiple layer incision, when the blade cuts through the crust of human skin. Then the uterine incision, slicing into the uterus, sliding through slimy liquid, stopping the point of the blade before nicking the babe himself. This is the danger point, when, unless you suction the amniotic fluids from the baby's mouth, he can quickly drown. His little face, unable to take a breath, like a naked water vole plucked from a sewer.

That's why Caesareans don't work at home. You need the right equipment.

The cries begin as I walk upstairs with the romper suit.

"Ssh. Be quiet."

Scratching against the door. Little paws with claws.

"You're not coming out."

I walk past the spare room door, the whimpering behind

it. I should not have bought a dog. They do not mix with babies.

I push open the door to the nursery; its yellow walls make me feel warmer as I enter the calm space. A waft of air tickles the mobile above the cot, bright birds and butterflies spinning.

Adam is lying on his back, and if his eyes were open he could see red admirals and robins up above him. I read a book that said babies cannot see that far, but I'm not sure I believe it. I'd rather he had something to look at, not just an empty ceiling.

"How's my baby, hey? Are you all right?"

I hang the romper suit over the side of the cot and reach in to lift him out. I know some people think newborn babies wrinkly and ugly, that only a mother can love them. But they are wrong. He is beautiful. His thin, hopeful lips. His eyes, so dark that they are almost black. His bubble of a nose and dimpled chin.

"My boy."

I carry him to the changing table and carefully lay him down. I un-pop the press-studs on his clothing and peel it all away.

"This one will suit you better, don't you think?"

I'm sure that he just smiled.

He likes it. Sailor boy.

11.15. Nothing to report.
Other than that the police should be doing this, not him. He'd told them, his wife would never have gone off and left the dogs. She was eight months pregnant. They looked at him, nodded, said he could put in a missing person's report, but he knew what they were thinking. She has left because you are a loser. Perhaps it's not your child.

"She would not have left the dogs."

When he came home from work five days before, the pugs were barking and twirling their question-mark tails, and Helen wasn't there. She hadn't left a note. It didn't look like any of her clothes were missing, but in truth he couldn't tell. Her car was gone. Her handbag. Her purse. Her mobile, which wasn't on, so he left a garbled message. He imagined that she was at the supermarket, then lost hope when he saw the fridge was full. He rang her friends, her mother. They all told him not to worry. But they were worried now.

He'd been driving around looking for her, even took the dogs for walks, not that they could walk for long, with their legs being so short. That's when he realized that there *was* something missing. He was sure there were five puppies. He only counted four.

I close the nursery door and let Adam rest in peace. I stop outside the spare room, can hear sniffling by my toes.

"You want your mummy? Bet you do."

The first time that I saw Helen McNiece she was in the local newspaper, her smiling face alongside a smug pug. Both of them proudly pregnant, but only one a winner at Crufts. I remember touching my own belly as I looked at them, feeling a nervous kick against my hand.

I'd wondered if this was her first child. If she'd had years of trying.

That monthly dribble of disappointment.

It was easy to track her down, as the newspaper gave the name of where she lived, and there was only one McNiece listed in the phonebook. She said it was lucky that I rang; it gave me the first pick of the litter. She would call me back when they were born. We became quite chatty on the phone, not that I told her anything personal, but we bonded. She emailed me photos of the pups when they arrived, and then, on the big day, we met.

Helen McNiece was blooming as she welcomed me into her home and asked how far along I was. I told her just six months, though in my head it's less than five. She rubbed her own belly in a soft, circular motion, and I copied. Though I'd tried to move my hand in the opposite direction to hers it somehow wasn't possible. She laughed.

I pulled my rubber gloves on in her kitchen as she went to

fetch the pups. I avoided touching door handles and surfaces. I need not have brought a knife with me, her utensil jars were brimming. I felt blood rush to my head as I waited for her return. I had forgotten the rope; I'd left it in the garage. My eyes skirted round the surfaces, but all I could see was a roll of clingfilm and a spaghetti jar. I considered using clingfilm, I could have got behind her, stretched it across her face and started to wrap. Pulled it tight around, again, again, her mouth gulping like a giant carp. Hanging on until the air dripped out of her and she dropped on to the floor.

I flicked my arms behind my back as she returned with an armful of pug pups. She tipped them on to the kitchen lino and they bumped around her ankles, sniffing her shoes, snapping at her laces as she laughed. Their smudged faces rippling with heavy thought lines on their brows.

I could do it now, I plotted, as she leant over, the pups jumping up and snapping at her long hair.

I could move round behind her.

Do it.

As I took a step, the largest pup bounded towards me, yelping. Helen smiled. "I think she's chosen you."

The pup dribbled on my boot. Dark chocolate eyes looked up at me, trusting. I thought I heard a growl, then realized it was a car engine approaching. Tyres crunched along the gravel drive. We had company.

Helen noticed my rubber gloves and gave me a quizzical look. "Urine," I shrugged. "Just in case."

She didn't understand. I felt conspicuous.

"I have allergies." I smiled. She looked relieved, as if I wasn't mad.

Her husband barely glanced at me as he came through the door, mumbling something about work. I patted all the puppies, and made a big show of taking photos on my mobile phone, saying I needed more time to decide. This was a life-changing decision, after all.

She had looked disappointed.

*　　*　　*

11.30. Action needed. About to approach the house.

He had arrived at number 47 through the work of a detective. Not any of those he had spoken to, but something he had once seen on the telly. He'd gently rubbed a pencil over the notepad by the phone, and made out the indentations of the last words his wife had written.

baked beans
coleslaw
worms
47 Atherton Rd

There were two Atherton Roads within a twenty-mile radius, and he had been to both. He'd parked outside, in the hope that his wife would step out of the front door.

He slid from the driver's seat, taking his notebook with him. Snapped the door shut and locked it. Walked towards the house and rang the bell.

Nobody answered so he rang again. He considered going through the little gate at the side of the house and knocking round the back.

The front door opened.

Ian was heavy with disappointment. It wasn't Helen. He had so wanted this to be her, but deep down knew it wouldn't be. He hadn't wanted to ring the bell because he knew that she was lost to him. He'd had that feeling, since the moment he came home to an empty house. That he wouldn't see his wife again, and that he'd never meet his son.

The woman on the doorstep looked uneasy. He tried to explain himself.

"I'm looking for my wife. I wondered if you'd seen her?"

He pulled a photo from his wallet, the one he'd carried with him for eight years.

"Her name's Helen McNiece. She's pregnant. Not in the photo, but now. And she's younger then. But she still looks the same."

The woman's eyes flickered as she took a closer look. Ian stared at her, his eyes stinging. There was something vaguely familiar about her, but he couldn't place it. He guessed that she was older than Helen, who was thirty-five. This woman was at least forty, not that he was an expert on these things. But she was familiar . . . He realized. She looked like a plumper version of that American actress, the one in the film with the boiling rabbit and the knife.

She passed him the photo back.

"I'm sorry. I've not seen her. Why are you asking me?"

"I found your address."

"Oh. I don't know why that would be." She looked like she was considering saying something, but then changed her mind.

They stood in silence for a moment, him not knowing what to say, and her seeming embarrassed.

"Do you want to come in?"

He thought she looked sorry for him.

"I can make you a coffee?"

His mind was buzzing. Scratching. He could hear a distant cry.

His mobile rang.

"Sorry, I'd better . . ." He clicked it open. Listened. His stomach lurched. "Really? You're sure? Yes – that's the number plate. Thanks."

The woman was staring at him. "Your wife?"

"They've found her car. It's in a car park, about ten miles from here."

She sighed.

"Thank you, for your time. I'd better go."

He hurried back to his car and drove away.

I feel pity for that man, McNiece. I get a sense that he would have made a decent dad. Better than my boyfriend Martin. When I rang to tell him I was pregnant, he asked if it was yet another false alarm. If I was lying to him again. There was a quiver in his voice, and I sensed a gleam of hope. I knew he would come back. He told me to ring him when the baby was born, to organize a blood test. I'm not sure what to do.

I think I need a walk, to get some air inside my lungs. I may go to the shops. I am out of everything, apart from jars of

baby food. I hadn't realized you couldn't feed those straightaway. I have eaten several jars myself. I wasn't keen on the steak
and kidney mush, but rather liked the raspberry pudding. I
think Adam would have liked that too.

Helen McNiece had everything prepared. She'd read
books, gone to her classes, bought a breast pump and bottles
to sterilize. She was ready to be a mum.

I phoned her up and said I wanted to buy the smallest
pup. His name was Peregrine Montague the Third, but
went by the name of Monty. I prefer to stick to Dog. I said
I had a transport problem, so I couldn't get across. Helen
offered to drive him over, so I gave her my address. I
assumed she'd be alone, as her husband worked all day. I
had already decided on where to take her car, with an easy
bus route back.

It seemed to go to plan. She arrived, I led her through to the
back room, and she put the puppy into the tartan basket that
I'd bought as a way of showing interest. I had envisioned
making her a cup of tea, but the distraction wasn't needed.
She was so engrossed in the little pup, its punched-in face
making her oooh and aaah, whispering to him that he would
be very happy. That he had a lovely home.

She was kneeling down, her swollen belly almost resting on
her thighs. She put her arm out as I approached, expecting me
to help her up. I focused on her silver necklace as I ran the
knife across her throat. Pushed her head back with my other
hand, and red spurted upwards, hitting my face and spraying
spots into my mouth.

Her wide eyes staring.

The pup yapping.

Yelping.

I had sterilized my instruments.

Caedo. I cut. *Caedere*. To slaughter. *Cecidi*. I slaughtered.

I cut.

I cut.

I cut.

*   *   *

He was waiting at some traffic lights, foot hovering over the accelerator. They'd found her car. Not her. Her car. That was a start.

And then it came to him. The actress was called Glenn Close. That was the exact thought that had popped into his head when he saw the woman in his kitchen. She was a fat Glenn Close.

The light turned green. A car horn pipped behind him.

She had lied. She knew his wife. She had been there in his kitchen.

He had to turn.

He had to go back.

He switched the stereo off as he drove, he wanted to concentrate, and he needed to work out what to say. If Helen was there, why was she there, why had she left?

"Please be there."

Her car was in a car park ten miles away.

"I love you."

As he approached Atherton Road a woman's shape got his attention. It was her again, walking away from the house. He hoped she hadn't seen him. Her head was down, she probably hadn't.

He parked opposite number 47, looked up the street as he crossed the road. Saw the back of the woman's coat as she reached the corner. He flicked the catch on the side gate and walked along the length of the house to the back door. He tested the handle, and was surprised to find it open.

"Helen?"

He stepped inside.

"Are you there?"

He heard a whimper. Scratching.

"Hello?"

He recognized the sound and walked towards it, past a closed door on his left. He peered into the front room. Empty. The whimpering grew louder as he walked upstairs. The scratching became more frantic.

"Helen? It's me."

Ian pushed the door open, to be met by the sight of a hungry pug. He had never been so happy to see a pug before. He scooped him in his arms; felt a fast heart beat against him, echoing his own.

The pink carpet was littered with little shits, spread like slugs across the floor. Ian covered his mouth. Helen wasn't there.

He walked along the upper hallway, past the bathroom, towards a closed door at the end. His stomach flipped when he saw the cot inside, a happy mobile tinkling above it.

The pup was whining. There was no noise in the cot.

Ian felt hot sick rising in his throat as he looked down. He dropped the dog; it scurried out and ran downstairs.

He couldn't tell if the baby was a boy, but guessed so from the outfit. Saw tiny fingers curled together, making fists. The light caught cobwebs of fine blonde hair on his bare head. A fly buzzed round his face, landing on his cheek. His lips were blue, as if painted with a wash of colour. His skin was mottled, his face translucent on one side, but darker on the other.

Another fly flew from the dead baby's mouth.

Ian retched, was sick into his hand.

He couldn't look again, but had to.

He needed to see if the baby looked like him.

Ian slowly walked downstairs, head spinning, almost drunk. The pup was scratching at another door, whining to get in. He knew something was wrong.

The buzz of flies immediately hit him as the door pushed open. The room was filled with them, black snow flying through dank air.

He saw Helen's shoes. Her feet. Her legs. He felt his own give way as he saw the shape of her. It was as though she had exploded. Flaps of skin folded out from where her belly used to be, leaving a cavernous hole inside.

"No. No. No . . ."

Ian closed his eyes, sank his head into his hands, but the image was still there.

"No. No. No."

His knees were stained dark crimson from her blood.

"No. No."

The pup was barking loudly. It had heard the front door open.

"No. No."

Footsteps behind him. He looked up and saw the woman's face. A flash of leather as she pulled a dog lead round his throat. Pulled it tighter. Tighter.

He didn't have the hope to struggle. He could feel hot pressure building in his eyes, and focused on his wife beside him. On that dark gash, like a ruby-coloured scarf across her neck.

The leather pulled harder against his throat, breath squeezing out of him as he tipped backwards to the floor. Looking up at the cream Artex ceiling, covered in a swarm of spots.

Flies.

Black flies.

Black.

There was a man parked outside in a blue car. He is now in the dining room. I am glad that this is over. I can keep my Adam safe. You cannot underestimate a woman's need to love.

My father used to say I was the kind of person who wouldn't get noticed unless I made a fuss. No one ever asks me how I am, or what I'm doing. And I am glad of that.

In a few days' time the clampers will come. They will tow that car away.

Anything Can Happen

Christopher Fowler

Killing someone is no big deal. Did it, got told off, so what?

I was on the number 75 bus coming home from school. It's not a long journey, just six stops through Blackheath, South London. I could have walked. The bus was crowded because I had to get off near a train station, and it was rush hour.

There was an old guy with wispy white hair in a navy-blue raincoat, standing right in front of me. A bunch of small kids behind. The driver opened the doors before the bus had completely come to a stop. The kids behind pushed forward and I was forced into the old man's back. He was thrown off balance, wobbled, missed the step, fell out of the bus and landed face-smack on the pavement. Old bones, really hard, *whappity-crack*.

A London Transport cop saw the whole thing and ran over. I heard her say that the old man was dead. The kids pissed off, leaving me. Some old bag shouted that it was my fault. The LT cop tried to grab me and I started complaining, so she got nasty and I kicked her. Dumb move.

They couldn't question me there because we were blocking the station entrance. The next thing I knew, two more cops had arrived along with an ambulance, and I was chucked against a wall and then bundled into a white van. I looked back through the window and saw the old guy. His nose was pushed all the way in. No blood, which was odd. A medic was lying with his head on the guy's chest. Then we turned a corner and I was taken to Blackheath Police Station to be interviewed.

I was left in a corridor that smelled of chips, sick and disinfectant for two hours while they tried to find my folks. The Amazing Invisible Sister was supposed to be at school, but I knew she had bunked off with some of her single-cell girlfriends to go to the mall.

I asked the desk sergeant for something to read and he looked at me as if I was mad. Cops don't half swear a lot. A policewoman handed me a warm 7 Up and even brought a packet of cheese biscuits. Finally I was taken to a gloomy cream-coloured room with a barred window and asked to write down what had happened.

I talked to a detective sergeant, then my mother turned up. She kept saying things like "I rilly *rilly* don't have time for problems like this in my life right now, Christian." The police let me go home with her, but only after we had both signed a load of paperwork. The policewoman typed with two fingers and didn't know how to work her computer.

I figured I would either be found:

A: Innocent

B: Guilty of Manslaughter (that means unlawfully killing without the intent to kill. It can be Voluntary like getting into a fight, or Involuntary like driving too fast and crashing into someone)

C: Guilty of Second Degree murder (that's death resulting from an assault where you mean to hurt the other person but not kill them)

D: Guilty of First Degree murder (where you deliberately kill someone)

I know about this stuff because my mum's addicted to cop shows.

Come on, I bet you're thinking A. But you don't have all the evidence, because I didn't tell you everything. In fact, I missed out one very important detail.

The old man I knocked off the bus was already dead, but I didn't find out he was dead until later.

That night I watched a really ancient film called *Dawn of the Dead*. My best friend Track brought over the DVD and we ran it in my room (Track had switched the sleeve of the DVD box with a Spiderman film so her dad wouldn't know she'd swiped it).

The movie wasn't scary because it was in old-school muddy-vision and was really cheap and badly acted. It's about what happens when the dead come back to life and are still wandering about looking for people to eat. The living shut themselves in a bunker and spend the whole time arguing with each other, but there was a good bit at the end were the bad guy got torn in half and told the zombies to choke on his innards.

It turned out the story had already started coming true. All over the country, all over the world. It spread very quickly, a thousand times faster than the last avian flu epidemic. I was online right through the whole thing, and the speed was amazing. It was all over the networking sites I visited. You've never seen so much panicky unfriending going on, like they could catch it over the internet.

In films the Deads come out of their graves and stump around in waist-high mist with their arms stretched out like sleepwalkers. And they moved about more slowly than Mr Sangjhavi down the road, who has something wrong with his legs. Even my sister could have outrun them, and she won't even get off the sofa to change TV channels when the cat's asleep on the remote. In a few of the *Living Dead* remakes the Deads shift really fast, but that seems kind of silly because their muscles would actually be all dried up, and they'd have to move slowly. Basic biology, duh.

Compared to the real thing, the Deads in films aren't accurate in other ways. Think about it; when gravediggers bury someone, the coffin is sealed and put in a hole that's packed with earth and stamped flat. So we're talking about a hundred pounds of dirt to push up, assuming that you could get the lid of the box open in the first place, which you wouldn't be able to do. There's not enough depth in most coffins to use your arms as levers and the lid is usually screwed down.

The truth is, nobody came out of the ground. When the Dead came back to life it was only the ones who had died in hospitals and morgues or their own homes who could get up. If any others were lying around above ground, like in funeral parlours, I guess they rose up too. And how could you tell they were Living Dead and not just, you know, someone's gran?

At first there weren't any to see on the streets. When they did finally appear, they didn't walk around with their arms raised like sleepwalkers. Their hands hung limply at their sides and they didn't move about much, although they did sometimes bump into things and fall over. But they weren't funny, like in *Shaun of the Dead*. I've seen every living-dead movie and TV show going now, and I'm kind of an expert. And the main thing is – they were just kind of sad and smelly. The main difference from the films is that they didn't try to eat people's brains. If you think about it logically, how could they? They were Deads, and that means brain dead. They only had the vaguest memory of their old habits, which didn't include eating other people's brains. Eating a brain isn't going to restore your own. That's like saying if you eat part of a cow you'll grow four stomachs. I did see one eating a Pot Noodle, though.

The trouble with the real Deads was that they weren't from horror films. They weren't creepy, just boring. Some of them could do really base-level stuff they remembered from when they were alive, like reading the *Daily Mail*, queuing in WHSmith for a Galaxy bar or humming old songs. Most of them could put their clothes on because that's something you do every day of your life. But you couldn't train them any more than you can train really stupid insects or our biology teacher's dog. You could point up in the air and they would follow your finger but then they'd stay like that for hours, like chickens expecting rain. And it's because they were Deads, end of story. I mean, after you're one of the Deads you don't understand jokes or follow complicated Swedish detective shows on TV, and the only way you can play football is by being one of the goalposts.

My encounter with the dead bus passenger had prepared me for all of this. I'd had first-hand experience of what the Deads were like after they came back to life. But part of me still didn't believe it was possible. It felt like we'd slipped into an alternative universe, one where an unbeating heart and a blank mind wasn't quite enough to keep people from rising up and walking around. I mean, half the kids in my class act like they're Deads anyway. Teachers ask them questions and they just stare back as if someone just spoke to them in Italian or something. Maybe the living and the Deads had more in common than I thought.

What was *really* weird during that first week, though, was the reaction of the adults. They didn't think about how or why the Deads returned to life, they didn't run around waving their arms and screaming their heads off in panic like they do whenever there's a petrol strike. They just looked embarrassed and kept out of the way, and waited for the government to tell them what to do. Actually, my nan blamed the immigrants, but she blames the immigrants for everything, and "political correctness gone mad".

The news crept out very slowly. I watched TV late that night in my bedroom, and the Sky newsreader reported from outside a hospital morgue about a patient who had been found wandering about in the corridors. Doctors had run tests and said he had no heartbeat. The newsreader looked like she didn't believe a word of what she was having to read out. She kept patting her hair and looking off to the side of the screen, whispering, "Are we still on?"

Then it cut back to the studio and some ecology guy who looked like he'd just got out of bed said it might be to do with global warming, and I thought *As If*, I mean, you don't have to be a rocket scientist to figure out there's no link between the ozone layer and the reanimation of dead tissue. It's like saying PlayStation games give you rabies or something. Get a grip.

I kept hoping they would cut to footage of the Deads lumbering along roads and bashing into walls and generally looking thick. I rang Track and told her to turn on the TV but her dog stepmother answered and told me off for calling after 9 p.m. I watched TV all over the weekend and looked at all the newspapers, but found nothing more reported.

The day I bumped into the old guy on the bus was the day I connected with the Deads. The police told my mother that the old man had passed away several hours earlier, and nobody was going to press charges, but I should watch where I was going in future. No wonder they all looked so confused as we left the station. Looking back at the day I committed "murder", it wasn't especially creepy or weird, just something that happened from time to time, like my dad bashing his wing mirrors when he's trying to park at Sainsbury's.

The next time I met a Dead it was creepier. It was the following Monday, and I was getting home late again from school. I'd been caught selling mobile phone covers during Social Studies and had to stay behind. I remember cutting down a shadowy tree-lined avenue and seeing a guy shuffling ahead, dragging his feet. The sky was the colour of wet newspaper and it had started to rain hard. I had a hood on my jacket, but the guy was getting soaked. He hadn't noticed that the heel of his right shoe was hanging off, but apart from that (and getting wet) I guess he looked normal, a bit like my dad. Then he turned around, and I saw that he had a toothbrush sticking out of his mouth. Maybe it was because I'd already come into contact with the unliving but this time I knew I was in the presence of a restless soul trapped in a corpse. One who still remembered how to brush his teeth.

The figure before me was drifting more than walking, his feet barely lifting from the ground. As far as I could see in the fading light he was wearing ordinary street clothes, although they were dirty and one sleeve of his jacket was torn, and he looked like he'd been in a fight. But you often get people like that in my neighbourhood. I even wondered if maybe he was advertising a new killer-zombie videogame, but he wasn't interesting enough to be doing that. Then I realized something; he was behaving *exactly* like the man on the bus, as though his brain wasn't controlling his movements, but rather a distant memory of how to move.

As I drew close I caught an overpowering stench of chemicals, as though he'd just heaved himself up off a mortuary slab. His face was grey and dull, the colour of old computer plastic, but his eyes were the real giveaway. They had a fixed, dry look, like a doll's eyes, I guess because there was no fluid to lubricate them, and they were stuck in one position. The colour had faded from his pupils, so that his eyes looked like a pair of dirty peppermints. I kept pace with him as I passed, and it was then that I realized I wasn't scared of him so much as grossed out. He opened his mouth as I passed and the toothbrush fell out. I saw that he had no teeth left.

I kept my distance. It's a bit like when you see a blind person coming toward you. You can either stand really still until they've gone past or move out of their path. You feel a bit guilty for being there at all. The same with the Deads. When someone is dangerous they give off warning signals, and if you catch the signals you know when to keep away. It's like the older kids who hang outside the Am-La 24-Hour Grocery Store near my school. I always cross over the road when I see them standing together. You don't need to go looking for trouble.

But this guy was dead and there weren't any signals good or bad, and I knew the worst thing that could happen was he could fall over and block the pavement, like a drunk tramp. The street was quiet and the few people who passed us didn't see anything wrong. I guess in the dim rain there was nothing unusual to see except that the old guy was really getting soaked.

I arrived at my turning and the guy just shuffled onwards into the gloom. I missed the early evening TV news but asked my mum if there had been anything about the Deads, and she made a face and said of course not, Alfie, go and clean your trainers, you're walking mud in.

I remembered noticing that her eyes were red and she kept touching the corners, as if she'd been crying and was trying not to let me see. I figured either she'd had another fight with my dad on the phone or she'd seen something on TV about the Deads.

The next day I tried to discuss what had happened with friends at school but no one was interested except Simon Waters, and he believes anything so he has minus zero credibility. He thinks crop circles are made by Venusians, not a couple of sad guys with a piece of rope and a plank. He's desperate to believe in anything less miserable than his own existence, which consists of getting beaten up all the time by "Bulldog" Jake Drummond and going home to a father who is dating a foot specialist.

Nobody had seen anything. I might have begun to think I was imagining all of this if it hadn't been for the man on the bus. The police wouldn't have lied about him, would they? And there was the wet guy in the avenue, and the news item. But I had no real proof it was happening apart from a bunch of nutters on Twitter and Facebook, including the American girl who sends me Likes ten times a day and thinks there are voices in her mum's dishwasher. Maybe I was tired when I watched the TV and had fallen asleep and dreamed it. That left the bus incident (maybe the police lied for reasons of their own) and the wet man (maybe he had been wearing contact lenses and they had steamed up, and had just forgotten about the toothbrush).

It wasn't much to go on.

That was when I decided to begin my Deadwatch, which is an old school notebook marked out so that I could record each dead sighting as it happened. I thought this would be a good idea because nobody could leave comments on it like they can online.

For the first few days I had nothing to write about. Then I saw another one, not up close but at a distance. At first I thought it was a woman, but then I realized it was a bloke in a hospital gown. He was stumbling across the park behind our house. I wasn't imagining it either because Fang (our Jack Russell terrier) started pulling at his lead and scrabbling his claws on the path, making horrible choking noises. I figured he couldn't tell the difference between a walking dead man and a rabbit. There was a rustle of leaves as the hospital man blundered into the bushes. I ran after him, but the bushes had closed up again, and I could only see and smell earthy darkness.

Cautiously, I moved forward, pushing the branches out of the way. Fang started to whimper and pull back. I took another step, opening the leaves and looking inside the bushes.

There was nothing; just leaves, soil and damp.

Suddenly a huge white face jumped up before my eyes and roared at me. I yelled and fell backwards, Fang slipped the lead and bolted, and the man vanished. I shouted "Peedy" and ran home with my heart knocking against my ribs.

With each passing day there were more and more sightings as the Deads took to the streets. Soon I was recording as many as six or seven on a single Saturday morning (the girls liked standing up against the window of Accessorize). I stopped bothering with the book because there were too many to keep up with.

One Saturday I was cutting through the park just as it was starting to get dark. There were dozens of Deads sitting under the rustling oak trees. They were seated in deckchairs near the bandstand with their hands in their laps, quietly waiting for the music to start. As I got to the outer perimeter I saw two of them sitting on the railings with their arms around each other like lovers, except that the railing spikes had gone right through their thighs, pinning them in place.

It was a kind of fucked-up sight. I stopped going to the park after that.

At the start, most Deads were in pretty good condition, I mean their jaws and ears weren't hanging off or anything, but once in a while you'd see one in a really bad state. There was another guy in the park wearing a hospital gown, and the stitches down the front of his chest had burst open so you could see his innards move from side to side when he nearly fell over. There was no blood though, and his guts were grey-brown like piles of uncooked barbecue stuff. That was pretty gross.

I guess the police were stopping us from going near the Deads because I kept seeing all these signs that said roads were shut. It felt like the adults had all been talking together, and had decided to keep the news from their kids in case we freaked out. You'd expect this nervousness from my mother, who had a total nuclear meltdown when I brought a dead sparrow into the house, but not from Ted, our revolting ancient next door neighbour who lost an eye in a gas explosion at work and talked about sending blacks home, even though the woman who delivered his meals was from Africa and he thought she was great. Ted was shitting himself, I could tell, because he was at the window all day, looking frightened.

Obviously the Deads were going to stick around, so the government had to do something to hide them away. This is guesswork, but I think they probably arranged for coffins to be buried at a greater depth and for doctors to put padlocks on the mortuary doors. Maybe scientists were looking into ways of freezing the Deads or vacuum-packing them like Tesco's lamb shanks so that they couldn't return. I kept a watch on online forums, but could only find rumours and nut-rants.

I think the government's plans must have proved too expensive, because suddenly it seemed like more and more Deads were walking around the streets every day. Either someone was letting them out or they were finding new ways to escape.

Then I found a website called WalkingDeads.com that said the government couldn't work out what to do about the Deads. They'd set up a team to investigate, and cut a few open to have a poke around, but the Deads were just meat that wouldn't lie still. They had no heartbeats and dried-up blood and hardened veins and leathery skin and dry staring eyes. At first the scientists thought they were being reanimated by radiation in the atmosphere, then they thought it was a rogue virus, and finally they started to blame the EU.

Anyway, none of this really touched my family or our lives. We carried on as if everything was normal. Whenever I started to raise the subject, my parents killed the conversation before it could get interesting. It was like they were afraid.

I posted a few messages on the website, but never got any sensible replies. After a while, I lost interest. If adults and even my classmates were going to pretend there was nothing wrong, I could too. But I wanted to talk about it with someone, so I decided to talk to Track.

My best friend Track was christened Tracy because her dad was a big fan of *Thunderbirds* and there's a character on the show called Tracey (boy spelling), but it's also a girl's name so it could be used either way. That way he only had to bother thinking up one name when his wife got pregnant. But Tracy hated being called Tracy so she shortened it to Track, which worked as she only ever wears tracksuits. Track is pretty easy to convince about most things, so I decided to start with her.

"I want to show you something," I told her. "I want you to make up your own mind about this, okay?"

I took her to see the Deads sitting in bus shelters, looking neither happy nor sad (looking like they were waiting for a bus really). I took her to shopping malls where the Deads stared vaguely at window dummies, like they wanted to make friends with them. I pointed out the multiplexes and pizzerias where the Deads stood around in a state of shock (they never ate food but enjoyed being in queues). We saw them swaying backwards and forwards watching football in PC World and sunbathing in the park even when it was raining. I felt sorry for them.

Finally Track said the words I'd been waiting to hear all month.

"Okay, I believe you. The dead are coming back to life. Now what?"

I looked at her blankly. It was the first time anyone had ever really believed me about anything. "I don't know," I admitted.

"I mean, it's not like they're doing any harm, is it?"

But now that everyone could see that the Deads weren't going to hurt anyone, all kinds of trouble started. For one thing, no matter how harmless they were, they tended to creep people out. It was only natural; the way they looked and smelled was kind of depressing. Track heard that the police wanted special powers to round them up, because they were always falling on to railway lines and wandering into busy traffic, but I figured people had begun protesting, arguing that because the Deads were still walking around they had human rights.

Then the doctors began worrying that the bodies would decompose and put everyone at risk from germs, but they didn't really rot. First they leaked a lot, then got drier and more leathery, and this was helped by the fact that it was winter and a lot of them had taken to sitting in libraries with the central heating turned up high.

They got damaged and tattered from constantly bumping into things, and some of them lost fingers and clumps of hair, which made them even creepier-looking. One of them sitting on the train seat opposite me tore his trousers, and tugged the hole around so that the other people on the train wouldn't have to sit facing his willy, like he remembered being embarrassed.

So now it was all out in the open. And while TV shows and newspaper articles preached respect for the Deads, teenage gangs began going out and messing with their bodies, cutting bits off or dressing them up in crazy outfits to make them look stupid. I saw one old guy in the high street wearing a purple glitter wig, a ballet tutu and mismatched wellingtons. Sometimes if you were out with a bunch of friends and saw one shuffling along ahead of you, someone would run up and pull his trousers down, then run away laughing. Also, some companies hung advertising signs on them to sell stuff, but it didn't look clever, just creepy. McDonald's ran a series of really bad-taste posters on the Deads that had pictures of hamburgers and the slogan "Try some fresh meat" over them, but everyone complained so they stopped doing it.

A few Deads travelled on public transport because they remembered how to use their Oyster cards, but they tended to fall under the trains. They fell in the river and would float about for a few days, getting run over by motorboats, but eventually they would drift to shore, climb out and begin aimlessly walking around again. Hospital crews collected the most disgusting ones and took them away somewhere.

Track and I checked all this out together. It was great having someone to share it with. It was like having a best mate and a girlfriend rolled into one. We started keeping a proper journal about the Deads, writing everything up after each event.

I remember we saw an old woman fall out of the back of a van and get dragged down the street on her face. I followed her just to see what would happen if her coat strap managed to disentangle itself. When the poor old love finally hauled herself to her feet, the remaining part of her face fell off like burned wallpaper, leaving her with tarmac-scraped bone and an expression of annoyance, like she'd just been short-changed in an Oxfam shop.

A few weeks after this, one wet Saturday afternoon, my grandpa died. He had lived in the house with us for years even though my mother had never liked him, and at first nobody even realized that he had died. He just stayed in his armchair all day staring at the TV, but I knew something was wrong because he would normally start shouting at the screen when the football came on, but today he didn't. And he was still there watching *Strictly Come Dancing* later, which he hated. He did make himself a cup of tea, but he left the teabag and spoon in the cup, drank it scalding hot and immediately peed it all back on to the floor, which was gross.

My father wouldn't let my mother call the hospital and they had a huge row. It was decided that grandpa could stay for a while so long as he didn't get in anyone's way. My mother refused to change his clothes, but Dad argued that they didn't need changing very often because his sweat glands were no longer working.

The best thing about the Deads is that if you sit on a chair they've just been sitting on, it still feels cold. When a living person has been sitting on a seat for a while and you sit on it after them it's still warm, and feels kind of creepy. A toilet seat is the worst because someone has been sitting on it with a bare butt and that feels disgusting. But the Deads don't leave warm seats because their body temperature is about the same as winter tap water.

The worst thing about the Deads is that they don't sleep. So if I went downstairs for a glass of water in the middle of the night I was likely to find my grandpa sitting at the kitchen table with the light off, and this gave me the creeps.

Still, it was difficult to break the old geezer out of his tea-drinking habit. I guess when you've been making thirty-five cups of PG Tips every day for sixty years it becomes a ritual you can't break. Grandpa wasn't allowed out by himself because he had a tendency not to come back and we would have to go looking for him, so my dad came over and made a fake bus-stop out of painted wood and put it outside the house, and Grandpa would go and stand by it, patiently waiting for a bus that never came, until we brought him back in. Sometimes he got away, though.

A few days later I took Grandpa to the cinema. I guess it was an odd thing to do, but I was supposed to be looking after him (we took turns) and there was a film that I really wanted to see, a supernatural PG-13, which meant it would be creepy but not very gory. I managed to pass myself off as over thirteen and pass Grandpa off as alive, but the woman on the counter watched us suspiciously.

Halfway through the film, just when the star had gone to the cellar to look for her cat even though she knew there was a maniac loose, I turned to find Grandpa staring at me with wide eyes. He wasn't breathing of course, and his mouth hung open to reveal a thick dry tongue that looked like a slice of boiled ham. What bothered me most was the way he repeated something he used to do when he was alive, tilting his head to look at me with narrowed eyes, so that for a moment I couldn't tell if he was really a Dead. It was just the illusion of life, of course, but an unsettling one.

A few weeks later, Grandpa somehow managed to sit down on the top of the electric cooker while the burners were on, and branded himself. My mum threatened to leave us if my dad didn't arrange for him to be put somewhere. The next morning I stood on the doorstep and waved goodbye to Grandpa as he stared sightlessly back and stumbled off across the flowerbeds, led away by a hospital porter.

Two days after he left, I was walking home from school late, and took a short cut past the backs of the houses a few streets away from where we lived. Ahead, only half visible in the grey fading light, a Dead was standing with his head tilted to the sky, staring at something. As I drew closer he sat down with a thud, as if his legs had suddenly given way, and I realized that it was Grandpa. He'd come back.

It looked as if something had been eating him, cats perhaps, or foxes. There were little bite marks all over his face and neck, and one of his arms had hardly any skin left on it. Then I realized where we were, and what he had been looking at.

He'd slipped out of the hospital and come back to the house he had shared with Grandma when they were first married. I could tell he'd been hoping to see her pass the windows. But she had died long ago. He was standing before the glowing kitchen windows of his youth, staring up through half-remembered dreams of a happier past. Old people often talk about the past, which is boring because you weren't there. But he was remembering something from a past *life*.

I never saw him again. I just went to school and stayed home at night. There were too many Deads around, and it disturbed me. They blundered into the garden at night and followed me to the shops and fell down the steps of public lavs and floated past in the river looking confused and sad. One day I knew there would be more Deads walking around than the living.

My parents didn't seem bothered by any of this. They carried on with their jobs as if everything was normal. People had stopped caring or even noticing. My world was gently rotting apart just like the Deads. So I forgot about Grandpa being taken away and people coming back. I erased them from my mind and just got on with my schoolwork. I put away my Deadwatch, and stuck to the house rules. But they came back to haunt me in a different way.

I got an idea that something was wrong when I was summoned to Mrs Bleeker's office. Mrs Bleeker is our Deputy Headmistress, and she's kind of pyramid-shaped and has really yellow skin so we call her Angry Bird, after the one you can make go really fast. She teaches Spanish and Metalwork, which is a really off combination unless you're thinking of becoming a welder in Madrid.

I waited until her light switched from red to green, then knocked on the door.

"All right, you don't have to knock it down, Alfie, come in and sit over there." She gesturcd to a really low purple beanbag on the other side of her desk. I dropped down into it and knew I wouldn't be able to get out easily again. She had me where she wanted me.

"Alfie." She leaned forward on her elbows and wedged her fingers together under her chins, looking concerned. "I thought we should have a little talk."

"Have I done something wrong?"

"Well, it rather depends on how we define the word *wrong*. Your mother tells me ..." *Oh shit*, I thought, *she'd been talking to my mother?* "... that you have a rather overactive imagination. And of course, this can be a very good thing. Our finest poets and artists have wonderful imaginations that allow them to see the world in all sorts of new ways. But there is a time and place for everything, and we have to be very careful that it doesn't cross over into our ordinary lives. Because then it starts to look as if we're telling lies, and if people think you're telling lies, they won't be able to trust you. You wouldn't want that, would you?"

What the flying flick was she on about? I wracked my brains trying to imagine what my mum had said to Bleach-head Bleeker.

"She explained to me how very upset you were when your grandfather was taken away to Sunnymead."

I still couldn't see where old Bleacher was going with her case. She took off her glasses and tiredly rubbed the top of her nose. "Is this where you first got the idea? Or did it come from the films you and Tracy Mullen watched?"

I widened my eyes, stuck out my lip and gave her a blank look. I was trying to tell her I had no clue about what she was asking.

Mrs Bleeker leaned so far forward that the desk creaked in protest. "When did you first get this notion into your head that the dead could come back to life?"

"It isn't a 'notion'. It's the truth."

"Alfie, Mr Al-Fhazhi tells me you're one of his best pupils." Mr Al-Fhazhi was my English teacher. Al-Fhazhi is the English version of his name, which is unpronounceable. He's an exiled Iraqi and he's really cool. Simon Waters's parents complained about a man from Iraq teaching English, and they can't even string a sentence together in their own language without swearing.

Bleach-Brain checked the notes on her desk, tapping them with her pencil. "He says you have a highly developed sense of imagination and that your essays are first-rate. But you must be able to distinguish what is real and what is made up. Or," her eyes narrowed suspiciously, "are you just making things up to cause mischief?"

"No!"

"Then why have you been going around telling so many lies? I believe you told your friends you were arrested for murdering a dead man on a bus." Even she must have noticed how bonkers that sounded. "When in actual fact a passing policeman happened to see a poor old man slip and fall off the bus as the doors opened."

"No, he was a Dead—"

"And that you told people your grandfather was dead . . ."

"He is!"

"No, Alfie, he is not." She shook her head sadly. "He had a

stroke and was taken to a special nursing home because your mother couldn't care for him at home."

"No, if Mum had done that she would have told me. She would have taken me to see him."

"She tried to tell you, but you didn't want to listen. She said you can visit him whenever you want, but the trips must be specially arranged in advance."

I wanted to explain about the Deads in the park and everything else, but knew now that she would never believe me. My mum had grassed on me about the horror films I'd watched, and Bleach-Brain thought it had affected my imagination.

"I'm not going to ask you about what you consider to be the truth, Alfie. You know what's real and what's made up. I know that some boys have big imaginations, and that sometimes their imaginations run away with them. But did you never stop to think about the hurt it might cause? Your mother is very upset. You can't go around telling everyone that the dead are coming back to life. This is a very serious matter that could affect your future here. Come and see me tomorrow afternoon – I'll have decided what to do by then."

I left her office very confused, because there were things I was sure about. An old man really did fall off the bus. There really is an old film called *Dawn of the Dead*. My granddad really has lost his mind and lives in a place full of dried-up people. But maybe some of the rest got sort of exaggerated.

I got into the same sort of trouble when I told my sister Lucy's stupid boyfriend that she had been attacked by bees and was so disfigured that she couldn't see him for six weeks.

Track was waiting for me on the wall of the sports ground after school. I told her what had happened with the Bleach-Monster, and she decided that we were both right. "Everyone exaggerates," she said, dropping into step beside me. "Facebook, TV, movies, our families, everyone. It's not your fault. Leave this to me."

The next day I went to see Mrs Bleeker again. I felt sure I

was going to be kicked out of school, but Track had promised me it would be okay. And she was right.

"Your classmate Tracy Mullen came to see me, to explain about your creative assignments."

What creative assignments? She must have meant the books we drew together and the diaries we kept.

"Tracy explained how you were looking at everything around you and exaggerating what you saw, in order to write about it."

"Well I suppose so," I said. "I mean, I thought they were Deads, but I guess they're just old. See, to someone my age, older people are kind of dead because they're so wrinkly and move around at tortoise-speed."

"I think you need to have more respect for your seniors . . ."

"It's not like I don't respect them, Miss, I guess it's just the way the old and the Deads look so alike. That and the smell."

"Even if you think that, Alfie, I really don't think you should say it out loud. I want to make a deal with you. If you promise not to keep pretending to other people that these ideas are real, Mr Al-Fhazhi and I will set you some special writing assignments, where you can really use your imagination to the fullest, and maybe we'll be able to put this special talent of yours to good use. How about that?"

Some deal. I struggled out of the Bleacher's purple bean-bag and left her office with piles of extra schoolwork, and a warning not to infect anyone else with my weird made-up ideas. But Mrs Bleeker and Mr Al-Fhazhi thought that my creativity shouldn't be stifled.

Maybe you'd be happier if this story ended with me and Track fighting off armies of the Deads, but that wouldn't be very believable, would it? And besides, you've seen that in movies like, only a quintillion times before.

I thought about it carefully, and what I realized was this; my life is pretty boring, but there are things in it that interest me, and I'd like more of them. So I think maybe I wish them into existence, and they become real. That is, they're real to me, but not to adults. And maybe that's what being a kid is all about, having adventures that are bigger than real life because you can add the missing ingredient; your imagination. And adults can't access that stuff after a certain age because they have to think about work and bills and getting chewing gum off the back seat of the car.

Besides, I've discovered something else that's going on, and this is weirder than the Deads.

There's a new kid in our class called Tony Maroney, and he looks like a hungry wolf. He's the tallest kid in the class by about a foot – it looks like he's been kept back a year. He has thick, low hair that's so black it almost looks dark blue, and by the end of every day he needs a shave. He keeps so still and quiet in class that everyone is afraid of him. See, by keeping really still and not saying anything he makes you do all the work, and so kids who cross him go into long panicky explanations about why they do things, and he just stares at them in dead silence, and they lose their nerve even more until they say something stupid, and then they're doomed.

Although he's English, Tony grew up in Sicily, which is an island off the coast of Italy where the Mafia comes from. I know this is true because Mum heard about it from the man who painted his uncle's bathroom. Tony has cold blue eyes like chips of iceberg, and wiry black hairs on the backs of his hands. He's supposed to be eleven but looks about eighteen. Even the teachers watch him warily, as though he might do something terrible behind their backs.

Me and Track have finally figured out his secret. We know what he is; he's a werewolf, and we think there's a nest of them living under the school gymnasium, and he's the king of them. He didn't start in our class until after the full moon, so we're waiting for the next one before we strike. Last night I melted my gran's silver crucifix into a ball on the cooker hob (we ruined the saucepan, so I had to hide it in the garden), and now we have to find something to fire it from. I'll let you know how that turns out.

Meanwhile, I'm filling in my secret blog. I've moved on from the Deads. The werewolf thing is going to take up all my time. Mrs Bleeker said imagination is a wonderful thing, so it needs a capital "I". And there are other words that need capitals, like Real and Strange and True and Brave.

I'm young, I can make anything happen.

The Hotline

Dreda Say Mitchell

Rukshana Malik wasn't angry when she was passed over for promotion at the London bank where she worked. It was true that Sarah, the successful candidate, wasn't as well qualified. It was also true that she was a bit younger, but Rukshana didn't want to draw any conclusions from that. After the selection process was over, her manager had given her a debriefing in which he explained that it had been a very close thing and that Rukshana still had a very bright future with the company – after all, she was only twenty-nine. He also suggested that the next time a position came up, she should go to him so he could prep her with some interview practice. Rukshana liked Jeff; he was a great boss. So she was disappointed and a bit puzzled, but she wasn't angry.

Her family was, though. They suspected that the reason she hadn't been given the promotion was that she was a Muslim who wore a headscarf. Her sister, Farah, asked, "This girl who got the job, what does she look like?"

"Well, she's young and blonde . . ."

"And very good looking, I imagine?"

"I suppose."

"Oh, wake up, Rocky." Farah waved her hands in the air. She was wearing her pale blue soft leather gloves with the fancy fringe at the end and the three white buttons on the tops, one of her newest fashion accessories.

"It's not like that; they have strict policies on race, religion, gender, and the rest of it."

Her sister sighed and shook her head with pity. Sometimes it was easy for her to forget that Rukshana was the older of the two, and an outsider could be forgiven for not realizing they were related at all. Farah wore her faith lightly, dressed in Western clothes, and was a party girl with dark brown eyes that flashed and sparkled like her gold jewellery.

The following week, Rukshana was called away from her desk to see a guy from Personnel. As soon as he told her that she was a highly valued member of the staff and a key member of the team, she knew what was coming, and sure enough she was right. He went on, "Unfortunately, in today's harsh financial climate, tough decisions have to be taken . . ."

Rukshana was let go, but she still wasn't angry. She was handed a letter that included a nice payoff and a glowing reference, and all her co-workers said that they were sorry to see her leave. But she was nonetheless let go. She was in tears as she cleared her desk and didn't see an angry Jeff appear from his office.

"Is this true, what I've heard?" he asked.

"Yes."

"This is outrageous. I'm going up to Personnel, they're not getting away with this." He started walking toward the elevator.

She grabbed his arm and dragged him back. "Please, don't. It's all right, honestly."

"I don't care."

He stormed off, and she didn't see him again before she left. Farah was equally angry when Rukshana told her what had happened. "You should sue the bastards."

"For what?"

"Like Marlon Brando said in *The Wild One*, 'Whaddya got?' There's race, religion, gender – sue them for all three. Make them pay. Drag their arses through the courts, embarrass them in public, chuck dirt at them and make them wish they'd never heard your name."

"It's not worth it."

Farah was genuinely baffled. "What's the matter with you,

Rocky? Why aren't you angry? I'd be fizzing if people treated me like that."

"I'm just not angry."

And it was true – she wasn't. She was upset, scared, shocked, and confused. London could be a tough city at the best of times, and when you had no job and bills to pay, it was a very frightening place indeed. But she still wasn't angry.

That evening she got a call from Kelly, her best friend at the bank. "Rukshana, I can't believe they've done this to you. You've got to get them back."

Not another person telling her to sue . . .

"You can't take an employer to court for letting you go. That's not how it works."

"I'm not talking about the bank. I'm talking about Jeff and that bitch Sarah."

Confused, Rukshana answered, "It's got nothing to do with Jeff and even less to do with Sarah."

There was a long silence before Kelly said, "Oh, of course, maybe you don't know . . ."

"What don't I know?"

"About Jeff and Sarah. About them having a bit of slap-and-tickle."

Rukshana was horrified. "They're not having an affair. He's married with kids; he's got a photo of them on his desk, he's always going on about his family."

"Oh, Rukshana, puh-leeze – you can't be that naive. They're carrying on, everyone at the bank knows that."

"I didn't know that."

Kelly hesitated. "Well, people didn't like to tell you gossip, what with you being a Muslim and everything – they thought you wouldn't like it."

Rukshana was disgusted. She loved gossip. Kelly went on to tell Rukshana what everyone knew. "It's been going on for months. They think it's a big secret, but of course everyone knows. That's why he fixed it for her to get the job, to keep her sweet. Then he advised Personnel to get rid of you, so in case you sued them about missing the promotion, they could say you were just bitter because you'd been fired. That's what everyone's saying happened."

"That's what everyone's saying?"

"That's what everyone's saying. He was on your interview panel, wasn't he? He goes up to Personnel every five minutes, doesn't he? Every lunchtime at noon, Jeff and Sarah meet up. He goes out and waits a couple of streets away, and then five minutes later she follows and they get a cab to some Holiday Inn, where they do their dirty business. Then at two o'clock on the dot, he comes back, and five minutes later, she arrives on her own so no one will guess that they're at it. I mean, can you imagine? It'd take a lot more than a promotion to persuade me to shag that fat ugly bastard. Talk about lie back and think of England. Rukshana? You've gone very quiet. Are you still there?"

Rukshana was still there. She was just very, very angry.

Rukshana didn't do anything the following day because she was still too angry; she wanted a clear head when she decided what to do next. Twenty-four hours later she was still too angry but had decided to ring a couple of lawyers anyway to see if she had a case against the bank. They were a bit sceptical but thought she might be able to do something on discrimination grounds. They were less sure about Kelly's preferred option, that Rukshana sue Jeff for being a lying, cheating, disloyal, fat ugly bastard who'd taken her job away. Rukshana was glad the lawyers didn't advise that. She didn't want to sue anyone; that wasn't what she was after.

She couldn't relax. The only person in the house during the day was her granddad. He was in his eighties. He got a little confused sometimes, but on other occasions he was very sharp. Whatever – she didn't feel like chatting. She tried doing a little housework to calm down. That didn't help, but she did it anyway. In Farah's room, she picked up the clothes her sister had scattered around after she'd come in from a party the previous night. Rukshana held a miniskirt against her hips; it really was immodestly short. A few months ago, their cousin had come from Pakistan to visit and had shared a room with Farah; what a culture shock it must have been for her. Their cousin refused to leave the house without wearing a burka, so when she went out, she was covered in black, only her eyes visible to the outside world. When she returned to Pakistan, she'd left one of her burkas behind, and it was still sitting on a shelf, possibly meant to serve as a reproach to her wayward cousin. Rukshana picked it up.

From the bedroom window, she could see the towers of the City, London's financial district, looming over the rooftops; down below those towers was the bank where Jeff and Sarah were having a good laugh at her expense. She looked at the clothes in her hands and then out over the city, and she bit her lip.

Rukshana knew what she was considering was a serious criminal offence and that she'd go to prison for several years if she was caught. She'd have to get everything right and not make any mistakes. There were a lot of things that could go wrong, and there was her family to think about. Then she thought about Jeff appearing from his office and telling her how outrageous her sacking was and how he wasn't putting up with it. She gripped the clothes tightly in her hand. Every single day she spent staring out the barred windows of a prison cell would be worth it. Jeff was going to pay. She smiled and whispered to herself:

"It's on."

It was a Thursday. Rukshana had everything prepared and all the timing worked out. She was wearing one of her sister's short skirts, a low-cut top, and ballet shoes on her feet. In her shoulder bag were silver high heels, a pair of fashionably outsize Jackie O. sunglasses, and her cousin's burka. Out in the hall was the family bike that she'd oiled and left ready. And she'd picked the day very carefully.

Her grandfather was a cricket fanatic. He was already in his armchair with various fruit juices and nibbles in easy reach, getting ready for the first day of the England–Pakistan Test match being played in London. Every ball would be shown on the TV, along with the replays and analyses. Rukshana knew her grandfather; he wouldn't be moving from that spot all day. He might briefly go upstairs for a call of nature, but even that wasn't certain. Where cricket was concerned, he had very firm bladder control. And there was a house rule – no one disturbed Granddad when the cricket was on. Knocks on the door went unanswered, the phone was left to ring, and any attempt to start a conversation was ignored.

When the first ball of the match was bowled, Rukshana looked up at the clock on the wall. It was half past eleven. She had thirty minutes to complete the first part of her plan.

"I'm just going upstairs to read a book."

She was met with silence. Out in the hall she put on her cousin's burka and wheeled the bike out on to the street. Very, very gently, she pulled the front door shut. She mounted the bike and began pedalling, the burka wrapped around her, only her eyes visible. She rode to the end of her street and turned on to the main road that led to the City.

On a typical day in London, you could see almost anyone dressed almost any way, but even so, a woman cycling in a burka was unusual. Truant schoolkids laughed as she flew by. Some drivers did double takes when they saw her, which were quickly followed by contemptuous stares directed not at her but at her burka. Rukshana almost wobbled on her bike, she was so shaken by the response to her clothing. She'd heard women in her family talk about how they were sometimes insulted and verbally abused on the street when they wore their burkas, but Rukshana hadn't thought it was as bad as this. And – perhaps it was inevitable – one guy leaned out of the window of his van and yelled "Terrorist!" when she stopped at a traffic light. She threw off her shock. She began to feel mad and bad. She felt like an outlaw.

It took her twenty minutes to arrive at her destination, a quiet side street two blocks away from the bank where she'd worked. She parked the bike, locked it up, and checked the street. There was no one looking. She pulled the burka off over her head and put it in her bag before swapping her slippers for the high heels. She put on sunglasses. She used a mirror to apply some make-up and arrange her long raven-black hair so that it waved and flowed around her face. She smiled at her image. She looked fantastic, nothing like her normal headscarf-wearing self. She couldn't help thinking that she could give her sister a run for her money in the looks department.

Unsteadily at first, but with growing confidence, she clip-clopped down the street on her heels and then turned on to the main road. With her new look, she might as well have been in a different country. The same sort of male drivers who had given her dirty looks when she'd been on her bike were now slowing down to admire her bronzed legs. When a man leaned out of a van's window and shouted, "Oi, oi! Do you fancy a portion, sweetheart?" Rukshana avoided eye contact and kept walking. She wondered if it was the same man who'd shouted "Terrorist!" at her fifteen minutes earlier.

She walked the two blocks. On the left was the bank, and on the right was a small park where the staff sometimes went to eat their lunches. Rukshana took a seat on a bench that gave her a view of the entrance to the bank. She crossed her long bare legs and looked at her watch. It was 11.55 a.m. She'd made it. A bicycle courier walked past her wheeling his bike; he clocked her legs, and she heard him whisper "Asian babe . . ." as he went by. She smiled and looked at her watch. It was noon. She looked over to the entrance and sure enough, just as Kelly had foretold, Jeff emerged from the bank and walked down the steps. He adjusted his tie and ran his fingers through his hair a few times before trotting off and turning down a side street.

Five minutes after that, Sarah too came out of the bank. She turned and walked down the same side street as Jeff had. Rukshana shook her head and whispered, "Bastards." Then she stood up, adjusted her hair again, and walked across the road. There were hundreds and hundreds of employees in this building, so she was sure she would get away with it. On the steps of the bank, she took a deep breath and said to herself, "This is it," before walking into the lobby.

In front of her was a security gate that you needed a swipe card to pass through. To the left of it sat Mark, a security guard, a big barrel of a man in a peaked cap. She fished around in her shoulder bag and took out her now-invalidated employee swipe card along with another one that she used for her local library. She wriggled her shoulders like her sister and giggled at Mark; he smiled back. When she got to the gate, she used her library card to try to get through. A red light flashed and the machine honked at her. She tried again. Another red light and another honk. She looked at Mark helplessly and waved her swipe card at him. Like a middle-aged knight, he got out of his chair and came over to help.

The bank had strict procedures about access. Mark's role was to examine her card and see whether there was a problem and, if necessary, refer her to the security office. But Rukshana knew Mark well. His view was that strict procedures didn't apply to ditzy, sexy women with long legs. And today, Rukshana was a very ditzy, very sexy woman with very long legs. Mark towered over her.

"Is there a problem, miss?"

"Oh, yes, Mark," she breathed. "My card is always letting me down."

Mark slipped his own security card into the machine, and there was a green light, a ping, and the gate swung open. She squeezed his arm.

"Oh, Mark, you're such a sweetie . . ."

Mark saluted and Rukshana walked through with the almost physical sensation of his eyes drilling into her backside. She walked to the elevator and went up to the fifth floor, taking out her sister's blue leather gloves and putting them on. When the doors slid open, she was face to face with Renata, a colleague who knew Rukshana as well as Rukshana knew her. Rukshana stiffened; everyone who might have recognized her, with or without her headscarf, should have been out at lunch. Renata smiled at her.

"Do you really need those sunglasses in here, dear?" For a few seconds Rukshana thought it was all over. Renata held the elevator door open for her and said, "If you don't get out, you're going back down." Rukshana got out, fingered the sunglasses, and stammered, "G-got to look cool . . ."

Renata got in the elevator, smiled, and said, "You look very cool, darling. You'd better watch out or you'll have that sleazy lecher Jeff after you."

The elevator doors closed. Rukshana hurried down the corridor to Jeff's office and peered in the window. It was empty. With her gloved hands she pulled the handle and went inside. She sat at his computer. On the screen was a website featuring romantic breaks for two in Paris: *The city of love . . . a weekend of amour . . . for that special person in your life . . .*

Rukshana had the feeling it wasn't Jeff's wife who would be going. She took a list out of her handbag and began typing in the web addresses of radical Islamic websites, one after another, so that a casual observer of Jeff's computer history might think Jeff spent all his time looking up death-to-the-infi-del!, death-to-the-great-Satan!, death-to – well, death-to-pretty-much-everyone-really! websites. Then she changed his screen-saver from a sugary snapshot of Jeff's wife and kids to a photo of a radical Islamic cleric.

She decided to skip the elevator and took the stairs down to the lobby. Mark didn't wait for her to try her card this time; he jumped up smartly and opened the gate for her, assuming her card still wasn't working. She gave him a long, sultry look with the promise of the East in it – a look her sister had perfected – and with that she was back out on the street.

She walked the two blocks to her bike and changed into her burka and ballet shoes. She checked her watch. It was 12.40 p.m. She had to move. She pedalled furiously away from the glass and glitz of London's financial district to a poorer quar-ter of town and parked her bike in the yard of a disused workshop. Over her loomed a minaret. She walked a couple of streets until she was standing in the shadow of the tower.

Al-Nutjobs Mosque. That wasn't its real name, of course. It was called Al-Nutjobs by the British newspapers; they claimed that every Muslim extremist in London was a regular there, but the members of the Muslim community weren't so sure. Their view was that most of the people who hung out at Al-Nutjobs were undercover newspaper reporters, police spies, and operatives from various Western intelligence agencies. Whatever the case, Rukshana knew the street was plastered with CCTVs and other forms of surveillance and that all the local public phones were bugged. She had to be very, very careful.

She walked up to the pay phone opposite the mosque. She checked that her gloves were on and then went inside. She picked up the phone, put some coins in, and called the special police anti-terrorist hotline. When she got through, she faked an Indian accent, the sort that had been thought very amusing on British comedy shows in the 1970s but that in these more liberal times wasn't considered funny anymore.

"Please, please, this afternoon, bombs, bombs! *Bombs!*"

Rukshana explained in her accent that she'd overheard a campaign being planned in Al-Nutjobs, and the ringleader was an undercover white convert who worked at – and she gave them all Jeff's details. As the operator desperately tried to keep her on the line, Rukshana shouted, "Please, please, this afternoon, bombs, bombs! *Bombs!*"

She hung up and walked smartly down the street. Rukshana collected her bike from the disused workshop and checked her watch. It was 1.15 p.m. Time was short. As she jumped on the bike to pedal back to the bank, a siren wailed through the air. Shit – she hadn't expected the cops to move that quickly. A police car screamed down the street heading toward the mosque. Rukshana didn't look back as she cycled to the bank. Once there, she parked her bike in the same spot as before, took off her burka, and slipped into her heels.

Her old bench opposite the bank was still available, and she sat down and checked her watch. It was 1.55 p.m. She was just in time. At 2.00 p.m. precisely, just as Kelly had said he would, Jeff appeared and walked back into the bank. Five minutes later, Sarah arrived, looking a little red-faced and with her clothes askew, and followed him in. Now Rukshana just had to wait.

If you reported any ordinary crime, the police would assess the evidence and decide what, if anything, to do. If you reported a terrorist bombing from a pay phone outside Al-Nutjobs, the police couldn't wait. They couldn't investigate the threat to see if it was serious; they couldn't weigh things up. They had to act fast and worry about it later.

At 2.15 p.m., the police acted. In the distance Rukshana heard sirens, and then more sirens as other police vehicles joined the chorus, and then they all came around the corner, brakes squealing, lights flashing, careering down the street. A police van mounted the pavement and juddered to a halt; it was followed by police cars and motorbikes. The doors to the van flew open and a half a dozen cops in black-and-white-checkered baseball caps, submachine guns slung over their shoulders, jumped out. Pistols were pulled from holsters; safety catches were disabled. The police raced up the stairs and into the bank. Other vehicles arrived, and soon there were so many flashing blue lights, you might have thought you were at a carnival.

Five minutes later, Rukshana rose to her feet to enjoy the view. Jeff was dragged down the steps, being frogmarched by two burly cops. He was thrown to the ground and spread-eagled; one cop kept a pistol to his head while the other cop pressed his knee into Jeff's back and handcuffed him. Down the steps came another officer holding Jeff's computer. Then the doors to the bank flew open as two policemen tried to stop Sarah from running after Jeff. She screamed, "Leave him alone, he hasn't done anything, what's the matter with you?"

Rukshana winced as Sarah punched one of the policemen in the face, after which Sarah was bundled to the ground, long legs akimbo, and thrown into the back of a van. Then the two suspects were driven away.

Rukshana sat back down. An old teacher of hers had once quoted a French saying: revenge was a dish you ate cold. Perhaps that was true. But it certainly filled up the belly.

"Oh, Rukshana, you should have been there!" Kelly rang that evening to tell Rukshana about the day's events. "The cops turned up and nicked Jeff. And they took Sarah away too, it was so funny."

Rukshana put on her best sympathy voice. "Poor Jeff . . ."

Kelly couldn't believe it. "Poor Jeff? After what he did to you?"

The following evening Kelly updated Rukshana. "It was all a hoax! The police released Jeff in the small hours without charge. Now we've had a team of detectives in all day trying to find the hoaxer. They're drawing up a list of suspects. It'll be pretty heavy for the guy who did it. The police don't take too kindly to that sort of thing – the cops say it'll mean jail time for the culprit. That won't help Jeff, of course, now that it's all out about him and Sarah. The bank's really embarrassed. Word is that when it's all calmed down, they're going to sack him. And Sarah."

"Poor Jeff."

"Poor Jeff? You have more reason to hate him than anyone . . ." There was a long pause before Kelly added, "I don't want to worry you, Rukshana, but I think you might be on the list of suspects, what with being let go." There was another long pause, and then Kelly asked, "It wasn't you, was it?"

"Of course not."

"That's what I told the police! A nice inoffensive Muslim girl like Rukshana – no way was it her. The thing is, though . . . I'm not sure they believed me."

It was the following Tuesday, the last day of the cricket match between England and Pakistan. The commentators agreed it was going to be a thrilling finish, and Rukshana's grandfather was in position in his armchair for it. Rukshana was jumpy.

Every time she heard a noise outside, she got up and looked through the window. Then at about noon it happened. A silver sedan pulled up outside her house and a man got out and walked up the garden path. There was a knock on the door.

Rukshana's grandfather snapped, "Ignore it."

Instead Rukshana ignored him and went to the door. She opened it to a man with a flashy suit, sunglasses, and slicked-back blond hair. He'd obviously modelled himself on a character from an American cop show. He showed her some ID.

"Rukshana Malik?"

"Yes."

"Detective Constable John Martin, Metropolitan Police. I'm investigating a very serious crime and I'd like to ask you some questions."

She looked into his eyes. He knew. And what's more, he knew that she knew that he knew – but could he prove it? Rukshana had been ultra careful. She'd made sure she was unrecognizable in the burka and in her sister's clothes. She'd burned all the evidence and left the bike on the High Street, where some kids had promptly stolen it. She'd worn gloves. She had a story worked out and she was sticking to it. She knew what to do; she watched the same American cop shows as DC John Martin.

"You'd better come in."

John Martin said good afternoon to her grandfather and was ignored for his trouble. Rukshana whispered, "He's watching the cricket, he doesn't like to be disturbed."

"I see."

They sat down on a sofa. John Martin went through the preliminaries, explaining why he was there and giving Rukshana the chance to avoid wasting everyone's time.

"Is there anything you'd like to tell me about the events of last Thursday?"

"I'm sorry, I don't know what you mean."

John Martin sighed. He knew. But could he prove it?

"Could you tell me where you were last Thursday?"

"I was here all day with my granddad."

John Martin looked over at the cricket fanatic. "Could you confirm that, sir?"

Martin was ignored. Rukshana explained, "He'll confirm it when the cricket's over."

John Martin was disgusted. "I'm sorry, I'm not waiting seven hours for the cricket to finish."

Rukshana shrugged her shoulders. "I'm sorry."

John Martin moved on. "You must have been very disappointed to be passed over for promotion at the bank?"

"Not really, no."

John Martin feigned surprise. "Not really?"

"I'm a person of faith, Detective Constable. Do you know what that means?"

John Martin looked blank. Islamic theology obviously wasn't his strong suit. Rukshana went on. "I accept everything as part of the divine plan. So, no, I wasn't disappointed."

"Very commendable, I'm sure. But you must have been a little upset when you were let go? Angry?"

She smiled at him. "That's for atheists, I'm afraid."

John Martin had the feeling he was being put down, but he pressed on. "Were you aware that the successful candidate was having intimate relations with your manager?"

"Jeff and Sarah? I certainly was not. I had no idea. People don't pass gossip on to me. It's because I'm a Muslim, you see."

John Martin pursed his lips and produced a photo from a file. He handed it to Rukshana. "Do you know who that is?"

It was a CCTV still photo from the lobby of the bank. It showed Rukshana at the security gate in her heels, short skirt, low-cut top, and sunglasses. Rukshana passed it back.

"No, sorry."

John Martin passed it back to her. "Have another look. Rack your brains."

Rukshana studied it again before handing it over.

"Still no."

John Martin moved in for the kill. "It's you, isn't it?"

Rukshana feigned outrage and tugged at her headscarf. "Certainly not. I'm a good Muslim. That girl looks like a prostitute. Totally inappropriate clothes for any decent Muslim woman."

John Martin passed her another photo, asked her if she recognized the subject. This one was a CCTV still of Rukshana in her burka outside Al-Nutjobs. But Rukshana had hit her stride. "I doubt her own mother would recognize her. If it was a woman, of course; perhaps it was a man in disguise? We don't wear burkas in this house."

John Martin played her the tape of the phone call to the anti-terrorist hotline. When it was finished he said, "That was you, wasn't it?"

"It sounds more like a white comedian making fun of Asians. There's too much of that sort of racism in our society. I don't know why the police don't crack down on it."

And so it went on. For an hour, John Martin probed and Rukshana parried. But Rukshana could see the detective was getting frustrated. He knew, okay, but he couldn't prove it. Eventually, John Martin accepted a cup of tea and a couple of samosas that he found "very tasty". Then, with obvious reluctance, he returned to the attack.

"Our inquiries have revealed – oh, I say, good shot!"

John Martin was looking over Rukshana's shoulder at the cricket. A young Pakistani batsman had just hit the ball clean into the cheering crowd. Granddad turned around and said to him, "What about that kid, eh? What a prospect!"

John Martin returned to his questioning, but he began going around in circles. He admitted the photos could have been of anyone. He also confessed there was no fingerprint evidence and that the tape didn't really prove anything. He admitted – off the record – that the police had quite a list of people who didn't much like her ex-boss Jeff, so they had a lot of others to interview. In fact, some of his fellow officers suspected Jeff's wife was the real culprit, and, frankly, they didn't blame her. The wife was certainly a more promising suspect than a nice Muslim girl like Rukshana.

"Okay, Miss Malik, I think we're about finished for now."

But as he got up to go, he noticed something on the mantelpiece. He walked over and picked up the large pair of sunglasses that Rukshana had worn the previous Thursday when she'd framed Jeff. They were sitting where she'd left them when she'd got back. John Martin looked at the shades and then fished out the CCTV still of Rukshana in the bank lobby and studied it. They were obviously the same distinctive pair. Rukshana felt her stomach tense. She'd been so careful, and now this . . .

But before John Martin had a chance to ask Rukshana for an explanation, her granddad snapped, "What are you doing with my sunglasses?"

"Your sunglasses?"

"Yes. They're medicinal, I use them to cut out the glare from the TV."

Granddad got up, took the sunglasses from the cop's hand, and put them on. He looked quite natty in them. John Martin was not convinced.

"You use them to cut out the glare from the TV?"

"That's right."

"So why weren't you wearing them when I came in?"

"I was. But I take them off when we have visitors. I don't want to look like a prat, do I?"

"I'm sorry, sir, but . . ."

Granddad angrily turned on the unfortunate police officer. "Are you calling me a liar? And by the way, the girl is right – she was here all day last Thursday and I was here all day watching cricket in my sunglasses and I'd like to see you prove otherwise. Now, why don't you clear off and catch some real criminals?"

When John Martin was gone, Rukshana sat down in the front room by her grandfather.

"So you were listening then?"

"I can listen and watch cricket at the same time. I'm not stupid. And that was a very foolish thing you did. You could have gone to prison."

"I know. And thanks, Granddad. For backing me up."

Her granddad nodded and then said, "If you'd wanted revenge on someone, you should have spoken to me. I know all about that. When I was a child, a British prime minister came to our village and was a little bit rude and arrogant." Rukshana's granddad forgot the cricket for a moment and became lost in thought. Then he added, "Now, that was a revenge story . . ."

The Zatopec Gambit

Roger Busby

When the bold chess player sacrifices a piece, usually a pawn, during the opening in order to secure an advantage, the move is called a gambit.

The day the burka bandit hit the King Kebab mini mosque and sparked an international incident, Detective Constable "Metal" Mike Malloy was raiding his brother-in-law's scrapyard. It was good solid CID work, the sort he enjoyed, so whenever the stats needed a boost he would borrow a couple of PCs from the relief, a handful of PCSOs and a dog handler for good measure and they would roar down the Old Kent Road in unmarked cars and a couple of vans, blues-and-twos going full blast, and turn the place over in fine old style.

Over his twenty years in the job "Metal" Mike had become a past master in the technique of raiding premises, and every time he would burst into the office, scowl menacingly and announce: "Okay, everybody stay put – this is a police raid!" And Alex Donnelly, his brother-in-law, would look up from his desk with tired, patient eyes and reply: "You got a warrant this time, Michael?" To which Malloy would invariably respond: "Since when did I need a warrant, Alex? This is family business." With a sigh Donnelly would push his work aside, produce a concertina print out of his scrap register for official scrutiny, and exchange pleasantries on family affairs while the raiding party, suitably equipped in loaned hard hats and steel toecaps to avoid infringing Health and Safety, scrambled over the acres of junk in the yard outside.

When it was all over, "Metal" Mike would return to the station, debrief his team, crank up the system and input the "dynamic intel" in meticulous detail. The borough had never had a more conscientious crime intelligence analyst than DC Malloy and nobody seemed unduly concerned that the monthly crime profiles uploaded to the Yard's number-crunchers appeared to relate exclusively to the activities of Southside Ferrous Factors, Alex Donnelly's scrap-metal business. Malloy could be relied upon for big number crime stats which kept the dream factory happy, and that was all that mattered.

Of course "Metal" Mike's preoccupation with his brother-in-law's scrapyard was not as simple as might appear at face value. For one thing, Detective Constable Malloy was bliss-fully ignorant of the fact that Donnelly really was a high-class villain and that was why he never complained to the brass about the seemingly unwarranted intrusion into his busi-ness. Similarly Alex Donnelly, who felt quite confident in his ability to hoodwink his numbskull brother-in-law, was unaware of the fact that the borough's glowing crime stats had risen through the system and had impressed NSY's Serious and Organized Crime Command. So much so that, unbeknown to him, Donnelly had been elevated to the rare-fied status of a Zatopec target and circulated to all London-wide crime squads.

Otherwise, this example of familial symbiosis ticked along quite nicely to each other's advantage; such as the time "Metal" Mike earned his sobriquet by recovering two war-memorial plaques, a giant bronze sculpture and a mile and a half of copper signalling cable which had closed the Northern Line for a week thanks to a whisper from his brother-in-law. While DC Malloy basked in the glory of a two-page spread in the *South London Press*, and twenty seconds on BBC London, Alex Donnelly was quietly satisfied that the media vilification and subsequent court case had put a troublesome rival out of business. Yes, in filial fashion, the unlikely brothers-in-law rubbed along in blissful ignorance until the day the burka bandit hit the King Kebab mini mosque just as Lawson Hollingsworth MP, Minister of State for International Affairs and the Third Secretary to the Pakistani High Commissioner, dropped in for a cultural visit, and all hell broke loose.

Alex Donnelly cut a fine figure for a South London scrap dealer with his penchant for pinstriped business suits and hand-tailored shirts. His thick dark hair was greying at the temples, adding a distinguished touch to his appearance, and he would have passed in the Square Mile for a merchant banker or stockbroker with his meticulous Old World manners and careful attention to the niceties of social etiquette. He had long since disposed of the amusingly alliterative South Side Scrap sign over the gates to his yard in favour of the more upmarket Southside Ferrous Factors, a respectable cover for his flourishing business exporting other people's antiques concealed in shipments of processed metal. He had built up a lucrative Euro-business on the booming continental metal exchange which qualified for all the EU subsidies, but to his criminal associates who specialized in plundering country mansions, Alex Donnelly was a 20 per cent of market value take-it-or-leave-it fence and, as such, a leading light of their fraternity.

If only his waspish younger sister hadn't upped and married that pride of the local law, Michael Malloy, the chain of events, which eventually elevated Alex Donnelly to the exalted criminal rank of Zatopec target, might never have happened. But as was his nature he took the bumbling attention of his detective-relative philosophically and in the course of "Metal" Mike's frequent visits to his premises even found him a useful, if unwitting, source of police information. While the raiding party rummaged half-heartedly through the mountains of twisted metal and gutted car shells, he would lubricate their conversation with Scotch and American sipped from cut-glass tumblers in quite a convivial manner.

In sharp contrast to the fastidious Donnelly, "Metal" Mike was studiously slovenly, favouring the *de rigueur* attire of the plainclothes street cop, scuffed leather jacket and jeans more often than not topped off with a woollen watch cap which he considered added a raffish touch to his street cred at the factory as an all-about-no-nonsense thief-taker. Quite what his sister had seen in him, Donnelly was at a loss to comprehend, but despite their singular incompatibility things went tolerably well as each played his own game with the other. Then, as so often happens when much has been invested in preserving the status quo, an unrelated event snuffs out the sun and changes everything forever.

By a coincidence of geography, Alex Donnelly's scrapyard sprawled across a vacant tract of Southwark hinterland between gaunt high-rise estates and clutches of low-rent retail and street markets once earmarked for a grandiose shopping/ leisure complex, then abandoned as the civic planners fled before the hot breath of the transplanted slum dwellers who had made the neighbourhood their own. And central to this cosmopolitan milieu was the King Kebab and mini mosque where the devout could satisfy both their earthly and spiritual hunger under one roof. Thus it was that at the moment of alignment as the Minister of the Crown and his diplomatic guest from the land of the Wazir sat down for a convivial cultural lunch, the runes were cast in the form of the burka bandit bursting in from the street and emptying the twenty-round magazine of a stubby TEC-9 machine pistol into the ceiling with a deafening rasp of automatic gunfire. As the tableau froze under a haze of plaster dust, the bandit calmly flipped another magazine into the assault pistol and growled: "Infidel goat-fuckers, you is being robbed . . . *Inshallah*."

Deputy Assistant Commissioner Tom "The Cat" Parker cast a jaundiced eye over the zoo-like chain-link fence which protected the yard of Peckham's central police station from the denizens of the neighbourhood, breathed a despairing sigh and exclaimed: "Rank hath its privilege, Bobby, and for a

DAC just four rungs from the top of the ladder, mine happens to be a nice warm office on the fifth floor with plenty of passing eye candy and a good lunch in the Commissioner's mess, not slumming it out here in the backwoods. So before I put this down to a sad bad dream, get back in the car here and tell Simon to whisk me back to the Yard, and please remind me what the hell I'm doing here."

Grinning from ear to ear as he held open the door of the DAC's Range Rover, Detective Chief Inspector Bob Jones, who ran the borough's robbery squad, replied with studied insouciance: "You're the guv'nor, guv'nor; me, I'm just a foot soldier toiling in the weeds, so you tell me."

From anyone else the flippant response would have brought a sharp rebuke, but despite the gulf of rank, the pair were old friends from back in the eighties when they had stood shoulder to shoulder in full riot kit repelling the hordes as members of the Met PSUs dispatched north to quell the miners' strike, a plum tour of overtime duty which had enabled Bobby Jones to pay off his mortgage and "The Cat" to buy a pied-à-terre in the Barbican as a hedge against inflation. Both men were career cops with time in, but loath to sever the umbilical. Jones inclined his head towards the mesh-enclosed tunnel, which accessed the factory through the custody suite, and swept a hand: "Shall we?" he said.

In the squad chief's office Jones drew the Venetian blinds and produced a bottle of Bells from his desk drawer. He poured two glasses and for a long moment they sipped whisky. Then "The Cat" said: "I was in the outer office admiring Charlene's legs – the pelmets they wear for skirts these days are enough to give a man palpitations – when I got called to the presence and the Old Man was stalking around the office like a caged tiger. Apparently Hollingsworth is tipped for promotion to Home Secretary in the next reshuffle and the Old Man's terrified he'll be out on his ear and no chance of the promised K, so he practically pleaded with me to get over here and sort this little job of yours pronto so he can get back into the heir apparent's good books."

"So a penny-ante stick-up, which might have rated a DS top weight, suddenly gets five-star treatment, eh guv?"

"You know the game as well as I do, Bobby. The Old Man says jump, all I say is "How high?" I'm not dying in this ditch, and neither are you. So let's take it from the top and see if we can't wrap this up pronto, before it all hits the fan."

Jones fed a disk into his laptop and swept a theatrical hand. "Meet the burka bandit," he said as the black-clad figure appeared in blurry monochrome. "Got him on the Mickey Mouse street CCTV."

"Not much to go on there then." The Cat peered at the fuzzy image. "Looks like a walking tent."

"Oh, it gets better," Jones said, as the briefest glimpse of the bandit entering the King Kebab and mini mosque flashed up and then the screen went blank. "That's when he shot out the camera."

"Weapon?"

"TEC-9 on full auto just to make sure he'd got their undivided attention."

"Part One prohibited weapon," the Cat sighed. "Where do they get them from? We've been running Trident like an express train, and still they keep coming."

"South London, guv'nor," Jones shrugged, "You could get yourself anything from a Saturday-night-special to an RPG if you needed one. All Trident's done is make 'em smarter; nobody keeps their own shooter anymore, you hire 'em out from rent-a-gun."

Jones tapped the mouse to pause the DVD. "He gives 'em the gypsies while they're paralysed in shock-n-awe and good as gold they turn out their valuables on the tables, mister scoops up the goodies, empties the till and he's on his toes in thirty seconds flat. Good old-fashioned no frills stand-and-deliver blag."

"Score?"

"Twenty grand top whack. Cash and the brethren's bling."

"Including the third's classic platinum, diamond-studded Day-Date Rolex Oyster on President Bracelet presented to him personally by one-time El Presidente himself, Muhammad Zia-ul-Haq, for services rendered when he was the ISI section chief in Waziristan."

"Spook?" Bobby Jones raised an eyebrow.

"Probably still is," the Cat said. "Not unusual for the right-hand man to the High Commissioner. So he's giving it bunny to Hollingsworth that this is a Taliban-inspired attempt on his life; thinks they've got a fatwa on him and Hollingsworth gets the hot prickles under his collar and starts melting the Old Man's dog-n-bone."

"Give me strength, guv," Jones sighed. "Next they'll be saying it's the Klingons."

"Al-Qaeda was mentioned," the Cat said.

"More like Al Capone," Jones said. "This tickle isn't a jihad, it's a gee-up."

The Cat folded his arms: "Enlighten me further, Chief Inspector."

Jones tapped the mouse and the laptop came back to life. "We got a blizzard of niners and the rapid response van got there first." A kaleidoscope interior of a speeding transit caroomed around the screen. "Head-cams," Jones explained. "They're doing a reality doc for Channel Four, *Cops-n-Robbers*."

"Who authorized that?"

"Fifth floor, guv," Jones grinned. "All part of the Commissioner's hearts-and-minds programme. Remember 'Dull it isn't'?"

"Yeah and 'Badge of Courage', classics from the DPA cringe-makers."

"One good thing though," Jones said. "We got witnesses on tape."

A wild-eyed Pakistani waiter lurched into view. "Suicide bomber," he wailed, "had on bomb belt, blow us all to kingdom come!"

"Too much information," the Cat said. "Turn it off, Bobby, and just give it to me straight."

Jones closed the laptop and refreshed the DAC's drink. "Well, we gave all the usuals a tug. Rikeman was favourite, fitted his MO to a tee, he pulled a job just across the pavement one Christmas dressed as Santa and he's got form as long as your arm."

"And . . ."

"Looked tasty too, if he hadn't got a cast-iron alibi, playing poker down at the Showdown with a bunch of the borough's finest."

"ID parades?"

Jones shook his head. "Nobody really got a good look at the bandit; one burka's much the same as another. One thing though, on his way out the bandit pulled up the hijab and took a big bite out of Hollingsworth's doner kebab. When we were putting the usuals through the hoops we tried for a regurg order so we could stomach pump 'em, but the CPS wouldn't wear it, so in the end they all walked."

The Cat laughed. "That would've been a first." He took a pull on his drink. "Back in the good old days, Bob, when you and I were rip-roaring young Ds we'd have nicked the lot of 'em and let 'em draw lots to see which one was going on the sheet. All the villains knew the score; if it wasn't the one you were nicked for it was for the one you were plotting up. What was the old slogan?"

With a big grin Jones said: "Don't bother with Burton's, the robbery squad'll fit you up."

"Happy days."

"Long gone, guv'nor. CPS said stomach-pumping a suspect was a definite no-no, would infringe their human rights and we'll all end up in the dock at Strasbourg."

The Cat chuckled at the thought: "So basically, Bobby, you're still on square one."

"Have a heart, guv'nor, it was hardly the crime of the century, and if it hadn't been for a couple of top-weight string-pullers jerking the Old Man's chain, we'd just be giving it a crime number and you'd be nice and cosy admiring Charlene's legs."

The Cat thought about it for a moment and then he said: "Look, Bob, no offence and no criticism of your lads, but I've got guiding light on this so I'm bringing in the Sweeney, full throttle."

Jones blinked, "Jesus, guv, talk about a sledgehammer to crack a nut."

"The way it crumbles," the Cat shrugged. "Look on the bright side, actually I'll be doing you a favour because you won't have to take the flak when the heavy mob start treading on toes; your squad can take a back seat while my lot squeeze the local villainy until the pips squeak." The Cat finished his Scotch in one swallow. "Summon the troops," he said, popping a mint, "I'll do the briefing myself. Who've you got on intel?"

"DC Malloy."

"Any good?"

"Crackerjack."

The Cat nodded, then he said: "Oh and just to smooth any ruffled feathers, Bob, you can give 'em the good news."

"Oh yeah, and what would that be guv'nor?"

"Brakes are off overtime." The Cat rubbed his hands. "Could be a nice little earner, like the good old days."

When Detective Constable Malloy returned to his partitioned cubbyhole in the CID general office he found a familiar face lounging in his chair puffing on a Bolivar Corona which he had purloined from the cedarwood cigar box "Metal" Mike kept tucked away in his desk drawer.

"Hey Mike, how's your luck?" the face, a DC on the Flying Squad, greeted him with easy familiarity. They were old section-house buddies who used to play snooker together back in their single men days, but Malloy considered the interloper helping himself to one of his prized cigars a dead liberty.

"Not allowed to smoke in here, Dave," he said pointedly. The cigars had been hand-rolled on the inside of a dusky maiden's thigh, or so he had been led to believe.

The Sweeney DC blew a smoke ring. "No problem, matey, I was never here, so I don't count." He grinned. "Anyway, my team just got called in on this little tickle of yours so I thought I'd drop in, sort of on the QT as you're an old buddy, and let you have a goosy at these smudges." He spread a selection of photographs across the desk.

Malloy stared at them in stunned silence. They were shots of Donnelly's scrapyard. "This one in particular," said the DC, dropping ash as he slid the last picture across the desk. It was a close up of Malloy himself coming out of the office.

"What's all this?" "Metal" Mike wanted to know, blinking in surprise, and the detective winked conspiratorially. "Thought I'd just mark your card, amigo; my guv'nor would crucify me if he knew I was telling you this, but it would be a poor state of affairs if we couldn't help each other out in the job, eh?"

"That's me there," Malloy couldn't help blurting the obvious. "What's going on?"

"Alex Donnelly," the DC confided, leaning forward.

"Alex Donnelly?" echoed "Metal" Mike, his voice rising in alarm.

"Shh, not so loud, this is need to know only."

"What about Alex Donnelly?" Molloy asked in a hoarse whisper.

"That's what I'm telling you," said the DC. "He's a Flying Squad target."

"What?"

"Twenty-four-hour surveillance."

"What for?" "Metal" Mike put the question with an edge of desperation.

"Zatopec," the DC whispered.

"Jesus," Malloy breathed the expletive; it didn't bear thinking about.

"Just a word to the wise, old mate," the DC counselled with a wink as he dropped the cigar into the wastepaper basket, "in case some guv'nor up the line starts wondering how come you're so pally with a squad target, puts two and two together and comes up with five and you've got the rubber heels from Professional Standards breathing down your neck. So like I said, I was never here, okay? If anyone should ask, you haven't seen me in years." With a sweep of the hand he spirited the pictures into an inside pocket and was gone before the incredulous "Metal" Mike could question him further.

With a low moan, Malloy slumped into his chair, his mind reeling. Alex Donnelly, his brother-in-law, a Zatopec target! It wasn't possible. Had he just dreamed it? Had it been some apparition there in the office? Some quirk of his overheated imagination? "Metal" Mike rubbed his eyes. Yes, that must be it, the adrenalin rush of his contribution to the burka-bandit briefing was playing tricks on him. His wife's brother a Sweeney target? It wasn't possible, he must have dreamt it. He wrinkled his nose; what was that acrid smell? Something was burning! His eyes fell on the wastepaper basket from which blue smoke was curling.

The Sweeney came down like Byron's wolf on the fold and as any self-respecting villain will testify there is nothing quite like a full-on police dragnet to shake the mice out of the woodwork. No sooner had DAC Tom "The Cat" Parker cranked up the operation, fuelled by the prospect of limitless overtime, than the neighbourhood was crawling with detectives, much to the chagrin of the criminal fraternity who immediately began to batten down the hatches to weather the storm, but not before the sweep had stumbled across a lock-up crammed with stolen TVs, a hydroponic cannabis "farm" bathed in the glare of 600-watt grow-lights in a foil-lined roof void, and a thermic lance plus a full kit of housebreaking implements concealed under a loose floorboard in a spare bedroom. Several of the brotherhood found the frenzied police activity just too much for their blood pressure and took off for a belated holiday in Tenerife. Alex Donnelly declined a seat on the chartered jet. It would, he told his colleagues, take more than the Old Bill busting a gut over a tupenny-ha'penny blagging to crack his nerve. Besides, he was to all intents and purposes a legitimate businessman with interests and a reputation to protect.

So he was just a mite surprised when a hoodie sidled into his office, long-billed baseball cap pulled low over his eyes, and announced in an anguished tone: "My God, Alex, you've made a right monkey out of me!"

Donnelly, who was in his customary place behind his desk, sighed, sat back from his computer on which he was assiduously tracking the EU metal market and looked up expecting the usual motley raiding party to materialize behind "Metal" Mike Malloy. But to his surprise, his brother-in-law was alone and his pained expression, odd appearance and injured tone seemed to indicate something was seriously amiss.

"You don't look so good, Michael," he replied mildly. "You'd better take the weight off and tell me all about it."

Tugging the hood further over his head in the hope of concealing his true identity from the prying eyes of the Flying Squad's long toms, Malloy flopped heavily into a chair. After extinguishing the fire in his wastepaper basket he had headed directly for the scrapyard to have it out with Donnelly.

"You've made me look a right mug," he complained accusingly.

"Mike . . . Michael," Donnelly replied patiently, "I haven't the faintest idea what you're talking about."

"And what's Linda going to say, eh?" Malloy grumbled. "Answer me that?"

"Look," Donnelly remained unruffled even at the mention of his sister, "you've got the advantage over me, what am I supposed to have done?"

"All this time and you didn't even tell me . . . me, your own brother-in-law. You let me keep on coming here without so much as a nod or a wink. It really is too bad, Alex."

Donnelly leaned forward, resting his elbows on the desk, and asked gently: "What's too bad, Michael?"

"And to think I had to find out for myself."

"Find out what?"

"That you're a Flying Squad target, that's what!" Malloy exclaimed hotly. "There's Ds on rooftops, in TV repair vans and pretending to dig up the road, taking pictures of everything that moves around here, including ME!"

Alex Donnelly sat up and spent a moment composing his facial muscles. "A Flying Squad target, eh?" he mused, shifting his mind into overdrive to assess the ramifications of this piece of information.

"Not any old target either, a Zatopec target," "Metal" Mike scowled miserably from the depth of his cowl, "the one that goes the distance."

Careful to avoid betraying a hint of emotion, Donnelly asked: "How did you find out?"

"From the horse's mouth," Malloy replied, "from the squad itself, and how d'you think that made me feel? My own brother-in-law a Zatopec target and I'm the last one to know. I'm telling you, Alex, you've made a right monkey out of me and no mistake; what's Linda going to say?"

"You haven't told her then?" Donnelly inquired, merely to keep the conversation going although he really couldn't have cared less about his sister's opinion at this juncture. He had enough to worry about on his own account.

"Of course not, I only just found out myself and I came straight over. You've spoiled everything, Alex, you know that. I was going to do a raid today and another tomorrow. I'm on this burka bandit job, you know, on the hand-picked team and we're pulling out all the stops. It was my big chance to shine, but how can I do it now with those jokers from the Squad perched all around? You've queered my pitch good and proper."

They talked on in this fashion a while longer: Malloy accusing; Donnelly placating as he extracted more and more information from his brother-in-law. The picture certainly looked gloomy, but he was a resilient and resourceful villain, and now that the first flush of shock had passed he began to examine the problem as a chess player, with a cool analytical approach. There had to be a gambit he could play, the Donnelly defence; all he had to do was figure it out.

The more Donnelly thought about it, the more he pinpointed the burka bandit bit of nonsense as worthy of consideration. Here was a single event stirring everything up, exciting the forces of law and order, turning a damned great searchlight on the shady areas of the manor. It was of constant amazement to a realist like himself that a nondescript crime could still cause such an uproar. It was all over the TV news and you could hardly move for woodentops prowling the streets. But that quirk of bureaucratic imbroglio could at least give him a starting point in his search for bargaining power, for he had no intention of remaining a Flying Squad target for a moment longer than was absolutely necessary and he was astute enough to understand that, with the right commodity on offer, you could bargain your way out of anything.

So by flattery and subtle questioning he proceeded to pick DC "Metal" Mike Malloy's brain clean on the subject of the burka-bandit blagging.

"All right," Donnelly said at last, "let's see if I've got it right. This comedian pulls off an armed robbery." He was always careful never to slip into the criminal vernacular in conversation with Malloy. "And it so happens that a pair of VIPs come a cropper and start yelling blue murder. Your lot get the bit between their teeth and haul in some likely candidates. Is that about the strength of it?"

"It was down to that toe-rag Ricky Rikeman, pound to a penny, got his MO stamped all over it, only he'd got a cast-iron alibi backed up by a bunch of upright citizens, so he walked."

"And now you're beating the undergrowth looking for some other prospect, eh?"

"I don't know why you're so interested in this case," Malloy replied morosely, "not now you're a big deal Flying Squad target who can't even play fair with his own brother-in-law."

"Just humour me," said Donnelly easily. "Did I get it about right?"

"I suppose so."

"This alibi," Donnelly mused, "can you get me a look at the statements?"

"Well I don't know about that," Malloy bridled, "that's official police business and besides . . ."

"Michael, look at me, this is a family thing. Would I ask you otherwise? Besides, you're an important bloke, the crime intelligence analyst. So don't go selling yourself short. Besides, you wouldn't want to let those glory boys from the Yard put your nose out of joint now would you?"

"What if I could get 'em?" Malloy scowled miserably and Donnelly eased himself back in his chair, a gambit beginning to take shape.

"Wouldn't you like things to get back the way they were, like the good times," he waved a hand, "when you had the run of the place and no hassle from snoopers taking liberties with "Metal" Mike Malloy?"

"Yes, but . . ."

"Trust me, Michael, get me those statements and I'll see what I can do to put this little mix-up to bed." Donnelly rose and walked over to the cocktail cabinet. "Now how about a drink to calm the old nerves?"

Malloy heaved himself to his feet. "No thanks," he turned the offer down emphatically, "I've been here too long already. Associating with a Zatopec target! Jesus, they could boil me in oil for that."

Donnelly shrugged; mentally the chess pieces were already in motion. "It'll be all right, Mike, you'll see," he said persuasively. "Just get me a shufti at those statements, okay?"

"I can't bring 'em here." Malloy shrank deeper into his hood and Donnelly laughed at his pained expression.

"Why not? You're always down here. Break the pattern and you'll be the next under surveillance."

An involuntary groan escaped "Metal" Mike Malloy's lips as he imagined the Squad staking out the Greenwich mews townhouse, which was his wife's pride and joy. Linda would crucify him.

"Just get the statements," Donnelly urged, reaching into his desk drawer to fish out a thumbnail-sized flash drive. "Use this, and trust me Michael, it'll be okay."

*   *   *

It was, Malloy discovered, surprisingly easy. As the local intel analyst on the case, his password gave him total access to the need-to-know database. The cranked-up investigation was now running on Holmes, the acronym for the Home Office (Large) Major Enquiry System, which churned out the actions and crunched all the input into something the SIO could get his head around. As any old-time detective would bemoan, before computers came along, it was vital to get a job by the scruff of its neck within the first forty-eight hours or drown under an avalanche of paper, as the card index grew like Topsy. It took the debacle of the Yorkshire Ripper to concentrate the minds and come up with something that doyen of Baker Street would have described as elementary.

When he was confident he was unobserved by the incident room support team, "Metal" Mike pulled up the alibi statements on his terminal, slipped the key into the USB port and in the blink of an eye downloaded the file and exited the system before the gaggle of inputters could spot an interloper and start asking awkward questions.

The following day he was back at his brother-in-law's yard sitting across the desk, gnawing his knuckles anxiously as Donnelly read through the statements on his laptop, hoping for a change of expression which would indicate a ray of hope. He had slept badly the night before, plagued by nightmares of vultures circling as he staggered, exhausted, across an endless desert. Donnelly read in silence, absorbing the stilted prose, taking particular interest in the details of the alibi which he reread several times.

"These people," he broke the deep silence finally, "they've got damned good memories."

"Unshakable," the detective replied gloomily. "All-day poker at the Showdown, he couldn't have planned it better if he wanted to. They all tell the same story and if you're thinking collusion, forget it, they've been checked out."

Donnelly smiled. "But that means if one cracks, they all go out the window?"

"They won't," Malloy replied. "There's enough witnesses there to sink a battleship, people at the tables, people at the bar, statements all tally and the CCTV is time-coded. That's the best alibi I ever saw, it's fireproof."

"This one," Donnelly said, alighting on one of the names, "Oliver Bodkin, what d'you know about him?"

"Metal" Mike frowned, dredging his memory. "He's the garage owner with the Bentley, big wheel at the golf club, likes to play a little daytime poker with his cronies."

"Didn't know Rikeman from Adam either," Donnelly mused.

"That's right," Malloy agreed, "how'd he put it? Oh yeah – just helping out like the Good Samaritan and doing his public duty assisting the police, that's what he said."

Donnelly's smile widened. "Nice touch," he said, and, to himself, the chess-master murmured checkmate.

When Malloy had gone, Alex Donnelly called in two of his biggest and ugliest yard hands and dispatched them to Bodkin's Deptford garage with an invitation the man couldn't refuse, unless he fancied a length of lead pipe bent over his cranium. They returned with a pasty-faced man who seemed to be having some trouble with his breathing.

"Hello Odds," Donnelly greeted him affably. "Long time no see." He rose, smoothing down the jacket of his pinstripe suit, and nodded to the minders to release their grip on the man's arms. "Good of you to come at such short notice."

Bodkin gasped for air like a stranded fish, breath wheezing from his lungs. His voice was a nasal whine: "I thought you and me were mates, Alex. You didn't have to send these gorillas to work me over. Busted half my ribs."

"Tried to leg it out the window, boss," explained the larger of the two messengers. "Got so excited we had to give him a slap to settle him down."

"All right, lads," Donnelly told the pair, "just wait outside a minute while I talk to Mr Bodkin here. I'm sure there's no hard feelings."

When they were alone, Donnelly poured his guest a drink. "What I want you to understand, Odds," he said apologetically as he handed over a generous tumbler of whisky, "is there's nothing personal in this whatsoever, it's pure business."

"What's going on, Alex, what'd I do?" Bodkin yelped, gulping at the Scotch in an endeavour to fortify himself.

"It's a long story," Donnelly told him in his quiet courteous manner, "but let's put it this way, you're a good careful villain, Odds, I've got to give you that, nice thriving little firm ringing bent motors and shipping 'em out without the law getting so much as a sniff. Nice sensible living with plenty of prospects, just the kind of entrepreneurial spirit the government's always banging on about." Donnelly's voice grew cold. "So why, oh why, did you have to go and spoil it by getting mixed up with this toe-rag Ricky Rikeman, eh?"

Bodkin's eyes widened, but he still tried to brazen it out. "I don't know what you mean, Alex."

"What I mean," Donnelly explained patiently, "is you fitted this scum up with an alibi stuffed full of porkies."

"Hey, Alex," Bodkin cried, "what d'you mean, porkies? What would I do a thing like that for?"

"And the trouble is," Donnelly went on, ignoring the protestation, "owing to certain adverse circumstances affecting me and my associates, although it does go against the grain, I'm going to have to get you to throw this scumbag Rikeman to the wolves."

"For God's sake, Alex," Bodkin blurted, his face ashen, "it wasn't my idea, I just went along with it. He was a loser, owed us big time and promised to ante up if we pulled him clear of the Old Bill. Jesus, if I'd known it was going to cause you grief, Alex, I'd've told 'em to shove it, straight up, on my baby's eyes I would."

A faintly regretful smile touched Donnelly's lips. "No sense in getting all worked up, Odds," he said. "As I explained, this is purely business. We've always got on well in the past, you stick to your side of the street and I stick to mine, but you see it finally comes down to a question of priorities."

"What do you want me to do, Alex?" Bodkin asked desperately. "Anything you want, just name it."

Donnelly examined his fingernails: "Like I said, I want you to dump Rikeman, make a new statement to the police; say you were confused, mistaken. An honest mistake, eh? Must have been someone else. I'll take care of the arrangements."

"Anything you say, Alex," Bodkin gabbled. "You're the boss, anything you say."

"You're still missing the point," Donnelly spoke quietly, polishing his nails and inspecting the shine. "I'm going to have to make an example of you, Odds, so that all those one-eyed-jack cronies of yours get the message and follow suit. But I want you to believe me when I tell you there's absolutely nothing personal in this at all. You've got to look on it as a business transaction, a little sacrifice in the name of goodwill."

Bodkin yelped in fright as Donnelly recalled his henchmen and they dragged the man out to his car, a midnight-blue Bentley Continental GT, and deposited him behind the wheel. "Nice jam-jar," Donnelly admired the soft cream hide interior and sleek lines of the luxury limo, sitting there contented in sharp contrast to the dirty yellow HyMac yard crane which loomed over it, its four great rusty claws poised over the roof.

"I'd belt up if I was you, clunk click," Donnelly advised as he stepped back and nodded to the crane operator. The talons swooped down and seized the car, rocked it on its suspension then swung it effortlessly into the air, glass and paint flakes showering down as the hydraulic grab bit into the roof. Roaring and belching smoke from its exhaust stack, the HyMac jiggled the car in midair then crashed it to the ground. A wheel spun off and went bouncing into the scrap pile. Bodkin was screaming in terror as the crane heaved the car into the air again, shaking it like a terrier worrying a bone. The bonnet flapped and the boot lid lurched open on impact as the crane let go and the Bentley crashed back to the ground.

At Donnelly's signal the process was repeated several times until, bent and buckled, the no longer sleek Continental looked very sorry for itself and from inside the wrecked car Bodkin could be heard wailing hysterically. After a while Donnelly gave the order for the claws to relax their grip, setting the car down for the last time with a shriek of tortured metal. Odds Bodkin had screamed himself hoarse as, battered and misshapen, the once epitome of luxury automotive design had been effortlessly reduced to scrap. He was gibbering like an idiot when they hauled him out of the wreck and deposited him at Donnelly's feet. Spittle drooled from his lips and his eyes swivelled in his head as he scrabbled about in the dirt and ended up clinging to Donnelly's leg.

"Like I said, no hard feelings, Odds," Donnelly told him solicitously as he plucked a bejewelled Day-Date Rolex from Bodkin's limp wrist. "Oh, and I hope this fancy motor of yours is still under warranty, otherwise I think you just lost your no-claims bonus."

Tom "The Cat" Parker caught up with his old sparring partner in the steam room of the Elephant Turkish Bath and Sauna on the Walworth Road.

"My God," he exclaimed, towel wrapped around his waist toga-like, "this place hasn't changed a bit." He cast an eye over the veined white tiling and bleached-out benches. "I used to come here with Michael Caine, before he was Michael Caine."

Bobby Jones, looking distinctly the worse for wear, blinked uncomprehendingly. "Before he was Michael Caine?"

"Mm, he was Maurice Micklewhite in those days and the Elephant and Castle was his stamping ground. We used to have a laugh. If I'd kept in touch I might have got a part in *The Italian Job*. I was a bit of a thespian myself in those days." He peered at the naked form through the mist of steam. "You don't look so good, old son."

"Sweating neat alcohol," Jones said. "Last night was a marathon, like none other. I've got jack hammers going flat out inside my skull." He winced, recalling the scene. The Commissioner had sent over a case of champagne and a

limitless bar tab, so the party had spiralled out of control in
time-honoured fashion. He had awful memories of DCs
throwing up in the alley adjoining the pub; another, attempting to drunkenly seduce a barmaid, fell down the cellar steps
and broke his leg; a usually staid DS danced a jig on a table
wearing only his underpants and then led the assembly in
community hymn singing before collapsing into a paralytic
stupor. Jones shuddered at the memory.

"Well, you cleared the burka bandit job, Bobby. Feather in
your cap all right. The Old Man was cock-a-hoop. Hollingsworth gave him a pat on the head and maximum brownie
points, so his K looks safe again. Of course he says he only
wants it for his old woman so she can swank around as Her
Ladyship to compensate for all the time he was away keeping
this fair city safe for honest folk."

"Now where have I heard that before?" Jones muttered as
the Cat perched on the bench beside him.

"You know what, Bob," he remarked brightly, still strolling down memory lane, "This reminds me of when we were
up at Orgreave, knocking miners' heads together and using
the old coking works bath house for a scrub-up. Seems like
only yesterday, eh, when we were young and keen as
mustard?"

Jones groaned. "Not so loud, Tom, my head can't stand it."

"Well, you'd better fill me in on this burka-bandit job. Good
bit of work by your lads, commendations all round. So what
happened, some sharp D get lucky?"

The groan faded into a sigh. "Damnedest thing," Jones
said. "Rikeman's cast-iron alibi blew up in his face, just evaporated."

"Get away."

"He had all those witnesses in his pocket, backing him up
at that all-day poker game."

"So who pulled the rug out from under?"

Jones winced as the pain stabbed behind his eyes: "Local
crime intel, would you believe? That old warhorse Mike
Malloy . . ."

"Metal Mike as I recall." The Cat had a good memory for nicknames in the job.

"The very same. Been out to grass in crime intel longer than I can remember, then bang, he's got this one sewn up and covered himself in glory."

"Luck of the draw, probably," the Cat said. "What did Metal Mike do, rub his lamp three times and get himself a genie?"

"Something like that," Jones agreed. "Turns out he's got a bloody good informant, some guy he's been cultivating for years suddenly came good, got a nice citizen's commendation coming from the Commissioner for his public-spirited action. We gave Rikeman a pull on the strength, and when we put it to him he didn't have a prayer, he folded his hand and coughed it. Not even the CPS is going to balk at a confession. Oh, and we're putting the poker school up for conspiracy to pervert. They'll probably go down for longer than burka man."

"That's the spirit," the Cat said, "that'll get the old sphincters twitching." He turned to face Bobby Jones: "This informant of Malloy's, wouldn't be some superstar called Alex Donnelly would it?"

"How'd you know that, Tom?"

The Cat scratched his ear. "That explains it," he said. "I got a steer from the Old Man on him. We'd got him marked down as a Zatopec target."

"What?"

"Just one of those things," the Deputy Assistant Commissioner shrugged.

"What'd you do?"

"Oh, we dropped him like a hot potato. How'd you like to explain away a Flying Squad target who's just cleared a major high-profile crime with a Metropolitan Police Commissioner's commendation in his pocket to prove it?"

"I wouldn't."

"Who for good measure personally returned the presentation timepiece to our friend at the Pakistani embassy, earning himself the grateful thanks of the representative of a friendly nation to boot."

"Ouch!"

"Oh yes, quite the man of the moment, our Mr Donnelly. So to answer your question, I had his stuff yanked out of the system and the file erased back to the Stone Age so fast you wouldn't have known he ever existed."

"Self-preservation," Jones nodded.

"Name of the game," the Cat grinned. He looked around again at the wraith-like figures materializing through the mist of the steam room and got to his feet, pulling his towel tighter around his waist. "Well, they're open, Detective Chief Inspector Jones, so how about a jar, hair of the dog?"

Bobby Jones lowered his head into his hands. "Go away, guv'nor," he pleaded, steadying his brow and waiting for the spasm of nausea to pass.

Funeral for a Friend

Simon Kernick

There's always the low murmur of whispered conversation at a funeral. The men, unsmiling, acknowledge each other with terse nods and stiff handshakes; the women kiss and hold one another in tight embraces, as if somehow the strength of their emotion will protect them from a similar fate. It won't. The end, I can tell you from experience, is lurking round every corner.

I'm pleased with the turnout today, though. I didn't think that I was that popular. I am, or was, a pretty brutal man. But I was powerful, too, and power tends to attract followers, I suppose.

I'm looking for one man in particular, but so far he's conspicuous by his absence. Most of the people have already taken their seats, and we're only five minutes away from the 2.30 p.m. start time. The door to the church opens, but it's not him. It's Arnold Vachs, my former accountant, here with his wife. Creeping unsteadily down the aisle, like the bride at an arranged marriage to King Kong, he's small and potbellied with the furtive air of a crook, which is very apt, since that's exactly what he is. His wife – who's a good six inches taller and supposedly an ex-model – definitely never married him for his looks. But Arnold Vachs earns big money, and that makes him one hell of a lot more attractive.

Finally, with one minute to go, the man I'm waiting for steps inside. Tall, lean and tanned, with a fine head of silver hair, he looks like an ageing surfer who's suddenly discovered how to dress smart. It's my old blood brother, Danny O'Neill, looking a lot younger than his sixty years, and as soon as I see him, I'm transported back four decades, right to the very beginning.

The year was 1967, and I'd just come back from a twelve-month stint in Nam. I was still a kid, barely twenty, with the remnants of an unfinished high-school education, and no job or prospects. The difference between me and every other Joe was that I was a killer. A few months earlier, our unit had been caught in an ambush in a jungle near the border with Laos, at a place called Khe Sanh. We were forced to pull back to a nearby hill and make a stand while we waited for the copters to come and pull us out. Nine hours we were on that hill, twenty-nine men against more than 300. But we stood our ground, took seven casualties – two dead, five wounded – and cut down more than forty Gooks. So, when I came back home, I'd lost any innocence I might have had, and pretty much all my fear, too. I was a new man. I was ready to embark on my destiny.

I teamed up with another vet called Tommy "Blue" Marlin, and Tommy's friend, Danny, who'd also served in Nam, in the 51st Airborne. The three of us went into business together. And our profession? I'd call us Financial Advisors. The cops, though, they preferred the more derogatory term of bank robbers.

We liked to hit smalltown outlets. The money wasn't as good as the big-city branches, but the security was minimal to the point of non-existent, and the staff tended to be too shocked to resist. We'd walk in, stockings over our heads, and I'd put a few rounds from my M16 into the ceiling, so everyone could tell we were serious, before pointing the smoking barrel at the employees. They always got the message, and filled up the bags we provided like they were OD'ing on amphetamines.

Sometimes we'd hit the same bank twice; sometimes we'd hit two places on the same day. But you know what? Nobody ever got hurt. In nineteen raids we never had a single casualty.

It was an enviable success rate. Problem was, it all changed when the cops decided to poke their noses in.

The target was a branch of the Western Union in some nowheresville town in north Texas. We'd been scoping it on and off for a couple of weeks and knew that the security truck came to pick up the takings every second Wednesday, just before close of business. That meant hitting the place early Wednesday afternoon for the best return. Everything went like it always did. Blue waited outside in the Lincoln we were using as a getaway car, while Danny and me rushed inside, put the bullets in the ceiling, and started loading up with greenbacks. But while we're doing all this, a cop car pulls up behind the Lincoln because it's illegally parked. The cop comes to the window and tells Blue to move the car, but just as Blue – being a good, dutiful citizen – pulls away, the cop hears the gunshots, draws his own weapon and goes to radio for back-up. He's still got the radio to his ear when Blue reverses the Lincoln straight into him, knocking him down. The cop's hurt but still moving, so Blue jumps out of the Lincoln and puts three rounds in his back while he's crawling along the tarmac towards his radio. Problem is, this is the middle of the day and there must be a dozen witnesses, all of whom get a good look at our man.

Two minutes later and we're out of the bank with more than twenty grand in cash, only to see the corpse of a cop on the ground and no sign of the getaway car. Blue's lost his nerve and left us there. Lesser men would have panicked, but Danny and me weren't lesser men. We run down the street to the nearest intersection and hijack a truck that's sitting at a red light. The driver – a big, ugly redneck – gets argumentative, but a round in his kneecap changes all that, and we turf him out and start driving.

We're out of town and out of danger long before the cavalry arrive, but the heat's on us now. A dead cop is a liability to any criminal. His buddies are going to stop at nothing to bring the perps to justice, but me and Danny figure if we give them the shooter then maybe we'll be less of a target.

Two days later, we track down Blue to a motel on the New Mexico/Texas border. He's in the shower when we kick down the door and, as I pull back the curtain, he begs for mercy. Just before I blow his head off, I repeat a phrase one of the officers in Nam used to say: *To dishonour your comrades is to deserve their bullets.* He deserves mine, and there are no regrets.

Danny and I both realize that, with Blue's death, the armed robbery game's probably not one for the long term. We've made a lot of money out of it, getting on for half a million dollars, most of which we've still got. So, we do what all good capitalists do: we invest, and what better market to invest in than dope? This was the tail end of the sixties, the permissive decade. The kids wanted drugs, and there weren't many criminals supplying it, so Danny and I made some contacts over the border in Mexico, and started buying up serious quantities of marijuana which we sold on to one of our buddies from Nam – Rootie McGraw – who cut the stuff up into dealer-sized quantities and wholesaled it right across LA and southern California. One hell of a lot of kids had us to thank for the fact they were getting high as kites for only a couple of bucks a time. It was a perfect set-up, and as more and more people turned on, tuned in and dropped the fuck out, so the money kept coming in. And Rootie had a lot of muscle. He was heavily involved in one of the street gangs out of Compton, so no one fucked with our shipments.

Rootie's in the church now, dressed in black from head to toe, looking the height of funereal fashion, but he was always a snappy dresser. He might be pushing seventy with a curly mop of snow-white hair, and just the hint of a stoop, but the chick with him would have difficulty getting served in the local bar, and you know what they say: *You're only as old as the woman you feel.* This girl's a beauty too, with a skirt so short she could hang herself with it. A couple of people give her dirty looks, including my long-term mistress, Trudy T. Trudy's always been a good woman – we had something going on and off for years – but she's turned a little bit conservative ever since she found the Lord a couple of years back, and I think she's forgotten what a wild one she was in her day. Seeing that miserable look on her face now, I want to pipe up and remind her of that home-made porno movie we made on the 8 mm back in the mid-seventies – the one in that hotel room in Tijuana where Trudy was on her hands and knees snorting lines of coke off the flat, golden belly of a nineteen year-old Mexican whore while I brought up the rear, so to speak. Religion, I conclude, has a lot to answer for, although I sympathize with Trudy for wanting to hedge her bets now that the end's a lot nearer for her than the beginning.

Talking of coke, that's what really made us. There was money in marijuana – no doubt about it – but it was nothing compared to what could be made trading in the white stuff. By the end of the seventies, we were bringing close to a thousand kilos a year into the States, using Rootie's distribution network to market it to the people, and clearing ten mil in straight profit. We could have got greedy but the thing about Danny and me was that, first and foremost, we were businessmen. We pumped our profits into legit businesses – construction, property and tourism, in the main – and eventually we were able to pull out of the smuggling game altogether.

Just in time, as it turned out. Within months Rootie got busted and, because he showed loyalty and refused to name the people he was involved with, he got shackled with a fifteen to twenty-five sentence, and ended up serving twelve.

It served as a good lesson to Danny and me. Always be careful. And we were. We built up an empire together – one that was turning over thirty million dollars a year – and we staffed it with men and women who showed us the same loyalty as Rootie had shown. We were a success story. I can look back and claim, with hand on heart, that I truly made it, and you can see that by the numbers of people in this church today. Three hundred at least. Friends, employees, lovers. Lots of lovers. Trudy T was one, but I've always been a man with appetites – they used to call me the Norse Horse, back in the day – and there were plenty of others. Row six, to the left of the aisle, sits one. Claire B was a movie star once upon a time, with the kind of perfect good looks made for the silver screen. She's eighty years old now and used to call me her toyboy. We had a lot of fun together, and that's why she's weeping quietly into her white handkerchief now while an old geezer, who must be close to a hundred, puts a wizened arm round her shoulders.

I scan the room and see Mandy H – a former Vegas show-girl I had a fling with back in the summer of '79 – beautiful once, now cracked and hardened with age, her face as impassive as an Easter Island statue as she stares straight ahead; then there's Vera P who took up with me for a while in the late eighties, after the death of her husband, a man who was one of my longest-serving employees. She was lonely and I was horny, a combination that was never going to work, but I guess I must have had some effect on her because she's sobbing so ferociously it's making her hair stand on end. And the service still hasn't even started yet. I should be impressed but I'm forgetting it already as I catch sight of Diana, as regal as an Ice Queen, sitting right down at the front.

Diana. My wife; my widow; my one true love – still as beautiful in her fifty-ninth year as she was the day we met on a snowy New York afternoon, twenty-five years ago. I was in Central Park for a business meeting with one of our Manhattan-based partners that I didn't want anyone snooping on. Not only because we were talking details that weren't entirely legal, but also because we were giving the guy a bit of a beating on account of the fact that he'd been cheating the organization. I'd just broken a couple of his fingers and was leaving him to two of my most trusted men to finish off, when as I came out from behind some bushes, I saw her gliding along the path in my direction – this gorgeous willowy blonde with a fur hat perched jauntily on her head and a little dog on a lead – and this cool, languid look in her eye. Man, I knew straight off, I had to have her. Within an hour, we were sharing cocktails. Within three, we were sharing a bed. Inside a month, we were man and wife. I'm nothing if not a fast worker.

I always wanted kids, but Diana couldn't have them. That's why there are none here today. It doesn't matter. We had each other, and for me, that was good enough. Everything had come up roses. The money was rolling in; the cops could never touch us; and I was married to the woman of my dreams.

Life was good. All the way up until last month it was good.

And then it all went wrong and twenty-five pounds of plastic explosive placed on the underside of my Mercedes Coupe, directly beneath the driver's seat, ended the life of Francis Edward Hanson, aged fifty-eight: lover, friend, businessman and killer.

A homicide investigation started right away, and there are currently plenty of suspects, but no one who really stands out. We'd killed or bought off most of our rivals years ago. The two homicide cops are in here now, sitting at the back of the church, trying without success to blend chameleon-like into their surroundings. They're wearing cheap suits and furtive expressions and they couldn't really be anything else. One or two of the guys turn and give them the look. No one in our organization likes the cops.

The service lasts close to an hour. It's too long really, especially in this heat. They sing my favourite hymn: Cat Stevens's "Morning Has Broken", and I remember I once amputated a man's leg to that particular song, which brings a smile; and Danny does a reading from one of the psalms. I've never believed in a Supreme Being, I've seen too much injustice for that. But I've always hoped there was some sort of afterlife, somewhere you can kick back and take it easy, and I'm pleased to announce that there is one, and that so far it looks like it might be pretty good.

And then it's all over. My coffin moves effortlessly along a conveyor belt to the right of the pulpit and disappears behind a curtain. In keeping with my express wishes, my remains are to be cremated rather than buried. The cops aren't too happy about this, you know, seeing their evidence go up in smoke, but they've finished with my body now, so they haven't got any grounds for refusal. There's a final bout of loud sobbing

– mainly from the women – and then the mourners file slowly out into the furnace-like heat of a New Mexico afternoon.

I see Danny move close to Diana. They talk quietly. It looks to the untrained eye as if he's offering her comfort and condolences, but I know better. His hand touches her shoulder and lingers there a second too long, and they walk through the graveyard together, continuing their conversation. Several people turn their way, with expressions that aren't too complimentary, but they don't care. Danny's the boss now and I'm reminded of that old English phrase: *The King is dead. Long live the King.* Life goes on. I'm the past. Like it or not, for these people, Danny's the future.

Except he isn't.

There's going to be a wake back at the ranch that I've called home for these past twenty years. They've got outside caterers coming in and it sounds like it'll be a huge party. I'm only pissed off I can't attend. And look at this: Danny and Diana are travelling back there together. They ought to be more careful. The cops are going to get suspicious. But they seem oblivious.

Diana gets into the passenger seat of Danny's limited edition, cobalt-blue Aston Martin. I've always liked that car. He gets in the driver's side and then, three seconds later: Ka-Boom! There's a ball of fire, a thick stream of acrid black smoke, and when it finally clears, a burnt-out chassis with four spoked wheels, and very little else.

People run down towards the site of this, the second assassination of a member of our organization in the space of a month. They want to help, but there's nothing they can do. Trudy T, she of Christian faith and Tijuana hotel rooms, lets loose this stinging scream that's probably got every dog in a ten-mile radius converging on the church, and the two cops shout for everyone to keep calm and stay put, one of them already talking into his radio. They are roundly ignored.

I just keep walking, ignored by the crowd, knowing that my disguise, coupled with the plastic surgery I've recently undergone, means that no one will have recognized me.

Now that I've got my revenge, it's time to start my new life. I always trusted Danny, and I think that's been my problem. I don't know when his affair with Diana started, but I guess it must have been a while back. Me and her haven't been so good lately and this has been the reason why. I think it was a bit much that they wanted to kill me, though, and make it look like an assassination. Not only is it the worst kind of betrayal, but it was stupid, too. How did they think I wouldn't find out about it? Maybe love makes us all foolish.

Anyways, I did find out. A friend of Rootie's knew the bombmaker and it didn't take much to get him to tell me when he was going to be planting his product under my Merc. Diana's got an older brother, her last living relative, but a guy she rarely sees. His name's Earl and he lives alone. At least he did. He's dead now. Being roughly my height and build was a bit unfortunate for him. I had him killed, just to spite her, and his body planted in the Merc on the morning that I was supposed to die. Rather than being ignition-based, the bomb was on a timer (something the cops'll probably work out eventually, not that it'll do them much good), and when it went off, tearing the corpse into a hundred unrecognizable pieces, everyone simply assumed it was me who was dead in there.

Not wanting to give anyone the chance to disprove this theory, I disappeared off the scene, having already opened bank accounts in false names and bought a house for myself in the Bahamas. Only thing was, I couldn't resist coming back to watch my own funeral and, of course, see the bombmaker's talents put to work for a second time. And it was a nice bonus, too. Getting both of them at once. Saves me tracking down Diana later.

As I get in my own car, and leave the scene of carnage behind, I think back to the friendship Danny and me had, and it makes me a little melancholy that it had to end like this. Like the time with Blue, though, I don't have any regrets. Danny knew the score. It had been banged into him from our earliest days.

To dishonour your comrades is to deserve their bullets.
And now he's had mine.

I think that if he wasn't splattered all over the sidewalk, he'd probably approve.

A Three Pie Problem

Peter Lovesey

Peter Diamond wasn't Scrooge, but Christmas could be a pain. For one thing, he missed Steph more than ever at this time of year. For another, people took pity on him and invited him to stay. His in-laws, Angela and Mervyn, asked him each year to go up to Liverpool for "a proper family party" and he was forced to think of excuses. He'd tried saying Raffles, his cat, needed looking after, but they didn't regard that as a reason. "Put him in a basket and bring him with you," Angela had said. "We'll fuss him up, same as you." Raffles, like Diamond, wouldn't relish being fussed up.

This year, Angela had a different strategy. "You know what I'm going to say," she told him on the phone about the second week of December, "and I know what you're going to say, so forget it. If you won't come to the party, the party is coming to you. It's ages since we visited Bath and we do so enjoy looking round. Don't panic, Peter. I'll do all the cooking and Mervyn will organize the games."

Games? He almost dropped the phone.

"It's fixed, then. We're arriving the Saturday before and we'll stay until the New Year."

"I could be on duty," was all he could think to say.

"Come on, you're the boss, aren't you?"

"A major incident."

"At Christmas?"

This Christmas, please, he thought.

There was no stopping Angela. They arrived with their

hatchback stuffed with suitcases and all the festive paraphernalia, including a plastic tree. Raffles took refuge in the airing cupboard.

For reasons nobody cared to go into, Angela thought the police in general were beneath contempt and her late sister Stephanie – she always used the full name – should never have hitched herself to one of them, let alone an overweight slob like Diamond. His rank did not impress her. His skills as a detective were disregarded. He hadn't papered the walls since they'd bought the house. Hadn't weeded the garden, washed the windows, mended the Hoover, removed the tidemark from the bath. He pampered the cat and cheated at cards. All this was pointed out to him on the first evening.

So the call from Bath Police Station on Christmas Eve came as glad tidings, even great joy, to the beleaguered head of CID.

"Sorry to disturb your Christmas break, sir."

"No trouble at all. Do you need me there?"

"It could be nothing at all."

"But on the other hand . . ." he said with a rising note.

"There's an outside chance it was murder."

"Say no more. Duty calls."

Angela rolled her eyes upwards and Mervyn looked aghast at the prospect of being alone with his wife. "Could I come with you, as a sort of observer?"

"No," Diamond said. "Too horrible for a man of your good taste. Why don't you redecorate the Christmas tree? Angela thinks my effort was crap."

He was gone.

Bath police had been alerted to the death of one Fletcher Merriman, aged seventy-eight, the senior partner in Merriman & Palmer, a small firm of accountants with an office above a shop in Gay Street. Old Mr Merriman had died two weeks ago of heart failure in the Royal United Hospital.

"There are suspicious elements," Georgina Dallymore, the Assistant Chief Constable, told Diamond. "I wouldn't put it any higher than that. He wasn't admitted with a heart condition. They treated him for gastroenteritis following an office party. He was in considerable pain, I gather. The heart attack came later."

"Poison?"

"The post-mortem was inconclusive. They tested for the known poisons and found nothing of note. He was on medication for a heart problem anyway, so there were traces of various substances in the stomach contents, but nothing lethal."

"So what's the problem?"

"I hope we're not wasting your time, Peter. It's just that the circumstances could have come straight out of Agatha Christie. He wasn't a nice old man at all. In fact, he was appalling. Everyone at the party had reasons to knock him off."

"Everyone? How many is that?"

"Three."

"Small party."

"All the easier to question them. It could wait until after Christmas, but you left the message saying you wanted to be notified if any serious crimes were reported."

"Absolutely, ma'am. Maybe if I spend Christmas on this one I can take days off in lieu at a later date."

"You mean when the in-laws have left?"

He grinned.

The surviving partner, Maurice Palmer, had agreed to be in attendance at the office in Gay Street, but it was a woman's voice on the entry-phone. Diamond gave his name and entered.

"Sylvie Smith, junior accountant," she said. She was smart, in her twenties, with dark, intelligent eyes. "He's expecting you."

"And did he ask you to come in on Christmas Eve just to show me in?"

"It's a chance to tidy my desk."

"Don't go away, then. I'd like to speak to you later."

Palmer appeared from an inner room and introduced himself. Fiftyish, in the obligatory dark suit and striped tie, he looked well capable of tangling with tax inspectors. Or police inspectors.

"Decent of you to see me," Diamond said. "I hope this hasn't messed up your holiday plans."

"Not as yet," Palmer said, "but I hope we can clear up any questions now. I'm booked on a flight to Tenerife tonight."

"Is that a tax haven?"

"If it is, it doesn't come into my plans. I'm going for some winter sunshine, I hope."

Diamond glanced about him at the filing cabinets and computers. "So is this the room where the party was held?"

"No, in point of fact. This is the office where the ladies sit," Palmer said. "The party was in here." He swung open the door he'd come through. "My room."

Diamond stepped in. "Nice."

It was oak-panelled, with a high corniced ceiling and a marble fireplace with gas flames that looked realistic. Leather armchairs, an expensive-looking carpet and a rosewood table with matching chairs testified to the status of the firm. "Fletcher Merriman used it for many years before he retired from the practice in 2001." He went to the doorway and said to Sylvie Smith, "Why don't you finish off what you were doing?" Then he closed the door.

"So old Mr Merriman came in just for the party?"

"His annual visit. It became a tradition. Every December he'd zoom in – you know he used a wheelchair? – with all the seasonal fare, three bottles of sherry, sweet, medium and dry, a dozen mince pies and a huge branch of mistletoe, and tell us it was party time. He loved surprising people."

"Surprising them? You just said it was a tradition."

"We had no idea which day he would arrive."

"From what I hear, he was better at springing surprises than receiving them."

"His heart condition, you mean? Yes, he had to be careful.

He'd had two coronaries since retiring. He withdrew entirely from the business. I've been running it for years."

"But he remained the senior partner?"

"Sleeping partner is a better description, but 'partner' is the operative word."

"So he still had a slice of the profits?"

"Fifty-fifty. We're still Merriman & Palmer, a respected name in Bath. He deserved some reward for all the years he put in."

"And will his family get a share of any future profits?"

"There is no family."

"So it all comes to you now?"

Maurice Palmer turned deep pink above his striped collar. "Unless I take on another partner."

Diamond glanced around the room. "Let's talk about the party. What kind of bash was it?"

"I wouldn't call it that."

"Did you finish the sherry between you?"

"Not entirely."

"Three bottles between four of you would have been good going. Were they all freshly bought?"

"Yes, indeed, from the wine merchant in Broad Street."

"Who opened them?"

"Fletcher – and he did the pouring as well. He liked us to be aware that he was the provider."

"You didn't keep the bottles, by any chance?"

"The dead men?" He shook his head. "They went out the same evening with the rest of what was left."

"And was the mistletoe put to good use?"

Palmer glanced towards the door and lowered his voice. "You must understand that my esteemed ex-colleague belonged to a generation before PC came in, when a little of what you fancy was no offence."

"He was an old goat?"

"I wouldn't say that."

"Would the women?"

"I'm sure they wouldn't be so disrespectful."

"But *you* didn't have to be kissed under the mistletoe."

"Hardly."

"I'll speak presently to someone who did. Tell me, Mr Palmer, did you try one of the mince pies?"

"I had three. And very good they were. He always bought them from Maisie's, the best baker in town. They were still warm."

"No ill-effects?"

"None whatsoever."

"And how did the party end?"

"With Fletcher complaining of stomach pains and saying he needed to get home. We called a taxi. Next morning I heard he was in hospital and some hours later he had a fatal heart attack. Sad, but not unexpected, allowing for his medical history."

"You didn't shed any tears, then?"

"He was not an easy person to have as a business partner. But that doesn't mean I wished him to suffer."

Diamond had heard all he needed at this stage, so he asked to Palmer to send in Sylvie Smith.

"In here?" Palmer said in surprise.

"The scene of the crime – if, indeed, there was a crime. Where better?"

"You wish to interview her in my presence?"

"No, I suggest you wait outside and see if her double-entries are up to the mark."

Sylvie Smith looked nervous, and more so when Diamond waved her towards her boss's high-back executive chair. "Give yourself a treat. One day all this could be yours."

"I doubt that very much." She perched uneasily on the edge of the chair.

Diamond preferred to stand. "So how many of old Mr Merriman's surprise parties have you attended?"

"This was the second. I joined the firm after leaving college, towards the end of last year."

"The first time it happened you must have wondered what was up when he rolled through in his wheelchair primed with mistletoe and sherry. Did he insist on a kiss?"

Her mouth tightened into a thin line. "He called it his Christmas cuddle. I'd hardly ever met him."

"He took it as his right?"

"It makes me sick to think of it."

"If you'd complained, your job would have been at risk – and there aren't many openings in Bath for freshly qualified accountants."

She rolled her eyes upwards. "That's for sure."

"Did you know this was an annual ordeal?"

"Donna said something about it, but I thought she was winding me up."

"Donna is the other woman who works here?"

She nodded. "She's been here six years. She'll be chartered next year if all goes well."

"But she isn't in today?"

"Decided to take some of her annual leave."

"Gone away for Christmas?"

"I don't think so. She has a flat in Walcot Street."

"Lives alone, then?"

"Yes."

"What age is Donna? All right. Indiscreet question. Is she under forty?"

"I expect so."

Diamond looked up at the bare ceiling. There was no central light. There were wall-lights representing candles. "I'm trying to picture this party. Presumably the old boy sat in his wheelchair under some mistletoe. I can't see where it was attached."

"We had to tie string across the room, from one of the wall-lights to the one opposite. Then the mistletoe was hung over the string just above where you're standing."

"Got it. When you say 'we' . . . ?"

"Me and Donna."

"I'm getting the picture now. So whoever attached the mistletoe to the string must have stood on this table beside me to do it. Who was that?"

Sylvie rolled her eyes again. "He insisted it was me. Said I had the longer reach." She hesitated and turned as red as a Christmas card robin. "I happened to be wearing a short skirt."

"The picture is even clearer. Where was Mr Palmer while you were on the table?"

"Mr Palmer? Some way off, by the fireplace, I think. It was Mr Merriman who had the ringside view, almost underneath me in his wheelchair."

"Did he hand you the mistletoe himself?"

"No. He was far too busy looking up my skirt. It was Donna who helped me."

"So when he'd got over that excitement, and the mistletoe was in place, the party got under way. Drinks all round, no doubt?"

She nodded. "I needed one."

"The sherry was where?"

"On the table."

"And the glasses?"

"Mr Palmer keeps some in his drawer."

"As every boss should. Did Mr Palmer pour?"

"Mr Merriman did."

"Did you notice if the sherry was new, the bottles sealed at the neck?"

"I'm certain of it. He had to borrow scissors."

"You know why I'm interested? Something upset his stomach and if the sherry was new I'm thinking it must have been the mince pies."

She shook her head. "They were fresh, too, fresh as anything, in boxes from Maisie's. Actually they were delicious."

Diamond felt his stomach juices stirring. "So you had one?"

"Three, at least. We all did."

"And could anyone have slipped the old man a mince pie from anywhere else?"

"I don't see how. We were all in here together."

"Making merry?"

"Making a stab at it."

"I expect a few glasses of sherry helped."

She took a sharp breath. "Not when he grabbed me and forced me on to his lap for the kiss under the mistletoe. That was disgusting. His bony old hands were everywhere." She shuddered. "It went on for over a minute. I could have strangled him."

"But you didn't. Did Donna get the same treatment?"

"Not quite the same. She was wearing trousers."

"And did you also get a kiss from Mr Palmer?"

"That was no problem. Just a peck on the cheek. He doesn't fancy me, anyway."

Diamond thanked her and returned to the outer office. "I'll need the address of your other member of staff," he told Palmer.

"Donna? There's nothing she can add."

"How do you know? Maybe she saw something you and Miss Smith missed."

"You're barking up the wrong tree, superintendent. Nothing untoward happened here. Fletcher died from natural causes."

"I'll let you know if I agree – after I've heard from Donna."

First, he returned to the police station and asked his eager-to-please detective sergeant, Ingeborg, to get on the internet. Encouraged by her findings, he called the forensic lab that had analysed the post-mortem samples and suggested a second specific examination of the stomach contents. He was told the chances were not high of finding anything they hadn't already reported and anyway it would have to wait until after the holiday.

"Typical," he said to Ingeborg. "We're working. Why can't they?"

The third surviving accountant lived in a classy flat. Donna was a classy lady with a sexy drawl to her voice. Not at all unfazed by Diamond's arrival, she offered him coffee. While she was in the kitchen he used 1471 to check the last call she'd received. It was timed just after he'd left the Merriman & Palmer office – and that had been the source of the call.

It was no crime, of course, to tip her off. Any colleague
would do the same.

"Here's my problem," he told her over the coffee. "Old
Fletcher Merriman was taken home ill at the end of the party.
The pains got worse and he ended up in hospital. I've seen the
medical notes. Abdominal pain, blurred vision, nausea and
low pulse. We're bound to check if he was poisoned, triggering
the heart attack that killed him."

"*Poisoned*?" she said with a disbelieving smile.

He nodded. "Yet we aren't sure how the poison could have
been administered, allowing that he brought his own food and
drink to the party and everything was fresh. Poured the drinks
himself, in full view of everyone."

"Did they find poison inside him?" she asked as calmly as
if she were enquiring about last night's rain.

"Nothing obvious, but the traditional poisons like arsenic
and strychnine are so easy to detect these days that they aren't
often used. I've suggested something else and they're testing
for it."

She didn't ask the obvious question. Instead, she said,
"Why would anyone want to kill a retired accountant?"

"This is pure speculation and shouldn't be repeated," he
said. "Maurice Palmer stood to gain financially. The old man's
death leaves him in sole charge of the firm."

"Surely you don't suspect Maurice?"

Diamond didn't comment. "And Sylvie Smith told me she
felt like strangling him after the groping she had to endure."

"She's young. She's got a lot to learn about men."

"His behaviour didn't bother you, then?"

"I've been six years with the firm. I know what to expect
from Fletcher the lecher." She ran her fingertip thoughtfully
around the rim of her cup. "Here's a theory for you, Mr
Diamond. Is it possible during a kiss to pass a capsule into
someone's mouth?"

"I expect so. Nasty."

"Something like digitalis that is taken by heart patients, but
dangerous in an overdose?"

"Ingenious. What gave you this idea?"

She shrugged. "He insisted on a full mouth-to-mouth kiss. In the absence of any other theory . . ."

"Ah, but I do have another theory. A better one than yours. The mince pies killed him."

She shook her head. "We all had mince pies. Rich food, I'll grant you, but the rest of us felt no ill-effects. There was nothing wrong with them."

"Something was wrong with at least one of the pies Fletcher Merriman ate."

"I can't see how."

"It was laced with poison. Bear with me a moment." He took a notebook from his pocket. "Tyramine and betaphenylethylamine."

"Never heard of them."

"But you've heard of mistletoe. These are the toxic substances contained in mistletoe berries. The symptoms are similar to enteritis, but with blurred vision and a marked lowering of the pulse. In a tired old body susceptible to heart problems, as Merriman's was, the poison induced a failure of the cardiovascular system. Killed him."

"But the mistletoe was above our heads."

"Not when he arrived. You and Sylvie fixed it up."

"Excuse me. Sylvie tied it to the string."

"And while she was getting all the men's attention in her short skirt, you were stripping a number of the white berries from the branch before you handed it up to her."

She frowned. "Untrue."

"You waited for the next opportunity, and it came when the old man was kissing Sylvie. You lifted the lid of the mince pie on his plate and tucked the mistletoe berries under it. Lethal and almost undetectable."

She was as silent as a child waiting for Santa.

He stood up. "Might I look into your bedroom?"

"Whatever for?"

"To test my theory. This door?"

She was in no position to stop him.

"So you're planning a holiday?" There was a packed suit-case on the bed.

"People do."

He stepped closer and looked at the label. "Tenerife. Shame. You're not going any further than Manvers Street nick. I'm arresting you on suspicion of the murder of Fletcher Merriman."

"So she's singing?" Georgina, the Assistant Chief Constable, said.

"She sang. Better than the Bath Abbey choir."

"You sound positively festive, Peter."

"It is Christmas Eve, ma'am."

"What was her motive?"

"She's a cool lady. Worked hard at her accountancy, fill-ing in the columns, promising herself a promotion when she's chartered next year. She saw the young woman, Sylvie, bright and ambitious, and decided she wasn't will-ing to wait and be overtaken. Cosied up to Maurice Palmer and promised to spend Christmas in Tenerife with him. She reckoned she could persuade him to take her on as his new partner, but first old Fletcher Merriman had to be sent to the great audit in the sky. She knew his annual ritual, so she could plan how to do it. A mince pie contains a rich mix. After digestion is anyone likely to detect some mistle-toe berries in it?"

"Did they?"

"Not yet, but she thinks it's a done deal, and she's confessed."

"Murder by mince pie. Who would have thought of it?"

"An ambitious woman with time running out."

"You don't think Palmer had a hand in it?"

"No, ma'am. He's not that brave, or bright."

"Case solved, then, and all in one day. You can get back to your family and enjoy the rest of Christmas."

Diamond took a sharp, audible breath. "Not for some time. There's all the paperwork."

"Leave it for later."

"No, I don't trust my memory. I'll be here for a while yet. I know where to put my hands on a beer or two. And the odd mince pie."

"Not too odd, Peter. We need you."

Dead Man's Socks

David Hewson

1

Peroni bent down to take a good look at the two bodies in front of him and said quite cheerily, "You don't see that every day."

"Actually," Silvio Di Capua replied. "I do. This is a morgue. Dead people find their way here all the time."

The cop was early fifties, a big and ugly man with a scarred face and a complex manner, genial yet sly. He frowned at the corpses, both fully clothed, lying on gurneys next to the silver autopsy table. One was grey-haired, around Peroni's age, short with a black – clearly dyed – goatee beard, tubby torso stretching against a dark suit that looked a size too small for him. The other was a taller, wiry kid of twenty-two or so with a stubbly, bruised face and some wounds Peroni didn't want to look at too closely. Dark-skinned, impoverished somehow, and that wasn't just the cheap blue polyester blouson and matching trousers. Rome was like everywhere else. It had its rich. It had its poor. Peroni felt he was looking at both here. Equal at last.

"What I meant was you don't see *that* . . ." He pointed at the feet of the first body. "And that . . ." Then the second.

Di Capua grunted then put down his pathologist's clipboard and, with the back of a hand cloaked in a throwaway surgical glove, wiped his brow.

Peroni was staring at him, a look of theatrically outraged disbelief on his battered features. Di Capua, immediately aware of his error, swore then walked over to the equipment cabinet, tore off the present gloves, pulled on a new pair.

It was 9 a.m. on a scorching July morning. Peroni and Di Capua had just come on shift. The day was starting as it usually began. Sifting through the pieces the night team had swept up from the busy city beyond the grimy windows of the *centro storico* Questura. Today was a little different in some ways. The head of the forensic department, Teresa Lupo, had absented herself for an academic conference in Venice, leaving the Rome lab in Di Capua's care. Leo Falcone, Peroni's inspector, was on holiday in Sardinia. Nic Costa, his immediate boss, was taking part in some insanely pointless security drill at Fiumicino airport. Their absence left Peroni at a loose end, with no one to rein in his inquisitive and quietly rebellious nature.

"Don't try to distract me with minutiae," the pathologist said.

"I like minutiae," Peroni replied. "Little things." He looked down at the kid in the cheap blue bloodstained clothes and thought: little people too. "Who are they?"

Di Capua glanced at his clipboard and indicated the older man. "Giorgio Spallone. Aged fifty-one. An eminent psychiatrist with a nice villa in Parioli, fished out from the river this morning. Probable suicide. His wife said he'd been depressed for a while."

"Do psychiatrists do that?" Peroni asked straightaway. "Wouldn't they just climb on the couch and talk to themselves instead?"

Di Capua stared at him and said nothing.

"Where?" Peroni continued.

"Found him beached on Tiber Island."

"That's a very public place to kill yourself," Peroni replied. "Bang in the centre of Rome. I've never known a suicide there in thirty years."

"He probably went in elsewhere," Di Capua said with a shrug of his spotless white jacket. "Rivers flow. Remember?"

"Time of death?" Peroni asked. "He's dried out nicely now. Shame it's shrunk his suit. That won't do for the funeral."

"I don't know. I just walked through the door. Like you."

The cop glanced at the second corpse. "And this one?"

Di Capua picked up his notes.

"Ion Dinicu. Twenty-two years old. Some small-time Roma crook the garbage disposal people came across in Testaccio."

"Small-time Roma crook," Peroni repeated. "It sounds so . . . judgemental."

"He lived in that dump of a camp on the way to Ciampino. Along with a couple of thousand other gypsies. We got him straightaway from the fingerprints . . ."

"Oh yes," Peroni said, smiling. "We printed them all, didn't we? Man, woman and child, guilty of nothing except being Roma."

"I'm not getting into an argument about politics," Di Capua told him.

"Fingerprinting innocent people, taking their mugshots . . . that's politics?" Peroni wondered.

"Don't you have work to do?"

"I knew his name already," Peroni went on, ignoring the question. "Got here before you. Looked at the records downstairs. The kid never went inside. Couple of fines for lifting bags from tourists on the buses. Got repatriated to Romania when we were bussing people there. Came back, of course. They never take the hint, do they?"

"Maybe he should have done," the pathologist suggested.

The cop went to the other end of the body and leaned over Dinicu's bloodied, bruised features.

"What killed him?" he asked. "And when?"

Di Capua sighed.

"You've worked here a million years, Peroni. You know what a man looks like when he's been beaten up. When did it happen? I apologize. The battery died on my crystal ball. Come back later when I've got a new one."

"Some big tough guy who liked to use his fists," the cop said. He pointed at the corpse of Spallone. "The other guy's got a messy head too."

Di Capua folded his arms.

"Not unusual with river deaths. Could have hit the stone-work falling in. Got washed around by the swell. When we've done the autopsy then I'll tell you."

Peroni leaned over the dead psychiatrist and said, "Nah. If you hit stonework you get grazed. The Roma kid could have gone that way. He's cut. Spallone here . . ." He looked more closely. A bell was ringing but too faintly. "He's bruised. Swollen. No blood."

"Blunt force trauma," Di Capua said.

"That tells me a lot."

The pathologist folded his arms and looked a little cross.

"Why should I tell you anything? You're not dealing with either of these guys. Not as far as I know. Inspector Vieri's been round seeing Spallone's widow. He sent some wet-behind-the-ear *agente* to wake up the little hood's camp at seven. No one talking, of course. If it wasn't for the prints and photos we couldn't even ID him. *Agente* said even his own father wouldn't help. Chances are it's a gang rivalry thing and some other Romanian hood will wind up dead a couple of days down the line . . ."

"Dead quack gets an inspector and the full team. Dead immigrant gets a visit from an infant. The Roma mourn their dead, Silvio. Just like we do. Also you're forgetting the deal."

"The deal?"

"You don't do cop work and we don't dissect your corpses."

Di Capua was starting to get mad.

"Yeah well . . . One drowned doctor. One beat-up street kid. And you hanging round here as if you care. Don't you have work to do?"

"There's always work if you look for it," Peroni answered. "Right now I'm . . ." He searched for the right word. "Foraging."

"Then why don't you go forage somewhere else?"

"What next?" the big man answered, ignoring him again. "Slice and dice. Weigh the organs. Check the spleen and things. Peek inside at every last little bit of them, working or not, until you get something to write down on your report . . . what? Tomorrow? The day after?"

Di Capua opened his arms wide.

"That's the way it goes. Custom and practice. One mistake and we all could hang. As you know. Now . . ."

"Just a favour," Peroni said quickly, coming close, putting a huge arm round the skinny, balding pathologist.

"Why should I . . . ?"

"The socks," Peroni interrupted. "Those . . ." He pointed at the two sets of feet in front of them. Shoes off already. Ankles splayed. Very dead.

"What about them?" he asked.

Peroni laughed, took away his arms, clapped his big pale hands. Then he retrieved a pair of scissors from the kidney bowl on the silver autopsy table and carefully cut up through the front of all four trouser legs. Spallone's expensive dark blue barathea didn't give in easily. The Roma kid's garish polyester was so flimsy he could slice it apart just by lifting the lower blade.

"Are you kidding me?" he asked when he finished.

Both men were wearing long socks pulled up close to the knee. Odd socks. The one on each right leg light blue and unpatterned. The other pale grey and ribbed so subtly the markings were scarcely noticeable.

The fabric of the blue socks seemed as cheap and thin and artificial as the kid's shiny jacket and trousers. The toes were close to going on both. The grey ones were newer, wool maybe. Expensive.

"I never knew a young guy who wore long socks like that," Peroni murmured. "Curious . . ."

"Gianni . . ."

"But not as strange as the fact that two dead men, found the same morning in different parts of Rome, seem to have dipped into the same sock drawer before they went out for the night."

"You don't know that!" Di Capua protested.

Peroni retrieved his phone from his pocket and took a picture of the dead legs. Then he reached forward and very lightly tweaked Spallone's dead big toe.

Di Capua shrieked.

"That was the favour," the big man added. "I don't leave till I get it."

The pathologist grumbled. But he still went and got a pair of tweezers and, very carefully, pulled each sock from each dead limb, depositing them in four separate plastic envelopes.

Then the two men peered at the plastic bags. One set, the grey ones, had a brand, a pricey one from Milan. The others looked the kind people picked up three pairs to the euro from a street stall. No name. Nothing to identify them.

"I can check on the fabric to see if they're the same too," Di Capua said, serious now. "Give me till the end of the afternoon."

"Thanks," Peroni said, and slapped the pathologist hard on his white-jacketed shoulder. "That would be good."

2

Inspector Vieri's team worked on the floor below, in an office next to Falcone's unit. Peroni's customary home was empty now. Costa had taken everyone except him to Fiumicino for the drill there. Peroni knew why he'd been left behind. He always found it difficult to keep a straight face when the management decided to lead everyone in the merry dance known as role play.

Vieri had arrived the previous month sporting the finely tailored suit and standoffish manners of a young officer eyeing some rapid progress up the ranks. He had all the traits that mattered when it came to catching the eye of promotion boards: a couple of degrees from fancy universities, a spell at business school, periods in some of the more fashionable specialist units involving terrorism, organized crime and financial misdemeanours. The man was all of thirty-three and had never, Peroni suspected, punched or been punched once in his entire life. To make matters worse, he hailed from Milan and spoke in a gruff, cold northern voice that matched his angular pasty face. He never set foot in the Questura without shoes so polished they looked like mirrors. No one ever saw a hair out of place on his bouffant, gleaming black-haired head. The general opinion in the Questura bar round the corner was he'd make *commissario* before he turned forty, maybe even thirty-five. After that the direction of his golden future was anyone's guess. Just to rub salt in the wound the man's wife was a beautiful redhead who worked as a producer for the state TV company RAI. All things considered, as far as the average grizzled Roman cop was concerned, Vieri might as well have worn a sign saying "Shoot me" on his back.

This morning's suit was dark blue barathea, not unlike the shrunken jacket and trousers clinging to the corpse of Spallone upstairs. Peroni, who had barely met the man, strode over smiling, introduced himself and asked if he could help.

Vieri gave him a taciturn stare. He'd brought a handful of officers from Milan with him when he arrived in Rome, turned them into his personal confidantes, people he spoke to before any of the locals whenever possible. An unwise decision for such a clever man.

"Don't you have work in your own unit?" Vieri asked. He didn't look in the least grateful for the offer of free manpower. Just suspicious.

"Sure," Peroni replied pleasantly. "But sometimes a little local knowledge can help an officer who's new around here. I hope you don't mind my saying. Rome's a village really, sir. The peasants tend to stick with their own and . . ."

Vieri wasn't listening. He was staring at his phone, a model that was decidedly fancier than anything handed out as stock issue to the average Questura officer. Another innovation from Milan.

"The socks," Peroni added.

The young inspector scowled and waved him down. He was reading his emails. It seemed to Peroni he was the kind of man who thought every message, whatever its contents, was of overriding importance, if only because it was addressed to him.

Vieri barked out a couple of orders to two men across the room. Local guys. Peroni knew them both. One of them nodded. The other briefly stared at Peroni with hooded eyes.

"The socks," Peroni repeated. "If you'd care to come upstairs to the morgue I can show you. Better to see than try to explain sometimes." He scratched his ear. "I keep trying to work out how many possible solutions there might . . ."

"I don't approve of police officers interfering with the work of the forensic department," Vieri said rather pompously, not once taking his eyes off the phone.

Peroni felt his hackles rising and wondered whether he cared if this man noticed or not.

"It's cooperation, not interference, sir . . ." he began.

To Peroni's surprise Vieri's hard stare managed to silence him.

"I know it was once fashionable for police officers to watch and sigh and groan as pathologists go about their business," the inspector declared. "Truthfully it's a waste of time. Theirs and ours. When forensic have something useful to tell us, they will do so and I will listen. In the meantime . . ."

Peroni watched him bark out yet more orders. Hunts for CCTV images. Mobile phone records. Car details. A call to the media to see if anyone had seen a man answering Spallone's description near the river the previous night. Nothing about the Roma kid.

"You don't think it was suicide?" he asked when Vieri was finished.

"I don't know, *agente*," the man replied curtly. "I have no preconceptions. His widow assures us he was a troubled man. He absented himself from home at regular intervals." Vieri shrugged. "I have no reason to disbelieve her. Spallone was a widely respected man. He sat on the board of several public bodies. He was a patron of the opera. Known in political circles. We will investigate and report in due course." For the briefest of moments his stony, ascetic face displayed something approaching doubt. "I imagine she's right. They were a wealthy couple, well connected. Hard to see anything else."

Peroni stood there, wondering whether to point out that Vieri had contradicted himself already. Instead he said, "I would really appreciate two minutes of your time to see these socks."

"You didn't listen to a word I said, did you?" Vieri snapped.

"On the contrary. I hung on every one."

The young inspector turned away from him. He was listening to someone else speaking on the phone.

"The Roma kid . . ." Peroni began, not moving a centimetre, speaking a little more loudly to regain Vieri's attention.

"If the father can't even stir himself to come and identify the body there's very little I intend to do at the moment. They can stew until they want to talk, or sort it out between themselves and then we'll pick up the pieces."

Peroni blinked, struggling to believe what he was hearing, though, with a moment's reflection, he knew the man's callous words should not have come as such a shock. This was the modern force, not the one he'd joined thirty years before. Priorities, procedures, resource management . . . and the keeping sweet of bereaved relatives of men who sat on public boards and patronized the opera. All these mean, inhuman practices had come to swamp the previous shambling chaos through which officers sifted hopefully, trying to sort good from bad, the crucial from the inconsequential, with little to help them other than their own innate intelligence and knowledge of their fellow men and women.

"You'll never get a thing out of the Roma if you send kids to talk to them," he said with undisguised brusqueness. "It doesn't work like that."

Vieri's eyebrows – which were, the old cop now noticed, manicured and shaped – rose as if in a challenge.

"You think you could do better?" the man from Milan asked.

"I know it," Peroni replied straightaway. "You want me to go there?"

"You don't work for me," Vieri said, looking him up and down. "Frankly I prefer younger officers. My problem, not yours . . ."

With that he turned and started talking to his men again. About phone records and databases, video and intelligence. Peroni guessed this team could try to work two cases – no, one and a quarter at best – for the rest of the day and never set foot outside the building, never do a thing without having a phone to their ear, their fingers on a keyboard, their minds tuned for a call from the morgue and the delivery report that said: it's fine go home, there's nothing you can do.

One of the men Vieri had brought with him from Milan was watching Peroni with a look that spoke volumes. It said: get out of here.

"You know," Peroni said, touching the guy's arm and nodding at the sunny day beyond the window, "it's really not scary out there. You won't even get sunburn, I promise. You should try it some time."

Then he marched out of the room, along the corridor, back into his own empty office, looked at the vacant chairs there, the silent phones, the desks, the computers, papers strewn everywhere.

Years before, Peroni had been an inspector himself. As arrogant as Vieri. Maybe more so. Maybe with better reasons. He was good at that job, a leader, a man who let people run with their own imagination at times, and always – or usually – managed to reel them in before they went too far. Then his job and his private life collided and when he woke up from that crash everything he held dear was gone: family, career, a good few friends. He was lucky to keep any kind of position in the police after that, even one as a lowly *agente*, maybe the oldest, lowliest officer there was by now. Lucky too that, for some reason he could never understand, love came back into his life in the shape of Teresa Lupo, the morgue boss now in Venice. And friendship in the form of Costa and Falcone.

But they weren't here. He was, and he could do what he damned well like.

Afterwards Peroni would try to convince himself it was a considered, reasoned decision, one weighed and balanced, pros and cons, before he made up his mind. But this was, he knew, a lie, a conscious act of self-deception. The proof already lay in his pocket. On the way out he'd subtly lifted a very full notepad from the desk of one of Vieri's taciturn Milanese minions.

There was one sentence in it about Ion Dinicu and three pages about the eminent psychiatrist Giorgio Spallone and his businesswoman wife Eva. They lived in a fancy street in Parioli. It seemed a good place to start, but only after he'd checked a couple of things on the computer first.

3

The villa was, like everything in the couple's quiet, rich, suburban cul-de-sac, daintily perfect. A three-storey detached home from the early twentieth century, soft orange stone with colourful tiled ribbon decorations over the green shuttered windows. A small orchard of low orange and lemon trees ran between the ornate iron gate and baroque front door with its stained glass and plaster curlicues and gargoyles. In the finely raked gravel drive stood a subtle grey Maserati saloon and next to it a lurid red Ferrari.

He glanced through the window of the low sports car. There were magazines on the passenger seat, titles about women's fashion, a few coarse gossip mags and, somewhat oddly, a glossy about men's health, with a cover of a muscular bodybuilder type straining at a piece of exercise equipment. There was nothing on the seats or the dash of the Maserati. The car looked clean and tidy. And, like the Ferrari, not much used except as some icon placed behind the iron gates, one advertising the wealth of those to whom these vehicles – so unsuited for the busy, narrow roads of Rome – belonged.

Showy jewellery for the drive, and it wasn't hard to work out which was his and which hers.

Parioli, he thought. The place was such a byword for bourgeois snobbery that the term "pariolini" to describe its residents had become, for some, an insult in itself. It was a little unfair. But only a little.

He walked up to the door, rang the bell and showed his ID when a maid in a white uniform answered. She was foreign, of course. Filipino he guessed. The name "Maria" was embroidered on the uniform. She'd been crying recently and didn't look into his face after she read the ID.

"I know we've been here already. How upsetting this is, Maria," he said. "But I do need to check a couple of small details with Signora Spallone. Please . . ."

She wasn't there, the maid said, still staring at the ground.

"Where is she?"

"Down at the gym."

Peroni was thinking about this when the woman sensed his puzzlement and added quickly, "It's Signora Spallone's job. She and the signore own it. She wanted to break the news to the people there. They all knew him."

"Of course," he said, nodding. "This is such a very small thing. I just need to check some clothing in their bedroom. Giorgio's. One quick look. The boss won't let me off shift until it's done. Can I . . . ?"

She opened the door and he walked in. The place was beautiful, spotless and palatial, walls covered in paintings, old and new, corridors dotted with what looked like imperial-era statues.

"Their bedroom?" he asked.

"They sleep apart," she said quietly and led the way upstairs.

The first bedroom they came across was huge, the size of many working-class apartments. It had its own separate lounge and a bathroom with two sinks, one toothbrush by the nearest.

He opened a wardrobe and saw line upon line of elegant dresses there.

The husband's room was as far away as it was possible to get. Right at the back of the house. He could hear the drone of traffic from the busy main road. It was small and functional and hadn't been decorated in years.

"When did Giorgio move in here?" he asked.

She looked at the bed, all perfectly made for a man who'd never sleep in it again. Then she brushed some stray cotton fibres off the sheets and said, "Two months." Nothing more.

Peroni opened the wardrobes. Plenty of expensive suits and shirts, drawers with underwear and socks. All wool or cotton. Nothing cheap or artificial.

"He was a careful dresser," he said.

She nodded.

"The signore took pride in his appearance. He was a gentle-man."

"A depressed gentleman?"

Her chin was almost on her chest.

"I am the maid, sir. You ask those questions of the lady."

Peroni got the address of the gym, a backstreet near the Campo dei Fiori in the city centre, not far from the Questura. An awkward place to get to from Parioli, twenty-five minutes if the traffic was light. Then she showed him to the door. He couldn't help noticing a pile of unopened letters on a side-board next to it. A few looked like bills. Several bore the names of banks.

He stood on the threshold for a moment, gazing at the Maserati and the Ferrari.

"Those are not cars for Rome," Peroni said. "Too big, too expensive. Too easily scratched by some stupid little kid who hates anyone who's got the money to buy them. Why anyone . . ."

"They hardly use them," the woman said. "Only when they leave the city. Every morning I wash them down. But when those big ugly things last went anywhere . . ."

She shrugged.

"How do they get around then?"

"I call a driver," she said as if he was being dim.

4

Peroni didn't approve of exercise. So gyms didn't impress him much. The one the Spallones owned was called the "Palestra Cassius" and occupied the first floor of a vast palazzo in the Via dei Pellegrino, the old pilgrims' street from the city to the bridge to the Vatican. The name intrigued him until he saw plastered behind reception a black-and-white picture of the man most people knew as Muhammad Ali, not Cassius Clay. There was a debt to history being paid here, but it wasn't a Roman one.

The place smelled of aromatic oils and sweat. There was a blank-looking girl with a ponytail behind a computer, rows and rows of unused exercise machines and, close to the small windows at the back, a boxing ring. A sign leading off to the right said "Sauna".

"Exercise I can do without," Peroni told the kid behind the desk when he walked in. "But sitting around sweating doing nothing . . . that I can manage. Is it good?"

She gave him a leaflet. It boasted of the biggest, most traditional Finnish sauna in Rome. She had her name embroidered on her T-shirt: Letizia. Someone, Spallone's wife he guessed, liked to tag the things they owned.

"I could break into a good sweat looking at the prices," he said.

"We've got great introductory discounts," she piped up. The girl looked around at the lines of empty machines. "And discounts after that if you ask nicely."

"I always ask nicely. How many people work here? Trainers, fitness people and the like?"

"Ten, fifteen guys. Plus me. We're good."

"I'm sure you are," Peroni said, showing her the police ID. "But I'd really like to see Signora Spallone now if you don't mind."

The woman was in her office with ten or so of her men. Every one of them was big and fit, under thirty he guessed. Names embroidered on their shirts. Mostly foreign from the way they spoke and muttered as he showed his ID. More than half of them blond, Nordic. Like Eva Spallone herself, he now saw.

Shc ushered them out and gave him a hard stare, the one civilians used when they thought the police were paying them too much attention.

"You're not Italian," he said.

"Is there something wrong with that?"

"Not at all. It's just that I always try to place people. It's a game."

Eva Spallone looked no more than thirty-five. She had short blonde hair, the face of an angel, bright blue eyes, and the curvy, almost carved kind of figure Peroni normally saw in the magazines, not real life. She didn't look as if she'd been crying recently.

"Finnish," he said.

"You guess well."

"Not really." He pointed to the books and trinkets behind her desk. "You've got that blue and white flag there. The sauna makes a thing about being Finnish and not many do that. Two and two tend to make four. Usually anyway."

On the desk stood a picture of her with a man he took to be the living Giorgio Spallone. She was in a wedding dress, he in a suit. The Colosseum was in the background. So many weddings used that location for pictures after the ceremony. From the look of her he guessed this couldn't have been more than four or five years before.

"I went to your house," he said. "There was a detail to be cleared up. We thought you'd be at home."

Her eyes misted over then. Very quickly it seemed to him.

"This was Giorgio's business too. It was how we first met."

A tissue came out of a very expensive rose-coloured leather handbag so small it couldn't have contained much else. She wiped her pert nose then rubbed her bright blue eyes with the back of her hands.

"In a sauna?" Peroni asked.

"He loved the silence, the tranquillity. When his mind was troubled it was the place he went. On his own."

She didn't want to answer that question.

"So you two started the business?"

"It was a wedding gift." Another dab of the eye. "He was the kindest man. Everyone here loved him. I had to tell them myself. Lately he'd been so . . . melancholy."

Peroni found he couldn't take his eyes off the wedding photo.

"What detail?" she asked.

"Was your husband a fastidious man?" Peroni asked.

Eva Spallone blinked.

"Fastidious?"

"Was he careful about what he wore? How good his clothes looked? How neat they were?"

"Very much so," she said.

"Thanks." Peroni got up.

"You came all the way for that?"

"I don't need to take up any more of your time, signora. Will you be here long? Just in case my boss thinks of anything else."

"I'm having lunch with a friend. Round the corner. So many people to tell. And you won't let me do anything with poor Giorgio. No funeral arrangements. It's okay. I understand."

He asked himself: was that what most widows did the day their husband was found floating in the Tiber? Have lunch with someone to tell them how awkward things were?

He wondered. Most people reacted by staying close to the home they shared. A few found that too full of memories. Too painful.

"Here," she said and gave him a business card for the gym with her mobile number on it.

On the way out he stopped by the ring. Two of the hulks were sparring, landing not-so-gentle blows with puffy brown leather gloves.

Peroni watched them, thought about the gloves and said quietly to himself, "Boxing."

The rest of the hulks stood around watching, commenting in a variety of accents, none of them native Italian. None of them looked to be in mourning. Next to the ring was a glass door marked as the sauna entrance. Peroni wandered over and took a look. He'd no idea what a sauna was like really so he opened the door and found himself gasping for breath almost instantly. It was like peering into a hot, damp fog. All billowing steam, so thick he couldn't see his hand in front of his face.

"You wanna try?" asked a hulk, taking him by surprise when he walked up behind.

"Isn't there someone in there already?"

The hulk laughed.

"Who knows? You share a sauna, man. That's what it's about. Togetherness." He squinted at the fog. "But no. I don't think there's anyone there. Thursdays are quiet."

"Spallone used to come here alone, I thought," Peroni told him.

"Yeah well . . ." The hulk shrugged. He looked and sounded East European, Russian maybe. Peroni couldn't quite make out the name stitched on his shirt. "That's more business than choice I guess. Sauna's a sociable thing." A big elbow nudged Peroni in the ribs. "A place for men to talk. Get things off your chest."

"Maybe I'll try next week," Peroni told him and walked out of the building, back into the bright day. It was just after noon now. Lunchtime. He wondered what Teresa was doing in Venice, how the play acting was going at Fiumicino, what kind of culinary delicacy the ever-picky Falcone had chosen for his solitary meal in Sardinia. All this speculation made Peroni hungry so he bought a *panino* stuffed with rich, salty porchetta from the market and ate it from his big left fist as he drove out to Ciampino and the Roma camp.

5

He didn't need any directions for this place. Every cop knew where the Roma lived, dotted around the city in shifting encampments, bulldozed from time to time by the authorities only to reappear a few weeks later, a kilometre or so down the road. Several hundred, even a thousand men, women and children lived in these places, crammed together in hovels built out of scrap wood and corrugated iron, huddled around makeshift braziers in winter, sweating out in the open in the scorching summer. For years now the Italian government had been trying to push them back into Romania and Hungary. It was like trying to sweep away the tide with a broom.

Peroni pulled through the camp gates and found his car immediately surrounded by scruffy urchin kids, hands out begging for money. He pushed through them and found himself confronted by a tall, surly-looking man with a beard. Grubby clothes, dark, smart eyes. Security around here.

"Police," Peroni said, showing his ID. "I need to see Ion Dinicu's father."

"Not here," the man said immediately.

Peroni sighed, looked around. There were eyes glittering in the dark mouths of the makeshift homes, all watching him. He'd dealt with these people many times in the past. It was never easy. They liked living apart from everyone else. They didn't want the police to solve their problems, offer them protection. In their own eyes they were a separate nation, detached from a world which failed to understand them. That didn't mean they were without rules or principles or beliefs. Faith even.

"If Ion isn't identified . . . claimed by someone . . ." Peroni told the man, "then it's up to us to deal with his funeral. If that's what you want, fine. But bear this in mind. We'll pass the work on to a charity in all probability. A Catholic one since we're in Rome. If anyone wants an invitation . . ."

The bearded man stood there, silent.

"If Ion's father speaks to me now, just for a few minutes, I will make sure a request goes through for an Orthodox service. Romanian Orthodox if you like. It can be done. It won't be unless I ask for it."

He waited.

Orthodox and Catholic. It was like football. Same game, different teams. Bitter rivals.

Two minutes later he was in a corrugated shack at the end of the camp, seated at a low plastic table with an elderly bent man who smelled of cheap dark tobacco and wood smoke.

"What do you want?" Ion Dinicu's father asked.

"To find out who killed your son."

"Why?"

Peroni shrugged and said, "It's what I do. Don't you want to know? Don't you want some kind of . . ." He hesitated. The word sounded odd, wrong, in these circumstances. "Justice?"

Dinicu's father had the same kind of eyes as the man on the gate. Dark and intense. Blazing now.

"Find me the man who killed my Ion and I'll show you justice," he said. "He was a good boy."

Peroni sighed.

"He was a pickpocket. A petty thief. Petty. But a thief all the same."

"That was then!" the old man cried. "Not now."

"Now he's dead. I want to know why."

The Romanian was silent for a while, then he murmured, "Everyone hates us here."

"Why did Ion come back then? After we deported him?"

"Everyone hates us there too. At least here there's money. Work."

"Tourists on the bus. Women with purses in the park."

"No!"

"Then what?" Peroni wanted to know.

"When he came back he was a chauffeur. People wanted to go somewhere, they called. He was good. Cheaper than those taxi guys. Reliable. He had his own car."

This was interesting.

"Where's the car?"

"Gone. He went out on a job yesterday. Next thing you send round some kid in a uniform to tell me he's dead. What am I supposed to say?"

Peroni folded his arms, stared out of the opening of the shack, watched the kids playing with their grubby toys, the women sitting round, darning clothes, hanging up washing.

He couldn't shake from his head what he'd seen in the morgue that morning. How many possible explanations were there?

"This is going to seem an odd question," Peroni said. "What kind of socks did your son wear?"

The man blinked and looked at him sideways.

"Is this a joke?"

"Not at all. What kind? Short? Long? Medium?"

Ion Dinicu's father rolled up the legs of his cheap black trousers. His socks ran all the way to the knee.

"These socks," he said.

The cop nodded.

"I mean," the man went on, "*these* socks. We shared. Socks. Shirts. Was cheaper. Easier that way."

"Right," Peroni murmured and found his mind wandering back to the city.

"What happens to my son? You won't let the Catholics have him? Don't do that to him. He don't deserve it."

Peroni said, "Give me some way I can get in touch with you. When his body's released I'll make sure they know he needs an Orthodox service. If you want to come in to the Questura . . ."

The father was shaking his head briskly.

"Then give me some way . . ."

The man reached into his pocket and handed him a card. It read, "Deluxe Ciampino Limousine Service" and had two mobile phone numbers printed beneath a colour photo of the front of an elderly but very shiny Mercedes, a young man standing beside it, smiling.

"The second phone number's mine. First was Ion's," he said.

Peroni said thanks then walked back to the car.

6

By the time he was back in the city, looking for somewhere to park near the Campo dei Fiori, most of the smell of tobacco and wood smoke had left him. Peroni squeezed the battered unmarked police Fiat into a diagonal space that left the front wheels up on the pavement of the Via dei Pellegrino and would, to his regret, force pedestrians into the cobbled street. He hated doing this, but there was work to be done.

He got out and called the Questura. Prinzivalli was the duty *sovrintendente* running the uniform officers out on patrol. This was good news. He was an old-time cop, a colleague going back three decades.

Peroni said, "If I asked for five strong men outside an address near the Campo dei Fiori in twenty minutes would you want to know why? Time's a little short, see."

There was a pause on the line. Trust was an odd thing. Delicate, easily broken.

"I've got officers round there all the time," Prinzivalli said. "I'd still need to give them some idea what exactly they're looking for."

Peroni told him, then passed on Eva Spallone's mobile number and some more instructions.

"You know the new guy from Milan? The inspector? Vieri?" he said when he was finished.

"Mr Cheery we call him," Prinzivalli replied.

"He's the one. Well Mr Cheery's busy right now. It's best he doesn't know. Not straightaway."

There was that pause again, then Prinzivalli said, "Vieri hates being interrupted when he's busy. I've learned that already."

"Me too," Peroni said, then finished with a few more details and cut the call.

He read the notes he'd made on the computer that morning. Detailed notes. There was a stationery shop on the way to the gym. He went in there, bought the things he needed, then walked down the narrow street to the Palestra Cassius.

7

It was now close to four o'clock. Peroni smiled for the girl on reception and said, "It's me again, Letizia."

She was chewing a nougat from the bowl on the counter, looking bored in the way only teenagers knew.

Eva Spallone wasn't there. Must have been a long lunch. Prinzivalli could deal with her then.

There seemed to be one customer in the place, a fat guy sweating and grunting on an exercise bike. The hulks were still crowded round the boxing ring. Peroni walked over. Two of the biggest blonds were in boxing shorts, bare-chested, tanned pecs and biceps gleaming with oil, sparring lazily off and on the ropes. They looked bored too.

Peroni clapped his hands and brought the fun to a close. Ten sets of eyes turned on him. He waved his ID card high, chose his most authoritative of voices and ordered them all into Eva Spallone's office. That instant.

They obeyed straightaway, shambling over to the far side of the gym in a long line. Peroni watched them. Bodybuilding did something bad to the way people walked, he decided. It was like health stores. They always seemed to be full of sick, sniffy people.

The ten hulks filled the small office. The smell of sweat and oils and liniment was a little overpowering. None of them spoke, which he found interesting.

"This is a simple, routine check," Peroni announced, forcing his way to the desk. "I want . . ."

He began coughing. Kept on coughing. The hulks stared at him. They looked worried they might catch something.

"Sorry . . . sorry," Peroni said, gasping. "Got a really bad throat today. Hurts like hell. Tell you what . . ."

He pulled out the dark grey paper he'd bought in the stationery shop and the blue pen then scrawled a single word in large capital letters.

"Any of you guys ever been . . ." He coughed and roughed up his voice even more. "Here?"

Then he walked down the line showing them the paper. Eight of them shook their heads. A thuggish-looking guy, with the name Vladimir embroidered on his T-shirt, glared back at Peroni and said, "Was years ago. In Russia."

"Must have been fun," Peroni replied.

Only one, halfway down the line, didn't answer at all. He was the biggest of them all, one of the boxers, a good deal taller than Peroni, muscle-bound with a flattened nose, dim close-set eyes and a stripe of Mohican-cut blond hair. His chest gleamed with sweat and oil, his muscles looked as if they'd been sculpted somehow.

There was a name embroidered on his bright red satin shorts. Eva Spallone did take great care to tag her possessions. Peroni looked down at it and said, "Sven?"

"What was the question again?" the man asked.

Peroni held up the paper. The close-set eyes glanced at it nervously then darted round the room.

"The rest of you leave," Peroni ordered, and he didn't take his attention off the man in front of him for a moment as they filed out of the office.

"Swedish?" Peroni asked when they were gone.

"Finnish."

"Like Eva Spallone. Isn't that nice?"

The hulk just stood there. Big, stupid Sven, with his beady blue eyes and blond cockatoo stripe.

Peroni looked at him and said, "You know when my daughter was four years old the doctors thought there was something wrong." He indicated his eyes. "Here. With her sight. We went through all these tests. Pretty nurse in the clinic." He grinned. "I never said no when it came to running her there."

"What?" Sven asked.

"Bear with me," Peroni went on. "One of the things they thought was maybe to do with the way she saw colours. That perhaps she was colour blind." He sighed. "Scary when you think there's something wrong with your kid. There wasn't. She just needed better glasses. But that nurse was so pretty, so careful, I kept going back and talking to her. I thought I knew everything then, of course. Colour blindness. Red and green. People couldn't see traffic lights and things. I was a smartass. She put me straight. Sure they can't see red or green. But they can see something, which light is on for one thing. So they can drive if they want. No problem usually. And also . . ."

He reached into his pocket and found his own notepad where it sat, next to the one he'd stolen from Vieri's guy that morning.

"It's not just red and green. That may be the most common kind there is but you find lots of others. Like one called . . ." He glanced at the note. "Tritanopia. You heard of that, Sven?"

The Finn stood there stiff as a gleaming rock, saying nothing.

"I looked it up. They call it blue-yellow colour blindness but it's not that simple. Specially with the blues. Anyone who's got this thing really struggles with those. Can't see the difference between blue and black easily for one thing."

"What're you talking about?" Sven asked.

Peroni's eyes narrowed, "I'm talking about you. How did it go? Let me guess. Eva's been monkeying around with you for a little while. She says, 'Oh Sven, oh darling Sven. If only it was the two of us. You and me running the gym. Then we'd be together and make lots of money too. But Giorgio won't ever divorce me . . .'"

Beads of sweat were beginning to build on the Finn's broad, tanned forehead.

"So all you've got to do is wait one night until he's in the sauna on his own. Walk in there, boxing gloves on, beat him about the head until he's out stone cold. You got those gloves on, remember. No serious marks. No cuts. Dump him in the river. Eva says how sad, how depressed he was. Suicide. Stupid cops nod and then you're done."

Sven cleared his throat and stared down at his own broad chest.

"I guess Eva thinks a sauna's a clever place," Peroni went on. "All that evidence – sweat and blood and everything – gets washed away down the drain. Not sure about that

frankly but it doesn't matter. You see Giorgio Spallone's a
nice guy. Really. His maid in Parioli calls him cars from some
poor Roma kid called Ion. He likes Ion. Feels sorry for him.
Sneaks him into the gym for a sauna last night as a favour.
And there's the Roma kid, hidden in all that steam, when you
go wading in with the boxing gloves, punching Giorgio in
the head."

Peroni reached down and lifted Sven's vast fists. He undid
the lace ties of the boxing gloves at the wrist and gently tugged
them off his enormous hands. There were cut marks on the
knuckles. He touched them. Sven flinched. Then he looked
more closely at the hulk's face. There was a graze near the
right cheekbone.

"Middle-aged psychiatrist's a piece of cake for a thug like
you. A Roma kid like Ion doesn't go down so easily. I guess the
gloves came off there. But he was a little guy. You punched
him out in the end."

"This is stupid . . ." Sven murmured.

"It was," Peroni agreed. "See when it's done you now have
two bodies in all that steam. Both naked. One, Ion, dead I
guess. Giorgio out for the count. You got to dress them – Eva
won't do that for you. You got to get them out of there."

He cocked his head and looked up at the Finn.

"Ion's car, I guess. You got his keys, beat where it was out of
him. Put the two of them in there. Giorgio goes in the river
somewhere near the Ponte Sublicio in Trastevere. Then you
drive over and dump Ion with the trash near the nightclubs in
Testaccio, the sort of place a Roma kid might find himself in
trouble."

"Stupid," Sven said again.

"Here," Peroni told him, "is the problem. Tritanopia. You
got to put their clothes on and it's hot, you're scared, you're all
alone. And you don't see what everyone else can. Those two
guys are wearing different-coloured socks. They'd know it. I'd
know it. But not you."

He pulled out his phone and showed the hulk the photo
from that morning: four dead legs, two sets of odd, long socks.

Peroni put the phone away and picked up the paper sheet he'd written on.

"See this? The paper's just about the same colour as Giorgio's socks. The pen the colour of Ion's. You can't read what I wrote there, Sven. Because it all looks the same to you. Here. Let me help."

He took out a red pen and scribbled over the letters he'd written earlier in blue.

"How's that?"

Sven could see the word now. He stared at it with his tiny, frightened eyes.

"P. R. I. G. I. O. N. E," Peroni spelled it out. "Prison. Jail. Incarceration. That's the place you're headed. One murder's bad enough. But two."

He sighed, put away the paper, reached up and lifted the Finn's chin so he could look into his face.

"Two is so much worse. My advice is this. Tell the truth. Think about cooperation. Tell everyone how Eva put you up to it and led you by your beat-up nose. We'll find out anyway. You don't think you were the first one she made goo-goo eyes at, do you? We'll talk to all the other guys. But if you help us now you're talking years off the sentence. Otherwise . . ."

He stood back and looked up and down at the shining, sweating man in front of him, quaking in his tight red satin shorts.

"Otherwise it's just more fisting time in jail, and really I do not recommend . . ."

The Finn pushed him out of the way and raced across the gym towards the stairs.

They run oddly too, Peroni thought. Arms pumping, legs going up and down like mechanical dolls.

He walked over to the receptionist, watched by the line of wide-eyed, open-mouthed hulks who'd stayed behind and the fat customer now stationary on his exercise bike. There he picked up a couple of fistfuls of nougats from the bowl and stuffed them into his pockets before calling Vieri.

"There's good news and there's bad," he said when he got through to the inspector still in his office in the Questura. "The Spallone case and the Roma kid are done. Bad is ..." He popped a nougat in his mouth. "... you're going to have to unplug yourself from your Blackberry and take a walk outside."

8

When he got down the stairs he found Sven cuffed, hands behind his back, face pressed against a blue police wagon blocking the narrow street. Prinzivalli was there, seven men with him. Peroni handed out nougats from his jacket pockets.

"I only asked for five," he said. "You didn't need to come."

Prinzivalli watched the hulk make one last effort to struggle then give up. The Finn looked shocked and a little teary-eyed.

"It's on my way home. End of shift." He popped Peroni's nougat into his mouth. "I thought perhaps this was something I didn't want to miss."

"It's just an arrest," Peroni answered.

Eva Spallone was being marched down the street in the custody of two women officers leading her firmly but politely by the arm.

"Wife?" Prinzivalli guessed.

"The ice queen of the north," Peroni murmured.

Moments later a Lancia saloon drew up behind the van. Vieri got out, face like thunder, with three of his minions from Milan.

Peroni looked at the men holding Sven, nodded for them to let go a little. The hulk looked up, saw the Spallone woman and started to squawk in broken Italian, "Was her idea! *Her idea!* I tell you ..."

"Tell him," Peroni cut in, indicating the approaching Vieri.

"Her idea!" he yelled again, at Vieri this time. "Not mine!"

By now the Spallone woman was close enough to hear.

"Shut up you moron!" she screamed at him. "Shut the . . ."

She glanced at Peroni, looked as if she felt stupid for a moment. Then the abuse started again, this time in an incomprehensible stream of gibberish, a language so strange Peroni couldn't begin to guess a single word.

He took out his phone and hit the record button. When she was done he stopped the phone, walked out in front of the van and said to the officers there, local and Vieri's crew from Milan, "Listen to me. I want these two taken into separate custody. No chance they get to talk to one another. No shared lawyers." He held up the phone. "I want a Finnish translator. Call Di Capua and . . ."

Vieri broke stride and leapt in front of him then roared, "*I* am the inspector here!"

Peroni put a hand on his shoulder and said, "Of course." Then he turned to the men again and said, "The *inspector* wants these two in custody. No contact. Finnish translator. Forensic are going to seal off the sauna in this place. The Roma kid was killed there, Spallone got beat up. Whatever this woman thinks, there's got to be some trace left. Check bank records and the financials for this gym of hers. This place was bleeding old man Spallone dry. Talk to the maid. She's got the Roma kid's number and called him when Giorgio needed a ride. There's your link. And the car." He pulled out the business card Ion Dinicu's father had given him. "This is an old Mercedes. Dinicu used it as an illegal cab. Spallone was his customer. My guess is Sven here ferried them away in it after he hit them then dumped the thing. Find this . . ." He squinted at the picture and read out the licence plate. " . . . and we're in court come Friday. My guess is start looking around Testaccio." He glanced at the Finn. "Sven here's not the brightest button in the box."

The Finn squeaked.

"And you," Peroni added, glaring at the hulk in the red satin boxer shorts, "remember. Tell the truth. One word. Fisting."

They all stared at him in awed silence. Peroni eyed a minion from Milan. The man had his notepad in his hand. He hadn't written a word.

"I'll repeat the licence plate once more," he said. "After that . . ." He touched Vieri on the shoulder again. "The inspector gets cross."

They all scribbled it down that time. Peroni looked at Vieri and asked, "Anything else?"

The man's hair didn't look as perfect as it had that morning. He was lost for words.

"I'm off shift in thirty minutes," Peroni added, glancing at his watch. "Take off the fact I never got a lunch break in truth I'm done now." He eyed Prinzivalli. "Beer? The usual place?"

The uniform man stripped off his uniform jacket, turned it so the lining was on the outside, and said, "The usual place."

"Come . . . with . . . me . . ." Vieri ordered, gripping Peroni by the arm.

9

They walked round the corner, back towards the Campo, and Peroni filled him in on the details along the way.

To the man's credit, Vieri listened, furious as he was.

When the explanation was done, Vieri shook his head and said, "I could have your job."

"No, no." They stopped by the place Peroni had bought his porchetta *panino* that morning. "I've done much worse than this and I never got kicked out then. Besides I've only got a few years left. What's the point?"

He looked Vieri in the face.

"Anyway what are you going to say? Fire this man because he tracked down a couple of double murderers on evidence I wouldn't even walk upstairs to look at? Not when he pleaded with me? I was too busy on my Blackberry, see. Too tied up watching CCTV and waiting for the mobile phone records to land in my inbox." He scratched his head. "Is that how you get on the up escalator in Milan? If so, let me offer some advice. Don't try it here. Won't work."

Vieri stiffened.

"We would have found all this," he insisted. "When forensic reported, when we got round to the detail . . ."

Peroni felt a little red light rise at the back of his head.

"You didn't need the detail. Two dead men, odd socks, same pairs. How many questions does that raise? How many possibilities? They didn't get up that way. All you have to do is work out how they got naked. Then ask yourself why whoever dressed them didn't spot the socks were wrong. Really. That's it."

The man from Milan was silent, a little down in the mouth.

"You use your eyes," Peroni added. "Watch what people do with theirs. You know the only person who's looked me straight in the face all day? That poor Roma kid's father. He didn't have anything to hide. He wasn't choking on some stupid obsession with systems and procedures and idiotic theoretical—"

"Okay, okay," Vieri interrupted. "Point taken."

"And yes," Peroni added. "You would have got there in the end. But this case maybe hangs on our golden boy Sven getting scared enough to cough it all up and put Eva beside him in the dock. Get his confession and before long she'll realize she can't wriggle out of it. You won't have to prove a damned thing. You could have spent months trying to do that, and I'd bet a politician's pension somewhere along the way Sven would have gone missing, by himself maybe or courtesy of some other hulk Eva was keeping sweet between the sheets."

Vieri nodded. He seemed to agree.

"It's Toni, isn't it?" Peroni asked. "I'm Gianni."

Vieri glanced behind him to make sure no one was watching. Then he took Peroni's hand.

"The trouble is, Toni, all that northern crap doesn't really cut it here. Not sure it does anywhere frankly. Walk around staring at your Blackberry and your computers all day and you're as blind as that stupid Finn, to a few things, maybe ones that matter. At least he's got the excuse he was born that way."

"The paperwork—" Vieri began.

". . . is your problem. This is your case. You get the credit. Tell them you sent me out to see Dinicu's father on a hunch. It all fell into place from there. You've got someone itching to confess to two murders and cut a sentencing deal. No one's going to ask a lot of questions."

The inspector nodded.

"And if none of this had worked out? All your hunches came up empty?"

Peroni grinned.

"Then you'd never have been any the wiser. Here."

He gave him the minion's notepad, the phone with the recorded exchange in Finnish between Eva Spallone and Sven, and the keys to the unmarked police Fiat.

"I stole the notebook from your guy. A translator might find something useful on the phone. And me and Prinzivalli . . . it may be more than one beer. You get someone to deal with the car."

"Fine," Vieri said and started to turn on his heels.

"Hey," Peroni called. The man stopped and looked at him. "You should come for a pizza with me and my friends. Falcone, Costa, Teresa. Well . . ." He shrugged. "She's more than a friend. You'll like them."

Inspector Vieri laughed. It made him look human.

"Oh," Peroni added.

He reached into his pocket, took out a nougat, held out it for the man from Milan.

"Welcome to Rome."

Daytripping

Gerard Brennan

Mattie squinted at me through a cloud of smoke. I wrinkled my nose at the stink of burning weed. My wake-and-bake friend didn't acknowledge the disapproval. He pulled a huge hit and offered me the joint. I waved it away.

"It's eight in the morning, man. I haven't even had a coffee yet."

"Caffeine's bad for you, James."

I shook my head. "And what are you? The picture of health?"

Mattie's build would have given Buddha stomach-envy. He was big before he started toking, but since those marijuana munchies took hold he must have doubled in size. I patted my own flat stomach and once again felt grateful that I'd left drugs behind me in my early twenties.

"I'll be around a long time after you're gone, James." He knocked a length of ash on to a saucer on his kitchen table. "That heart of yours won't hold up to the stress of the rat race."

I thumped my chest. "Nothing wrong with my ticker, Mattie. It's your lungs I fret about."

"There's no tobacco in this spliff." His lips bowed into a disgusted frown. "I gave up that cancerous shit ages ago. I roll them with dried parsley now."

I sniffed the air again. That cloying dope scent was prevalent – and okay, maybe it held a nostalgic charm – but I could smell something more subtle underneath. It reminded me a little of the stew my ma used to make.

"Parsley?"

He pointed to a little glass jar on the table. Honest-to-God dried parsley.

"Can you use any herb?"

Mattie shrugged. "I haven't tried anything else. Some Scottish guy told me he used it so I gave it a go. Stick with what works, you know?"

I realized my leg was pumping up and down under the table. Jitters. I wanted to leave, get on with my day. Already it was going to be hell finding a parking space anywhere near the office.

"You invited me for breakfast," I said.

Mattie leant forward. "Right enough. Sorry, man. How do you want your eggs?"

I glanced around Mattie's kitchen. Dirty dishes in and around the sink, crumbs on the floor, bin overflowing with takeaway cartons and blackened banana skins. I noticed muddy paw prints on the worktop. Mattie didn't own a pet. I suppressed a shudder.

"Boiled, please." They'd be harder to contaminate that way.

The stoned behemoth rocked himself out of his chair and trundled across the sticky linoleum. He tugged a pot from the unwashed stack in the sink. The dislodged crockery settled with a clatter. Without so much as a rinse, he dropped six eggs into the pot and poured hot water from the kettle on them. He dumped it on the ceramic hob and dialled up the heat.

Slapdash bastard.

"Do you want some tea?" he asked.

"No coffee?"

"I told you about that caffeine."

"Tea it is, then."

Mattie rummaged through the crap on his worktop and found a teapot. It was covered up with a knitted cosy in Rastafarian colours. I didn't pass comment. Too easy. He plonked the teapot on the table and I heard the liquid contents slosh.

"Brewed this earlier."

"Ah, man, I've been here for ages. It'll be like cold piss."

"Don't worry, James. This is proper herbal. It needs to soak for a while to diffuse."

He pulled off the cosy with a magician's flair then fetched us two cups from a cupboard. At least *they* were clean. The teapot, not so much. Brown stains formed thin rivulets down the spout and something was fused to the side. The something looked like it might have been a condom, but in what circumstance . . . ?

"Maybe I'll just have water, Mattie."

"Water here's stinking. You're better off with this. The badness is boiled out."

Mattie slopped the tea into the cups and pushed one in front of me. He eased himself back in his chair, graceful as a sumo wrestler, and raised his cup.

"Chin, chin, James."

I forced a tight-lipped smile and lifted my cup. The murky liquid had greasy patches on the surface, like petrol in a puddle. I sniffed it but couldn't distinguish a scent other than the heavy stench of dope so thick in the air.

"Come on, James. Drink up."

"No harm to you, Mattie, but this looks pretty rank."

"Never mind how it looks. Just swallow it down. I promise it'll knock your socks off."

"I don't—"

Mattie slammed a meaty hand down on the table. The wallop shocked me. I almost threw the cup in the air.

"Drink the tea, James."

My friend smiled at me. He gave me those eyes I remembered so well. It was how he looked at me over that first joint we shared in his mum's garage on a rainy Saturday afternoon. His stare was soft, unthreatening, and it held something else. A deep kindness, I suppose. And then I remembered that time he lent me money to pay rent when I'd lost my first job after uni. This was before I cleaned myself up and put some distance between us. I couldn't be a proper grown-up with friends like him.

Mattie had called me the day before. First time I'd heard from him in years. He needed to see me. There was something big going on. And I had figured he'd been going through some sobriety programme and a quick visit to check in on him was the least I could do. But he hadn't changed at all, except for the extra weight he carried. But then, in some cultures that was a sign of wealth and good fortune. And I always liked Mattie. He wasn't a bad influence so much as somebody who thought he could show the world a good time. And he'd just offered me a cup of herbal tea that was spiked with God-knows-what. Maybe I'd gotten a little high off his second-hand dope-smoke but it suddenly seemed very important that I drink Mattie's tea.

I gagged on the first sip. It was lukewarm green tea with some weird aftertaste.

"All of it," Mattie said.

I tipped the cup back and gulped. That brutal flavour hit me hard and I retched but managed to keep it down.

"What was in that, Mattie?"

"The key to a higher understanding."

"I can't believe you spiked me." But of course I could.

"I'm trying to help you along. It's evolution in action, baby. This is the stuff that'll bring us up to the next level."

"But what was it?"

"Psychedelics. Mostly magic mushrooms but I got a little DMT in there too."

"What the fuck's DMT?"

"You don't need to know. Just trust that it's harmless and as long as you stay calm and feel safe, you're in for the experience of a lifetime."

"And what if I don't stay calm?"

"You will. I'm here to look after you. Put negative thoughts away. The tea's inside you now, reacting. Go with it. You're safe and comfortable and nobody can hurt you."

"I don't do drugs anymore. What if this kills me?"

"Be cool, friend. Nobody ever died from psychedelics. If anything, they're medicinal."

"All medicines can kill you if you take the wrong dose."

"Positive thoughts, James. Enjoy the trip."

Mattie leant back in his chair. The joints creaked. I wondered how quickly this stuff was going to hit me. I felt strange already but didn't know if it was the drug or panic.

"Why would you do this to me?"

"It's a gift, brother."

"Stop calling me brother."

Mattie laughed. It sounded wrong. Something was definitely happening to me. The gear was kicking in. My stomach cramped. I didn't know if that was normal. The spiteful wooden spindles in my chair dug into my back. I wanted to elbow them but was afraid they might bite me with splintery teeth. Time got weird. I checked my watch. Ten minutes since I drank the tea. Or was it? When did I start? Had my watch stopped?

Work.

I was going to be late.

Scratch that. I couldn't show up in this state. I'd get fired. I had to phone in sick. But the phone would tout on me. Scream over my protestations and tell my boss that the words tumbling over my lips were dirty rotten lies. Aborted foetuses from my dank brain. Would an email be acceptable? My phone buzzed in my pocket. The tingle spread through my body. Reverberated in my core. No. That wouldn't do. My phone was going to break my spine. I fished it out of my pocket and tossed it on to the tabletop. The vibrations skated it across the surface. Then it stopped dead. Did the caller die too? I wanted to ask Mattie.

He looked at me, his head cocked like a curious dog. No, cats are curious. But dogs do that head tilt thing better. They're nicer creatures too. Loyal. A bit smelly. I wanted a dog. He'd keep me company at night, curled up beside me on the sofa. But I had allergies.

"Some dogs are hypoallergenic," Mattie said.

He was in my mind. I ignored him. Figured he'd get back out again if I didn't acknowledge his presence.

A sharp cramp attacked my gut. I imagined it torn asunder, ropey intestines spilled to the floor. It scared me a bit.

"I don't feel safe here. Can we try your living room?"

"Best if we face each other, James. Your eyes will keep me anchored."

What the fuck does that mean?

Mattie didn't answer. I didn't know if I'd said it out loud. At least he was out of my brain.

I noticed I was breathing faster. My head was a little light too. Cool sweat pinged up on my forehead and trickled under my arms. I thought about the melting icecaps. It wasn't global warming doing that. The world was shifting. Preparing for a new Ice Age. This I knew. It was hardwired knowledge. I clung to it like a lump of driftwood at sea. Ice. It sank the unsinkable and it would end us all. Like shaking an Etch-a-Sketch. Restore factory settings.

"Not today, though."

Mattie nodded.

I scratched my arm. Then my neck. I pushed down on my elbow to force my scratching hand between my shoulder blades. The itch kept moving. Do magnets repulse or propulse? God knows. Yes he does.

Mattie was still nodding. I thought he might be broken.

You're going to lose your job.

"Good. I hate that fucking job."

Mattie stopped nodding. He tilted his head to the left, then the right.

"Are you okay, James?"

"Etch-a-Sketch." Why did I say that? Oh, icecaps.

"Your skin's going a funny colour."

I didn't know how to answer that.

"Can I touch your face real quick?"

He didn't wait for me to answer. Mattie was beside me though I didn't see him get up. His clammy hand brushed my cheek.

"I think I'll grow a beard."

"Sure, James." He cleared his throat. "I don't think this is right."

I tried to clear *my* throat. Couldn't do it as well as Mattie. I wanted to ask him for advice. The words got stuck.

"James, listen to me. I need you to slow down your breathing."

Mattie looked worried. I scratched my arms. Sped up my breathing just to fuck with him a little then I realized I couldn't slow it back down. I squeaked. The hamster fell off the wheel.

What hamster?

The room shifted. The floor was on my back. No, wait, I was on the floor. Yuck. Sticky lino. Mattie knelt beside me. He tugged on my tie.

Don't choke me, Mattie.

He looped the tie around his wrist. Did I put two on that morning? I felt at my collar to see what was restricting my throat. Nothing there. I could smell shit. Did I shit in my boxers?

"I'm taking you to a hosp . . ."

I sat up, wondered what the fuck a hosp was. Looked around me.

Hospital.

How did I get here?

Mattie stared at me from a chair he could barely fit into. "You're awake."

"When did I go to sleep?" I asked.

"Why didn't you tell me about your allergies?"

"Did I not?"

"I'd have remembered." He twisted a rolled-up newspaper in his fat hands. "Who the fuck's allergic to magic mushrooms, like?"

"What kind of man puts shit like that in his friend's tea and tricks him into drinking it?"

"It was a present. I was doing you a good turn."

"But instead . . ."

"Anaphylactic shock. You fucking wimp."

A nurse drew back the curtain. She scowled at Mattie. An impressive Nurse Ratched impression.

"Could you moderate your language please, *sir*?"

I smirked and Ratched caught sight of it.

"You needn't laugh." She rested one hand on a sharp hip. "A grown man taking . . . that rubbish. On a *Tuesday*."

What could I say? A bigger boy made me do it? I cast my gaze down to my chest, meek as a lamb. Ratched huffed air through her pinched nostrils and marched off.

"Bitch." Mattie's voice was so low I barely heard him.

"You know, Mattie, you always got me into trouble at school."

"And what?"

"Nothing. I just assumed we'd grown out of it."

Mattie gave me that Buddha grin of his.

"So, I'm allergic to magic mushrooms?"

"Something similar to penicillin in them or . . . I don't know. Yeah, you're allergic."

I closed my eyes and thought for a second. The bed rocked and I dug my fingers into the edges of the mattress. Counted to ten and tried to figure out if I was still tripping. Couldn't tell for sure. I envisioned myself peeling back cobwebs from my brain. The image sharpened my mind. I focused on Mattie.

"Can I feel like that again without the mushrooms? Maybe something people aren't likely to be allergic to?"

Mattie double-blinked. He tugged on his earlobe. "Probably, yeah. I can look into it, like."

"Yeah. You do that."

The End of the Road

Jane Casey

He never had any luck; if there was trouble going it found him, wherever he was. Even halfway to the middle of nowhere, there it was – that lurch in his gut. Things had gone against him again.

He pulled off the road on to what passed for a hard shoulder, loose gravel that lost itself in a half-hidden ditch. The car shuddered to a stop. Stones peppered the underside like shot. He turned the engine off and opened the door, a quick glance over his shoulder confirming there was nothing coming over the brow of the hill. He'd have heard it, anyway. The silence was complete, after the scratchy growl of the hire-car's engine. It was thrashed – too many tourists going too fast on unmade red-dirt roads. They'd be the last ones to use it, the man had told him at the airport, grinning widely like it was something to be happy about.

"What's wrong?"

"Flat tyre." He got out of the car before she could respond, slamming the door on the start of a sentence. He could see her lips moving, her face hard behind the giant sunglasses. Nothing he needed to hear.

The tyre must have been damaged already. He hadn't seen anything on the road. Hadn't been looking, though. It was a straight road that ran over gentle hills, cutting through farmland, and there wasn't any traffic to speak of, or anything else to take his attention away from the hazy blue mountains in the distance and the neatly parcelled fields – green, yellow, fawn, iron-red. The livestock were cream-coloured sheep with upholstered legs, far too hot in the spring sunshine, and Friesian cows that looked weirdly familiar under silver-leafed trees. Then there'd been a field of ostriches and he'd nearly driven off the road staring at them. He'd seen blue cranes huddled motionless by round green ponds, and birds of prey hunched on power lines, staring out over waves of rushing grey grass, and he couldn't get enough of it. There's been an animal too, a sand-coloured thing that streaked across the road before he could focus on it, low to the ground. A stoat or a weasel or something. Hunting.

He hadn't said a word to Lisa about any of it. She'd been asleep most of the way, her head tipped back against the seat and her mouth slack. She hadn't slept on the flight. She'd kept him awake too with her complaining. Wasn't used to the back of the plane anymore. Couldn't forgive him for downgrading their tickets from champagne and flat beds in business class. And hadn't laughed when he pointed out there was no business anymore. They were lucky to be going at all.

Luck wasn't why, though, he admitted to himself, hunkering down with the wheelbrace and the instruction book as if he knew what he was doing. Pride, more like. He couldn't admit to Conor that they wouldn't be using his holiday home in South Africa after all. He had to keep up appearances. Conor with his easy, hands-in-pockets manner, his eyes that missed nothing, that never laughed even when he was roaring at some joke he'd made. He couldn't let him find out the truth or it would all be over. The fragile pretence that everything would come good again would crash down around him.

And it sort of made sense to go. It was a free holiday, apart from the flights and the car. A trip to the end of the world, as Conor put it. A little white cottage with a reed-thatched roof, very simple, Conor said, as if it was nothing to him to have a holiday home 6,000 miles from Dublin. Which was all part of it, of course; you had to act like it was no big deal. He'd been half-listening as the words rattled out of his friend's wide, lipless mouth. It was a cruel mouth, he'd been thinking. A wry twist to it, as if he knew the truth.

"I mean, we thought about the west coast."

He'd been a second away from making an eejit of himself, saying something about Galway or Sligo or fecking Clare, when Conor had gone on, no encouragement needed, in that South Dublin rugby-playing drawl.

"But then we decided we'd prefer the Indian Ocean. And when we found the place it was a done deal. You can really get away from everything, you know?"

The sun was burning the back of his neck. Jesus, it was only October. Spring for them. What would it be like in the summer? The silence was starting to take on new shapes as he tuned into it: the breeze in the grass, insects whirring in the undergrowth, something clicking away to itself busily like an oul' wan telling her rosary. And he was sweating, grunting with the effort as he loosened the nuts and lugged the dead wheel off. He felt like heaving it into the ditch but he didn't quite have the nerve, even if there was no one to see. It would be a shame too; there was no litter anywhere. No plastic bags hanging in the barbed wire. No piles of rubbish by the road. He still hated himself for being a good boy, putting it back in the well where the spare tyre had been, tucking it in like a sleepy child.

He flinched away from the thought before his brain had properly formed the words and slung the bags back into the boot fast, slamming it shut with a tinny sound. The heat from the sun-warmed metal scorched his palms.

"All okay?" She sounded drugged, half-asleep again. The car was airless.

"Fine." *No thanks to you.*

"Is it much further?"

He ignored her, pulling out into the no-traffic with a flourish. The windscreen was splattered with tiny bodies, smears of red and green and clear liquid like water. Another handful scattered against the glass as he crested the next hill and swooped down, the tarmac smooth under the wheels so even in that fucking jalopy he felt as if he were flying. The road looped and ran in front of him like a roller-coaster track and all he had to do was follow, follow, and feel his stomach disappear when it dropped over the edge . . .

Jesus. Concentrate. The sun or the stress or the travel had given him a wicked headache. No proper sleep for weeks now, the thoughts chasing each other around his skull like a pack of sex-crazed squirrels. The glare off the tarmac was fierce.

"Is there any water left?"

She shook the bottle at him in reply, the last few drops running down the inside. Oh, she was pissed off with him now. That was fine, wasn't it? What did she have to be pissed off about? The anger stirred, rolling over inside him and he was glad of it. He needed it.

The car roared down the empty road and little birds darted through the dusty air behind it, chasing the insects that survived his passing.

"Is this it?" She was sitting up, looking out, her face already falling into the sulk that was never far away these days. For once he could see her point. The cottage was halfway to falling down, low and sagging on its small plot of grass, the white lime on the walls rubbed and cracked. A small brown boy was squatting on the doorstep, poking in the dirt with a stick. Six, maybe seven. Shorts and a jumper that didn't fit him properly, winter-thick despite the hot sunshine. He looked up, wary as a stray dog, and disappeared in through the green-painted door.

"Oh, my God." Her head was swivelling, taking in the tumbledown walls, the weeds growing up the middle of the road. She had slept through the last part of the drive, missing the moment when the fields faded to rough grass and white sand began to edge the road instead of rusty soil. She hadn't seen the line of the horizon resolve itself into dunes glinting in the sun. Where he'd parked they were out of sight of the sea but salt in the air smeared gauzy dirt on every window and he could smell it on the wind. The tide had to be coming in, he thought, listening to the waves. The sound was disorientating. It seemed to be coming at them from everywhere, buffeting the car.

"There's nothing here. I mean, *Jesus*."

He waited a moment longer, enjoying her dismay a little too much to put an end to it. She had wanted to go to Dubai. This was about as far away as you could get from air-conditioned luxury. Her bottom lip was actually quivering.

"This isn't it. This is the village. The holiday houses are over the hill. I've got to get the key."

He left her sitting in the car again and swung into the cottage with a rap on the door, the big smile on his face, how are ye and aren't ye great to have the key ready for us and oh that Conor is a great fella altogether. A lot of nodding and smiling from the old woman, even though she probably understood one word in fifty. She was old, dignified, her face lined like a dry riverbed. Dirt poor, literally. Like an Irish peasant in famine times, he thought, scuffing earth under his foot, a catch in his throat from the wood smoking sullenly on a pitiful fire. She did the cleaning at the cottage. She'd be in every day. She'd look after them. He found a note in his pocket, knew it was too much, put it on the table anyway. Conor was the big man, was he? Well, it was easy to be the big man to people who had nothing. You didn't have to have very much at all yourself, to look rich to them.

He had his foot over the threshold when the thought occurred to him that Conor felt that way about him and Lisa. Deserving poor. *Give them a holiday. Let them see how well I've been doing for myself.* He wanted to drop the keys in the dust and go, drive away, back to Cape Town. He could book them into a disgustingly lavish hotel and max out the final credit cards for ten stupid, self-indulgent days of spas and five-course meals and flowing wine. Fuck Conor; fuck the lot of them. Fuck the bank and the mortgage he couldn't pay. Fuck the stupid house that was worth a quarter of what they'd paid for it.

It took him the length of the slow walk back to the car to get over it, to get control of himself. He needed to be there. Because the way out of his predicament was sitting on her arse in the passenger seat with the window down, her stupid ignorant face turned up to the sun.

And he couldn't tell if it was hatred or pity that was lodged in his throat.

He opened his eyes and the room was already light, white sliding in around the edges of the shutters. The sea was quiet, the waves slurring as they washed over the rocks below. The tide going out, he supposed, without really knowing. Somewhere outside a bird was chanting, a wood pigeon or some such, and he couldn't help fitting words to the six-note call. It was plaintive, reproachful. And insistent. *You said you'd come with me . . . you said you'd come with me . . .*

He risked a look. She was still asleep. Her face was flushed, her mouth pressed against the pillow so it slid sideways. Sweat darkened her hair and her skin glistened damply. She looked younger, asleep. She looked different.

He got out of bed carefully, folding back the duvet around her so she didn't notice him going. Just after seven, according to his phone. He shut himself in the bathroom, hoping the noise of the shower wouldn't wake her. Three days they'd been there and he'd developed a routine, walking around downstairs, opening the shutters. He'd go to the shop for milk and the paper. Back at the house he'd make coffee and sit outside, watching the sea while he ate breakfast. The white-painted house was poised on the edge of high ground with nothing between him and the water. He could never get used to it, no matter how long he stared. The colour of the water – that pure cold green like the heart of Antarctic ice. The searing white of the dunes marching into the distance, immaculate and untouched. And the miracle of the whales: a black back suddenly arching from the valley between two waves, or a V-spray of white water snorted at the sky, or best of all, a great surge far out to sea as one of them heaved itself up and out of its element before slamming back down and disappearing. He couldn't tear himself away.

Lisa didn't get it.

"You can't see much, can you? Just a black speck. That could be a rock, sure."

"They're the size of ten bull elephants lined up end to end," he'd told her, reading from a book he'd found in the sitting room. "The adults, that is."

"Is that how they measure things here? In bull elephants?" She was ripping the piss and he didn't mind, sort of – he laughed back at her. It was nice. A shared moment. And then she ruined it. "Can we not go somewhere to see them properly? Get a boat?"

"They only do land-based whale watching here. Not to spook them, you know."

She pulled down the corners of her mouth. "That's shit."

They had been hunted to the edge of extinction, but that had stopped years before. They might have a memory that men in boats spelled disaster. Or did they? Did they suspect the low concrete sheds along the shore had been used to cut them up? Did they tell tales to the young ones of the blood-stained sea, the boats riding low in the water with their giant haul, the harpoons and the nets and the killing frenzy?

"They have to feel safe so they can mate and give birth. The next bay along is a nursery for them, it says here. You can see the mammies and their calves. Look." He turned the book, showing her a picture from overhead of a small whale swimming beside its mother.

"I thought it would be like Fungi the dolphin. D'you remember? Down in Dingle? And you could go out in a boat and say hello to him."

"I never did that." He put the book down, but not to talk. To end the conversation. Fucking Fungi. It didn't begin to compare. He'd go into the kitchen for a bit. Make tea or coffee. Or pour a drink, if it was time yet.

"I wanted to see him." She said it softly, to herself. "I always wanted to."

He had left her sitting there, on her own.

She slept on until after he had eaten, after the first pot of coffee was empty and the second lukewarm in the sunshine. He'd read the paper. Done the crossword. Folded it over and made shite of the sudoku. The day wasn't that hot after all; there was an edge to the breeze that fluttered the pages of his paper. He shivered in his T-shirt, looking for fives on the little grid. Every time he looked up he saw the barbecue built against the side of the house and imagined Conor standing there grilling fish caught that morning. *This is the life.* Oh, Conor would know what he was doing. *He* wouldn't. He'd set fire to the thatch or something. He imagined it, imagined himself screaming. *My poor wife. Lisa. She's all I've got.*

How very true that was. She'd told him after they were married that she couldn't have children. He'd gone away and cried for them both, but mainly for her. Poor Lisa. It had brought them closer together, at first.

Then her sister let it slip. "Couldn't have? Didn't want, more like."

She'd tried to backtrack but it was out, and all she could say when he pursued it was, "Ah, sure you know Lisa."

He didn't. That was the first time he'd realized it. And realized that she liked it that way.

He got up and walked to the edge of the lawn, to the pathetic shin-height fence of wooden sticks that was all to stop you from going right off the edge. It wasn't a cliff; it was a hill, but steep. It was covered in tussocks of grass that might give you a handhold if you fell, if you had the presence of mind to hold on.

Further down the coast, there were rocks. Proper cliffs the colour of wet cardboard. Sheer drops. It was worth considering.

The bird was still going mental. *You said you'd come with me. You said you'd come with me.*

People had accidents on holidays. Every year, people didn't come home from honeymoons. Trips of a lifetime. The papers were full of that stuff. Falling off balconies. Car accidents. Bus crashes. Cliff-top walks ending in disaster.

He chewed his lip, feeling the headache start up again.

It was because you couldn't say what was dangerous and what wasn't, when you were away from home. His father had a theory that you were in most danger on the last day of a trip when your guard was down. Could he wait for the last day?

If he did anything.

His palms were wet and he wiped them on his jeans surreptitiously, even though he was alone.

How else did people die? He went back to the paper, flicking through the news pages. Reversed over by a car that didn't stop. Strangled and left by the side of a road in a township near the airport. There was a picture. A 747 hung over the huddled shacks as it came in to land, the locals staring down at a body in a pink dress that lay at their feet. The main story was about a white couple who'd been shot during a burglary. The picture was a Tamboerskloof mansion with the security gates standing open, police vehicles filling the driveway. Poor bastards.

He threw the paper down and rubbed his hand over his head, hating himself. He couldn't do it. He had no gun. The knives in the kitchen were too blunt to cut bread; they'd never saw through skin and muscle. He couldn't imagine strangling her. He would fail, as usual. He would fuck it up and end up in prison, back in Ireland if he was lucky. Sitting in Portlaoise beside some ex-IRA gangster.

A sound from above: he leaned back to see her opening the shutters, squinting. He raised a hand.

"Is it warm?"

"In the sun."

"Not shorts weather, though."

He shook his head.

"I packed too much." She disappeared from view and a minute later water gurgled down the pipe, into the drain. He could hear her singing to herself, as if she were happy.

They got out of the house that afternoon, driving around, aimless. Lisa put the window down and leaned her head against the car door, the wind blowing her hair around her face. She'd found a radio station that played oldies. It cut out constantly but she wouldn't let him turn it off.

"I like it."

It reminded him of when they got together. He had his first car, a third-hand Peugeot, and he'd drive her up to the Hill of Howth or along the Vico Road – anywhere you could see the sea. All of Dublin stretched before them, cradled in the mountains. Theirs for the taking. He'd done his best, he really had. He'd given it everything. His hands and arms ached; he had to keep making himself relax them on the wheel. He just wanted it to stop.

"Did you say something?"

He shook his head.

"I thought you said you wanted to stop."

"Here? There's nothing here."

"Where are we going?" She sat up. "Where even are we?"

A red back road cutting through farmland, wire fences on either side of the earth track. Nowhere at all.

"Doesn't matter."

"It doesn't?"

"We'll know it when we get there." He took the next turn to the right, and the next, ending up on a dirt road that was bumpy enough to loosen fillings.

"This is insane."

"We're exploring."

The road twisted and snaked through miles of nothingness and he lost himself in the driving. He stopped thinking about where they were going, or anything else. He'd forgotten she was there until she spoke.

"Look." She was pointing through the bleary windscreen, now crusted with dust as well as insect innards. "Is that a lighthouse?"

"So it seems." He said it as if that was what he'd planned, as if he'd known it was at the end of the road.

"Oh . . ." She put a hand on the dashboard. "Oh, let's go to the sea. I want to see the sea again."

*   *   *

The beach was perfect – miles long, pure white sand, deserted except for a man line-fishing from the rocks in the distance. The wind was cutting across it, ripping through the low green shrubs on the dunes.

"Will we walk along the beach?" he asked.

"As far as we can go."

"To the end?"

"To the end of the world." She grinned at him, her eyes very blue, and he almost kissed her then, even though he hated her. He loved her too – that was the hell of it. He turned and stumbled away from her, horrified by himself. The ground was slipping out from under his feet and he couldn't seem to stop it.

"What's wrong?" She caught up with him, holding on to his arm. "What's the matter?"

"Ah, I don't—" He almost sobbed.

"Are you not well?"

He shook his head. "It's nothing. Just too much sun." The beach was so white it dazzled him.

"We'll go back to the car."

"No. We said we'd walk." He pointed at something black on the sand, in the distance. "I want to know what that is. Come on. I'll race you."

He outdistanced her easily, the wind searing his eyes. Poor bitch. He'd made her what she was. He'd promised her the world.

By the time he got close enough to the dark shape on the sand to see what it was, he'd pulled himself together again. He put up a hand to stop Lisa.

"Wait there."

"What is it?" She wrinkled her nose as she reached him. "Is it dead?"

"It's a penguin."

"It stinks."

"It's rotting."

"Lovely." She pulled at his arm. "Come on. Leave it."

"I'm just looking."

"Don't touch it. Are you mad?" She was dragging at him. "Let's go."

He couldn't stop looking at the bird. The feathers, rough and spiky on its breast. The cloudy eye garlanded in flies, the ones that weren't slipping in and out of the half-open beak. A penguin. Honest to God.

"You wouldn't get this on Dollymount Strand, would you?"

"I'm cold." She'd taken a step away from him. "It's too cold here, with the wind. No wonder there's no one here."

"I don't mind it."

"I do."

"So you don't want to walk on the beach?"

"What else could we do?"

He couldn't think of anything. "Go back to the house?"

She looked away from him, her hair blowing around her face so he couldn't see what she was thinking.

"We'll be grand once we're walking." Why he was trying to persuade her, he didn't know. He'd be happy enough with his seat in the sun, watching for whales. The beach was no good for it. They were too low down and the surf was running too high.

She started off without him, walking fast. He matched her pace, slipping in the sand that gave under his feet at every step. Tiny flies rose up from the ground to fling themselves at his face. The wind carried handfuls of grit that found his eyes and his open mouth; he spat a couple of times, until she turned around and gave him the look.

"It'll be easier on the way back. We'll have the wind behind us," he said.

"Why do you have to be so fucking cheerful all the time?"

"I don't know," he said, hopeless. "I'm not."

"You are. You won't even admit the truth to yourself. This is horrible. I hate this place and I wish we'd never come."

"Yer man'll hear you." He was looking over her shoulder at the fisherman, a still, upright figure, dignified in rubber boots and a heavy jacket.

"Why would he care?"

"I don't know." He didn't know how to explain it. To that man, they probably looked privileged. He fished for a living, standing there on a deserted beach, casting his line into the surf. A simple life. What would he make of the two of them with their petty squabbles, their need to spend money to feel happy? He looked at the fisherman's lean silhouette, black against the greeny-white chaos of the waves, and felt like weeping.

"You've cracked. Fucking looper." The anger had gone out of her voice. She turned and started walking back, following the wavering line of footprints they had left. He gave her a couple of minutes before he followed, shoving his hands in his pockets and walking with his head down, pretending to whistle.

He'd parked where the road ended, a patch of tarmac walled in by dunes on three sides. It was sheltered from the wind and he was conscious of the heat from the sun again as he trudged across the car park, pulling the keys out of his pocket. His face stung – either he had burned or the wind had seared his skin. The car would be roasting when they got in, and Lisa would complain. She had her back to him, standing beside the passenger door, looking at her phone. Her back was hunched, lumpy with emotion. The white trousers had been a mistake, he almost said. Her arse looked twice its usual size. What could she do to him, anyway, if he said it? She'd wanted him to start telling the truth.

"All right?"

"No." She threw the word in his direction without turning around.

"What's wrong with you?"

"We've got a flat again."

"Shit." He crouched down to look, poking at it with a wary thumb. "Shit. We used the spare tyre already."

"I told you to get it fixed."

He hadn't thought it was worth it. He'd been planning to tell the car-hire people it was damaged when he got the car. Trying to save money again.

"Is your phone working?"

"No reception. You?"

Not a bar of it. He flung himself at the nearest sand dune, slipping and sliding. He held his phone up, trying to catch a signal – as if it was floating around on the breeze somewhere above his head and he might manage to snag it. There were snakes in the Cape, he recalled, feeling vulnerable. Cobras. Lethal, they were.

"Nothing." The dune half-collapsed behind him as he ran back down. "I'll have to go for help."

"Go where? We didn't pass any villages or houses even. And you can't leave me here on my own. I could get raped."

"You'd be lucky." Her face went a terrifying shade of purple. "Listen, Lisa, I'm only messing with you. I just mean that there's no one here, and—"

"I know what you meant. Go fuck yourself."

"You have to laugh, though. I mean, what are the chances? Two flat tyres in one holiday?"

"I'm not laughing. It'll get dark soon. And cold." She folded her arms. "I'm not staying here on my own."

"I'll go and ask that fella. The fisherman. He might be able to give us a lift."

"He probably doesn't even speak English. And he might not have a car." She looked around. "We're the only people here."

He started off towards the gap in the dunes, ignoring her. He could make himself understood. He had cash on him. That usually worked wonders.

It took him a second to take it in, squinting against the wind and the low sun. The rocks were empty. The beach was deserted. He ran forward a few paces, trying to catch sight of him, but there was nothing.

"Fuck." For the first time he felt afraid. He didn't know how to survive away from the modern world. For all his shite about wanting the simple life, he needed his phone. He needed a man to come and fix the tyre. He wanted a recovery truck to rescue them, or, failing that, a car with tourists in it like themselves, who'd give them a lift. They could have a laugh about what bad luck he had. He could hear himself now, playing up to it. *Ah God, sure I'm a disaster altogether.* And Lisa would nod, meaning it.

She saw his face as he came back towards her. "What?"

"Not there."

"I don't believe you."

"Go and see for yourself. He's gone home."

"How?"

"Maybe there's another car park. Maybe he lives nearby but I don't know where. In a sand dune or something. There's no houses."

"Go and find him." She was half-sobbing.

"I can't."

"What'll we do? We can't stay here. There's nothing here. No light, even. No water."

"Stop panicking." He spoke sharply, wanting to shut her up. "I have to think."

He opened the boot to look at the other tyre. Maybe it wasn't so bad. He levered it out and bounced it on the ground experimentally. No. Worse. He let it fall, left it lying there.

"You could try to drive on it."

"I'll wreck the car."

"I don't care about the car. It doesn't matter if it wrecks the car."

"We'd get stuck, Lisa. That road is all loose sand and gravel."

"Then we'd better start walking, because I am *not* staying here." Her voice had risen and the edge in it sawed across his nerves. He just wanted her to stop talking. To stop.

He became aware that he was staring into the boot. At the wheelbrace, specifically. It was heavy, he recalled. Metal. It could do damage, with enough force behind it.

He ached to swing it. He imagined the impact. The force travelling back up his arm, vibrating away to nothing in his very bones. Her knees, crumpling. Her body folding. Her head turned away from him, so he didn't have to see her face.

He could drag her on to the beach. Into the surf. The waves could take her. This was a shipwreck coast. It had killed hundreds of times over. The sea had enough power to explain a cracked skull; she would be in tatters by the time she was discovered. If she was ever discovered.

She had turned away from him again, muttering to herself.

He had his hand on the wheelbrace, his fingers curled around the cold metal, when he heard the engine in the distance. His first reaction was disappointment, before relief surged in like the tide. It was a bakkie, a pick-up truck with two men in it, travelling fast. He came out from behind the car waving his arms, conscious of Lisa doing the same. *Stop. Don't drive past us, wherever you're going. Don't leave us here. Something terrible might happen.*

The driver braked hard, opened his door and jumped out, all in one quick movement. "What's up? Got problems?"

He was white but he had a strong accent. Blue eyes. Lined face, though he couldn't have been older than them; the sun would do that to you. Sandy hair. And the other man, the passenger, he was the same. They could have been brothers. Farmers? Or fishermen too? Something physical – they were lean as running dogs. They made him feel fat and pale and useless.

"Our car . . ."

"We've got a flat tyre." Lisa stepped in, straight down to business. "Can you give us a lift back to the nearest town?"

Two pairs of blue eyes switched to her, assessing her. The driver grinned, showing gaps in his teeth. "No town near here."

"There must be somewhere. Somewhere our phones would work." She waggled hers at him. "This thing is dead."

"Can I see it?" The passenger held out his hand.

"Nothing to see." Lisa was putting it into her bag.

"Give it to me." There was a strange tone in his voice.

She looked up. "What?"

He got there before she did. Not rescuers. Hunters, like the weasel he'd seen on the first day. "Give him the phone, Lisa."

"Why?"

"Give it to him or he'll take it."

Lisa looked at him, then back at the passenger. And back to him. He could see the fear on her face. He could taste it in his own mouth. Nothing he could do. Nothing he could say to them. She handed it over.

"Give me your jewellery."

"Give it to him," he said when she hesitated. "Go on. It's not worth it."

"Not my engagement ring."

"Everything." The man was implacable. The driver hadn't moved. He was watching the two of them. Waiting for someone to try to fight back. He'd be waiting a while.

"Where are you from?" the passenger asked.

"Ireland." They said it in unison. Waited for the chorus of approval, the one you always got. People loved the Irish, didn't they? The world over.

"Got your passports with you?"

He did. And his driver's licence. And yes, they could have his watch. His camera. His MP3 player. His wedding ring. His cash. It all went and he didn't care. He didn't need any of it. He felt numb. Lisa was crying. He couldn't understand why.

"It's all right," he said to her, as the passenger finished going through the car. "It'll be all right."

She shook her head, her face twisted like a child's. "I want to go home."

The driver moved at last. "We'll leave you good people. You stay."

"Will you let someone know we're here?" They wouldn't, he knew.

"Someone will come." He pointed to Lisa. "Go stand by him."

She came to him, whimpering with fear as she passed the men.

"Turn around."

"Why?" He was genuinely curious. He didn't feel scared, he realized. He felt nothing at all.

The passenger was holding something behind him, so they couldn't see it.

That wasn't good.

"Turn around." The driver was grim. "Walk forward, slowly. Fifty paces. Go onto the beach and keep walking. Don't look back."

They did as they were told; they had no choice. The sand was pale pink as the sun slipped towards the horizon. The blue in the sky and the sea had faded to lavender. All of Africa lay behind him and the wind that chilled his face came from the end of the world. He'd never seen anything more lovely.

"What's going to happen?" Lisa whispered. "What's going to happen to us?"

Her hand found his and he let it lie there, warm and human, as they walked towards the pitiless sea.

A Nice Cup of Tea

Christopher J. Simmons

On the day she was going to die, Edith found the dead rat in the garden. It lay there on the garden path for all to see, curled and doubled up. It had obviously been writhing in agony for the last few seconds of its life. The body was bloated and it was quite stiff when she nudged it with the toe of her shoe. Timorously Edith lifted it slightly and then withdrew her shoe, watching as the tiny body simply rolled back into its original position.

Edith fiddled with the phial of arsenic. The chemist had been right. The stuff had worked a treat. If there was one thing she couldn't stand, it was rats. As she looked down at the deceased, a squadron of aircraft flew overhead. She looked up and wondered what part of Hitler's citadel they had been bombing the night before.

Edith's heart gave a lurch and her chest felt tight, her eyes watering. Suddenly, killing vermin seemed minascule compared to other things that were going on in the world, but daily life had to go on and the rats had to be deterred. Her father was old and she had too many jobs to be able to keep the large garden in trim. It had become a playground for vermin. One had scampered over her foot only the other day as she pegged out the washing. They were getting too bold. If nothing was done about them soon, then they would overrun the place in no time.

She had even caught one squeezed under the kitchen door, its front in the kitchen, and its behind still in the backyard.

She had felt guilty afterwards when she had screamed and started hitting it with her brush as the animal squealed with pain whilst trying to wriggle back out from under the door. But it was added pressure – she didn't need any more stress what with looking after her aged father who ordered her about ever since her mother had been blown sky-high when a bomb had torn apart the friend's house she had been visiting at the time.

"Edith! Edith!"

The banshee wailing only added weight to her already overburdened shoulders. It was exactly the same reaction when she heard the screeching of the klaxon – a sharp grip of fear followed by an overpowering lethargy at the thought of spending hours in the confined space of the Anderson shelter with her father shouting and complaining, mainly about the Germans, although Edith, just for good measure, still came in for criticism from her father's tongue.

Edith had obviously not reacted quickly enough, and lost in her thoughts had not moved from the rat.

"Edith! Edith!" came the continued wailing from upstairs.

Really, her father was becoming quite tedious in his old age. If she ran up those stairs once, it was a thousand times. Leaving the dead body to deal with later, she quickly marched into the house.

Up in his bedroom, Edith listened attentively to her father's latest request. He wanted another cup of tea.

"I have already made you two cups of tea, father. That will make three cups of tea this morning. The doctor said all this tea isn't good for you."

"Blast that fool of a man." said Albert venomously, which led him on to a fit of coughing. "I don't care what he has to say. I know my own health better than anybody. Now, get me that cup of tea, girl!"

In frustration and sheer exhaustion, Edith looked at her father and, deciding that it would be far more trouble than it was worth to argue with the cantankerous old sod, she slowly descended the stairs to start the preparation for his tea.

Where he put it all, she did not know. Edith had taken after her mother who, like her, had been big boned. Her father was a scrawny man with sunken features, his facial skin stretched tight over his skull. And despite all this liquid he never needed to go to the loo.

It was another of Edith's numerous tasks to escort her father to the outside toilet opposite the kitchen and then wait by the door while she listened to him huff and strain inside.

Then, after flushing the toilet herself as he also seemed incapable of doing even that, she helped him back up the stairs and into his bed. But that was only twice a day and although he had a commode, it was rarely used.

So how did he hold in all those pints of tea he drank throughout the day?

It was a mystery to her.

Down in the kitchen Edith began to make her father another cup of tea, rescuing the tea leaves that she had used for his earlier two cups that morning. Did the old fool not realize there was a war on? Tea, like everything else on this island, was rationed and most times plain unavailable.

Edith sat at the kitchen table and began to flick through a magazine she had managed to pilfer from her friend, June.

Edith gazed longingly at the pictures of people on the beach, laughing and having a wonderful time. Where were these people who had time to gambol across the bright golden sand beneath a huge yellow globe as their skin turned a luscious mahogany? They certainly didn't look like anyone Edith knew as everyone, herself included, had pasty complexions from the harsh winters, short summers and lack of a proper diet. They couldn't be on this planet – the whole world appeared to have been sucked in to Hitler's mania.

She turned the page to look at a photograph of some bananas growing in their plantations and ripening under the sun. Edith longed to taste them. What she wouldn't do just to taste that exotic fruit one more time.

Edith had tasted banana once and she tried to conjure the taste in her mind and transfer the memory to her tongue without success. She was sure that her lips would tingle if ever they could taste the treasure within that yellow skin. Edith wished she could be transported to such a decadent and beautiful paradise where she ate richly coloured fruit and played on the beach all day.

Here in London, with the constant traffic during the day and the constant fear of being bombed at night, Edith could only wonder what she was going to concoct with the frugal vegetables she had in her almost bare larder.

It was at that moment that there came a thumping from upstairs. The old man was banging his walking stick on the floor, impatient for his third cup of tea. She tried to ignore his banging, but soon the screams of distress and agitation started to float down the staircase.

"Where is my tea, girl?" her father shouted for all the neighbours to hear. "Have you gone to Ceylon for the tea leaves, girl?"

Edith roused herself from her chair and bit back a clever remark she could have shouted at the ceiling above her. Having squeezed the last of the tea out of the leaves, Edith took up her father a cup of very weak tea, knowing that he would make the inevitable comment.

"No tea left to put in the pot, girl?"

Edith, feeling beaten and faded, declined to give her father any fuel for the fire he was so hopefully stoking. Instead she simply turned and headed for the bedroom door.

"I will want to go out sometime today. Midday will do me perfectly well. You can come and dress me in about fifteen minutes and help me down the stairs."

"You are perfectly capable of dressing yourself." Edith remarked at the door. "I will help you down the stairs, but I know you can dress yourself quite happily."

"You will help me on with my shoes, girl. You know I can't reach."

"Fine." Edith sighed. "I will be back to help you on with your shoes."

Before her father could start any other argument, she left and sharply closed the bedroom door behind her.

It was midday and finally, after much fussing, Edith and her father finally got out on to the street. Making sure that her father's blanket was properly secured across his lap, she started to push her father along the pavement in the dilapidated wheelchair that had once serviced her mother during a spate of illness.

The sunny day had turned cloudy and a wind that had started up fought against Edith as she pushed the great hulking monstrosity and her father along the street.

The streets were busy as people hustled and bustled around trying to make the days seem normal despite the numerous airplanes humming overhead. Sometimes, if it was enemy aircraft approaching, then the wail of the siren that broke through the air was enough to send a shiver down every spine.

Lumps of masonry and glass were scattered about the street, the shrapnel from bombed-out houses that had yet to be cleared. Anything of any worth would have been swept away by the scavengers who dodged the bombs and headed towards – rather than away from – any raging fire to see what pickings there might be.

It disheartened Edith that despite Winston Churchill's rousing speeches, at the end of the day people always looked after themselves.

Thankfully, Edith's father had only wanted to go to the newsagent's at the end of the road for a newspaper and a packet of his favourite tobacco, which he secretly smoked against the doctor's orders.

Edith wondered why he didn't simply let her go and buy his daily paper and tobacco. He said he needed to get out of the house and get himself some fresh air, but Edith felt he enjoyed being awkward making her push him through the streets.

Sometimes her father liked to go further, which left Edith

feeling completely exhausted. And yet still the man made more demands on her. She herself knew she was no spring chicken being in her late thirties with the possibility of matrimony far behind her.

Soon they were trundling back down the street when a small ball smacked into the side of her father's face. He let out a great cry swiftly followed by an exclamation which filled the air and embarrassed Edith so that her face burned red. She prayed that the neighbours hadn't heard her father's expletive.

"What the hell blazes do you think you're playing at?" he shouted at a group of boys who had been chasing the small red ball and stopped dead when they saw it hit the old guy in the wheelchair.

"Could have had my eye out, you little bastards!"

"Are you all right?" Edith asked leaning over her father. He shooed her away, his hand nearly poking her own eye out in the process.

"Get away from me, girl. No, pick that blasted ball up instead."

Edith hesitated. These boys were children of her neighbours and she didn't want to upset any of them. She had enough without aggravated parents giving her grief on her doorstep.

The boys had obviously been throwing the ball against one of the numerous brick walls that had previously been someone's home when it had gone wide and taken its unlucky course.

"What are you waiting for, girl? Do as I tell you. Pick up that ball!"

As if poked by a red-hot poker, Edith involuntarily jerked away and collected up the ball, her nervousness making her fumble and drop it the first time. On the second attempt she had it firmly in her hand.

"Give it me," growled her father through gritted teeth. His claw snatched the ball from Edith's and, with a force that only hate made possible, he clenched and squeezed the small ball, the effort nearly making it burst in his fist.

"See this, you little sods. This is my ball now."

There was no response from the group. There wasn't one among them that had the cheek to answer her father back. Edith inwardly pleaded that one of them would stand up to the vicious old man in the wheelchair.

Unfortunately her father's reputation seemed to precede him and the boys turned and ran off over a derelict site where a row of terraces had been razed to the ground a fortnight before. Edith did think she caught a few words from one of the elder boys as he headed away with the rest of the pack. It sounded like "miserable old swine", which shocked and pleased Edith in equal measure. Serve the old fool right.

"Did you just hear what they said, girl?" he cried indignantly.

Edith said nothing and with a smile touching her lips began to push back towards home.

In the hallway, Edith had the devil's own job of getting the old man up the stairs. As part of his enjoyment he liked to lean his whole weight on Edith and felt a deep satisfaction as she struggled with him up the stairs.

He never told her that when she went for the food shopping, he quite happily went up and down the stairs under his own steam.

"Don't throw me on the bed, girl. I'm not your dirty washing," he barked. "Now take my shoes off."

Edith bent down and untied his laces and with difficulty removed his shoes – only to be rewarded for her labours with the pungent odour of the old man's sweaty socks.

"Now, all I require is a nice cup of tea, girl. And then you can leave me to have a smoke and read of the paper."

With further effort, Edith manoeuvred him to the easy chair next to the bed. Her father made a noise and then shifted his body sideways, his hand diving into his trouser pocket. He pulled out the small ball and placed it with pride on his bedside cabinet.

"Don't you think you should give that ball back?"

"Near took my head off," he replied as he shook his newspaper in preparation for reading it.

"They didn't do it deliberately," Edith replied, trying to be benevolent.

"They're not having it back," he grunted like a recalcitrant child himself.

Edith turned and stood in the doorway.

"You do realize the neighbours will most probably be round later to complain about your behaviour towards their boys."

"And you'll deal with it as usual," her father sneered.

"Not this time. I'll send them straight up here even if you're in your pyjamas."

"That's right. Abuse the weak, why don't you?"

It was then that Edith had a moment of strength pass through her bones. She really felt she'd had enough of him today. He had really been the absolute limit. Edith straightened herself up and pinned her father with a malevolent stare.

"You are anything but weak," Edith declared. "And you are an embarrassment to me."

Her father slowly looked up from preparing his first roll-up and eyed his daughter properly, something he hadn't done since his precious Phyllis had been killed outright two years before.

After a few moments that felt as solid as steel her father questioned Edith.

"So, you think I am anything but weak, do you? And what does that make you, Edith?"

A *fool* is what Edith wanted to say. *An absolute fool for kowtowing to you all this time.*

But it was his look that silenced her and Edith's moment of strength quickly ebbed away. It was the knowing gleam in his eyes that made Edith believe he knew something she didn't and it made her feel a fool of fools.

"I'll go and put the kettle on," was all Edith could murmur as she went to close the door and escape this hateful man.

"Oh, and Edith?" her father called.

Edith opened the almost closed door to hear her father's latest command. With a split second to react the red ball flew inches past Edith's face, her shocked expression making her father howl with laughter.

Edith didn't see where the ball landed but could hear it ping about on the landing.

"There you go," her father said through laughter, before his face quickly changed to its usual death mask. "You can take the bloody ball back to your little friends. Happy now?"

"You could have . . ." Edith cried, before her throat constricted. She gave a swallow before being able to continue. "It nearly hit me in the face!"

Her father wafted his hand about by way of answer and settled the paper on his lap.

"You horrible, spiteful man!" Edith cried as she slammed the door and stormed downstairs.

Standing over the kitchen sink, sobbing, Edith looked out of the window. It was with a sharp shock that she saw the rat still lying swollen on the garden path. She had forgotten to pick it up this morning and dispose of it properly.

Then the second thought entered her mind. One she tried to push away, but it kept taking centre stage. No matter how hard she tried, it would not go away.

Edith had never been one to act irrationally. Every moment of her life had been carried out with forethought. *Probably too much*, she thought, although that couldn't be helped now. But her personality would not stop her from doing something that may well catch up with her in time.

Twenty minutes later, Edith was still sitting at the kitchen table, the glass phial directly in front of her on the scrubbed tabletop. She had sat immobile all that time deliberating what to do. Never in her whole life had she countenanced such thoughts, but the idea of being free from her father's tyrannical reign was not allowing her a moment's peace.

She pushed the phial away from her as though it were a poisoned chalice, just as the banging started on the ceiling.

"Edith! Where's my tea?" came the usual battle cry, seconds later.

Mechanically, Edith swept up the glass phial and placed the kettle on the stove. She didn't know how much would be acceptable and how much she could use without it distorting the taste. She would put some sugar in it and tell him he needed the sugar after his "near death" experience with the children's ball. Ridiculous little man!

Edith was still hesitant, the phial in her hand, when the banging started again. Growling to herself in desperation, Edith flicked some of the poison into the teacup.

"Your tea," said Edith as she grimaced at the old man.

Her father gave no response as she laid the cup carefully on the bedside cabinet next to him.

Edith hesitated at the door. Should she stay and make sure he drank it or should she leave, let him die in peace?

Finally the old man noticed her presence and looked up.

"What are you dithering for, girl?" he snapped.

"Nothing." Edith replied with a wan smile. She decided to leave him. Let him pass away alone. She wanted nothing more to do with him. Edith closed the door gently and started down the stairs.

It was then that she stepped on the small ball her father had thrown earlier.

The fall headlong down the stairs killed Edith instantly.

Later, the doctor would give Edith's father a sedative to calm him down. The old man had heard his daughter's scream, but no amount of running could have saved her. She broke her neck the moment she hit the bottom of the steep stairs.

"A terrible tragedy," commiserated the doctor. "And you didn't get to finish your tea, either," he crassly commented.

"Not to worry," the old man sneered. "I never drank it anyway. I only asked for it to give Edith something to do. I always poured it into the plant pot. Edith never made a decent cup of tea in her life."

Out of Bedlam

Stephen Gallagher

It was late in the afternoon when one of the ward orderlies appeared in the doorway to Sebastian Becker's basement office. Sebastian had spent most of the day clearing a space to work. They'd given him a desk and a chair, and a hook for his coat. He would have appreciated a window.

The orderly, clearly not expecting to find the room occupied, said, "Oh."

"Is that my welcome letter?" Sebastian said, eyeing the envelope in the orderly's hand.

"That would depend, sir," the orderly said. "Are you the Visitor's man?"

"I'm Sebastian Becker. Special Investigator to the Lord Chancellor's Visitor in Lunacy."

It was the August of 1912. Sebastian had been the Lord Chancellor's man since the beginning of the year, and Sir James had been promising him an office for some time. Until now Sebastian had worked from coffee shops and corner tearooms, collecting his messages from a pie stand under the Southwark Bridge Road railway.

And now he had a room of his own, this grim little chamber under the Bethlem asylum, a space that he shared with suitcases and trunks storing the effects of deceased patients. Despite it being within walking distance of his home, he'd already resolved to spend as little time here as possible.

The orderly said, "Then this is for you. From the Director, sir."

It was no welcome note. It requested Sebastian's immediate presence in the male patients' gallery. The orderly led the
way.

Lambeth's Bethlem Royal Hospital had separate wings for
men and women, separated by an administration block in the
middle. The men's gallery was light and airy, with pictures on
the walls and the atmosphere of the roomy but relatively
spartan hotel that some of the more deluded patients believed
it to be.

The Director was standing outside one of the private
rooms, in an animated argument with a tweed-suited man and
an equally well-dressed woman. Curious patients had gathered to watch.

"Mister Becker," said the Director. "You're the Lord Chancellor's man. Will you please explain the law to Mr Raby's
relatives, here?"

"The law as applied to what?" Sebastian said.

Raising a hand to forestall interruption from his two well-
dressed visitors, the Director explained that inside the room
lay the body of John Raby, a Chancery lunatic who had been
a Bethlem patient for more than two years. Though Raby had
always entertained hopes of release, the hospital's Consulting
Psychiatrist had declared him incurable. Raby, who was harmless but inclined to wander, had been locked into his room for
his regular afternoon nap and had died in his sleep.

Sebastian turned to the visitors. "And you are . . . ?"

"I'm Mrs Willis and John was my brother," the woman
said. "We're here to claim his property."

"A Chancery lunatic's property is under the protection of
the Crown," Sebastian said.

Mrs Willis was about to reply, but her husband cut in. "You
call it protection?" he said. "I call it control. Everybody knows
that once the Masters of Lunacy get their hands on your
fortune, you can wave it goodbye."

Sebastian said, "Who found him?"

"I did, sir." It was the orderly who'd brought him the note.
"I went in to rouse him at four o'clock, for his afternoon tea.

When he didn't respond I sent one of the patients to fetch the Supervising Physician. I did not leave his side until Doctor Stoddart and the Director arrived."

"Is the Physician with him now?"

"He is," said the Director.

"Excuse me." Sebastian left them to resume their argument, and let himself into the private room.

Dr William Stoddart had finished his examination. A heavily built man of some forty-four years, he was drawing the sheet across John Raby's face as Sebastian entered and closed the door behind him.

"Becker!" Stoddart said. "You wasted no time in getting here."

"I was in the building," Sebastian said, "but the relatives got here faster. Did Raby keep much of value in the room?"

"Mostly sentimental objects."

"His sister and her husband don't strike me as a sentimental pair," Sebastian said. "What about those books?"

Stoddart looked around at the bookshelf. "I wouldn't know," he said. "They're fine enough bindings, I suppose. But I'm hardly an expert."

Nor was Sebastian, but he moved to the shelf and took down a volume at random. Chancery lunatics were people of wealth or property whose fortunes were at risk from their madness. Those deemed unfit to manage their affairs had them taken over by lawyers of the Crown, known as the Masters of Lunacy. It was Sebastian's employer, the Lord Chancellor's Visitor, who would decide their fate. Though the office was intended to be a benevolent one, many saw him as an enemy to be outwitted or deceived, even to the extent of concealing criminal insanity.

It was for such cases that the Visitor had engaged Sebastian. His job was to seek out the cunning dissembler, the dangerous madman whose resources might otherwise make him untouchable. Rank and the social order gave such people protection. A former British police detective and one-time Pinkerton man, Sebastian had been engaged to work "off the books" in exposing their misdeeds. His modest salary was paid out of the department's budget. He remained a shadowy figure, an investigator with no public profile.

"What do we know about Raby?" he asked Stoddart.

Raby had been a bachelor of some prosperity. A shrewd investor who had lived well off his dividends and indulged his hobbies. He read, wrote bad poetry, and received few visitors. Sebastian leafed through the fifteenth book of *The Odyssey*, Pope's translation, in full leather boards. It was dated 1724, and its bindings were spotted with age.

Stoddart was preparing to leave. Without looking up from the book, Sebastian said, "Was it a natural death?"

"He died alone in a locked room. There are bars on the window. No one could approach through the gallery without being seen by at least a dozen people. There's no trace of poison and the body's unmarked. I know you're paid to be suspicious, Becker, but in this case you're wasting your time."

"Can you tell without dissection if a rib has been broken?"

"Why?"

"*Can* you?"

One minute later, Sebastian stepped out into the gallery. A book – not the Pope translation, but a different volume from the same shelf – was in his hand.

Mrs Willis said, "Are you satisfied? Can we go in now?"

"I fear not, Mrs Willis," Sebastian said. "Your brother's room must be kept secure until the police arrive."

"The police?" the Director said, and Willis echoed him in almost the same breath.

Sebastian was looking at the orderly, who was standing behind and apart from the others. Sebastian said to him, "Does the prospect worry you?"

"Why should it?" the orderly said, with no change in his expression.

Sebastian said, "You unlocked the room and discovered the body. You stayed with the body after sending for help. You took care to be the guarantor against any suspicion of foul play. Unfortunately, if foul play should then be discovered, your own position becomes awkward, to say the least."

The orderly said nothing.

Sebastian said, "Is anyone familiar with the term 'burking'? No?"

No one claimed familiarity. But the Director was taking a keen interest.

Sebastian said, "We can thank Burke and Hare for its coinage. The Resurrection Men would dispatch a victim by putting their considerable weight on the chest while pinching the nostrils and clamping the jaw shut with the heel of the same hand. It caused rapid suffocation with no obvious mark. I asked Doctor Stoddart to check Mister Raby for any broken ribs. There were none, but he did discover several ribs separated from the sternum. I believe a post-mortem will show that pressure forced a tearing of the ligaments."

To the orderly, again: "I would hazard that Mister Raby was merely asleep when you unlocked his door. In full view of the other patients you pretended to discover him dead and called for the supervising physician. Then while alone with the 'body' you took his life without waking him."

"Oh, my poor brother!" Mrs Raby said with a sudden and explosive show of grief.

The Director said, "But what possible advantage could one of my staff gain from the death of a patient?"

"None," said Sebastian. "Unless someone paid him to do it."

Willis was about to speak. Sebastian didn't miss the subtle nudge from the man's wife that made him stop.

"Raby was a man who received few visitors. I dare say the hospital's signing-in book will show exactly how often his sister and her husband came to see him. Yet on his death, they were here within the half-hour. I'm sure there's an explanation, of course. Perhaps they live locally. Or had some business in the area. Any explanation other than that they knew the likely time of their relative's death, and stood ready to swoop."

"This is an appalling slander, sir," Mrs Willis said. "And my brother not yet cold. We have nothing to gain by being here."

"No?" Sebastian said. "Then this must be a surprise to you."

He let the book fall open in his hand, and from between its pages took a sheet of folded paper.

"A share certificate," he said. "There appear to be two or three hidden in every one of Raby's books. By this means he kept some portion of his fortune out of Chancery control. A fortune that you would have inherited in time, if only you'd had the patience to wait."

"A fortune bled dry and squandered by then," Willis said.

And his wife said, "Say nothing."

The Director said, "Perhaps we'll await the police."

"Indeed," Sebastian said. "You can denounce my speculations to them, and have faith that they'll grasp your obvious innocence in the matter. In the meantime I'd remind you that this is a secure establishment. An early departure might be difficult."

"To my office?" suggested the Director.

"I should think so," said Sebastian. "I don't fancy the smell in mine."

Bentinck's Agent

John Lawton

I was a dodger. I do not mean by this that I have ever played baseball for Brooklyn or LA. I mean I was a draft dodger.

I was also a jumper. "Jump" adds class to what was, in fact, no more than a crawl. I had all but crawled on my belly into Canada in the autumn of 1972. Autumn? I mean fall – of course I mean fall – I have played too long the Englishman.

The matter was simplicity itself. Nixon had been elected in '68 on a promise of getting us out of Vietnam. What he did was introduce a lottery: every male of age was given a number between 1 and 365, one for every day of the year. The lower your number, the greater your chances of being drafted, and mine were as high as my number was low – 32. Only a college deferment had kept me out and that lapsed as soon as I graduated. Hence Canada, hence England, hence London. Jack Turner, BA (Tufts), twenty-two years old and flat broke. I'd got by for a year in Toronto and blown everything I'd saved on the ticket to London.

As I said, I was lucky. I gambled on the inefficiency of any bureaucracy and applied for a Harbright scholarship. The people running the Harbright Foundation back in Washington had neither the brief nor the inclination to cross-reference their applicants' list with the FBI's wanted list. I got one. A year's funding – fees plus an immodest living allowance. All I had to do was find a college that would accept me and the cockamamie proposal I had knocked out for the Harbrights: "The Use of Imagery in the Poetry of Hart Crane." Vague as fog and not entirely original. To my amazement, Lincoln College, Oxford University, accepted me.

I had a year to write whatever it was – I honestly didn't give a damn about getting another degree – and learn to play the Englishman.

I soon toned down my accent, and if asked I said I was Canadian – this more often than not brought "Ah, draft dodger, eh?" So I stopped saying it and just let everyone assume what they liked. Anonymity was hard-won. I was aiming to be a mid-Atlantic nonentity. Never quite made it.

By 1974 I was back in London – straight after the Three-Day Week, smack between the two elections – possessor of one degree (a second looming) and a work permit. London was my oyster. Alas in the post-Heath, post-diluvian England of 1974 the oyster was rotting on the shore. It was a sour time.

Entirely to my surprise, I found I hated English hippies. Parental recrimination, personal incompetence, political shallowness, pseudo-religious gullibility . . . all wrapped up in a tie-dyed T-shirt and played out to the sound of pompous stadium rock. Please. Gimme a break.

I was living with my girlfriend, Jess, same age, same rising sense of dissatisfaction, same sense that we were doing what we always boasted we'd never do: fuck up as our parents had fucked up.

That autumn she turned out every cupboard in the flat – the English had yet to invent the closet – and I found myself staring at a heap of tie-dye shirts, flared jeans and crushed velvet jackets.

"What a load of tat!"

I reached down to rescue my bong. She kicked it away from me.

"Tat, Jack. A load of fucking tat."

I saw an ideology shrivel in that heap.

If this was what we had been, what were we now?

*   *   *

I did what my father would have told me to do, had he the faintest idea where to find me: I got a job. I got a job without him bellowing the instruction in my ear. Jess and I burnt all the tie-dye tat in the backyard. She wanted to throw on her Incredible String Band and Pink Floyd albums as well, but I pleaded the stink it would make and put them out by the trash. They were gone the next morning. And so began the new game. No more playing at hippies. From now on we'd play at being grown-ups.

"Are we straights now?" Jess asked me.

"Nah. We could never be straights."

"Then what are we?"

"We're . . . in disguise. We're . . . subversives."

"Oh Jack, you're so full of shit."

Time and again Jess came back to me about that assertion.

We went into advertising . . . Y'know, selling shit and saying it's toothpaste . . . Boogle, Biggle & Boggarty. Whatever.

I did not stay the course. After less than a year Boogle or Biggle or it may have been Boggarty (whatever) suggested in that understated English way that perhaps I might be better suited to some other profession. It might have had something to do with my slogan for a campaign to relaunch Ranger bicycles: "Go to work on a bike."

Fine.

I cleared my desk.

I went into publishing. Atterbury & Sykes. At the interview Atterbury (or maybe it was Sykes) told me the firm prided itself on publishing a book on – he did not say "life" or "biography" – "Jimmy or Marilyn" every year.

"Who?" was my reply.

"James Dean and Marilyn Monroe," was his.

My heart, scarcely buoyant in the first place, sank beneath the banality of my new trade.

After less than a year, Atterbury (or maybe it was Sykes) suggested in that understated English way that perhaps I might be better suited to some other profession. Clearly I had not taken Jimmy and Marilyn into my sunken heart.

So I moved to Hopkins Dean, where I lasted longer, long
enough to get the message. London publishing was a game of
musical chairs. Scarcely worth unpacking the metaphorical
briefcase.

Jess stayed in advertising. She did not stay with me. Every
so often I'd get a call, "This is your straight speaking."

She hated it. Opted for a policy of Take the Money and
Sneer.

"They're idiots. Utter fucking idiots. They call themselves
'creatives'. They're about as creative as my left buttock."

All the same, she kept up the disguise. And the subver-
sion dwindled to gossip and drunken cynicism as we
propped up bars all over London and she rubbished everyone she ever met in the cling-wrapped, plasti-coated world
of the ad man.

Our habitual first clink of the glasses was "Fukkemall."

Either they'd get her in the end or the bottle would.

By the mid-eighties I was with Hamilton Hardy, a small house
with a big reputation. I didn't have a big reputation. I'd move
from one job to another without any seeming promotion even
if the salary went up. I was a concierge . . . the doorman of Lit
Fic. I edited on autopilot while the kettle boiled.

I think my boss at that time, Sebastian Hardy, tolerated me.
He would not have been heartbroken if I quit on him. All the
same he was unlikely to come to me with the understatement
about my suitability. Sebastian would never "have to let me
go". He'd fire me or I'd quit.

My indifference to my own fate was shattered one day in
1985 by a telephone call from Syd Meadows – to give the old
man his full whack, the Hon. Sydney Price-Meadows, senior
partner in one of London's oldest literary agencies, Hawes
Greene. Syd had been there so long he'd even known Ebenezer Hawes, a man born in the 1860s and often dubbed the
last Victorian in London publishing, if not in London itself. I
liked Syd. I'd done business with Syd, bought half a dozen
books off him and watched contentedly as he racked up boozy

lunches on my expense account that would one day surely plunge Hamilton Hardy into well-deserved bankruptcy. I liked Syd. I'd not the remotest idea why he liked me.

"You saw my ad in the *Bookseller*?"

Actually I'd seen it and ignored it in the *Guardian*.

"The one for a new book agent."

"Yes. I've been interviewing."

"Aha?"

"A shower, an absolute shower. I've just listened to a dozen wet-behind-the-lug'oles graduates in Eng Lit rehash their education for my benefit."

Syd had never been to university – Sandhurst and the Guards – and degrees never impressed.

"Not one I'd dare leave alone with Tom Maschler for two minutes."

"Bad as that, eh?"

"Fucking awful. They could all spot the next Byron, but they wouldn't know the next Ian McEwan if he fell on them. The hard men of Bedford Square would skin 'em alive."

"Syd. Why are you telling me this?"

"Simple. Job's yours if you want it. I'll pay you whatever you're on now plus three grand."

I said nothing. He filled my silence.

"Don't take too long to think about it. Your days at HH are numbered and you know it. You've no future with Sebastian Hardy. And if you stay I predict he will bore you to death in less than two years."

He rang off without another word.

I typed a brief note to Sebastian: *I have to quit. Can we just forego the thirty days' notice?*

And then I cleared my desk. I would love to have typed *Fuck you* or something equally "subversive", equally childish, but – dammit – I was going to be an agent. I might to have sell the old bastard a book one day.

I dropped in at Hawes Greene's office in Henrietta Street the next day, thinking I'd tell Syd I had accepted and agree a starting date.

Syd wasn't there. Instead I got his secretary, Vera Buckett –
Dagenham Vera, the prototype of Essex Girl. I'd never met
Vera, talked to her frequently on the phone but never face to
face.

"Well, dearie, you look just like you sound."

So did she – more than a little blousy, a tad to the fat, a fag
glued to her lower lip and a hint that she might have been a
looker fifteen or twenty years ago.

"He ain't 'ere, but you was expected."

"I was. I mean, I am?"

"Fourth door on yer right. That's your office."

"When do I start?"

"You have started. The Hon. Syd's in Libya. You'll handle his
clients till he gets back and until you've got a few of your own."

"Libya?"

"Tobruk, dearie. Another of his bleedin' army reunions. If
he goes to one he goes to a dozen. There are times I think he
was in every bleedin' battle from Waterloo to Arnhem."

All morning figures, faces would appear at my door.

"Oh, has the photocopier been moved?"

Men in suits, mostly. Nobody asked who I was.

Vera phoned.

"Mr Mailer, for Syd. You'd better take it."

Oh shit. Norman Mailer. Oh shit.

"Er . . . er . . . Mr Mailer, what an . . . er . . ."

"Dennis Mailer here, son. *Daily Express*. I was looking for a
quote from Syd . . . your rivals at Curtis Brown are rumoured
to have got a seven-figure sum for Francis Freeman's new
one. I mean, funny money or what?"

"Er . . . I er . . . no comment."

I put the phone down. It rang again at once.

"Butterfingers," Vera said.

"What?"

"You dropped the ball. The point was to deal with him, give
him something pithy, not hang up on him. Unless, of course,
you declare this an FO day."

"Foreign Office day?"

"Fuck Off day. A day when Syd says I can tell the press to fuck off."

"In those words?"

She hung up on me, the sigh all but audible over the dialling tone.

Two minutes later she dropped a couple of dozen manila files on my desk and said, "Read and learn."

I passed an hour in silence. Reading and learning. She rang through again.

"Mr Vidal for Syd. Just deal with it, will you?"

Fred Vidal of the *News of the World* or Bert Vidal from the *Observer*?

"Hello?"

The aristocratic, Virginian voice, slightly drawly, affected and affecting. Oh shit, da man.

"I was hoping Syd was free this evening, but I gather not. Why don't you come over to the old boarding house at six-thirty? New blood is always interesting, for the first half hour at least."

"The old boarding house?"

"The Connaught."

The Connaught. Posh posh posh.

"Any . . . er particular dress code?"

"No. But Princess Margaret is a stickler for titles, so HRH her until she's drunk and then you can call her your honeybum and she won't care. And if you bring Vera Buckett you'd better bring your own gin, too. I'm rich . . . but not rich enough to refloat the *Titanic*."

He didn't say goodbye. I got Vera in an instant. Giggling down the line.

"Dress code. Hahahah. You twat."

I got a few minutes with the Great Man. It went the way most conversations with fellow Americans went . . . ending with the inevitable . . . "Draft dodger?"

For once I could take it as a compliment.

I chatted with the boyfriend, Howard – a short, Bronxy guy who reminded me of nothing quite so much as a gumshoe – and I watched Vera Buckett and Princess Margaret get shit-faced without addressing a word to one another. And very soon I began to see that they were almost identical, displaying the same disdain for all around, divided only by an accent. Although to be fair, I'm pretty sure Princess Margaret didn't buy her frocks in the M&S on Oxford Street.

Then a familiar face appeared. Tony Marks of the *Daily Beast*. A pleasant enough hack of limited talent. I'd bought a couple of books by him for Sebastian and as far as I could remember he'd been at work for years on a life of Maurice Oldfield (the M in MI6) that I was pretty certain he'd never finish.

"Jack boy. I hear you jumped ship."

"Jumped ship?"

"Y'know. Gamekeeper turned poacher."

"Ah. Yes. I'm an agent now."

"'Scuse me if I talk shop for a bit, but there is something I'd like to ask you."

Oh no. I did not want Tony Marks to become my first client. I didn't ever want Tony Marks to become a client.

"Tony, I thought you were with Curtis Brown."

"I am, Jack boy. Not about to ask for meself. Chap I've met writing a book needs an agent."

"So why not introduce him to your man at Curtis Brown?"

"Are you kidding? Introduce a friend to your agent and you'll end up losing both. No, this could be right up your alley. Chap named Roger Bentinck. Ring any bells?"

"Should it?"

"MI6. Dodgy business behind the Iron Curtain. Bulldog Drummond. James Bond. That sort of thing. He wants to write a memoir."

"Will they let him?"

"Precisely why he needs an agent. I'll get him to give you a bell at old Syd's."

He ducked out so fast I didn't have time to say no. But I was an agent without any clients. Why would I say no?

The following day the telephone rang a couple of dozen times. Routine stuff and most of the people who wanted to talk to the Hon. Syd weren't prepared to talk to me. He was the sorcerer. I was just Mickey Mouse.

Around five, Vera put Roger Bentinck through. I had no real idea whether I had wanted him to call or not, and expectation simply didn't enter into it.

"Bentinck here."

"Mr Bentinck, I—"

"Newmarket, tamorrer."

"What?"

"Meet me in the Owners and Trainers Bar at Newmarket in time to study form for the 2.30. I'll leave your name with the johnny on the door. Just ask for me."

I did not get another word in.

Two minutes later Vera Buckett appeared in my doorway, fag adroop.

"Just say it."

"Say what?"

"Go on, ask me."

"Vera, for Christ's sake!"

"Ask me what the Hon. Syd would do."

"What would Syd do?"

"What, Syd? Turn down a day at the races? Not bloody likely."

A Day at the Races. Wasn't that a Marx Brothers movie?

I'd never been to a racetrack in my life. I wasn't about to risk another burst of derision from Vera on the matter of dress code, so I went dressed in workaday sports jacket and grey pants, assuming that an ordinary summer Thursday would not be a top-hat gig and I would not be meeting royalty twice in one week.

The bowler-hatted jobsworth looked me up and down,

but that's what jobsworths do. He showed me to Bentinck's table.

Bentinck gave me the merest glance.

"Golden Boy."

Who? Me?

"My old dad would always bet on any horse with the word gold in his name."

"Not exactly scientific, then?"

"No, lost more often than not."

The eyes came off the racing pages to meet mine. They were soggy eyes, the eyes, I thought, of a deeply sad man. The face was jowly and red – a joyless red, a red that might have been acquired in good times that were long, long gone and now was merely a painful reminder, glimpsed in the mirror while shaving.

"When were you born?"

I hadn't even sat down yet.

"29 August 1951. It was a—"

"No. You're not supposed to tell me. Ruins the bloody game. It was . . . hang on . . . it was . . . a Wednesday. Am I right?"

"Yes. Wednesday's child is full of woe. My mother was forever quoting that at me."

"And are you?"

"No. I'm a cheerful soul."

This made him laugh. I pulled out a chair and sat down while he sniggered.

"American?"

"Yes?"

"Draft dodger, I suppose. All you blokes are draft dodgers aren't you?"

I said nothing to this. It didn't seem to require an answer.

"Of course, in my day you'd have been shot."

I tacked away. "How do you do that?"

"Do what?"

"The trick with the birth dates."

"Oh that would be telling. But it is just a trick . . . a simple mental . . . algorithm. Yes, that's the word. Now who do you fancy in the 2.30?" He shoved the racing pages across to me.

That was okay. I like a challenge. I am up for what is new.

We walked down to the members' enclosure near to the winning post. I got a good look at him for the first time. He was a head shorter than me, stout to fat. A sheen of sweat across his face that made him look very unhealthy. I'd put him at a well-worn, lived-in sixty. A sixty looking as though it would not make sixty-five. Breathless and baggy. Gung-ho and world-weary at the same time.

"You own a horse?" I asked.

"No. Why do you ask?"

"Owners' bar? Members' enclosure?"

"There's an English notion you need to grasp, dear boy. Ligging. The noble art of bullshit. Everybody here thinks I own a racehorse because I act as if I own a racehorse. So many things in life are pretence. Nothing wrong with it. It's not a moral issue . . . It's just the way things are."

I wondered about what I had just heard. The manifesto of a spy schooled in deceit or of a con man as likely to pretend to be a racehorse owner as a spy? The former was easier. A big pair of binoculars, a bespoke suit worn incongruously with a crumpled felt hat, and a racing paper folded under your arm. What were the props of a spy? Would a spy ever say he was a spy? Was anyone who did say he was a spy least likely to be one?

Any question I might have posed was drowned out.

Racing was like all sport: a bit of a thrill, followed by prolonged boredom. A kid in high school once tried to explain football to me as being like chess. Big guys in armour crashing into one another is like chess? Right. And many a London pub bore has attempted to entice me into an appreciation of soccer . . . or cricket . . . and all I can say is that both move marginally faster than baseball or glaciers.

No problem with speed at Newmarket, but it is arcane stuff requiring study or feigned interest. Having no knowledge at all, I opted for the latter. Bentinck had the knowledge, Bentinck studied "form" . . . firm going, soft underfoot, trained by X, ridden by Y, had won the last Z times out and so on. I bet whenever he bet and as he bet and came back £479.50p richer. And not once did we bet on a horse with "gold" in its name. He hooted, he cheered, he waved his fat little arms in the air and he gabbled at me in incomprehensible fervour.

What he didn't do was mention a book. Or the possibility of a book. And the saggy sadness in the eyes never once matched the waving arms or the throaty cheering.

I went home bookless and richer, secure in the knowledge that I would never go to the races again and that I would never hear from Roger Bentinck again.

The Hon. Syd returned from Libya.

"Got me knees brown for the first time since 1943."

I thought I'd have to bring him up to speed on anything and everything, only to find Vera had already done it.

"Who's this Bentinck character?"

I told him.

"D'ye reckon he's kosher?"

"No. He's ligging."

"Ligging?"

"A word I just learnt. He's a freeloader. I think he's someone having fun playing a game with Fleet Street and with me. He probably spun Tony Marks a line in exchange for free drinks all evening. He acts like a spook, so people think he's a spook. He's the most unlikely-looking spy I've ever met."

"Not that you've met all that many," said Syd. "But what does he look like?"

"Toad of Toad Hall," I said. "He looks like Mr Toad."

"Poop-poop!" Syd replied.

A week passed.

Men in suits still asked me where the photocopier was.

Vera Buckett called me a twat at least twice a day.

Roger Bentinck rang.

"Lunch, Thursday. Meet me at my club."

Club? What fucking club?

"Guards in Piccadilly. Did it never occur to you to look me up in *Who's Who*?"

I kicked myself. It had not crossed my mind to find the fat fraud in any work of reference. It was another English notion I needed to grasp, an absurdly English notion. The antediluvian hippie in me silently subscribed to the *other* notion, that anyone who was really anyone would not be in *Who's* fuckin' *Who*.

Syd had *Who's Who* (and for that matter *Who Was Who*) for every year going back to 1938 in his office.

He didn't even look up from his desk.

Just said "Who're you after?"

"Bentinck."

"If you find him, read him out to me. The potted version."

Who's Who is nothing if not potted. Life reduced on the simmer plate.

"Roger George Cholmondoley Bentinck. CMG. Born 1925. Younger son of George Bentinck and Laura *née* Cholmondoley elder daughter of Viscount Cholmondoley of Callow. Sherborne, a year at Keble, Oxford, reading Geography, volunteered for the Coldstream Guards in '43. Just caught the tail end of the war. Ended it as a captain. Discharged 1946. Bit blank on anything since. No mention of wives or children. Clubs, Guards. Hobbies, racing and Meccano. What's Meccano?"

Syd ignored the question.

"A Cholmondoley, eh? I don't suppose you've heard of his grandfather. Mad Mike Cholmondoley, led an absolutely suicidal cavalry charge in the Boer War. If Tennyson had been around there might even have been a poem about it. Alas the old boy had gone to Poets' Corner by then, so all Cholmondoley got was a court martial and no verse. It would have paid him not to survive the charge, but there you are. Dead heroes, living idiots. Two sides of a coin."

"Syd, does any of this make you think he might be, as you said, 'kosher'?"

"Perhaps. The silence after 1946 is telling. That's when they'd have recruited him if they did recruit him. There are people I can ask."

Syd, at that time, represented Marcus Frey, acclaimed writer of spy novels under the nom de plume James McVey. All McVeys went to number one. A good half dozen of them had been filmed. He alone would bankroll Hawes Greene if every other client dried or died. And, of course, Marcus Frey was "kosher" – his real name was an open secret and the books sold as being the work of an MI6 insider. The secret was that Syd ran every book by MI6 before even the publishers saw them. Hence no controversy, no comeback, not even a hint of censorship. All done, as Syd would have said, on the nod. A few discreet phone calls. Nothing on paper.

"Leave it with me," he said.

I was . . . I was . . . antsy. That could be the word. By Thursday morning I was antsy. Once more on the whirligig with Bentinck and not a word from Syd.

Ten minutes before I was due to leave, he came into my office and looked around as though despairing of the décor.

I pointed to the long Plimsoll line of dirt three feet off the ground along the side wall.

"Used to be the photocopier room," I said.

"Good Lord. Must get you something for the walls. A book or two wouldn't go amiss. Now. Roger the Lodger. He is the real thing. Ran our chaps out of Berlin in the forties and Vienna in the fifties. Been on the retired list since '66. Picked up his gong the year after. One hundred per cent kosher."

Hell. I had rather hoped he wasn't and that perhaps this would be my last outing with him.

"So maybe there's a book at the bottom of all this?"

"It may well be there's one hell of a book at the bottom of all this."

I played the straight.

I wore the suit.

I had not asked Vera.

Another jobsworth, another fleeting moment of utter disdain. I was shown to the bar of the Guards Club on Piccadilly.

Bentinck was perched on top of a bar stool with his back to me. Not an item of furniture that favoured his particular morph. He looked like a toffee apple on a stick.

He swung around, slopping his whisky and soda, and said, "Y'little shit. You've had me vetted!"

If I had any doubts about Bentinck the spy they just flew out and splashed down as fast as his whisky. He was kosher. I knew he was kosher. He knew I knew he was kosher.

"How d'ya do it?"

"That would be telling."

Hard to tell when a red man is about to explode with anger. The wheezing rising in his throat presaged something, but as seconds ticked by I wasn't certain whether he would erupt in rage or laughter.

The wheezing rose half an octave, a tad shy of whining; he slipped from the bar stool, clapped me on the back and I realized that this was as close to laughter as Bentinck got.

"Let's eat. I'm fair famished."

At lunch I learnt why Roger George Cholmondoley Bentinck was the size, shape and hue he was. He loved his grub. I come from what might be termed the muesli generation. Rabbit food, my father used to call it, glaring at me across his plate of ham 'n' eggs. I have eaten muesli for breakfast, lunch and dinner. Never in my life had I sat down to beef Wellington. Bentinck was insistent. It was what the club did best. It would be criminal not to try it.

Have you ever seen beef Wellington? The look alone is worth a hundred words. Suffice it to say it is the nearest thing you will ever find to Desperate Dan's cow pie. It is beef, expensive beef, wrapped in layers of pâté and mushrooms and encased in pastry. No need to leave the horns on the side of your plate. The Guards club would never have been so vulgar as to leave the horns on.

And . . . and . . . it is disgusting.

All the same, it explained the teetering on the edge of aneurysm and apoplexy that was by now the natural condition of Roger George Cholmondoley Bentinck.

I picked, trying not to show revulsion.

"Hippie, eh?" Bentinck said in precisely the same tone he had said "draft dodger". "Give it here."

And he speared the remains of my beef Welly with his fork, hoicked it on to his plate and with his free hand beckoned to the sommelier for a second bottle of claret. Most of the first had gone down him, not me.

"I'm wondering," he said. "Can I work with a chap like you?"

"Why wouldn't you?"

"Can't tell a three-legged nag from a Derby winner. Drinks like a girl. Eats like a bird. What more do I need to say?"

"How about that I can turn Post-it notes into polished prose and pitch you to the best editors in London? Or I could if you ever got around to mentioning a book."

He munched. Staring at me. Flakes of puff pastry showering down like the first delicate snow of an early winter, dusting the napkin tucked into his waistcoat like a bib. Always the mark of a serious trencherman.

"You cheeky little bugger."

"My point remains. Cheeky or not."

"Well, I'm hardly going to blab about it here, am I?"

"I'm asking myself: is he going to blab at all?"

Silent munching ensued.

He finished his plate with dedicated elbow work, and a swift though delicate action on the fork that put me in mind of watching Muhammad Ali float like a butterfly.

"Tell you what. We'll have pudding and adjourn to my place. If it's blabbing you want, it's blabbing you'll get."

I had a 3.30 meeting with Graham Garside, a first novelist fresh out of Leicester Polytechnic, who had written a "promising" novel depicting his life and hard times growing up in a suburb of Nottingham. My first real client. Clutching a real kitchen sink. I wasn't going to pass that up for more Bentinck blather. I had yet to learn that "promising" is one of the most unreliable terms in the English language.

"I have to work this afternoon."

"O'course, wage slave. I do hope it's worth it. Tell me, how much do you rake in? Twenty-five grand a year? Thirty?"

Thirty grand was more than twice what Syd was paying me. Yet the tone in which Bentinck uttered the word implied it was peanuts to him.

"I get by."

"Well get by my house at seven-thirty tonight."

He flipped a card across the table.

A house in the Boltons. No wonder thirty grand was peanuts.

"Now," he said. "To matters of state, to cabbages and kings . . . to pud."

A waiter set dessert menus in front of us.

I opened mine and read nothing. I wasn't going to eat another mouthful. Bentinck rolled his eyes down the page and muttered, "The things I do for England."

And when he looked up he was smiling, and a friendly light seemed to flicker in those saggy eyes.

"Call no man unhappy with a pudding menu in front of him."

Graham Garside was twenty-two. He'd have been about fourteen by the time punk penetrated Nottingham *Profond*. And if there was one thing he hated in life it was hippies. What was it? Could he smell patchouli on me? I had washed off the last residue round about 1967. Whatever . . . his lip curled at the sight of me. A sub-Elvis sneer that conceded that he might just let me represent him, a quiz on who I read and liked (utterly irrelevant) . . . leading to undisguised contempt when I replied "Iris Murdoch".

After twenty minutes with him I was almost looking forward to the sneers and contempt of Bentinck. They at least were accompanied by a modicum of curiosity.

He'd get back to me.

Of course.

I held out a hand for the kid to shake. He looked at it as if I'd presented him with a cold kipper.

"It's been a pleasure, Graham," I lied.

"It's Gaz."

"Okay, it's been a gas."

"No, I mean I'm known as Gaz. Only my dad calls me Graham."

Well, that was me put in my place.

I thought at first I had misread his address, but I checked the card. I was in front of the right house, possibly the only house in the Boltons, that hugely expensive loop of Chelsea real estate, in need of paint and joinery. A three-storey house of flaking stucco and rotting window frames. God, the neighbours must hate Bentinck.

I pressed the bell. No sound of ringing. Where the Victorian knocker had once been was a deep scar in the paint. I pushed. The door drifted in and music drifted out.

At this point in my life I had long forsaken the Grateful Dead – once the LSD wore off, who didn't? Not much had replaced them. Music was that stuff happening in the background. Happening everywhere, elevators, coffee bars ... I could not even get a haircut without some MOR pap burbling away from tinny speakers in the ceiling. Free champagne, sir? Free coffee? Free ear-ache? Most of London's public places left me craving silence. After Jess left I'd unplugged the record player. Nothing would induce me to turn it back on. And I could not have told you if the crackly sound coming from the back room of Bentinck's house was Mozart or Messiaen.

I reached the end of the corridor, opened the door into a small back room aglow with western light, crammed with furniture. Bentinck was slumped in an armchair that had suffered a volcanic eruption of stuffing. There was a tumbler half full of whisky next to him, and a can of tinned custard, most of which was spattered down his waistcoat. His eyes were shut. He was humming along with the music.

"Do you like Brahms?" he said, eyes still closed.

"I've no idea."

"This is the Third."

"Third what?"

The eyes opened.

"Oh God, do you people know nothing?"

He got up with some difficulty. Noticed the custard dribbles down his front, muttered "shit" a few times and shuffled across to the record player.

I'd never seen anything quite like it. A turntable over a foot across, a strobe read-out, an arm counterweighted with pre-decimal silver coins, a yard of wires trailing from pre-amp to amp and a 78 rpm record spinning.

"Brahms's Third Symphony, Berlin Sinfonia, 1946. First recording they made after the war. Among the first violins you'll hear Klaus Boehm. Talented young chap. I ran him in '48 to '49, right through the airlift. Till the Russians tumbled to him, that is. Left him hanging from a lamppost in the British sector. They broke his fingers first. Bastards."

At last . . . a fact. The merest shred of spooky-doo.

He turned the volume down a fraction. Found a second tumbler, blew off the dust and handed it to me with a nod towards the open bottle of Bells.

"Lend an ear. On the last side. Over in a jiffy."

I lent the ear. I looked around.

It began to dawn on me that there was more than one Roger Bentinck. The dapper if somewhat gross man who had bought me a gourmet lunch, and the slob who got shit-faced in the afternoon, ate cold custard straight from the tin and appeared to live in a haze of dust and cobwebs in the back room of a huge and neglected house in one of the most prestigious streets in Chelsea.

Which one was trying to teach me about classical music? Which one had just teased me, however inadvertently, with the possibilities in his tale?

Brahms's Third is not one of those symphonies that ends with a clash of cymbals. It dwindles to nothing through the plaintive call of woodwind. I watched dust motes, jerked to life by two colossal bass speakers, dance in sunbeams. I looked at what I was certain was the detritus of several lives, as though Bentinck had less furnished the room than simply allowed stuff to gather around him.

There is an old Tory tale . . . Fred Smith, MP, has the old blue-rinse bags in his constituency over for tea. He thinks it has gone well and that he, nouveau-riche and nouveau-Tory, regional accent dropped, suits newly tailored, past duly buried, has pulled off the stunt. As they are leaving, one dowager says to another, "But my dear, his furniture is bought!"

In Toryland you do not buy furniture, you inherit it.

It seemed to me that every item of furniture Bentinck had inherited was now stacked around him, leaving a small pool for his occupation in the centre.

"Being a Yank I expect you'd like to ruin your scotch with half a pound of ice."

"Two cubes would do."

Bentinck went to the kitchen. After a bit of banging and smashing he returned with a pudding basin full of ice.

Helpfully I held out my glass.

"Not so fast, Sonny Jim."

He took the glass off me. Set it down on the table about eighteen inches away from the basin.

Behind them at about the same distance stood a toy crane made of pressed steel in a flaky red, held together with brass screws. I'd spotted the crane way before. I just didn't know what it was. Bentinck pointed to the battered cardboard lid of a toy box on the floor.

Meccano No. 10 Kit. 12 years and over.

Ah, the hobby listed in *Who Gives a Fuck Who's Who*.

Two boys in the pre-war garb of grey shorts and sleeveless pullovers were making a crane twice the size of Bentinck's in the dim arc of a reading lamp, all watched over with loving care from the sidelines by a benign, pipe-smoking dad.

"Indulge me."

He cranked levers, wound cable. The crane gently grabbed a couple of ice cubes, swung across the table and plonked them down in my Scotch.

Bentinck was grinning, then he was laughing that explosive, wheezing laugh of his. Then I was laughing, too. It was so . . . so . . . so wonderfully silly.

I felt it was the first time we'd actually been on the same wavelength.

"Down the hatch, eh?"

"Of course," he said apropos of nothing. "We could go anywhere we liked in Berlin in '46. International zone and all that. We could hang out in the caffs in the Russia sector, and they could simply whizz a jeep into any of the Allied sectors and kidnap who the hell they liked off the streets. If they nabbed one poor bugger that way they nabbed a thousand. People could simply vanish. They got Klaus on his own doorstep not 200 yards from the Tiergarten Station. Tortured him in their own sector, dumped him back in ours. I doubt there was much he could have told them. Such a bloody waste."

"He could," I ventured, "have told them about you."

"Oh, they knew about me. They had a wall chart up with mugshots of every British Intelligence officer. As an Intelligence officer in Berlin you were marked. You could run a field agent. You couldn't actually be one. Set foot in the Russian sector and you had a tail in less than a minute. I even had the buggers follow me to the gents. Come to think of it, that was a sure way to find out if you were being followed. Nip to the gents. He follows. Might just be coincidence. So next time nip to the ladies. No German male would ever dare follow me in there. And if the bugger was still outside when I came out, then I knew for certain. If I went into a bar they'd usually park their elbows a dozen blokes away. I'd pay the barman to send a beer down to whoever it was and raise my hat to him. All rather open. A waste of their time, not mine. The only mission I was on was to see how many tails I picked up in a night on the booze."

"Not exactly a secret, then?"

"Oh there are secrets aplenty. Just not in Berlin in '46. You'll get your secrets all right. After all, it's what you came for, isn't it? It's what you blokes want, isn't it?"

Was this the moment to remind him that it was he who had come to me?

"Us blokes?"

He ignored this.

"I think I'll spin the shellac again tomorrow. If you're free, come back for Beethoven. The Seventh. Furtwängler, 1943. Recorded in Berlin while we bombed them to buggery. Not that you can hear the bombs, of course."

Could I be surprised that he had nothing better to do on a Friday night when I had nothing better myself?

It was 3.30 p.m. again. There's one every day. I was getting used to them. I met with Lucy Devlin, recently down from University College, Dublin, and the author of a "promising" first novel depicting her life and hard times growing up in a Dublin suburb – much of the dialogue rendered in a challenging phonetic transcription.

Who was my favourite author?

I felt I was on safe ground with Iris Murdoch, a Dubliner herself, and stuck with "Iris Murdoch".

She'd be in touch.

Of course.

Two days later I received a postcard saying she didn't feel comfortable with a man as her agent.

Well, that was me put in my place.

It was not that Bentinck offered any explanation of music. There would have been little point if he had, and I think he subscribed to the same notion I did: either you get it or you don't – or, as they said in my teens, "Can you dig it, man?" Telling me to listen out for a cadenza in Beethoven would have made as much sense to me as pointing out the engine manifold in Mozart.

What he did – all he did – was create a space in which I was not fussing about anything else. No one was trying to talk; no one was doing anything other than sitting fairly still and listening. An all but impossible condition, unless imposed from without.

It worked. Furtwängler's Beethoven blew me away.

"It was different in Berlin in '63. Different world, different players. Same game."

"What made the difference?"

"The Wall. Going East became . . . I dunno. More of a risk? Hardly. It was always a risk. They'd never snatch one of *us* off the streets of West Berlin. But we could always meet with contrived accidents. I suppose the difference was uniforms and side arms became cloaks and daggers. Now, isn't that just what you wanted to hear? But . . . fifteen years on, fifteen years away from Berlin, fifteen years older, a bag full of fake identities . . . they didn't know me anymore. I went East without a tail for the first time. I was Georg Feinmann from Charlottenburg, visiting his dear old auntie in Hellersdorf. I was Peter Grosz from Steglitz simply exercising my West Berliner's right to a stroll in the East.

"The last big run, the one that did for me, was in the autumn of '65. The Russians used to have Warsaw Pact troops rehearse taking West Berlin. Every time they did it we didn't know whether it would stop at the dress rehearsal or carry on for a first night and a curtain call. Would have been curtains for us. We couldn't stop 'em, after all. Jack Kennedy had stood up in Berlin and declared himself a Berliner in public. In private he'd told Willy Brandt there was no way America would go to war over Berlin. So everything we could find out about their intentions was vital.

"We had blokes in the East who'd deliver full details of the battle plan as such . . . everything down to the menu in the commissars' canteen. That October they rumbled us. We were in Bernau . . . big Russian Tank Division HQ in Bernau. I was meeting my snitches. We walked into a trap. Bit of a shoot-out. Both my blokes go down. What they know dies with 'em. I kill three of theirs and run for it. Bernau's only just east of Berlin, but going back via Berlin looked like suicide. I went south and west. Took eight days. But I'd used up eight of my nine lives. I wasn't a lot of use to SIS after that. I was gracefully retired. Can't complain. They were bloody decent about it and I knew I was blown. Blown to the point where any Soviet agent probably had a mandate to shoot me on sight their side of the Iron Curtain. Hence I am as you see me now."

As he was now was Bentinck in evening mode – and evening mode seemed to begin straight after lunch. Pissed as a fart with half a tin of Ambrosia creamed rice, cold from the tin, down his waistcoat. "As you see me now" had no tinge of regret to it. A remark that was not tongue in cheek. Not a hint of irony.

"And is this a secret?"

He snorted into his laughter mode.

"Secret? Of course it's a bloody secret!"

Three-thirty. I met with Izzy Cowper, recently down from Girton, who had written a "promising" first novel depicting her life and hard times growing up in St John's Wood.

I switched my answer to Muriel Spark, feeling that Iris Murdoch was jinxing me. A bare-faced lie. I'd never read a book by Muriel Spark. I'd just seen the film *The Prime of Miss Jean Brodie*, with Maggie Smith.

I liked Izzy. I could represent Izzy.

Never heard from her again.

I had sat through the Brahms Clarinet Quintet in B minor. If Bentinck had said it was in Q major I would have believed him.

"Adolf Busch and chums. Recorded in '36, I think. Dunno where."

I had become his amanuensis as well as his student. He spun the shellac, but I got up and turned the records over. Up and down like a jack-in-the-box. No 78 would play longer than about five or six minutes, and even a relatively short piece of classical music would take up six sides.

I never had any idea how long Bentinck would play for. When the music finished he usually had a can of something canned and a large shot of something bottled and began his performance after a couple of dessert spoons and one large slug.

"Radio Free Europe. Radio Free Europe. Radio Free Fucking Europe . . . was a fraud from start to finish. You lot . . ."

My lot? Ah, now I wasn't a draft dodger anymore. I was just an American. A representative of my upstart nation.

". . . You lot encouraged rebellion, encouraged it in sixteen different languages. You broadcast support and reassurance to people willing to put their lives on the line and then you did nothing. Berlin: nothing. Hungary: nothing. Czechoslovakia: nothing. The promise was hollow . . . America was never going to go to war in Europe again. You could kill all the little yellow rice-munchers you liked in Laos and Vietnam, but you'd never fire a single shot at anyone wearing a Red Army uniform. People died for you."

If I'd had a flake of patriotism it might have surfaced at this moment, bobbing on the buoyant hypocrisy that is the moral scheme of your average human being. It didn't. Why else was I in England? So as not to have to shoot little yellow rice-munchers. C'mon Jack. Tell the truth. I was in England so as not to have little yellow rice-munchers shoot at me.

"It's a betrayal beyond measure. You sold a promise, you sold an idea. And even after the great betrayal they cling to the idea."

"Mr Bentinck, what idea?"

"That everyone in the world can be an American. You sold them the promise of the Lone Ranger, Perry Como, fridges, air-conditioning and takeaway pizza. Who the fuck needs ideology? That is your ideology. Of the pizza, by the pizza, for the pizza."

Can't argue with him on that one. Indeed, I couldn't. He'd

passed out again. The custard tin slipped from his hand, the little yellow river started out across his chest on its long journey to the groin.

After Brahms several days passed without any further invitation to drop by. I took my 400-odd in winnings from Newmarket and found a used hi-fi dealer in the Edgware Road. How much would it get me?

It got me a pair of matching Quad 405 monoblocs, a 34 pre-amp, Rega turntable and a pair of rather battered Rogers BBC monitors. All British – it would pass any Bentinck test. And all gobbledegook to me, but the man in the shop helped me pile it all into a cab, assuring me I'd got a bargain. Either that or he just cleared all the crap out of his back room in one fell swoop to one fell idiot.

All wired up on top of my desk – not piled high with all the manuscripts sent in by all the clients I didn't have – I found one failing. No records. No vinyl and most certainly no 78s. I'd used the last album, *Tea for the Tillerman* by Cat Stevens, as a frisbee on Primrose Hill. The golden retriever who caught it would not give it back. I should care.

In Harold Moore's shop in Great Marlborough Street I bought Schubert's *Death and the Maiden* by the Busch Quartet that Bentinck had introduced me to. After that I was out of cash. I went home clutching a record I'd never heard to feed an addiction I'd just discovered.

It was brilliant stuff. It was miserable stuff. After two consecutive playings I was suicidal. Death and the Dodger.

Lunch with Syd. The Caprice in Arlington Street. A stone's throw from the Guards Club.

I had not taken on a single writer. I could be apologetic. If needs be. But I knew to let Syd make the first move. And if I was due for the sack, would he have taken me to a restaurant as classy as this?

"I'm glad you're not rushing into this. An agent needs no more than fifty clients. More than that is unmanageable. And at minimum they should be earning ten grand a year from their work. Make that fifteen, on second thoughts. Had one young chap a few years ago who'd taken on twenty-two writers in the first six weeks . . . most of 'em no-hopers. As I say, glad you're not rushing into things."

The repetition told. Of course he was glad, glad and a little concerned. He knew I'd no clients. The Buckett woman would have told him that.

"How are things moving along with Roger Bentinck?"

"Well . . . he's certainly kosher. Enough gung-ho tales to convince me of that."

"But?"

"But he is a wreck of a man. I'm not sure he'll ever write any of it down."

"But if he does?"

"If he does . . . it's as you said. One hell of a book. He was there . . . He appears to have been there . . . at most of the major incidents of the Cold War."

"Do you wonder why he wants to tell all?"

"Yep. Can't fault his patriotism. Thinks Margaret Thatcher is God's representative on earth . . . takes the *Telegraph* every day just to see who's died . . . and hates Americans. How patriotic can you get?"

Syd mused on this one.

"Well I'm sure he'll come clean eventually. Something will . . . burst. Meanwhile, it's getting a proposal out of him . . ."

Mea culpa.

"And when you do, and when you start pitching it, that's when the shit will hit the fan."

We both paused. I knew what he meant, but I wanted to hear him state what we'd both known all along.

"They won't want him to do it, of course. But we don't give up that easily do we? I just wanted to warn you. It could get a bit nasty if they set the Branch on to you. I want you to be prepared."

"Branch?"

"Special Branch. Military Intelligence has no powers of search or arrest. A bit like the CIA not being supposed to operate within the USA. So, they have a squad of Scotland Yard bully boys at their disposal. They kick down doors, crack skulls, arrest people . . . and so on. You won't like it if Inspector Plodder calls. They can make quite a mess, I gather."

"Why me? Why not Bentinck?"

"No. I don't think they'd do that. It's you they'll come after."

"Do you want me to drop it?"

"No. I just want you to be ready."

"How do I do that?"

"Until you actually get a proposal out of him, keep no notes. Store it all in your head. When you get the proposal, keep it in the open where anyone can see it. Conceal nothing. Leave the folder on your desktop."

I got it, but I had one last question.

"Syd. Why did you hire me?"

"As opposed to whom?"

"As opposed to an Englishman who might have grown up sharing your values and your tailor."

"Well you've seen 'em. The chaps Larry Greene stuck me with between old Ebenezer's death and my taking over. Perfectly capable men. No reason to fire any of them. They do their job. But they're stuffed shirts in three-piece suits. All Oxbridge educated. PPE and Greats and all that nonsense. But if brains were flint they couldn't light a fart. No. It was time . . . time . . . to put a cat among the pigeons."

"Or an old tie-dye hippie among the stuffed shirts?"

"I'll need a translator for that one, I'm afraid. Anyway. I must dash. Stick the bill on the company card. And keep me posted."

"D'ye know that chippy by the Earl's Court tube?"

"No."

"Well, I'm sure you'll find it. Cod, chips, mushy peas, easy on the vinegar and don't forget the tartare sauce."

"What?"

"Eight o'clock. My place. Get what you fancy for yourself, but no Coca-Cola. American muck. Disgusting smell. I'll give you the ackers when you get here. Schumann tonight. Artur Schnabel at the joanna. Don't be late."

He rang off.

Thus ended ten days of silence.

I had been summoned.

Cod, chips and Schnabel.

Just as well. I was wearing through the grooves on Schubert.

As ever, Bentinck's choice in music was impeccable. Schumann op. 44, a piano quintet. For all I knew *the* piano quintet. A decidedly vigorous work. We ate fish and chips with nothing more significant than his saying what a pleasant summer it had been so far. Food and music did not overlap. He listened without distraction.

And after Schnabel.

"Good fish was it?"

"I guess . . ."

"Would you care to guess why?"

"What?"

"Why did I send you out for fish and chips like a twelve-year-old running an errand?"

Perhaps because you're a fat, idle bastard?

"Ah . . . I'm supposed to see a symbol here."

"Indeed you are. Ever heard of the British Baltic Fisheries Protection Service?"

"Of course not."

"I was part of the team that set it up after the dust settled in Berlin in '49."

"Fisheries protection? Codfish in danger?"

"Black entry. Dropping agents into the Baltic states. Dozens of them, literally dozens of them. The poor buggers were tripping over each other in the forests of Courland."

"Poor buggers?"

"Well . . . they none of them lived, did they?"

This was my cue to shut up and listen. And, forbidden to write anything down, to take all the mental notes I could.

"It was your lot came up with the idea. Fucking CIA. So happens that at the end of the war we had ships from the Reich navy intact. Everything Jerry hadn't managed to scuttle in the Baltic. E-boats mainly, light, fast surface craft. Used to skim along at one hell of lick.

"It was a Russian irritation to harass fishing in international waters in the Baltic. The CIA decided we could redeploy these boats in the pretence we were protecting local fishermen working out of the British Zone, and every so often we'd nip right up to the coast and drop off agents. I can still smell the sticky mud banks on the Latvian coast, standing up to me ankles in it in pitch darkness. All I have to do is close my eyes and I can smell the shit and seaweed stench. Ah . . . me . . . that bit worked fine. Clockwork. In and out before old Ivan could blink.

"Operation Plumduff. I called it that. It was designed to get agents into the Baltic states, gather intelligence and become . . . I dunno what to call them . . . rallying points for resistance? The spearhead of a counter-revolution? What were we thinking of? Seventy-four men to start a counter-revolution? Madness, utter madness. For a year or so I kidded myself it was working well. I suppose it's possible they weren't on to us from the start. But they were. They knew our every move. They set up a fake resistance group in the forests; they'd make contact with the people we dropped, nab 'em, turn 'em or shoot 'em. Worst of it is I reckon some of our chaps are still in Russian gulags to this day.

"We used blokes we'd gathered up in the war years. Some of them had been refugees in England since the thirties. And we used blokes who'd fled west as the Red Army took everything in its stride in '45. And we used Germans. We used Nazis. One of them was an SS Standartenführer. Y'know what that is? Full-blown bloody colonel. Jackboots, death's head insignia, the whole caboodle. A man with the blood of thousands on his hands. He told me he'd torched entire villages in Poland as they retreated.

"Anyway . . . a few came back to us with cock-and-bull stories the KGB had hammered into them, most we never saw again. By 1951 it was obvious to me it had all gone to hell in a handcart. Our blokes were telling the KGB everything they knew once they got nabbed. But there was more than that. The KGB knew everything. They'd known everything from the start. Looking back I think the only reason they didn't grab me is because it would have wound up the operation on the spot, and the longer we went on sending men in there the bigger fools we were making of ourselves. If I hadn't called a halt to the op we might well have sent hundreds of agents in there. I mean, why would they shoot the goose that was laying golden eggs for them?

"Of course, your lot played hell. I pulled the plug ten days before Burgess and Maclean packed their bags. Great timing on my part. Utterly unplanned. The CIA droned on about England leaking like a sieve. And MI6 had the perfect cover story. Two spies who were already out of the bag. No need to look further."

A pause while he topped up his Scotch. In too serious a mode now to bother with the toy crane. He didn't offer me one. He was totally self-absorbed and silent, sitting with both hands wrapped around the glass.

"Mr Bentinck. Which one was it? Burgess or Maclean?"

"Neither. Maclean didn't know about this and Burgess didn't know about anything. I think the silly sod saw defection as a kind of holiday. Thought he'd be back when his traveller's cheques ran out. No, it was neither of them. And before you ask, it wasn't Philby either. And it wasn't that tosser Blunt. I knew who it was. I just couldn't prove it."

Another long pause. Another gulp of Scotch.

"He's still alive. Not in the service anymore, of course. Bit long in the tooth for that. No. He picked up his gong a few years ago. Enjoys a touch of fame. Plenty of boards to sit on. A small role in public life. Enough to make his wife the darling of the WI and keep her opening church fetes for the rest of her days. No peace for the wicked, eh?"

At last the penny dropped.

"And you're going to name him?"

"Of course I'm going to fucking name him!"

"So," said Syd. "We might have a libel problem."

"Not according to Bentinck. He thinks the guy will just come clean."

"What makes him think that?"

"He's been in touch, apparently."

"Apparently?"

"I have only his word for that."

"And the book proposal?"

"He's working on that."

"Apparently?"

We met in time for the 2.30 at Sandown Park. A Thursday, early that September.

Likely Lad came in at evens. Bentinck had nagged me to put a hundred on the nose. So, I doubled my money.

Then he urged me – I needed no nagging by this time – to join him in backing an outsider. Scary Mary at 16 to 1.

"A hot tip."

"From whom?"

"That would be telling."

"Aha."

"For fuck's sake, boy. I'm an old spy. People tell me things. Bit like being a priest when you come to think about it. Every bugger's always bursting to tell you something. Spies don't have to spy, they just have to listen."

I was riffling through – counting would not be the word – a wad of notes amounting to 3,000 pounds when he slapped down an envelope in the middle of my stash.

"There you go, hippie. Your cup runneth over. Call me tonight."

He went his way. I went mine. I found myself alone on the train back to Waterloo.

All the same the power of paranoia was overwhelming. I couldn't take his proposal out in a public place. Could I? But the public place was empty . . . just some tweedy piss artist snoring off a racing lunch at the far end of the carriage. But what about the Official Secrets Act and all that guff? I had always assumed Bentinck and I would be breeching it. Not that I'd ever been asked to sign it. It's an odd law that you have to sign up for. Not guilty of theft, rape, murder . . . can't catch me. I never signed on the line. Made no sense to me.

I read it when I got home. This made no sense to me either.

Two double-sided, handwritten A4 . . . no, two foolscap pages, the old rogue was still using fucking foolscap . . . that said absolutely nothing.

I called him.

"Mr Bentinck. What happened to all your stories . . . I mean about life in the field?"

"Bit early for that, don't you think?"

"No, I don't. We have to give them something. I mean something else."

"My childhood didn't interest you?"

It did. I realized how he'd acquired his facility with languages. An English childhood cut short when his shit of a father wrapped two and a half tons of 4.9 litre Armstrong Siddeley round a tree and his mother married her lover on the spot and whisked young Bentinck and his baby half-sister off to Zurich. But . . .

"And Oxford?"

No. Oxford had bored me silly. My own year there, as well as his. His had been spent necking yards of ale and lobbing bread rolls at oiks. Mine had been spent scrabbling around for meaning in *the syphilitic selling violets* . . . whatever.

"And banking?"

Absofuckinlutely not. Boring, boring, boring.

"Not really."

"It's a major part of my life. Or did you think I paid for a house in the Boltons by selling whelks from a stall in the Mile End Road?"

"Mr Bentinck . . ."

"Send it out. You have the contacts. You've done bugger all else but boast about your contacts. And if you haven't got the contacts, then what fucking use are you to me?"

He hung up.

This was before the invention of the PC, and well before the invention of the laptop. I sat up that night and typed out, cleaned up, polished Bentinck's pitch on my Olivetti manual typewriter. I could write it for him . . . Tell what he had told. I could not square the morality of that. He was my client . . . Syd had impressed upon me the duty of care. I could send out his proposal. I could decline to send out his proposal, but I couldn't overrule him on the matter of content. Besides, one curt, snappy rejection letter and I could get him to revise and rethink.

I'd send it to Jenny Broome at Nathan Wolowitz and Parker. I'd no idea who Parker was or ever had been. Nathan was one of those Eastern Europeans who'd landed in England as refugees from Hitler and had come to dominate London publishing in the post-war years. Nathan was the kind of man to publish Bentinck, and Jenny was the kind of woman not to. I'd hear from her pretty quick. And it would be curt and snappy.

Paranoia tiptoed up to my window yet again. I delivered Bentinck's proposal by hand. Walked over to Great Russell Street in my lunch hour and dropped it off at reception.

At seven, when I stepped through the door of my flat in Primrose Hill, a cop sucker-punched me and I went down and out. I flatter myself a smaller man might have been down for longer. But down is down. When I sat up the world was topsy-turvy. They'd thrown everything I owned on the floor and kicked in the cones of my new speakers.

The cop set a chair upright with one hand and with the other grabbed me by the shirt front and hauled me into it. I weigh 180. I was tossed like a leaf.

"Where is it?"

The temptation to ask "Where is what?" I readily dismissed. He'd only hit me again.

"On the desk in my office."

"All of it?"

"All there is. Nothing I imagine you haven't seen already today."

"Meaning?"

"I have Mr Bentinck's handwritten proposal and a carbon of the typed version. They differ only in so far as I cleaned up the custard stains and his punctuation."

Another cop emerged from my bedroom. Smaller than the first, but dressed the same. Like two comic coppers in a *Daily Express* Giles cartoon – trench coat and trilby, regardless of the weather, and shoes I had learnt were referred to as beetle-crushers.

He was higher in rank, I guessed, but they weren't offering any introductions.

Cop Two righted another chair and sat opposite me. I could smell pipe tobacco, Old Spice and NHS dentistry.

"Delighted to hear you're not trying to be a smart alec, son. Sensible of you not to be asking about warrants and such. National security, after all. Warrants mean nowt where the defence of the realm is concerned. So happens I've read nowt. So, why don't you tell me what's on your desk?"

"If this is business, why not make an appointment and come to my office?"

An exchange of glances between them. One of them definitely meaning "Shall I thump him again, boss?" . . . the other more quizzical. He was weighing up the idea.

Then:

"Why not? We've found bugger all here."

"I'm free at ten."

"Make it nine, you lazy little sod."

He leaned in closer. Dropped his voice.

"And don't think you're getting off lightly. We know all about you. Draft dodger. Fuck with us and you might find yourself on a plane to Vietnam."

Please. This was a red rag to a bull.

I whispered back, "The war ended ten years ago. Carter pardoned me in '79 and if you know of any extradition treaty between the UK and the USA that covers military service . . . then you're way ahead of me."

There. That was telling him.

There. That was his pal knocking me sideways with a punch that lifted me off the chair. Me and my big mouth.

I lay there, tasting blood, staring at the beetle-crushers.

"Dearie, dearie me, just when we were getting along so nicely. Nine o'clock, son. Don't be late."

I was up half the night clearing up the mess. I could weep for the speakers. I could weep for the albums. One of the bastards had taken a pocket knife to *Death and the Maiden*.

Roger George Cholmondoley Bentinck, this had better be worth it. Don't be late? Damn right. There was three grand in cash locked in my desk drawer. I wasn't going to let the flat-foots get their hands on that.

I got in at eight.

Vera Buckett damn near dropped her fag when I handed her the money.

"In the ladies, Vera. Take twenty for your trouble."

On the dot of nine, she phoned through that two gentlemen were in reception.

They came into my office. I had the Compleat Bentinck in a brown cardboard folder on the desktop. I spun it round so they could see the title.

Unnamed Memoir by Roger Bentinck.

They sat at the back of my office. Boss read the file, Thumper scraped his nails with a pocket knife – doubtless the same one he'd taken to Schubert.

"Is this it?"

"Yep."

"School and Oxford and his dad and all that?"

"Yep."

"You let us turn your gaff over for this? You're a twat."

"So people keep telling me. And I don't recall being able to stop you trashing my flat."

The file was slapped back on my desk. I could see the cogwheels turning. He was weighing whether or not to search my office. I put my money on "not". I might be a piece of Yankee shit to him, but the Hon. Syd was known to them. He had his reputation. Not that they wouldn't mess with him, but they'd not do it lightly.

When they'd gone, the Buckett woman stood in my doorway, blew a smoke ring and moved on, just as the phone rang.

It was Jenny Broome.

"Jack, is this some sort of joke? You've been hyping this to me for over a month. It's . . . it's bollocks."

"I know."

"Then why send it me?"

"Jenny, would you mind putting this in writing? Give me something I can show Bentinck."

"What?"

"Just a quick critique and rejection on headed paper."

"You bastard. You're just using me to flush him out."

"Yep."

A pause. She was seriously considering telling me to get lost. I was wondering whether I dared tell her that Bentinck knew the name of the Fifth Man. Burgess, Maclean, Philby, Blunt and Guess Who.

"You owe me, Jack Turner. You fucking owe me."

"Agreed. Jenny . . . you haven't had any . . . visitors today or yesterday?"

"Eh? You mean the filth? No . . . Why would they bother with this?"

"Only because they don't know what it is yet."

"I suppose you're right. Deal with that if and when it arises.

Meanwhile, you owe me lunch. Syd never has any trouble getting into the Ivy. You can damn well take me there."

About an hour passed. Syd was never in before ten. Why not? He owned the "joint", as they say in Hollywood.

He looked at my bruises.

"Anything I should know about?"

"Nothing you hadn't predicted."

Around 11.30 Syd returned with his Bart Simpson mug full of milky coffee and a packet of McVitie's Hobnobs, to which he was all but addicted.

"It's not an Official Secrets matter."

I could not hear a question there.

"We may take it as read, Bentinck has signed. You haven't, and never should. But there's this new thing . . . the Obligation of Confidentiality or some such guff. He hasn't signed that either. Be amazed if anyone who left the service in the sixties had. So, what have they got?"

"The suspicion, chasing the certainty, that what Bentinck has to say will violate the Official Secrets Act. The identity of a Russian mole is a secret . . . but is it an official secret? Is it a British secret or a Russian secret, and if the latter, who gives a toss?"

"Couldn't have put it better myself. Do have a Hobnob."

The following day I got Jenny's rejection letter, raised an eyebrow and forwarded a copy to Bentinck. The day after that Bentinck rang me.

"'Unrevealing to the point of tedium'! 'The life and times of another old English bore'!"

Weeeell . . . I did feel Jenny had overdone it just a tad.

"Who is this fucking cunt?"

"Quite possibly the best young editor in London."

"Then who's the best *old* editor in London?"

"Mr Bentinck, that's not the—"

"You sent it out half-cock to some young twat who doesn't

know she's born yet . . . You pass me off as an old bore with nothing to say for himself. What in God's name do you think you're playing at?"

"Mr Bentinck, you asked me to send it out as it was. I told you beforehand . . ."

"You told me fuck all. All you've done is boast that you know every fucking publisher in fucking London. And who do you know? Some man-hating fucking bluestocking!"

"Mr Bentinck, that proposal needed more work. I told you that."

"Then why did you send it out, Sonny Jim?"

"Because you told me to."

"Fuck you. Fuckyoufuckyoufuckyoufuckyoufuckyoufuck-you!"

The fuck yous would fill a page and why waste paper? I listened, and when he finally paused for breath I attempted another polite interjection, but he charged in with . . .

"You're fired!"

A couple of minutes passed.

Vera Buckett appeared, fag adroop on lower lip, carrying an ashtray. She always carried an ashtray if she came into my office. Her one concession to a non-smoker was not not to smoke, it was not to flick ash on the carpet.

"Okay, Vera, let's hear it."

"Are you glad he's gone?"

"Relieved might be the word."

"I see. But now you've no clients. You are, in fact, a waste of space. Literally so."

"You have anything else you want to share with me?"

"Share? Share! Oh you fucking hippies. Yes, I'll 'share'," both hands went up to frame the word in speech marks, "this with you: there's no victory in him firing you or you firing him. The only success was getting the bloody book out of him. Any less and it's a waste of your time and a waste of Syd's space. We might as well move the photo-copier back in."

"What would you suggest? I already go through the slush pile every day to so little purpose."

"Move yer arse. You're supposed to be the Crown Prince of Lit Fic. Take on some clients and do it quick. Stop messing around with no-hopers who don't want to know you . . ."

"There were only three."

"Stop messing about and start building your list. Forget promising and go for established."

"And how – from the elevated view of a secretary and receptionist – would you suggest I set about doing this?"

"You little gobshite! Poach 'em! Get out there and nick other buggers' clients! And you dare talk to me like that again and I'll rip yer bollocks off!"

Well. That was me put in my place.

Poach 'em.

So I did.

Writers are fickle creatures. Most have no loyalty whatsoever. Most live in a constant state of feeling ill-served and unappreciated.

I rang half a dozen writers I'd published in my two years at Hamilton Hardy and announced that I was jumping ship. Not – note – that I had already jumped ship. That in itself might have appeared disloyal. And since all had reasons aplenty to be dissatisfied with the service they thought they weren't getting from Bloggs and Brown or Bottle and Briggs (make up a name, it really doesn't matter) . . . by the end of the week Hawes Greene had six new clients on the books, including a Somerset Maugham winner, a Hawthornden and two hotly tipped to win the Booker one day.

I felt free of a quagmire . . . a quagmire that was Bentinck. I don't think I can honestly say that I liked any of these writers any better than I liked Bentinck, but they weren't going to suck me into a bog of contradictions. Just flatter their fragile egos with soft lullabies of genius and all would be well.

I received a postcard from Toby Mornay's agent. A postcard in an envelope. It read: *Fuck you!*

I received a postcard not in an envelope from Jeremy Crich's agent: *You're welcome to him, and I hope you lose as much sleep over him as I have.*

And as I'd managed to bag Crich at the point when he was ready with a new and uncontracted novel, I was in business. Or as they say back home, I wuz cookin'.

Yes. All would be well.

Two weeks or more passed.

I was in the office late. Even the Buckett had gone back to Dagenham.

Whoever was last to leave ended up with the direct line. So when the phone rang I answered.

"Is that Hawes Greene?"

"Yes."

"Sorry to be calling at this time of night. I'm trying to find Jack Turner."

"Speaking."

"Mr Turner . . . I'm Molly Bentinck."

A young voice . . . a beautiful voice . . . a daughter omitted from *Who Ain't Who* . . . a sister?

"I'm Roger's wife."

Fuck me!

He was wedged halfway up the stairs, where a small landing enabled a 180-degree turn in the staircase. He'd fallen, collapsed, taken a snooze, whatever, at this point and Mrs Bentinck could not budge him.

He was wearing shirt, Y-fronts and socks. No trousers. She was wearing a neat little black skirt and a highly starched white blouse. She'd kicked off her high heels to get more purchase on 200 and more pounds of Mr Toad.

She was maybe five years older than me. A looker.

"He just flopped," she said. "I tugged and shoved for a bit, then his eyes opened once. He said, 'Get Jack', and I was left wondering who Jack was. I found your letter from a week or two back among the rot and rubbish on the dining table and took a chance."

Get Jack? Why, for God's sake?

"You want to move him now?"

"If you wouldn't mind, Mr Turner. He is between us and the loo."

We got him to the next floor, into a bedroom, on to a bed that screamed with his weight.

It was, in utter contrast to his small back room, clean and ordered.

She caught me looking.

"It's my house. Been in my family since it was built. I told him when he wanted to move in all the crap from his mother's house after she died that he could have two rooms on the ground floor, and that's all. The rest he is to keep clean and tidy. He pays for the cleaner, who is never allowed into his pigsty at the back. He's also responsible for the exterior. But you can see for yourself how conscientious he is about that. I don't suppose you know what happened to the door knocker?"

"I don't. And I can assume you don't live here?"

"Good Lord, no. I live in Tuscany. I left Roger six years ago. Let me put the kettle on and I'll fill you in. I suppose he'll have tea. Somewhere."

Back in Bentinck's allotted portion of the house, among a lifetime supply of tinned desserts . . . custard, rice pudding, tapioca, semolina and some stuff called Angel Delight, which he whipped up in a Cuisinart – I had known him to spatter both of us in butterscotch – she found a packet of Typhoo.

"You may imagine, I was not the first Mrs Bentinck."

"Well, there are no Mrs Bentincks in *Who's Who*."

She said nothing to this – a "so what?" shrug.

"He married Penny when he was twenty-five. She was taken ill while he was running some daft mission in the Baltic. He put the job first. Assumed she'd pull through. Dashed back at the last minute to find she'd died a couple of hours earlier. Never forgave himself. He had betrayed her – that was his word. Betrayed her in the service of a cause that in itself was a betrayal.

"Had plenty of girlfriends after that, but he wouldn't marry anyone until he was out of the service. Didn't want to see the pattern repeated. Either something would happen while he was away or something would happen to him. Married again in '67. Swiftly followed by an acrimonious divorce in '69.

"We met in '72. You may find this hard to believe. In his late forties, he was still slim. Harder still, he was still charming . . . still . . . intriguing. Or perhaps you can see that. Perhaps that's why you're here?"

A few teacups later a voice from above bellowed, "Molly!"

Molly said, "The kraken awakes." And went to see what.

Five minutes later she returned with half a dozen foolscap sheets – handwritten on both sides.

"For you," she said.

I leafed through them.

"No," she said. "Read. I'll make more tea. I might even warm up a can of tinned milk mush."

"If I'm to read more Rogerisms, I'd prefer a whisky."

"Why not? Why not, indeed?"

Instead of reaching for the half-empty bottle of Bells, she reached into her travel bag and pulled out a duty-free litre of Laphroaig.

Okay, for Laphroaig I might just get through twelve sides of Bentinck-scrawl. By page four I was asking for a top-up.

It was rant. Twelve pages of semi-coherent drivel ending with "MAURICE OLDFIELD WAS NOT A POOF!" in capital letters.

"Well?"

"Mrs Bentinck, did you know Maurice Oldfield?"

"Yes. And I was at his funeral only a couple of years ago, as it happens. A good friend. So, Roger's springing to his defence is he?"

"Lurching would be more the word."

I showed her the last line.

"Oh. Well, there has been a lot of nonsense put about by those third-rate hacks who specialize in writing about MI6,

hasn't there? Maurice was gay . . . ergo Maurice was a security risk . . . ergo Maurice was a double agent. All bollocks, of
course."

"That's pretty much what Mr Bentinck says."

"And that's his book, is it?"

"No, Mrs Bentinck. It's not a book. At best it's a letter to
The Times."

"Bad as that, eh?"

"Why is he doing this?"

"What? Defending a mate?"

"No . . . that I do understand. The rest of it. Wanting to
write a book at all. I don't know what he believes. I don't know
what he's saying."

She crossed the room, picked up the cover of Bentinck's
Meccano kit and handed it to me. The two little boys in the
half-light, the paternal gaze of a loving father.

"It's all there. Everything he believes in is in that picture.
Everything about the England he defends. Look at the boys.
Socks pulled up, garters in place, ties straight, hair combed . . .
Dad's even wearing a suit. And they produce something
practical and useful and probably grow up to be District
Officers in the far reaches of the Empire."

"All that in a box lid?"

"Yes, all of it."

"Then why betray it?"

"Ah . . . you think writing about it is betraying it?"

"I . . . don't know . . ."

"Roger is defending it. If he ever writes his book he will be
defending these values by exposing their betrayal."

"And that was . . . ?"

"I think you'll find he blames you people for that."

"He already has."

"Which is why I was surprised he wanted an American
anywhere near this. But . . . you're one of the very people he's
trying to get through to, aren't you? It's addressed to you. It's
personal. After all, so much of it is. The betrayal is personal.
He is so unforgiving."

"The first Mrs Bentinck?"

"Exactly. A private betrayal matched by a public one. He cannot write about the former, so he writes about the latter. He berates the West and America in particular for betraying Eastern Europe. You should hear him on the subject of Berlin."

"I have."

"Or on Vietnam, for that matter."

"That he doesn't much mention."

"Draft dodger, eh? This may surprise you, but in Roger's eyes the only honourable thing to do about Vietnam was dodge. To go was to betray. To give false hope was to lie. To pitch in and pull out was to lie. He's no respecter of cowards, don't get me wrong. But he honestly believes it was better not to have got involved in the first place. I watched the final evacuation of the embassy in Saigon on the BBC with him. He was in tears. All he could say was 'Betrayal'."

Molly Bentinck kept a flat in St John's Wood. We let Bentinck sleep it off and she drove me home. Just before I stepped out of the car she asked, "There's nothing you can do with what he's writing?"

"Mrs Bentinck, he fired me."

"I think you'll find not."

Oh God, could I bear his "not"?

"Do keep in touch, Mr Turner."

For 200 quid the guy in the Edgware Road replaced my woofers. Woofers? I know. Don't ask. Then I went back to Great Marlborough Street and spent another 200 on albums.

Pasta and punctuation. Lunch with Jeremy Crich. A man with an infinite ability to manipulate the comma. I had known him to ring up, asking to revise over the phone, only have him move commas around, swap semicolons for en-rules, en-rules for em-rules and blah-de-blah.

He handed over *Hackney Year Zero*, a hard-hitting satire of his life and hard times at the proletarian "coalface" in one of

London's less fashionable boroughs (where they can't spell "cappuccino"), to which he had moved from Hampstead (where they can spell "cappuccino"), with, "Can you get me a hundred grand for this? I need to get me teeth fixed."

When I got back to Henrietta Street there was a note on my desk from the Buckett:

Bentinck phoned for you.

Said something like "Mozart, 2 Joannas. 8.30 tomorrow night."

Is this spook code of some sort? Vera.

I took Mr Bentinck a present. Two tins of Bird's Custard. That'll learn me. He pulled a face at the conjunction of two words on the label I'd never even noticed: "low" and "fat".

Molly had left the Laphroaig. He poured for us both, said, "Pin back yer lug'oles," and pulled a long-playing Microgroove 33⅓ rpm record from its dusty paper sleeve. We had moved up from shellac to vinyl. I did not ask what. Mozart, that much I knew. Two pianos, that too. He'd fill in the rest later.

A lively piece. Lots of elbow on the strings. But no pianos. A couple of minutes pass and just as I'm thinking he might have picked up the wrong record a piano crashed in with a riff (rock 'n' roll has riffs, why not Mozart?) that knocked me for six. Twenty minutes of bliss followed. I cannot even hear him breathe. I can forget that I am, for reasons which passeth the understanding of Our Freud, a prisoner of a fat toad with an inordinate ability to get under my skin. I am . . . bound by the beauty.

"Well, what do you think, hippie?"

"I think: can I live without this? Who was it?"

"Concerto for Two Pianos in E flat. K whatever. Clara Haskil and . . . and . . . and some other bloke whose name I can't read without me specs. Recorded about thirty years ago, I reckon."

He didn't mention his hymn to Oldfield. I could only assume that Molly had told him what I'd said and he'd shelved it. He made no reference to passing out – trouserless in Chelsea

– halfway up the stairs. I could only assume he had little or no memory of it. He made no mention of screaming bloody murder at me down the phone and I was damn sure he remembered that.

We played the Mozart again. He showed me a dumper truck he was building with his Meccano kit, and as the evening struggled to its grateful close I said, "Mr Bentinck, about the book idea . . ." with every intention of concluding on "Let's just forget it", but he cut me short with:

"Working on it."

I got Jeremy Crich his hundred grand. (What fools these mortals be.) Syd congratulated me, and the Buckett, for once, refrained from calling me a twat.

Syd said to bring him up to speed on the spookery. I related to him much of what Molly Bentinck had told me.

"It's a Chinese box. Layer upon layer. I'm not at all sure I understand the half of this."

Syd said, "Perhaps I do."

"Betrayal is not the simple word I thought it was."

"Oh, I think it is. You'll recall I said Bentinck's grandfather Mad Mike Cholmondoley had been court-martialled in the Boer War. Cashiered. That is military justice. Much more prevalent is military injustice. The textbooks record the fate of Mad Jack . . . retired to his estate in Rutland and spent the rest of his life slaughtering pheasants and careering across the farms of his tenants in pursuit of the uneatable, till the day he fell off the horse and broke his neck. No book records the fate of the eighty-odd enlisted men under his command who came back wounded . . . half of them missing limbs . . . but you can bet your last farthing there were no pensions, no free medical care . . . no nothing.

"I think your Mr Toad probably feels the injustice inherent in military folly. It is possible, though I doubt he would say so as clearly, that Bentinck regards everything MI6 has done since the Cold War began as folly, that they waste people just as surely as any crazy cavalry charge. That's the betrayal.

'Homes Fit for Heroes' was a betrayal. If you served in my war, most of the fifties was a betrayal. If you served in that farce down in the Falklands, you're being betrayed even as we speak. Bentinck is a patriot. I see no reason to doubt that. Bentinck is betraying those who politick with patriotism and the safety of the realm. He believes in both, needless to say. In his own mind Bentinck is only betraying the betrayers."

"Wheels within wheels."

"No. It's simple, far simpler than you think."

Bentinck's next choice, the next module in my education in music, was simplicity itself. He had me sit through all six of Johann Sebastian Bach's suites for unaccompanied cello, played by Pablo Casals, relieved (but that honestly isn't the word) by a Brunello di Montalcino 1976 and a bowl of butterscotch Angel Delight.

"There's an arrogance comes with the job. I know you think I'm an arrogant prick, but the kind of man who'll do what I did will always think he's right, otherwise he wouldn't bloody do it. But it goes beyond that. The Deputy Head of MI6, back in the fifties I mean, took arrogance to a new level. He spoke for many of us. You might even think he spoke for me. He sent around a memo, this would be twenty-five and more years ago, so leaked I'm amazed it didn't end up in the *Daily Mirror* . . . It said that SIS was now the guardian of moral and intellectual integrity, that the Cold War had induced a moral stalemate as deadlocked as the nuclear stalemate of Mutually Assured Destruction. It was down to us. We were the front line, the Home Front . . . We were . . . everything."

"Stealth knights in Teflon armour?"

"Sneer if you like. Indeed, you may be right to sneer. It was in itself a delusion. It's like a law of physics. Some action and its inescapable reaction. We set up an organization like SIS . . . whose job is to serve and protect. How many police forces in the world have that as their motto, I wonder? But . . . the laws of physics prevail. Once set up, any organization has as its first principle its own survival. It can flip from serving the state to become the internal enemy of the state if it feels itself threatened. But since it still is the secret servant of the state it will feel wholly justified in its actions and in keeping them secret. Secrecy is not just its modus operandi, it is its very nature."

A phrase from my student days came back to me: Lit 101.

"'The law is the law, even when it's wrong.'"

"Eh?"

"It's Kafka. Either in *The Trial* or one of the short stories. Writing about the secret police."

"German?"

"Czech Jew. But he wrote in German."

"Hitler get him?"

"No. He died years before."

"Ah . . . one of the lucky ones."

I had no idea where this was going and left the next moment to him.

"And so . . . you see . . . we have a self-perpetuating, self-justifying body that has arrogated to itself the moral guardianship of the state . . . and what you end up with is a state within a state. A secret state. It will work against our enemies, wherever perceived, and because, as you said, it does not cease to be the law even when it is wrong, it doesn't question what it does. It doesn't question what it achieves."

"And you do?"

"Shall we say I have come to?"

"And you question what has been done? You question the achievement?"

"Let me ask you . . . You're a child of the Cold War. It's your world. What do you think thirty-five years of espionage has achieved? Are we a safer world? Are we one inch nearer to Moscow? Does a single Russian soldier stand one inch beyond the spot he stood on in May 1945?"

Why hesitate? He surely knew exactly what I was thinking. "I think it's all a game that wasn't worthwhile, that achieved nothing. And if you now tell me that this is not stalemate, it is equilibrium, I shall say horse-puckey."

"So you think I wasted me time?"

"You did ask."

"Well. At last we see eye to eye."

I left, clutching a new foolscap summary of the book he still intended to write.

Inspector Plodder was on my doorstep. I'd sat in the back of a cab and read. Plodder had nipped ahead of me in his cop car and stood waiting, while his thug of a sergeant sat at the wheel of the car.

"You turned over my flat so soon? I'll be mightily pissed off if you trashed my hi-fi again."

"Haven't been in."

"Such restraint."

"You'll be showing it to me all the same."

"Yep. I will. In my office. Tomorrow."

"Nine o clock."

"Noon. I have to get it typed up first. There'll be a copy waiting for you. Smile at Mrs Buckett, you might even get coffee."

"Glad you're being sensible, son."

Yeah. Two hundred quid sensible.

He read it through. So slowly that his coffee went cold.

His opinion might matter. His judgement didn't. Bentinck had delivered much more – thumbnail sketches of all the old missions he'd told me about, enough to ring alarm bells – but Plodder would not be the judge of that. He could see spilled beans, but he'd no idea how big a crisis this might amount to. He'd have to take this back to SIS.

"I'll need to keep this."

"S'okay. It's a copy. I have the original. Don't ask for it. You're not getting it."

He weighed this up. He knew damn well he had what mattered, got up from his chair, knocked back his cold coffee in a single gulp and crammed his hat back on.

"I could make you, you know that."

After he left, the Buckett came in and plonked a small tin

on my desk – Fuller's Full Strength Laxative Sugar – "No nasty aftertaste!"

"He asked for two sugars, so he got 'em. I 'ate coppers."

Imagine this. A month has passed. We are into autumn. The rain is pelting down against the windows of Syd's capacious office.

Around the table are Syd, me, Nathan Wolowitz, Jenny Broome, the Deputy Treasury Solicitor and a Mr Briggs, who has described himself merely as being from the Ministry. He doesn't say which ministry, but it's a phrase the rest of us take to mean spook.

Syd has made it clear that neither Jenny nor I should speak. He introduces himself as being . . . "in the words of Bismarck, an honest broker". The matter is between the government and Nathan. Between the government and Roger Bentinck, whom I have advised not to attend, as I'm worried about words like "arselickers" and "bunch of utter fucking gobshites" clouding the discussion.

Nathan Wolowitz rarely made house calls. His man picked him up at home in the Bentley, drove him to the office and drove him back. He was not known to visit, but when he did it was an imperial procession. In my office two flunkeys and a chauffeur sat sipping what I hoped was unlaced Buckett-brewed instant coffee.

Nathan had not yet spoken. He was fond of nods and gestures and seemed sparing with words.

The DTS spoke first.

"I'm afraid we can't sanction publication of this."

Nathan addressed his reply to the spook.

"Why so?"

"I'm afraid we can't go into detail. Official Secrets Act and all that. You have signed the Act, I believe, during your time in Allied Propaganda during the war, and of course, needless to say, Mr Bentinck has signed it."

Nathan looked briefly at Syd as though the two of them were cued.

"Then I await your court order so restraining me. I bid you good day, gentlemen."

He got up slowly. English manners made them rise at once. Nathan was maybe five foot four, they towered over him, but he'd wrong-footed them already. They'd not expected to be shown the door in less than two minutes.

"Mr Wolowitz, you surely don't *want* to go to court over this?"

"Yes. That is exactly what I want. If I do not go to court then you, an unelected official and a secret policeman, will be allowed to decide what is in the public interest. I'd be happier with the courts deciding that . . . in public, such is the public interest."

When they'd gone, Syd passed the single malt and said, "Jack, you have the list?"

I had. One sheet of A4 with the names of twelve other publishers who'd agree to say that they, too, intended to publish Bentinck and to share the legal costs.

Nathan glanced down it.

"Magnus Reiter? We haven't spoken in years. Peter Shaw? I should have said he would not deign to piss on me if I were on fire. However . . . perhaps the matter is bigger than the men. You must have done some silver-tongued persuading, young man."

I had, but it was no time to boast.

Syd said, "A common front, Nathan. When it's all over I'm sure normal service will be resumed and we can all go back to hating each other."

Jenny Broome didn't wait for normal service. Syd whisked Nathan off to lunch. She stood on the pavement in Henrietta Street and called me a shit.

"Jack, what I wanted was a book. What have I got? A fucking lawsuit. You promised me the Fifth Man. What have I got? A fucking lawsuit."

"There's a principle here, Jenny."

"Principle my arse. It's just another boys' game. Why don't

you stick to pissing through that damn thing instead of trying to think with it?"

Well, that was me put in my place.

The next thing, having scarcely recovered from the utter contempt of our putative editor, was to get Bentinck into the papers. If they were taking us to court, they would be doing so in the spotlight.

The Buckett came to see me. She knew my phone was searing hot from all the Fleet Street hacks that had called me in the last two days.

"Don't let it go to your head," she said.

I was not aware that I had.

"It's not about you. It's about him. The agent is never the star. That's the author."

Okay. Where was this leading?

"They're pestering you for interviews. Don't give any. Get all you can for Mr Toad, but none yourself. You're not the star . . ."

"I heard you the first time."

"You're just a facilitator. You put people together, you make a connection, you take your 10 per cent. Literary agent, estate agent. Not a deal of difference."

"What about secret agent?"

She told me to go fuck myself and left.

Well, that was me . . . and yadda yadda yadda.

There were dues to be paid. Tony Marks got first crack at Mr Toad. Bentinck was relaxed with him. He'd talked to him on half a dozen occasions about Maurice Oldfield. What he could talk about this time was limited: his motives for doing what he was doing; his conflict with the government over it; but not what he was actually going to say in the book.

It went well. Tony was not the brightest bear in the woods and once or twice I stepped in to suggest a question to him, but apart from that I didn't speak. If you look at all those photographs now, there's usually two men in suits: Bentinck in a good bespoke that fitted, and some hack in an off-the-peg that sagged; I'm the figure usually half-cropped off by the frame – the one not wearing a suit.

After half a dozen such interviews Bentinck's suit was fine, but the man sagged.

We went back to his house. He was muttering to himself about Rachmaninoff . . . or it could have been buggeroff . . . a confusion only solved when he fired up the hi-fi and stuck on Rachmaninoff's Third Piano Concerto in D minor by Vladimir Horowitz. For once someone I'd heard of. He'd come out of retirement a few months ago to take up performance again at the age of eighty-two. The papers had been full of him.

"First LP I've bought in years," Bentinck said. "Pour the booze after side one, will you? I need to get me feet up . . . God, I hate the Press" . . . and his "fuck 'em, fuck 'em, fuck 'em" was just audible over the brass that opened the piece . . . sounded like a French horn to me . . . but what did I know?

We sipped Scotch in silence between the first and second movements. After the third . . . well that was when he'd usually talk at length, about the music, about his time in the field, whatever was uppermost in his mind.

Tonight he said, "Forgive me, dear boy, I must to me pit."

And he went upstairs, leaving me to switch everything off and let myself out. I turned down the volume and played the piece over again, helped myself to a can of creamed rice pudding from his stash and left half an hour later.

It seemed to me that I had watched a kid's balloon go pffft.

The next time we met was about ten days later. He rang me. I could no longer get him on the phone and I had assumed he'd left it off the hook because he was getting hack-pestered.

"Tonight, 8.30. You bring a record."

First time he'd suggested that. Perhaps he was finally certain I would not show up with the Incredible String Band or the Grateful Dead or whatever generic term stood in his mind for all the bands he'd never heard of.

I took him a novelty . . . not that I mean a joke. I mean I tried to take him something that might otherwise never have occurred to him: Debussy Preludes. Okay, I knew he had them. I'd seen Walter Gieseking's version from the fifties gathering dust in his vinyl stacks. I took Debussy's own version, from God-knows-when. A "gem" I had found in Harold Moore's shop.

After the custard, Bentinck said.

"How did they do it? He never made any records. Conducted a lot, but he never recorded, and if he had they'd sound like crap."

"Piano roll."

"What?"

"Debussy made piano rolls. Someone has found a way of playing the roll and recording the sound. It may be a machine, but effectively it is Debussy's music as the man himself played it."

"Amazing," Bentinck said without a trace of pleasure. "O brave new world that has such people in't."

And I got ne'er a word more out of him.

More dues. I owed Jenny Broome lunch at the Ivy on Syd's ticket. There was no way she would not collect.

"And how is the man of the moment?"

I wasn't sure if she was talking about me or Bentinck. She read my mind.

"I don't mean you. Of course I don't mean you."

"Mr Bentinck is . . . down. Pffft."

"Really? Can't say I'm surprised."

"It surprised me. It's as though he's lost interest. After all this time. As though he can't be bothered anymore."

"Try this on for size, Jack. Did it ever occur to you that your Mr Toad might be a ringer?"

"A what?"

"Oh God, you've never read a word of Edgar Wallace have you? Zero for Lit 101, Jack. A ringer. A fake. A plant. A . . . double agent, for fuck's sake."

"Jenny, I'm really not following you here."

"Suppose he's still working for SIS. Suppose he is a plant.

A cat put among the pigeons. Put there to flush out the Left in London publishing. Well, you gave him exactly what he wanted, didn't you? A list of every left-of-centre publisher in London who's prepared to take on the law, the government, the Establishment. He's won, hasn't he? So why wouldn't he lose interest? Why wouldn't he give up?"

"Everyone knows who's who in London publishing. What was there to be learnt?"

"Everyone in London publishing thinks Left and lives Right. They read the *Guardian*, and then they vote SDP. They give to Band Aid, but they worry more about the catchment area for the local schools. It's a quantum leap from making all the right sympathetic noises about the deserving poor to actually defying government. What have they gained? They know the sheep from the goats now."

"And me?"

She was stirring her soup now, not quite looking me in the eye, but I knew when the eyes lifted she'd fire point-blank.

"You? You were his dupe."

"Okay. Okay . . . and why wouldn't he dump me?"

"Eh?"

"He hasn't. I admit I see less of him, but he hasn't dropped me. Just at the point when you say there's nothing more to be gained."

"He told you he'd name the Fifth Man, didn't he? Well, has he? No . . . and he's never fucking going to. He's used you, Jack . . . and you, as ever, have used me."

It is a happy man who sits before a pudding menu with his company credit card. Alas, that day I never got to. Come to think of it I was lucky I didn't end up with onion soup dumped over my head. Jenny liked to freeload. To storm out of a lunch I was paying for must have stung.

Fifth Man? Worm to catch a sprat?

Jack Turner? Sprat?

Jack Turner? Twat?

The Buckett was standing in my office door, looking at me.

I'd no idea how long she'd been there. The ashtray was poised in her left hand, the fag equally poised on her lower lip.

"You was miles away."

"Was I?"

"Penny for them."

What? A penny for my thoughts? Endearment from this fucking Essex harridan? Did I look that bad?

A week or so passed.

The usual call to music came.

I went.

I have no recollection of what was on the turntable.

I watched Bentinck without hearing. The face that once had relaxed under music now had a line scored down the forehead to pinch the flesh together right between the eyes.

When whatever it was had finished, I said, "You've given up, haven't you?"

One eye opened before the other, sized me up without the head turning.

"Perhaps. I'm tired, my boy. Oh so tired. And I find myself ill at ease as a cause célèbre."

"Then what was the point of it all?"

"The point was to make a point. The one thing we haven't managed to do. Spin it again, Jack."

Suddenly it all added up.

Sprat. Twat. Dupe.

I could call him out right now . . . You set me up . . . You used me . . . You *betrayed* me.

I didn't. I put the record on again, his eyes closed and I slipped out silently before side one had finished.

The next summons, he said, "What do you have post-Stravinsky? I find I have next to nothing?"

I said I was really very busy right then, but I'd look.

I didn't.

Sprat. Twat. Dupe.

Another couple of weeks passed.

He sent me a postcard. A photo of a man walking away from the Brandenburg Gate on the Soviet side – coincidentally the same photograph used as the cover of the new James McVey spy novel. And on the back . . .

Jack, dear boy . . . ?

It was Christmas 1986.

We had lost our court case, embarrassed Her Majesty's government worldwide, made a reluctant celebrity of Bentinck . . . but we had not published a book. What we had done was boost the "integrity" of London publishing with a common cause that was topped only by the stand against the fatwa on Salman Rushdie a couple of years later.

The week before Christmas a small book arrived in the mail. I received books every day. Opening a book package was hardly a priority.

The Buckett slapped a pile of envelopes on my desk, but flipped the package and put her finger on the name on the back – one word, *Bentinck*, and a post code. After all these months.

He'd had it privately printed and was sending it out as a sort of Christmas card. Making his point. The note inside hoped I was well and added that he'd also sent copies to Jenny Broome and Nathan Wolowitz.

Thirty seconds later Jenny was on the phone.

"Well . . . that's the end of that then, isn't it?"

"I guess so. Jenny . . . I didn't know he was going to do this."

"Yeah, right. Jack, the next time you have a fat toad from MI6 who tells you he'll name names . . . take him somewhere else, will you?"

It was the evening of the next day. I was last out again, so the direct line rang on my desk.

"Jack? It's Molly. Could you come over to the Boltons right away?"

"What's wrong? Is Roger ill?"

"No. He's dead."

*   *   *

He was in bed.

Old-fashioned enough to wear a nightshirt.

It seemed he had died in his sleep, a book on the counterpane, the reading light still on when Molly found him.

"Have you called anyone?"

"Just you. There's no hurry. Is there?"

"I suppose not. And . . . and . . . nothing suspicious?"

"Let's not go there, as they say these days. Roger's health was appalling. Penny to a pound he died of natural causes . . ."

"There are people who might find this very convenient. And just one day after he finally gets the book into print."

She took my head in both her hands, made certain my eyes were looking into hers.

"Don't even think it. You hear me? Don't even think it."

We opened the Laphroaig and a tin of custard in Bentinck's honour.

We sat in silence. I'd have put on music for him, but I had not the first notion of what I should choose.

After a while, Molly said, "Roger was a crap husband, you know."

"Why did you marry him?"

"The question no woman ever wants to be asked. But since you do. I had been married once before, at what might be an early age, but what was probably typical of the early sixties. And what I took from that marriage was a list of conditions. A checklist of that with which I would not up-put. I would not marry a boozer. I would not marry a slob. I would not marry a man who could not cook. I would not marry a man who could not support me and my, theoretical, children. If he was good in bed, that was a bonus. If he was good at DIY – jackpot. Neither was essential."

"And Roger?"

"And Roger met none of those conditions. So I married him anyway."

"And?"

"And . . . *amor vincit omnia* . . . and *amor* is plain fucking wrong. Roger was a crap husband. When I left him he became a friend. Not a great friend, not even a good friend, but . . . a friend. And now . . . I have lost him."

What had I lost?

A friend?

Such a notion.

Had it ever occurred to me to think of him as a friend?

A grotesque, upper-class, right-wing English Tory . . . a fat, rude, greedy drunkard . . . who despised everything I stood for . . . *without despising me.*

A friend I had abandoned and left to die alone . . . sprat, twat, dupe . . . betrayer.